WAS SHE ABOUT TO LOSE EVERYTHING SHE HAD WON OR GAIN MORE THAN SHE HAD EVER HOPED TO HAVE?

Dori Gray had been married and divorced. She had accepted the fact that she could never bear children. Restless, vibrant, she had had lovers. She had built a successful career. It hadn't been easy, but she had done it—won celebrity and respect in a tough "man's world."

That was when Dori found herself an astonished, unwed mother-to-be.

That was when all the certainties turned into questions, and no one could answer them but Dori.

THE TENTH MONTH

THE TENTH MONTH

Laura Z. Hobson

A DELL BOOK

*Again to Mike and Chris
and now to Sarah*

Published by
Dell Publishing Co., Inc.
1 Dag Hammarskjold Plaza
New York, New York 10017
Copyright © 1970 by Laura Z. Hobson
All rights reserved including the right
of reproduction in whole or in part
in any form. For information contact
Simon & Schuster, Inc.
Dell ® TM 681510, Dell Publishing Co., Inc.

ISBN: 0-440-18605-6

Reprinted by arrangement with
Simon & Schuster, Inc.
New York, New York 10020
Printed in the United States of America
First Dell printing—May 1972
Second Dell printing—July 1972
Third Dell printing—November 1978
New Dell printing—April 1979

ONE »è»

THE MOMENT was to stand out forever in her memory. There she stood, alone and naked, thinking of nothing except the minutiae of the bath, toweling herself dry, gazing idly about the warm steamy room, then at her image in the long panel of mirror in the closed door.

Her breasts looked fuller. She had gained no weight, but her breasts, always small, looked fuller. Below her navel, there was the faintest globe of fullness too.

She stood motionless, staring. Had the years of longing fused into some betraying lens of illusion? Or could it be at last the moment she had imagined so many thousand times?

She stepped closer to the mirror, looking away for an instant, then suddenly back to her image as if to trap something before it could escape. The same impression, of a most hesitant distension, tentative, a curving outward thrice over.

Oh God let it be true.

She stood, searching the glass. She saw the tight-muscled body of a girl, but she was forty. She saw the lifting spheres of a virgin's breasts but she had been married and divorced. She had never remarried and if this were true—oh let it be true.

She moved a step closer to the mirror but this time she looked only at her face, her eyes, too eager now to be her ordinary brown eyes, at her mouth, compressed now as if to clamp down on any word of pleading, and therefore not her ordinary mouth either. Then swiftly she looked again at her body and suddenly laughed aloud, as a child laughs.

She flung her arms wide and the towel billowed out behind her like a sail caught by a gusty wind.

Don't. It'll probably be all over by morning.

She let the towel drop and went to her telephone. It was late afternoon and Dr. Jesskin would not be there, but his two nurses knew her and when she said, "This is Theodora Gray, could I possibly see the doctor tomorrow morning?" she was given an appointment at nine thirty.

"I'm working you in," Miss Mack said, "so if you could get here a few minutes ahead?"

"Of course I will. And thanks."

She held on to the crossbar of the telephone after she had put it into its cradle, gripping it as if at a lever to propel herself into action. What she wanted to do was lie still, silent, commanding her mind not to leap ahead, yet yielding to her mind's rebellion, and for a while go on regarding this possibility as if it were already fact.

But it was nearly six and she was being called for in half an hour, for dinner and then a concert. She had been looking forward to the evening with eagerness, that special insistent eagerness that came from extended periods of loneliness. Loneliness came only at long intervals, but then it lasted a long interval too, like the changing of the seasons, never sudden, never over in a day or a week. There was a foreboding first, of the advent of another spell, like the lowering of a sky as the barometer drops and the winds gather, and then when the sun went, there was the knowledge that the bleak darkness would remain and remain and remain.

She hid these bad times, with success now, unlike the first year after her divorce when she could not possibly have fooled anybody, but the effort was still depleting and destructive and she always emerged as if from an illness, unsure of herself, except for her work, wary, yet eager for new people, for all people. Friendships that she had let lapse were picked up again, and new friendships welcomed with a readiness she for one knew was excessive.

She had accepted a date for the concert from a man she scarcely knew—had that alacrity seemed excessive? She had met him only the week before, at Celia's, and because it was there, it was easy to get talking about music; she had thought he might be involved professionally with music as Celia and Marshall Duke were, but he turned out to be a lawyer. His name was Matthew Poole; he called himself Matthew, not Matt. She liked the name that way, uncondensed. Her own name unconcondensed was pretentious; Dori made it usable.

She still signed her pieces *Theodora V. Gray,* and though she was not one of the big names in the newspaper world, there was enough value in her by-line to make it foolish to consider changing it. *Dori Gray* in print would look cozy or cute or chic like *Suzy Knickerbocker* and her special pieces were not even remotely related to the cute or chic nonsense so many editors parceled off as the special province of their women writers. She had never considered going back to her maiden name (I'll decide what to do about my name when I marry again") and by the time she began to see that she wasn't one of those women who remarry easily after a divorce, so much equity had been put into the name Gray by her own effort that she felt she had earned her own title to it.

"Haven't I just read something of yours?" Matthew Poole had asked when Celia introduced them. "In a magazine?"

"The Spock piece. I don't often do anything political."

"That's the one." Suddenly he added, " 'Dr. Spock Brings Us Up Short.' "

"You remembered the title."

"Half my cases right now are conscientious objectors."

"Oh good."

She always felt drawn to, and safer with, people who were what was so scornfully called "liberal" these days by the extreme left. She was used to the scorn of the extreme right, but this new scorn was harsher. She had never been very good at talking politics; she got furious at the camouflaged racists who were such devotees of law and order, and at the black-power toughs who talked so glibly about shooting whitey, and at the doctrinaire Communists who went livid over free speech in New York or Washington but remained sublimely untroubled by jailing or shooting of dissenters in Havana or Moscow or Peking.

Matthew Poole had shown himself more controlled when they had talked of these things. It was odd that she could remember this part of their talk that day at Celia's but not how they had got around to the concert. She was glad he was a lawyer and not a writer or editor or newspaperman. She always liked meeting people not connected, however tangentially, with deadlines and early editions and newsbreaks. The Press—capital T, capital P—was an ingrown world where you were too close too often to the same people, covering the same stories, eating in the same restaurants near the paper, falling in love with the same men in a kind of inky incestuous turn and turn-about. She had from the first made it a point never to get involved with any of them; not once until last year, during the endless newspaper strike that had finally killed off her paper and made her for months, as Dick had said, "a press orphan"—

For the first time since the mirror she thought of Dick. Dick Towson. If this were true, what would Dick do? How would he take it, what would he say, what would he feel? They had been drifting apart, without rebuke and without misery, amiable toward each other as they had been before he left on his assignment in Vietnam, and though she had felt the same apprehension anybody would feel about his going into the danger of battle-reporting, she had almost welcomed the trip, as he probably also had, as a most tactful *Finis* to their dwindling affair.

"By Dick Towson." It was a by-line known in dozens of newspapers the country over, the by-line of a first-rate reporter with a brisk, vivid style. If it was by Dick Towson, it would never be dull.

She glanced toward the open door of the bathroom, the blank mirror now reflecting only the edge of the tub and a strip of flowered wallpaper above it.

Unexpectedly she laughed again. If it were true, it would be "by Dick Towson."

On her dresser a small clock chinked six times and she jumped up, reaching for her underthings. As she drew her thin girdle up over her knees she suddenly stopped and, hobbled as she was, crossed the room to her low dresser. The beveled glass cut her off at mid-thigh, but above, embedded within the jut of her hipbones, was again that tentative orbing.

* * *

The concert turned into background music for her thinking, which meant that as a concert it was a failure. Usually she listened to music as she read a book, note for note, as it was word for word on a page, skipping nothing, her mind never wandering. But tonight there was no stillness in her for listening, nothing passive and receiving, though it was good to be there and good to be there with Matthew Poole.

At dinner he had talked of himself and his family for the first time, of his two teen-age children, Hildy and Johnny, whom he spoke of with a pleased satisfaction as if they were good children to have, and of his wife Joan, elliptically and briefly as if there were some disaster there that had best go untold. And then he had turned the talk to her, putting the inevitable questions, not trying to sound casual as he did so, not trying to disguise them as small talk.

"I know you're divorced," he had said. "But I didn't

want to ask around about whether you're tied up emotionally as of now, or reasonably uninvolved."

She was glad he hadn't tried to make it sound offhand. This sort of question never was. But what a time for it! What a time for her to get interested in somebody new. Sitting here, watching the baton, focusing on it as if its tip were the one solid point in a light swarm of fever and unreality, she half wished he hadn't been at Celia's last week. What a time! Tomorrow morning would be only the first step, a quick examination and then waiting for the lab reports. But she would be saying the words aloud to Dr. Jesskin, not just hearing them in her own mind, but really saying them out into the air: I think I am pregnant.

"Reasonably uninvolved," she had answered Matthew at the table, and had gone on to say too much about herself, about how she seemed to go through awfully long stretches of *uninvolved,* like some vexing stubborn anemia, how irritated she was at times to be making so little use of her so-called freedom, how she sometimes swore she was going to turn promiscuous and have affair after affair after affair.

"But?"

She could still hear his amused "but." Now she glanced at him quickly and then back to the orchestra. He was absorbed in his listening, eyelids half lowered though not music-lover shut, his whole look one of repose and pleasure. She understood that; but tonight, for her, was something new. She tried again to listen as she always listened but the phrase "I think I am pregnant" went on repeating itself, a soft pedal-point against which the flow of sound went streaming by, rhythmic, mobile and somehow kind.

*   *   *

In the morning she was ten minutes early and the first patient had not yet arrived. "Then I might as well sneak you in ahead," Miss Mack said, as if she understood very well that this was no routine visit, no dutiful checkup. She opened the office door, said to the doctor, "Since Mrs. Reeves is late again," and withdrew instantly. She always remained in the examining room, with an obviousness that had always amused Dori. As if without this starchy and omnipresent chaperon no female patient could feel safe in the presence of Dr. Cornelius Jesskin. He was already preoccupied as she entered his office, reading his own notations in the folder opened and spread before him on his desk. She recognized it without looking at its slightly worn tab that would say Mrs. A. Gray, with the *A* crossed out and a *T* written in above it. Its last entries were over two years old; she had even been neglecting the annual Pap test.

The doctor had motioned her to the chair beside him and she waited until he looked up at last from his notes. Then in a rush she said, "Oh, Dr. Jesskin, it seems to me, yesterday I was having a bath and I— I think I may be pregnant. I think my breasts are a little different, and I began to think—I realized I might have skipped a period again. Do you remember when I began to be irregular about my periods? And then—"

"Just a moment," he said. "Suppose you start at the beginning, and tell me." He was looking at her carefully and she thought, He has to stay neutral, and then, making herself speak slowly, sounding almost docile, she began her recital once more.

He fingered the pen in his hand as he listened, not using it to jot down any note of what she said. His face wore no expression except his usual one of concerned interest, an intentness that shut out every other importance in the world except the one importance brought in by his patient. When Dori ended, he said, "I'll have a look at you soon, but tell me again when your skipped period, if you did skip, when it should have started."

He began to write and she gave him dates but again broke off and spoke in a rush. "Don't you remember the first time I skipped? You said it wasn't usual at that age, but that it did happen, and might again."

He searched his notes. "That would have been about when?"

"Two years ago. I was thirty-eight. In the spring, April."

He was nodding now, reading his minute, perfectly legible writing. She had gone to him then only because she was trained to go to doctors when the inexplicable showed itself, and it was inexplicable enough at thirty-eight to have no period for five weeks. "Early menopause," she had joked to herself, but might it not be some symptom of—of what? A tumor, a cyst, the first fearful sign of malignancy. You didn't ignore it; you went to your doctor and faced it fast. That time there had been not even a stir of hope that it might be this; it had been one of the interminable stretches of total aloneness.

"Yes," Dr. Jesskin said, looking up from the folder. "You then returned to being regular. 'More or less' is the way you put it. You reported in by phone for four periods, then stopped calling in."

Suddenly tense she said, "You aren't going to tell me this may be just another skipped period?"

"I am not going to tell you anything as yet, Mrs. Gray. After I examine you, we will arrange for laboratory reports. But even before that, I think I should remind you of something you already know—we must remember it now—the possibility of pseudopregnancy. We see it, not very often, but enough to have to consider it. The menstrual break, the swelling of the breasts, even engorgement of the uterus. You know of such cases, do you not?"

Like a thin coating of sleet, his speech constricted and chilled her. "You told me, that other time."

He tapped the old-fashioned buzzer beside the phone and at once Miss Mack appeared.

"Mrs. Reeves is here now," she said.

"I'll see Mrs. Gray first."

Miss Mack ushered Dori into the examining room and indicated the curtained alcove where she was to undress. "He never likes it when patients are late,"

Miss Mack said fussily, "and this one always is. He wants to teach her a lesson."

That's not why, Dori thought. He also wonders if it could be true. She stripped quickly, not hearing Miss Mack's friendly babble, and then stepped back into the examining room. Again the table, she thought, again the stirrups, again the sheets draped so carefully over your raised knees as if it were immodest to let a gynecologist see your knees or thighs but sobriety itself to open the core of your body to him. The idiocy of the rules. Miss Mack always staying right through, just to *be* there.

Her heart began to pound. It was a new sensation, disagreeable and heavy. I'm afraid, she thought. Through the closed door she could hear the doctor speaking, on the telephone probably, leisurely, contained, the same Dr. Jesskin he always was. Suddenly she remembered her very first visit to a gynecologist, long before she had heard of Dr. Jesskin. She was afraid then too, but in a different way, the orthodox way. She was twenty-two, then, and she and Tony had just been married. Less than two months later, she missed her period. She was stupefied with unwillingness, with unreadiness. They hadn't even talked of children except as a vague possibility in the future; she was not ready to stop being a girl, to stop being the young bride, the girl reporter on the paper. When she was certain she was pregnant, she told Tony. He was unwilling too. "We could stop it," he said. Filled with relief, she cried, "Oh, let's, till next year."

And next year had flown, and another and another and by the time she had sought out Dr. Jesskin, a specialist in sterility problems, had told him her history, she had faltered, "So you see I'm not sterile, Doctor, I'm not barren, I mean I wasn't, but this is the sixth year of our marriage and we've begun to be terribly afraid we can't ever have children."

She was not sterile. She was not barren. She had been injured by the abortion, Dr. Jesskin's examinations and tests had finally revealed, the slow tests, the careful tests, some painful, like insufflation to see if the Fallopian tubes were blocked or still open, others routine. She had been too harshly curetted; now she could not sustain a pregnancy. "I might be getting pregnant every month," she had explained to Tony, "but the ovum can't get embedded—it's like clinging to a wall of paper."

But this was reparable, the doctor had said, this damage that need never have happened, though the repairing would be slow, and progress for a long time indiscernible and unprovable. "You will bear a child someday, I think," Dr. Jesskin had said, and she had trusted him and had been faithful with her visits, never missing one for two full years, sharing in his patience, sharing in his confidence when he said at last, "Don't count on this, Mrs. Gray, but this might be your year, it might be. The uterine lining is getting back to normal."

But before another week of that year was out, Tony was gone and everything they had tried for was gone too. Later—she couldn't remember how much later— she had gone to Dr. Jesskin once again, and told him of her divorce. She promised to resume her treatments soon, knowing that if she stopped for good there would be retrogression, a loss of everything gained these two full years, a defeat forever. But even as she spoke, she wept uncontrollably, and Dr. Jesskin had counseled her not to commit herself as yet to any program, that shock and grief in themselves were often enough to upset all the body's chemistries and powers.

"But if I stop, I'll have lost my last chance."

She had made one appointment but when the day came she could not bear the going, could not stand the continuing of a purpose which now was off in the distance of "when you marry again." To marry at thirty was not as easy as it had been at twenty-two; her needs had taken on shape and firmness; she could no longer live in a vague happy cloud of girlish responses to a man because he danced well or because he took you to all the smart places. And by thirty-five, by forty—

Suddenly Dr. Jesskin opened his office door behind her. She lay inert; unafraid; simply waiting. Miss Mack reappeared, offered him a small tray with instruments and the examination began. It proceeded in complete silence, as always in the past, and as always, Dr. Jesskin's expression was one of total absorption. When the examination was over, he asked Dori to sit up at the side of the table, her legs dangling, and Miss Mack quickly rearranged her drapings, over her shoulders, scooped low over her navel, revealing only her breasts. As the doctor began the careful palping and prodding, Dori thought wildly, It's like the annual check for cancer—he never says anything then either.

"Would you please stand now?"

She slid off the table, with Miss Mack swiftly redraping her once more, this time leaving her torso bare, but gathering the white folds tightly around her hips into a bunched rosette for Dori to clutch to herself, an elaborate and coiled fig leaf.

It's so stupid, she thought; why can't I just be naked? The words were angry, but she could not have said them aloud. Dr. Jesskin was looking at her in profile, below her navel, up to her breasts, below again, and then he moved around to see her full on.

On his face was that familiar expression, absorption, nothing else. "When you are dressed," he finally said, "I will see you again in the office." He nodded, almost formally, and she hurried to the alcove and into her clothes. As she knocked and opened his office door a few minutes later, he dropped his pen on the page before him—it was still her folder—and said, "Well, my dear girl," and before she could interpret the words or the half-permissive tone of them, he added, "there is no way to be sure, as I said, until the tests are complete." She sat down, silent. "But it does seem, there is some slight evidence of change." Before she could speak, he raised his index finger an inch or two, a polite, cautionary inch or two, in renewal of what he had asked her to remember. "Some slight change, not only the apparent enlargement which you reported, but also perhaps a change in the cervix. It is out of the question to be certain, so early, but a change suggests itself, I must say."

"There is at least a possibility that I'm pregnant?"

"I must not answer in any way until the reports are in. I'll have the Drav Index done, which is faster, but also the A-Z test, totally conclusive."

"How long do they take? Could you tell them to hurry?"

"They always hurry, on pregnancy tests." He stood up and she did too. "But the A-Z won't be in until the day after tomorrow."

"Two whole days? Till Thursday?"

Suddenly he lost his look of absorption and controlled care; he put his hand on her arm and said, "You must try not to think about it."

She laughed, at him, at his suggestion, and said, "Oh, thank you, Dr. Jesskin."

*　　*　　*

Try not to think about it indeed. She stopped at a drugstore counter for toast and coffee and thought, Thank God for Martha Litton, and glanced at her watch. She was to be at Miss Litton's at eleven for the interview that had been so difficult to set up, now that Miss Litton's third comedy, *Time and a Half,* was a greater smash than her first two, and though she never worked at deadline heat for these special pieces, she could plunge along on this one for the entire day, and into the evening. She often did her best work in the evening.

Don't think about it. She walked to Miss Litton's apartment quickly, and was again too early, and walked around the block several times before going up. From Miss Litton's testy greeting—"I tried to reach you this morning but you were out. It's turned into the worst sort of time for an interview"—she knew she was in for a difficult session. Thank God for that too.

She rarely took notes beyond particularities of spellings and dates, but today she did, using not a notebook but copy paper folded and propped against her purse. Twice in the first minutes she had to say, "Sorry, could you tell me that again?" and twice Miss Litton repeated what she had said, showing an impatience that it should be necessary.

It was all useless stuff, the official gabble of publicity releases, but Dori hid that estimate of it. At the first chance she said, "Could we go back *before* your first play? You were born in Philadelphia, I know—"

"*Av ovo?*" Miss Litton said primly, but began nevertheless to talk of her childhood, and for the first time Dori listened without bothering with her folded copy paper. Here it is, she thought, the only kind of thing that ever explains anybody, if you can ever get at it.

The interview went on for an hour and when Dori left she had the first paragraph of her piece clear in her mind. She would go straight to the typewriter and stay with it and not let herself think, and though she rather thoroughly disliked the current Martha Litton for her self-love and self-praise, she ought to be able to use that dislike judiciously and write something that had insight and some feeling.

"Anything by Dori Gray will have warmth," her editor at the paper had once said in her presence, "sometimes enough to singe your eyebrows."

It must be true; enough people had said so by now, enough letters had told her so. It wasn't a trick; it must come through her effort always to see into, to look for character instead of characteristic. She was never facile and easy with a phrase anyhow; that was what had ruined her the one time she had tried out for a panel show on television, that and the fact that she had gone stiff with self-consciousness, what with the whole production staff and the other panelists, experienced charmers all, waiting hopefully for some clever little mot.

Yet the light turn of phrase came readily when she was with one congenial person. Dick Towson always laughed when they were together, and had even asked why she didn't try writing light pieces or a humor column in some women's magazine. He was the one with the light touch, really; perhaps that was why he brought it out in her when they were together. If he were here right now she would probably burst out with her news; she was always apt to tell things to anybody close to her, close in the special closeness that came only with making love over a long period of time. D. H. Lawrence had talked in Lady Chatterley of the deep peace that came from steady lovemaking, only he had used the word, the lovely thick Anglo-Saxon word which she liked and approved of in theory but could not easily say, despite the uninhibited language of 1967.

But Lawrence was right; there was a peacefulness and closeness from a continuing sexuality, if it was satisfying and solid for both, and she and Dick had known that closeness and knew it still, even though they also knew, each of them and without verbalizing it, that they were coming to the end. Paradox, paradox. She had never ended anything with hatred and blame, except after Tony, and she still felt warm toward Dick and linked with him.

Linked. A surge of feeling surprised her, for his share in what had happened—*it has happened, the reports will say yes*—a leap of grateful love, the best sort, for it asked nothing. Suddenly he seemed newly appealing; she remembered how exciting it had been, almost a year and a half ago, how flattering, that he should be demanding her time, her emotion, her body, when he could have chosen almost any younger or prettier girl. That first time they were in the apartment alone, she had said something about those possible other girls, and he had suddenly and roughly taken her hand and held it against himself and said, "But you're the one does this," and watched her as she felt the bulk of him rising to her palm, arrogant and sure.

They had gone to bed that night and it had been right and good and equal for them both, and there were none of the insufferable little coynesses and uncertainties and she had known she would see him whenever he was in New York and not off on an assignment. "Is it all right, about your family?" she had asked once, and he had shut her off, not brusquely, but with a decisiveness that removed all responsibility from her, and any need for guilt. "I've got a damn good marriage in all the usual twenty-five-years-of-it ways, steady, and no surprises, and all the kids know Dad's a newspaperman who's away half the time but won't ever go for good, and nobody's got any kick coming, so it's okay all around and you and I don't ever have to worry about it."

They had never worried about it. At the beginning he would telephone her late at night when he was covering some story in London or Washington or Tel Aviv, but though he never labored the point, she knew that he also called his wife from those same places and that overseas phone calls were almost matter-of-fact to his four children.

At the beginning he would come straight to her from Kennedy Airport when he returned; for the past few months, though, he often went home instead and came to her the next day or perhaps the day after. It was one of the small signals of the passing of time, the passing of the first heat and press and gluttony of a new affair, and she saw it for what it was with a strange willingness, a wisdom she did not know she possessed but which she welcomed with a faint pleasure as if she were awarding herself the mildest of accolades for avoiding that most dreaded feminine failing, being too demanding.

Yet at this moment, if he were to phone and say he was just in from his assignment, impossible since he was off in that fierce part of the world, if he were by some fluke to phone and say, "Towson here, I'm at Kennedy, can I come over?"—

She glanced at the telephone as if it actually had rung and suddenly rose from the typewriter. She hadn't gone beyond the first paragraph of the piece on Martha Litton; she had let her mind wander, undisciplined and wanton, because the first major problem she would have when all the reports were in would be centered in Dick Towson and his right to know or her decent obligation not to let him know.

Suddenly another one of Dick's pronouncements popped into her mind, this also spoken with that brusque decisiveness that lifted all responsibility from her. "Either of us can want out and all holds by the other barred—yes?" She had laughed at the adroitness and thought how exactly his mood had suited hers. As for this kind of hold, it was not only barred but unthinkable.

She began to prowl restlessly around the room. Anyway, she thought, I don't have to decide now. He may be there for months. I'm going to take this just as it happens, one day at a time.

She went back to the typewriter and wrote hard for another paragraph and then once again pushed back from her desk and began to move about. It was a pretty room, her bedroom and study combined, a room she felt easy in when she was alone, and a little proud of when she was not alone.

Suddenly she wished she were not alone. Remembering that first night with Dick had made her remember how marvelous it was to be made love to, how normal and sweet and good she always felt. She wished she were newly in love, newly in bed, for the first time with somebody new, caught in that fresh wild passion of beginnings, where you could never stop to think of any future—

The wrong moment for ruling out futures, she thought wryly. Again she went to her typewriter; another paragraph spurted from the keys and then the telephone rang. It was a shrill loud bell which she had often resolved to ask the phone company to mute or diminish and the sound of it scarred her mood. She lifted the receiver and heard Matthew Poole say "Hello?" and her heart lifted too.

"I thought you were going to Boston," she greeted him.

"I'm in Boston."

"Calling me from Boston?"

He laughed. "Long distance—it's a new invention."

"I've heard."

"I'm taking the five o'clock shuttle back," he said, "and I wondered if you'd have dinner with me."

"Tonight?"

"That's why I'm using the new invention."

"I'm not being too bright, am I?" She hesitated. "I was going to finish writing an interview I'm doing."

"That sounds disciplined and worthwhile. Don't be. Say you will have dinner with me."

"I'd love to. I'm in no mood to be disciplined and worthwhile."

"Good. Can I come by at about six thirty? And you tell me where to take you for dinner?"

"I'll give you a drink while I decide."

As she hung up she thought, I oughtn't to. Until I know for sure, I ought not to see him even once more. Suppose he—but he won't. He's not the sudden lover like Dick. And if he is, I'm not. But my God, there I go. If it's not hindsight-thinking, devious and destructive, it's forward-projection, equally dangerous.

She moved toward her desk and boredom invaded her. Who cared about Martha Litton and her self-importance and vanity and mannerisms? There were days for working and days for restlessness and God knew this was a restless one. She went to the kitchen to ask Nellie to put out ice cubes and a few things to have with their drinks.

"I could stay on if you want," Nellie offered in a dubious tone. She always sounded dubious, a rather surly Swedish girl who arrived daily at three and left at five except by special arrangement.

"Never mind, thanks. We're going out."

The kitchen window suddenly streaked across with rain and Dori was dismayed. The afternoon sky had gone purple-gray and wind was whistling around the corner of the building. His plane would be storm-bound or detoured to Washington or Richmond and the whole thing would be off. The telephone would ring again and he would explain and ask if they could make it another time.

They could but it would be different. Right now was the time, right now when she should be saying no; this mood was the mood, this restlessness the yeast that was rising—all part of the wild impossible present, with those technicians off in an unknown laboratory, starting their tests to find an answer they didn't care about one way or another.

She went back to her own room and stared out at the storm. The sky darkened further; streetlights came on and people raced along the edges of buildings, tenting sopping newspapers over their heads. She watched them minutely as if they were terribly important to her, as if they were her dearest friends suddenly attacked and hurrying toward her for safety. What made Matthew Poole so important, so suddenly important? Last night's dinner and concert added little to what she actually knew about him, but he somehow had revealed himself more freely; there had been about him a pleased and contented air that compelled attention, as if he were not often happy. She hadn't seen it except during the music, but now she realized that it had been there through all of the evening. He had taken her home and come up for a nightcap and talked again about the boy he was going to defend as a conscientious objector; he talked with the calm tone of a man who knew she agreed with him, and an inordinate pride had ballooned in her for the Spock piece that had told him so. And then, with no word of whether they were to see each other even once more, he had said good-night and left, without so much as an extra pressure of her hand.

Now this. She turned abruptly from the window and went to work. This time she wrote without pause, telling herself it was only first draft anyway and better than hanging around waiting for time to get itself spent. When she wrote this way, without pause or question, she slid the spacing lever to position 3, so that she was doing triple-spaced pages, and they flew by. Time enough to improve them tomorrow. Or, if the storm went furiously on, this evening, when there would be nothing else. A fine lonely evening in the home.

Finally she bathed and dressed, and thought the rain and wind had abated, and could not be sure, and then a bell rang and it was not the shrill telephone but the front door.

She opened it and stood aside, letting him pass by her into the square little hallway, each saying hello as if they were constrained.

"Was it a rough flight?"

"Not to speak of."

"I thought—I always think everything is grounded if it rains. What can I give you for a drink?"

She started for the living room and he followed but he did not answer. At the small chest that served as a bar she turned to him questioningly. He was watching her with what looked like sternness; his mouth was drawn as if in disapproval, his eyebrows drawn as if in anger. Suddenly he put both his hands on her shoulders and said, "I cannot stop thinking of you," and drew her toward him, his face seeking hers, but his mouth not. "It's been years since anybody's mattered this much."

She heard her breath as it was sharply drawn inward at his words, felt the weaving churning move of passion rolling, and thought, But I mustn't, not now, not now of all times. He turned his head to kiss her, and her breath sucked inward again and something wavered and fell within her and she was invaded all at once by the lovely helplessness of acquiescence.

Suddenly she pushed hard away from him, wheeling away, saying lightly, "Something to drink," lightly, falsely, the social tone she hated in others. "Martini? Or Scotch on the?"

"Scotch, please." He watched her put two cubes into a glass and then pour the Scotch, accepting the drink in silence when she offered it, waiting until she prepared one for herself. Then he said, without emphasis, "Why did you suddenly decide no?"

"I didn't decide. I just had to *not* go on."

"There was one moment when you suddenly stopped. Up to then you were as moved as I was."

"I was," she said, "oh, I was."

He waited but she did not continue. She sat down on the sofa and in a moment he sat down too, well away from her. "Last night you said you were reasonably uninvolved," he said finally. "Does it turn out you're not as uninvolved as you thought?"

She shook her head in denial.

"But if that *is* it, I'll wait around until you are."

"It's not being in love with somebody. It's something else. I don't think I can talk about it. For now anyway."

"Then don't. You needn't ever."

She turned quickly away and set her drink on the coffee table. Even his voice stirred her, the negation in it now. Just this once, she thought. Give in; don't make up rules about what you should do, what you shouldn't, when you should, when you shouldn't. Without knowing she was going to, she put her hand out behind her, reaching toward him. In another moment she was in his arms and there on the sofa, like two fumbling adolescents, they made love.

*   *   *

They stayed together for all of the next day, and through a second night, in the discovery and rediscovery of passion each felt was deeper and more meaningful than all the onetime passion of first youth. They talked, they told each other as much of autobiography and truth as they could tell, and they withheld far more than either knew, the censors at their lips unsuspected by either one.

"I'll be more expansive about this someday," Matthew said once when he was talking of his marriage and of his wife. "I'm difficult to live with, I guess."

"Who isn't?"

"Marriage is difficult, is what you're saying."

"It also has its good things."

He nodded and seemed to be deciding what those were but he did not speak. They could sit silent and remain at ease; already they had discovered this about each other. The truncated form of their self-revelation was, they each understood, only for the present, for this newness which was still so enveloping that though they were not inhibited in seeking each other's bodies, they still were restrained, as strangers might be restrained, from too ready an outpouring of revelation involving others.

It's one difference between being a girl and being older, Dori thought in the middle of a silence after she had swiftly told him of the sudden ending of her life with Tony. When you're older you summarize, you don't lavish detail on every scene, even the huge ones; there's been too much piled up by the time you're forty. She could remember the readiness with which she would tell everything there was to tell about herself when she had gone out with her first dates, tell about herself as a girl at school, at college, tell of her first experiences with boys. When she met Tony, they had sat for hours in some booth or at some table in one of his favorite restaurants, each telling the other "everything" in the first generosities and trusts of new love, a new love that was going to last forever. Tony had been equally ready to tell everything about himself, details of his first dates, his first discovery of sleeping with a girl—a woman, twenty years older and kind and gentle, with a healthy attitude toward sex so that he was at his best with sex, never furtive, never ashamed, and had in turn doubtless trained her to be the same, brought her up to be the same, as it were, since he had been her first lover.

But now with Matthew, narrative was synopsized as she went along. It was almost as if she were gliding rapidly over most of her marriage to tell of its abrupt ending, and even that she told in a hurried way as if she were recapitulating something he already knew, as if she were fearful lest she sound the stereotypic whining woman, the hurt and injured woman she would hate to be, and hate to be thought to be.

She fell silent then, remembering its ending and the aftermath with disbelief that it could have been so terrible. Through month after month she had been a creature in the positive and cunning control of a thing stronger and more skillful than she, an almost animate savage that could spring at her, direct her thoughts, her sleep, her instincts. For all those months, twenty, thirty, nearly forty months, her own will could beat back that savage only when she was actually working; in the first minute after she whirled the last page out of her typewriter, the other took over, the boss other, the controlling other, reminding her not of pain but of the happy hours they had had before he had left her for Hazel, reminding her of sweet and good evenings, of lovemaking that had gratified each of them and both of them.

Twenty, thirty, nearly forty months, and then somehow she had realized that she was what people called "over it," as if one ever were truly over one's first great wound, as if the fading scar tissue were not permanently part of one, livid no longer but toughly existing forever.

Sex had begun to be possible again, not love but sex. Quite suddenly she had stayed overnight with a man who made fun of her refusal—"You're afraid you might feel happy again"—and it had been a night of violent sexuality that she had violently responded to, suddenly restored to life and appetite.

She had seen the man a few times more, aware that for her it was loveless as it was for him, mindless, no memories or hopes or past or future, nothing but the throbbing wet wonderful rise and fall again and again.

Soon enough she had refused to see him and he had not believed that she meant it. "Why not? Who's going

to get sore at you?" Nobody, she had agreed, and admitted that she ought to make better use of her free status, but she had gone on refusing, sinking again into the old unwanted and arid continence.

Why didn't she get married again, her friends had asked again and again. "You're so attractive and you can't really like living alone."

Nobody had understood that either and she had had no easy explanation. Hidden within her, doubtless, was the real answer; she had assured herself that she could reach down, find it, uproot it if she tried hard enough, if she needed to enough. But later, when searching for answers would no longer cause upheaval all over again.

But as time passed, her private creed had become, Let it be, leave it, don't touch, fragile. And now suddenly with Matthew, now in these two days and nights those wise admonitions no longer were necessary.

Now with Matthew—as she thought it, she touched his hair and closed her eyes in deepening intensity— she was finding again for the first time in all the lost long years the indescribable interweaving of sexual love and romantic love, both threaded through now with the gigantic new *perhaps* which those impersonal technicians off in some aseptic laboratory had already put their official negative or positive to, in some report that was surely in the mails at this very moment.

"No, we never had children," she had said in her swift account of her marriage. She did not say it airily as if it had never mattered but neither did she permit the tone or inflection of some major sadness that would flag his attention. Later, if it were pronounced true tomorrow by Dr. Jesskin, she would decide whether to tell him and how to tell him. Already she wanted him to know that she was no benighted barren woman; already she found herself wondering whether this might change her in his mind from the desirable unattached woman he thought her into a— into a what? A problem? A shock? An untouchable?

Just for now, she kept telling herself. Just this

couple of beautiful days. During the first evening he had telephoned his house, talked to his daughter, and the clear young voice of Hildy had sounded out to her across the room. "Are you still in Boston, Dad?" He had answered only "I won't be home until Thursday," and they had talked of other things. Her own telephone calls had been as free of explicit falsehood because nobody existed to whom she need tell or explain or alibi or dissemble. And she had thought, in extenuation she had not dreamed she needed, Otherwise I'd never never get through until Thursday morning with Dr. Jesskin. Now if something *is* wrong Thursday morning, now I could bear it.

To be hit by two such beginnings at one time! Almost it seemed that fate had sent Matthew to her now as a shield against the wildness of disappointment that might await her in the morning. And equally it seemed that this same fate was slyly asking her whether now she would still be overjoyed if the reports said yes, you are pregnant.

TWO »కు

THE TELEPHONE RANG and her hand whipped toward it. Matthew had left at eight and she must have fallen asleep again. Asleep when this was Thursday?

"Good morning, Mrs. Gray." It was Dr. Jesskin. It was the first time he had ever called her himself.

"It's positive!" Her words seemed to jump at the telephone.

"Let's not talk by phone. Can you come in at eleven?"

"Of course I can. But you have to tell me—it *is* positive, isn't it?"

"Yes."

"Oh God."

Instantly everything else receded into the background, even Matthew. She was electrified by the core knowledge of that *positive* and yet was quieted by it too. A quiet seemed to flow through her veins and along her nerves, like the quiet shared after making love, completed, willing to put aside whatever required attention, saying "not now" to would-be interrupters: questions of work undone, of infidelity, of what weight and value their sudden lovemaking would prove to have in the days ahead.

Nothing else matters, she thought, her hands flying to her hips, the fingers splaying out, their tips touching over her navel. Nothing else. Suddenly she doubted herself about Matthew. Had it been as real as it had seemed? Was it so irresistible because it would help get her through all the deliberate hours until Thursday morning?

She fled from that idea, but it was possible. She could not know now; now was dressing and getting over to Dr. Jesskin.

She thought of all the past years of Dr. Jesskin, all the visits, all the tests and treatments, the biopsies of uterine tissue to check on progress, the familiar steel speculum still warm from the gleaming sterilizer —it was curiously pleasant to remember, even, as she entered the waiting room this bright Thursday morning, suddenly new again, vivid, present, and yet strangely remote from her nerve centers where pain and envy could twinge, peaceful now as she glanced around at the other women waiting too.

All those years ago when she sat in this same waiting room, she had looked at the girls and women in their various stages of pregnancy, not with envy, but with a mute amazement that each of them could so easily accomplish what was so impossible for her.

Then, she used to avoid looking at Miss Mack or Miss Stein, the doctor's appointment secretary, both of whom knew all too well that she was one of his "other patients," who were there not because he was the obstetrician who would guide them through pregnancy and one happy day deliver them, but because he was also a "sterility specialist," a phrase he always quietly amended to "a specialist in so-called sterility."

I'm not sterile, I'm not barren. Dori could still hear her too earnest assurance to him on that first visit, as she had faltered through her recital, see him writing in her folder; it had held only a first page then.

Had he already added a notation this morning after the report had come in? Had he already written down the gist of what he was going to say to her today? And the questions he planned to ask? But she had no answers yet—except one.

Miss Mack signaled her, and ushered her directly into his office, closing the door with a soft snap behind her. Dr. Jesskin rose, silent, studying her as if she were a new patient whom he had never seen before.

"Oh, Dr. Jesskin, will you help me?"

She had rehearsed what she would say, but these were not the words she had ready. She had meant to thank him first for persistence and the rightness of his beliefs, and then only to speak of the present.

"Sit down," he said slowly, sitting down himself. "This is no time to hurry. That's why I said not to talk on the telephone." Before him was her folder, closed, but atop it was a single sheet of heavy stationery. He glanced at it and handed it to her.

She scarcely saw the letterhead of the laboratory or the half-dozen notations typed in at intervals, but the word *positive* leaped at her. Just seeing it there on the paper added stature to it, made it more true, no longer a guess or a possibility, but a fact.

"May I keep this?" she asked, her voice shaking.

Unexpectedly he smiled, and she put the report into her purse. "So," he said slowly, "you are pregnant."

"Will you help me?"

"Are you sure what you will do?"

"Of course I'm sure."

He nodded but his face was expressionless—a routine look, one of interest and attention that he would give to any patient. Neutral, Dori thought, he's being neutral again, and an undefined disappointment invaded her. "Are you able to take me as a patient even though I haven't married again?" She was neutral too, determined to keep pleading or apology out of her voice.

"Let us see these dates again," he said as if he had not heard her, and opened the folder. He seemed to be preparing his thoughts, laying them out neatly, as his instruments were laid out neatly on the tray by Miss Mack.

"You had intercourse only once since your last period," he said simply, "and that was on October sixteenth. The first period you missed was due about November third. You may have missed a second, since today is December seventh."

"A date that will live in infamy," she said, smiling,

but he only nodded.

"Usually we are uncertain about the precise date of intercourse and thus of conception, so to arrive at the most probable date of confinement we calculate backward three months from the onset of the last menstrual period, and then add seven days. But since you are sure of October sixteenth—"

"Quite sure. It was the date he was leaving for—"

He waved this aside as if he did not invite so personal a revelation. "In that case we can reckon forward two hundred and eighty days, which takes us to July twenty-third, nineteen sixty-eight. A few days earlier or later, but July twenty-third is our theoretical date." He was obviously reading from the page.

She drew in her breath. He had already put down the probable date: that simple act, that new notation in her twelve-year-old folder of struggle and frustration, suddenly was more convincing than a dozen laboratory reports.

"Are you able to take me, Dr. Jesskin, even though this will be what they call an illegitimate birth? It's not only that I am not married now but that I won't be. I don't want to fool you about that."

He closed the folder once more. "Why are you so sure? I do not wish to interrogate you, please understand."

"I do understand. I myself want to tell you. He— the man with whom I was having an affair—it was an affair, nothing more—we both knew all along that it was that, and we both knew it was ending."

"Now that you are pregnant, though?"

"I haven't told him. I don't know whether I should tell him. He's an awfully decent man, no scoundrel betraying me, and he assumed I was on the pill like everybody else until I told him once I wasn't because I couldn't get pregnant anyway."

His expression changed slightly; for an instant he looked gratified. "Has he, perhaps, the right to know?"

"I suppose it is a right, yes. But he's married and has four children, and we never talked of marriage,

never. Anyway he's away now, abroad, so I can take
enough time to think that out."

"Time, yes." He leaned toward her earnestly. "This
is why I asked you to come in so we might talk, the
way it is impossible to talk on a telephone. You haven't
yet taken enough time to think of all the other matters you must think about."

"But I have. I've thought about everything."

"About everything as it is now, yes. But have you
thought of six months from now when you will be
big? Or a year from now when you will have a four-
month-old baby? An adopted baby? A friend's baby?
A relative's baby, after some fatal accident to the parents? You have to think through all these things, talk
and discuss them, with whoever is the right person
to discuss such matters with."

"Why, Doctor, I already know—"

"We think sometimes with our minds, at other times
with our emotions, at other times only with our instincts. It is important now to give you enough time
for all three thinkings, and I am going to ask you to
go off and come back in two weeks for another visit."
He saw her face change and added mildly, "Did you
imagine I would then refer you to another doctor?"
He touched the buzzer and as Miss Mack appeared, he said formally, "Please set up an appointment for Mrs. Gray for week after next." He nodded
goodbye, and again Dori felt strangely disappointed.

*   *   *

All three thinkings. Only at rarest intervals did he slip
into a foreignism that revealed his Scandinavian
childhood, Danish, Swedish, whatever it was, but there
always was a pleasing measured way he used language and occasionally a phrase that stayed with her.

All three thinkings. The mind, the emotions, the
instincts. But she had already engaged them all, she
thought, and the results were final. I can't possibly
conceive of changing my mind, even if I were to think
for months instead of weeks.

I can't possibly conceive. That word—mysterious, powerful, ordinary, gigantic. I have conceived. I could never conceive, I did not conceive, but now I have conceived. What a conjugation for a woman of forty.

Think and discuss and consider. If Cele were in, she could go right over and, perhaps tonight, she would tell her brother Gene.

In the pale winter sunlight a glass telephone booth glinted at her from the corner of Madison and she opened her purse for a dime. Suddenly she felt an irrational impulse to call Tony and tell him. To telephone him this minute, though she had not spoken to him for ten years, call him right at his office and say, I told you I could, I always knew that someday it would be all right again as Dr. Jesskin said; it might have happened years ago but you ended that chance when you ended everything else. As quickly as the idea had come it fled. Tony? Why Tony at this late date? She stood contemplating the glass booth and remembered Tony's voice that last night, telling her he had been having an affair with Hazel for nearly a year.

"And letting me go right on with Dr. Jesskin?" she had cried out. "How could you, oh why didn't you make me stop trying? Letting me watch my ovulation dates? Making love to me on our special schedule? Oh God, how horrible, that you let me go right on."

She turned quickly away from the booth. Dignity, the straitjacket. She would no more make such a call than fling a rock through the nearest shopwindow. Yet she had been lost for a minute in a reverie of revenge that she had long thought done with forever.

Another booth beckoned to her from the next corner. What she really wanted to do was to tell everybody in the whole damn world. She wanted to phone the paper and tell them, she wanted to call all her friends who had always been so polite about her being childless, she wanted to wire Alan and Lucia in San Francisco and cable Ron in London.

Matthew. Matthew Poole.

Memory filled her: the sound of his voice, his touch, the feel of his hands, his body, the way he took charge, solicitous yet taking charge—that male authority that made it so wonderful to be female. The morning had falsified something; from the moment Dr. Jesskin phoned the word *positive,* she had pushed Matthew aside, and distrusted their two nights as an episode to speed time along. An episode? For her who had never been able to go in for a two-day episode, never in all the years?

It's more, she thought, and for the first time an unwillingness dragged at her. A few weeks was the longest they had. How many weeks? Two, three? At home, alone, naked? She saw again the way he had looked at her when she was last naked before him, when they had left the sofa and the living room and gone decently to her bedroom, undressing, standing revealed to each other. She knew about her body, her one vanity perhaps, certainly her least wavering vanity.

He saw nothing of her "tentative orbing," knew nothing of its newness, its meaning. But in two or three weeks—how soon would she be too changed to let him see her?

Don't, she thought, don't think ahead. She went into the telephone booth and called Cele. "The most incredible thing has happened—can I come over?"

"Sure. The plumber's here. Give me twenty minutes."

"I'll walk."

*   *   *

She walked along trying to decide how to tell Cele—spring it at her? lead her slowly along and let her guess?—and she found herself thinking of a thousand other things instead. *Ab ovo,* Martha Litton had said so archly in the interview and she had put aside her notes, knowing that here it was at last, the only kind of thing that ever explained anybody. But did her own childhood explain her?

If so it eluded her, for when she tried to think back about her own beginnings she found herself skipping from the story they always told—"I was born the night Lindy flew to Paris"—a story that struck her as sickening in its little-girl cuteness, skipping all the way to that line on the application blank for Wellesley when she had so hurt her mother and infuriated her father. "Episcopalian and/or Jewish," she had written, thinking herself so witty. What a row had ensued, what a frightful fracas with her father, one of the many and one of the worst. Though she was the youngest and the only girl and thus the supposed easy favorite with her father over her three brothers, she was in actuality a constant irritant to him from the moment she was turned New Dealer almost overnight by the simple act of going to a fine rich college where virtually the entire student body worshiped Franklin Delano Roosevelt and all his works. She who would tell anybody anything could barely admit to her new friends that her father hated labor, that he was part owner of a factory which fought unions, that he was rich and Republican and revolting about the poor.

She did admit it to her freshman roommate, and the sterling advice she received about "how to handle reactionary parents" was the first political solidarity she had ever experienced. That was Celia Kahn and that solidarity had never wavered thereafter. Perhaps that was why she felt that her real history began not with childhood but with Cele, although college too was like a prelude history, a preface, with the real Chapter One beginning four years later in the little furnished apartment Tony had on East Tenth, the first time she went there with him and knew that at last she was not going to pull back and say no. In 1948, three years after the end of war, she was still not only a virgin but a girl who had never much wanted to stop being a virgin. At twenty-one she had never really been in love. All through college, whenever she and Cele had one of their all-night talking bouts about boys and sex and how far you could go, she had never really had the kind of wild juicy episode that Cele so often told her about. "You're a slow starter, Dorr," Cele had once told her with great authority. "When it finally hits you, glory hallelujah."

It hadn't been glory hallelujah until Tony. Cele, then, was already married to Marshall Duke who was just starting out with a recording company and they quickly drifted into a related but quite different status. They were two married couples, whose separate, past loyalties confused and complicated the new demands of marriage. But soon enough she and Cele had rediscovered their older closeness and it had never again lost its private vitality. When Tony left, Cele saw her through those first empty weekends, the first summer and, the first Christmas. Later, when her life had become normal again, it was Cele who played matchmaker, a role she had always avoided. Whenever she or Marshall met an interesting new person, young or old, married or single, she had asked Dori over for drinks or dinner to meet him.

It was Cele who had first urged Dori to quit the newspaper grind for good, particularly since the journalistic debacle that had robbed her of the daily paper she had been with for fifteen years and put her on a rather amateurish, though well-meaning, weekly. "You've got some cash stashed away," Cele had said, "and you're rent-controlled, so you could ride out even a bad break in free-lancing."

"Thank God for that." Her fervent tone had sprung out of her proprietary sense about her four-room apartment, not inexpensive since it was two hundred a month, but protected from the wildly rising prices all about because it was in an old building, still under rent control. She cherished its large square rooms, its thick walls and doors, its windows looking down on a sunny quiet street, even its slightly worn look that told of ten years of her life in it.

But she was glad too that she did have some money, about thirteen thousand dollars, from money left by her father, minus death taxes, which had come in

equal shares to her brothers and herself on their
mother's death three years ago, minus further death
taxes. And she had, more importantly perhaps, the
equally solid fact that her special pieces had appeared
in many magazines, little ones, big ones, occasionally
in political ones and in the more literate women's
magazines, though never in the ones that prided themselves on being "service magazines" as if they were
roadside service stations for offering the most hum-
drum of provisions to keep you going. Nor did she
write for the fashion magazines, with their satiny
vocabularies, or for the one magazine most young
writers looked upon as their one particular goal, *The
New Yorker.* She had sold one piece to it when she
had just begun to write, a caustic tale about a smart
hostess, and when they bought it she had been as
elated as she was supposed to be. But then she had
tried other pieces in her more natural vein, with
some feeling, with some emotion, even indignation,
and these had been turned down—with kindly notes
instead of printed rejection slips, telling her the editors still remembered the nice irony of "The Party" and
hoped to see more of her work soon. She gave up sub-
mitting to *The New Yorker;* nice irony was not what
gave her pleasure in writing, though she made a
mental note to check that for sour grapes when
enough time had elapsed for perspective's sake. She
did so several times and each time decided it was true.
"Keep your cool" was not her life slogan.

"You're too intense, Dori," her mother had once
told her during the first year of her divorce. Then, before she could reply, her mother had added, "And
thank God you are. It's the best, on balance."

"You blow your cool about this damn war," Dick
Towson had said more recently.

"I have no cool. I hope I never do have."

Cool, coolth, cool it—the great desideratum of so
many people in today's world. It was a living-in-ice, a
living away from, never impassioned about right or
wrong, never hot under the collar, never half sick with

pain or pity. Keep your cool—a whole generation was chanting the slogan and they thought it was just an *in* phrase of the young, never seeing the paucity within their own lives that led them to this revealing admiration.

Not a *whole* generation. Not the young protesters on the marches and picket lines, not the boys refusing to kill, not the fathers and mothers who supported them, not the lawyers who defended them in court. Matthew—

She wouldn't tell Cele about Matthew. Not now. Not until she knew what it meant, what it would mean. Never had they confided to each other in the small tattling ways about men or marriage or sex, never since the half-bragging talk of college days. Cele did know about Dick Towson, vaguely, in large outline, and also knew that it was over or virtually over.

Poor Cele, she suddenly thought, she's so sure it will be at least a year before anything new starts up for me. She's probably all set for another one of my celibate years where she worries her head off about me.

"Mrs. Gray." It was Cele's maid, standing in the open kitchen door of the house to accept delivery of a parcel. "You going right past me like that?"

"Why, Minnie, I didn't know I was already here."

*   *   *

As she listened, Celia Duke's face went bright with pleasure. "Then what?" she would prompt if Dori paused in her recital. "What did Dr. Jesskin mean by that?" At the end she said, "So you have two weeks to think and discuss. Think and discuss what?" She looked around the room, searching, and they both laughed. Then she suddenly went over to Dori and hugged her. "It's so great, Dorr. Congratulations."

"Oh Cele. Dr. Jesskin was so professional and neutral, it's lovely to have somebody happy about it."

"He wanted to stay tentative so you could still change your mind in the next two weeks. It would still be safe two weeks from now—"

"To go back and say, 'After all I think I'll have an abortion'? He knows I'd never—God, it's nearly thirteen years since I first went to his office. No, it must have been something else; maybe he wondered if now I'd be getting married. Maybe he was thinking about his own position. What do I really know about him? He might be the most churchgoing moralist alive."

"Want to bet?"

Dori apparently did not hear her. "Cele, when will I begin to show?"

"Let's see, this is the seventh week? Three more to New Year's, four in January—not till February at the earliest. He'll order you to watch your weight and stay thin anyway. They all do now."

"Can you remember when you began to look big?"

"Well, me." She looked down at herself. "I look a leetle bit, right now." She was wearing her usual stretch pants despite the ten pounds she had gained in the last few years. "But you're not weak-minded like me and you'll stay thin for ages."

"You mean I can keep on seeing people for another month, month and half?"

She said this so eagerly that Cele laughed. "What's wrong with you? Do you think you get pregnant one minute and start bulging the next? What about all the nineteenth-century novels where the dear servant girl goes unsuspected right up to the time she bears the child?"

"Hoopskirts. Crinolines."

"So now we've got tent dresses and shifts. Nobody will suspect for ages unless you tell them. Are you going to tell them at the paper?"

"Of course *not*."

"I didn't know. You didn't say."

"You mean—" She examined Cele's expression with sudden interest. "You mean, be the emancipated female and not keep it secret at all?"

"I didn't mean anything."

"Do you think I *should*?"

There was a pause and then Cele said slowly, "Look, Dorr, that's maybe the biggest of the three thinkings Dr. Jesskin meant. And it's got to be all yours. I would be ghastly to try to influence you."

"I guess I just took it for granted this wasn't something you announced on a loudspeaker." She hesitated. "I was already thinking of where to go until it was over, what name I'd go under, how I'd get mail, all sorts of cloak-and-dagger stuff like that."

"Did you decide on a place?"

"Remember how crazy we were about the Grand Tetons? Not right in Jackson Hole where I'd run into people from the ranch, but some small town around in there."

"Wyoming? With your doctor in Manhattan?"

"I guess I overlooked that small matter of mileage. How often do I see Dr. Jesskin? Once a month?"

"About." She looked perplexed. "Isn't it weird, the things you forget that you were sure you never would forget? Me with three kids and I can't be sure. I guess once a month, to start with anyway."

"Apart from Dr. Jesskin, I wouldn't go that far because then I'd be cut off from the only people who know about it." She hesitated. "How will Marshall take it?"

"The way you and I take it." She spoke with vigor, but she looked uncertain. "Well, I don't know, at that. He can be pretty square at times. He didn't use to be, but he does seem to be changing."

"Lizzie starting to date. That would do it."

"The damn pill. He assumes Liz has a prescription on her own."

They exchanged looks that said, Men. "Maybe it would be better not to tell him for a while."

"I'd blow my top," Celia said, "if I couldn't tell somebody." As the words were spoken, as they became entities, alive, she drew back from them, disowning them. "There's the rub, isn't it?"

"I suppose."

"Who else is going to know?"

"Only Gene and Ellen."

"Oh."

"What does 'Oh' mean?"

"Nothing." *Oh* meant, Too bad Ellen has to be in on it, and Dori knew that it meant that, so there was no point in elaborating. "What about Ron and Alan?"

"I hadn't even thought of them. Isn't that family love for you? If my mother were alive she would have worried but been happy and I think my brother Gene will be, but Ron and Alan?" She made a face.

Gene was the only one of her brothers whom she admired completely and for whom she felt a family warmth that was not briefly assumed at Christmas. He was older than the others, being fifty, and the only one who had always lived in New York, but her separateness from the other two was due to far more than geographical distance.

Ron, three years younger than Gene, had long ago settled in London where he was a partner in some fine neocolonial oil company operating in the Middle East, and Alan, who was only about a year older than she, was farthest away in everything that mattered to her. He lived in San Francisco with his wealthy wife Lucia, who seemed another species, come from another world, the world of the Social Register, of the D.A.R. and genealogy, and he seemed to enjoy that world with her, enjoy their status as Important People, going to the right dinner parties, belonging to the right clubs, sending their children to the right schools and camps. When it came to books and ideas, Lucia was close to being an ignoramus, and Alan didn't even seem to mind, which made him incomprehensible to Dori.

Alan was the only one of the four who had opted for the answer "Episcopalian" when the question "Religion?" turned up on a printed form; the other three wrote "None," meaning it. Even that had not really satisfied her father, though he had merely grumbled with the others, reserving his explosion for her and her inspiration of "Episcopalian and/or Jewish." Her mother who was Jewish by birth had only said, "You're making it seem like a joke," but her father had shouted, "if you're ashamed to write 'atheist,'" shouting it with a huger wrath than one indiscretion could have earned, even so monstrous an indiscretion. She had thought then that he was taking out on her all the rage he had suppressed over the boys, and had been infuriated at the injustice. Actually the one area of life where she could and did admire her father was religion: the amazing fact that he, Eugene Arling Varley, son of an Episcopal minister, had had the independence to declare himself not an agnostic but an atheist, to declare it as a youth and maintain it throughout a long life among traditionalists and conformists of every kind.

Suddenly Dori smiled. How predictable, that she thought of her mother and father now, in these first hours of discovery about herself. She looked at Cele as if she too must be smiling, but Cele was not looking at her at all. Her face had changed; it was somber.

"Look, Dori, here's something I probably ought not to say, but I have to."

"What?"

"It's none of my business."

"I've made it your business. Say it."

"It's something that's been bothering me a lot, but I might—"

"Cele, stop fussing."

"Okay, you don't want to say who the man is, I'm not going to guess. But if it's somebody who's married and has lots of children and can't get free, then how about finding somebody else?"

"Somebody else?"

"Lots of women in the history of the world have told somebody who wasn't the father that he was."

"But who? Just pick somebody off the street?"

"You could start an affair now, and then a month or so from now, tell him and get married."

"Celia!"

"I don't mean some stranger, but I thought just now,

What if there's somebody she likes, somebody she's drawn to, who isn't all tied up with a family?" She saw Dori's look and drew back from it. "Oh, skip it. It's a rotten idea. I'm the one could go in for finagling, not you, so forget it."

Dori said nothing. The right words would not come. She could not say, That's such a cheap trick; but she could not stop the words from forming in her own mind. There was a sudden sweetness pulling at her too, a sudden longing to try it, to do what millions of other women had done in the history of the world, the traditional silence to a husband when a child came from an adultery, the traditional means of snaring an unwilling boy into wedlock. In her mind's imagery there suddenly appeared, tiny, floating as if they were suspended in a golden bubble, herself and Matthew, their hands extended toward each other as if to hold a sudden happiness, unexpected, unsought, all at once theirs. "If I thought I could carry it off," she said at last. "But I'm such a rotten liar, I'd be sure to blurt it out sooner or later, and then what?"

"Forget it. It's an n.g. idea. What about some small town around Washington? You could fly here on a shuttle to see Jesskin, I could meet you at the airport and drive you. How many people do you know down there that you'd run into?"

"Apart from Lyndon and such? Not anybody, and with Lyndon it's not reciprocal." She laughed. "If we're talking of an hour by plane, then how about Boston somewhere? Or the Cape?"

"It would be all right in February or March, but what about hot weather when it's mobbed?"

Dori was already rejecting the Cape. "It ought to be some place you get to by car; you always run into people you know at airports."

"Oh let's skip all that for now. We'll hit on the perfect hideout when we're not so jazzed up. Oh, Dorr, it keeps coming at me: it happened. After all this time, it finally happened."

THREE ›੩❧

HE TRIED AGAIN, and again there was no answer. Off
and on all morning Matthew Poole had tried to reach
her to say whatever there might be to say, what he did
not know. She was out. Each time he tried to call her,
he had left his office and phoned from the row of
booths in the lobby, though his secretary would never
lift the receiver once the bulb on her desk glowed red.
Knowing that was not enough. It was not security he
needed but a sense of unrupturable privacy which he
could not have in the realm of his busy office with the
door opened at precisely the wrong moment by one of
his partners.

Dori was asleep when he left at eight, not really
asleep rather, for she was still smiling—smiling and
happy, her eyes closed and sleep drifting into her
again, or was it she who was drifting into sleep? He
liked the first phrasing. She had begun to wake while
he was dressing and he had told her not to let herself
really wake—it had been nearly five when they had
gone to sleep, a loss of rest he might have deplored or
resented at some other time but which now was one
more token of success and fulfillment. She had drowsily nodded at his words and her eyes had closed and
she had smiled.

Why should he be so touched by this one small point,
this small embellishment? Finding no answer, he at
once felt impatient and desirous, a loutish need to go
straight back to her and, almost without greeting, put
her down on that sofa, or the bed, or the floor, and
fall upon her as if he had not been near a woman for

a year. There was something in her own passion that roused him beyond restraint; it was not merely that she was new, nor that they were ten thousand miles removed from the fatigue of familiarity—

He dismissed the thought, as a treachery, a lie, a tawdry falsehood. Not everybody experienced the lessening of desire in marriage, at least not to the extent he knew. Jack and Alma were still good together; Jack Henning was his closest friend and he had said so, unequivocally with a thumping robust lewdness that he, Matthew, had called a boast, a brag, all the while knowing that it was exactly the truth. Jack Henning was his age and had been married as long as he, and would not bother to say they were good together if they had long since lost the impulse toward one another that sought and was satisfied, sought and was satisfied, even at lengthening intervals as was inevitable with the passing of time. No man in his forties was fool enough to hope that after years of marriage and familiarity there would be the initial frenzy of need, the same insistence and insatiability. But if one could sustain that in marriage, how fortunate that man would be.

Man or woman. He thought of Joan. Perhaps she also had found that sexual delight—not merely sexual satisfaction striven for and achieved, sometimes arduously achieved, but spontaneous sexual delight—was to be had now only with another man. Had she anybody else? He had asked himself that several times in the past few years, for she was as tactful as he about not going near any situation between them that would normally lead them to bed together, and each time he asked it with less need to know the answer.

Once again he left his desk, this time for a luncheon appointment with two clients, about a contract that had been abrogated, not a case that caught at his deepest interests. His years of self-discipline in the practice of his profession, however, marshaled his full abilities to their discussion, but interrupting his concentrated attention there was the knowledge that there was a girl in the world he was suddenly entwined with, a girl he would soon be talking to again, seeing again, taking to bed again. He had gone home in the morning for breakfast with the kids, letting them assume he was coming from the airport; then he had changed and shaved and left for the office. That night the Hennings were due for dinner; he considered calling it off and seeing Dori again but it was so rare that they had people in for an evening that he had let it alone.

After luncheon he tried her number again; she was still out. Suddenly he was vexed and angry. She had mentioned some morning appointment; she must have gone straight to the paper after it. She had talked about her job, not very fully, as if she had only partial interest in the new arrangement on the new paper, compared to the years of attachment to the troubled *Trib* which had finally gone under. He called the paper. She was out, perhaps on assignment. "She doesn't keep staff hours," a voice said, and he replied with a brisk "I know, thanks."

Persistent—he had always been called a persistent devil by people who did not like him and he supposed it was true enough. He had been called self-centered too, and that was doubtless equally true. Even in love that seemed the most outgoing and generous, the love for one's children, was there not in fact an enormity of self-interest? Was there any joy he had ever known comparable to the joy he felt in Hildy and in Johnny?

His father must have felt that about him, but he was ten when his father died and he had virtually no memory of him. His mother, a lawyer like his father, most certainly had felt— He stopped quickly; he did not want to think of his mother just then.

He tried the telephone again and gave up. He would send some flowers and try to put Dori out of his mind. Each hour made her more vivid, made their two days more important in retrospect. This was no simple affair; he had had affairs ranging all the way from a quick easy encounter to a complicated convoluted entanglement from which he soon had need only to escape; he knew affairs and needed them and valued them for the part they played in keeping a none too happy life going.

The Hennings made the evening easier. He marveled again at how pleasant it was to have good friends in one's own house, at one's own table, with one's children there, scrubbed and sweet and clever; in a year Hildy would be off to college, and God knows what rebellious young Johnny would take it into his head to be doing. But it was good.

Usually the people Matthew valued he saw away from the house. In the office, over luncheon, over drinks, during the summer months when Joan and the kids were away at Truro—his own personal friendships, except for the Hennings, were normally carried on in the world outside. He no longer struggled to change that, and no longer struggled to remake Joan. How could a man be angry at a wife because she was shy? He could, at the beginning, try to get her past it, try to help her overcome it, try to coax, urge, wheedle, give her moral support, but if finally he saw that there was some incurable, some neurotic cut to her character that made her half sick with apprehension about meeting people, welcoming them, entertaining them at home, why, then, finally he had to accept her as she was and change his own expectations and his own ways of behaving.

Long ago he had learned that it was too difficult to have friends come to the house for dinner or the evening. Inevitably they felt so chilled that sooner or later they remained away, as one remains indoors in inclement weather. Not that if was Joan's purpose to freeze them out. At the beginning, in the first year of their marriage, she had tried to make all his friends welcome, and with the Hennings she had succeeded. Jack was so easygoing himself, with such equability and good nature, that he was easily able to ignore Joan's manner, able indeed to admire Matthew for handling it so adroitly. Alma Henning was not so equable; for a long time she had been confused by her own inability to get through to Joan but she had finally seen that there was no point in pushing for a level of easy camaraderie that wasn't within Joan's grasp, and she had let it go at that. Matthew was interesting enough by himself, she had once told her husband, and he and Matthew together took over the evenings anyway, so that she could relax into a low output of effort and get by. While they were young, with no maid in either household, she would help Joan with dinner and washing up, and since they had their first babies in the same year, a surface kind of talk was easy. Later it was harder but Alma kept on managing and Matthew had been grateful. With lesser friends than the Hennings it had always been the same depressing cycle: the hearty first visit, the less hearty second, a straining and striving, and sooner or later an excuse offered and an invitation turned down.

"She's shy," he had said in those early days when he loved Joan with a young man's fervor. He had said it to his own mother again and again, his mother who had been so happy when he married, so quick to praise Joan's looks, to approve their apartment, admire Joan's cooking, Joan's taste. "It's only that she's shy." For a while it had been enough, though long afterwards, after his mother's death when it was too late, he had seen it could never have been enough, that his mother had been far too intelligent not to see the small wounds Joan gave her for exactly what they were, Joan's nonappearance the first time they were asked up to meet some of her friends, Joan's last-minute backing out as they were about to go to a funny movie; Joan's withholding of any sign of warmth.

But at the time he had seen only the week-to-week particularity, never the total that was putting itself together. Gradually—who could trace back these minor sadnesses?—every visit from or to his mother had become a tension, with the span between arrival and departure growing shorter and shorter, with a sort of gelid determination keeping the talk going.

Once when he had chided Joan for never calling his mother week in and week out, she had wept, and in the first year of marriage a bride's tears could outlaw any other consideration. "Darling, nothing could be worth your being so unhappy."

He would do the phoning himself, he had decided, but somehow he did not. As time piled itself on time, he had begun to think that when they had children, all would be well; Joan would not be so shy, there would be the natural talk and shared love that everybody could partake of. But Hildy's birth had deepened the chasm. Joan by then had yielded totally to her own aversion for her mother-in-law, still denying the aversion but no longer making even one phone call a year to her.

He should have put his foot down hard—now he saw it—should have turned on Joan and said, Damn it, suppose I treated your mother this way? Make do, put on an act at least with mine; she is getting old and she loves me and she has never hurt you and this damn cliché of daughter-in-law antipathy is not going to be our cliché anymore. Millions of families the world over have the mother-in-law–daughter-in-law problem, and somehow they cope, so damn it, you cope.

But he had never said it. When Hildy was born, his mother had come up once or twice; each time had been stiffly formal, like a state visit, with everybody knowing it would last no more than half an hour.

"Would you like to hold the baby?" He could still hear Joan saying it, politely, distantly, could still see his mother sitting alone on their sofa, holding her first grandchild, looking mostly down at the baby, sitting there as if she were a stranger in her son's house, which of course she was.

The last such visit had ended with Joan saying at the closing door, "Thank you for coming," in the tone one would have used to a visiting teacher from the neighborhood school. He had seen his mother's face change, but his one emotion was relief that the door was closing and the miserable visit ending.

Again months passed and again he determined to institute some communication between them. But the sight of the telephone would make him wonder what to say; the pen in his hand would pause after "Dear Mother." She did not call him either; only occasionally did he let himself know that her silence was a dignity. Then he would wonder if he were being callous with his own silences, perhaps even cruel, but the very idea of having it out with her made him uneasy. Reproof, the rebuke of women—he had always hated it and instinctively turned away from it.

Hildy began to talk, Hildy began to walk, Hildy was one year old and then two, enchanting as all two-year-olds are enchanting, and never once did he decide, It is too much, whatever is wrong between Joan and her, she doesn't deserve this from me. Only during the last weeks before Johnny's birth did he finally tell Joan he was going to start seeing his mother alone, taking Hildy along too, but before he actually did it, there was a phone call from her office that she had had a severe coronary and had died. The unknown voice had added tonelessly that of course it was the third attack in little over a year.

"Yes," he had said as tonelessly.

He resented her death. His mother had never told him of any of these attacks, had robbed him of the chance to set things right between them, had left him with words unsaid that would now stay unspoken forever. But he had sobbed that night when he was alone and forced himself to put names to his actions and his non-actions, still rejecting "cruel" or "callous," but seeking on, as if he were in a courtroom, himself both the accuser and the accused.

Only later, a long time later, could he accept the first fringe of truth in his unwilling fingers. He was not cruel or callous, but he couldn't handle emotional problems close to the nerve. He reacted badly, he could think only of how to end them, deaden them, escape them, nullify them. It was a weakness; he did not like it in himself. In any marriage it could become a major danger. In any love affair it was a danger too.

He had been married for eight years when he had his first affair. It released him from a thousand docilities and a thousand blindnesses; he felt a man renewed, his own man. Joan knew instinctively that he was no longer the same Matthew, and he agreed that she was right. "You're having an affair," she had said. "Am I?" he had answered, and she had accepted it for the statement he had meant it to be.

The idea of divorce must have occurred to Joan in the next nine years, as it had occurred to him; in the most banal of all phrases, they had stayed together because of the children. They had each stayed married because neither could consider giving up the one true pleasure left. The children were, to him, the full source of happiness and pride; to leave them, to see them only at preordained intervals, to drop out of their daily living, was not to be contemplated. The children and his work—that was enough.

And then he went to Marshall Duke's house and met Dori Gray. How could one know so surely that here was haven, here was a readiness for warmth, to receive it and to give it, here was eagerness and need? He had known it and had felt himself respond to it and had known that his life was going to change.

Now sitting silent over coffee with the Hennings, he thought of her again as she had been when he left her that morning, saw again the faint curving of a smile on her sleepy lips. Something had stirred in him at the sight, had touched him, and he had been unable to catch it. He had wanted to waken her, to tell her again how he felt, but he had kept silent, staring down at her, saying nothing. Was it that silence that had brought him twelve hours later to remembering his mother and the words unspoken forever to her? How strange, how harsh and unbidden, the associative freaks of memory, and how helpless one was against them. Yet this harshness now did not repel him; it seemed to speak to him with an urgency he did not yet understand, in a code he could not yet decipher.

* * *

Eugene Bradford Varley, named after his grandfather, was well aware that he was Dori's favorite brother and equally aware, he asserted, that he deserved to be. "If I were a low-minded oil tycoon like Ron," he had once said, "I wouldn't expect anybody but oil wells to like me, and if I were a high-minded snob like Alan, I'd not even expect that."

This amiable self-esteem was one of the characteristics Dori found so likable in him and one she wished she shared. Gene never needed reassurance from anybody about anything. He never needed to explain himself, justify himself, defend himself. If you disapproved of something he said or did, you disapproved; it was your right. If you tried to persuade him to change, he might try in turn to persuade you that he need not change, that you might have overlooked this or that aspect of the matter, but his attempt at persuasion would be mild, low-keyed and brief. If you opposed him outright, and showed scorn or anger or, worst of all, indifference, he drew down a windowshade in his eyes and closed you out, and you knew that you would not have the chance again to show scorn or anger or indifference because you would not be likely to see Gene Varley even one more time.

Which made him, Dori had once told him, a despot. A nice despot, a rational despot, but a despot nevertheless, because his rule over his emotions and his mind was absolute. "Most of us poor benighted folk," she had said, "are always taking Gallup polls of our own constituent opinions before we can finally point to one as the probable winner." He had agreed that he generally spared himself the wear and tear of inner conflict and had said it in a way that told her she would do well to start doing the same.

But all that was a long time ago and a general observation. He wouldn't need to admonish her now, she thought, as she picked up the telephone to call him. She was still at Cele's. How the day had vanished she did not know; they had gone out to lunch together and ordered celebratory champagne cocktails; they had gone to a music store for some records they each wanted for Christmas gifts and then to a bookstore as well. Now suddenly it was four and the early twilight of winter had begun and she was afraid she had waited too late in the day.

"Professor Varley, please." She almost never called him at the university, for she never knew his schedule of classes, seminars or student meetings. He picked up the phone, sounding affable. "It's me, Gene. I wondered if I could come over tonight. There's something I'd love to talk over if you're free."

She heard him ask his secretary whether there was anything on his calendar and knew there would not be. Ellen long ago had learned to compress their social life into the weekends, since he was so opposed to any ordained activity during the evenings of his bursting workweek. The university aside, he was a voracious reader; he loved music; he could spend hours in his darkroom, developing the dozens of extremely good pictures he had managed somehow to take since his last bout with his cameras. Bout was the wrong word, for his addiction was chronic and endless, with nothing intermittent about it, though with Jim and Dan both grown and gone from home, his favorite and handiest subjects were no longer easily available and his addiction harder to support.

"Looks okay tonight," he said. "Around seven?"

"I'd thought about eight, eight thirty. I'm at Cele's for dinner but I can leave right after. They're going to the theater."

"Fine. Then come whenever."

"Thanks. I hoped it could be tonight."

"Anything wrong?"

"Quite the opposite. Something great."

"You got fired!"

"You idiot." She laughed and thought, How like Gene. He was even more unequivocal than Cele about urging her to try free-lancing, and with a tougher practicality in his argument. "You've got a certain leverage, Dori, though I wish you'd cut out from that savings bank and into this boiling bull market. But even so unless you want to try for the *Times* or the *News,* neither of which would have the sense to want your kind of stuff, what sort of future is there for newspapering in New York?"

"No future, but don't crowd me."

He never crowded her. She did have a certain leverage—and some part of her training by her businessman father made her hold back from chipping it away on frivolity or risking it in the market like everybody else. She had never regretted rejecting alimony; to her lawyer's astonished protests, she had only said, "I happen not to be the alimony type."

Over the years she had discovered that she liked having something solid, liked seeing the interest mount up, a few hundred dollars a year, liked it when intangibles like inflation forced banks to raise interest rates on loans she had never yet made and on deposits she had never yet depleted. Oh hypocrisy, she sometimes thought. It's a wartime inflation because of an undeclared war you despise. But you don't refuse the interest, you don't give it away, you would be embarrassed to be such a crank, such a high-principled nut. You like it. You like the feeling it gives you. Especially when something comes up that takes money. Like now.

If she had had to go to Cele asking for a loan, how different today would have been. If she were going now to Gene to ask for support, how she would dread this visit. If she were penniless, unable to give up her weekly pay, how fearful a problem would be facing her. Suddenly she imagined a procession of frightened girls, as if they were figures on a frieze, their heads bowed, their faces tight with terror, all caught in the horror of unsought and unwanted pregnancy. Was it only money that made the difference?

"What's the big news?" her brother asked as she arrived. "Here, I'll take that." He took her coat, and then threw it at one of the chairs in the square entrance hall of the apartment.

"You're a help," Dori said, retrieving it and hanging it up in the coat closet. From the living room Ellen called, "Coffee—come on in," and almost at once Dori was repeating the opening words she had used that morning with Celia. "The most incredible thing has happened." But as she went on swiftly to tell them, Ellen said, "Oh, *no*," her eyes wretched. Gene said, "Good Lord, that is news," and did something she had never seen him do. He began to pace the room. Up and down, back and forth, in silence, he crossed and recrossed it, going off to the windows, coming back to them on the sofa, but turning quickly as if he were forbidden to sit down.

Dori thought, For once it's me who's without conflict. Under the bravado she felt a distance from them, not unexpected from Ellen but lonely and unlooked-for from her brother. He was now standing at the windows, drawing the draperies back and looking carefully out at the night as if the slow drift of snow had become a matter of professional concern.

"The one thing I do know," he said at last, coming back to them, "the one sure thing is that keeping it a secret won't work. Whether you go to Wyoming or some town in Vermont or even go visit Ron and Maude in England—no matter where you try to hide out, this is bound to get out."

"Why? Who'd want to do me in the eye enough to tell it?"

"Nobody would want to. Say you don't have one enemy in the world. Say you don't know one gossip in the world. Say you don't even know one careless person in the world. Just the same it's going to get talked about somehow, by somebody, either viciously or innocently as hell, with no faintest ulterior motive. In any case, goodbye secret."

"Then okay," Dori said vigorously. "If it's 'goodbye secret,' it's goodbye. I can't see why it has to, though. Only you two and the Dukes are going to know. Maybe not Marshall—Cele wasn't sure she'd tell him."

"Why not?" Ellen said, not looking at her.

"He's pretty conventional, under all that modern talk."

Ellen seemed about to defend Marshall but changed her mind. "What about Jim and Dan? You don't want us to keep it from them or their wives, the way Cele intends to keep it from Marshall?"

Before Dori could answer, Gene put in mildly, "Dori hasn't had time to even consider Jim and Ruth or Dan and Amy. What we do about them can be put off for just now, can't it?"

"I was only thinking," Ellen said quickly. Then she addressed herself to Dori once more. "Not that they couldn't be trusted to keep a secret. I'm sure nobody would *want* to do you in the eye. Heavens. But I think Gene is right—somebody is bound to forget and say something—"

"Would you forget?"

"Don't sound that way," Ellen answered.

"What way?"

"I don't know."

But Dori knew. She had been so sure of warmth and approval, and she had been suddenly reminded that neither warmth nor approval was as automatically bestowed as one wanted them to be. She glanced up at her brother, but he had resumed his pacing. There was again a silence and Ellen said, "We all need a drink. I'll go get ice cubes." Dori looked after her. There had always been some basic distance between herself and Ellen, what she jokingly called "the in-law mile," but usually it was bridged over by the civilized cement of good manners because of Gene and the boys. To find Gene distant as well was another matter entirely, and inside her something ached and something else was angry.

As if he had suddenly realized that Ellen had left them alone, Gene turned and spoke hurriedly. "The grocer might talk, in whatever small town you go to, the postman, the next-door neighbor, the druggist, whatever story you tell them about your missing husband. That's what Ellen meant, that somehow it would get out and start being a nice juicy scandal. Why can't you come here?"

"Here?"

"Right here with us, for the duration. You can have Jim's old room, or Dan's, and if we have guests, you can lock your door and stay put."

"Oh Gene." Unexpectedly her eyes stung. She should have known, through all the pacing and all the silence. "Thanks for asking me, but of course that's impossible."

"What's so impossible about it? Here, you'd never have to go near a postman or grocer or druggist—"

"But what about Norah—are you going to fire her and let me be the cleaning woman? What about your nice talkative doorman? I would have to get out to street level once in a while, wouldn't I? And what about your Miss Pulley, when she comes here to work?"

"None of that is what you mean. You mean Ellen. I can make her see it; she was caught short just now, but she'll adjust. I don't think you ought to hold it against Ellen that her reaction time is slower than ours on something like this."

"I don't, I really don't." She looked at him earnestly, but she knew he did not believe her, and could not believe her because of course she did hold it against Ellen. "If I were a hippie or yippie, Ellen would say, 'Oh, well, what do you expect of those dirty long-haired slobs?' and then she'd be tolerant about it. But being *me*—good family, New England background, forty years old—why, it's unthinkable."

She broke off. She never permitted herself the in-

dulgence of complaining to any man about his wife—
why should she think it permissible with her own
brother? He must know, as she did, that Ellen's "reaction time" was rooted in a kind of class snobbery
—"people like us simply don't have illegitimate children"—and knowing it about his wife, he must regret
it. Aloud she said, "Excuse it, please. I didn't mean
to give a lecture about Ellen. I do think it would be
tough as all get-out for both of you with me here,
locked away like crazy Aunt Hattie up in the attic
when guests come." He laughed and she went on,
hurrying to consolidate her small victory over her
blunder. "Once I find the right place to go on the
lam, Gene, you'll agree it's best all round."

"Maybe so." He looked dubious and then suddenly
more positive than he had looked all evening. "Why
isn't it better yet to tell the whole world to go to hell?
Then you'd stay right in your own apartment, lead a
normal life, see people you like, get help from anybody who gives a damn about you and stop all this
clowning about hideouts and secrets."

"Oh Gene, it sounds so wonderful. Today, in a
phone booth, I imagined just that. I imagined calling
the paper and telling them, calling everybody I know,
telling them, even calling Tony just to say, Look, I did
it, I always knew that someday I'd be able to."

Ellen came back with the ice bucket and there
were drinks to be made. Dori's expression signaled
Gene not to reopen the subject and he talked of student restlessness at Columbia and at half the other
campuses in the land, liking it. Students were fed to
the teeth with "the biggest bureaucracy there is except the army." From students they went to the restlessness among civil rights leaders, the growing fury
of the blacks—"I still can't say 'blacks' without forcing myself," Dori said—and by the time she left, she
had nearly forgotten the constraint between herself
and Ellen, thinking instead of what Gene had offered
as the best plan of all.

Why don't I? she thought as she walked home. He

had put into words just what she had felt as she saw the shine of the telephone booth on the street that morning. Cele had wondered about it too, obliquely raising the point and then backing away from the risk of influencing her. But why not tell the world to go jump in the lake and have nothing to do with the whole complicated twisty business of living a secret?

She glanced around as if expecting a sign, a directive. It was still snowing, easily, and the city lay in the white hush any snowfall lends its streets. Why didn't she? Why shouldn't she? She was no poor frightened girl in trouble. She was not ashamed. Nobody on earth could make her feel this as disgrace. Then why did she not obey her instinct and shout it from the rooftops? She glanced up at the snow-touched terraces atop the apartment buildings. From right up there—why don't I?

She had thought there was no need for Jesskin's three thinkings. She had made the one decision, the only decision: to go ahead. Wrong—she had not made it; it had sprung full-blown, a new being in her life, strong, firm, beautiful. There had been no gestation period needed, no elapsing of time, no birth pangs. In the same instant that her mirror had gleamed its faint signal to her, in that instant the *yes* was born.

Now came conflict. A secret or not a secret? Keep silent or shout it out? She had taken it for granted that this was private, that this wasn't something you announced on a loudspeaker, but all day today there had come the pull of other desires, to tell Tony, to phone the paper, to agree with Cele, with Gene, with those snowy terraces up there in the sky. Would there be other conflicts? She wanted no others, she would hate them if they came, hate herself if she shilly-shallied until they took on size and shape and substance. There were matters to be solved, certainly, the logistics of the whole thing, all sorts of matter-of-factnesses to be disposed of, but these were merely the practical considerations, not to be dignified by the concept Conflict.

She must not let real conflict get a foothold, she knew herself well enough to know that. She had gone through periods in the past where she couldn't be decisive about the simplest things, whether to wash her hair, whether to go for a walk, how to phrase a letter, and she remembered them with a horror and a dread. Of course they had come only in times of sadness and depression, not in a buoyant time like this, but perhaps the mysterious process of growth was the same—she mustn't risk it—perhaps if the seed of conflict were embedded at all, it would attach itself to the flesh of life and expand and grow until there was no way to abort it.

Her own metaphor made her suddenly smile. When to tell Matthew, how to tell him, that was also a problem to be solved well and thoughtfully, with care but without conflict.

She glanced at her watch as she drew near a streetlight. It was nearly eleven. Off and on, all day long, Matthew had kept returning to her mind, kept claiming part of her through the excitements and celebrating and discussing, Matthew the unnamed, Matthew the unspoken. Even with her entire attention apparently on Cele, on Gene or Ellen, he had been there, an interior presence to whom she would any moment return. Now that she was alone, tired from the massive day, eager for bed and rest and silence, it was as if she were going fully toward him once again.

*   *   *

There was a letter slipped under her door when she got to her apartment and for a moment she thought, The Christmas rush already? Does it start this early in the month, and so late in the afternoon? This must have come after Nellie had left for the day.

It was a business envelope, its upper left corner engraved *Weston, Solomon, Jones and Poole,* over which, in longhand, he had written "Poole—personal." Her name was handwritten too, and there was no stamp on the envelope; he had sent it by boy or come by and left it himself. She lifted the flap easily; it was barely glued, as if it were not very private, and there was no salutation.

> I tried several times to phone you today, but this may be better. Have you any idea how remarkable you are? How beautiful and how responsive? At forty-two a man is not likely to be misled about love. I know that it is not a constant, that it can diminish or grow, and that at the start nobody can be certain which of the two it will do. But having bought in this careful coin an alibi for the future, I think I may tell you that I am not a diminisher by nature. I will be telephoning tomorrow.

> MATTHEW

It was written in a strong flowing hand easy to read except for the *m*'s and *n*'s which looked like linked and topless *o*'s in the middle of words but not at either the beginning or end, so that she did not have to pause over "man" but did over "diminish" which rippled along as if it were *diminish.*

Somehow this was endearing, and she looked at the two words, diminish and diminisher, with a fondness that set them apart from all the rest. Then she began to read his note at the beginning once more, but suddenly realized her neck was moist and knew she was still in her snow-wisped coat, standing there inside her front door reading her first letter from Matthew. She slipped out of the coat, threw it down on a chair, remembered saying "You're a help" to Gene and hung it up properly in the closet, finding some small amusement in this repeated ritual. Then she went into the living room, sat down on the sofa—the sofa she could never look at without remembering him there with her—and read the letter once more.

—Lots of women in the history of the world have told somebody who wasn't the father that he was—

—Just pick somebody off the street?

—You could start an affair and then tell him and get married.

—I'm such a rotten liar. . . .

Again conflict, again, another kind, a horror in it and a sudden magnetic power, pulling her forward, beckoning, tempting. She started slightly as if at a noise and went to her room quickly, tossing the letter on her turned-down bed and tapping the tiny ON switch of her radio. Mozart came into the room, fresh and bright, and again she started, for it was so similar to the quintet they had heard Monday evening. Monday, Thursday—three days, seventy-two hours, and an entire new world spinning in the infinite space of the unexpected? All at once she felt unreal, felt unable to manage, not fitted for so profound a change in all her patterns and all her abilities. What made her so sure she could go ahead? How could anybody manage alone and in silence? Nature had never intended it for solitude, God had never.

Oh cut that out, she thought roughly, the one damn thing you're never going to do is go sentimental. You can feel good or bad, happy or horrible, afraid or not afraid, but you can never, not even once, feel sorry for yourself.

She felt better at once. She went to her desk, took out from the upper drawer a small oblong package which her newspaper and stationery store had delivered earlier in the week. She opened it and drew out a refill for her desk calendar and also a narrow little book in a red cover that matched a row of ten or twelve other narrow little books in red covers in a small bookcase behind her. *Daily Reminder* was stamped on all of them, and on this, in bright gold letters, the numerals *1968*. The combination looked strange and she paused over it for a moment. She leafed through the pages quickly until she came to July, and then more slowly until she came to the twenty-third. It was a Tuesday. She remembered Dr. Jesskin's warning that July 23rd was "a theoretical date," that it might be a few days earlier or later, but she stared at that one page and then, in the upper right corner she wrote, very lightly, very small, 280. She smiled at the figure as if in salute and began to undress. Without looking directly toward her bed she could see Matthew's letter, a small white marker lying there as if to denote a particular presence.

How completely good it was, to have a letter like this, and how long it had been since she had received one. Dick Towson rarely wrote because he was a telephoner. When she did hear from him it was by a telegram, cable or picture postcard, and she had never even remarked on it until now, so usual had nonletter-writing become in this age of speed and terseness. ARRIVING NINE THIRTY STOP FLIGHT EIGHT FOUR ZERO STOP LOVE YOU STOP

She laughed and glanced again at the letter waiting for her on her bed. Out in the kitchen the house buzzer sounded its raucous clatter and she went to it, surprised. The kitchen clock showed eleven thirty; unexpected callers didn't appear at eleven thirty, and she had long ago told the doorman not to announce people he recognized as her friends. "Some flowers," he said now, pompous as always. "They're in the package room. I missed you when you came in, so will I send them up now?"

"Thanks, please do."

They were odd spidery-looking great discs, as round across as large chrysanthemums, white and tall and fragile, their hearts edging into a young yellow green. She had seen them in florists' windows but did not know their name, and now she touched them with her fingertips as if some tactile recognition would suddenly inform her. She arranged them in her tallest vase, an etched crystal vase that had been a wedding present—the continuity of physical things—and carried them into the living room, to set them upon the coffee table in front of the sofa.

Flowers and a note from your lover. How old-fashioned, how outmoded; as the young would have it, what a drag. She could hear the derision in the word and automatically moved toward her dictionary. One of her hobbies was language, the derivation and shifting usage of words and phrases, and she knew all the *in* slang because it was part of her writer's need to know it. She rarely used any of it when writing or talking, but tracking it down was always amusing. She remembered how astonished she had been, on reading a Trollope novel recently, to see that one of the fashionable words a century ago, borrowed from the people in the pubs, was "gammon." Gammon as an expletive, gammon as a rebuke, gammon as a mild oath. Then too she had gone straight to her bedroom where, on a tallish mahogany stand, her great unabridged dictionary reposed, always open, and found eight or ten meanings for that surprising word. Now as she turned the left-hand pages back to the *d*'s, the telephone rang. Before she reached it, she knew it would be Matthew, and before she answered, she knew she would say, Oh, of course, even for an hour.

FOUR ᎭᏃ

"I'VE THOUGHT OUT all the things you told me to
think out, Dr. Jesskin. You were right, there were so
many more than I had dreamed there would be. But
I did. I've talked to my brother and to my closest
friend."

"And the result?"

They looked at each other in silence. His face was
still what she had thought of as neutral. It was a waiting face, an interested face, not the face of an advo-
cate or of a dissuader. Suddenly she looked again at
this calm, unruffled man and found what she had always found. He was involved forever with life in its
most primitive facets, conception and then birth, and
nothing, nothing at all, would make him put up ob-
stacles to either.

"And I am going ahead. Will you help me?"

Awkwardly he put his hand out on the desk and
took hers as if in a handshake. "I am proud of you."

"And will you?"

"You have known that I would." His voice was still
without stress but an animation shone in his eyes.
"We will work it out step by step, between us."

"Oh thank you." Her voice shook but he did not
notice. "Is it going to be awkward for you in any way,
taking me? Miss Mack and Miss Stein knowing I am
not married—"

"We will not start by worrying about me," he said.
"What are the worries about you?"

"Well, I do wonder about one thing. I've heard it's

a little risky to have a first baby as late as forty—is that true?"

"Certainly not. You are a fine healthy girl and forty is not regarded as anything but young today. Medically, that is. Cosmetically—that is perhaps another matter."

She laughed outright. He was talkative. He sounded happy. "And another thing. I haven't had any morning sickness yet—when does that start?"

"It is a variable. Sometimes it is immediate, sometimes it is never. In my own belief—I have no scientific data, just my belief—it is worst where the pregnancy is resented or unwanted and it is often not experienced at all when the woman is overjoyed to be pregnant."

He made a note in the folder; she knew it was the medical equivalent of "no morning sickness," and in her mind added a parenthesis: "(overjoyed)." She suddenly had a need to confide in him about matters more real than these two, and the certainty that he would permit it, find time for it, perhaps welcome it. "I do have one problem that I get a different answer to every day," she said. "The biggest one so far." He nodded, silent and expectant, as if he knew perfectly well that once the preliminaries were out of the way the real questions would come. "Things like where to go, when to go, what name to go under—those aren't answered yet either, but I know they will be. The great big one pushes them all to one side." Again she paused.

"You cannot quite make yourself tell me?" He put the pen down and shoved the folder away.

"It's just that something in me doesn't want this to be a secret, wants to tell it to everybody, wants to let everybody see me later on, big and pregnant, and let them think whatever they want to think."

"Then why do you not?"

At once she felt combative as if he had said, "That would be better; that is the best thing to do."

"Because where everybody knows," she said with

new stress, naming a famous actor, a famous painter, a famous movie star, all of whom had, willingly or via scandal and law suits, proclaimed to the world their indifference to conventional marriage—"because their children grew up to be neurotic wrecks. At school they must have been called 'dirty little bastard' from the first minute, and been taunted and whispered about and goggled at."

"School-age children are savages," Dr. Jesskin agreed, but unemphatically as if again he were turning neutral. His eyes strayed to the two photographs, easel-framed, standing on his desk before him, and he seemed to be studying their faces for reasons of his own. One was of a pretty woman, whom Dori took to be his wife, and the other was of a boy and a girl, about ten or twelve years old, looking enough like him to proclaim themselves his children. Were they savages too?

Dori felt rebuked by his speculative look as he gazed at the photographs. The stress and ardor of her words seemed girlish, the point she had raised suddenly tangential in this office, before this man.

"Oh, Dr. Jesskin, forgive me. These are things I shouldn't bother you with at all; I forgot for a minute. I'll decide for myself, and I suppose you will not disapprove either way."

"That is so. I will not." He pulled the folder back within writing distance and briefly she wondered what he had expected to hear from her that would not bear the recording in her history, already so full of other unrecordables. "In a moment," he said, "I will have a look at you for some measurements, for the technical chart. For the next three months, I will want to see you every fourth week. Miss Stein will give you an appointment card and Miss Mack will take a blood sample, for hemoglobin, for an Rh test and so forth. This is all routine. Have you any directives to ask of me? Most patients do."

"Directives?"

"You want to know whether you may continue to

have intercourse. The answer is yes. It is normal. Indeed as the pregnancy progresses, the increased production of hormones is stimulating to sexual activity. That is, unless there is anger over the pregnancy, when resistance, even hostility, becomes a factor."

This was so surprising a dissertation and so precisely to the point, though she would have had to make a conscious effort to raise the point herself, that she felt a remarkable surge of new confidence in Dr. Jesskin. Always before he had avoided any overlay of psychoanalytical talk; today he had spoken twice of resistance and hostility, or of the good normal opposites. He was giving her his blessings to go ahead and be made love to, but he was thinking of the "awfully decent man, no scoundrel betraying me," while she was thinking of Matthew. She suddenly felt wanton, promiscuous and secretly pleased, but she looked down as if she were too shy to meet his glance.

"For the moment," he went on with no perceptible change in tone, "I have only two prescriptions for you, but they are both important and both to start at once, please. First, to begin a regimen of long walks, daily walks, brisk, not ambling, but a positive kind of walking. Three miles a day would be best. Second, begin now to do this." He stood up, turned half away from her so that he stood in profile, unceremoniously held back his starched white coat, and then visibly pulled in his slightly flabby stomach, pulled it in with a sudden jerk, then released it, then pulled it in again, released it. Tall and thin, he was totally free of self-consciousness as he performed for her, and it was all she could do not to laugh. Automatically she imitated him, sitting as she was, watching him, fascinated at the unexpected sight. He saw that she was keeping time with him and nodded in approval.

" 'Suck in the gut' is the not so elegant way to describe this exercise," he said, dropping his hold on his coat and sitting down again. "The effectiveness is remarkable. You want taut muscles, strong, tough, and if you work faithfully at it, you will have them.

As you see, you can do this exercise standing or sitting, wherever you are, in a car, at the movies, at your desk, when you are watching television, even in bed. I want you to do it ten, twelve times a day, beginning today, in batches of ten or twelve times each."

She did laugh. She put her hands on her stomach and sat there practicing. She saw her hands jerk inward and she felt an immediate tightening of her muscles.

"The best maternity girdle of all," Dr. Jesskin said with satisfaction. "You will build it right into you, just this way, and keep strengthening it and toughening it right to the end."

"Couldn't it do any damage to the baby? Pulling in that hard?"

He waved the baby out of consideration. "You can't compress fluid," he said as if he had suddenly turned physics teacher. "You can't squeeze or pinch or decrease it." He touched the buzzer and Miss Mack appeared, competent as always, her manner as always, her eyes revealing nothing.

* * *

School-age children are savages. As she walked home the phrase sounded again and again in her mind, spoken in the mild voice designed neither to urge nor to exhort, and each time a phrase of her own replied, I won't let them be.

She had it within her own power to prevent those school-age savages from hurting, perhaps damaging, a five- or six-year-old boy or girl, and there was suddenly no question that she would exercise that power in the one sure way open to her.

Those future tormentors would never know. Their parents would never tell them because their parents would never know. Nobody would tell the parents. No shred of gossip would inform them, no hint would be whispered to them, no weapons would be handed them to be handed over to their school-age offspring. This much was at last settled.

Dori felt relieved. She walked quickly past shop-windows bright and commercial with Christmas green and red and tinsel, seeing no particularities, only a brightness to match her mood. As she reached her front door she could hear her telephone ringing brass-ily inside and she dived for her keys, sure she would be tantalized by silence once she reached her desk. But the ringing persisted, patient, stubborn, and when she breathlessly said "Hello?" it was Ellen, sounding embarrassed, sounding serious, asking if they might meet, perhaps today.

"Of course. Whenever."

"Are you working? Or could I drop in now?"

"Come on, I haven't even started." But she braced herself and looked at her watch as if time had become a factor. Had Ellen ever before come over alone to talk to her? She could not remember even one occasion in all the twenty-four years she had been married to Gene. They had usually been congenial enough in a loose casual way that was only a cut above indiffer-ence, but private talks between them, private visits, private anythings, never happened. Since the night she had told them her news two weeks ago, she had heard several times from Gene, asking how she was, asking genially, "Anything else new, for God's sake?" but from Ellen there had been only silence.

The sensation of being braced for trouble grew as she waited for Ellen's arrival, and during their greet-ings and their exchange of mechanical cheer about Christmas shopping and Christmas plans, it became acute enough to be uncomfortable. "What is it, Ellen?" she finally asked. "We seem to be duck-ing it."

"I've tried to avoid it altogether," Ellen said. "For two whole weeks I've gone crazy trying to just put it out of my mind. But I had that awful feeling that time was running out—"

"Running out on what?"

"On telling you the truth about this. Gene won't,

not ever. Your friend Cele won't either." She looked
defiant but also wretched.

"What truth?"

Ellen remained silent, managing to give off an aura
of reluctance as if her being there was no doing of
her own, as if this conversation were no choice of her
own but rather a distasteful trap into which she had
somehow been inveigled.

"Is this some truth about including Jim and Dan?"
Dori prompted. "And their wives?"

"That too," Ellen said with such a pounce that
Dori knew she had not even been thinking of her sons.
"You can't ask Gene and me to tell lies to our own
children."

"I didn't ask you."

"It's far more involved than just keeping this to our-
selves for now. For now that might be possible, but
then there comes one lie, and then another, a whole
series of fakes—we've *never* led them up the garden
path—they would never trust a word we said from
that minute on."

In her indignation at being asked to behave so
abominably, Ellen raced on about bringing up two
boys like Jim and Dan, how basic, how indispensable,
complete trust was between parent and child, until
Dori finally interrupted to say, "You were going to
tell me what it was that Cele would never tell me, or
Gene either."

"Yes I was. Somebody simply has to, and of all the
things they're saying, they absolutely are not coming
out with what they really feel down deep, what they
instinctively feel—that you're making the most awful
mistake, that this is the most terrible thing you can
do."

"Terrible?"

"Yes, terrible."

"Terrible for whom?"

"For everybody. For yourself and for Gene and
me, for—for the future."

"The word you can't say is 'baby,' " Dori said. "A terrible mistake for the baby."

"All right then. For the baby. For the whole family. For yourself most of all. A terrible mistake."

"I don't think Cele feels that and isn't telling me. Or Gene either." Ellen looked away. "Does he? Does Gene? Or are you guessing?"

"Apart from Gene—look, now that you know you *can* have a baby, don't you see how different things are? You wouldn't ever again have the awful feeling you used to have, don't you see that?"

"Now wait a minute." There was a warning note in her tone but Ellen missed it and again raced on, immersed in her own earnestness.

"You would know that you're cured at last and just knowing would make a whole new situation. So even if you—there's still time, it's still safe—even if you didn't go on with this now, you'd know you could, and you might even marry faster, knowing it. And be so much happier in the long run."

"You are telling me to have an abortion."

"I'm only pointing out the true—"

"Did Gene know you were going to say this?"

"I don't discuss everything with him."

"Does he know you feel this way?"

"I've told him, of course I have. We're family, Dori, what affects you affects all of us together."

"Oh no it doesn't, not from now on it doesn't." Dori stood up, her voice suddenly loud. "This is nothing you need have one more minute of, not one more word of, not one more bit of news about. I will see you when it's all over, a year from now, two years, but now let's for God's sake call it quits." She started from the room.

"You might consider the way other people feel," Ellen said behind her.

"And vice versa."

"You're being utterly selfish."

"And vice versa."

She waited at the door from the living room, not

looking at her sister-in-law, not thinking, wanting only to be alone once more. As Ellen passed her, saying, "I should have known," she answered, "That's right. You should have known," and opened the hall door. A moment later she was leaning against it, feeling for the first time the rise and swell of nausea.

School-age children are savages. They're not the only ones, she thought furiously. Just now in these few haggling minutes, here in her own house, she had heard the taunt of "Shame, shame!" Damn it, Ellen, shame on *you*.

*   *   *

She had stood her ground, she had said the right things. Off and on for the next hour she warmed to a small private glow of accomplishment, and then suddenly she accepted the truth: she was shaken through and through.

How many thousands and thousands lived through shame, humiliation and contempt because they were pregnant without being married? Why wasn't there a worldwide campaign to remake attitudes and emotions about it? They tested for the Rh factor, they watched for it, they knew it could be fatal to new life, but did anybody in authority check for the shame factor, the poisoning guilt that could be equally lethal, if not in the physical sense, then lethal to pride and self-worth?

The shame factor—if it were absent, how few young lives would be wrecked, how few hideous abortions there would be, the awful self-inflicted ones, the filthy unsterile ones, the slicing agony at the hands of the doctor who would not risk an anesthetic?

Dori shuddered. She hated Ellen for plunging her into these thoughts. Then she knew Ellen as Ellen wasn't the point, only Ellen as symbol. If Ellen, why not somebody else? Not Matthew, of course not Matthew. But was Marshall Duke saying this sort of rubbish to Cele? Was Ellen giving Gene a nightly burst for being so easy and acquiescent?

Matthew was no Ellen, not even a Marshall Duke, but he was in love with her, or, to be properly wary of large phrases, he was falling more surely in love with her, and any news of this magnitude might jar him through and through too. It was such a fragile process, that transition from "I'm in love with you" to the simple solid "I love you." Was it foolhardy to put it to any unusual strain so soon?

Day after day for the past two weeks she had been playing with opening phrases for the moment when she would tell him, but it had been a pleasant sort of daydreaming, with no sense of haste to prod her. Not just yet, it was too near Christmas, which he would be spending with his family; not right after Christmas either—he had promised to take his family off on a skiing weekend over New Year's. He had told her all this with a care, as if in a wish to say *"en garde"* to her, do not let these family patterns distress you; they were established long before we met. She had understood, had told him that she knew why he was telling her so carefully, so far in advance, and that she liked his doing it. And she had thought, liking this too, that after the holidays were done with at last, the timing would be just right for her news, and that she also would use care and love in the telling, and then had gone on half luxuriating in imagining the moment when at last he knew.

Her hand felt again the pressure of Dr. Jesskin's fingers, as if he were reaching out to congratulate her. *I'm proud of you.* She could hear the words again, but this time they were in Matthew's voice.

She drew back. Over them, through them, around them, a shrillness sounded: *You are making a terrible mistake. Terrible for whom? Terrible for everybody.*

Oh yes, she had stood her ground, she had said the right things, but Ellen had won something just the same. If Ellen had not come over, would there now be this sudden anxiety about what Matthew would say?

She was seeing him this evening and for a moment she wished she were not going to.

Almost automatically she turned to her desk. Work, the anodyne. The piece on Martha Litton was too long and she had been having trouble cutting it. Usually she could be dispassionate about cutting her own work, looking at each sentence with a skeptical eye that asked it, What's your reason for existing? But this time that stern editor within her had gone fishing and a friendly defender had remained, rooting for each phrase, urging her to see its charm, if not its necessity. Now she turned on it in a violence of energy, slashing out entire paragraphs, rearranging sequences, slinging in new transitions as if she were back on the defunct *Trib,* on some late-breaking story, with a copyboy waiting at her elbow to rush each take down to the pressroom. When she saw that she was at last on the edge of completing the job, she telephoned the paper and told Tad Jonas she was in the neighborhood and could she drop in at four with the completed piece?

"Sure, come on. Remember—I liked it the way it was."

By the time she got there she felt sure of herself again. She again had a sense of accomplishment, but this time it was real and it lasted. This came from work, her own work, and she knew how to do it, and when it went wrong she knew how to set about correcting it. This was not taking a good stance, striking the right note, this was her own self in operation, and despite her occasional envy of people with bigger talents, the mysterious something that might make her more than the writer of good pieces for a paper or a magazine, she found a full satisfaction in what her own self did manage to do well.

"Hi, Tad," she greeted her editor, "I think you'll like this better." She opened a flat manila envelope, drew out about fifteen typed pages and laid them on his desk. "Two thousand words shorter and less wobbly." He read the first paragraph and the last before he looked up.

"I didn't think it was all that wobbly."

"Maybe it's me who's wobbly. Or just plain stale. I think I need a vacation."

"When are you taking off?" He sounded mock resigned to it. "Tough, not having enough dough in the bank to swing a winter vacation."

She laughed. She liked Tad; they had worked together for years on the *Trib* and he had never let their friendship interfere with cutting her work when cutting was indicated. He was an editor with a built-in discontent, for he wanted either to be on a huge city daily again or else to have a fat advance from a publisher to write the novel he was always talking about, but he did precisely nothing about either desire except suffer over its denial. Despite his own failures, he was pleasant enough to work for, generous about telling you he liked something, never needling or mean-spirited about finding fault. If he disapproved of a piece of work he said so, roundly, vulgarly, but straightforwardly to you, with his reasons for thinking so, usually cogent. It didn't happen very often with Dori but she was good at forestalling it by behaving just as she had with the Martha Litton piece.

"Maybe longer than a winter vacation," she said. "Tad, don't get caught short if I do something wild one of these days. I just might."

"Like what?"

"Like quitting."

"You've got to be kidding. I thought you finally decided you liked working here on a nice slow weekly schedule."

"I do, in that sense. But of late I seem to think of treadmills awfully often, and of getting into ruts. That means something, doesn't it?"

"I guess it does. Maybe that you're in love or that you're going to write a book."

"Heaven forfend. Forfend the book anyway." She

saw him look at her with the sudden attention that the first whiff of news or gossip commands in the human animal, especially the human animal trained to sniff out news. She slapped together the sheets of the Litton piece again and said, "Well, we'll see. I hope you'll agree this thing is better for all the rewrite."

As she left, she thought, Laying the groundwork, that's what I was doing. Write a book indeed. Poor Tad, that's all he thinks of, so he ascribes it to me. He can't face the fact that if he really wanted to, had to, he'd have done it years ago, the way other people have done, after hours, mornings, weekends. But me! Never.

This sounded a little defiant to her, a little dishonest, for she recognized, and had for a long time, that it was something she regretted, that her natural scope was the smaller scope of articles, that she would never be able to encompass a sustained piece of work, hundreds of pages of work, on some given subject. What if she had to write a whole book about a Martha Litton, or even about a Benjamin Spock? There must be some mechanism within the talents of other people that kept them wound up for a longer duration of interest and energy, but that mechanism was missing in her.

Fine. It was good to know what your limitations were. Knowing kept you comfortably back from the abyss of frustration that so many people lived with. She had had her one private abyss for too many years to play around the edges of a second one. She felt superior and it was delicious. Let Tad know frustration, let everybody and anybody; for the next few months at least she was safe.

Laying the groundwork. It might be wise to follow through rather quickly, before she needed to leave the paper. She might line up one or two actual magazine pieces right now, with some actual editors and some actual deadlines; the deadlines could always be extended if enough notice was given. She could choose topics which she would have to research abroad, so when somebody said, "Where's Dori?" the answer would be "Oh, she's doing a piece in Rome," or Honolulu or Africa. People accepted such answers without paying too much attention; she had done it herself, except for people who were close to her. Casual people could be gone a year and when she saw them again, she had no idea of whether it had been a month or a few weeks or a matter of days.

Matthew was not one of the casuals. Matthew would know to the week how long she had been gone, just as she would know if he were to step out of her life now with some story about a law case that would take him away from New York. That could work with Tad Jonas and the staff, with most of her acquaintances and friends—how much fewer were the people one called friends with the passing of the years and the pruning of the tree. Was that merely a concomitant of maturity, or was it a dark kind of inturning that robbed one of companionships and parties and amusements?

She didn't turn from anybody who mattered. Her heart thudded as she looked at her watch; in three hours, soon after dinner, she would see him. He came to her deep in the evenings usually, about ten, staying until midnight. Saturdays and Sundays, not. She knew that pattern so well; like the big holidays, the weekends were for his children. It had been that way with Dick Towson too; before Dick, she had not yet been wise enough to accept the pattern. It used to affront her that she had to spend weekends and holidays alone, and all the timeworn clichés about affairs were really true. Then for no reason that she could name, some buried good sense had struggled up through the gravelly muck and had come to her rescue with Dick, making her see without rancor or confusion that this was part of the contract one made with life if one had an affair with a man who was married. And the only men any woman was likely to be drawn to, once the carefree teens and twenties were gone, were men who were already married. Conveniently widowed men were for television serials; in actual life the only bachelors of thirty or forty were the neurotics and misfits, the mothers' boys, the homosexuals, the cranks.

It was intelligent, then, not to be confused or "insulted" by the necessities about weekends and holidays, and Dick had remarked on the fact that she wasn't, complimenting her for "not being a Friday squawker like most dames." Matthew had never spoken of it, but he couldn't have felt any unspoken pressure upon him to see her over weekends, for it was nonexistent. Nor could he have felt any pressure to tell her about his family either, for she knew better than to ask about them. He still said little about Joan; it was his children that he enjoyed telling her about, and his work. When he spoke of his life apart from his kids or his cases, he still seemed watchful and less than free. One night he had told her a little about his boyhood, but he had grown somehow nervous and hurried and had ended, "I think I was so anxious to prove that I wasn't drawn to the law by two silver cords that I got pretty rough about it at times."

"That sounds natural enough," she had said.

"Maybe so. But I can be a selfish bastard—better not expect too much of me in the nobility line."

"I never expect nobility nohow." They had laughed, but she had listened with all her antennae out, searching for the unspoken message behind his words. Now some faraway signal seemed to say, Don't rush, take it a day at a time, think of the right way, there are plenty of other things you haven't decided yet either. She actually enjoyed keeping some of them in suspension; it was pleasant to leave pending the matter of where to hide out, a kind of game as if she were thumbing her way idly through travel folders, trying to choose between a vacation in Jamaica and one in Europe.

By the time Matthew came, the anguish that had begun with Ellen in the morning had disappeared and Dori felt euphoric. It was the day before the Christ-

mas weekend and tonight they would exchange their
first presents. She could give him nothing that needed
to be hidden or explained at home. After hours of tele-
phoning and scurrying around and searching out of
reliable opinion, she had collected for him the best
recording known of each piece of music they had
heard at their first concert. Actually, though she
would only tell him this later, she had bought a du-
plicate of each of the four records for herself, so that
she too might have that same concert whenever
memory and emotion combined to ask for its rebirth.

He was touched, as she had hoped he would be,
and he offered her his gift hesitantly, as if it were
banal compared to the thought that had gone into
hers. It was a pair of earrings of smooth white coral,
domed and shining, thinly outlined in gold; she loved
his wanting to adorn her, loved the earrings themselves and though she did not say so, loved him for
knowing that she would have been disturbed if he
had brought her something that cost more than she
could have spent easily for herself.

She put them on and turned toward him. "How did
you know I'm mad for white coral?"

"I know things about you."

"How *did* you know? You couldn't have asked
Cele." Before he could answer, she said in a rush,
"You *do* know about me. That I'm Victorian about
things like too expensive presents, for instance."

"Books and flowers only?"

"And something lovely like these, but—"

"Not a mink coat?"

"Not a mink coat. Oh Matthew—you know so
much about me, but there are some things still that
you don't and—"

"Important things?"

She suddenly went somber, and for a moment there
was silence in the room. The records lay spread on
the carpet, four glistening squares of color and design, and on the coffee table the small elongated
jeweler's box in which the earrings had come. He saw

her hand go to her throat as if to quiet a too lively pulse there and he said, "Don't answer that, darling." It was the way he said it that moved her, the offer of patience and trust. "Don't even try until you're good and ready," he went on. "If ever I start cross-examining you, on anything, no matter what—"

"You weren't cross-examining. I brought it up in the first place, and it was a perfectly natural question with anybody you're this close to."

"But don't answer it anyway." Slowly he added, "Let's try not to make all the young mistakes, Dori. We can't crawl inside each other's minds and feelings, and past and present, the way kids think they can. We can't be in the same cocoon."

"We'd fit though."

They made love then and later, lying beside him, curled inside the curve of his body, she thought again, We would fit. A vision flashed bright, of herself tucked in an arc within the arc of his being while, unknown to him, another being, not yet an inch long, was curving within her own.

Suddenly she felt a sweeping singing sureness that everything about this would go well, would go smoothly, would be happy and good. She turned toward him again. "Oh, Matthew, even without you on Christmas or New Year's, it's being the happiest Christmas and New Year's of my life."

*   *   *

It was past midnight when Matthew got home; Joan was still dressed, waiting for him, though normally she was either asleep or in bed, watching some television celebrity show or an old movie.

"You weren't at your office," she said. "I tried three times."

"No. Is anything wrong?"

"The school suspended Johnny."

"Damn it. For how long?"

"The rest of the semester."

"Does he know?"

"I told him. He raised the roof."

"Did he know it was coming?"

"No more than we did. A fine time for them to do it, just to make sure we had a happy Christmas. I had a lovely evening with Johnny, you can believe it."

"I'm sorry I wasn't here too."

"You're never here."

She sounded bitter and he could not blame her. Not ten minutes after he had left to return to the office, she said, Mr. Garry, Johnny's homeroom teacher, had telephoned and told her the news. A formal letter was in the mail, apparently lost in the Christmas rush, since there had been no response from the Pooles before school had closed for the vacation, and finally, though Garry had left town on his own holiday, he had decided he ought to make sure they were notified without further delay.

"Was it about the hockey?"

"That and all the other things. 'Repeated insubordination,' Garry said."

His heart contracted. He had seen it coming, had talked it out with Johnny, not too insistently, not too often. The boy had been in a roil of rebellion against going out for hockey practice, just as in the fall he had refused football practice and in the spring, baseball. "All that crap about team spirit, Dad, just makes me puke."

"Suppose everybody at school just dropped things they didn't like—what kind of school would you have?"

"You didn't dish out that kind of stuff up in Boston to Jim Benting—the draft makes *him* puke."

Anger had flared between them, but in him admiration too. Formidable at thirteen, that kind of logic. Johnny was growing into a loner anyway, aside from his rebellion against authority in any of its forms. His abiding interests were making ship models and reading, the one unexpectedly expert and detailed, the other unexpectedly catholic and widespread. In the past two years he had raced through not only all the

Hornblowers but also *Lord Jim* and half a dozen others by Conrad, also *David Copperfield* and half a dozen others by Dickens. But making friends came hard; most boys made him bridle, most girls bored him, and except for his favorite subjects, his chief comment about school was, "Forget it." Most of his teachers he dismissed as finks. The school rebels were his heroes, and the university rebels beyond them his gods. He was never going to be anything but a rebel himself, and like all rebels anywhere in any period of history, in any milieu, he was going to be hurt. And the people who loved him and valued him were going to be hurt with him.

My turn, Matthew thought, not pausing over the phrase. All parents knew pain as well as joy through their children; he had often wondered whether there was any greater joy in the world than that which came through a beloved child; now he thought that if that was true, then the corollary and opposite must also be true.

"Let's have some coffee," he said to Joan, "and talk. I'm sorry you had to take this on by yourself. I didn't dream anything like this was about to descend."

She didn't answer and he knew he had protested too much. He either did that in troubled times or fell silent, speaking as if to somebody he hardly knew, as if speech came hard to him, as if he were a man of monosyllables.

"When things go wrong, you just clam up." That had become her accusation of recent years and it was true enough, particularly when a quarrel threatened. He could not stand the discussions, the explanations, the repetitions, but-you-said, but-you-never-said. The maddening paraphernalia of a quarrel stifled him, choked down his capacity to yield, to understand, and left him in stone-hard silence.

Except when it came to a fight for a client. In court he could feel the flow of power and will to proceed as the attack deepened; it was like a perceptible surge of adrenalin that he could see, a bright emission, life-rich and potent. Perhaps because he was himself not under attack, that withdrawal never occurred in court; on the contrary, words bubbled up, arguments, rebuttal, all urgent, clamoring to be spoken, leaving him with a sense of release and elation.

He felt again the racing exhilaration that had flooded him as he had argued for Jim Benting; he had felt an endless strength, to fight all the way, right up to the Supreme Court. Whatever one thought of Benting's turning in his draft card to symbolize his protest against war, surely no just man could condone the draft board for wiping out his student deferment, reclassifying him for immediate military service, using the draft as a whip to flog a dissenter.

No, he hadn't clammed up on the Benting case, he never did on something that deeply mattered to him. Perhaps that was the key clue, that phrase "deeply mattered." He glanced at Joan, silently drinking her coffee. As she habitually did when she entered the kitchen, she had flicked on the switch of her record player and he tried not to see the pile of song records on the turntable, or the upper stack, pegged up in the air waiting. The volume was low as it always was and it should have been easy to ignore the ceaseless thread of sound, but an unwelcome snobbery climbed within him. From morning to night she listened to this kind of thing, twelve hours a day as a background for cooking and cleaning and knitting and sewing and all the things she said she really enjoyed. It mystified him, this difference between them about music, to name just one difference that had not been there at the beginning; for years her music had seemed mindless to him, automatic, just there, like humidity or sunshine, cloying or pleasant but mindless. He thought of the four records in his briefcase.

Again he was mystified at the many other distances that had grown so inexorably between them—music was only one of twenty such distances. How had it all happened, when they had started out as closely knit as any young couple in the first rapture of love?

And since it had, then how could any reasonable man ever expect any love to endure beyond its first beginnings? Could it endure between him and Dori? Given enough time, given life together in one household? In the deepest sense he was glad that this one valid test could not be made, would never be made. He was in love now with the insistence of a young man's love, the continuing desire of a young man's passion, and the fantasies and imaginings of a boy. But he knew, as a boy could not know, that there was no future for this kind of love, and that knowledge was his protection.

The affairs in between had never raised these questions; they had been for the most part brief and manageable; he was, he supposed, a selfish man when it came to emotional entanglement. He had been quick always to sense the shifting of the gears, as it were, in the mechanism of any affair; when the going was effortless and smooth, all was well, but when it became necessary to shift into middle gear and then into low because ease and smoothness were disappearing, then he grew watchful and unwilling. He had wanted no basic entanglements. He wanted no guilt. He wanted never again to reproach himself for being callous or cruel.

"I'll call Garry in the morning," he said at last.

"He's in Ohio for the holiday. He called from there."

"I can call Ohio. I'll talk to Johnny first."

"I've shopped so, for Christmas."

He saw through the non sequitur, and again he could not blame her.

*   *   *

If it wasn't Christmas night, he would phone Dori, late as it was. It had been an exhausting and endless effort to keep the semblances of a happy Christmas day; the two days before had been bad for everybody, edgy at best, violent and hostile at worst. Johnny was miserable and infuriating. Today had been a farce of

Tolstoy's happy family, all the proper sounds of joy and surprise and gratitude at each new present, and underneath always the heaviness. And there had been no sudden collapse at suppertime into baby-sleepiness; Hildy was still awake in her room and Johnny had just slammed off to his.

Joan was exhausted too. Matthew sat sprawled in a big chair, silent. To say now that he was going to the office would be insulting, so palpably untrue would it be. Yet he had to get off for a while; he had been with them all through every moment of three nights and days and he needed to get off as he needed to breathe.

"I'm going for a walk," he said. "Want to come?"

Joan looked up in quick surprise and said, "I think I'll straighten up the rest of this mess."

He was glad and knew it. Outside he walked in the direction of his office—so much for habit—but for the first time in all that troubled stretch of days he could think fully of Dori. It was going to be a crowded week, one trip to Washington, another to Boston; if it were not so late now he would call her, but she probably had had a strenuous time of it too. Any number of times during yesterday and today he had longed to talk with her, to hear her voice, to tell her about Johnny and the blow it was, not for anything practical like advice or counsel, just for solace and the sense of sharing a problem. But how much could she understand this sort of thing, since she had never had children? How much could anybody understand who had never known the sweeping pride or the fierce dismay your child could give you, so dissimilar from any other pride or dismay in the world? How much did she regret not having children? The one subject she rather shied away from was this one of children; she had told him of her marriage and her divorce with enough completeness to make him see both clearly, but about the marriage being childless she had sounded constrained and somehow artificial.

"We did want children," she had said. "The one mistake was the timing. Practically the first minute after we got married, so we stopped it. But then when we did want to start a family—"

He could still see her palms outflung, to gesture "nothing." He remembered his discomfort at having embarrassed her and again thought, as he had then, But why embarrassed? He would have understood regret, or relief that there had been no child to suffer from the divorce, but there had been something else that he could not understand.

He glanced once more at his watch. Twenty after eleven. Much too late. It was a clear cold night, dry and frosty; around the streetlights, the air seemed to sparkle and the crisp night renewed him. At Fifty-eighth he paused and looked about him. A block to the west, across Fifth Avenue, the old bulk of the Plaza rose to its modest height, dwarfed by the new skyscraper being flung up across from it, and he turned toward the hotel, planless except for the idea of stopping in for a drink to feel better. Inside he ignored the bar and made for the row of telephone booths. A drink with her instead, a half hour of talk, no bed, no sex, just being with her for a little while; suddenly he wanted nothing else.

Five minutes later she was opening the door to him, a short wrap of some kind over her brief nightgown, her legs bare in the abbreviated wisp she wore, as short as a little girl's party dress. How beautiful she was this way, without makeup, with her hair loose, and how important in his life, and in so swift a time.

"The school suspended Johnny," he said abruptly. "Once before they warned him, but it's bad to have it really happen."

"Oh Matthew, why did they? When?"

He told her about the last two years of growing worry over his son, finding comfort in the intensity of her listening, the absorption of her listening. As if she'd been through it herself, as if she knew the sinking of the heart that came with this sort of trouble.

"Dori, don't you get bored hearing about somebody's kids?" he asked unexpectedly. "Most people get bored; you can't talk to them about that part of your life at all."

"Of course I'm not bored. If I had had children, I can't imagine—" She broke off abruptly as if the thread of her thought had been snipped by shears and now fluttered, dangling, in separated halves.

"What is it, Dori?" He reached for her hand and held it between his own. "There's something that makes you change, whenever we talk about kids. What happens? What sort of thing is it?"

"I didn't know I changed. What do you mean, 'change'?"

"I can't say exactly. But two or three times already I've come smash up to a stone wall closing you off. If you want that wall there, all right, but if it's something you want to talk about—"

She felt her eyes sting, and she thought, But don't blurt it out, not now, not ever. Wait one more day, wait until tomorrow—just to be sure you're not acting on impulse, not now, not ever.

"Oh, Matthew," she said, "you don't know about one of the greatest parts of my life, that started when I was married, when we began to want children, and didn't have any, and didn't, and didn't, until I finally went to a doctor to see why I wasn't getting pregnant, a Dr. Jesskin, who was specializing in that branch of medicine. Nearly thirteen years ago, it was, the first time I went."

Now it was Matthew who listened with the intensity of total absorption. Talking, she lived again through the long-ago tests, the long-ago promises, the disappointment and hope and disappointment again, the fearful pendulum. She felt again what she had so often felt as she watched women and girls going and coming in Dr. Jesskin's office, some happy, some disgruntled, some with an anxious look about them that made her sure they were there not because they were pregnant but because they could not be.

"My poor girl," he said once.

At his words, at the tightened handclasp, her eyes filled with tears. But she felt good because she hadn't lost control, hadn't blurted out too much; now when she did tell him about being pregnant he would know the whole story of it, know the years behind it, see it as she saw it.

"Did you ever think of adopting a child?" he asked at last.

"We had even set a timetable. We were going to give Dr. Jesskin one more year, and then if it was still nothing, we were going to start seeing adoption agencies. But after the divorce even that was finished." She looked at him in sudden curiosity. "Could I have gone ahead? Could a woman alone adopt a baby? Or is it true that only couples are allowed to?"

"Not that I know of." He became the attorney, alert, wary of the quick reply. "I'd want to check out New York adoption laws at the office with people who specialize in them, but I seem to have read of cases where single women did adopt."

"Don't bother looking it up. I just wondered." She suddenly sprang to her feet. "I haven't even given you a drink. We got talking right at the front door. But oh Matthew, I'm so glad we did."

FIVE »⅜ラ

I SHOULD HAVE TOLD HIM, she thought the moment
he left. This would have been such a natural time to
tell him, when he was hearing all the rest of it, caring about it, knowing how it must have been. He
would have known about this too, he would have
seen why, he would have been as sure as I am about
it.

Why didn't I? What made me pull back? I've got
this fixed idea about waiting until the holidays are done
with, but what's so sacred about that particular timetable? I'm using it as some sort of excuse. I'm big
and brave when it comes to Cele or Gene, but I run
like a rabbit—

Oh nonsense. You didn't know what it would do to
him if you went on then and there, you wanted to give
him time. You still don't know whether it will infuri-
ate him or hurt him or put him off you completely.
You daydream that he will understand and approve,
but suppose he did just the opposite?

How little she knew of him after all, despite knowing so much. Twenty days of being in love made you
positive—if you were twenty—that you knew an entire human being, but at forty you had learned better,
at forty you knew how complex and involuted and
shifting any love could be, at forty you knew the awful risks in the unexpected.

Unexpected? That was understatement for you.
Poor Matthew.

The brush of depression feathered across her mind.
It wasn't only with Matthew that she was being timid;

she was putting off a dozen lesser problems that were still there to be solved, leaving them strewn all around her like assorted notes and reminders on a crowded desk, waiting to be picked up and disposed of. Suddenly that tranquil "one day at a time" seemed to be approaching its end, a bright bubble floating toward a brick wall.

In a week a new year would start and she would be in the eleventh week; her own body would be forcing her to positive action. She stripped off her nightgown and crossed to the dressing table, staring with clinical detachment as if at a stranger. She still looked, in this dimmed light, much as she had looked the first night Matthew had seen her, Matthew who had already wondered that she liked them to make love in the dark, who would one day hear that she loved to be made love to in the blazing sunlight. But even in the half-light there was more definition to the orbing, instantly seeable perhaps only to her own eyes but surely there. In a few days more he would see it too.

She slept restlessly as if she were in transit, in a plane or ship or train, always on the surface of sleep instead of burrowed down in the good depth of it. In the morning she woke suddenly, with a decisiveness of relief, as if she had at last solved some mystery while she slept. She jumped out of bed, thinking, If ever I was on an inexorable schedule, I'm on one now, and I'd better go in for some inexorables of my own. She crossed to her desk, dated a sheet of typing paper 12/26, and wrote:

DECISIONS TO BE MADE BEFORE Jan. 2, 1968

The tingle of danger ran along her nerves. This was no document to leave blithely around for Nellie to find. Nellie! What to do about Nellie was one of the decisions, minor, but one of them.

"Minor," she wrote. "Nellie to go; two weeks' notice today."

Major: Hideout for Feb. 1 through ⅂ ¹y.

Major: Costs? Jesskin's fee? Hospital? Can't use Blue Cross under false name.

Major: Tell Dick T in letter? Wait till return? Not tell at all?

Minor: When Cele to shop for maternity clothes?

Major: Matthew.

My poor girl. He had felt how it must have been for her, he would know that following all those years there could be now no alternative for her, he would see that she had to go ahead, unmarried, married, alone, not alone, rich, poor, no matter any of those outer things. The primitive thing is what he would have seen, would have felt it as anybody feels the choice of life over nothingness, of birth over nothingness, of the filled vessel over the empty one.

She looked at the telephone. But he had a crammed week ahead, with only snatches of time between clients and flights and whatever bouts he would be having with Johnny; there was, after all, some good sense in the timetable she was following; it had to be right for Matthew too.

How different love was from sex itself, and how this with Matthew had transformed her life and needs in just three weeks. All the years with Tony seemed shorter in retrospect; Tony and she had been so young during their marriage—she saw it now and could even forgive him for tossing it all aside, for he had been operating then on the same young values. The young were always so sure they alone knew about love, but when they got to be thirty and then forty, they would see how much their lives had drawn from the passing years, how white and innocent and thin their first youth had been, and how muscled and complex and durable love could become.

She returned to her list. Major: Matthew. Her mind balked at anything beyond Matthew, but she thought, Oh no you don't, no more stalling.

Minor: Pseudonym, alias.

Major: Mail forwarding; answers mailed from where?

Major: Bank and checks. New account under new name.

She stood up, read her list through with satisfaction and then went to the front door for her morning newspaper. In the kitchen for breakfast, she shivered; the window had been left open by Nellie and a nightful of blasting cold had come in through the careless half inch of space. She went back to her room for a long flannel robe and thought of flats in the ghetto with inadequate heat or no heat, their tenants endlessly calling up janitors to complain and threaten and beg.

Suddenly she knew where her hideout would be.

Not the Grand Tetons, not the Cape, not Washington—all these were fantasy places, absurd, impractical, valid in the first days of dream unreality but not worth serious thought now in the sure status of the third month. She was not the type to go unnoticed in any small town at any time; suddenly she remembered the vacation that had made her fall in love with Jackson Hole and the Grand Tetons so long ago. One sentence from her and somebody would ask, "Where are you from in the East? Boston? New York?"

Her clothes, the license plates on her old car, her letters, all from New York—everything would give her away now, and in the big months ahead. Alone, not staying at any dude ranch with a lot of other Easterners but really alone, living in some small rented cottage in a small town, she would within weeks trail question marks wherever she went. No matter what story she told—husband off in Vietnam, husband killed in an air crash—she would soon turn into a mystery lady, a personality, a Somebody Interesting.

Where did criminals go when they had to hide out?

Suddenly she laughed aloud. Why, she had had the answer all along, had seen it in a hundred movies, in a hundred crime shows on television, had read it in a hundred detective stories.

They hid out in the biggest city of all.

Not her own New York, not Madison and Park and Fifth, not in the Village, not in her own attractive neighborhood where all her friends were. Certainly not. But what about a furnished room in the Bronx for the six big months? How many of her friends would she run into in a grocery store up on Mosholu Parkway?

New York—it would be New York. There was something momentous in the decision. To stay right in New York, to abandon the travel folders of her imagination, to know she was half an hour away from Matthew, that she could phone Cele and ask her over, see Gene—

So of course, New York. If not the Bronx, then Brooklyn, out in Bay Ridge or near Coney Island. Perhaps good old Manhattan, just across the park, over on the West Side. Apart from Lincoln Center, she could probably wander all those side streets and avenues for hours every day without seeing one soul she knew.

The fact startled her. Life in New York was stratified, sectionalized, "segregated" not only as to black and white but also as to income, general style, general background. That awful word *status*. She knew her own segment of the city, that one narrow strip of attractive clean streets just east of Fifth and Central Park, where she had always lived, and where most of the people she knew had always lived too. There was a snobbery in it, suddenly horrid, a snobbery she had never caught before. She was angry at it now, glad to awaken to it at last. She would break through it, had to, wanted to. It would be part of the newness and goodness of everything else so suddenly happening.

She turned to the back pages of the *Times,* but at once realized she would do better with the Sunday *Times* where the real estate ads would be in the hundreds instead of in the weekday dozens. If not this Sunday which was the always shrunken post-Christ-

mas paper, then in the next. Too early to look seriously, but just about right for some self-education.

She returned once more to her list of minors and
majors and telephoned Cele. "Hi, I've decided to do it
for myself. Do you want to come with me?"

"Do what yourself?"

"Get my own clothes."

"Suppose you run into somebody, from the paper
or wherever?"

"Couldn't I be in a maternity shop buying a gift for
a dear pregnant friend?"

"Sure you could. Okay, I'll go along and buy one
for a dear pregnant friend."

They met in an hour and by noon Dori had chosen
everything she would be likely to need for the half
year ahead. This was a new world to her, a world of
the young, judging by the other customers, a world
she had never even shared beyond a passing glance at
some coy headline in an advertisement about "lady-
in-waiting" or "blessed eventuality." She was not surprised that the clothes were so pretty, but their prices
astounded her. A navy dress in a ribbed silk was a
hundred dollars; a red checked housecoat, sixty;
there seemed to be nothing for anybody poor. Suddenly she thought again of the girl who "got caught"
and had to go on with her job, thought of her looking
at these clothes, these price tags, thought of her going
away empty-handed. There were thousands of such
girls at this very minute of time, maybe hundreds of
thousands, with their fear, guilt, shame, anger at the
man who had "knocked them up." She could suddenly
see them as a group, as a part of society out there in
the city, in all the cities.

There's a minority for you, she thought; I guess it's
my minority from now on. She wondered how big
it really was, what the world really knew about it.
She might find out for herself, right away while she
could still go to libraries and newspaper morgues,
save up the research until she was ready to write a
piece about it.

"That's enough," Celia said firmly. "You try these on before you get swamped." The saleswoman showed them into a cubicle of fitting room, said, "When you decide, call me," and disappeared.

Another surprise caught Dori as she tried on the navy dress, a distant pleasure she could foretell as she imagined herself bulky inside it one day, and an impatience for that bulk to come, meaningful, unmistakable, a commitment from which there was no escape except the good escape of completion.

A sudden desire to show herself to Matthew in this dress seized her and she unexpectedly announced, "This one I'll take home with me, Cele. I just might wear it right away."

"A preemie," Cele said, laughing. But to herself she thought, Is she still seeing him? I thought they were winding it all up.

* * *

At home that evening, with some vague talk of cutting expenses, Dori gave Nellie two weeks' pay in lieu of notice and then checked off on her list the *minor* about Nellie and the *minor* about clothes. Minor or not, victories. In the morning she slept late, relaxed and warm and free of wake-up compulsions; then, remembering, she dressed quickly and went to the library.

It was the main branch at Forty-second and Fifth, the very sight of which always gave her a rising sense of expectation. In the vast catalog room, she went to the B and C sections and searched the cards for *Birth* and *Childbirth*. A subhead on one card caught her eye: "Illegitimate birth; 302,400 in yr." Three hundred thousand in one year, she thought, in this country alone; my God, are any of those three hundred thousand girls *happy* about it? She started for the reading rooms to get the book, but as she passed the A cards, she hesitated. *Ab, Ac, Ad.* She pulled out the *Ad* drawer and riffled through it half guiltily, telling herself that Adoption Laws could wait for another time. But she kept on, pausing at last over a card for a magazine article on "Single Parent Adoptions."

As if she had no choice, she filled out a blank for it and went straight to the Periodical Room. She was excited, tingling and warm along her temples as if a pleasant headache were possible, and she began to read. Too quickly at first, her eyes racing ahead of her mind like searchlights on a road trying to pick up some valuable object far ahead. After a moment she made herself start again at the beginning.

There was nothing in the statutes of New York State that prohibited a single person from adopting a child, though it rarely happened. The public adoption agencies still clung to their old standards of what constituted acceptability in adoptive parents; the optimum still was the married couple with a reasonably good income, happy in marriage, stable in personality, still young though not so young that they had been childless for fewer than three years. But an experiment begun in Los Angeles a few years aback had proved that single-parent adoptions could and did work, and that they were often the only way to place the children most optimum parents didn't wish to adopt: the handicapped child, the Negro child, the Mexican child, the child of mixed bloods or mixed religions.

After Los Angeles the new concept had been ventured upon in half a dozen other cities; by now eight states had shifted from their rigid two-parent rule, and New York was one of them.

Change, changing, she thought, new mores, new wisdoms. She read the article once more, this time taking notes. The agencies all were officialdom itself—she would never go near officialdom. Would that make a difference?

Matthew would know. Or a partner in his office would know. The moment she told him, he would begin to help her. Suddenly she wished this was not a crowded week for him, wished there were no clients, no crisis with Johnny, no three-day family weekend off there in the snow.

Cut that out too, she thought a moment later. Futile wishing is one more thing you're never going to do.

* * *

"So, somewhere in this city," Dr. Jesskin said slowly, "you will get thee to a nunnery, so to speak. That is very good. Certainly for the sake of this baby who will be your child, it is very good. You have thought it out, in my opinion, to a decision that is wise. I am glad."

The grave tone, the unexpected quote, inappropriate to the point of being ludicrous—there was something so straightforward and so simple in the way he used them that she thought, I love him. He is so good and kind I really love him. He reached for his calendar and she waited.

"I have thought out some matters too," he said. "In April, the start of the sixth month, you will no longer come here to the office, even as my first morning appointment. I will instead start making house calls. Hideout calls, you might say."

"Oh, Dr. Jesskin."

"And for your confinement in July," he went on, glancing at her open folder, "where do you intend to go?"

"I hadn't even thought that far ahead."

"I already have to. Now that you do think of it, have you any idea where you will go to give birth?"

"Some small private hospital, I suppose."

"My dear Mrs. Gray, no. You are not going to have this baby in some little medical setup somewhere, and certainly not in your rented room."

"Then where? You have it all decided!"

"Yes, I think so. But it depends." He checked himself. His face was animated again and she thought. He's not only good, he's quite good-looking.

"It depends on money," he said firmly. "We must first consider money. My fee of course will be at your convenience, but I do not know if you can—if you are pressed—"

"I have thirteen thousand dollars in a savings bank," she said simply. "Not from alimony—I hate alimony. My father left us each—" She broke off in confusion. She wanted his help and his approval, but why was she telling him this much, why putting in her proud little bit about no-alimony? She glanced at him in embarrassment. He was again his usual self, attentive, waiting, absorbed. "I mean, within reason I can afford whatever you think best."

"Well then," he said, "we can dismiss the rented room and the little medical setup." The first hint of irony sounded. "In that case you are going to have this baby right in Harkness Pavilion, right on the eighth floor, the maternity floor. That is where."

"Harkness?" She could not think he was joking, but Harkness? City editors always kept an eye on Harkness. The wealthy went to Harkness, the celebrated, the illustrious, people who made news, whose deaths and births and illnesses and recoveries were minutely reported in the press.

He was watching her, with delight in her disbelief. "One does not expect an illegitimate birth at Harkness, so that is where you will go, one of the pampered ladies there."

Suddenly she laughed. "How marvelous! I wouldn't have dreamed of it."

"The one thing different from the other ladies is that you will not be on orders to walk the corridors for exercise. You will stay behind your closed door all the time, before and after, and a NO VISITORS sign on the door. You see I am considering matters." He held up his hand to ward off her thanks. "One more thing. On that door, along with the sign of NO VISITORS, will be two names. One will be Jesskin, but yours will be—what?"

"My false name? I've thought of a dozen—"

"I will need to know soon, to reserve a room for July twenty-third or thereabouts."

Suddenly she leaned toward him, her eyes anxious. "There will have to be a false birth certificate, won't there? Under whatever name I choose?"

"Yes."

"But you will be signing it?"

"Of course."

"Couldn't you be disbarred or whatever it is, for signing a legal document you know is false?"

He picked up the paperweight, apparently examining its many facets. When he spoke, his voice was dry, remote, as if he had all at once become very nearly a stranger.

"We will be very clever," he said, "and this will remain our personal business. But if I am found out, and charged with signing a false birth certificate, I would have to find a way to manage that."

"But have I the right to let you run such a risk?"

"My dear girl, it is not you alone who are involved." He rose and she thought, It's the first time he's sounded sentimental about the baby. "The other person now involved," he continued as he nodded to her in farewell, "is me."

*　　*　　*

It was a wild idea but she could not resist it. She had to see it, look up at it, imagine herself there on a hot blue summer day. The bus to take was the No. 4, and she walked from Dr. Jesskin's office to the bus stop on Madison and waited.

Harkness, eighth floor, the maternity floor—just saying the words made July twenty-third closer. Everything since she had made her list had done that, piling reality on reality. How much more there was to tell Matthew tonight than there had been one week ago.

At nine or ten tonight she would be telling him. This time there would be no backing away. She was suddenly impatient. If only it could be this moment instead. Or at lunchtime or at five. A No. 4 bus was bearing down on her but suddenly she drew back from the curb. They had never had luncheon together and they had never even met for cocktails.

She found a phone and dialed his office. She had called him only once before but she recognized his secretary's voice and said, "Is Mr. Poole in? This is Theodora Gray."

"Yes he is, Mrs. Gray. Just a moment."

It was several moments before he came on and her heart began its familiar thudding. She must not think now of how he would take it; she never should have wondered how he would take it.

"Hello," Matthew said in the receiver, and she said, "I hate disturbing you at your office. Happy New Year," and he said, "I like to be disturbed," in an artificial bright tone that was for his secretary. "Happy New Year to you."

"I wonder if—I wanted to talk to you about something and I thought maybe you could drop by for a drink after the office."

There was a pause, and then, almost formally, he said, "If you think best, I could make a free hour right now."

"You could? In the middle of everything?"

"Of course I could."

"Oh, Matthew, thanks."

"I have a couple of phone calls first, and then I'll be there. Let's say about twelve. Perhaps you'd give me a sandwich."

She hurried home and changed into the navy dress, finding a rightness in wearing it now for the first time. He was dropping everything, perhaps canceling a luncheon appointment; he had instantly understood that this was no idle impulse and he was responding without pause. It was part of him, part of what drew her to him, this responsiveness in him awakening total response from her.

The navy dress seemed frivolously short, shorter than she had thought it when she had tried it on in the store, shorter than her usual clothes, but she rather liked the frivolity of it. And she liked herself in it—if she stood tall in it, holding in hard, there was still nothing but the flat straight planes of the navy silk.

Making sandwiches and coffee, she tried not to rehearse what she would say. Rehearsed lines were always false, glib, revealing a poor thin worried tension in the speaker. But she rehearsed it anyway, framing the first thing she would say, then the next, hearing her voice speaking to him, his answering her, until by the time he arrived and asked, "What is it, darling?" she felt confusedly that she had, by some telepathic miracle, already revealed everything she had to tell him.

"It's something I've been wanting to tell you, but kept putting off and off."

His face was sober and he looked at her with a concentrated attentiveness. She said, "Oh Matthew, thank you for coming right over," and preceded him into the living room. His concern was so total. Men always expected total attention from the girl they were with, but so few returned it when it was the girl speaking. Her throat was dry but she ignored the bar table and sat beside him on the sofa, suddenly floundering for any words at all.

"What, Dori?"

"Oh Matthew, I'm suddenly so nervous, it's so important to me."

"Is it about us?"

"Not really, and yet it is, the way anything is now." She saw her own fingers interlacing and clutching at each other. "You were so marvelous when I told you about all that time of my trying to get pregnant, you understood it, you really saw how it must have been."

"Darling, are you pregnant now?"

He said it so swiftly, the impression of eagerness in his way of saying it was so fleeting, that she could never be sure it was there. For one flashing moment she thought, Women all over the world, but she flinched from it and the instant was lost.

"That first night we made love, I didn't know yet—I was afraid to believe it. I had been to Dr. Jesskin that very morning for tests but the results weren't in yet and it could have been nothing, a skipped period, it's happened before—"

"That first night?"

"I'd seen Jesskin in the morning but he couldn't know without tests—"

He stood up abruptly. He seemed very tall standing above her, tall and rigid and alien. He was not looking at her, he was not looking at anything, he seemed not to be breathing. Then he said, in a rough voice she had never heard, "Are you pregnant by another man? Is that what you're telling me?"

"If I'd already known for sure that first night, I would have told you then and there—no, I couldn't have told you yet, but I wouldn't have let us start."

"Are you saying you *are* pregnant?"

"Oh yes, and I—"

"Pregnant by somebody else. You are saying that too?"

"You see, I was coming to the end of an affair, and usually with me, a year or so will go by before I even meet anybody who interests me again, but this time you—"

He caught her wrist. "You are going to have a baby from that other affair and you've known it and you let us go ahead, deeper and deeper, with me not knowing one goddam thing about it. Christ!"

He flung her wrist free and she was hot with anger at the rage in his words. She squeezed her lids shut as if to hold back tears but she heard him cross the room to the bar table, heard him open the whiskey carafe and pour a splash of Scotch and drink it, without bothering with ice or soda.

"I meant to be more careful," she said, "about the way I told you, I didn't dream it would suddenly be said. For a long time I meant to write something to you first, or maybe just say I was going away for a while because of something that had happened before I ever met you." He said nothing. His hand rested on the neck of the whiskey carafe, fingers tight around its filigreed silver collar. "But ever since I told you the first part of it I wondered what had made me pull back and then it all seemed banal to wait and try to think how to say it, as if I were afraid or ashamed."

"Damn it, you're thinking exclusively of what you felt and how you feel."

"I'm not. I've thought a million times about how you would take it, I've worried so about the way you might feel, I kept thinking, 'Just for one more week, and then I'll find the right way to tell him—' "

"So you blast me with it like a load of buckshot."

Dori winced at his roughness, but thought, You did blast him. How had it happened? How could things go so wrong? "I didn't mean to blast you. I'm sorry—oh you have to know I'm sorry it came out that way."

He made no reply. He went to the window and stood staring out at the raw winter day, the streets grayed with sooted snow. She suddenly thought of her brother Gene staring out the window that night she had told him and Ellen, and the dearness of Gene ever since, even after Ellen's visit. But Gene was her brother.

She felt sad and compassionate toward him, a new sense of Matthew despite his rage. She started toward him, but halted. Everything she said now came out wrong.

He suddenly left the window. "Why don't you look pregnant?" He looked pointedly at her stomach. "How long has it been?"

"I do look it when I'm not standing this way, straight up this way, holding myself in. It's part of the exercises I do, it's sort of a habit already." She hesitated and then said, "See?" As she let her muscles relax, the flat planes of the navy dress altered; a delicate sphere took shape.

He looked away sharply. "How long has it been?"

"This is the eleventh week."

"Then every time we've been together—oh my god-dam Christ."

She remembered his talk about cross-examining and nearly cried out that he had no right to put her through this quizzing. But he did have the right. She had given him the right by loving him and letting him love her.

"Are you going to marry the—the—whoever he was?"

"I haven't even told him. He's away now."

"Going to blast him with it too?"

"I don't know whether I will ever tell him at all."

He started to speak but thought better of it. He went to the bar again and splashed more Scotch into the glass he had left there, still not bothering with ice or soda. Then he said, "I'd better not stick around. I'll call you when I get this into some sort of shape."

Dori watched him go to the front door where she had so often met him with an upsurging of pleasure, and the drag of depression pulled downward throughout her body. He took up his coat and hat, not putting them on, and left.

She turned back to the living room. On the coffee table the pretty plate of sandwiches, the fruit and coffee suddenly repelled her. She remembered the way he had looked at her after asking why she didn't look pregnant. Again she squeezed her eyelids shut but this time the tears came anyway. She went to her room, took off the navy dress, hung it deep in her closet as if it were something to be hidden even from herself, and went back aimlessly to the living room. The thought of food was repugnant. She drank a cup of coffee, took everything out to the kitchen and started to wash the dishes. It was important at times like this to have something essential to do.

*   *   *

An hour later she was on the street once more, on the corner of Madison, waiting for the No. 4 bus. This time she took it eagerly, as if it contained some miracle comfort she could find nowhere else. She watched the store windows go by, watched the people, watched the traffic lights, her mind emptied by some primitive mechanism, draining it of pain and guilt. She felt guilty because she had failed in the way she had told him. Matthew deserved more of her, anybody deserved more of the person he loved, for there was an unwritten treaty between two people in love, to spare the other needless pain and shock. Pain and shock there might have been for him no matter how gentle she had been in the telling of this news, but she had multiplied them both by "blasting him with it."

Defensive, Dori, always defensive. For such a long time now those words had not sounded in her mind, not once, but here they were again, like old antagonists one had hoped to be rid of forever but who persisted in coming back at unlikely times, unbidden but undismissable. But this time she could not ignore them.

This was a *major,* more major than anything she had written into her happy list. She knew that losing Matthew for good was what she had been afraid of all along, the threat through all her delays and timetables. And she also knew that to lose him for good would entail no minor adjustment; it would be no peaceful and willing ending of an affair as it had been with Dick Towson, but total upheaval as at the end of her marriage. She shuddered.

Outside the bus window the streets grew unfamiliar and strange. Dori tried to pin her attention to them, like some sightseer from a foreign land, but she could not concentrate. Delay was so false, so much the opposite of what she really was. She should have told him that first night, before they had ever touched each other, there on the red sofa; she should have blurted it out right then, "It's probably all a mistake, but there is one chance in a billion that I am pregnant, and I won't even know until Thursday." That would have been shock too, but a protective one keeping them back from a worse danger.

Instead she had thought, Just this once, and then through the hours that followed, just these wonderful days. No matter how natural that had been, no matter what her motives, the delay and then the planning were so out of character for her, she should have known better than to rely on them even for a short while. She had been called tactless too often not to know that she lacked the small graces of subterfuge. And she had been called oversensitive too often not to know that she was not one of the thick-skinned of the world who never got hurt. Faults, both of them, but together they added up to something that was the basic truth about her.

For the first time, Dori felt comforted, and by the time she left the bus and stood looking up at the great blocks of white buildings between her and the river, she began to recapture at least part of the eagerness she had felt that morning when she had left Dr. Jesskin's office.

There was Harkness Pavilion, a separate unit from the main hospital, closer to the river. She counted upwards; there was the eighth floor. The maternity floor. The arctic wind whipping at her from the Palisades across the Hudson suddenly lost its meaning; she could imagine a July day of piercing blue sky and yellow morning light and somewhere in there herself in the very act, the everyday, commonplace, unbelievable act of giving birth.

She began to walk toward the river. She stood at the crest of Riverside Drive and looked up once more. One, two, three, four, five, six, seven, eight—one of those windows on the eighth floor may belong to my room. She could see herself standing by the window, looking out at the water, and something in her seemed to stretch forward toward that distant day, as if one could crane toward a point in time.

She retraced her steps and again stood on the Broadway corner where she had left the bus. But she was too restless to enclose herself in the specific space of a taxi or bus, and she began to walk, not the crisp positive walking she did every day as part of her orders, but an aimless, sightseeing walk, not ambling only because the wind was too sharp for meandering along. The stores interested her, the movie houses, the neighborhood in general. For all she knew she might find her furnished room somewhere near here; this might become the hideaway.

A store caught her eye because of its name, Tots and Toddlers, and though she smiled at the mawkishness, she stopped to look at the window display. Then with no prior decision to do so, she went in and said to the only clerk there, "I'd like to buy a present for a newborn baby."

"Boy or girl?"

"I don't know." She laughed in confusion and said, "It just happened and I haven't even heard that much. Does it matter?"

"Not if you don't care about blue or pink. What sort of present were you thinking of?"

"Anything, nothing fancy."

The woman looked at her with less interest, as if she had received a code message that this customer was not ready to be lavish. She turned to a series of shelves behind her, stacked one above the other, but each open on its front face like a bookcase. "A wrapper," she said. "Like a bathrobe, you know?"

Dori accepted the scrap of white flannel she had handed her and instantly said, "Why, the whole sleeve isn't as long as my middle finger."

With a voice tinged with the faintest scorn, the woman said, "Have you ever seen a real newborn baby?"

Dori laughed outright. "Only from a distance," she said. "This will be the first time close up. I'll take it."

SIX

MATTHEW WOKE UP as if a fire alarm had shot off at his ear. It had happened every night for the ten nights since she had told him. Each time he heard a voice jeering, her voice, often his own, sometimes an unknown's, but always taunting and raucous.

"That's right, buddy, always blame the other person." This time it was his own voice, needling, insulting. Here he was blaming Dori for this ripping tearing clawing of his entrails, as if she had planned this butchery of jealousy, had planned it weeks before she knew he existed, had begun to plan it with Jesskin years before.

But he could not stop his anger. Hour after hour he could not; try as he would to return to thought and clarity, he could not. There was no way. He would have to forget it, forget her. He would have to get over her, never see her again, rid himself of her once and for all.

For almost a week he knew that this was what he had to do. It was a nightmare matched by the alternative nightmare of continuing with her. See her again? Love her again? Glory in her body?

He shook with fury at his own fury; he should not have let himself fall into this pit, should have stayed remote, a man having an affair with a damn sexy responsive appealing female, but nothing more, as with all the other affairs. He had instead let this become different, let his whole being become fettered and tethered by need, by love, by some positive sense that here again was the thing he had never thought to know again.

Pain, goddam it, pain and grief and suffering always, when you had done nothing to deserve it, when you knew yourself free of causing it. Every damn life anywhere had its damnable quota of it, not to be exorcised, only to be endured.

Like one of the split-second images flashed across a movie screen, he remembered his mother holding a tiny Hildy, looking down at her, sitting alone there looking down at her first grandchild.

Jesus, why now? Why see that lonely posture now, springing into reality again? Over the years at mad irrelevant intervals, that image would suddenly stand before him again, clear, silent, there. He would flinch and it would go, but for an instant it was there. His mother who had never hurt him had hurt him indeed in the end.

And now Dori, whose gleaming slender body possessed his mind and filled his memory. She was no longer his, basically she had never been his, not even that first time on the red sofa.

Be fair, be fair. That first time she didn't know herself. You came down from Boston with one determination, admit it, you couldn't wait, you wanted her then, that night, she did hesitate, you felt it and spoke of it to her and nobly offered to wait if she wasn't as uninvolved as she had thought. But *this* was what was holding her back, and you gave her as much chance as a snowball, so now you're blaming her for going ahead. You knew all along you wouldn't let her fight you off on that damn red sofa. You knew it then and you know it now, you always have made love to the women you wanted to make love to, you always make them want you to, and now—goddam it, damn it, damn it, damn this for happening.

He would call her when he got this into some sort of shape. That's what he had said, thinking that if only he could get off by himself, away from the sight of her, the God-given processes of reason and enlightenment would come into play and help him accept this as another one of life's problems, to be handled, absorbed, reconciled to, like a verdict gone against you, like Johnny's suspension from school. But he didn't really believe it.

I'm not a diminisher by nature. He had written that to her in his first letter, faintly enamored of the sound of it, but meaning it, feeling sure of himself with her, sure of them together. Now he was truly diminished, withdrawn, dry with coldness and fevered at the same time, half of himself gone dead and still.

The word *diminished* infuriated him. Abruptly he got up from bed, slid his feet into his slippers, nearly gasping at the first sting of their frozen leather, and went into the kitchen. Night after night he had done this also; twice Joan had waked too, to admonish him not to be too concerned about Johnny or even about Hildy's sudden demands for a bigger allowance when her next birthday came. "It's more than that," he had said, but when she had looked attentive, interested, he had quickly added, "You know how things stick in your mind and won't come unstuck."

Now he waited for a moment to be sure she did not wake and follow. From the icebox he got half a glass of milk, took it into the living room, and then he unlocked his briefcase. In an inner compartment was the letter that had come yesterday morning at the office. He had read it a dozen times already:

> DEAR MATTHEW,
>
> I would give anything not to have started with you without telling you first that Dr. Jesskin had just begun tests and that I would not know for sure until Thursday. I cannot, even now, be sorry about *it,* but I am wretched about you.
>
> Always,
> D.

A dozen times, too, he had tried to answer it, but he would write, "Dear Dori," and then his pen would go still. He would look at the phone but wonder what possibly to say. The specific idea of going to see her, of talking to her, of trying to put into words—he could do nothing.

He needed more time. He could not think of these new complexities. Never had his own life been so filled with complexities: Johnny, the Benting case, the sudden vision of Hildy as a sixteen-year-old and all at once not a child any more. Maybe later on, the time would come when he was calm enough again to see this about Dori in an acceptable light. But not now.

He tore her note across and then again across. He looked about for a place to throw the scraps, then aligned them, put them back into his briefcase, and locked it once more.

*　　*　　*

On the fifteenth, Dori told Tad Jonas she was quitting to try herself at free-lancing. She would of course stay as long as he needed her, but because there was one piece with an early deadline, she would appreciate it if she could pull out pretty soon. Jonas said, "Anytime, cookie, I knew it was coming," and she left the office for the last time.

She had heard nothing from Matthew.

The one note she had written him was short, almost too short by the time she got through tearing sentences from it. She had sent it to his office, marked *Personal,* wondering how sacred that word on an envelope was in his secretary's opinion. The very next morning she had waited for the mail; he had not answered it. Nor the morning after, nor the morning after.

It's a fascinating time to be alive anyway, she told herself, not only because of being pregnant and watching it happen, but because of a million things outside me. There was hideous news or wonderful news every day: hideous, like the indictment that week of Dr. Spock and the four others, with trial to come in April or May; wonderful, like the story from South Africa about transplanting the heart of a man newly dead into the body of that dying dentist. Her own blood had pumped in some wild hope at this bizarre story; a new world was opening for the future, with new chances, new possibles. Maybe by the time any 1968 baby grew up, there would be a hundred such miracles, a cure for cancer found, the end of pain, the end of war.

The end of pain? Not since the despairing days just after Tony's departure had she felt this gnawing sensation of emptiness, and this seemed sharper now, more unremitting. Or was that because you could only remember past pain, never reinvoke it? Every moment of thought now said *Matthew,* the soft hush at the core of his name like a brush across her heart. Never before had she heard the sound made on the ear by Matthew's name; now she heard it constantly, and constantly it brought with it its cousin sounds, *breath, death, ethic, ethical.* Ethic, ethical— what was right here, what wrong?

She had foreseen that he might leave her when he knew but she had never believed in it. She had been vain, loving his praise of her body, wondering only whether that would lessen, and by how much. She had told Cele what Dr. Jesskin had said about sex and pregnancy and Cele had said, "Oh, yes, right up to maybe the last few weeks." There was a special quality, Cele had told her, a new intensity. But Cele was remembering herself and Marshall as a young couple; it had been "their" pregnancy and had made them both happy.

That flash of eagerness in Matthew's first question, "Darling, are you pregnant now?"—she had not imagined it, and now it was too poignant to bear. If she had been able to let him think it was "their" pregnancy, that instinctive eagerness might have expanded and grown, thrusting, strong enough to endure through all the clutch and twist of problems that would face him because of it. He would never leave Hildy and Johnny; his devotion to them was an absolute. But he would have become involved too with *this* child, would never have walked out this way, would not now be silent and absent and lost.

But oh God, I couldn't. I couldn't lie to him and pretend and go on letting him think, and then go through with the terrible lie about a premature baby in July.

There were women who could and she marveled at them and also despised them. She half envied them their shrewdness and ability to manage life and she also detested them for it. She herself had had no choice. Her options had lain only in method, and there she had proved a failure.

She could not sleep. At each shrill ring of the telephone she told herself it would not be Matthew, but when it was not she had to force her "hello" to sound normal. Irrationally, she summoned telephone repairmen to muffle the ring, but the new sound was no less rasping. The doorbell, the morning mail, a florist's delivery boy in the elevator—each became a hazard to be met and overcome. Within hours of mailing her letter to him she began rewriting it in her mind, adding phrases she had not thought of in time, letting herself argue with him, plead, even at last accuse him. *Don't let us make all the young mistakes?* But at the first real difficulty, Matthew, you cut away in a rage like a boy of twenty, ignore a decent letter or throw it into the nearest trash basket.

Rebuttal at once, defense of him; perhaps he needed silence and absence to regroup his forces, to rearrange his life with Joan—

Come on, cut that out, she thought, the one damn thing you're never going to do is to think about any future with Matthew. You can love him or hate him, see him or not see him, fight or make up, but the one thing you are never going to do is to think about being married to him.

She felt better. Vaguely she was reminded of something else that had once comforted her, but she could not catch hold of what it had been. It had come at some other time when she was becoming overemotional, and she had seen then that she need not give in to it.

Weekends were easier; she had never seen him on Saturdays or Sundays. On the third Sunday of his absence she turned determinedly to the voluminous real estate ads in the paper. Houses—Manhattan, Houses—Brooklyn, Houses—Queens, page after page of houses for sale, for rent, everything houses. Also apartments: Furnished, Unfurnished, Six Rooms, Four Rooms, Two Rooms, Apartments Wanted, Apartments to Share. At last she came to Furnished Rooms, East Side, West Side. There were only a few of each, and most of these in hotels, hotels with unknown names in side streets, but all belonging to the same family of third-rateness. Hotels were out anyway; she had to do without even a shabby lobby, without a front desk and elevator man.

That meant a room in a brownstone. In half an hour she had underlined half a dozen. One was in the Bronx, on West 253rd Street, and she wondered if it were near Bronx Park; another was rather close, on West Ninety-fifth, definitely near Central Park; another was in a remodeled brownstone in the old Chelsea district. That was too close to the Village. If she could find something near one of the great parks, she could do her brisk three miles in the early morning or evening; she was free of the usual fears and alarms about the dangers of the streets and the parks. She had always been a lone walker in the city, and not once had she encountered anything more suspect than a weaving drunk.

She reread the ad about the place on West Ninety-fifth. It was not a furnished room but a "2 rm studio, gd. fl, all new furn," and suddenly she thought, On the ground floor I'd never have to meet people on the stairs. The $180 rent astonished her but she stared at the telephone number which served as signature to the ad and almost without volition dialed it.

A foreign voice answered, perhaps Italian, perhaps

Spanish, but there was no difficulty in understanding. Yes, just renovated, repainted, new icebox, new bed, new everything, very big studio room and kitchen. No roaches. Nobody had lived there since the new furniture. All first time for the new tenant.

"When could I see it?"

"Anytime. Ring the super's bell."

"I'll be there in about a half hour."

"What name, please?"

She hesitated. She had been choosing and discarding names for so long and now suddenly she had to decide. "Grange," she said. "Mrs. Grange—I'll be there right away."

"If it's rented, don't blame me. First come, first served."

"I'll hurry."

She dressed quickly, a spurt of new interest lifting her spirits. The time ahead is still good, she thought, nothing can change that. How strange that she could feel, at the core of surrounding pain and loss, this persistent quiet rightness. It was almost as if she were, somewhere, still happy.

As the taxi turned off Central Park West into Ninety-fifth, she looked out in anticipation. The street looked bare and almost clean; with the temperature below twenty, the bareness was not surprising. In summer there would be ear-piercing children screaming to each other as they played, music blaring from open windows, jammed traffic, the usual hullabaloo of city streets in hot weather. But by then, with only days to go, why should she mind anything?

Dori stopped in front of the house. Its brick front was already shabby, mean, its windows dirty against an assortment of lace curtains, chintz curtains, drawn shades. Two great garbage cans stood at the curb where the taxi stopped, lidded and faintly odoriferous, a pair of horrid welcomers. She ignored them and went into the small vestibule where an astonishing expanse of brass letterboxes stretched across one wall. She counted sixteen and thought, At these rents, peo-

ple room together. She pressed the bell over the typed
card, *Steffani, SUPER,* and at once the foreign voice
of the telephone queried through the round grating in
the brass: "Who is it?" And she made herself wait a
second, rehearsing, before she said, "Mrs. Grange."

A moment later the landlady appeared and without a word of greeting led the way to a door at the
rear of the hallway. "Everything new," she said as she
opened it, and as Dori went by her a chill of disappointment seized her. It was a large room, with low
ceilings and two windows on a cement-paved back-
yard; it might once have been the kitchen of the house,
as at Cele's, and the floor was covered with yellow-
and-brown linoleum as if it were still a kitchen. But it
was furnished like a studio bedroom-living room in
the drab good taste of a bargain furniture store. A
stiff squared-off sofa that the landlady proclaimed "a
convertible, a double," was flanked by a pair of lad-
derback chairs in a shiny veneer, obviously new, and
there was a corner table, also shiny new. Where a
fireplace might have been was one armchair near a
home-made platform of wood, oblong, twelve inches
from the floor, empty, devoid of meaning until the
landlady said, "For the television."

"And is there an outlet for an air conditioner?"

"Don't need no special outlet." Mrs. Steffani gave
her a closer look, a scrutiny as if to make some judgment. A television set was expected, but not an air
conditioner? By what yardstick? This was no slum
neighborhood; actually it was a rather pretty street,
with several other remodeled houses, and she certainly
would not be the only tenant on the block with an air
conditioner. Then why that second look as if she had
asked for a private garage?

Mrs. Steffani led her to the kitchen, a sliver of a
room, also facing the cemented yard, and then to another sliver, the bathroom, the walls of both a staring
dead white. Here too was the same unused look, with
no fingerprint, no frayed edge, no smudge.

"Did you just paint it?"

Mrs. Steffani nodded. "All the furniture new, every stick. Look here, this new stove and icebox. Brand-new."

"Lovely," Dori said, going back to the big room. But how ugly, she thought; I'd simply die in such an ugly place.

Behind her Mrs. Steffani said, "You want it? Or you don't want it? The lease is one year. First and last month in advance."

"I won't need it for a whole year. My husband—"

"A year's lease. Here, nothing by the month. You want your husband to see? Okay. It could be rented the next twenty minutes. First come—"

"Yes, I know." She cast one last glance around as if trying to decide. "I'll let you know. I have one other place to see."

At once Mrs. Steffani dropped any show of interest, going back into the hallway, Dori dismissed and forgotten even as she passed by her to the front door. Out in the street she paused, relieved to be away from the unspoken pressure she had felt inside. A hundred and eighty a month for *that*? Because it was remodeled and not subject to rent control! This dreadful housing shortage let such rents happen. But a year's lease would run over two thousand. Unthinkable to start off that way. She certainly could find something that cost less.

In the bus uptown to her next address she reminded herself that there was still no great rush; she could look again next Sunday and the next. But the moment she arrived at the furnished room on West 253rd, she was nervous. A smell of mildew and frying fat rushed out at her, filthy walls appalled her and she fled, suddenly exhausted, her one thought to go home. But she did not go home. By bus, subway, taxi, she continued on the rounds of her addresses, from one impossible to another.

Her nervousness deepened. Suppose that a place like Mrs. Steffani's really was unique, and that after a few more Sundays when there was no more time for being choosy, suppose that then she could find nothing but the ones with frying fat and filth?

Suddenly the "just renovated, everything new, no roaches" seemed a treasure she had wholly underestimated. Suddenly the linoleum on the floor, the varnish, the bargain-basement taste seemed admirable, utterly desirable. Quiet, clean, a few of her own things strewn about—why had she ever left this paragon of a place for somebody else to snatch up? Perhaps after July she could sublease it—better not raise that question now. She hailed a taxi.

"Is it rented?" she asked over the brass announcer in the hall, and then said, "Wonderful," at Mrs. Steffani's reply.

Mrs. Steffani demanded a deposit until the lease was ready tomorrow or Tuesday. "Check or cash, twenty-five down."

Dori opened her purse. But I can't write a check signed Grange, she thought, and nearly said so out loud. "Here's the cash," she said. "May I have a receipt?"

For the first time Dori felt optimistic. Tomorrow she would find a bank in the neighborhood and open an account in the name of Dorothy Grange. A bank account under an assumed name. She might move in right away, this week, the moment the lease was signed and a telephone connected. There would be a sense here of a new start, of getting down to it, of cutting all the trains of thought to the past. Here if the phone rang, she wouldn't leap for it as if it might be Matthew. He would not even know her number.

*   *   *

Four evenings later, she glanced around her bedroom, disheveled as it was with its still-open suitcases and a dozen odds and ends. The telephone rang and a voice said, "Towson, home from the wars."

"Dick! When did you get in?"

"Yesterday, and does this city look good."

"You've been gone, let's see, three whole months. Your pieces have been great."

"Thanks. I just heard you'd copped out on your paper. Is that true?"

"Tell me I'm crazy. I'm going to free-lance."

"Why didn't you drop me a line about it? I'd have told you then."

"I should have written." She added quickly, "But I've thought of you lots."

"I'll bet."

"I really have."

"When do I get to see you? How about a drink tomorrow around five?"

"I can't, Dick, I'm sorry."

"Then when? How about after dinner? Have you a date tomorrow night?"

"I can't think. Wait a minute." Automatically she turned toward her calendar as if she really were looking for a free afternoon or evening in a crowded life. But her eyes were closed. Automatically too, as she did so many times every single day, she tightened her muscles over her stomach, feeling the good tautness, releasing, tightening, knowing that now even when they were tight there was no bland flat planes any longer. "Dick, could I give you a raincheck?" she said at last. "I'm sort of swamped with things right now."

For a moment there was no answer. Then he said, "Well, okay, if that's the way it is." His voice brightened as he added, "Have fun, whatever."

"I'll do that."

"Think of me."

"Oh I will." Suddenly she laughed a little. "I truly will."

So are decisions made, she thought as she hung up. It's as if your active mind had nothing to do, as if you just put the problem into the miracle-computer of your unconscious, fed it in, left it there through all the mysterious whirrings and clackings and tumblings, and then as if there came, at the proper time, the desired *output,* your decision, firm, clear, authoritative.

Input and output, technology's new words for a process as old as man, as old as conscience. How could it possibly be right to tell Dick Towson that I am going to have a baby that he unwittingly sired? To what end? To make him feel guilty? Responsible for its support? Honor-bound to get a divorce and make an honest woman out of me? I am an honest woman.

And suppose he did, what about that other honest woman, his wife?

She left the telephone and returned to her packing. She was moving in the morning, and Cele had been over all day to help. Clothes were easy; two suitcases were ample. There had been a problem about the pots and pans and dishes and books she wanted, because cartons or a barrel would scarcely go with her official story to the building, that she was off on a world cruise by plane and ship for ten weeks, but Cele had solved it by lending her a huge plaid carryall that concealed awkward shapes. Cele was known to the doorman; she would be coming over every few days to pick up her mail.

"A hard and fast itinerary is out," Dori had explained. "It's a crazy kind of trip with a crazy schedule."

"I wouldn't mind taking a trip like that myself, Mrs. Gray."

"I'm dying to get started, Bill." It would be the longest ten weeks on record. The stretchingest, she thought, and smiled.

Now she checked once more to see that she had overlooked nothing. She glanced longingly at her record player; it was a fine true system and she wanted it with her. But one didn't take hi-fi equipment on world cruises and Cele was going to lend her one of Marshall's the moment she was installed. Into the carryall she had slid half a dozen records; now, almost as a final rite, she added her set of the four she had hunted down so happily to give to Matthew at Christmas.

The packing had tired her but she was too keyed up to consider sleep and she made one last tour around each of her four rooms, in one last search for some forgotten object she would sorely miss. This was what made packing difficult, the selecting and choosing, this I must take, that I needn't, yes, but I might need it. Now, looking down at the mahogany stand near her desk where there reposed in all its grand solidity her vast unabridged Webster's, she hesitated once more. Cele had ridiculed her for considering it an essential on West Ninety-fifth Street, and she had yielded. "But don't I deserve one or two fetishisms?" and Cele had raucously declaimed in an exaggerated Jewish accent, "Fetishisms yet! On a world cruise she needs a hundred-pound dictionary, plus whatever else she's carrying."

They had laughed and now Dori smiled, remembering. Cele was that rarest of creatures, a friend who was there when help was needed. She would be there in the morning for the actual move; she would do the unpacking at the new place, she would do the first marketing for her, stow supplies in cupboards and cabinets. "Sugar and soap flakes and canned goods weigh tons, Dori—you can do nice things like fruit and steak."

This final rambling search for any forgotten object was oddly pleasing. Closing her apartment, locking the door behind her, and leaving everything behind was soothing, as if she were leaving her pain about Matthew there too.

She glanced at the silent telephone. After tomorrow if he should try to call her, it would ring and ring and ring. That maddening secret sound of a telephone ringing on and on and on, giving no reason for its futility, offering only a "no comment" to the caller—a sudden sympathy for Matthew awoke in her, quenched by an ironic query somewhere: "And what makes you think he'll be calling?"

She had vetoed the frugal step of stopping service for half a year just to preserve that "no comment" and prevent the singsong revelation that service has been temporarily discontinued. Frugality could be costly on the scale of real values; she had already begun another list of majors and minors headed "Possible Tattlers."

Had she overlooked any? Her suitcases were monogrammed TVG, as were the towels and napkins and few pieces of silverware she was taking, two knives, two forks, two soupspoons, four teaspoons; it would take more than a Mrs. Steffani to prove that those initials had ever stood for anything other than Dorothy V. Grange, though she might, in a brilliant moment, pause over the *T*. The dozen or so books she had to have with her were not so perfect, for in them all had once been written either T. Gray or Dori Gray or D. V. Gray, this from a school-bred ritual of writing her name inside the front cover of any book or notebook or exercise book she had ever acquired, but she had methodically inked them all out and written Grange in, instead, using various pencils, pens and marking crayons to avoid obvious similarity.

Her new checkbook on a big neighborhood bank on Columbus Avenue would be the only one kept in the shiny new desk, her real checkbook for her "real bank" being stored in one of her suitcases, always locked. Deposits in her Grange bank, as she thought of it, would never be her own checks, signed Gray, drawn on her real bank. She would write out her real checks to either Cele or Gene and get their checks in return to be deposited or mailed to her Grange bank. She would even have to pay her hospital bills by Grange checks.

When she had first realized that she could not use her Blue Cross hospital insurance, she had been worried, but it was a brief worry vanquished by the reality that nowhere on any public record in any bank, store, organization, nowhere on any punch card of any computer, could the connection between Gray and

Grange ever be set forth for even impersonal eyes to see. Except in that one ultimate document of adoption which, she knew somehow, was to be held *in camera* forever by the courts and the laws of the land.

But for the rest, it was to be Gray and Grange. It was all legal; her newspaper years told her that. You could take any pseudonym you wanted, any pen name, any stage name, do anything in that name and still be legal—unless you planned to commit a crime or did commit a crime. All she planned to commit, she thought cheerfully, was one small baby.

She had overlooked nothing. If Mrs. Steffani and her passkey ever did enter the apartment while she was out, she would find not one detail that could point to any tenant except Dorothy V. Grange. And if she should overhear Gene or Cele call her Dori or Dorr—who said that every Dorothy had to be nick-named Dot?

Only once so far had she made a slip that might have raised a question. For a moment only, at the signing of the lease, there was the fleeting pause over a question not properly answered, and it had gone by quickly enough to be nothing.

"Your husband to sign here," Mrs. Steffani had said, accepting the first and last month's rent and pointing to a dotted line on the document.

"He's in the Air Force," she had replied, a split second late. "I'll sign."

Mrs. Steffani looked uncertain. Then she shrugged, accepted her copy of the lease and departed. Dori had intended to say that he was in the Air Force and off on duty in Vietnam, and how awful that he had to be away at such a time, but her half answer, sufficing, taught her something: the less you explain the more real it sounds. She had determined to be frugal with her words.

At last she undressed and went to bed. As the light went out, she thought of Matthew. Why had he done this? She had imagined every kind of reaction from him, but this continuing silence, this continuing absence, with never an answer to her letter—this she had not foreseen.

I can't be sorry about *it,* she repeated silently, remembering the words she had written, but I am wretched about you. Wretched. What a word, what a cheating, mealymouthed, uncomplaining word. I resent the way you've taken this is what she had really meant, I'm shocked by it, and frightened too. I am forty and this may be my last passionate love, I will not be a girl any more, I will be a woman with a child, and you loved me, and now you stay away and say nothing, not a word, just this silence and absence and more silence and more absence.

I'm not wretched; I'm sore and insulted and let down. Not sore meaning riled, but *sore,* full of ache and hurt and woundedness. And you—what about your insight and care for other people and all the fine things I thought you stood for?—that you do stand for if it comes to a law case?

But this was sarcasm, hitting out, hitting back. Suddenly the thought of tomorrow was no longer a soothing thought; it became a desperate longing for the new beginning in the linoleum-floored room across the park.

*   *   *

From the beginning she liked it. It was a different world but she liked it for being different. She did not feel removed from regret or pain about Matthew but she did feel somehow insulated as by a protective cooling layer. It was more than that, she thought after a few days in her new place; here she felt encapsulated somehow, the cocoon again and safe. I am creating my own womb for me to curl up inside, that's what I'm doing. There was a harmony in the notion; she let herself think about it.

She had Cele for dinner the first night and Gene the second. She had always liked cooking and now she gave herself to all the lengthier processes of it, ig-

noring the shortcuts she used to stoop to in the press
of time, the pre-prepared seasoning, the pre-chopped
chives, the canned and frozen and freeze-dried every-
things. She never felt too tired to market and cook,
she even liked washing up afterward and doing the
daily housework. She had promised Cele that she
would exchange her weekly cleaning woman for a
daily part-time maid "later when I'm a big hulk," but
for now she could manage very well alone and for
some obscure reason needed to. It was part of the
different world she had come to.

Not physically different so much; there were just
as many streets like this half-tended, half-neglected
one over on the East Side, if you walked away from
Fifth and Madison and Park over to Lexington and
Third and Second, just as many there where the snow
still stood blocked and solid and graying in the gutters.
In fact this new street of hers, this West Ninety-fifth,
was rather handsome, certainly the near-the-park half
of it which included her house. The old apartment
houses on the corner gave way on each side to a quartet not of brownstones but of white stone houses, pale
and clean as if they had been newly sandblasted.
There were signs of remodeling, but fortunately the
old bay windows on their upper floors and their man-
sard roofs were unchanged, and on one or two there
were wrought-iron picket fences around the step-down
areas at the kitchen entrances, with window boxes or
privet hedges dusted with snow. At the street level all
doors and windows were barred with iron grillwork,
but brass knobs and number plates and bells gleamed
from faithful polishing.

Off to the west at the Columbus Avenue end of the
long block, a modern apartment house was nearing
completion. It promised to be attractive, with its tan
brick and white stone walls, its picture windows and
terraces, and she was relieved to hear that it wouldn't
be ready for tenants until the end of the year. This,
and some other new or nearly new buildings sticking
up out of the rubbish of old tenements up and down

Columbus Avenue—why had she not noticed them when she came to answer the ad?—all these new buildings, tagged "middle-income housing," all looked inviting. She'd better keep an eye out for friends and acquaintances after all.

Walking, marketing, going to Broadway to a movie, she kept a particular watch on passing faces. In an old fur coat lent her by Cele, needlessly ample thus far, and from under the flopping brim of a dated felt sports hat, she looked out at all approaching people, ready to cross the street at the first sight of anybody familiar. The faces too were different from the faces of home across the park; there were many dark faces here but so were there on Madison and Park. But over there they were the faces of delivery boys and maids whereas over here they were of people living in the neighborhood, mothers with small children, school kids tearing along with their books or on skates or sleds, old people. There still were more whites here than blacks and Puerto Ricans, but for the first time in all her life she was living in a really integrated neighborhood. Better than talking about it, she thought vaguely, not stopping to inquire what she meant. It all added to the sense of difference, of actually being a traveler, as if the lies about the crazy world cruise were in part true and she were far from home and greedy for new sights and new experiences.

When she said "home," she never thought of the linoleum-floored studio room she now lived in. Home still meant the apartment she had locked up and left, still meant her books, her music, her desk, her dear familiar paintings and furniture and colors. But soon she came to see, embarrassingly enough, that home also meant certain other things which brainwashed you with a subtle sense of privilege and upper-classness.

At home you mailed a letter right up on your own floor, going down a carpeted hallway in your dressing gown to the brass chute ten steps from your own front door; here you dressed and went outdoors to the corner mailbox, and if it was late at night you didn't go at all until next morning because of the horrendous tales you were always hearing about crime in the streets. At home you ordered food from the grocer and butcher by phone and had it delivered, the tomatoes, the perfect pears, the apples, the lettuce wrapped separately in glossy white paper before being put in the carton, to isolate and protect it; here you went out yourself in good weather or foul, to the stores on Columbus, saw all your vegetables and fruit dumped into one great brown bag, and were careful not to choose too heavy a load to carry. At home there was always the doorman to tell you the weather or whistle up a cab; here there was the bolted door and the announcer beside it and the peephole through the door and the latch chain always slid into the groove before you opened more than an inch to anyone whose voice or face you did not know.

And yet day by day she liked it more, liked it for being different. In daylight hours at least she disregarded the horrendous tales and walked freely in the nearly deserted park, striding out as she had been ordered to do, feeling immune to danger as if nobody ever could possibly hurt her.

* * *

And then one Sunday morning in early February, she suddenly found herself shaken by something else she had heard horrendous tales about. In the twenty days that she had been walking in the park, she had always turned south, instinctively turning toward the skyline which stood clear and sharp and beautiful at its southern rim. She would walk hard, as Dr. Jesskin had ordered, following the winding, dipping, curving walks to the old casino near Sixty-seventh, and then with more than half her mileage accounted for, leave the curving route within the park and return outside on the special pavement of Central Park West, six-sided stone plaques cemented together, like gears meshed one to the next. In bitter weather, with the temperature in the twenties or below, these daily three miles were test enough of her will and stamina, but there was a sense of accomplishment afterward as well as a glowing well-being. So far she had had not a minute of illness; early in the fourth month it was still too early for any discomfort of bulk.

On this particular Sunday morning she idly turned north instead of south when she entered the park, her back to the skyline, nothing ahead but winter-stripped trees on mildly rolling hills and the sky itself. It was an easy sky, a blue sky, wind-cleansed of soot and haze and lowering gray. It filled her with longing for spring and then summer, for trees leafing gently and then richly, for shade arching again over green park benches, for movement and sound everywhere instead of this sparse winter stillness and emptiness.

Because it was the weekend, with the roadway closed to automobiles, she walked in the road itself, long cleared of the last snow which still lay patchily on the ground and pedestrian paths. An occasional cyclist, dressed like a skier against the cold, came whistling by, and on the shallow slopes still under snow, a few children were tumbling around on sleds or skis.

She had gone in at Ninety-sixth as she always did and soon found that there were more people about than she had at first thought. Off at her right lay a vast playing field that she had never in all her years as a New Yorker seen before; there was a game in progress, voices rose shrill and bright, largely in Spanish, and she wondered if today were some Puerto Rican holiday or field day. The roadway led up a sharp hill and then down; she glanced occasionally at the aluminum light poles, each marked with numerals and letters to guide police or repairmen or park maintenance men to a specific site. The playing field ended at about 100th Street. She had worked out the system of the poles for herself in the first days of her walking; W 9601 meant that it was the first pole inside the park

at West Ninety-sixth Street; if it had read E 7202 it
would have meant the second pole inside at the East
Seventy-second Street entrance, and M 6703 would
have meant the Mall around Sixty-seventh, the third
pole in a cluster of half a dozen.

This small decoding for herself had given her a
spasm of childlike pleasure; every day she found some
new small pleasure in the park, always with a thready
surprise stitching along her senses, for she had always
lived near it and had assumed that there was nothing
about it that was new or unexpected. Now she was
seeing things one did not see from taxis racing
against the lights to get you to a theater or concert,
and up here to the north and west it was like finding
a new park entirely. Here were playgrounds she had
never seen, playing fields she had never seen; there
ahead now, down far below in a great hollow, was the
first shine of the new skating rink she had heard about
in the past year or two but had never seen.

Dori heard voices, sharp young voices, gleeful,
laughing over nothing, the climbing shouts of children
at play. It was a large rink, and crowded, somewhere
music was playing, and she thought of the older rink
down at the other end of the park near Fifth Avenue
and Sixtieth, where she herself had so often skated.
Hans Brinker, or the Silver Skates; there was always something shining and lovely about gleaming
ice and twinkling blades, red scarves and mittens, eyes
aglow, ruddy faces whipped by the wind. She was being sentimental and knew it and did not chide herself.

The roadway curved sharply and as she came
around a bend she was suddenly close enough to the
rink to see it not as panorama but as a specific scene.
There was something strange about it, and she did
not know at once what it was. She looked beyond the
roadway toward the rusty old tenements fringing the
far border of the park and even without consulting
the nearest aluminum pole she suddenly realized that
she was approaching the northern boundary of Central Park at 110th Street. Harlem. The skyline here

was Harlem. And then suddenly she knew what was strange about this skating rink on this shining blue morning.

All the faces were dark. All the children were Negro or Puerto Rican. Perhaps one child was white, perhaps two, out of the hundreds down below the rising ground where she stood, but it was a whole world of brown and tan and black young faces.

De facto segregation. Once somebody had asked her what, exactly, de facto segregation meant and she had thought it a stupid unwilling question, as if anybody could possibly not understand what de facto segregation was. Now suddenly she thought, If you were here this minute you'd never have to ask that question again.

She shuddered. Those Spanish voices back at the playing field weren't celebrating some fete day, they were there because that was about where it started, in the Nineties on the West Side, and she had passed it by without thinking. All over the rest of the park these past twenty days, wherever she had passed some group of kids out with a teacher for athletics, she had seen how many faces were dark, except when the group wore the blazers or uniforms of some private school, when the faces were nearly always white with only a few black—as tokens? She had always known all about the city's population, had always assumed there could be no surprises.

But this was a surprise. This was solid and ugly and she wanted to turn quickly away and would not let herself. She walked closer, listening now as well as watching, hearing the young shouting voices, hearing the excited cries and laughter, seeing the little playing animals on the ice who did not even know that on this lovely sunny Sunday morning there was something hideous in their shining skating rink.

*   *   *

"Can't we have one hour without that damn music?" Matthew demanded.

"Why of course," Joan said. "I didn't realize you minded."

"This whole damn weekend we haven't had five minutes without it."

"You might have said so before you got this worked up about it."

Both children stared at him as their mother left the table and went out to the record player. There was the crisp click of a switch and a declining wail as the turntable came to a stop. The mournful sound told the story, for normally Joan pampered the machine and would have lifted the tone arm properly, and pressed the stop button only when the needle was safely disengaged. Now she did not even wait for the record to stop; she went out of the kitchen and down the hall to her own room.

Matthew grunted. It had been a foul weekend all round, foul roaring wind and rain, the children indoors, the house roaring with their voices, their intermittent spats, their incessant motion. When he was a boy and landlocked by weather, he had had none of the noisemakers that were the appurtenances of today, no transistor radio, no television, no stereo; he had doubtless been a nuisance in whatever ways children can be nuisances to their parents, but he had no recollection of incessant noise accompanying every activity. I used to read, he thought, everybody used to read.

Hildy rose from the table, her face wearing the injured look that told him she found life hard to bear in this household. She started from the room and he said, "What about the dishes?" She turned back, still injured, not answering but beginning to clear the table. "I'll dry," Johnny said, and disappeared. With the new semester he was reinstated at school, impenitent, still saying that basketball and hockey made him puke. The school had "compromised" by capitulating. He would do shop and painting, favorites both, instead of sports.

Matthew watched his daughter as she moved be-

tween the table and the kitchen. She was wearing a
skirt so short that it barely cleared her tiny buttocks,
and again it startled him that he lived in an age that
permitted its young girls such flagrant narcissism. For
he was sure that the ever-briefer skirts of Hildy and
her friends revealed not only their desire to attract
boys but their own enormous self-approval; they knew
very well how delectable their slim young thighs
could be to the male eye, the young male eyes of their
sixteen-year-old admirers as well as the startled eyes
of their fathers and uncles and other supposedly immune observers. But they also found them rather
delectable themselves, when they gazed into shopwin-
dows or long mirrors.

Next week, on the first of March, Hildy would be
sixteen; recently she had put a definable distance between herself and her parents, natural enough, not
meant to be hostile, not meant to be troubling. Yet to
him it announced a milestone. She was grown up. In
an earlier age, sixteen would have been merely another
stage in the gradual process of becoming an adult, but
in the rushing years of the late nineteen-sixties, the
message to most parents was "I'm an adult now." In
Hildy it had come abruptly; last year she was still his
loving little girl, now she was at best an amiable
relative, at worst a cool remarker of his faults and
frailties and a cooler critic of his decisions.

Alienation. The word was all over the place, already a nonce word, a slogan, a piece of verbal clap-
trap uttered so easily and so often it had forfeited its
original force. Blacks and whites, alienated; doves
and hawks, alienated; young and old, alienated. It was
a kind of shorthand no longer fully decipherable by
people who sought meaning underneath the hooks and
curves and dots and squiggles.

It was a world in turmoil and here he was, alienated
right out of it. His turmoil was his alone; he seethed in
it; it seethed in him; he could not control it and rejoin
that other world, those other turmoils, could not get
back to living as he was living before—before—

Damn it, he had ordered his mind not to do this, and his mind kept doing it anyhow. Before Dori, before wreckage, before catastrophe. He was pierced with longing for that flashing of happiness in the first instant of her telling him, before he caught what she really meant, and he was pierced too with desire, not sexual desire but a desire as poignant, to be back before this had happened, back there somewhere with her before, before, while there was still time for them. This backward-longing was something he had never known before, a something not in the schedules and manifests of life as he knew it.

Last night he had spent two hours drinking with Jack Henning and Jack had finally said, "What's eating you, for God's sake?" To his own complete astonishment, he had told him to go to hell. But then, in a few brusque sentences he had told Jack about Dori, not naming her, told it harshly, the essentials only, of their affair, of her swift importance to him, of her sudden announcement that she was already pregnant when they met, and that he had found himself staggered in a way he had never known before.

Jack had been staggered too. "You offered to help her." It was a simple statement, bearing no question mark.

"She wasn't looking for help." He had then summed up her history of doctors and tests and waiting, and had ended, "so help was the last thing she wanted. She was happy about it." He had seen Jack's eyes fill with some new expression that he meant to query him about, but in another minute Jack was ordering more drinks for them both and the moment passed.

Later, alone and in a half-drunk reverie, he had thought, Alienation, that's it. Dori and I are alienated —what a farce of a word. Distance from, distance between, separation and silence, that is alienation. We are alienated one from the other.

The phrase still haunted him, even now, weeks later. It was feeble and false, but it was also true. Why? Why did it remain true? Over and over he had assured himself that this was no typical male jealousy but something else, yet he could not find what that something else was. Over and over, like a scientist, like a detective, like a trial lawyer preparing for court, he had searched through the whole body of evidence for the one clue that had evaded him, and each time he wound up defeated. If she had lied to him about her life these past years—but she had told him all he needed to know about herself and men, more than he had told her in return. He hadn't felt a qualm about those infrequent and apparently none-too-meaningful affairs of hers, had known she was just getting over one. He had wasted no time thinking of them, any more than if she had told him about her first kiss, though he had not let himself visualize her responsiveness to anyone else, knowing as he did that if it were required of him that he answer yes or no as to whether sex had moved her, he would have had to say, Yes, always. It never was possible to think of her as unmoved about sex, cool, remote, contained about sex. One of the holds she had on you was the depth of her response, the readiness, the complexity, like your own, the totality of drive toward the top of it and then the totality of the moment itself.

Remembering was still a savagery, and then fury that she should have—

Should have what? He still could not state it, this crime he charged her with. If he once could frame it in the containing rim of words and phrases, he might at last manage it, accept it, view it as reality and then come to terms with it. But he could get no closer than his own certainty that what looked like an onslaught of male jealousy was more complicated.

He still did not know what it was. And until he did, he was immobilized.

SEVEN ⸙

SUDDENLY IT WAS WARM and in Central Park the first green tinged the winter-brown earth. Spring had not officially arrived, but each day offered another indicator that the equinox was coming, the season filling. Dori began to go out earlier in the morning, no longer needing to wait for the sun to cancel rawness and cold; she stopped at bushes to stare at their thickening buds and wonder when the first burst of color would come. Her daily walk became a sought pleasure now, and though she pulled herself at intervals out of her lazy watching and renewed the ordained briskness of her step, she saw proof each day that she had always libeled the city by saying that the change of seasons was imperceptible in it.

All at once the yellow feathering of forsythia sprayed the bushes she had been pausing before, and a day or two later on the last Sunday of March, a small tree was pinkly white with blossom. Was it dogwood? She had always been too much a city dweller to be sure, and she wanted to stop a mounted policeman and ask, but as she approached him she could imagine the words "Officer, is that dogwood?" and was embarrassed and passed him by. Other trees were budding, and with a start she noticed that every one gauzy with green was a young tree, still slim in its trunk, still slender in the spread of its branches. The old trees remained dead with winter, the great oaks and elms and maples, all caught tight with their years, slower to move and change, stolidly patient amidst the burst and thrust of life around them.

At home she telephoned her brother at the university. "Gene, don't laugh at me, but could you ask Miss Pulley to get the name of the best book on trees and plants and flowers from the Botany Department? A beginner's book, what things are named and when they bloom, that kind of thing. I've gone all-over interested and could order a copy."

"My God, Dori, I thought it was pickles or something you were supposed to crave."

"That comes later. Please do, Gene, and let me find out when a dogwood really blossoms. Maybe it's magnolia."

"If Pulley can swipe a copy up here I'll drop it off on the way home. Have courage, hang on."

She took his teasing cheerfully and felt an elation of interest. Who knew where hobbies had their genesis? Maybe this would become one of the lifelong kind that would never leave her. She was reading everything else these days, she might as well read about trees and shrubs.

She picked up the *Times* which she had only glanced at during breakfast, and prepared another cup of coffee to read it by. This had become a small ritual for the morning return from her walk; she recognized that it was quickly forming into a pattern, perhaps an unvarying pattern, and could only feel indulgent toward it. Surely you had the right to help things along with little rituals?

And then she stopped reading. She held the paper as if it were a bar of metal to cling to in a moment of weakness. She did not move. She forgot to breathe. It was true—she had not imagined it.

The smallest thump. Not a kick, it was nothing as firm and sure as a kick despite everything anybody had ever said or written. From within her, against the wall of her being, there was a small thump. The first one.

She waited unmoving. The newspaper slipped to her lap, the coffee was forgotten, she was electric with the waiting and then there it was once more. She suddenly realized that she was grinning like a maniac.

This was where the happy young wife was supposed to take the happy young husband's hand and put it over her swelling body so that he too might feel the kick. But she wasn't young and she wasn't a wife and she hadn't a husband. It must be marvelous, to share it. But it was also marvelous all in itself.

She sat on, immobile, inviting it, pleading with it to happen again. It did not, and she thought, Stubborn, hey? and a swell of feeling loosed itself in her.

It wasn't a kick. It was more like, like—she tried to reproduce the sensation. With the knuckle of her index finger she tapped the muscle of her left arm; that was something like, but not exact. With the flat part of her thumb, she gently poked at her hard rounding and still small stomach, as if she were prodding a melon. That too was something like, but still not right. With the edge of her hand she lightly struck her kneecap, a doctor testing reflexes, and dismissed the result: too bony. It had been a tap, firm but not bony, a thwack, a tapped signal, a magic telemetry across the incalculable space between nonbeing and being.

She had an impulse to call Dr. Jesskin and tell him, but she held back. He had told her it would be happening soon, "the end of the fourth month, the beginning of the fifth, these are individual matters also." She had been expecting it and yet it was totally unexpected in its arrival. It would happen again, but whether in minutes or in hours, there was no one to say. She would report to Jesskin after it had gone on for another day or two.

Once more she tried to remember just how it had felt. Without knowing it, she again sent her fingers tapping at her flesh and bone, seeking, testing, trying for approximation. And then, her lips accidentally apart, she tapped her right cheek with the middle finger of her right hand, and thought, That's it. She tried it again, this time opening her mouth wide and stiffening her cheeks so that the cavity within made a small hollow shell. She tapped again with a stiffened finger and at once thought with delight, If it came from the inside that would really be it. Life.

*   *   *

The movie would end in three or four minutes and as always she rose and made her way to the exit before the house lights came on, seeing the final scene standing, poised for instant departure. Under the brightness of the marquee, she paused, swiftly looking about her, seeing the faces of passing strangers with the familiar sense of satisfaction. All as it should be. It always was.

The sky was clouded and once she moved away from the lights of Broadway, the night was murky, warmer than early April evenings usually were. As she turned into her own street, the din of radio and TV voices seemed more insistent than usual, but she had already trained herself not to listen to them. Cars lined the curbs, their consecutive bumpers faintly shining, inches apart, but the usual beehive look of early evening was missing, the street empty of children as if some Pied Piper had passed through only a moment before and seduced them all away. Far ahead, at her own corner, a car deliberately double-parked, and she wondered at the gall of the driver until she remembered the doctor's shingle in the window.

"The assassin's bullet—"

One of the radio voices suddenly cut free from the surrounding din and pierced her wall of non-listening. The air was always vicious with shows of crime or terror or bang-bang-you're-dead, but there was a horror in the voice speaking these words, a shaken excitement that proclaimed that this was truth, not playacting, and an answering horror and excitement rose in her through the jerking next words until she heard "Martin Luther King was shot."

Oh God no. She heard her own cry, wrenched from her, torn out of her throat, and suddenly the circumambient din of voices that had been overlapping in the evening air turned into an unbearable repetition: Martin Luther King, Martin Luther King, Martin Luther King was shot and killed, Martin Luther King, Martin Luther King—

She began to run in a dark invisible need to get behind walls, to close out the voices. Running reminded her that she must not run, and she changed to a rushing, gasping walking. She was filled with fear, with pain, with hatred for the killer, for all killers, for all haters except the haters of haters; they were different, they were the good, the decent, the reasonable and loving, the ones who were flooded with fury at hate and death and killing.

She unlocked her door and bolted it instantly behind her and saw the night gleam on the shiny linoleum but before she clicked the switch of the lamp, she crossed to the low wood platform and clicked on the television instead. In the seconds that had to elapse before sound and image could appear she sank into the armchair as if she had been wounded, and when the first words came they were spurts of words clustered around the same shaken excitement she had heard on the street. "The assassin's bullet" . . . "ambulance rushed to the hospital" . . . "possible conspiracy." She was hurled back to that November day not five years before when other shaken voices were telling of bullets and blood splashing and assassination and conspiracy, and the two became one and she could scarcely see the small lighted screen through the scald of her sudden tears.

After a time she remembered that the room was still dark except for that one oblong at her knees and she rose to turn on the lights. The telephone rang. It was Gene.

"Do you know?"

"Oh Gene, I can't bear it."

"I'll come over. I tried to call you before."

"I was at a movie. Oh please come, Gene, it's so horrible."

She heard her voice waver, the "horrible" broken in half by the suck of her breath, and she thought, It's the first time, and did not ask what first time she meant. Relief poured through her belatedly; this was no thing to bear alone and Gene had known it and was coming to sit it out with her, a loving wisdom making him do it. The telephone rang again. It was Cele.

"Are you all right, Dorr?"

"Yes, are you?"

"It's brought back the whole thing about Kennedy."

"For me too."

"Where were you, how'd you hear it?"

"Coming home from the movies, I heard it on somebody's radio and didn't take it in until his name."

"We were just leaving the house and Minnie began to scream, 'They shot him, they shot Martin Luther,' and we both rushed into the kitchen to her radio and the kids heard it on theirs and I've been trying to calm them all and wondered about you."

"Gene is coming over."

"Then I'll come tomorrow night. God, do you remember at school, everybody telling just where they were when they heard about Roosevelt?"

"But that wasn't assassination. He was old and sick and he died, but Kennedy and now—oh Cele, what's *happening?*"

There was a pause. Then Cele said, "Don't go out for a day or two, will you? They say rioting is starting in Washington and Memphis already."

Long after she hung up, she sat staring at the television set as if in hypnosis. Gene was slow getting there, and obscurely she was glad. She needed time; she had to absorb, hear, let the tears come unheeded through the rerun of old scenes where Martin Luther King alive was speaking in the curiously rhythmic chant of his careful enunciation—move-ment, children, moun-tain—words grown familiar and dear by repetition. She had been right there in Washington on that hot August day in 1963 when he had first said those words and she had gulped over his dream. *One day on the red hills of Georgia . . . one day even the state of Mississippi . . . a dream that one day my four little children*—now she listened again to a replay of the same words and her throat locked. She had gone on the great march without knowing exactly why she went, knowing only that she had to be there too, had to walk with strangers too, bearing witness, peacefully. She remembered their walking, almost amiable along the wide and beautiful stretches of the capital's avenues, remembered the sudden sting of tears when up ahead somebody started, "Mine eyes have seen the glory," remembered the new song, "We Shall Overcome," whose words and melody she had never heard before and could not then know she would hear so many times again.

And now this, unbearable. Again she thought, It's the first time, but now she knew suddenly what the phrase meant. It's the first time since Matthew that anything horrible has happened in the world, and he's not here to go through it with me, not here to talk about it, not here to help me bear it, or want me to help him.

Her heart pounded, but this was not the happy beat of excitement and expectation; this was new, this was a heavy acknowledgment of disappointment, of disapproval. Could it be of something more than that? Of, perhaps, dislike?

She quivered at the thought, shrinking back as if she were the recipient of the word instead of its bestower. "Dislike" was too strong, but there was something. It was fine to say that you should never put your own yardstick along the stretch of another being's acts, ticking off in a kind of lineal moralizing how much you approved and how much you found less than worthy. But that was theory. And right now at this harrowing moment there *was* something for the first time that made her draw back.

Gene arrived then. She was dry-eyed as she opened the door to him, but the first sight of his darkly somber eyes filled hers. "Oh, Gene, what's happening to us?"

"It's a good question, damn it." He slung his coat off unceremoniously and asked for coffee. He sank into the armchair in front of the television set and began to listen again to the details he had already heard and heard and heard again, the white car speeding away, the Lorraine Motel balcony, the dirty brick flophouse across the street, the tall white man who was particular about the dollar-a-day room he had rented that afternoon, turning down one that faced a blank wall and choosing another that looked across the bare mimosa trees to the porch of the motel, owned by Negroes, for Negroes only.

"If he'd been able to stay anywhere he chose," she said, "they might not have known where to go to pick him off."

"It was bound to happen. He knew it. I suppose we have all known it all along."

"Here's coffee. Would you like a drink too?"

"Not yet." He continued to watch the screen and she pulled a cushion from the sofa and sat on the floor to one side. There was silence between them and she thought, This is all anybody needs, to share it, not to take it square alone. But that was going back to her accusations, and she cut sharply away from that direction of her thinking, like a driver taking a corner on squeaking tires.

For perhaps an hour they listened and talked, listened again and talked again. They talked of violence and nonviolence, of the whiplash of white hatreds and the new militants in the ghettos, of the growing rebellions of the young everywhere, on every campus, in every nation, and of the burden those young felt, to put to right the world into which they had been born.

"Gene," she said, sure he would follow the unspoken transition, "do you know a good lawyer I could go to, for the actual adoption?"

"Not offhand, but I'll ask Dave Weiss. I think it's a special field."

"How much would you have to tell him?" Professor Weiss was on the law faculty and a close friend of Gene's, but she had never met him.

"That somebody I know wants the name of a lawyer for adopting a child. What else did you think?"

"He'd assume it would be through the usual adoption bureaus."

"I'd tell him it wouldn't be."

"He'd assume it was a married couple."

"I'd tell him it wasn't."

"Wouldn't he need to know anything more than the simple fact that 'somebody you know' wants a lawyer for adopting some little old baby?"

"Probably whether I'd got myself into a jam, but he wouldn't ask me." Unexpectedly he laughed. It was a blessed relief to be talking of this instead of the other. "I'd assumed this was all arranged by now, the way you've arranged everything else."

She looked suddenly away. "I sort of had assumed it too, that a man I know, a lawyer, would help me with the legal part of it. But I—I've lost touch with him."

He glanced at her inquiringly but said nothing. For a moment he turned back to the television screen, thought better of it, and without asking her, went to her small kitchen for more coffee. She followed him with both their cups.

"He's not the villain who's responsible," she said, too lightly.

"I didn't think there was a villain."

"There isn't. I don't know why I'm trying to make jokes."

"I do."

"Oh, Gene, thank God you came over tonight. Was it all right for you to be here with me all evening?"

"Ellen isn't pregnant," he said shortly. He heard the snap in his own voice and added, without emphasis, "Anyway, she has more sense than we have about something like this. If you call it sense."

He stayed for the eleven o'clock news and then on

for another hour until he saw that she was getting sleepy. She had not pretended the sleepiness but the moment he left, drowsiness vanished and she turned compulsively back to the set. There was a necessity she could not explain, to hear all of it again, and once more, and then once more, as she had done during the hours and days after Kennedy was assassinated, right through until the first flicker of flame upon his grave.

At one thirty she went to bed exhausted. But the dreaming began, as it had begun that other time, the sudden start came again, the clutch of shock, the piercing longing that it had not happened, that it was only nightmare. The horror had been greater over President Kennedy's assassination because he *was* the President, but the jagged edge of this shock was just as bloody, and the next morning on the street when she passed a Negro woman she wanted to stop and say, "I feel just the way you do." But she thought, It would sound patronizing and I would die.

*   *   *

It was during the final mile of her walk that morning that she was suddenly driven by the need to settle the matter of the lawyer. She had not even thought of it as one of the problems during those early days when hideouts and false names and new banks and mail had preoccupied her. So sure had she been then that her lawyer would be Matthew, or if a specialist were needed in this field, then somebody Matthew would select and recommend and, in a sense, watch over.

All at once the thought of Gene's asking Professor Weiss was distasteful. If she herself knew Weiss, if he were her own friend, it might be good and right and natural to turn to him, but for her brother to be delegated by her as an agent to a stranger—suddenly the idea upset her. This was too personal, this matter of the attorney who would have to know all about it, who would guide her through the maze of papers and documents and laws and statutes—she should have realized that going to an unknown lawyer recommended by an unknown colleague of Gene's was an agitating notion at best. She had not thought the thing through at all; she had let it slide; never had she put it on any list of majors and minors, and suddenly it loomed very major indeed.

She hurried home and telephoned the university. Gene was in class; she said to Miss Pulley, "Would you just ask him to delay on that legal matter for a day or two—he'll know what I mean. Thanks a lot." She hung up, convinced that he had already had it all out with Professor Weiss, and her spirits fell. This sudden preoccupation with the matter of a lawyer was excessive, but that insight did not end the preoccupation. Was she still remembering Matthew's quick offer to check out New York adoption laws with people at his office? Was she still assuming that somehow, some way, it would still be Matthew who would see her through this final, and tremendous, chapter?

She drew back sharply. The one rule, the basis, the foundation: no sentimentalism, no daydreams, no girlish refusal to face whatever reality there was. And God knew one reality was that there was no Matthew.

On her next visit to Dr. Jesskin she could ask him about the final step of the adoption itself. Why had she not thought of asking Jesskin long before this— she had asked him about everything else. Probably, he saw ahead to it as clearly as he had seen ahead to that room on the eighth floor of Harkness and the two names on the door.

The knowledge soothed her, pacified her, and yet a few moments later she thought, My next visit is on the fifteenth, a Monday, and this is the fifth, a Friday. That's two weekends to get through and the week in between.

She dialed quickly. "Miss Mack," she said, "this isn't any emergency, but something's come up, and do you think I could talk to Dr. Jesskin before he goes off for the weekend?"

"Can we call you back? He's with a patient."

"Of course. If he's not too rushed."

"About one or one thirty then. You sure you can wait till then? Nothing going wrong?"

"Really not. Thank you."

She looked at the clock and then at the morning paper, black with headlines about the assassination. She still had not come to grips with it in print; she had read headlines and set it all aside for later, just as she had permitted herself radio news for a few minutes this morning and then set that aside for later too. The assassin had not been caught. Knowing that single fact, she had forced herself to wait through breakfast and through her walk. Now she edged toward the *Times,* unwilling to open herself to pain again.

The telephone rang and it was Dr. Jesskin. "Miss Mack said you sounded ill though you said you were not," he stated quietly. "I thought it best not to wait till one o'clock to call back."

"Oh Doctor, I'm not ill, but I had such a hideous night, I was so horrified, I couldn't sleep—"

"I think many of us couldn't sleep last night," he said. "Have you any physical symptoms? Miss Mack said you did not sound like yourself at all."

"No physical symptoms, only terribly upset, and that seemed to tie into something else upsetting and I—well, I wondered, Doctor, if I could possibly see you for ten minutes today, or if you weren't too rushed now to talk a little by phone."

"I'm not too rushed."

"It's just that I had thought at the start that a lawyer I know would take charge of the formal adoption process, in court or however they do it. But that's all been changed and I haven't faced up to it and when I got upset last night I also got awfully upset that anything so important should still be up in the air as late as this and I got wondering if by any chance you might know a good lawyer who—"

"Miss Mack was correct," he said calmly. "You do

not sound yourself. But you do know how one anxiety tends to trigger off another?"

"I'm sorry."

"Do not be sorry. Will it quiet that anxiety if I say that some weeks ago, for my own education, I did already discuss with a first-rate attorney how one would go about legally adopting one's own child? He does not know the name of my patient, but he is my good friend and he did educate me completely. It is entirely feasible and if you should wish me to arrange a meeting between you and him, that is simple."

"Oh Dr. Jesskin, there never was a doctor like you."

"There is a disadvantage," he said and she thought he chuckled. "As with Harkness, I seem to run to expensive solutions. This lawyer is a senior partner at Cox, Wheaton, Fairchild, Tulliver."

"I know of them." It was one of the great law firms in the country.

"Just as one does not expect an illegitimate birth at Harkness," he went on, "so one does not expect an illegitimate baby to become a client of Cox, Wheaton, Fairchild, Tulliver. Is that not correct?"

This time he did chuckle and she could only say, "It is correct and it's just marvelous. Would you go ahead and tell him about his new client and about me? Honestly, Doctor, I just don't know how to thank you."

*　　*　　*

The day became bearable. For a long time after she hung up, she sat in a benign relief, like warmth. Then she turned to the telephone book to look up Cox, Wheaton, Fairchild, Tulliver and wrote on the last page of her desk calendar their address and telephone number. Which one was the senior partner who was Dr. Jesskin's friend? Would she one day be known to Mr. Cox or to Mr. Wheaton, Mr. Fairchild or Mr. Tulliver? Would that day come before July twenty-third, or afterward? Soon after or not for six months after when the time came to go to court?

In her research for her two articles, still only roughed out and nowhere near completion, she had found out that in New York State, unlike certain others, a waiting period of half a year was mandatory, a six-month trial period between the time any baby went into any adoptive home and the time the legal process of adoption could be taken to court. The city of New York would send a social worker of some kind once or twice during that trial period, to judge the prospective parents, the prospective home, the general prognosis for the baby's future.

Suppose one of them came to see us, Dori thought now, and turned me down? She began to laugh. It was impossible, of course, but it was high comedy even to think of such a scene. Or high horror.

Cox, Wheaton, Fairchild, Tulliver wouldn't let it happen. They would know, or one of them would know, their archives would know, where secret papers were held *in camera,* and they would not let the State of New York interfere. God bless Cox, Wheaton, Fairchild, Tulliver, separately and aggregately.

She smiled and her eyes fell on the deserted *Times.* A sweep of guilt invaded her, that she should so soon be turning from its intolerable burden to her own good fortune. But that's it, she thought, that's all part of it, the systole and diastole forever.

*   *   *

Cele came late in the afternoon, bringing three days' pile-up of mail from home. It was mostly requests for donations, but the April rent bill was there, a department store bill, the telephone bill, and a note from Tad Jonas saying the Martha Litton piece was still pulling mail and why the hell didn't she drop people at least a postcard and a clue about whether she'd like it forwarded or not? "I must write him," she said, showing Tad's note to Cele, "or it'll twig his attention, but for now, let's get on with these." She opened her locked suitcase for her real checkbook.

Rapidly she made out the checks, addressed envelopes bearing her real return address, handed them to Cele to put straight into her own purse again for mailing on the way home. She also returned all the original envelopes that had her name on them and any letters where her name was typed to show through the envelope window. These Cele also put back in her purse, to dispose of in some street bin.

Then only did Dori say, "I can't talk about it anymore, can you?"

Cele shook her head. They had talked of it already, before they began on the letters, talked until they each felt spent. Through supper they watched the evening news in silence; they listened as if bludgeoned to the inevitable recapitulation and then the nature of the programs changed; now they were scenes of rioting in dozens of cities, of burning buildings in a dozen black ghettos, of crowds and looting and tear gas, of the smashing of windows, of screaming sirens and troops and police and the National Guard, called out by this governor and that mayor, of havoc across the face of the nation.

"Forty cities," Dori said once. "He said 'in forty cities.' Did you hear that?"

"I heard a special bulletin that said 'sixty or more.' "

"All in ghettos?"

"Of course, ghettos."

"But it's their own neighborhoods they're wrecking."

"If it were white neighborhoods, they'd be shot by the dozens."

"Sixty cities," Dori said, awed. "Could it be the start of another civil war? *Time* would promptly dub it Civil War Two."

"Let's quit talking about it. You look terrible. I'm going to get the fruit and cheese." She snapped off the television set and went to the kitchen. Dori went to the mirror in the bathroom, combed her hair and freshened her lipstick.

She did indeed look terrible, frowning and tight-faced. She also wanted to stop talking about it, and she made an effort to sound more cheerful. "I do look fierce, face-wise, as the ad boys might say. But figure-wise? It's five and a half months, and sure, you can tell I'm pregnant, but not the way I thought I'd be by now, not good and bulky and obvious. Are they holding out on me or what?"

"You're going to be the servant girl that carries on till the last minute, with the mistress of the house not suspecting a thing. You look great, if not yet 'great with.' So stop hurrying."

"First you say I look terrible, then that I look great. Which do I believe?"

"Both."

"Okay, it's easiest that way." Then matter-of-factly she added, "That lawyer I met at your house, Matthew Poole, have you seen him again?"

"Not since. Have you?"

"He asked me to a concert."

"Did you go?"

Dori nodded. "It wasn't long after I met him."

"We like him but he's not the social type and we don't see him often either."

"I liked him too." The brief interchange surprised her. Cele was gazing at her with the mildest air of encouragement but she ignored the invitation. She was not certain why she had never said anything to her about Matthew; she had known she would not talk about being in love, but she had not planned a specific reticence about seeing him. Now suddenly she was bringing him into the conversation without pretext of pertinence, just idly speaking his name, the trick of the loving—or lovelorn—and with, of all perceptive people, Celia Duke. She nearly laughed. Yet without meaning to, without even knowing how she had managed to, she certainly had given Cele the wrong impression. They didn't see him often either. Maybe if you once embarked on lies you became so adept at the techniques that you soon lied out of habit,

in a fine promiscuity including people you had never
deceived in your whole life.

There was a pause; they ate fruit and cheese.

"I wrote to my brother Ron in London yesterday,"
Dori said, again matter-of-fact, "and asked if I could
use him for a mail drop for six weeks or so. I didn't
say why, just asked if I could send him an occasional
letter to put British stamps on and mail out from
there."

"How will he take it?"

"He'll say yes. His secretary will do it—it won't be
more than a few times at most. He'll decide I'm having an affair and need a cover for that, and he
couldn't care less." She could see Cele trying to put
this train of thought together with the one that had
made her mention Matthew. But Cele remained matter-of-fact also.

"And Alan? Did you write him too?"

"I tried to write the same damn letter to him, actually typing off the same words. But it stuck tight;
I could imagine his passing it over to Lucia and the
look between them. I might just up and phone him at
the office some day. This note of Tad's—it's his second one."

Cele glanced at her watch. "It's only ten of five out
there."

"Call him now?"

"Obey my impulse, Dorr. Get it done. Get your
mind off everything awful, and back onto yourself."

For a moment Dori hesitated. Then she went to the
telephone. "Person to person to San Francisco," she
said and gave the operator Alan's name and office
address. "His sister calling." In less than a minute she
was saying, "No, not a thing, Alan, everybody's fine
here. I'll tell you in a minute why I called. How's everything with you?"

She listened and Cele, watching, thought how animated she looked again, how pretty; she had forgotten the TV set and the bulletins and the dead body
lying in that final darkness—God, why should she not?

She felt protective and loving as if Dori were her sister or her child.

"It's going to sound wicked as hell," Dori was saying into the telephone. "And I thought you might not want to tell Lucia, so I called you there instead of at the house." He said something that made her giggle. "Not a movie star, no, nor a millionaire. But for a few weeks I'd love it if I could mail a few letters to you, for you to mail out with a San Francisco postmark. Not many."

She looked even more animated; Cele thought, She's actually in a tizzy as if she really were going off with a lover. She waved a hand to catch Dori's eye. "Tell him it's secret even if he can't do it," she whispered. Dori nodded.

"Lucia of course, but not one single other? Oh your secretary, she'll have to—no, I know she won't. Well, thanks, Alan, thanks a lot."

When she hung up she said, musing, "It's the first time, I swear to you on the Koran, the Talmud and the Bible, the very first time he hasn't been a stuffed shirt."

"Then he will?"

"Yes, but he'd die of disappointment if he knew I wasn't having an affair at all." Suddenly she shoved away from the telephone. "Oh, Cele, I'm not having an affair, but I was, and it was real, and it meant everything and now it's over and—"

Her voice suddenly caught and she turned away so that her face was averted. Cele did nothing. It must be Matthew Poole. It couldn't be. Dori never had sudden loves; she was never casual about friends or politics or books or what she read in the morning paper, then how would she be casual about sex? With sudden concentration she tried to recall exactly what it was Dori had said about Matthew Poole and that concert, whether she had said that was the first time she had seen him or whether she had specifically said that was the only time she had seen him. Already it was too far back in the blur of the evening to remember precisely.

After another minute of silence, Dori said, "Let's see if there's anything new about it," and crossed the room to the TV set. The click of the knob was sharp in the quiet room.

*   *   *

Suddenly Matthew knew what it was. He was not thinking of Dori but suddenly there it was, the truth, the thing he had not been able to name. Perhaps because he had not been thinking of her, because he had not been at his relentless prodding of his thoughts about her, it suddenly skimmed along the surfaces of his mind, and he caught at it, netted it and held it carefully as if it were a fragile creature that could be wounded or destroyed.

It was an April night, raw, sensitive, and fresh, and he was walking home from his office, tired and dispirited. He had lost the Benting case; it would now go to appeal before the circuit court. He had never been trapped into hope on the first stage of the case and had been careful to prepare Jim and his parents for this first defeat, so that they too would know all along that the ultimate decision was still months off, perhaps even a year. The Spock indictment had, curiously, encouraged them, though he had tried to explain why the idiot charge of conspiracy in that case cut through any bonds of similarity with Jim's own. Jim saw it, but his parents persisted in feeling that even if the Spock trial, coming up soon in Boston, ended in conviction for him and his codefendants, the verdict would be so outrageous it would certainly be reversed someday by a higher court, and thus by some esoteric logic it was more certain that a reversal would someday be forthcoming for their son as well.

How strange, parents. How strange the persistence of his own hope that the bad times now with Johnny would reverse in some golden process as time went on, that in three years or so when Johnny the boy became John the college student, there would be a magic shift in his son's personality.

His intelligence told him not to hope but he went on hoping. He knew as surely as astronomers know three years in advance just where a star will be in the cosmos, so he knew that on a day in 1971 his son would be part of some great campus protest, would be arrested or suspended or expelled from the college of his choice, and that he would applaud him for his courage and his principles and at the same time know the stricture in his own heart at his son's newest struggle. When your kid's in trouble your heart is lead. A lifetime went into making your children happy and when they were happy your whole world was right. You knew what it was all for, you had done it, or helped do it—

That was when he suddenly knew. Dori was happy and he had had no part in it.

Suddenly he remembered the change that had come over Jack's face that night he had told him about Dori. *And you offered to help her,* Jack had said. It wasn't like that, he had answered, she didn't want any help. He had gone on to give Jack the whole background, all the years of tests and doctors, and Jack's expression had altered; a kind of comprehension had entered it, as if something had suddenly opened. But Jack had only ordered more drinks and they had got rather drunker than was usual for either of them.

All at once he knew what Jack had thought, knew why he had kept still about it, thinking it better for him to come to it himself. If she were crying to you for help, Jack had thought, you'd have stood by her, but you couldn't take it that she was happy about it.

She was happy in the profoundest sense and he had had no part in it. She was pregnant at last, and in the profoundest sense also, he was excluded from it. She had done this without him and she would go on without him. She was already, on that day she told him, already going on without him.

There was the crux of it and he had not faced it

until now. He had talked of a blast of buckshot, but that was only alibi for his protracted silence and absence. Buckshot? It was more like napalm, to sear and scar. But that was alibi too.

At last he had isolated the truth. He had at last "got it into some sort of shape." Twelve weeks had gone by in the attempt; it seemed twelve years, it seemed twelve minutes, so endless was it, yet so hot and new. He no longer sweated out nightmare hours, but he could not recall even one moment of peace, of pleasure. She was away somewhere; he had tried two or three times to call her, the last time the night of King's assassination. Not even that time did he know what he could say, once he got through talking of the murder. That he was still trying to get this into some sort of shape? That he was still on hell's own wheel? That this was merely an interim call, meaning nothing? Each time he had been relieved that she did not answer. Now he suddenly felt that he could wait not an hour longer to face her and say, God forgive me, I've been in hell because you're happy.

EIGHT »ક&

IT WAS TEN THIRTY that night when the phone rang and Celia thought, Dorr, something's wrong. The one worry that still fretted her was that Dori might suddenly wake up one night, sick, and be there all alone, without even a maid to summon help. But the voice on the phone was a man's voice, not very familiar.

"Celia, it's Matthew Poole. I didn't wake you, did I?"

"Heavens. In this house?" She laughed. "Even the kids are awake."

"I gathered you were night owls. Something Marshall said once about *Nachtmusik*."

"And not always *kleine*." She was ridiculously glad to hear from Matthew Poole. All at once she knew she had been right at Dori's a couple of weeks ago, though they had not referred to it since. "It's rather fun to get late phone calls, unless it's some drunk, so did you want Marshall?"

"As a matter of fact, it's you, not Marshall." He was keeping his voice light and wondered if she knew he was. "I've been trying to reach Dori Gray and having no luck, and I hoped you'd give me an address that would find her."

"She's away for a few weeks."

"That's what her doorman said; I went by there. Some sort of cruise, and you pick up her mail every few days."

"Yes, I do."

"But I'd like to wire or cable her and I wondered if you'd give me the next stop on her itinerary."

"I, well, you see—"

There was a pause. Like Dori she had rehearsed the answer to every foreseeable comment or question, but this was one she had not foreseen and she was caught. To say to Matthew Poole, You can't wire or cable her, all you can do is write her at her regular address and I'll forward it and she will get it in due time—this would be a rudeness so signal that it would flag his attention at once.

It was he who broke the silence. "Look here, Celia," he said, no longer casual. "I know about Dori. She told me the last time I saw her. So even if you're not telling anybody else where she is—"

"Know what about Dori?" It sounded cautious, and it was cautious. She did like Matthew Poole, but she did not know him very well, and how could she be sure that when he said he knew about Dori, he actually knew this? Dori certainly had not told her that he did.

"Know that Dori—I wish this weren't the telephone."

"We're not bugged. Are you?"

He laughed; the whole concept was uncomfortable. "It might be better if you could let me see you tomorrow or next day for a few minutes. Would you?"

"Tomorrow if you like."

"About five? For about ten minutes?"

"Even fifteen."

As she was putting up the receiver she glanced again at the clock. Only five minutes had passed; Dori would not be asleep. Of course she would consult her as to whether to tell him where she was; the only question was whether it would distress her to know he was trying to see her, and if so, whether she might not wait until morning so as not to risk Dori's having a worried night. Or ought she to keep it to herself until she had seen Matthew Poole, heard what he had to say and had something more informative to pass along to Dori than the mere fact of his telephone call?

She wished she could ask Marshall's opinion, but

that would only end by irking her, as she had been irked when she had finally told him Dori was pregnant. "Is this for real?" he had said. "I thought she couldn't." She could hear again the instant curiosity in his voice, very satisfying indeed.

"It will be born in July."

"Is the guy willing to get married?"

"He is married, with four children."

"Who is it?"

"My guess is that it's a newspaperman she's been seeing for a year or so, but you know Dori about what she calls 'he-said-I-said' talk. I did gather they were winding up their affair when it happened."

"Did he walk out on her when he knew?"

"She didn't tell him."

He nodded as if to say, Sensible girl. Then he had asked how people were taking it.

"Nobody's 'taking it' because nobody knows about it except her brother Gene and me, and now you. She's not going to play Emancipated Female for her own ego and have her kid called 'dirty little bastard' all its life."

"Good for her." He had glanced down at his work then, and she had known that his brief curiosity was over. He knew everything he needed to know; male-like, he now was returning to important things like the contracts being drawn up for a subsidiary company specializing in cartridges of taped music. She had been irked then; a hundred times since she had been irked again for he never showed more than a perfunctory interest whenever she gave him any further news about how things were going. Nor would he now if she asked his advice about Poole's call.

She was irritated at her dear beloved husband. He was still, after eighteen years, the one man she could imagine being married to, was still, among the hundreds of men she had met through his large business connections, the only one she could imagine as an abiding and continuing person in her life. Mainly he was easy to get along with, though they had the usual

number of spats and quarrels, and he was delighted
with the kids, though he never had enough time for
them. He seemed happy with her most of the time,
though he was quickly bored if she talked about politics,
and if he had ever had in those eighteen years an
affair with another woman, he had had the wit and
the skill to keep it to himself in every way, with no
telltale absences or careless shreds of evidence. So
he was a good husband and it was a good marriage
but at times she wanted to scream at him or hit him
for being so immersed in his big successful record
business that his attention span for anything else
was about four minutes long.

Now she gazed for a third time at the clock and
then dialed Dori. "You're not asleep," she greeted her.
"I can tell by your voice."

"Of course I'm not."

"Dori, for a minute I wondered whether to hold
this back until tomorrow, but I decided not."

"Hold what back?"

"Well, Matthew Poole just phoned and asked for
your address, and naturally I ducked and then he
persisted and asked if he could stop in tomorrow."

"Stop in where tomorrow?"

"Oh here. I didn't give him your address or phone
or anything, of course."

"Of course." She swallowed in a suddenly dry
mouth. "What did he say, Cele?"

"Just that he's been anxious to get in touch with
you and had phoned and phoned and then that he
went by your house and asked your doorman and got
the cruise bit and also that I picked up your mail to
forward. So he wanted me to give him the next stop
on your itinerary, as if he'd cable you or call you per-
son-to-person at the North Pole or wherever."

"What did you say to that?"

"I got around it, sort of gulping 'Well, you see,' and
not being too good about managing it. Then he
switched tactics and said he 'knew' about you, that

you'd told him the last time he'd seen you, so even if I wasn't giving your address to anybody else—"

" 'Knew' about me? Did he say what he knew?"

"He was as cagey as I, as if he didn't know if *I* knew. Anyway, then I decided I'd have to clear it with you before he gets here. He's coming at five unless you tell me to head him off."

"Oh Cele." She fell silent, and Cele waited in silence too. The telephone line was live between them, they each knew it, nobody had to ask, "Are we cut off?" yet neither was ready to say the next word. Dori was waiting for order to come, for her heart to stop its lurching, for a decision to be made about what to say, how much to say. "He does know I'm pregnant," she said firmly at last. "He also knows that it had happened just before I met him. Remember the Martin Luther King night when I suddenly told you I had been having an affair and that it was all over—"

"Certainly I remember. But you barely started and then you clipped it short."

"I know I did. Well anyway, I haven't seen Matthew Poole, or heard from him, since New Year's, and I don't know what this call of his means, but of course give him my phone number and address if he wants them, and after he's been, will you call me and—" She burst into an embarrassed laughter. "Will you listen to me? Clickety-clack, clackety-click, like some gushing adolescent."

Cele laughed too. "That's not what adolescents sound like. Liz would say 'groovy' or 'hey, man,' or something lyric and poetic like that. Me, I'm glad you're shook up. I hope he's worth it; I told you we didn't know him very well but liked him."

"I *am* all shook up. Cele, what I'm trying to say is all of a sudden there was Matthew at your house and then three or four weeks later, there was no more Matthew, and I do want to tell you all about it but now I have to wait and see what any of this means."

"Sure you do."

"Call me."

"I might at that. Good night. I have a feeling of being *deus ex machina* or something, big sense of power."

Dori tried to go back to the book she had been reading, but couldn't keep her mind on it. She was wondering what Matthew's sudden determined effort to find her might mean.

That he loved her, that he had at last "got it into shape," that he was going to come to her in remorse and longing and renewed passion.

Her body swirled with her own sexuality at the thought, swirled and spun and swooped as it had not since the day they had parted. Except in dreaming, she had been devoid of sexuality, despite Dr. Jesskin's pronouncements on the heightened presence she could expect. Now suddenly she saw that it was still possible, instantly possible, waiting only to be summoned forth from whatever locked and frozen cell it had fled to on that fierce day when he had gone off with his coat over his arm.

But that was the day after New Year's and this was the middle of April. Three months to get it into "some sort of shape"? Three months to come to terms with it? There was something wrong in the equation. A week, two weeks—she would have understood that, have read nothing into it, would never have needed to excuse it or make allowances for it. But three months? A quarter of a year? A third of a pregnancy? Something was excessive about it, something in Matthew was all twisted round or knotted up, else he would not have needed three months.

But remember the way you blurted it out at him.

Now don't go blaming it on yourself; you can't always be in the wrong. Don't you go twisting it around and knotting it up until it's all your fault. You've always been too damn ready to be the hurt instead of the hurter and he did hurt you, and then kept on hurting you, on and on.

She felt restless and uneasy. She jumped up from the big chair and reached for her coat. She had to move, stir, stretch, not sit bound in that chair in this limited space. Never since living here had she gone out for a walk at this hour but she was going out now. She threw a scarf over her hair, wondered briefly whether the heavy coat would be too warm, wore it anyway, and let herself out into the mild night.

There was still music drifting from open windows up and down the wide street but few people. She turned toward the park, knowing that she would not enter it, and began walking briskly down Central Park West. Ahead lay all the night splendor of the New York sky, the twinkling levels of whole lighted floors in some of the great buildings, the reckless fling of other lights as if they had been strewn from a wild hand at accidental windows. She loved it. No matter what happened to her in the future she would always live in New York. It was her city, her hometown, her world. For all its viciousness and crime and noise and filth and cruelty, it also was the core of all the life she really valued: music, theater, ideas, books, newspapers, people. London rebuked her at once, Paris, Rome, and she made obeisances and apologies to her memories of all three but still she walked on toward the great jagging skyline below the park, loving it.

She walked on the west side of the street, past one apartment building after another, their lobbies alight, nearly all presided over by doormen. She felt safe proceeding from one pool of lighted sidewalk to the next like a child jumping from rock to rock to cross a stream. If anybody did dart out at her from an intervening strip of shadow, one cry would bring help.

But nobody darted. Soon she felt foolish for having considered so dire a possibility; between the sheepishness and the exalted response to the night sky, she slowly regained an inner calm. The wariness was tempered, she suddenly saw; the rush of readiness for Matthew was still there but in some way it was tempered too.

She was changing. Not only her body, but she, the whole being that she was. These months over here alone had surprised her in some unfathomable depth of herself, far down, far below anything she had known of herself before. This loneliness of the three months over here had not been her old enemy, had not been arid, not a long spell of bleakness that would remain and remain and remain, not the old-style loneliness she had always fought off like a dark tenacious illness. This had been a factual aloneness, that was all. There had been many days and evenings when she saw not one soul but a grocery clerk, yet there had been no misery in the idea *alone*.

She was changing. She hadn't thought of that, but tonight, with Matthew once again entering her life, on whatever basis, tonight she wondered for the first time if it would be the same Dori Gray he would find.

*   *   *

She woke thinking, He may call me right after he sees Cele. But how to get through all the hours until five? She was due at Dr. Jesskin's at eight thirty and she was glad the day was starting with a specific task to do. Dr. Jesskin's house visits were to have started with this one but when she had seen him in March he had said, "You are splendidly thin and tight; your musculature is clearly of the highest order."

"The exercises you ordered. And the three hard miles every single day."

"It must have beeen there before the exercises. Are you an athlete?"

"I love tennis and swimming, and I've always done lots, but not as an athlete, on school teams or anything."

"They have served you. Sometimes it is simply a case of good health, and good construction to start with. At any rate you will still be able to come here next month and my house calls will start in May. So you see I have made one miscalculation already. I am glad."

Her good construction. Each time she had recalled the phrase again, she had smiled. That and the three thinkings were the things she would always remember about him probably, apart from the great thing. She knew nothing about him as a person, only as a doctor, and if there was any flaw in him as a doctor, either through the long years of the "so-called sterility" period or now during these incredible months since the day of infamy, then it was a flaw too microscopic for her unaided vision. She remembered the smiling faces on his desk, his wife and children, and thought, No wonder.

She had switched from the old fur coat at last, to an old loosely cut tweed of her own that was equally shapeless and nonrevealing, but as her taxi drew up to Dr. Jesskin's office, she still looked quickly about, up and down the avenue, fumbling for her fare so that if there were a familiar face anywhere she could sit back unseen until any danger of a meeting was past. Here on Park Avenue, there was still danger; over there where she lived, she had long since learned that there was none.

She had quickly given up the old sports hat pulled down far on her face, realizing that in the scarf-over-the-hair environment there she was merely calling attention to herself. She had taken to scarves too, because of the severe cold, but since the first thaw of March, she had even given those up most of the time. She never had her hair done any longer; that was her only disguise. She let it grow, washed it every few days, let it hang loosely around her neck, and at times thought, I'll never go back to the damn beauty parlor racket again anyway. That final rinse they always give you "for highlights," really! Now she saw that her own hair was slightly deeper in tone, more really brown, and she liked it. Some sketchy gray had begun to come in at the temples, for so long toned away by the "rinse," and she saw it with some surprise, with some displeasure, and then, upon reflection, with acceptance and even with approval. It was becoming, just a faint grayish feather above the outer corner of each eye, and she had never even known before that the paired plumes were there.

There was nobody in sight on the street and she stepped quickly into the office. Miss Stein was not yet there but Miss Mack said, "There you are, always on the dot," and led her in to change. "The doctor is ready. He's always on the dot too—you'd better believe it."

The locution amused her. She was more and more fond of Miss Mack, increasingly impressed with her behavior. Not once in all the visits since that day of the lab report had Miss Mack betrayed the fact that she knew Dori was pregnant. She seemed to have perfected some trick of seeing her only from the neck up; even when her hands were busily draping that sheet around torso and legs, she directed her gaze only at the upper part of her body, above the pregnant belly, above the enlarged breasts, above any and all evidence, even avoiding any direct gaze into Dori's eyes, settling instead on a point just below her chin.

Now as she stripped, Dori had the mischievous impulse to turn naked to Miss Mack and say, "Hey, look, I'm pregnant," but to Miss Mack it would have been a gibe, a jeer at the way she did her job, so the impulse died. In the togalike sheet, she stepped on the standing scale in the examining room, knowing in advance what her weight would be, and heard Miss Mack say, "Good, you're obeying orders; the fatties annoy us so."

For the first time Dori used the small step stool to get herself up on the table. A sign of progress! Again the stirrups, the hiss of the sterilizer, the clink of steel instruments, but how marvelously unrelated to the years of dogged persistence and fading hope. Even if she had been like some pregnant women, prey to a dozen ailments and miseries all through, this was what she would never have let herself forget, this blessed difference from that void time.

"Good morning, and how has it been going?"

"Good morning, Doctor." From the table, she twisted her head backward to where he was coming in by the door from his office. "Except for my panic call that day about a lawyer, I've been grand."

He ignored the reference. "No physical discomfort in any way?"

"Not really. I don't skip and hop and run, but nothing you could label physical discomfort."

"I expected not."

He began the examination, silent as always, swift, satisfied. Then he moved his stethoscope down from her rib cage to her protruding belly, gently pressing it here and there until suddenly he nodded and smiled. "Strong and clear," he said.

"Oh, Doctor!"

"Do you want to hear for yourself?"

"Of course I do. Can I?"

He reached for another stethoscope, saying, "This one is weighted, to amplify sound," and fitted the twin tubes to her ears. She raised her head, craning forward, and then sat up, lowering her head to shorten the distance. Dr. Jesskin was holding the rounded listening tip to the spot where he had heard the hidden heartbeat, and she waited to hear it too. But she heard nothing. She sat forward a little more. She could hear nothing.

"It is there," he said calmly. "Sometimes the untrained ear does not catch it, but it is there. Quite decided, quite clear."

She listened again and suddenly said, "I think, I really do think—I can't be sure."

"You undoubtedly did." Dr. Jesskin took the ear tubes back and turned toward the scale, stooping to read the precise quarter pound. Then he said, "When you are dressed," and returned to his office. Dori glanced in triumph at Miss Mack who returned the glance with her air of knowing nothing, as if stethoscopes placed on stomachs sent no message to her brain. Even her remark about fatties annoying "us" had not been a definite admission that she knew Dori was pregnant; twelve years ago during the "sterility visits," if her weight had been what it should be in the charts of Miss Mack's mind, she would have been as likely to say, "good, the fatties annoy us."

Dr. Jesskin stood as she went in to his desk. Sometimes he did this, with a courteous reach for the back of her chair, at other times he sat ignoring her entrance entirely, reading the opened folder and his last notations. Today his expression indicated that there were no notations on which he needed to refresh himself.

"You follow every textbook of normalcy," he said. "It would be extraordinary if any deviation showed up now. How do you sleep?"

"I take a couple of aspirin and then read until about twelve."

"You will later on want some help, and then I will prescribe." He looked at the ceiling as if to avoid a direct glance. "My friend Bob Cox is more than ready, I will say eager, to handle your case. This time I told him much, everything I know of you and the long history behind this birth. It is all in confidence, I need not say. Even from his partners."

She started to thank him but he waved off any such idea. "You will not need to consult him until much later, perhaps in September or October. And I miscalculated again; his fee will be no extravagance at all."

"But—"

"He feels some sort of vested interest: we are old friends. He was at Harvard Law while I was at Harvard Medical. Now his son and my son are finishing up at Law and in June they both become junior clerks in his office."

"Will they be working on my case too?"

"Neither one will ever hear your name or see your documents." He consulted his desk calendar, but only as a reflex action, hardly pausing over the riffling pages. "Now as to the next part of your schedule, the seventh and eighth months. You will of course no longer come to the office. I begin the house calls.

Eight thirty in the morning, May thirteenth, on my way here—will that be convenient?"

"Any time is convenient."

"Do you know what the advent of the seventh month means?"

"That it would live."

The four words were so simple, so strong, that the sudden waver in her throat startled her. It was like the first time she had felt the small firm thump; again there was that chasm between what she had always known and the moment it became her private knowing, within her own blood and bones and ligaments.

"That is so," Dr. Jesskin said. "It would have achieved completion in the biological order, but of course you will go to full term and not need to prove that."

He sounded genial, pleased with her as if this advent of the seventh month were an achievement she was to be praised for, and she left feeling that she had been applauded by the one mentor whose good grades and good graces she most wanted in all the world. Only when she was once more tucked safely into a taxi did she suddenly think, I wonder if he'll take Miss Mack along on May thirteenth, to stand there, during the house call. She laughed aloud, and then for the first time since she had entered Dr. Jesskin's office she remembered that this afternoon at five Matthew would be talking about her to Cele.

*   *   *

The doorbell rang but she moved automatically toward the telephone and then stopped, knowing it had made no sound. Ever since Cele had called her two hours ago, she had waited for his call, even turning the evening news program down low so that the volume left wide margins for hearing her muted telephone bell at its first ring.

"He's just left," Cele had said. "He really is determined to see you. He said right off and flat out that you were in love. That was almost the way he greeted me, sort of, 'Thank you for letting me come. Look here, you see, Dori and I are in love, were in love, no, let me say I was in love with Dori' and then he went on to say he'd been going through a—'bad time' is what he called it, and he didn't once say 'pregnant' as if he still wasn't sure I knew and wasn't about to give you away. He sounded as if it had been pretty rough, and that it had baffled him, I mean his own feelings had, and that finally something had clued him into another way of looking at it, and that he wouldn't want me to give him your address without checking first with you, but would I call you long distance then and there wherever you were, at his expense, and ask you, and then give it to him. He nearly fell apart when I said you were right in New York and that I had already had your permission and then gave him your number and your address."

Ten times she had wanted to interrupt Cele's tumble of words but so sure was she that Matthew would telephone within minutes that she was afraid to tie up her own line and had held back all her questions. But then nothing. She had tried to eat and could not; she had bathed quickly, ready to go wringing wet to the telephone, but it had remained silent. She had dressed in the navy blue silk and put on the white coral earrings, just in case his call included a question about when he could see her, and as if there were some guarantee of continuity if she appeared now to him as she had appeared on that wrenched-off last visit.

Not the same. Now there was nothing faint and hesitant and uncertain. There still was her own slenderness in arms, legs, face, throat, but now there was a hard shining belly, not soft or pudgy or fat, but hard and gleaming like stretched silk.

The doorbell rang again and this time she moved swiftly to the door, hand on the knob, eye to the peephole. "Who is it?"

"Me, Matthew."

The deep voice, the Matthew sound, like no other sound. She drew the bolts and opened the door. There he stood, thinner, older, his face not happy in greeting. "Cele said you were alone, so I decided not to talk first on the telephone."

"Oh Matthew," she said, and all the wary words were lost. She stepped aside and he came in, saying nothing, looking at her, looking at her face as if to draw forth from it something sustaining, looking openly down to the bulk he had never seen, openly and easily and without pretense. Then he looked up again, saw the brush of gray he had never seen in her hair, saw her intent eyes.

"My God, you are beautiful," he said. He still did not move toward her and she stood still, not wanting to make the first gesture, not wanting to offer him the first touch. "I thought you couldn't be the way I remembered, and you are."

He turned abruptly and looked at the room, also carefully and at length. "So here's where you've been all along." He made a sound that would have been a laugh at some other time. "And I was imagining you in England or France or Timbuktu. Celia Duke said you like being here."

"I've grown attached to it. Isn't it hideous?"

He suddenly laughed. There was a burst to the sound, a breaking of constriction, a freeing, and he stepped toward her and said, "Oh, my God, Dori." He put a hand on her shoulder and drew her toward him and felt her move within the drawing arm and suddenly she was tight against him and he felt the hard rounding bulk of her that he had never felt, and again he said, "My God, Dori," and the words were gritty in his throat.

"What about a drink?" she said, pulling back from him. "I need one too." He said, "Scotch, please," and the hesitant look returned. A thin strip of sympathy went around her throat like a cord, unexpected and tight, and she said, "You take the big chair. It's the only decent one in the place."

While she made their drinks he was silent and so was she. Then she sat down on the low wood platform and looked up at him and smiled. He was so strained and uncomfortable that the impulse rose in her to say, "Never mind, it's over now, don't feel awful about it, let's forget it." But something clamped down on the words—it was not over, not really, not until it was understood equally by each of them and accepted equally, if acceptable it proved to be. One could "understand" anything; long ago she had understood Tony and his sudden announcement that he was through, but that had been no protection from what lay ahead. Just the same she could not find it in her to insist here and now on an accounting.

"What about the Benting case?" she asked over her untouched Scotch. "And Johnny, is he all right again at school?"

He answered the second question first, and she saw his relief in the alacrity and detail with which he spoke. He talked of Hildy too, of her increasing aloofness and secretiveness; at her birthday party, he had not been astonished at the shaggy look of some of her friends, nor at the incessant twang of guitars, but he had once thought that he had smelled the acrid sweet smell of marijuana. He had wanted to go straight in and ask, "Is anybody smoking pot in here?" and had not done it, remembering Hildy's harsh scorn of "parents who thought they could run every minute of their children's lives." Had not done it, and felt not proud of his restraint but uncertain of his fitness for parenthood in the new universe of liberated youth. "If there was ever a classless society," he ended, "today's teen-agers are it—they're wonderful, they're impossible, all of them alike."

And then he told her briefly about Jim Benting and his parents, and the appeal, and again she heard relief in his voice, as at a reprieve. He really did not want to explain the three months, not yet at least; he did not want to go over the weeks of absence, he wanted only to forget them. He had come to some point with himself that had made him ashamed of his own behavior, and he was grateful that she was not standing

there invincible and demanding, a Juno figure of outraged womanhood demanding explanations.

"Oh, Matthew," she suddenly said, "you don't really
want to talk about it now. Cele said you called it 'a
bad time,' and I thought you'd want to tell me but if
you don't want to for a while, you don't need to."

He suddenly stood up, looking down at her. "It's
nothing I'm proud of."

She put her hand out as if she were going to touch
him but did not. "You once said we shouldn't make
all the young mistakes, remember?"

"Yes, I do."

"Then let's not."

There was silence and then he was down beside her,
his arms around her, his mouth against hers. "Darling,
I'll be careful," he said at last, and passion swirled
again in her, a vortex, rotating upon itself, not to be
resisted. She undressed, stood naked for a long time,
letting him see her as she was, turning down no light,
seeking no nightgown or covering. He looked at her
and nodded as if in acceptance, and she nodded too,
gazing down at her distended body, seeing gladly the
gourdlike roundness, so purposeful with its silken taut
stretch of skin.

*   *   *

Matthew stayed most of the night, making a telephone call after midnight which she could hear clearly from the bathroom where she had gone to give him
a semblance of privacy when he said he'd better call
home. "I'm sorry to call this late," he said almost
formally into the telephone, "but I won't be in for a
couple of hours yet." She wondered at the formality,
and wondered for perhaps the first time what, exactly,
was the actual status of his and Joan's relationship,
when staying out half the night could be managed with
one brief phone call after midnight. Obviously there
was very little of any tight proprietary hold left. On
both sides? Or only on his?

For the first time she wondered if this loose ar-

rangement made Joan unhappy and wanted to ask
him and could not. A swift memory flew across her
mind of Dick Towson saying of his own absences from
home, "I've got a damn good marriage in all the usual
twenty-five-years-of-it ways, steady, and no surprises,
and all the kids know I'll always be back, so it's okay
and you and I don't ever have to worry about it."
Perhaps Matthew could say the same thing about
Joan and his kids and say, too, "You and I don't ever
have to worry about it." As if he were saying, *That is
intact.*

The family intactness. As if he were saying, Sure,
I love you, but what's that got to do with anything—
meaning his continuing patterns, his true life at
home, apart from her. To her, *home* used to mean
that closed apartment; *intact* used to mean her other
life over there on the other side of the park, her
real life, with her books and paintings and colors and
continuity. Now home was here, right in this place
where she lived day by day; the truest life she had
ever known was this life, not the other one she had
accepted for so many years as the only one.

Change. People did change, life did change, not
everything remained intact and untouchable forever. She, in any case, had changed already. Was it
only temporary, delusive, not to prove real later on,
when July twenty-third had come and gone? It was
the first time the question had presented itself, but at
once it had stature and importance.

"Darling, are you all right?" Matthew called. With
a start she realized that his telephone call had ended
minutes ago, and that she had stayed shut away as if
to hide her skimming thoughts. In the instant she returned to him she forgot them, so wonderful was it to
see him there, sitting on the edge of the disheveled
bed, eager for talk, eager for her presence, eager soon
to make love again. He stayed until four in the morning and when he was leaving, he said, as if he had left
a sentence dangling a moment before, "But it's no

young mistake to put the 'bad time' on the record instead of evading it permanently."

"I meant only that you didn't want to talk about it tonight."

"Maybe tomorrow night I will. About nine thirty?"

But through the second evening he did not talk about it, nor on the third. He wanted to be "filled in" on everything she had done; she found it delightful to retrace each step for him, the dilemma of the hideout, the rejection of Wyoming and Washington and all the other far-flung ideas, the apartment hunt and Mrs. Steffani, the brotherly mail drops, the reservation already made at Harkness.

"If you want more exotic postmarks than California and London," he said, "we have some affiliate attorneys in Tokyo and Honolulu and Rio."

"That would really clinch it. I'm not keeping in touch with many people anyway; to let them forget about my being gone is better. But one or two judicious little letters from Tokyo or Rio would fill it in for fair."

Only afterward did she realize that she had said nothing about Cox, Wheaton, Fairchild, Tulliver and wondered that she had forgotten. She also wondered why Matthew had not asked her about her arrangements for the adoption. Was he still intending to check it out for her at the office, and proceed from there? And if he was, would she tell Dr. Jesskin to tell his Bob Cox that she wouldn't be needing his services after all?

She felt a most unexpected reluctance to do so. She had appealed to Dr. Jesskin in crisis, and he had given time and thought and care to this, which was no integral part of his function as her doctor. Now to brush it all aside—"the lawyer I mentioned has come back and will handle it for me, thanks anyway"—that was impossible.

Better not let it chivy her; better let time take charge, as time had taken charge of so many other things. She did not want to accost Matthew with it either: You're keeping awfully silent about lawyers on this adoption; are you trying to tell me something? Would you rather not get mixed up in it?

It was on Friday night, with the weekend separation facing them, that Matthew suddenly said, "I told you I could be a selfish bastard, and I guess that was the basis of this whole damn thing."

He had still not talked about the bad time; now she went quite still, waiting, a nervous longing in her to have it over with and let it slide backwards into the past again. But he was talking about the night Jack Henning had finally demanded to know what was eating him and how he had, to his own surprise, sat there and told Jack about her.

"Then Jack said, 'You offered to help her' and I said it wasn't like that, that you were a million miles from wanting help, and I told him why, and then a couple of weeks later, I suddenly remembered the way he had looked, comprehension dawning in him as if he had seen something basic and wondered what had kept me from seeing it. I knew he'd decided on the spot that it would be no good to spell it out for me, that I had to come on it all by myself. He was right."

He turned away from her, and she wished it were over. Resentment arose obscurely in her, that he was still in misery over this, letting her see he was, as if he were charging her with it still.

Tony had done that transfer too. The very day after he had smashed their marriage, he had sent a letter from his office, by messenger to speed it, saying he was sending for his clothes and moving to a hotel, that he could not "go through another such night." It was the letter of an ill-used man.

"And that basic thing," Matthew went on heavily, "was that if you had been in a state of misery about getting pregnant, I'd have come through like a brick."

"You would have. I never doubted it."

"I'd have stood by, I'd have been a hero. But you weren't miserable. You were happy, and I hadn't had a damn thing to do with it. There was the shutout right there."

"But Matthew——"

"I couldn't take it, that it hadn't anything to do with me, that it had happened for you before I even came along. That was the ultimate shutout, and nothing was going to change that, not ever."

"Didn't you know I'd have been ten times happier if you *had* been part of it? I wished so terribly that it had been you, I was on the verge of telling you it *was* you." He winced, but she could not be sure why. Was it simply regret that she had not lied to him?

"There's nothing about the whole damn story I can feel good about," he said at last. "I'm not going to cop any plea and rationalize my way out of it. Even when I finally saw it all, I also saw what it's like to love somebody the way you loved when you were a young man but without the freedom you had when you were young, to follow through and say, Let's marry." He compressed his lips; he looked angry. "I wish to God I could say it, darling."

"I wish to God you could, too." Joy leaped within her. It was as if he had said it. He wants to, she thought, that's what matters. It's like being pregnant; the primitive thing is what matters, not the social thing of having people know. This is the same now with Matthew; what counts is the primitive thing that he wants to say it: Let's marry. He wants to say, Let's marry.

Aloud she said, "But from the first minute you made it clear that you would never leave your kids. I've known it, you've known it, it's been part of everything."

"Yes, everything." He looked the way he had looked the first night he had come back, older, thinner, not very happy. Long ago she had thought of him as a man who was not often happy, and then she had forgotten that. Now she remembered it again and her heart went out to him.

* * *

Cele finally said, "Matthew Poole put me into it, so you might as well get over your reticences and tell me about it."

Hesitantly at first, then more easily, Dori did. It was remarkable that she had needed to keep silent for so long, for she discovered now that there was a definite pleasure in talking about herself and Matthew, in talking separately about him, about his life, his family, his work.

There was no impulse to confide intimacy of detail, nor did Cele indicate any eagerness for it. Indeed at one point Cele interrupted to say, "Remember at school how I used to sit up half the night giving you a blow-by-blow of some new date and how you finally stopped me?"

"How did I?"

"By being brutal."

"Brutal how?"

"It was sophomore year and I'd just come back from a football weekend in New Haven, fairly snorting with triumph. You looked at me coldly and said, 'Okay, but not one word about Then he tried to kiss me.'"

They burst out laughing, and Dori said, "I don't remember that at all."

"I used to be god-awful," Cele said. "No taste, no asterisks, I used to read love letters aloud to you until you said you wanted to throw up whenever I opened an envelope."

"I must have been god-awful too."

"There you go, defensive little Dori. I was a blabbermouth slob, is the truth, and it took me years to learn what you knew all along. Anyway, go on about you and Matthew."

Dori did not spare herself when it came to "blasting him with it like a load of buckshot." She told it all, astonished anew that what she had so thoughtfully planned in advance should have got so out of hand

and become so inept and abrupt. "I never blamed him for going off in a shock reaction."

"Oh Dori, you'll be the end of me."

Dori nodded as if in agreement. "The only thing I couldn't see was why it took him so much time to manage it. It took his friend Jack only that one evening to see what had hit him so hard and they were drunk."

"It's always easier to get to the heart of the matter when it's not your matter."

Dori was grateful, as if Cele were exonerating Matthew. It was all the more surprising, when she had come to the end of her recital, to have Cele say, "But there's something about your Matthew I don't quite get."

"What?"

"Why doesn't he get a divorce? Other men do."

"I know they do."

"Good men, not just rats."

"But Matthew—"

"Is he Catholic?"

"He's nothing. He was born Presbyterian. It's not religion, it's his children. Mostly his son."

"But his children are sixteen and fourteen."

"Even so. Johnny is a pretty troubled child and God knows what would happen if his father walked out on him now."

"Maybe one reason he's troubled is having a father who's unhappy, who hasn't been really happy for years."

"Matthew would never have said one word about that to either of them."

"He's not home much at night, is he? You think kids have no unconscious minds absorbing things like that?"

Dori was suddenly angry. Cele had no right to raise such questions; she didn't know enough about Matthew, could not know enough about him and his situation and his problems, yet here she was right spang in the middle of the forbidden territory of divorce and remarriage, territory Dori had put beyond the pale from the first moment, in her thoughts, in her fantasies, in her whole existence. Perhaps that was why she had been so reticent with Cele all along about Matthew, instinctively guarding those boundaries from casual assault, even with the most loving of motives.

They had to remain intact too.

Cele was apparently affected by her long silence. When she spoke again it was to say, almost carefully, with none of her usual good humor and vigor, "So much for that. You know more about it than I do."

"I do, Cele. I really do."

NINE ᕤ

MATTHEW WAS THERE on the Thursday of the following week when Ellen telephoned. So surprised was Dori that she nearly said, "Ellen who?" Not once since the ugly visit about her "terrible mistake" had Ellen called her, not once written, not once sent a message by Gene. Now at nearly midnight here she was.

"Gene isn't with you by any chance?" Ellen asked.

"No. Was he planning to come here?"

"I don't know. Have you heard that they may shut the whole university down?"

"I saw it tonight on the six o'clock news."

"Gene never got home and he never called. I've been trying to reach him or Miss Pulley. She doesn't answer her phone either, so then I thought maybe he had stopped by to see you."

"He's probably in some faculty meeting and perfectly all right."

"I asked the switchboard operator if there were any meetings this late and she said no." Her tone implied that Dori might have taken it for granted she would have thought of a faculty meeting. "Anyway, if he were at a meeting, he would have been able to get to a phone and call me. I keep thinking about their holding the dean prisoner for twenty-four hours."

"But they admire Gene and they know where he stands."

"I'd go up to the campus myself and see if I could locate him, but if he should get to a phone, I'd want to be right here."

Dori wondered briefly if Ellen was waiting for her to volunteer to go up and look. She imagined herself trying to push through the unruly crowds she had seen all week on the news programs, hundreds of students running, shouting, pushing, being pushed, blacks and whites, mostly men, many girls, as well as younger people from the city's high schools, determined to demonstrate too. "Have you tried Jim and Dan?" she asked.

"They're not in, either one. If you do hear anything, you'll call me, won't you?"

"Of course. I'm sure he's all right though."

She turned from the phone, wondering that she was so undisturbed. To Matthew she said dryly, "According to my sister-in-law, my brother Gene is missing." Then not so dryly she added, "Can you imagine even imagining a college professor missing on the campus? Wartime! It's all so unreal. So many things this year seem unreal."

He began to defend the student protesters but she thought, extraneously, One unreal thing is how much of my life happens now by telephone or by turning on a radio or TV set. That's what comes when you're in hiding; you're tied to the world by a thousand electronic umbilicals that you never thought vital before.

"I'm on the students' side too," she said. "You didn't think I'd not be? Except for two things."

"What two?"

"Their taking human hostages and their photographing private letters and documents. That just sticks in my craw." He nodded but she suddenly grew heated. "Matthew! If you half think it's okay, 'to get the proof they need,' then how can you ever object to the FBI walking in and photographing *your* private letters and documents to get the proof they think they need? Or Jim Benting's letters, or anybody else's?"

"Whoa, hold on," he said, heated too. "I never said it was okay, did I? Even though they weren't private letters and papers, but official ones proving the university's hookup to the Pentagon and the army. I'm no believer in the-end-justifies-the-means crap."

"But a lot of the students are."

"So they're wrong. Lots of them. But lots of them are also right. Who do you think forced Johnson not to run again, Lyndon Johnson, the most ambitious man in all politics?"

"I know who. And I love them."

"You're damn right. The young. The students. All those kids with their placards about Vietnam and the draft and napalm, all those students working day and night for Gene McCarthy, and now all the others backing Bobby Kennedy."

As he went on, staccato, more excited than she had ever heard him, she thought, This is the way he is at his best, when he gets most involved, with the things he believes in, or with Hildy and Johnny. Suddenly she saw that part of this defense of the young, of the rebellious young, was a kind of *a priori* defense for what might lie ahead for his own young rebel at home.

"Let's hear the latest," Matthew said and flipped on the radio.

". . . and an estimated one hundred," a voice was saying, "all wearing white handkerchiefs around their arms as signals that they are faculty, are maintaining their vigil before the five occupied buildings, to resist attempts by the authorities to eject students by force."

"Gene!" she said. "That's where he is."

"Professor," an interviewer asked, "could you tell us the purpose of this action?"

"Why, simply that we feel that with us out here, there's less chance of their getting rough with the students inside."

"Who, sir? There are no police here, are there? We were officially told not."

"But there are hundreds of private guards, plain-clothesmen, detectives."

"Have you proof of that, sir?"

"Plenty. And we hear the university may call in the police officially at any time."

Dori waited no longer; she dialed Ellen. "About a hundred faculty are standing guard in front of Hamilton and Avery and Fayerweather and Low—have you heard that?"

"No. Where did you?"

"No wonder Gene can't get to a phone." She told her what radio station to turn to, and could hear the relief in Ellen's voice. She accepted her thanks for having called back, and heard the grit of restraint enter as Ellen remembered the unresolved hostility between them. It suddenly didn't matter.

"If anything were to happen to one of those professors standing guard—" she said as she turned back to Matthew.

"Not with those armbands. What if any student got killed?"

"It's unbearable to think of."

"They'll probably shut down soon."

"Shut what down?"

"Everything. No classes. No lectures. No seminars."

"God, it's like a siege."

*　　*　　*

They shut down the next morning. It was Gene who told her, having stayed up there all night and arriving home, as he said, "on a few hours' leave."

"They did attack us," he added. "Sometime around twelve or one. They came charging right through us, and the hell with us being faculty."

"Who, the police?"

"University guards mostly. Savage too. A young instructor in the French Department, I don't know him, got a scalp wound five inches long and bled like a dying animal."

"Were you hurt?"

"Shoved a bit. God, something snaps inside you when they start to straight-arm you. I'll be fine right through, don't worry!"

"Right through? What does that mean?"

"I'll get some sleep and then go back. Twice as many will be out today as before. And if they do call out the regular police, with the nightsticks and tear gas and guns, they'll just galvanize ten times more supporters, students and faculty both."

"Oh Gene, be careful."

In the afternoon Matthew called to say he couldn't be with her until after the weekend. There was an agitation in his voice, despite his obvious will to control it. "Johnny's been hurt," he said, "and I'd better stay close tonight."

"Hurt how?"

"Not too seriously, but he's pretty worked up. Another kid had his nose smashed and was taken to a hospital."

"What happened? Where were they?"

"Up at Columbia. Another big contingent of high school boys, from lots of schools, like the crowd yesterday, to join the demonstrators. Five guys from Johnny's class went, they're all big enough to pass for freshmen. But he's the only one who got hurt."

"Oh Matthew, how awful. Will he be all right?"

"He's back from the doctor now. He had five stitches in his hand, in his palm under the knuckles, and he's a mass of contusions. I'd better stick around. Hildy and Joan are upset too."

"Of course. Oh darling, I'm so sorry. What a gutsy kid he must be."

"He's that, but what a time and place to show it! I thought we'd have at least three years' leeway before we got into this kind of thing."

There was a fatalism in the way he said it, outlawing any *if's* and *but's* about Johnny and the next years. Three years more of high school, she thought as she turned away from the phone, and then four at college; it would be 1975 before Johnny could be regarded as educated and independent. But somewhere in there would be the draft and Johnny's decisions about the draft board and whether to take that step forward or refuse induction and be sentenced to prison—

Her heart sank. In 1975 her own child would be seven, and she would be only three years from being fifty.

*   *   *

It's the way it was during the war, she thought, when every family you knew was affected by it. Gene was in the air force then, Ron in the navy; only Alan, just sixteen, had remained out of it. If anybody with two brothers in action could be said to be out of it. Heaven knows she hadn't been out of it.

Now here was Gene at fifty, haggard with his need for sleep, appointed to the new Senate of the Faculty in a nonfunctioning university and here was Matthew with no connection with campus or faculty, yet caught up in this violence because of Johnny. The stitches across the boy's hand would be removed soon and the contusions were in their final purpling, but for the first time the headmaster of Johnny's school had sent for Matthew and wondered aloud about the need for psychoanalysis for his son. It was Johnny, he said, who had argued the other four into going to Columbia the day the police were there; the others' parents had charged him with being "an organizer" and ringleader. That was probably unjust, but Johnny did have a long history of insubordination, persistent enough perhaps to be termed neurosis.

"I'm not scared off by the word *neurosis*," Matthew assured Dori, "I know better than the headmaster that Johnny isn't exactly a nice normal well-adjusted member of the establishment."

"You'd hate it if he were. A square, aged fourteen?"

He smiled without much amusement. "But the idea of professional therapy carries such an or-else in it, it puts me in a sweat."

"Just the same, it could be a great insurance policy against anything serious later on."

"That's what I keep telling myself." He was moody

tonight and she did not wonder. He had forbidden Johnny to return to the Columbia campus, but for the first time he knew that that would not keep Johnny from returning, if returning was what Johnny intended to do. To know that control was passing from your hands to your child's must be a good feeling if your child was eighteen or twenty, but when he was fourteen and willful and driven to some endless battle with those in authority—there was nothing gratifying about that.

"Johnny may have had enough excitement by now," she said without conviction, "to make him more amenable to what you tell him. Or enough of a scare." But there was no response from Matthew and she felt a little hypocritical. There was nothing to make a boy like Johnny lose interest in the Columbia revolt. A thousand city police had finally been called in, some of them careful, some vicious, seven hundred students had been arrested, over a hundred had been injured, and the siege was officially over. But that was "officially." Johnny still talked of nothing else.

"It's part of something so much bigger," Matthew said at last. "If it were only Johnny. Or only Columbia."

"Or only ten Columbias." Each day brought an explosion of student revolts, at Cornell, at Duke, at Ohio State and Northwestern and Stanford and fifty other campuses in the land; across the oceans other students were in rebellion in Prague and Rome and Tokyo and at the Sorbonne, especially at the Sorbonne, where people were already beginning to talk of "another French Revolution." Somewhere she had heard the younger generation called the new international underground, and she responded as she would to any other resistance movement. But what lay ahead? Danger, she thought, and worse violence and even war.

She ought to be afraid. She ought to be thinking, What a time to bear a child, what right have I to bring a new human being into such a world? But she could not think it. At a hundred other times in the world's turbulent life there were people who had said it, but birth had gone on undeterred by death. During the First World War there had been women giving birth; during the Second World War, during the first horror of the atomic bomb, there had always been those who cried, "What a crime to bring a child into so vile a world," but steadily, surely, conception went on, pregnancies went on, birth went on, as if to flout the killing and the death.

"If ever I did get a divorce," Matthew suddenly said, "you can imagine what it would do to him, therapy or no therapy."

Unexpected, unforeseen, his words caught her, miles from what they had been talking about, miles from anything to say in reply. She gazed at him as if she were trying to understand the separate syllables of some unfamiliar tongue.

"Darling, look," he went on, "you know by now that half of me wants to leave everything behind and start again with you."

"I don't think of it. I don't let myself."

"But I do. Especially since we've come back together. But then I immediately think of Johnny and Hildy, and of course Joan. There's not much left for Joan and me apart from the kids, but she's not one of these women who would be able to start again at forty-two and make anything of it."

He looked depressed, sodden with a sadness she had never seen so plainly. She tried to think of the right thing to say but found nothing. "Perhaps I'm the one needs the therapy," he added, and again she said nothing.

"I don't mean just in general," he went on. "I suppose everybody could use a psychic checkup just in general. But me—something's been bugging me recently and I can't shake free of it."

"Do you want to tell me?"

It seemed hard for him to begin. He didn't look at her when he spoke. "It's something I wrote you once, that's got into some cross-tangle with when my mother was alive. I see the connection and that's supposed to rid you of it, isn't it? Only it doesn't."

He had never said very much about his parents, but neither had she about hers, beyond sketching in her love for her mother and distaste for her father. In their first weeks there had been no time for reminiscence and anecdote except about themselves as adults, and in the month since Matthew's return, they were once again too full of their immediate life. She knew that his father had died when he was a boy, but she was not clear about when he had lost his mother, or whether they had been close or distant. He had admired his mother, that she knew, had called her a fine lawyer, a remarkable person to have succeeded some thirty years ago when the law was still regarded as a man's profession.

"Maybe talking it out would help," she said quietly.

"I think it started that first morning I left you in bed," he said almost irritably. "You were half asleep and I wanted to wake you and I didn't, and then I tried all day to get you by phone and couldn't, and I wrote you instead."

"I remember."

He surprised her by switching abruptly to his early life with Joan, to the slow realization that they were never going to have a large easy circle of friends, to the time Hildy was born. He began to hurry his sentences, he slid over their difficulties with his mother, hardly mentioning Joan's shyness or unwillingness, making it his own unwillingness to go through awkward scenes. At last he talked of his mother sitting in silence looking down at the infant Hildy.

"That was fifteen years ago," he said, "and for years I never thought of it, but now it keeps jumping out at me like a flash shot on a movie screen. So okay, I was thoughtless and stupid about family things, but how many young couples get in wrong with in-laws or parents? And why the hell should it start needling me at this late date?"

He broke off, angry, and she waited. At last she

asked, "Your letter to me. Where does that come in?"

"My letter? Oh that. It's mixed in somehow. Sometimes the connection is clear and sometimes it goes foggy, and right now the hell with it. I've said too much as it is."

She wanted to cry, It's not too much, Matthew, it's not enough. Why can't you say straight out, how and why your letter comes in? You must feel it or you'd never have mentioned the letter at all. But she thought of his friend Jack forcing his own words back. Jack knew you couldn't give insight to somebody like a gift. She knew it too.

*　　*　　*

The sense of frustration would not go away. Long after he was gone she continued an interior conversation with him, depressed that she had thought it hazardous to hold it openly while he was still there. At the end of his recital they had dealt only in the small banalities that often follow revelation, when, spent with the emotion of telling, he needed only comfort, a kind of retroactive absolution, and she, giving both comfort and absolution, had wondered whether he would regard the matter closed and never return to it, or pursue it the next time they met. To be unwilling or unable to talk things out, even after one had started to talk them out, was no way to reach firmer ground in any close relationship. She should have made it easier perhaps, should have asked the questions that would have helped him dig for the answers that were already his.

"Darling," she prompted him now in her mind. "Don't you see why everything is cross-tangling?"

"No, do you?"

"It's only a theory. It could be so wrong."

"Tell me."

"Why I think it happens whenever you're afraid of hurting somebody again."

"Hurting Joan?"

"Joan or me, either one. I wonder if you don't know

that it's better to face things with somebody you love than to avoid a scene just to keep the peace, that if you do avoid scenes about something important, you end up by 'diminishing' the relationship, and feeling diminished yourself too."

She could imagine his wincing at the *diminish*. Though he knew perfectly well about himself as a lover, the sexual association would be there, a major affront. She could see his look become distant, as if he had never mentioned the letter, the only letter he had ever written her, could see his look of distaste, of disbelief, then of a faltering acceptance. Yet it was Matthew who had cross-indexed the two lines of thought, he who had finally seen that he had been rather a weak man in that early crisis in his life and was perhaps uncertain whether he were going to go on repeating that kind of weakness. It was too difficult to say any of this to him; he did not wish to say any of it aloud himself. Not so far. If he were to end his marriage, he would again live with guilt, would again have the same inability to excuse himself for what he had done. And yet he also felt guilt about not ending his marriage, about keeping it "intact" while his real life was here with her. His instinct was to say, Let's marry, but he had to stamp it down; her instinct also said, Let's marry, but he had to stamp her down too.

So he lived with one guilt while fleeing from the other.

I was immobilized, he had told her when he talked about his three months away from her. *Until I understood it, I was immobilized.* Now wasn't he immobilized again?

He would not put it that way. He would not put any of it the way she had just put it; for one thing he would speak not of leaving Joan but of leaving Johnny. Tonight was the exception, the one time he had ever permitted the formation of those words about leaving Joan, and he had negated the idea instantly. Joan was not a woman who could start life anew in the forties.

She, Dori, was a woman who could, so she was elected to do it.

He would never have it out with Joan. He could not stand scenes, except in court where conflict was part of the *modus vivendi*. He would live on in silence, old guilt interweaving with new guilt, threading in and out of it, reinforcing it, warp and woof, dependent one on the other, inextricable. Poor Matthew. It was not a good way to feel.

And me? Dori thought. Am I immobilized too?

*   *   *

The summer came suddenly and she walked with a little less than her striding energy. The park was nearly at full bloom; wherever she looked there were flowering trees, cherry, peach, pear, apple, or so she named them in her new status as botanist. She had never known before that there would be so many banks of rhododendrons, so many beds of tulips; the deep pinks, the pale pinks, the shimmering white and newly fresh green delighted her constantly.

It pleasures me, she thought; what a lovely old verb. Around a curve she came upon a girl out walking too, walking toward her slowly, apparently not seeing her. She was a young girl, in her late teens probably, or her earliest twenties, slender, pale even for the lightness of her skin and hair. Her cheeks gleamed wet in the sun, with tears streaming from her reddened eyes and her face ugly in the distortion of grief.

"Are you sick?" Dori asked without thinking. "Can I do anything?"

"No, thanks." She looked up briefly but did not slow down or attempt to hide her face.

"Whatever it is, I'm sorry," Dori heard herself say and they passed each other and the girl moved off behind her, around the curve in the path.

It left her shaken. A husband lost in Vietnam? A boyfriend unfaithful to her? The news that she was pregnant?

She was suddenly convinced—it was that, the news just given her in some doctor's office or at some clinic. The lab report was in and it said "positive." ("Oh no, oh God, what will I do, where will I go?")

The words rang within her as if they were being cried aloud to her and again the extraordinary conviction came that she had guessed correctly. For weeks now she had forgotten that frieze of faces she used to think about; she had been too much immersed in herself, too grateful for the passing days and their ticked-off accomplishment, but now again, stark and vast, a multitude of unwilling frightened girls arose before her, three hundred thousand who were not grateful, who did not have the freedom she had to step aside for a while from jobs and salaries and offices and factories and earnings.

Of the two pieces waiting for her return to steady work, this one on the terrified and trapped was the nearest to completion, but she had put aside the final writing of it, afraid that in her continuing mood whatever she wrote might, despite herself, sound patronizing. Like that morning after Martin Luther King, she thought, when I wanted to talk to that woman I passed.

It would be better to set it aside until she began working again, in September or October. She was going to come back here with the baby after the hospital and live right here until she could show herself to the world once more, get to work once more for Tad Jonas and any other editor who needed pieces written. How fortunate that Mrs. Steffani had insisted on a lease for an entire year. She had known all along she could not be going straight from Harkness to her real apartment with a new baby in tow, had known she would have to return from that legendary world cruise as she had left, with the same two suitcases and the borrowed plaid carryall and nothing else. But she had also known that the shorter her total absence, the more acceptable her cruise story.

So, the interim stop would be right here in this

blessed ugly familiar place, and as soon as she could show herself again she would have to hire a maid to live here with the baby, while she went home alone and resumed her "normal life." She laughed at the words. Normal life indeed. With her coming over here every single day to spend hours with her own baby, and moving back in every Friday evening to take full charge while the maid took her two days off.

It was all part of her still-evolving plan. She was saving in every way she could and it was still going to be a big chunk out of her nest egg, but if ever there was a palpable nest involved in that phrase, this had to be it!

Two months would go by, three, and she would be seeing friends and colleagues again, magazine editors, newspaper people, and the vagueness of memory about other people's goings and comings would have set in among all of them. Then only would she break the news that she was adopting a baby and arrive at home one fine day, no longer alone, but with the classic blanket enclosing a very new baby.

Classic, except for the lack of the proud husband beside her.

She thought once more of the weeping girl with the distorted face. She should have stopped, not walked on, stopped and said, Look, I'm in a fix too. You don't know me, don't know my name and I don't know yours, so why can't we talk about it? It might help, it gives people a release to tell somebody else, that's why they go to priests, or analysts, or talk to strangers on a train or boat.

Daydreams. Fantasy. Fairy tales for the pregnant. Here she was holding unspoken conversation with Matthew, giving unspoken sympathy to the girl in disgrace, experiencing the outer world largely through radio and television news and the telephone.

But she was lucky. Compared to the weeping girl she had passed, how blessedly lucky. She *could* carve out a year of her lifetime and pay for it. That simple economic fact had made the difference between disgrace and delight.

Not just that, she thought in sharp rebuttal. There you go again, belittling, deprecatory, another way of being defensive. Damn it, you know perfectly well that even if you didn't have a cent in the world you'd still be having this baby.

*   *   *

She opened the door eagerly. "Good morning, Doctor."

"Good morning, Mrs. Gray. Mrs. Grange—I beg your pardon. You see I had no problem with the bell. You look splendid. How do you feel?"

"Splendid too."

He was alone, as she had known he would be. She had made up the bed in its daytime incarnation, and on one end of it she had flung an ostentatious sheet for draping. To get ready would take less than a moment; she was in a loose smock that was like a hospital garment, except that it was strewn with pink carnations.

He did not notice either her garment or the sheet. He was in street clothes, not in the starched white coat, and he looked different, not so remote as he did in the office. From his bag he was drawing out his stethoscope and sphygmometer, taking a swift look about the large room as he did so. He maintained his usual impersonal mien about whatever it was he thought of it and its decor, and already had managed at once to take charge of her the patient, as he did in his own office, signaling her to sit in the armchair while he drew up one of the small straight chairs.

"Good," he said after using the stethoscope, and "good" after its second placing, and "good" at her blood pressure, and "good" once more when she had stepped on her bathroom scale and he had read the dial. Then he had motioned, with one continuing gesture at the waiting sheet and the tidy bed, and said,

"I'll have a look at you now," and busied himself returning his instruments to his black bag.

The visit was brevity and authority and reassurance. Without more than his repeated "good" he had told her again that he was satisfied with her progress and that he had again ruled out even the most minor of complications. Therefore she was surprised when he seated himself at her desk, drew out a prescription pad, and began to write.

"Mrs. G-r-a-n-g-e, Grange," he said aloud as he wrote her name. "You see I practice too. When the time comes, I will practice on a birth certificate. These are Nembutal I am giving you, twenty should do it."

"I still don't need them, Dr. Jesskin."

"So much the better. But if you do, they will be here. One at bedtime, the label will read. Now as to your walking. You will probably continue the full three miles as yet, but if you should begin to tire too much, cut away half a mile, even a whole mile."

"So far that's all right too."

"I can see it must be. I am more than pleased with the way it goes." He rose and looked about for the door. She had an absurd impulse to make him pause, to offer him coffee or some problem that would detain him. "Next visit, there will be measurements again and a blood sample, and until then, of course, telephone me at any time."

"I will. Thank you."

He left. The whole visit had taken less than twenty minutes.

*   *   *

She thought of the Nembutal one night because she was unable to get comfortable, but decided to turn her light on again and read a little longer instead. Over her book she looked down at herself and thought, Soon we won't be able to. Except for the last few weeks, Cele had told her long ago, and it had seemed too far off to consider. But here it was the last week in May and soon it would be June, and after June, as everybody knew, there would come the magic of July.

She slept. In the morning, she walked past the gleaming windows of her bank and idly glanced at herself. She was big. She was startled to see how big, as if in the last week or two, when she wasn't watching, nature had played a trick on her. The pitch of her body had changed; she walked now as if she were canted back, solid on her heels, though she knew she had not altered her posture. It gets going, she thought amiably; it may take a long time but sooner or later the bigness is there. And it's saying, This baby's going to get itself born in a few weeks.

Nine weeks. For the first time she was thinking in weeks, instead of in months. Wrong. At the beginning she had also thought in weeks; the sixth week, the tenth week. But then the reckoning had gone over into the more solid unit of months; she could remember when she had first thought "the third month," and then "the fourth month."

And here was the eighth month already begun, and she was back again to thinking in weeks. An orbit, a circle, perfect and harmonious. Though on the twenty-third of June she would be thinking in months again, since it would be the beginning of the ninth month, the final month, the great month of termination.

The great month. She was at last great with child, for all the world to see. At the corner where she turned east to go home, she paused, then retraced her steps, to pass before the bank's expanse of plate glass once again. She wasn't all *that* big; she would get bigger. But nobody could for a moment doubt that she was pregnant. This was not being overweight, this was being with child, in the lovely archaic phrase she had always thought so remote and unattainable.

It's me, she thought now. Me and my good construction. She grinned at her image in the window and started for home.

That night she shifted about several times in bed; her body had begun to demand a little planning before it was comfortable. Always before, though she had never noticed it until it was gone, there had been a firm hard line of contact as she lay on her side, her rib cage, her hipbone, her knee, her ankle making the points of contact with sheet and mattress. Now, between rib cage and hip there was a rounded extension, as if she had put down a package close to herself, which lay beside her, obedient to her movement but quite definable and apart too. She liked its presence; she felt fond of it. It keeps you company, she thought, and felt completely satisfied.

*   *   *

"You promised," Cele said, "and you're welshing on it. 'When I'm a big hulk' you said, 'then I'll get a maid.' What do you think you are now, hey?"

"A big hulk. But, Cele, it's so pointless. It's nights you're worried about and the maid wouldn't be here then anyhow."

"There's no statutory regulation that things go wrong only at night."

"You know nothing is going to go wrong. You're just getting nervy."

"That could be."

"Well, I'm not and you ought to be ashamed of yourself. Maybe I'm not one of the crinoline types that nobody suspects until the last minute, but I sure seem to be the peasant type that squats down between the furrows."

"Some furrows. Harkness at a hundred a day."

"For only four or five days. Thank the Lord for that or I'd really go broke. It piles up, doesn't it?"

"Are you starting to worry about money?"

"Not 'worry,' no. I'll probably bear down hard for a couple of years to make some of this up, but that's okay."

"Don't talk so lightly about bearing down, Dorr."

They laughed and Dori said, "So stop nagging me

about a maid until I simply have to have one, to get working again. Where the devil would she stay in this place anyway?"

"You have a point there." She glanced at an open catalogue of baby carriages and cribs and strollers, lying open on the desk. "Especially after a few of *those* little items arrive."

"Cele, *do* be a goodie and go see them tomorrow and choose. In case there's any snafu or warehouse nonsense or any of the usual. This is the third of June, after all, and we don't want to wait too long."

"July third would be plenty of time. You just want to see a crib and a baby carriage under your own roof."

"That's it. Will you? Tomorrow?"

"Yes, pest, tomorrow. Glory, will I be glad when this is all over and I can ignore you."

Dori laughed. Matthew was again in Boston and she had asked Cele over for the evening. It was oddly pleasant, pleasant in some new way, and she speculated from time to time about what the newness implied. There was something in any good long friendship between women that was calm and solid, she thought, a shared knowledge that needed no mouthing or measuring, and this she had felt often before. She might even have fitted words to it in some piece or other that she had written; certainly this was not what gave her now a sense of discovery.

What was new then in this particular pleasantness of having Cele here this evening? She had told her of the girl in the park, of the vision of herself in the plate-glass window, of Dr. Jesskin's brief visit ("sort of austere, Cele, almost curt. And sans Miss Mack. I'm glad he wasn't that silly."). They had pored over the catalogue's pages of nursery equipment and Cele had been the old pro whose every nay and yea carried weight.

And then suddenly Dori thought, It's a vacation from problems, that's why it's so nice. Ethics, morals, duty to one's children, to one's wife, the opposing duty to the other woman, to me, to my life —poor Matthew, it all does weigh on him and he can't help it, and it also weighs on me and I can't help it either.

"Matthew and I," she said impulsively, "have been talking out some awfully big matters of late."

"That's good." She sounded guarded.

"Probably Johnny will start with a child analyst when they get back from Truro after the summer. They're driving up at the end of the week. School closes for both kids on Friday."

"Does Matthew fly up every weekend?"

"We've never had weekends."

"Suppose you—" She broke off, and Dori finished for her.

"Go to the hospital on a weekend instead of Tuesday the twenty-third? Then Matthew won't even know about it until it's all over."

"Soon enough," Cele said dryly. Then as if to cover up a slip, she swiftly added, "Do you still say you don't know which you'd rather have?"

"A boy or a girl? I still say it."

"Have you chosen the first batch of names?"

"For the falsies?" She laughed. "I'll have to write it all out for poor Dr. Jesskin. If it's a boy, his false birth certificate will be James Victor Grange, and if it's a girl, Dorothy Victoria Grange."

"That damned *V* in your monogram. Nobody's ever going to see your towels or teaspoons at Harkness."

Dori ignored this. "But on the permanent birth certificate, after the adoption—" she began tentatively.

"You've changed your mind."

"No. It's still Eugene or Celia. That's never changed, either of them, since I first told you."

"Eugene Bradford Gray. Celia Varley Gray. I've never let on how that pleased me."

"It's the middle ones I'm thinking of changing," she said uncertainly. "I'm not sure whether I ought to ask permission first or what."

"Whose permission?"

"I got thinking about this, Cele, and it won't go away. Suppose it were Eugene Cornelius Gray? Or Celia Cornelia Gray? I'm not so sure of that one—it sort of rhymes."

"Why, Dorr, it's quite an idea. When did you come up with it?"

"How do you ever tell a doctor thank-you for something like this? I got thinking about it and thinking about it and once the idea came it just wouldn't go away. Ought I to ask him first?"

"I wouldn't dream of asking him. Tell him when you're out of Harkness. Or let your Mr. Cox tell him." With sudden emphasis she added, "You're so right! If it weren't for Dr. Jesskin all those million years back, where would any of this be?" Her wave took in the room at large, the open catalogue and Dori herself in her ample smock of pink carnations.

Dori looked around too. "And not only the million years back," she said. "What about right now, and all along since it happened? Without you and without Dr. Jesskin, it would have been a whole other ball game."

Cele thought of Matthew Poole, but let it pass. In a switch of mood she said, "Apart from all that, I've got a surprise for you. In half an hour or so."

"What surprise?"

"Marshall's coming over. It's all his idea."

"Coming to see me? You're making it up."

"He's bringing you something. A hospital gift, call it. I could have hugged him, it's so right."

Automatically Dori started for the bathroom mirror and brushed her hair. Behind her Cele jeered and called out, "Don't forget the false eyelashes," but Dori went ahead changing her lipstick, which was all the makeup she used now on her tanned skin. Then she stepped out of the smock and into a brief white skirt with a thigh-length tunic of turquoise. Apart from the heat, the navy silk was now tightly obsolete.

"You do look good," Cele conceded.

"My party clothes." She was amazed at how much an occasion it seemed, to see good old Marshall so unexpectedly. Cele, Gene, Matthew, Cele, Gene, Matthew—for all these months since January, it had been these three and not once had she felt deprived. Yet now the advent of another friend took on importance and excitement as if she had been off in exile.

When he arrived, she let Cele open the door while she stood in the center of the room waiting. She stood motionless, in profile, as if she were assuming a pose for a painter, and watched him look her up and down before she said, "Hi, Marshall," and went over to kiss him. He returned her kiss with a warmth he had never shown before, and said, "This is blackmail night."

He offered her the package he had brought, and she said, "Ooh, a present. I love it already."

There was a solid heft to the oblong and she sat down to open it. As her present came into view, Marshall said, "The one sure thing is, you'll use it; there's something about them when they're new that drives you nuts. It's to take to the hospital."

It was a camera, complete with film pack, flashbulb, automatic light-setting, and almost instantaneous outcome. She was delighted and oddly touched that so practical a man of affairs as Marshall should have visualized her taking pictures of a just-arrived baby. She kissed him again and began asking how to operate it but suddenly interrupted to ask, "What did you mean 'blackmail night'?"

"Get up and stand the way you did when I came in." He took the camera from her hands. "I may sell you the negative for a hundred thousand and then again I may not."

"I never even thought of a picture of me pregnant," she cried, posing with alacrity. "But do I ever want it! I'll keep it in a safe-deposit box, but then I could always prove it, twenty years from now."

An extraordinary vanity permeated her and she had to restrain an impulse to lean backward and look bigger than she was. How long did you keep a secret like this from the baby you gave birth to? Twenty years? Twenty-five? Forever? She did not know, nor could she know; life itself would teach her the answer to this one. But all at once she felt a desperate need for a photograph for that distant day, proof, evidence that it was not fantasy, if in that distant day no other evidence would still exist.

Marshall was opening the camera and peeling off the picture. He glanced at it, showed it to Cele, and then Cele smiled and handed it over to Dori. "Real good-looking," she said, "except for being straight as a board."

TEN ⤳

IT WAS THE CAMERA that circuitously started her first
flare-up with Matthew. She had taken two pictures of
him, showed him the ones Marshall had taken of her
the night before, and repeated the jest about blackmail.

"What does *in camera* really mean?" she asked. "No
pun. I know the adoption papers will be *in camera*
and I thought I might put these pictures *in camera*
with them, and all my checks signed 'Grange' and the
false birth certificate and the hospital bill and everything."

"You can't use the courts like a safe-deposit box,"
he said, amused. "If any case is heard in private, in a
judge's chambers instead of in open court, then the
proceedings are *in camera,* and in your case, your
lawyer—"

"Matthew, I should have told you—"

"Your case will be *in camera,*" he went on. "So all
the documents become secret records for all time,
not open to the public at any time, remaining always
in the possession of the court." He went on to elaborate. Nobody could ever see the papers, neither friend
nor enemy, unless some court of law ordered them
to be shown. That could not be done at anybody's
simple request, not even at her own. No lawyer could
request them, no reporter could stumble on them,
not even the adopted person himself could get at
them. Only in the event that the adopted person were
involved in some criminal trial would the process be
set in motion whereby some future judge could rule

that the inviolable secrecy of that *in camera* might be breached.

"Not in any civil action," he ended, "no contract litigation, no divorce action, no libel or slander suit, nothing but a criminal prosecution could get at those private papers. See?"

She nodded. "Matthew, there's something else. I should have told you this, but the right moment never seemed to come up. One day while we were apart, I asked Dr. Jesskin if he knew a good lawyer to handle the adoption for me."

"A good lawyer?" he asked stiffly.

"This was while we weren't seeing each other and I sort of panicked and I asked Gene and then Jesskin, and Dr. Jesskin did."

"Did what?"

"Arranged it for me. It's a man named Bob Cox, a friend of his."

"Of Cox, Wheaton, Fair—?"

"Yes. It's a good firm, isn't it?"

"Very."

"Do you know Mr. Cox?"

"I've met him. He's good too."

"Are you annoyed? I could cancel it. I've never met Mr. Cox or even talked to him by phone so far."

"I'm not annoyed."

"It was just that—well, I hadn't heard one word from you and I had decided I never would, this was already April, and you had said you wouldn't be handling it yourself in any case."

"But I assumed you did want my firm to handle it."

"I did. I would have. Only all that time, it was already April—" The old defensive feeling, rising, infuriated her. Here she was explaining, repeating herself, offering extenuating circumstances. "You needn't look like that," she cried angrily.

"Like what?"

"As if I'd done something dreadful."

"I don't exactly enjoy being told off."

"You haven't said one damn word about it since

we've been back, either," she said. "Not one word, about courts, or what the proceeding is or when it's done or how long it takes, nothing."

"I didn't think it needed saying. When the time came—"

"You can't really think I could just let it slide happily along forever."

"Now, Dori, I never thought that at all."

"It's not the only thing you never thought at all. If I ever told you all the things you never think—" She turned fast, and slid both hands over her face. She saw again the slippery wet cheeks of the girl in the park and ground her fingertips into her eye sockets so that pain flashed. She felt his arm on her shoulder and angrily shook it free and sat there, huddled in on herself, hugging her bulk with her arms and elbows while her hands remained covering her face.

There was silence. He went to the kitchen and poured a drink of Scotch. She thought of that time in January when he had done that, not bothering with ice or soda, and the memory was sharp. Would he again go to the door and tell her he needed time to get it into some sort of shape? He had no overcoat to walk out with this time, maybe that would make it different.

"I'm sorry," she heard herself saying into her tented hands, "I don't know why I said all that."

"To punish me."

"For what?"

"Does it matter?"

"Don't take that injured tone."

"I didn't mean to." Suddenly he was beside her, telling her it was natural enough that she had been angry, that it was quite true that he had been legal-minded, knowing there was enough time, forgetting her very human need to see ahead, to have everything prepared well in advance.

"I'm glad you blew," he said. "It's not an easy time for you, darling, and you have the right to blow your top once in a while."

"It's better if I don't."

"But you did, so forget it. I'll start lining up the right man for the adoption at the office tomorrow morning."

But the reluctance she had already felt came back. "Please don't do it, Matthew." It sounded regretful, as if she were about to ask something difficult of him. "Maybe since it's all set in motion through Dr. Jesskin's friend, it might be best to let it stay that way."

"You mean not have me in the picture at all?"

"Not your firm." She thought he might be angry but a wild need transfixed her so that if she had wanted to change what she had said, she could not have done it. This was right. This was somehow native to her; if he had delayed so long on this, it revealed a reluctance in him too, one that he wasn't willing to see. It wasn't even very important, unless it indicated vaster reluctances.

Not only in him, but in herself as well. Insight. Nobody could hand it to you all done up in festive papers and gleaming ribbon; you had it or you had to dig for it until you found it. There was something here, some clue, buried, in retreat as yet from reason, deep in her own character, and for the first time she knew that she did not dare to sidestep the search any longer.

*   *   *

Early next morning she unlocked her suitcase, drew out a sheet of her real stationery and wrote:

DEAR MR. COX,

This is just to thank you in advance for taking on the case Dr. Cornelius Jesskin asked you about. Knowing that you have agreed to do so gives me a peace of mind I'm grateful for.

If all goes according to plan, I should be phoning for an appointment early in August. I can't tell you how much I look forward to it.

Sincerely,
THEODORA V. GRAY.

She addressed and stamped the envelope and went out to mail it from the nearest postbox. This letter needed no San Francisco or London postmark, or Tokyo or Rio either. She stood with her hand on the lid of the postbox, staring at the slot which had taken her letter. Her own name on her own stationery with her own return address, talking of a face-to-face meeting in early August. It was like leaning into the future.

* * *

June was the only bad month. Graceless at best, horror-filled at worst, Dori continuously felt a malaise that had no precise name, that lay somewhere between the heights of euphoria and the depths of depression.

She ascribed it to the newest assassination, she ascribed it to the deepening fears of racism in the election, she ascribed it to the pure physical deprivation of not making love. For the first time, she felt clumsy and plodding; she felt the slowness of time; she felt that none of this was the full sum, and this single certainty intensified everything else.

Matthew was never absent except on the unvarying weekends, eager always to arrive, loath always to leave, openly grateful for her rage at the sentencing of Dr. Spock and the others to two years in a Federal prison, talking to her hungrily about the plans for appeal, about his own appeal for young Benting. She understood for the first time that he rarely spoke of his work to Joan. He was taking on a new case, similar to Benting's but in New York, where he would not need to work through an associate lawyer as he did in Boston, this time without a fee, because this time his client was black and poor instead of white and well-to-do.

The argument about her own lawyer was all but forgotten. Neither of them ever spoke of it. When she did think of it she assured herself she was glad it had happened just that way, because she had been open and honest and free from the artifice that too often made a relationship pulpy and unreal.

And yet she also wished it had never happened. The slow elapsing days seemed to be a piling on and piling on of other things she wished had never happened. It was on the very night of the argument that she had been wakeful and restless after Matthew's departure and listened in the dark to an all-night music station, falling asleep to a Beethoven quartet. Through the music, tearing through the first thin veil of her sleep, had come a sudden voice, the voice not of the music announcer but the voice of crisis. "We interrupt this program to bring you a special news bulletin"—the news that out in California, on a night of triumph, Senator Robert Kennedy had been shot, perhaps fatally.

She was alone with it and stayed alone. It was three thirty in the morning here although half an hour past midnight out there; Matthew, Cele, Gene would all be asleep. That was good. She could not speak now to anyone, not again, not so soon again after April. If Matthew's family had already left for Truro, she would probably have called him anyway, but she was obscurely glad that it was out of the question. She briefly considered waking Gene or Cele, but at once, in a kind of pre-audition, she heard the words that would follow and knew she could not stand hearing them on her own lips and in her own ears. To be mute, to say nothing for a few hours—that was what she needed now, a reversal from that other time when she had wanted so much not to be alone.

It was as if she had suddenly become a sister of silence, a nun in some holy order with vows to remain without speech. She listened to all the stations in turn, her eyes dry, her throat clamped in a collar of steel, unyielding and pitiless, like a collar within the column of her throat pressing outward. It was like a maniacal replay of nightmare, a confusion and yet a sameness.

When at last her night-black windows began to fog into gray, she dressed and made up the room and then had breakfast. It was too early for the *Times;* that came at seven. Seven would also bring the two-hour news and interview show she sometimes listened to; she would hear only the bulletins and turn off the interpreters, the philosophizers, the assayers and the theorizers. Not again, not this time; there were limits to what you could stand.

But *they* stood it, his mother, his wife, his children, Mrs. King, her children, the people getting the official telegrams from Vietnam, the wives, the mothers, the children—

The life force. Birth going ahead in the midst of horror and death—why had she limited herself to the two world wars and the atom bomb? Why had she not begun with the Civil War, why not with the French Revolution, the Inquisition, why not with Christians thrown to the lions in the arenas of Rome, why not with Jewish children born in the Nazi decades, with Negro children born today?

The paper finally came, the television screen began its special reports and she yielded briefly to both and wanted only to get out to the quiet park and walk. At eight she called Gene and Cele, to say she knew and was going out, and when she came back an hour later she heard the flatted muted ringing of the telephone as she was opening her door and talked to Matthew in the same truncated way. He came in for a little while on his way home from his office and then again after dinner. Both times she seemed numb, unable to explain that she felt huge with it as if it were within her, another pregnancy, all of it, that long-ago November and then that night in April and now this one in June, that she felt filled with all of it and unable to accommodate the pull and drag.

"Take a sleeping pill tonight, darling," Matthew said. "You can't do this, not now, only a couple of hours of sleep the whole twenty-four. Take it now and I'll wait until you're in bed and then I'll go and know that you'll get some rest."

Obediently she went to the medicine cabinet, swallowed a yellow capsule, and in a moment was in bed. The latest bulletins still vacillated: there was a chance, there was little chance, there was the possibility that the body might live on without the functioning mind. She was riven by dilemma as if it were her responsibility, to decide which would be more tolerable, that or the finality.

"Darling," Matthew said, leaning over her from the edge of her bed, "I know this is a terrible time to think of us, but in a way, it's the right time too. There are no easy solutions for us, not ever, but I love you more and more and if you'll let me, I want to be part of your life from now on. And of the baby's life."

"Oh Matthew."

"I don't know that I've rung up any great success as the father of my own children," he went on. "But they keep telling us that a father figure is vital in any child's life, and if a father figure is all that important in this baby's life, and if you'll let me, I'll be that father figure always."

She wept, silently, not hiding her face, letting her cheeks glisten wetly as the girl in the park had done. She held tightly to his fingers, and when she fell asleep, he left her.

* * *

The crib arrived and was set in place, the carriage arrived and was given a corner of its own. And still it remained a bad month. Dori shortened her daily walk by half a mile and then lengthened it again whenever the mornings were cool. She resumed her work on her two pieces but then saw, with a slicing clarity, that she could not have these printed soon after her return without shouting to them all, Look, here are my new interests, illegitimate birth and adoption. There would have to be two or three other pieces first, another Martha Litton, another

Dr. Spock, and then in a year or two, but no sooner, these two.

This must have been a hidden reason for her delay in finishing either one; she who never blocked up on unfinished work. A brief cheer permeated her at this clarity. Clarity always was an asset, clarity about anything. She remembered the upward leap of her spirits when she had first made a list of majors and minors, when she had fired Nellie and gone forth for her first maternity clothes. From that minute on there had been clarity.

If only she could see what it was that remained unclear about herself and Matthew. That night when Senator Kennedy died he had moved her to tears and yet as the days inched by she knew nothing basic was changed. As long as she was herself alone, Dori Gray alone, Matthew was what she wanted, was what made her happy: his nearness, his presence as often as possible, his love and his making love.

But there would come the time when she could no longer think of herself alone, Dori Gray alone. To give birth was not to restore herself to being "herself alone." Wasn't that a state to which there was, thank God, no returning?

She was changing, but was Matthew? That night when he had finally told her about Jack Henning he had blurted out, "That was the shutout, right there. Nothing's going to change that."

But she would be even happier with a child growing up. Would that be a shutout too? Perhaps he would be close enough to the actual living developing child to feel a part of its life, a part of the future, feel that it was his too, and no shutout at all.

To a point, yes. To a degree, surely. In a partial version, an approximation, better than nothing, lovely up to the limits that their circumstances would permit.

"Why isn't he ever here on Saturday or Sunday?" An unknown little voice, high and unformed like all children's voices, sounded clear in her mind. "Why can't he ever be here on Christmas?"

Cut that, damn it, she ordered herself. Does it have to be all or nothing? Are you going to turn your back on what's there and moon around for what isn't there?

No, she wasn't. Yet she suddenly remembered the night she had gone down Central Park West at one in the morning, remembered the night sky ablaze, remembered her excitement over Cele's news that Matthew had called, and remembered too that on that threshold of their renewed life together she had wondered whether it would be the same Dori Gray that he would find.

*   *   *

"One more visit," Dr. Jesskin said, "and then I do not see you until the delivery room. Is that welcome news?"

"I can't believe it."

"Of course not." He began to put away his instruments but the austere brevity of his last visit was missing. His "good" and again "good" of last time was replaced this morning by "excellent" or "perfect," and he had asked how many sleeping pills she had left and had she any questions to put to him. "I see by the crib and the carriage that you plan to return here."

"Do you have a few minutes? Could I give you some coffee? I haven't any questions, no, but if I could take a minute and tell you what I'm going to do after Harkness?"

To her astonishment he said coffee would be fine and sat down in the straight chair, leaving the armchair to her. As she told him her "postnatal timetable," she saw him nod and thought how absurd it was that she should want his approval even on practical matters like these.

"That is a fine transition plan," he said, "ingenious and very sound."

"Then after the hospital, when I can start working again, I'll get a maid who likes babies—"

"Nobody under seventy," he said in a tone of sudden warning.

"Under seventy?"

"A reliable geriatric," he said calmly. "That is my plan for your private nurses at the hospital."

"Private nurses? Aren't they awfully expensive?"

"Only for the first night and day while you're coming out from the anesthesia." She looked baffled and he added, "In case you babble."

"Of course!"

"They will be seventy at least, still active, still in good health, but as much over seventy as possible. Eighty would be even better. Then even if you should hand them the whole truth, they wouldn't have too long a time left, poor things, to be indiscreet about it."

This was so deliberately spoken, and with such open self-approval, that she guffawed. He was pleased at her reaction and said slyly, "I would not wish old age on anyone, being already fifty-two myself, but an inescapable fact is that in certain circumstances a lack of longevity can be a great desideratum. Is that not so?"

"You think of everything. Oh, Dr. Jesskin, suppose I had never been sent to you, back in nineteen fifty-five?"

He finished his coffee and stood up. "Then I should have missed knowing a remarkable patient."

*　　*　　*

Long after he was gone, she heard the phrase sounding. Like his three thinkings, like her good construction, this about a remarkable patient struck for itself at once an indelible outline in her memory.

A remarkable patient. *Then I should have missed knowing a remarkable patient.* But surely he had gone through this entire business before, of the unmarried pregnant woman. He must have; in all his years of practice he must have had other patients who were with child but without wedding ring or husband. She could not, by the law of probabilities, be the only patient he had ever had who was having an illegitimate baby. Had he then turned the others away? Impossible. He had been through it all before.

That was why he was so ready with solutions, his suggestion about Harkness and the two names on her door, his readiness about the false birth certificate, his cleverness about geriatric nurses, all of it. He had not said so, of course; in a doctor's life everything was automatically *in camera*.

The knowledge that there had been others pacified her, mollified her, yet a few moments later she realized that it also robbed her. She did not know of what. Something. Something she valued, something she didn't want to give up.

She suddenly laughed self-consciously. Why, I want to be the only one, she thought, a goddam unique character in his whole medical career. But I'm not, I couldn't be. She could ask him someday, she supposed, ask in the most general terms, whether all gynecologists and obstetricians did not, in the course of a long practice, inevitably have a certain number of illegitimate births to cope with—but he would use the most general terms back at her and not tell her a thing. As for Miss Mack, asking her would be like asking the Great Stone Face.

Good old Miss Mack. Just yesterday she had telephoned to "remind" Dori of Dr. Jesskin's visit this morning, and had added, "And I'm to give you Doctor's telephone number in Huntington too, though the service always hops to it for anybody on the special list."

"What list?" she had wanted to say. "The list of people in the eighth and ninth months?" But all she had said was "Huntington?"

"His summer place. He's in town all week, but from June first on, he's still out there weekends."

"Thanks, I'd love to have it." She had taken it down, read it back to Miss Mack, and then later had thought, What did she mean, 'still out there weekends'? Anybody but Miss Mack would have said, "But from June first on, his family is out there and he goes out weekends." Like Matthew's family. Like all families. But Miss Mack would not commit herself to informing a soul that "Doctor" had a family, despite the photographs on his desk. If Dori herself asked her, Miss Mack would never admit that any Dori Gray had ever begun as a sterility patient and ended up having a baby. Miss Mack must have taken the Hippocratic oath all by herself.

Someday when all this was over, she would send Miss Mack a great big bunch of flowers with a card that told her some patients blessed their lucky stars for a doctor's staff too.

He's still out there weekends. It sounded as if the place in Huntington had been there for a long time. It also sounded as if it were in the past tense except for him. Did the rest of the family not go out there weekends? What about those kids and that pretty woman she was sure was his wife?

Kids? They were about ten or twelve in the photographs, and she had visualized them that way. But when he first told her of Bob Cox, had he not said that his son was finishing Harvard Law this summer with Bob Cox's son and that both of them were joining the firm as junior law clerks?

Then those photographs must be ten or twelve years old. Older. If you got out of any graduate school before twenty-five, you were an exception. A son of twenty-five and a daughter of twenty-three? Perhaps both married, and out at Huntington only for visits. That must be it. The inscrutable Miss Mack would never have mentioned it, any more than Dr. Jesskin himself.

But what about his wife? Why didn't Miss Mack say, "They're out there weekends?" And if that were the case, would she have inserted that enigmatic "still"? Wouldn't any couple keep going out to their summer place? Need one specify that the man went out there still?

She had never wondered about Dr. Jesskin's life, never visualized him as father, husband, brother, as anything but doctor and specialist. No, that wasn't quite so. The day after Martin Luther King's death when she had called him in agitation about lawyers, he had said, "I think many of us couldn't sleep last night," and like a streak of daylight she had had a flash of him as a political being, one who couldn't sleep either because of a hideous murder of someone he admired. She had forgotten that until just now.

She thought, I wish I knew more about him. When this is all over, I'll research the man! She wondered whether there were any medical articles written by him; that would be easy to find out at the Academy of Medicine. She wondered if the great big directory of physicians, which told all about a doctor's or surgeon's degrees and hospital connections, also told about his general life, as *Who's Who* did. In *Who's Who* the names of your children were listed, the name of your wife, the date of your marriage or divorce, and if there had been any death in the family, a lowercase *dec.* appeared.

Did the Medical Directory do the same—and would the lower-case *dec.* be there?

The embarrassment returned. More fantasy, more fairy tales for the pregnant. She really was beginning to show signs of the stress that lay in too much peace and quiet. What had started her on this remarkable train of thought?

Remarkable. The word in the context. *Then I should have missed a remarkable patient.* He had meant something by it. She was positive now that he had treated other unmarried pregnant women, so the "remarkable" did not have that sense. Nor was it another of his odd phrasings that betrayed his birth in Denmark or Sweden or wherever. She didn't even know that much about him. Here was a man who had become as necessary to her as breath and she knew not even the first detail about him as a man.

How absurd we are, she thought, how trapped in

good manners. Why had she never been able to sit
there at his desk and glance openly at the photographs and openly say, "Is that your family? The children look like you." What would have been intrusive
or rude about it if she had? He could sit there above
an open folder, and say, The last time you had intercourse was when? The period you skipped should
have been when? Could sit there and tell her, You
will want to know whether you may continue to have
intercourse. Of course, you may. It is natural, normal,
indeed, the stimulation of hormones during pregnancy—

But of course that was professional, every syllable
was spoken by a professional about professional matters. He knew everything about her that mattered,
knew of her having an affair that had produced this
baby, knew that she would be wanting to have intercourse and was thus having an affair still.

Had she made it clear to Dr. Jesskin that the pregnancy was antecedent to this affair? She couldn't remember. She thought that she had, at some point,
said quite definitely that that affair had been coming
to an end, and since he never missed anything, never
forgot anything, he must have realized that her interest in whether you were permitted to have intercourse
during pregnancy applied to somebody else and not
the man who had helped her achieve it.

Quite suddenly it mattered to her that it should be
clear in Dr. Jesskin's mind. If she were still involved
with the man who had, as they say, sired this baby
about to be born, then Dr. Jesskin would know that
it was a deep and abiding relationship, reaching backward in time, reaching forward, a relationship of
dimension, important and enduring.

But it isn't, she thought or at least I'm not sure.
How could she be sure of that reaching forward? Oh,
that was what was troubling, that not being able to
be sure of its reaching forward when this summer,
this year, next year were done.

Suddenly she was back again at the side of Dr. Jesskin's desk in Dr. Jesskin's office, before Christmas of last year, telling him she had done the three thinkings and was going ahead and would he help her. Again she felt the awkward touch of his fingers on her own, as if he were trying to shake hands. Again she heard his words, "I am proud of you," and all at once they fused with these words today, "I should have missed a remarkable patient."

He liked all this—that's what it meant. He liked her in the context of it. She was not merely a patient but a human being also and he had touched her fingers in a human code. This, today, had been the code still, undiminished all these months later.

Undiminished. That word again, she thought. It keeps at me and I wish it would let me be.

*   *   *

As it neared its end, June stopped being the bad month. Dori grew more adept at managing her bulk, as if there were a technique one could ease into. The discomfort of her recumbent body was there still but somehow she could "sleep around it" as if she could redistribute her entire body in secret ways to get the better of the bulk and awkwardness. When she woke at night, she took aspirin and slept again. She began to take afternoon naps as well, drowsy with weight and immobility, and for the first time her ankles, which had always been as tight to the bone as skin could be, grew puffy late each day, the thongs of her sandals cutting into the rising flesh. All this she reported to Miss Mack, to add to the record. She did not want to call Dr. Jesskin unless there were some emergency. Miss Mack sent her a prescription for pills for the edematous ankles but week by week there was no emergency.

"What day do you think this is?" she asked Matthew one evening as he came in, and before he could answer, "The first day of the ninth month."

"Hooray. Let's drink the champagne to it."

"You'll have to put another bottle by though."

"I guess I can manage another."

"Look over there," she said, pointing to the smaller of her suitcases, standing in the corner near the crib. "It's all packed for the hospital."

"Jumping the gun, that's known as. Let's drink to the gun too."

He was impatient to have it all over, to have her as she was when he had found her, her body tight and slender and beautiful, swift in movement, swift in response to him, to have her in bed again where all their problems were forgotten, where they either were conquered or appeared to be conquerable.

"I've been packing suitcases too," he said as he began to work on the cork of the bottle he drew from the icebox. "Metaphorical suitcases."

"Such as?"

"I told the family yesterday I wouldn't be up the weekend of the twentieth, that I couldn't make it." The cork popped and he rushed the bottle to the waiting glass. "Here, darling."

She accepted the sparkling glass and waited for him to fill his. "You thought of that," she said. "I'm glad. I had wondered, What if it should be early?"

He looked surprised. "Did you think I'd be off, that close to the official date?"

"I didn't exactly think about it." She raised her glass to him. "But I'm glad you won't be."

He raised his own glass. "Here's to gun-jumping," he said. "It would be most obliging of you not to be a stickler for the twenty-third."

"But I gather it's lots likelier to be late than early."

"Then at least Mrs. Steffani will have the thrill of seeing Mr. Grange here for one weekend anyway."

They laughed. Mrs. Steffani, after seeing him put his key to the door several times, had one evening addressed him as "Mr. Grange," and he had accepted the title without demur. Behind him, in the door that stood ajar, Dori had said, "I meant to introduce you," but Mrs. Steffani had given her a wary look that invited no further effort. They had tried to decide whether she knew he was no Mr. Grange and they had come down on the side of Mrs. Steffani's hidden wisdoms. "Otherwise, why would you show only Monday through Friday?" Dori had demanded.

"Because I have to be in Vietnam the rest of the time."

Now he added, "You mean, suppose you hang on till the following weekend? Then I'd have to say again that I couldn't make it, but my God, Dori, you wouldn't be that ornery, would you?"

"I'll try not."

She looked tranquil again and he became equally tranquil. The early part of the month, he thought, had been their worst time since they had been back together, and he was glad it was over at last. He now felt with Dori a blessed return of ease; she seemed to have resumed her early simplicity with him, the tangles smoothed away again.

"You're never ornery," he said with sudden warmth. "You are my lovely Dori and there's nobody like you."

"Matthew. You are a little drunk already."

"Not drunk at all." He kissed her. "Look, this damn rotten month is over and this is a good time again and there'll be lots of them. There'll be bad ones too, but we're stuck with each other, no matter. If we fight we fight, if we can't make love we can't, if we have to be apart, we have to. But none of that changes *us,* does it?"

To her surprise she asked, "Do you just say 'I can't make it' to Joan? Is that enough? Or 'I won't be in' or something like that?"

He set down his champagne and stared at it. It was the kind of question he resented, the kind any man would resent. It was rare, this sort of thing from Dori, but it struck a bad chord, left him aquiver with dissonance and minor key. She knew every essential about himself and Joan; he had never dissembled to Dori, never glozed over, never indulged in the tinny clichés of the wife-blaming husband. Then why such a question at all?

"I shouldn't have said that," she said as if he had spoken aloud.

"I agree. I don't think you should."

"But why not? I can't help thinking about it."

"Then why did you just say you shouldn't have?"

"I thought that too. I know it's illogical, but people aren't always all full of logic." He stared at the wine and his silence vexed her. "It's impossible not to wonder once in a while what *I* would do, Matthew, if you told me sometime, 'I can't make it' and let it go at that. I'd probably just up and say, 'Why can't you?' before I even thought not to."

"Dori, let's not get into this. There's no sense to it."

"I suppose there's not."

He returned to the champagne but the effervescence was gone. He was angry at her for flatting it out of existence and yet knew she had not done so purposely. She was troubled about many things ahead; he was also. Dori was not one of those mindless optimists who gabbled romantic nonsense about how glorious everything was going to be for them; she saw too intelligently the difficulties and crossed wires and crosscurrents—

Damn it, he thought, as long as it isn't cross-purposes and crossed swords. I'm crossed up and screwed up with too much analyzing, when all I want is to carve the possible out of the impossible. That's all Dori wants too. Then why can't we have it and let everything else alone?

"Darling, listen." He told her what he had been thinking and she kept nodding, phrase for phrase, though he felt that he was losing the point he wanted to make in the delicate task of transmission from mind to words. She had the look he had come to know, half of apology that she should have caused strain or tension, yet with it another half that maintained a point of view, her point of view, as if she were also saying, I'm tabling it for now, but not simply brushing it into the incinerator. It won't burn up.

It won't just conveniently disappear in smoke and a nice crisp smell of burning.

"So I think we have to take it as it comes," he ended. "We've solved it all so far. We'll solve the rest of it too."

"I know we will. Of course we will."

ELEVEN »&

A SHAFT OF STEEL speared upward and Dori woke with a small cry. She had never felt anything like it.

It was gone almost before she knew it. For a moment she wondered if it had been part of a dream, drug-induced, weight-induced, discomfort-induced. She glanced at the small clock on the table beside her; it was ten after one.

She closed her eyes thinking how it had been. It was like a metal wedge forced upward through the pelvic arch, a chisel driven into two halves of a boulder to break it asunder.

Then she knew. The image told her. It had begun.

She was wild with elation. She was to time the pains. That was the first order: Time the pains. How many dozens of repetitions had the admonition had, not only in the past weeks but all her life before, when the directive was not for her but merely part of the folklore of childbirth. You timed the pains; you didn't call for help until the pains were coming every five minutes. Her instructions were different because she was alone. She was to call Cele the moment she was sure there were pains at regular intervals, no matter how far apart; Cele would come over in a taxi and they would decide when to call Dr. Jesskin. She herself would decide at what point to telephone Matthew.

She looked again at the clock. The minute hand had scarcely left the ten-after position.

Perhaps this was something all by itself, instead of number one in a series. Again she closed her eyes thinking about it, thinking, For once somebody is going to describe it; I'm a writer, or I used to be a writer anyway, and I'm going to remember every bit of it so I can set it down for the record. All anybody ever writes about is the cries and groans and the beads of sweat. She smiled, superior. She was a better reporter than that.

Her thoughts grew hazy with sleep. For the past two weeks, she had meekly obeyed the doctor and taken one of the glistening yellow capsules each night as she went to bed. Since the final process had begun, that final re-positioning within her, her center of gravity was changed. A personal center of gravity was one more thing she had never contemplated before.

The wedge again—the chisel, the boulder. The same, the same splitting apart, the same, no deeper, no worse, the same.

She looked at her watch. One twenty. Ten minutes since the other one. Twice; not what you would call a series. Maybe it was something else, some mishap, the first. She hadn't expected this entering wedge anyway; she had been told she would have cramps, like menstrual cramps, yet deeper, and also toward the back. Something was going wrong, then, for there had been no cramps. But this was Monday, the—

She sat up suddenly, as suddenly as she could do anything. It was no longer Monday. It was Tuesday, the Tuesday she had waited for, the twenty-third of July.

There was no mishap, there was nothing wrong. She would wait for just one more, and if it came when it should, she would call Cele. She lay back, waiting, surprised in some far-off part of her, as if there were an exterior Dori observing her, surprised that she was so calm and so excited at once. She was alive with watchfulness, stirring with expectation, a little crazy with delight. If this should smooth out and go away and not continue, she would be savage with disappointment.

She glanced at the clock. Only a minute? Ridiculous. She closed her eyes. No woolly sleep now. The Nembutal might have flown clear out of her body. In another moment she once more sat up, but this time she left the bed and went to the kitchen. Tea or coffee? Or something cold? She put the kettle on.

She waited for the kettle to whistle, taking an almost clinical checkup on the way she felt. Shaken by anticipation and uncertainty, but otherwise good. If those two were the start, then nothing but good; if they were signs of mishap, then she was alarmed, since mishap had been so totally absent from all these nine months.

She started to glance at her wristwatch and stopped her eyes halfway in their journey. The timing would be reversed for this next one. She would look at her watch only if the third pain arrived, a confirmation after the event, not a possible psychic inducement beforehand. She felt very clever over this decision, poured scalding water over the tea bag in her cup and jeered at her self-approval as fatuous.

She took the tea carefully to her bed table, her eyes averted now from the little clock. She had left the camera for the last minute's packing and as her tea cooled she thought, Just for luck, and placed it next to the suitcase, on the floor beside it. The suitcase itself she did not touch. Everything was already in it but her toilet things and her Grange checkbook.

She went back to bed and sipped her tea. God, ten minutes could be long. If pain number three didn't arrive, ought she to notify Dr. Jesskin's service at least, that something seemed to be wrong? She was to call him at home if labor had begun, but if she were not sure?

Her breath sucked in on itself. The chisel, deeper, rocking her whole skeleton, prying the halves apart. The first sweat spurted from her pores. She looked at the clock. One thirty. She dialed Cele.

"Cele, it's me. It's started."

"How far apart?"

"Ten minutes, and I've had three. Not cramps at all, sort of being gored upward."

"Are you okay? You sound shaky."

"I'm terribly excited, that way shaky."

"I'll start out the minute I phone Dr. Jesskin. I think if it's ten-minute pains, I'd better call him first."

Moving slowly, Dori began to dress. The disappearance of the Nembutal amazed her; she might never have gone near it, so wide-awake was she, whereas her usual experience these past nights was to feel half drugged even the next morning when she awoke. That partly explained her aversion to sleeping pills; never had she taken them regularly except that one time when Tony left.

She dressed quickly, brushed her teeth and hair, and packed her toilet kit into the suitcase, along with the camera and checkbook. Then she looked thoughtfully about the apartment. There were last-minute checkups she had assigned herself to do.

The last page of her desk calendar; she tore it out and took it with her. She tried the lock of her other suitcase and felt for its key in her purse. She signed the note she had already written to leave for Mrs. Steffani, saying she would be back in a few days and would Mrs. Steffani take in her papers and magazines instead of letting them pile up at her door. She paused over her signature to be sure that in her excitement she signed it not Gray but Grange.

Again the shaft of metal, again the burst of sweat, this time an involuntary animal grunt from the back of her throat. She sat rigid, waiting for it to be over. Her wristwatch said one forty. Perhaps a fraction of a minute less.

With a start she realized she had not phoned Matthew.

*   *   *

She stared at the telephone, unwilling. The reluctance again. It was as if a hand had fallen on her shoulder, a light hand, a hint of a hand, accompanied by a voice saying, Stay, this is real, think about that.

She thought, Not tonight, not this one special night. As if someone were whispering on her behalf. Just don't do that tonight.

This dialogue had sprung from nowhere, perhaps from the sedation, still at work in her mind despite its apparent disappearance. Don't call Matthew; having him take you to the hospital is playacting and you know it, while this is real and you know that too. And her plea in reply: Let me alone, Uncertainty, let me alone, not tonight please, not on this one particular night.

She jabbed a finger at the telephone and dialed. "Matthew, it's happening."

"Darling. I'll be there the minute I can."

"Don't shave or anything. I waited to be sure, so now a lot of time has gone by already."

"I'll not shave. How are you so far?"

"Excited."

"Good girl. I'm on my way."

"Cele is too."

Again pain, different this time, like a blow, but still the feeling of cleaving, riving, splitting asunder. She was ordered to yield to it, not fight it, but she forgot the order until her whole body was clenched in resistance, when she suddenly let go, limp and collapsed. It was easier at once. Maybe her pains were harder right from the start because she was forty. *Forty is not old, not medically. Cosmetically perhaps is a different matter, but you are a fine healthy young woman and forty is not regarded as anything but young today.*

The bell rang and Cele's voice sounded outside the door, with Cele's key already in the lock. Absurd delight welled up in her; now it would be all right.

"Having one right now?" Cele asked as she came in.

"It's passing. How did you know?"

"Anybody would know. Sit down again." She crossed to the bathroom and came back bearing a bath towel which she tossed nonchalantly straight at Dori. "Dry off some of that. We might take it with us in the cab. I told him to wait."

"Are we starting right off?"

"Dr. Jesskin thought it might be wise to get you settled in."

"But Matthew's on his way."

"I told the driver we might be a few minutes. He's willing. He's got four kids and this doesn't faze him."

"What did Dr. Jesskin say?"

"He said, 'Yes' and he said 'Ten minutes?' and he said 'They will be expecting her, I will notify them myself.' Cucumber conversation."

"He's always cool. Did he say when he would be there?"

"Lord, no. He'll probably go back to sleep for a couple of hours. They'll call him in plenty of time. He also said he told the Admissions desk to hold back on filling out blanks until you were installed in your room."

"He didn't want them asking Matthew."

"Matthew? Does he know about Matthew?"

"Only that I'd be going up with you and a man, another close friend."

"Who he assumes is the father."

"He never assumes anything. Anyway I think I told him, way at the start." She waved all that aside. "Oh Cele, I can't believe that by tomorrow morning this will all be over."

"Hush your big mouth, Dorr. Forget about tomorrow, forget about everything, and when they tell you to bear down, you bear down but good. Now let's see: suitcase?" She took it and set it just inside the door. "Air conditioner? Let's leave it on for now; it's hell's own furnace outside. I'll not forget. When will Matthew get here?"

"Any minute. I told him I had already let a lot of time go by."

"Clever girl. Thank God you're not going in for natural childbirth—when it gets too rotten, yell for a shot of something. But for now, you just sit there and think how skinny you'll be next week."

When she stiffened with the next pain, Cele merely said, "Hang on, Dorr, I know it's rough." During the jagged clamor of the next moments, Dori thought, She does know; it's one thing women know and now I know too. It's not like *pain, I'm sick* or *pain, I hurt myself;* it's pain *for* something and you're not angry at it. She mopped her arms and the throat and face with the towel and the pain ebbed and the bell rang and Cele let Matthew in.

He went straight to Dori, leaning over her, free of self-consciousness despite Cele's presence, kissing her damp face. "Is that our cab out there? I held mine too."

They all laughed, Dori suddenly shrill in a mounting sense of occasion. "Oh, Matthew, I'm glad you're here. You and Cele—" She turned abruptly away. How could she have thought, even for a moment, of not calling him? What madness would that have been, what careless slamming of a door? He was real too and everything they had was real. Limited, bounded on every side, circumscribed but real. Was she to tear it down because it wasn't unlimited, like a frantic angry child?

"Matthew, why don't you pay off your guy?" Cele said. "Mine's all contracted for, big tip promised, I'm committed." He nodded and disappeared to dismiss his cab. Cele said, "Come on, Dorr," and picked up the letter for Mrs. Steffani and turned off the air conditioner. "Here we go."

It was all in somebody else's hands, Dori thought, in Cele's and Matthew's and Dr. Jesskin's and the baby's. The baby knew it was time to end the nine months inside and she was merely obeying, just as Cele was obeying and Matthew. From that first pain on, the baby had been in command. Nature then, but it was nicer to think, The Baby.

"What are you smiling at?" Matthew asked as he returned.

"Nothing. You feel good in between, that's all."

To Cele he said, "What's the schedule now?"

"We're starting right away. This girl is still on a ten-minute rhythm, but they do seem to be blockbusters, and the doctor said to get her up there."

"Right," he said. "Come on, darling." He held both his hands out to Dori and she pulled herself up and forward on their strength.

In the cab she sat between them, silent, listening to their spurts of talk, aware of their bodies close to her own. There was a core of detachment, though, a high pure knowledge that she was almost, nearly, not quite but almost at the culmination. She felt steady with the knowledge, steady within it, as if it were a frame built close around her within which she was tight and safe.

The pain came again, slicing through, sharper, more purposeful. It was no ten-minute lapse since the last one; she knew it without trying to see her watch. It was speeding up, it was fiercer, it was under way and nothing could roll it back now.

*   *   *

At the Admissions desk Matthew said, "It's Mrs. Grange, Dr. Jesskin's patient."

"Oh yes, Mr. Grange."

"I am not Mr. Grange."

The clerk glanced at Dori and then at a card. "Yes, that's right. 'Two friends.' You can go up with her for a while." She rang a bell sharply. "Chair, please."

"I can walk," Dori said, but the chair was arriving and obediently she let herself be put into it. Flanked by Cele and Matthew, pushed swiftly by an orderly, she did not speak. The huge empty elevator stopped at the eighth floor, and again the swift silent progress began, down a dimmed corridor. At the door of her room, she looked eagerly for the two names she had so often visualized. They were not there.

Inside Cele said, "I'll unpack," and Matthew gave her the suitcase, saying, "Here's where the useless feeling gets going." Dori said, "Oh no, if you and Cele weren't here . . ." and let her voice float away. In her ears it sounded strange, light and half muted. A nurse entered, young, smiling, saying, "I needn't ask who's the patient, need I?" and then a moment later, to Cele as much as to Matthew, "Would you wait outside for a while?"

This was no geriatric; Dr. Jesskin must know that the routine part did not matter; in a sudden flash of understanding Dori knew there would be many nurses tonight, many orderlies, the anesthesiologist, the people in the delivery room, to all of whom she would be just one more woman in parturition, faceless, nameless, except for the strip around her wrist saying "Grange" and bearing a number, her Harkness number which she would never use again.

She went rigid to another labor pain, deeper, more savage; this time her breath caught hard and the nurse turned at her gasp, nodding as if to give due recognition to pain, otherwise unimpressed, except to note the time. "We'll get you to bed," she said, "and prepare you. With first deliveries you never can be sure."

The pain did not stop. For the first time Dori screamed.

*   *   *

She could remember begging somebody for more anesthesia and she could remember being wheeled on a table and she could remember a brilliant light in the ceiling and she could remember voices but she could not separate anything from anything and she did not know whether it was still happening or whether it was over and she tried to open her eyes and could not and she went off again into a swarm of warmth and heavy softness. . . .

Somebody spoke and she could not answer. She knew it was a boy but she did not know how she knew, and when the voice came again it was Cele, calling to her, "Dorr, Dorr, it's Cele," and she tried to answer and nothing sounded and then she heard Matthew saying, "Dori, it's over," and she said, "Has he all his fingers and toes?" and fell back into the heavy dark softness again.

Quiet and darkness and a spurting upward like a fountain somewhere and it was happiness, the fountain, and she opened her eyes, and there was Cele bending over her and saying, "It's all over, Dorr, it's a boy," and she saw Cele and then Matthew and suddenly she knew them and her eyes opened wide and she said, "Is he all right?"

"Yes, darling," Matthew said, "and you're wonderful, and you can sleep if you want to—we'll be right here."

The spurting fountain again, and a rushing of warmth and she sighed and went away from them again but somehow knowing they were there, and wanting to be back with them, and being unable to do it as if she were sliding away into something thick and clinging and marvelously comfortable.

A door opened and she heard Gene's voice and everything went clear and she half sat up as he put his arm under her shoulder and said, "Congratulations, you," and she said, "Oh, Gene, you know Cele and this is Matthew," and she watched them shaking hands.

"Can I see the baby?" she asked. "What does he look like?"

"I'll go tell them you're out of it," Cele said. "He's huge and he doesn't look like anybody."

"How do you feel now?" Matthew asked. "Do you know what time it is?"

"What time?"

"Three in the afternoon." To Gene he said, "Cele called you when she went into the recovery room, around twelve."

"Did it take all that time?" Dori asked.

"Ten hours."

"When can I see him?" She half closed her eyes and when she opened them again the room was empty. The light had changed at the window; it was yellower and deeper, as if the sun were way down toward the rim of the sky. There was a rustle of newspaper and she turned her head. Rising from the chair in the corner of the room was a thin little woman, smiling, white-haired, pink-skinned, with a starched cap on her head.

"Hello," Dori said.

"I'm your four-to-midnight nurse, my name is Schulz. You've had a fine sleep and your baby is fine too."

"Can I see him now? I thought I was awake but then I went off again."

"That's not only postnatal but post-surgical."

"Surgical?"

"You needed some surgery at the end. Dr. Jesskin will tell you about it, but you're to rest in bed." She reached for her wrist. "No walking yet."

"Could I see my baby first?"

"Of course. I'll take your pulse later."

For the first time Dori was aware of her bound and tender breasts. She knew about the tenderness and the binding as she "knew" about everything; Dr. Jesskin had told her that since breast-feeding was out of the question, she would be wearing a tight bandage-bra arrangement to support her milk-filled breasts until the production of milk stopped. She had agreed without discussion; if she was to live apart from the baby for most of the first two or three months, what discussion could there be? Yet now, in one swift longing, she wished it might have been different. It was over as swiftly as it had come. You cut out all the *if-onlys* and *ah-buts;* she had accepted that from the start. Tender breasts were part of the bargain, useless milk part of the bargain. How little a price. She watched the door.

Matthew and his stubbled face—she suddenly remembered his bending over her and saying she could sleep, they'd be right there. Ten hours, he had said, and then hours more in the recovery room, and he and Cele had stayed right there, waiting for her, watching her sleep after she came back to her room, wanting her not to wake to an empty room.

The door opened. Mrs. Schulz entered backward, her thin spare back pushing the door inward. Then she turned carefully, her left arm a cradle, which she brought close to Dori, saying, "Eight pounds and five ounces, this young man. I'll go back for his bottle. It's not full milk yet."

Instinctively Dori's hands cupped together but the nurse said, "This way's safer," and placed the baby within the crook of her entire arm. Dori looked down.

Her tears burned her eyes, impossible, but there they were, a shimmer of distortion as she looked down at the red little face, the eyes closed, the skin shining, the wisps of hair faint against the red skull. She heard the door close and was glad.

In a moment she peeled aside the crossed corners of the encasing blanket and saw the tiny clenched fists. She raised one, and saw the bracelet around the wrist. *Grange,* and a number, the same number her wrist bore.

She stared at the tiny breathing morsel, the shimmer slowly passing, the grip at her throat slowly easing, a burst upward in her heart. She did not think in words, her whole response was an intuiting, not strung out in time like the beat of a pulse, but as simultaneous as a chord of music. This, this sleeping being warm on her arm, this new life, this continuing of her life—

Simultaneously she remembered herself before the long mirror at home, toweling herself dry after that bath, catching again the first unbelieving glimpse that said her breasts were a little fuller, looking down again to see between the jut of her hipbones a most tentative orbing.

Let it be true, she had thought, let it be true. And now there was this new morsel of humanity living the first hours of its own separate life. If she were to die this minute, he would not die, he would go on, he would live.

A new human being, she thought, her heart filling. Nothing else matters.

* * *

Sometime in the night, Dori felt pain and half woke, fuzzily thinking that she was still in labor. Then she remembered the tiny red face in the circling blanket and she knew she had already given birth and that it was over. She stirred and saw a dim light, reached out to her bedside lamp and saw that her wristwatch had not been returned. A voice spoke to her in a heavy accent.

"I'm Mrs. Czennick, your midnight-to-eight nurse. How do you feel?"

Dori sat up. She saw a plump old woman, massive compared to the spare little Mrs. Schulz, her hair a roaring henna above a face crosshatched with wrinkles and grooves. But she seemed pleasant enough, even glad to have her awake.

"I think I was dreaming, but I feel fine. What time is it?"

"Three, and you've been sleeping like a baby—like your own baby."

"Is he all right?"

"Wonderful."

"I don't suppose I could see him?"

"You better let the little thing get his rest, Mrs. Grange. He needs it too."

Dori nodded. She had been reading as much as she could lay her hands on about the care of infants and she gathered that nothing and nobody could possibly rob a healthy baby of twenty hours of sleep a day. But she was acquiescent, willing to wait until daylight. She accepted the pulse-taking and other attentions Mrs. Czennick offered, understood that the discomfort she had dreamed about had been real—I'll never use the word *pain* again, she thought, for anything less than *that* pain—and dismissed it since she knew it was a normal aftermath of the surgery, still unexplained but one of the matters Dr. Jesskin would tell her about when he came in the morning.

"You had several phone calls before I came on," Mrs. Czennick said, consulting a slip of paper she drew from her pocket. "Your friend Mrs. Duke, just to check in, she said she'd be back in the morning, and a Mr. Poole, also calling in the evening, to see if he could drop in for a few minutes, and also your brother."

"I can see people tomorrow, can't I?"

"Oh yes. Your early nurse told them all you were resting easily and that the baby was fine and that tomorrow you could have visitors whenever you liked."

"Any special visiting hours?"

"Here at Harkness, anytime unless the doctor says not, but he didn't. He also called in for reports of course."

"Did he say when he'd be here?"

"Early; that's his usual way." She offered Dori a glass of ginger ale and said, "You'll sleep again now; you'll be surprised." She turned the light out without asking and went back to whatever soft rustling pages she had in her shaded corner of the room.

Dori closed her eyes and waited for sleep. A silky comfort came over her, gentling, soothing. The surgery could not have been too serious; she could feel a tenderness, but it was part of the slightly battered aftermath feeling, and she accepted it along with everything else. She did not care whether she slept or not. It was marvelous to lie here knowing that it was over, that the great ninth month—

But this was Wednesday morning; it was no longer the ninth month. That was over and gone, as gone as the eighth month, as the seventh, as all of it. This was the tenth month.

Hazily she repeated the words. They had a new sound, unexpected, unexplored. The tenth month.

There was an appeal in that: the future. Once she had wondered whether the change in herself—not in her enlarging body but in her essential self, that change she kept catching glimpses of—whether it would prove delusive and transitory, would vanish when July twenty-third had come and gone. Now she knew it was still there; July twenty-third was not a finis but a beginning, not an ending but a becoming, a process—she had almost thought "a promise"—a process that would go on and on if she herself did not stifle it. The life process. Her own life.

In the darkness she thought of a phrase that kept repeating itself in her mind. You give birth, you get born. She was not sure what the words meant, yet she responded to the unseen equation within them. Cause and effect, the systole and diastole again. You give birth, you get born.

The tenth month. The first month?

*   *   *

The morning was a waiting for Dr. Jesskin's visit. She had awakened at first light and lay tranquil and silent, remembering. She was at last fully awake, her mind clear, her spinal cord and blood and brain no longer host to the blessed anodynes and opiates. The nurse had heard her move and at once Dori had asked, "Can I see my baby now?"

"The moment we take care of you, Mrs. Grange. Your medication and making you comfortable."

"Oh of course."

This time the baby came in crying, his face contorted with his energy, his skin damp with exertion, and as she took him, she felt a sudden admiration for the ferocity of communication from this mite. Eighteen hours old he was, not yet one day of life behind him, and yet a million years of instinct were guiding him in this demand for sustenance and survival.

She offered him the bottle and he kept yelling. She experimented, tentatively poking the nipple at his mouth until suddenly his lips closed about it and he began to pull, his ferocity draining away into gratification.

I think of him as he, or it, she thought as he was

again taken away from her. Or just the baby. I can't think of him by his name yet. Maybe that's good. I certainly don't want to get used to calling him James or Jimmy while I'm here, just for the nurses' benefit.

The private nurses. She had seen only two, but she was sure the third would give off the same faint aura of polite concern that she should be without her husband at this time. They had been briefed, she knew, by Dr. Jesskin, and the floor nurses would also be briefed, about the husband off in Vietnam, had been told that his absence upset her very much, that it would be wise to make no reference whatever to it, nor to her wish that he could be here.

Did any of them believe it—the private ones or the floor nurses to come? She glanced at the large woman and Mrs. Czennick instantly smiled back. Despite the garish hair and the raddled flesh, she looked like a friend and ally. Perhaps when you were generally considered too old to be employable you were thankful at being summoned back into the world of the needed, and showed your gratitude by pampering your patients.

Or perhaps it was simply that this was Harkness at a hundred a day. A cynical thought for so felicitous a time, but there it was.

At eight a Mrs. Smith entered and took charge. She looked older than either of the others, grayer, even a little shaky, but she exuded competence and greeted Dori by saying crisply, "Your doctor is down the hall. He seems good and chipper."

A moment later he was there, a tap on the door to announce him and a simultaneous entry. As she looked up from her bed, he looked taller than usual in the long white coat, smiling at her, nodding dismissal to the nurse, with no sign of his usual detachment. He said nothing at all until the nurse left the room.

"May I offer my congratulations?"

"Oh thank you. Have you seen the baby?"

"Long before you did."

They laughed together and then he became again

all physician. "You will want to know how it went, when I got here, all that."

"Do all your patients ask that?"

"All. It was about seven yesterday morning, and it went as it should go until I became concerned—after about nine hours of labor, quite within the normal range of labor—but I became somewhat concerned, not for you but for the baby, nothing drastic you understand, but concern."

"Was he in any danger?"

"Not to say 'danger,' but signs to concern one, heartbeat and such. We avoid forceps deliveries of course and so I performed an episiotomy."

"Which means?"

He explained and a swift imagined slash of the scalpel knifed through her. But he was continuing his explanation and her attention was riveted on it. "That is why you are not to get up for a day or so, and you may have to remain two or three days longer than I expected."

"It's nothing."

"I am sorry at the miscalculation. Once again a miscalculation."

"How can you be sorry about *anything?* Without you and the help you've given me all through—"

There was silence. She wished he would say something, move, change his position, but he did nothing and said nothing. She made herself glance back at him. He was simply looking at her. At the same time he seemed not to be seeing her, to be lost in some reflective gazing that focused nowhere except on thought. Soon he would say his usual "Now I'll have a look at you" and this visit, this single time when he seemed to be friend as well as doctor, would be over.

But he did not say it. Instead he said, "I have a colleague, a Dr. Earl Wingate, who assisted in the delivery. He will look in on you later this morning—I have asked him to."

She nodded and he began to move toward the door. Suddenly he smiled as if at some private joke. "I will hold the door wide, Mrs. Grange, so you can see that they are there."

He swung the door far back on its hinges and though she could not read the typed names she saw the two cards affixed, one over the other, and a larger sign which she could read. NO VISITORS, it said, and as she glanced once more at him, he murmured, "Except for the select few," and disappeared. She could hear his steps recede down the long corridor.

*   *   *

It was not only that morning that Dr. Wingate looked in on her, but every morning. Apparently, once the delivery was over, Dr. Jesskin assigned to others whatever postnatal and postoperative care was indicated, and remembering his crowded waiting room every morning she was not surprised. Dr. Jesskin, who had another patient on the floor already, still dropped by at about eight each morning to see her, reading the chart, asking how she felt, inquiring after the baby, giving an order to the nurse, but in five minutes or less he was once more on his way.

It puzzled her that he had not told her beforehand how it would be, he who had been so punctilious and so patient about preparing her for everything else. Dr. Wingate clearly stood high on his roster of colleagues; nevertheless a small feeling persisted that Dr. Jesskin was firmly moving her off center stage. She saw the folly of this but she could not quite dispose of it.

The baby was now center stage; center stage in the world of doctors would soon be occupied by the pediatrician, Dr. Baum, who had taken care of all three of the Duke children. She would probably have one final check by Dr. Jesskin after she left the hospital, but apart from that visit and the routine annual checkups, he too would be off center stage.

God, I'd like to start all over again this minute, she thought after one of his fleeting appearances. If only I never had to work again, if only I could stay in hiding for six years instead of six months! But, poor man, I'd never have the nerve to go to him for help a second time.

The door opened and there he was again, looking uncommonly pleased. He waited only for the nurse to leave once more and then demanded, "Do you not know a playwright named Martha Litton?"

"I wrote a piece about her, yes, and interviewed her for it."

"You see why I ordered no walks in the corridor?"

"She's not here having a baby?"

"But her daughter is, and the mother is here every day, and out at the desk giving orders and finding fault. I just heard the mother's name out there."

"But who told you that I know her?"

"The daughter is my patient, married to that young man who plays the lead in the mother's newest play, I forget the name."

"Time and a Half. But I still don't—"

"Miss Mack put it all together. She reads many magazines and newspapers and if anything involves a patient, she does not forget. She read what you wrote of Martha Litton, and put it on my desk."

"Good old Miss Mack." It came out spontaneously, and he said, "Yes, indeed," and laughed. Then, his mood changing, he added, "She also put on my desk the piece you wrote about Dr. Spock. That one, I'm afraid, she disapproved of. Which is where Miss Mack and I differed."

Her heart jumped at the compliment. Center stage or offstage, Dr. Jesskin would always hold his special place in her life. If she were young she would have wondered before this whether she were being romantic about him; as it was, she knew that her feeling was an admixture of gratitude and a kind of personal dependence she had never before felt toward anybody, not in her adult years. That would fade now, slide back into the past tense, recede as his footsteps receded down the corridor while the heavy door to her room was making its stately close.

*   *   *

Matthew motioned the cab away and turned toward the river. There wouldn't be any air there either, but he was restless and somehow dissatisfied with the way the hour had gone. Dori was allowed out of bed now, and the floor nurses never came in unless she rang, but there was no real privacy and tonight something stilted seemed to attack him, as if he were seeing her off at an airport, one eye on the clock.

But then it's always this way at the start, he thought heavily. Even with Johnny, I really didn't feel much of anything until he was beginning to walk and talk. It was different with Hildy because she was my first, and there was that damn ego involvement of knowing you had reproduced yourself out of your own genes and DNA and all the rest of the biological hereditary miracle.

Of course I can't feel it now, with a baby that's only a week old. Even if it were Dori and me together, instead of Dori and whoever the hell it was, I still would be feeling this void where emotion about the baby is supposed to be. I can't fake it, I'd better not try to fake it, not with Dori, she always knows what is put on and what is really there.

She's the one I'm in love with anyway, not her baby. I'm not letting her down if I do have this uninvolved whatever-it-is toward the baby. Interest in it, affection for it, love for it, all of that will come later; it must come. It comes to people who adopt children; after a while they love them as much as any parents ever loved their own child. You hear that over and over, you read it over and over. Even though you're sure it could never be more than an approximation, you have to admit that what evolves in these happy adoptive parents is apparently a mighty close second, so close that nobody in the world could tell you definitely whether it is the same or not.

He had no worry about a year from now, but right now, when he was at the hospital and the baby was mentioned, he had to force himself. Not that Dori gurgled or crooned over the baby; actually she rarely spoke of it herself. Perhaps it was he, Matthew, who brought the baby into their conversation. Self-consciousness, that was. She had shown him the several pictures she had taken, and others of the baby and her, but that was about it.

She didn't even talk very much about the birth itself, nowhere near as much as Joan had done. She had reported Dr. Jesskin's explanation of the surgery and had been rather funny and bawdy about it.

"I gather," she had ended, "that it was one swift zip of the scalpel in the right places, and if you won't think me vulgar, I gather also that the patient is stitched up tighter than ever, afterwards, so not to worry."

That was when he had said, "God, Dori, I ought to be arrested." Crassly, ignominiously, desire had roared upward through him. "I ought to go home before I rape you."

"In Harkness? Lovely."

Now it was almost time for her to leave the hospital, but it would be another month or so before they could make love again—he couldn't remember what the prescribed time for abstinence was. Too damn long. Dori would be impatient too. He saw again the gesture she had made the first day they were alone there; apart from patting her stomach and crowing over its flatness, she had suddenly said, "And look, all nice and skinny and no puff-up," and from under the sheet at the end of the bed she had extended one slender foot, the anklebones sharp under the taut skin. She must have known that this was a kind of sex shorthand telling him that she would be slim and firm and tight again soon, with the distension gone and the need for care gone and all the nay-sayings and prohibitions gone.

Dori, Dori. If the baby made her happy, then the baby made him happy. If it fulfilled the denied part of her, then he welcomed it. If he were to resist it, he would be a more selfish man than he was. He did not resist it. He would not let himself resist it.

*   *   *

"Better let me carry the baby," Cele said. "Then if we run into anybody, they'll think *I* just had him. Come on."

Something like outraged possessiveness streaked through Dori as Cele picked him up and started down the corridor ahead of her, but she followed, docile enough, carrying only her suitcase and a small shopping bag with a bottle of formula and some of his things.

"You're thinner than I am right now," Cele grumbled as they waited for the elevator.

"Still bosomy though." The arithmetic of it tickled her: the baby had accounted for over eight pounds of her eighteen-pound gain, and the amniotic fluid and placenta and all the rest for another four or five, so thirteen pounds had gone, whoosh, in that one night, and she herself had remained accountable for only five. Ten days of three-mile walks and then a new dress and let any doorman examine her all day long.

It was still too early for visitors and outside there was no taxi in sight. Already it was hot in the blaze of the July morning and they stood on the pavement, side by side, two women and a newborn infant. Momentarily Dori felt forlorn, thinking wryly, What's wrong with this picture? At last a cab drove up, discharging, first, a young man, and then slowly, carefully, a very young woman, her face tense, her shoulders constricted. Dori stared at her, as Cele hailed the cab, stepped inside, and gave the address on West Ninety-fifth. Automatically Dori followed, and there at last Cele transferred the baby to her arms.

Dori gazed down at him but she was thinking of the young woman just now beginning labor, being wheeled down to the elevator, being wheeled down the long corridor of the eighth floor. Was she afraid?

Did she have that wedge of steel cleaving her apart? Don't be afraid, she thought. It's not pain-I'm-sick or pain-I'm-hurt, it's pain *for* something. You won't even know what to call the something. You'll call it the baby and think that's what you mean, but it's something else too, something bigger than any baby, even your own baby. Much bigger, vague, all-the-world-big, the-whole-human-race-big, and maybe you'll be smarter than I am and not even try to find words for it.

TWELVE »&~

THERE WAS AN EERIE EXCITEMENT in being all alone with the baby. When Cele left in the late afternoon, Dori stood for a moment looking across the linoleum shine to the crib in the corner, to the small swathed creature within it, and she suddenly felt tense.

It was just the baby and herself now, alone for the first time behind a closed door. No friend to help, no nurse to advise or correct her or show her how, just that eight-day-old being and herself and whatever stumbling new knowledge she had about how to take care of him.

Suddenly she grinned. She was forgetting the baby's help, forgetting that he would let her know when to feed him, let her know when to change him, let her know whether he was uncomfortable in any way at all. Advise and consent, she thought, like the Senate. She started the record player and crossed to the crib to look down once more. This time she did not have to seem matter-of-fact about it; she could just stand there and stare for as long as she wanted. How little time it took to regard this one baby as the only baby.

The hum of the air conditioner, the faint noise above it from the street, the muted music in the room, the week's piled-up newspapers awaiting her, all combined to make a pleasing easy evening. Matthew was up at Truro early this week, something about a changeover in their house from the collapsing old furnace to a new oil heating system, though why that should be scheduled for the last day of July she didn't remember. In any case, she was half glad that he was away for several days, or at least half pleased at being quite alone for a few nights. One needed interims.

He knew already that they were under orders not to make love until September. Dr. Wingate's orders they were, on his last examination at the hospital. "You should not resume relations for another five weeks, especially if there is any discomfort." The discomfort was negligible, though she still had a faint surgical tenderness, but medical orders were to be followed, despite Matthew's quick protest. "Five weeks more? Good God, that's not until after Labor Day."

It was already two months since they had last made love, but for herself, she was not impatient at the dictum. Perhaps after the heavy final weeks of pregnancy and after the actual act of giving birth, it was instinctive for women to draw back for a while from any form of sex.

The trouble is, she thought ruefully, when there's no sex, you can think. The body's prohibitions of sex permitted problems to remain problems instead of letting them dissolve in the hot chemistry of passion. The word *passion* aroused her a little, but there was a tentative quality in her feeling, too, a willingness to evade it for a while longer.

I have to get used to everything first, she thought. It's like starting all over, with a new set of rules to learn. Once I get back to my own place, get working again, seeing people again, the whole special new feeling will merge with everything else but for now it's like being handed a whole new life.

Whatever had gone before was of course life, but now it seemed a half life, a partial life, full enough of love and pain and work and all the other ingredients of living, but it had always been her own life and now it was more than that. Now it was "our life," a family's life, a child's life interwoven with hers for the next twenty or more years, and there was nothing partial or halfway about that. In the hospital she had thought about the future, and here it was lying quietly, entirely in her care.

*   *   *

Before the weekend was over she felt as if she'd been in sole charge of a newborn baby a hundred times before and when Matthew arrived for dinner Monday evening, she was actually impatient for the baby to wake, cry, and need changing so she could display her effortless prowess in her new tasks.

But when he finally woke, she was so wary of being the effusive new mother that she stiffened into an impersonal efficiency, a nurse in a maternity ward performing the duty she was trained to perform. It was an idiocy of shyness, but she was caught in it. She changed the baby in silence. Matthew watched in silence.

"I don't think men react to them," he said, "until they start to walk and talk."

"I've always heard that. When I'm alone, I do react but I feel sort of funny in front of anybody, even Cele or you."

"It'll all shake down in a few days." He moved away and stood waiting for her. "Don't lose weight too fast, Dori, will you? You look the way you always did already."

"It's this new dress." She paraded up to and then back from him, like a mannequin modeling at a fashion show, delighted with the dress and herself. It was a bright wild print, short and full-skirted, swinging easily about her as she moved. She had bought it just that morning while Cele stayed with the baby. "If you were Bill the doorman welcoming me home, would you guess I'd had a baby?"

He shook his head and swiftly took her into his arms. "God knows how I'm going to get through until the third of September." She moved back and he at once changed his tone. "No doorman alive. Do you know when you can go home?"

"That's what I meant when I said I had a surprise. I'm going tomorrow afternoon."

"You got a maid!"

"I interviewed three on Sunday, and this one seems just right. She's no geriatric but she's not anybody I'm likely to meet in any friend's house later. She's not very good at English and she's sort of fat and sloppy, but she looks kind and the agency that sent her says she's reliable and good with children."

"Great. So tomorrow night I don't come here."

"I'll see how she is with the baby tomorrow and if she really is good, then I'll leave around five. I'm suddenly so impatient to get back there again."

"It will be damn good for me too." He moved toward her and again she stepped back. "I won't keep pestering you, Dorr, don't look so watchful."

"It's just . . . it'll be easier if we don't sort of inch toward things."

"No inching. It's a deal. But you have a date for September third, right?"

"Right."

He left after the eleven o'clock news and she was impatient for the morning and the arrival of Maria; she suddenly wondered whether she had chosen wisely, whether the woman, with her faulty English, had really understood what the arrangements were to be.

"I'm signed up for a two-bedroom apartment in that new building at the corner of Columbus Avenue," Dori had lied easily, "but that won't be ready for occupancy until around Christmas. And since there's no second room here, I'm turning the whole place over to the baby and you for now, and I'm moving in with a friend of mine, Mrs. Duke. She has a spare room."

Perhaps Maria hadn't believed a word of it, but she had accepted it without expression. Dori had explained too that she would be in to stay with the baby for part of every afternoon and Maria could do her marketing then and whatever else she wanted to do, because she, Dori, would be working (she had waved vaguely at the typewriter on the desk) and would probably be spending three or four hours right there every day.

In the morning Maria arrived an hour early, looking pleased to be there, apologizing in her mixture of English and Spanish for the huge suitcase she had brought, which turned out to be only a quarter full of her things. They were her regular clothes, with no sign of a maid's uniform, and Dori was oddly reassured. She was a workingwoman, not a proper maid, certainly not a baby nurse. Her own children were grown and married, and she was alone and needed the money, and that was why she worked.

The baby cried and it was Maria who attended to him, Dori watching, reassured again. Maria liked him. She was not constrained about showing it, either, but made little sounds and murmured over him and had an offhand way of turning him and diapering him that bespoke years of practice. Dori smiled. It was going to be all right.

Soon she went out for a walk. She was not yet up to any hard three miles, but she was on the way. She walked eastward through the park this time, nearing Fifth Avenue before she turned and began to go back. It was hard to believe that at last she was going home, back to the locked-up apartment where it had all begun. A sudden longing possessed her, to be there this very moment. She thought of her impatience to look up at the eighth floor of Harkness, of the bus ride uptown, of the way she had stood there on the street, counting the floors upward. And now she had the same impatience again, but this time for her own four rooms, the rooms that had been home for a decade.

If only she didn't have to leave the baby behind. Now he would be the one in the hideout, one small baby hiding out in a vast city! But you won't be in hiding from me, she thought swiftly, and it's only for a couple of months. I've just got to go back to the world the way I left it—just me alone.

She was apologizing to herself, she realized, not to her baby. She was making obeisances to the necessities as she saw them; she was in the final stages of the long plan now and she was not going to balk and undo everything. It was crucial to get the next part right or the whole thing would collapse. She walked more purposefully.

By four in the afternoon she was satisfied with Maria in every way, even with her slightly shuffling movement about the room. She seemed to be without nerves; she seemed calm to the point of being lackadaisical. Fine, better than hustle and bustle around the baby, she thought as she finished packing her suitcases and the carryall. At her desk she wrote out, in clear large calligraphy, Cele's telephone number, Dr. Baum's telephone number, and finally a number unattached to a name, her own. "Some evenings I will be at this number," she explained. "Just ask for Mrs. Grange."

In the taxi crossing the park she stirred to a high excitement. After all these months, after all that had happened, she was going home. As the cab drew to a stop, she watched the doorman spot her, and her pulse raced.

"Welcome home, Mrs. Gray. Good trip?"

"Wonderful, Bill, but it's grand to be home."

"Your friend said to expect you, when she was here with the cleaning people." He took her luggage, replete with airplane tags from Marshall's and Cele's bags, and as she followed him to the elevator, she felt the eagerness of a child.

But once upstairs silence greeted her. The place had been cleaned by a professional service, flowers stood on the low coffee table, sent by Matthew and arranged by Cele, but there was no voice to speak, no family or friend to greet her.

I want my baby, she thought, and I want Matthew.

She moved around each room of the apartment, seeing each picture as if she had just acquired it, sitting briefly at her desk, stretching out on the red sofa

listening to one of the many recordings left behind. It
was an old favorite; she might play it when Matthew
came this evening. Tonight would be their first time
here since that day in January.

No, she wouldn't play a record; it would be wrong
to create moods when there were rules and schedules
and prohibitions hemming them in. It would be better
to go out for dinner, much better, much less provoca-
tive and also rather fun. She suddenly had a vision of
a delightful restaurant, any delightful restaurant, with
large luxurious menus, gleaming silver, candles and
flowers. A young eagerness bubbled up. It was a hundred years since she had gone out anywhere. Going
out to dinner would be a symbol that her days in the
hideout were over.

*   *   *

"Oh yes, Mrs. Gray, Mr. Cox is expecting you. Would
you come with me?"

It was absurd to be seeing him so soon but the desire had been overwhelming and Dori had yielded to
it and telephoned for an appointment. Only with this
legal step under way would she be really ready to
face the dozens of appointments she was making with
everybody else.

The reception clerk led her past several heavy
doors of paneled walnut. Unlike most offices, there
was little of the slide and clack of typewriters, and
she had a whimsical vision of all those law partners
and junior clerks writing their briefs and letters longhand as they must have done whenever this venerable
set of offices was first established. It pleased her, this
lack of modernity at Cox, Wheaton, Fairchild, Tulliver, though she could not have said why. She even
liked its being way down here in this old building
near Trinity Church in the oldest part of the city,
where, some eighty years before, the original Cox,
Wheaton, Fairchild and Tulliver had begun their practice of law. She half expected her Mr. Cox to appear
in appropriate nineteenth-century raiment though she

knew perfectly well that he and Dr. Jesskin had taken their advanced degrees at Harvard together.

When he rose to greet her she was surprised. Far from being antiquated, he was amazingly young, seemingly in his forties, a little stocky and bald but tan, fit, smiling not with formality but with an outgoing warmth. "So you're Mrs. Gray," he said. "Congratulations."

"How nice of you. Thank you."

He indicated a leather armchair and moved around behind it to close the door before he resumed his seat on his side of the large table which served as his desk. "I suppose you know from Neil that I'm delighted to be your attorney. From Dr. Jesskin, I should say."

"He said you felt a vested interest because it was his case."

"That too. But I was also interested because it's interesting in itself."

"Is it going to be difficult?" She was opening her purse and now handed him an oblong of heavy paper, bearing a seal and official printing. "There's the certificate."

"Department of Health, City of New York," he read aloud as if for her benefit. "This is to certify . . . yes, yes . . . James Victor Grange . . . sex, male . . . date of Birth, July twenty-third, nineteen sixty-eight . . . place of Birth, Sloane Hospital." He looked up at her. "Neil told me he was going to fake the hospital too, since he was faking a few other things."

"He's on the staff there also, isn't he?"

He seemed not to have heard the question. He was folding the certificate lengthwise; he then reached for a long envelope into which he inserted it, sealed the envelope, and in ink wrote across the sealed flap on the back, *"Private. Not to be opened."* Below this he wrote the date and his signature, and then handed the envelope back for her inspection. When she had glanced at it, he offered her his pen.

"I don't need to," she objected.

"Just to be legalistic." He grinned. "Lawyers like to be legalistic, and new clients should pamper them, don't you think?"

"Without a doubt." As she signed her name under his across the sealed flap, she suddenly thought, But they were at Harvard together, they must be the same age.

"Now let's get some details straight," he said. "Your baby is not living at home with you as yet?"

She gave him the address on West Ninety-fifth and told him of her daily visits. "By the first of October," she ended, "when everybody's forgotten I've ever been away, I'll take him home for good."

"Ostensibly, then, he'll have been in a foster home since birth, with people on West Ninety-fifth. Then he comes to you on a trial basis of six months. When we appear before the judge, of course, he will know that this is your natural child, that you are going through these several steps to protect that child."

"I understand perfectly."

He went on to tell her about the routine of the social worker's calls, and the private documents, and she listened as if she had never before heard of any of it. "When the adoption is over," he ended, "you'll have a new birth certificate made out in the name of your legally adopted son."

"Will there be any connection, any provable connection at all," she asked, suddenly sitting forward, "between that new permanent certificate and this first one?"

He sensed her heightened concern. He ripped open the envelope they had each just signed and leaned toward her with the certificate in his hand. "See that big long number there?"

"Yes." She read the digits out loud.

"That same big long number will show up on his permanent birth certificate," he said slowly. "And nobody in this or any world could ever link the two together without going through some very stiff judicial procedures."

He talked about the procedures and again she listened as if she had never before heard any of it. When he had ended he repeated the ritual of the countersigned envelope and then picked up his pencil once more.

"And now, what are you naming your adopted son? That's the only name that will appear in your files here."

"Eugene Gray." She hesitated for a moment. "Eugene Cornelius Gray."

For a fraction of a second his pencil paused and she said, "It's a private way to say thank-you. You won't have to mention it, will you?"

"I will mention nothing of what either of us says in this office." He looked at her with a steady attentiveness that seemed new. "I wish it were not private, though, this one point. It would please him."

"But it is private." She sounded ill at ease. "I'm sorry, but otherwise I just couldn't——"

"Of course, then it's private," he said briskly, again writing. "Eugene Cornelius Gray—that's the permanent birth certificate you will receive and James Victor Grange disappears from the history books forever."

"And that will be—let's see, six months from October. That's November, December, January——" She burst out laughing. "There I go, counting on my fingers again."

He grinned at her as he had done before. "Better watch that habit—it can get you."

*   *   *

On her way to the subway she stopped and called Tad Jonas at the paper. "Okay, be mad at me," she began, "for not coming around before this. Can I drop by and say hello? It's Dori. I'm down on Wall Street."

"Who'd you think I thought it was? Sure, come on."

She made for the subway and once inside glanced at the list of names she had scrawled on a slip of paper in her purse. For today, three more after Cox and Jonas. So it was going, day by day. "Can I drop by?" "How about lunch?" "Come on in for a drink on your way home." The process of getting back into the stream of things with the peripheral people of a life was always easy, she was certain, because peripheral people did not care deeply about anybody but themselves; when she said she'd enjoyed her cruise, they asked a perfunctory question or two about where she had been and moved on to their own news, their own jobs, their own worries or triumphs or projects. Not one asked how long she'd been away. Not one, she noted a bit ruefully, had actively missed her.

With this visit to Tad Jonas she was very nearly through with the process. Earlier in the week she had even said to Gene, "I think Ellen and I might as well make it up now—how would you like to ask me over one night and *not* talk about having children?"

"What about a night when Dan and Amy are here too, or Jim and Ruth?"

"Do they know?"

"Not a damn thing. Ellen wouldn't go that far. She's not mean, Dori, just orthodox."

"An orthodox family evening suits me to the ground."

It had taken place just last night and she had enjoyed it. She had never faltered once over Dan's and Jim's queries about where she had been, shrugged off their "Long time no see," and even found herself smug because Ellen was uncomfortable when they met while she herself was nothing of the sort.

There would be nothing uncomfortable now, she thought, as she opened the door to the newspaper office, waving hello to a reporter she knew. Across the city room Tad Jonas shouted, "Hi, just let me get this off," and she went to his desk and watched until he finished marking copy for the boy waiting for it.

"Do you want to come back on the staff?" Tad finally greeted her.

"Thanks for asking, but no."

"Still the free lance. Well, I've an assignment looking for a writer."

"Election stuff? Mrs. Nixon or Mrs. Humphrey?"

He bridled. "There you go, charging me with the old crime! What I meant was a follow-up on Spock's conviction. The appeal will take a year or more. While it's hanging, what happens to kids resisting the draft? What are Spock's long-range plans? Like that."

"When would you want it?"

"Fast."

The word was a stimulant. A specific task with a specific deadline or an implied deadline, that was a stimulant too. She wanted to get back to work, to earning money. "If you don't crowd me, Tad," she said.

"Could two weeks do it?"

"Just about."

"And the price tag? Let's say three weeks of your old salary."

"Let's."

*   *   *

We all live at so furious a pace, she thought as her cab turned into West Ninety-fifth. She had forgotten such rush and hurry. She was exhilarated by the day, but tired too, and the stop here with the baby invited and beckoned as the promise of respite. As she saw the white stone houses leading away from the corner of Central Park West, geraniums in their green window boxes, their brass trimmings glinting in the afternoon sun, their stone still managing to look newly sandblasted and free of city grime, she felt nostalgic. There had been repose while she had her daily life here; there had been time to reflect, to think, to evaluate. Already the memory of it was slipping away; already she was looking back upon it with the faint poignancy of regret.

After leaving Tad Jonas, she had kept her engagement for lunch, put off her other two until next week and gone instead to the main library to begin work on her new piece on Dr. Spock. Two hours had fled, her eyes had finally wearied under the spotlight of the microfilm machine, her note-taking had edged off into the mechanical, a sign always to quit, and she had for the first time found herself wishing she were not seeing Matthew that evening, not seeing anybody, just going to the baby and then on home to a long cool tub and hours of just reading or hearing music while she remembered every word of Bob Cox's once more. And that involuntary pause of his pencil over "Cornelius." And why she had not said, Tell him if you like.

Maria opened the door at the touch of her key. "He's asleep," she said, "such a good baby," and at once Dori became Mrs. Grange again, the not fully explained woman who arrived every day without exception but who lived there only during Maria's two days off.

"You can go out for quite a while, Maria. I'll be here till about six. I'm dead-tired and it's so cool here."

Left alone, she took off her street clothes and put on the old loose smock with its pink carnations. It swung from her shoulders now, as free as a painter's smock in an old-time Paris studio, and she loved to wear it and be aware of non-bulk as she had once loved to be aware of bulk. She put a record on, fixed herself a "water on the rocks" and moved toward her typewriter. She might try a fast draft of an outline.

Midway she paused and returned to the crib. The way they slept! How short they looked, even long ones like hers, with their legs still folded up in the fetal position. Gene Gray indeed. She still thought of him as the baby, or he, or when she looked directly at him, as "you." Are you going to like the name Gene? Maybe you'll want to use all of it, Eugene, so you won't get teased as poor Gene always was about having a girl's name, Jean. You could use your mid-

dle name if you feel like it. But that would be shortened too. Neil, Bob Cox had said.

Neil. She would have guessed Nils as the Scandinavian nickname, or something like Nelius, to rhyme
with Delius. Her knowledge of Scandinavian nomen-
clature was a bit sparse, and she could at least have
asked Bob Cox that much. She had gone rigid at the
notion of asking anything about Dr. Jesskin.

The baby stirred. Everybody said how handsome
he was, but she never thought the word "handsome";
she could get no further than "marvelous," a kind of
all-meaning word she needed. He still didn't look like
anybody; he was no unmistakable image of herself or
of Dick Towson. The baby stirred again. Perhaps he
would wake and give her a few minutes—no, he was
already back in the depths of sleep.

She looked around vaguely, as if she had forgotten
the typewriter and were searching for some pleasing
activity to help her wait out the baby's sleep. Then
she crossed the room and called Matthew at his office.
He answered himself and at her voice he said, "Te-
lepathy. I've been trying to reach you."

"I've been out since nine. Has something come
up?"

"Not come up, but I'm a lunkhead and forgot.
Jack and Alma Henning are in town for the evening,
and it's been a date for a couple of weeks, so I
can't ditch them. Is it okay if I'm fairly late?"

"Well, not so okay. That's why I called you."

"You haven't a date *you* forgot?"

"No, silly, I haven't." The good old one-way street;
the enlightened Matthew preferred it the way all
males did. "What I have, though, is a headachy lot
of fatigue from this frantic pace I've been in, and I
thought I might go home and sleep from about eight
P.M. to eight A.M."

At once he was concerned. "You do sound tired,
darling. You really have been pushing it too fast too
soon."

"So maybe it's lucky you're tied up with the Hennings—some benevolent genie taking care of me."

"Then tomorrow night?"

"Tomorrow."

She hung up, suddenly aware that the air conditioner was very loud. Illogically she remembered that tomorrow she was to see Dr. Jesskin and that the day after tomorrow the baby would be one month old. Another milestone, a different sort, shared, existing not only in her life but in her son's.

*   *   *

Just after nine in the morning Miss Mack telephoned to say there had been a change in her appointment. "Doctor will be away until after Labor Day," she said, "and he set up an appointment for you instead with Dr. Wingate. Will that be satisfactory to you?"

She was taken aback. A broken appointment, broken by Dr. Jesskin? "He's not ill, is he?"

"No, nothing wrong. We've already cleared this with Dr. Wingate, but if you prefer somebody else—"

"Of course not. But I—that is, will you give me Dr. Wingate's address?"

"He's right near here." She gave her the address and said that eleven was still the time unless there was some reason to change it. "He expects you as Mrs. Grange, of course."

"Of course. Thanks."

"And your address on Ninety-fifth Street."

"Yes, I'll remember."

"Doctor said he would suggest an appointment here sometime after his return in September."

"If it's a vacation, give him a *'bon voyage'* from me, would you?"

"I'll do that."

Unpredictable disappointment invaded her as she hung up. Off center stage, of course, she had expected it, and this was merely the routine postnatal checkup, but she must have been looking forward to it as a chance to report on the baby, on her visit to Bob Cox, on being at work again.

Well, all right, sometime after Labor Day. Cele and Marshall were going away for the weekend, Gene would be away, Matthew of course. Suddenly the weekend loomed long and empty ahead of her. Labor Day was early this year, the weekend after this one, but she hoped to be finishing her piece for Tad Jonas before it ended, and then the day after would be the third of September.

She felt unsure suddenly, a throwback to her old self, not the new Dori she had been feeling recently, but the old Dori, aware of an empty weekend, lonely, aware of the need to get through time. Perhaps she too needed a vacation, a week or two away from everything and everybody, even the baby.

Another world cruise? She laughed aloud and felt better. Work was what she needed, and a nice tangible check in payment, something you could deposit in your bank and use to buy things with. No more transfer of money from savings, no more cheerful watching as the sum grew smaller. She had used about three thousand and that was enough. From now on she paid her way again. The money left in the bank would now become Gene Gray's college fund.

College fund! Instantly she saw him as a tall young man crossing some campus, hair tousled— would it be shaggy and long? would he have sideburns and wild clothes?—a member of the class of, let's see, Good Lord, of 1990, boys usually were twenty-two when they were graduated. Would he be a rebel like Johnny? Or by that time would there be new ways to register convictions, new mores for disillusioned youth? Probably. Techniques kept changing though protests there would always be. And Gene Gray, class of 1990, would never be a smugly satisfied member of the establishment.

She worked uninterruptedly for an hour, and welcomed the first cry from the crib. In the morning she went back to the library and time began to speed by again and she lost track of days, racing to finish her piece a day or two before her deadline.

Gradually August dwindled away in its own implacable heat, and on a Sunday morning September began. As she bathed and changed the baby she said aloud to him, "One more month and you quit hiding out and you come home with me for good."

*   *   *

It was the night after Labor Day and Matthew had phoned to say he would arrive early. His family was staying for another two weeks at Truro, and they were still able to start their evenings by having dinner together. This time she prepared the things he liked best, a sense of occasion tingling along her nerves. It's so damn girlish, she scolded herself, but the scolding changed nothing.

He brought flowers and a record, and talked of her piece for Tad Jonas and asked if he might read it.

"Of course, later."

"Later? I'd better read it now."

"We're going to have dinner now." She began to serve it, and told him that she had asked for, and received, Mrs. Steffani's permission to sublet the apartment from October first. " 'Mr. Grange is coming home from Vietnam,' " she had said, " 'but he's to be stationed in California, so of course I'm taking the baby there.' "

"Does Maria know?"

"I asked Mrs. Steffani not to say anything. I'll give Maria plenty of notice or pay her instead. I'd keep her on if it weren't for her knowing about Mrs. Grange."

"Did Steffani promise?"

"She just gave me one of those shrugs, and reminded me that the deposit of the last month's rent was all hers if I tried to walk out."

"Nice."

"Fine, as long as she won't stop a sublease. Four

weeks to go and he'll be living here for good. I can't wait."

They lingered over dinner and then he said, "Darling, let's go to your room."

Moments later she was standing naked, letting him look at her, hearing him say, "You're more beautiful than ever," letting him kiss her, letting him take her to bed.

They made love, carefully at first, tentatively, then more freely. They were greedy for each other and responsive and quick, each creative for the other, neither of them a selfish lover. Then came the silence they always permitted themselves, a communication in its own style.

"You're Dori again, the same Dori as before," he said at last and looked down at her. At once he added, "Does it hurt now? Is anything wrong?"

"Nothing, why?"

"You look a little, I don't know, sad maybe."

"I'm not sad."

"Thoughtful then."

"I suppose so." It's the first time, she was thinking, that it's plain and simple being in bed and making love. It's two people having an affair and that's all it is. It's not his fault that it's only that; it's mine. Nothing has changed for him, only for me. "Don't worry about it," she said lightly, "or I'll never look thoughtful again."

She closed her eyes and he lay beside her, silent. When he began again to kiss her, she said, "Please not."

"Something *is* wrong."

"Nothing, but please not again." I've caught up to him in a way, she thought; now he's not the only one with something else at the core of his life, coming ahead of us, coming ahead of everything. "Matthew, don't be mad at me," she said. "It's just—"

"I'm not mad at you. It'll be different next time."

When he left, she lay against her pillows, still thoughtful. She was not restless; she lay there pleasantly, willing and permissive as to the direction her thoughts took. They had come full cycle, she and Matthew, back to this same bed where they had made love at the start. They were still perfect as lovers, each for the other, attuned to the other, responsive, creative, still right together. She was the same Dori as before, he had said.

But I'm not, she thought. I seem the same, but I'm not. You give birth, you get born. You get to be surer about what is first-rate and what is a little less than that. An affair was not necessarily second-rate, but what was thoroughly first-rate was honesty, and an affair was anything but honesty. It could not be; by its nature it had to be hidden, laden with subterfuge, managed by lies and silences and absences unexplained.

She was not going to moralize about it; she could accept it, as Matthew himself accepted his own affairs, those others he had had, the ones that he had always brought to a close when the gears began to grind. Here at least she could be the emancipated woman, with as much ability as he to have an affair minus blindness, and enjoy what there was to be enjoyed. And now she could have the ability, as he did, to keep intact those other parts of life that needed to be kept intact.

*   *   *

Ten days after Labor Day Miss Mack telephoned to suggest an appointment. "I did see Dr. Wingate," Dori said automatically, "didn't he tell you?" and then quickly added, "I'm sure he did, and of course I'll come in whenever you say."

"Tomorrow at eleven then. Same time, same station."

Another of Miss Mack's locutions. It would be nice to see her again. It was months since she had done anything but talk to her by phone. Last April had been her last office visit, and here it was nearly fall, with the first crispness of autumn in the air.

In the morning Miss Mack greeted her as always, and Miss Stein also, but neither of them spent so much as two seconds gazing at her. She was not surprised; what did surprise her was that when Miss Mack signaled her turn, she barred the door to the dressing room.

"No need for getting ready," Miss Mack said. "Doctor says he will see you in his office."

He was standing as she entered. He was not wearing his long white coat; he was again in street clothes, and with a start she thought, he *is* as young as Bob Cox; I was making the family doctor out of him in my own mind, because the first time I ever came here I was in my twenties. She said, "Good morning," and he answered without smiling. This was one of the times when he held the chair for her, asking how she felt, how the baby was.

"I had a good report on you from Earl Wingate," he added, "and I gather that your visit to Bob Cox also went well."

"Oh very." She was about to go on, but he had picked up his pen, though her folder was nowhere in sight. He seemed more preoccupied than usual, and she decided this was not the time to talk either of Cox or of Wingate. He seemed to discover the pen in his fingers and hastily laid it down again.

"I have something I must say to you now," he said gravely. He looked at her carefully, and a prescience stirred in her. This was not merely a reversal of the usual routine; this was not to be a regular visit at all and that was why she had not had to change to the plastic toga.

"I have thought this out most carefully," he went on, glancing at her and then pausing once more. "I hope you will believe that."

"I do already. Whatever it is."

"I canceled our appointment and suggested Dr. Wingate as a temporary expedient because I was still not through thinking."

"I see." She had never heard him speak in this somber way. She sat immovable, waiting.

"It is not a simple matter, but now that your confinement is accomplished, I shall have to ask you, after all, to choose permanently another doctor."

"Permanently? But why?"

He seemed not to hear the question. "Once I poked fun at you, I recall, and asked you, 'Did you imagine I would refer you to another doctor?' Do you remember when I did that?"

"Of course I do."

"But now I do have to refer you to somebody else. Perhaps Dr. Wingate—but permanently, under your own name, now that Mrs. Grange is about to leave us."

"But why? How could I ever go to any other—?"

"It is not now a question only of wishes," he said slowly, his finger raised in that cautionary inch of his, asking her to consider, to avoid rashness. "It is now also a question of possibilities. My possibilities, perhaps I should say." He looked at her again, and then away. "Have you ever been analyzed?" he asked unexpectedly.

"No."

"Do you know anything about the relationship between analyst and analysand?"

"Only what I have read."

He picked up the pen again, but then he sat silent, staring down at the tip of it. She instantly was back at that concert so long ago, staring at the conductor's baton, staring at it as if it were the one point of solidity in a light swarm of fever.

"It is an unwritten rule of analytical ethics," Dr. Jesskin went on slowly, "that if an analyst should find himself beginning to be emotionally preoccupied with a patient, he should send that patient to another physician for further treatment. He could no longer maintain the necessary objectivity, could not maintain that professional distance which is so fundamental to any analysis."

"Oh."

"Each branch of medicine has its own unwritten rules—" He broke off and stood up, facing her in silence. She stood up also. She did not look at him. She swallowed and she heard the dry tight noise of the swallow and thought he must have heard it too.

"Fools and vulgarians," he went on, so carefully that it seemed it must be physically painful for him to speak, "think that a gynecologist takes some personal interest in his patients. Of course he does not."

She shook her head for no.

"But if he finds, in the course of circumstances, if he finds that he builds up an admiration for a patient, that over a period of time this admiration grows and even becomes tinged with—it is hard to say it clearly. I have probably said it all anyway."

"Oh, Dr. Jesskin." She turned sharply and went to the door. There she stopped, her hand on the knob, unwilling to open it. "When did you—could I ask when you decided this, about sending me to Wingate or another doctor for good?"

He did not answer at once. He was still at his desk, standing as if at attention; she had a moment to think his color had risen.

"I am not entirely certain," he said, choosing the precise words he needed. "It was after the baby was born, sometime during the next hours perhaps, perhaps during the next evening, surely before I returned to the hospital the following morning. As to the necessity that led to my decision—" He threw open his hands, palms up. "That is what I cannot be certain about, whether it was all at once there or whether it had been a long time developing. That I remain uncertain about, only that. Everything else is clear."

She nodded and quickly opened the door.

*   *   *

She could not go home. She had expected to put in several hours of work before going to the baby, but work was impossible. Orderly thought was impossible.

Her mind was like a starburst, in all directions at once, bright with light of some kind, bedazzled with it so that comprehension was shattered.

She crossed Madison and then Fifth and went into the park, dear and familiar over on the West Side, but still strange over here on the East Side. The morning coolness was already conquered, but she did not care. She had to walk, move, go from here to there, no matter where, just to give herself the illusion of direction.

What was he telling her? Probably nothing, except that he had become involved with her as a human being through all the long secret story of the pregnancy and the actual birth. He looked on her as a special patient, not just one more woman in his waiting room. "A remarkable patient," he had said that morning on one of his last visits, and it had sent her spirits on a rollicking spin. Now he was reiterating that and adding that it was improper to have patients one regarded as special in any way.

That's not what he was telling me. I know what he meant. Why am I running from it?

But I don't know anything about him and he knows everything about me. He knows about Matthew, but he can't possibly know whether I am totally happy with Matthew or partly happy or not happy at all.

And I am still happy with Matthew. I know the limitations on us, I've always known them from the first minute we met. There are always limitations, there are no simple solutions—

Limitations. God, there I go again, like the time I wrote "wretched." I am forty-one and this may be my last chance at finding something more than a love with limitations.

It would indeed be the final chance if she fell into a comfortable year or two or three with Matthew, with the sex drive satisfied, so that she would have no instinctive dynamo impelling her on to continue searching. A long affair, replete with those limitations, she had always accepted. That was the name of the game: my family comes first, you must accept that.

Why must I always accept? Isn't that being defensive too? Unsure, accepting what there is because you never really believe you can reach out the way other women do, to a life where you do not have to be willing to do without?

Suddenly she was crying. Where did these wild angry rushing tears come from? What longing and deprivation came with them, shattering her self-control?

All three thinkings. How long ago Dr. Jesskin had told her to take time, to think with her mind, with her feelings, with her instincts.

She thought, Oh, God, why did I never see it before?

THIRTEEN »ᢟ≈

SHE NEEDED TIME. She couldn't see Matthew tonight either; she would have to tell him so. Tomorrow was Friday and he'd be going straight to the airport from his office, so again it would be nearly five days before she saw him Monday evening. She needed that much time. Then she wouldn't be blurting things out. Then she could say that she was troubled, that perhaps they should not see each other at all for a month or two while she thought about everything that was still strange in her new status as a woman with a child.

"While I get things into some sort of shape." That's what she ought to say, with a fierce justice behind the words. She would not say it; it would be a spiteful echo of his own words, but if she did say it, if she could say it, it would be an avowal that it was not so simple to remain sweet and tranquil with an affair that could never grow to anything, an affair in whose limitation lay its own mortality.

Just an affair, just two people making love. Suddenly she shrank back from the vision of them in bed together, suddenly she felt that lovemaking was over between them, that she no longer could respond and share in a sexuality that held in it no conceivable seed of any future life. At the beginning, there had been a reaching, unexpressed, unexamined, toward something they said in words could never be, but which each kept wondering about nonetheless. Now in the last weeks she at least had come to accept the reality.

She walked on and on in the park, heading north,

past the reservoir, toward the pond that in winter turned into a shining skating rink. The wind rose and once she sat down to rest. At her right, through the fringing trees, were the buildings of Mount Sinai Hospital, of Flower, of the Academy of Medicine. She kept looking toward them. Then she rose again, found the nearest exit from the park and emerged on upper Fifth Avenue. To her left was the handsome building that was the Academy. She moved toward it and went inside.

* * *

Late Sunday afternoon, driving back from the country in their station wagon with three children and two dogs, Cele said to Marshall, "You might drop me at Ninety-sixth and the park."

"What for?" the children all demanded but Cele only said, "To visit somebody I know. I'll be home in half an hour."

"Who is it?"

"Do I always ask who you kids see or where you're going?"

That silenced them and as they neared the transverse that cut through the park, she left them and walked around to Dori's. Within minutes of her arrival, Dori was telling of the dismissal by Dr. Jesskin, careful to draw no conclusions for her, but telling. How long it had taken her to offer a word about Matthew! How natural it was now to tell of the broken appointment with Dr. Jesskin, of the subsequent one, of his careful choice of words, of her burst of feeling in the park, even of her trip to the Academy of Medicine and the directory that had yielded nothing of what she had gone to find out.

"So I still don't know and I can't be sure what he really meant, Cele, but I've just got to call everything off for a while."

"Meaning Matthew?"

"Meaning Matthew."

In an impatient non sequitur Cele demanded,

"But when you were with Cox that time, couldn't you have brought up the damn photographs on Jesskin's desk? Maybe during the bit about the baby's middle name?"

" 'Oh, by the way, Mr. Cox, is Dr. Jesskin's wife conveniently dead?' Like that?"

"Jeer all you like. You know what I mean."

"I just couldn't make myself; I'd have stood there with my mouth open and not a word coming out. And if I could, Cox would have told me nothing, not one solitary thing. They're all the same, every doctor, every lawyer, their basic training is *Confidential, Top Secret, In Camera.*"

"And who are we to complain?"

"Exactly."

"But suppose you were doing a story on Jesskin, you'd find out if he was married or a widower or whatever."

"Not unless he tossed it at me. His work would be the story, any papers he'd written—the directory did say he's published several, and I also found out in a couple of other places about various honors and degrees, even that he was born a Dane and came here when he was ten."

"But if it were a personal story, including family, you'd manage somehow. You'd never let yourself be stopped cold."

"I'd probably try bribing Miss Mack or Miss Stein and get thrown out on my ear. Or I'd go out to Huntington and ask his grocer and the gas-station attendant and the local post office if there was a Mrs. Jesskin around. Can you just see me?"

"Okay, okay. I was just speculating."

"And don't think I wasn't."

*   *   *

On Monday, Dori felt apprehensive as evening approached, and when the elevator stopped at her floor, she went to the door, opening it before Matthew put his finger to the bell. She was melancholy too, with a sense of impending change, perhaps impending loss and farewell.

Matthew didn't notice. He seemed troubled too, telling her quickly of "a rotten kickup with Johnny."

"He wants to change schools," he said. "And now that the analysis is only three weeks off, he's refusing to go."

Something unwilling rose in her, the reluctance again. She had never felt it before about his children. At once she felt herself a traitor, but immediately thought, I am not a traitor. But if I ever needed him at the same time Johnny needed him—oh, God, do I resent being second to a man's child?

That wasn't it. If there ever came a time when her child needed him at the same time his child did—

That wasn't it either. These were fragments of it, but no more. It was deeper, the something that had been growing within her for months, the willingness to say, This is playacting too. I have never seen Johnny, never had a meal with him, never heard you talk to him, never heard him talk to you—how then can he be real? And in all the years ahead, I won't ever know Johnny or Hildy either, then how can they ever be real to me? And if they are unreal, sort of half-people I hear about but never see, then you and I can never be real at the core, where our children live too.

"Matthew," she said when he ended about the kickup, "I want to talk to you about us."

"Us?"

"About me." She looked at him without speaking, as if she were searching for the precise words she needed, and she remembered Dr. Jesskin, as he had stood there by his desk, doing the same thing.

"I've been searching something out," she said, "and it's become awfully important. I'm not sure when it started, except that it was toward the end, before I had the baby."

"What sort of searching out?"

"It was about being big and pregnant, a good feeling, that *this is for something*. There it was, the opposite of aimlessness, the opposite of what's-the-useness, the feeling of intention."

Very slightly she stressed the word *intention* and then she glanced at him; his face was somber, reminding her of the many times she had found in it a look that said he wasn't often happy. For a moment she faltered, as if to discontinue, but this time a small shock of power, like a spark, prodded her to go on.

"Pregnancy, God knows, is intention, is promise, is the future tense, and if you think of a relationship between two people, you can carry over the concept. I got to feeling that without intention between two people in love, there's only the present and the repeating of the present."

"But there is intention, there is a future—"

"I couldn't get hold of any of this for a long time, and I kept turning away from it and telling myself to be happy in the present and not even look ahead at a lot of impossibles. I labeled those daydreams and sentimentality, and shoved them out."

"You know that half of me wants us to marry—"

"But the other half says Johnny and Hildy and Joan, and I am accepting that and always have, from the beginning."

"Accepting? You don't sound as if you were accepting it."

"All along I did accept it as the only premise we could go on. You know I did, we both did. But there was another premise for me, that accepting the limitations was better than losing you, better than going back to a year of nothing that used to follow the ending of any affair. That's where the change began to happen."

"Are you telling me you don't want us to go on?"

"I'm trying to tell you that I don't want to go on without any future tense."

"There is a future tense. There's always a future

tense. Do any of us know what may happen tomorrow, next month, next year?"

"You mean I can pin my hopes to some taxi accident, some awful disease, hoping that Joan will be conveniently dead?" She used the phrase purposely and he flinched and she saw it and knew she had meant him to flinch. She wanted him to see it now, not three months from now; it was nothing to stay immobilized about for week after week. "You moved me terribly that night," she went on, "when you said if a father figure was so essential in a child's life, you'd be the father figure in my child's life. But Matthew, that's playacting, isn't it? If he can't have a father, he'd better grow up with only a mother, like a million other kids in this world, but a real solid mother, not a combination of mother and make-believe father."

He was angry and she saw it, but there was no way to soften what she had said and keep it said. She felt an elation at not having faltered, an elation at managing words for this that she had been so slowly arriving at.

"Are you breaking with me?" he said. "Is that what it comes down to?"

"I think that's what it comes down to. I was going to suggest staying apart for a month or two, seeing what that did, but it would just be more difficult, that way, in installments."

He said abruptly, "Is there another man?"

"I don't like your asking it in that tone."

"Are you to call all the turns?" he demanded. "Haven't I the right to ask if you're having an affair with anybody?"

"I'm not having an affair. I won't be having an affair. I don't want any more affairs. I'm sick of affairs, even good ones like—like—the way ours was to start with."

He made a rough gesture as if to brush all that aside. "But I asked if there was another man and you don't answer that."

"I'm not sure," she said. "It may be that there is. I can't think about it too clearly, not yet, not right away."

"What does that mean? Have you met somebody new or haven't you? You must know one way or the other."

"Please, not that tone."

"What tone? Am I supposed to ask not even a simple question?"

"But not to cross-examine. You once said—"

"Right. I did say that. God, that was long ago."

"It isn't anybody new, it's somebody I've known for years and years but still don't know too much about."

"And you're in love all of a sudden?"

"I didn't say I was in love."

"Did he say it?"

"It's so vague. You're trying to box it, but it's still so vague." She turned and left him, going to her bedroom, going to the window, looking down to the street. She could hear him move about and she waited, to give him time to compose himself. After a while she went back and said, "This isn't easy for me either, and I'm sorry."

He put his drink down and stood up. "I suppose there's no point in talking it out anymore now."

She shook her head and they looked at each other. He moved toward the front door and she stood quiet, watching him go. Rue, she thought, what a lovely sad perfect word.

"Good night," she said. "It's true that I'm sorry."

*   *   *

She worked. Tad had praised her piece on Dr. Spock and immediately given her a second, easier to do, with less research. She wrote a first draft, cut it hard, rewrote it, and set it aside for a day and then attacked it for its final version. Work was part of life, a big part, a good part. She had been in hiding from work too, all those months of pregnancy, but now she had regained full citizenship in an open world, a world where intention was part of life, where the old satisfaction could be had, of starting from nothing and trying to make it over into something.

She thought of Matthew often, wondering about what she had done. She told Cele about it, and Cele merely shrugged. "One thing's sure, Dorr. If you wanted to prod him into some sort of definitive action, that's the way to prod."

"I didn't want to prod him into anything."

"Probably you haven't."

She turned her second article in; again Tad Jonas liked it and offered her a third.

"Am I pushing you too hard?" he asked. "You're going great guns, but you said not to crowd you."

"It's good for me, I'm waiting for something and getting uptight about it."

"Anything I can help with?"

"I might ask for a letter of reference."

"For what, in God's name?"

"Next month," she said, "a baby's going to get born and I'm supposed to be the one to adopt it. They might want references about stability and such."

"You're kidding."

"No, just waiting."

"Through who? Which agency?"

"None. A private adoption, through a doctor I asked to help me."

"God, Dori, way back on the *Trib,* when we first met, you were talking about adoption. You were still married. Remember?"

"Did I really? Well, it's taken me this long, so wish me luck, will you?"

"I'll be damned. Do you want a boy or a girl?"

"Either. I didn't specify."

"Well, good luck next month. I hope nothing slips up."

"So do I. Look." She held out two fingers, crossed hard against each other, and then left. It was the first time she had tried announcing it and it had gone easily, and with Tad of all people, tough and knowing Tad. She felt triumphant, the euphoria of certainty. She could do it and do it with conviction. One small final lie, a matter of three months off a baby's age. She wouldn't need to try it with anybody who'd be likely to see him close to, just with the world at large. And in a year or six or ten who would remember a little boy's exact birthday?

She went home and again started on the new assignment, pleased that it had nothing to do with the election campaign, which she could scarcely stomach. She had to force herself to look at the evening news programs, laden as they were with inanities and lies about peace, but one night she saw that four specialists in foreign news were to discuss last month's invasion of Czechoslovakia, and one of the four was Dick Towson.

Alone in her living room she watched him and listened to him. How long since she had thought seriously about him, yet how calm and fond her feelings were whenever she did. This was the Dick Towson who had made her pregnant; this was the man who was the father of her child, though he was not the father in any sense except the physical sense of being the donor. A sudden impulse burned in her to let him know, to thank him, to tell him if only "for the record" of his own life. But long ago the decision had been made about that, and she could not heed any sudden impulse. Warnings sounded like bells: Careful, this is a test, this is a time for control, for silence.

She studied the face on the screen, trying to see in its features any resemblance to the small face that looked up at her from that crib or from her arms. Nothing definitive; perhaps something in the eye socket, perhaps something in the chin, nothing more. She had done the same thing when her brother Gene had dropped in one evening to see the baby. Gene had held him, bent over him, examining, studying, and all the time she was comparing the tiny head and face with Gene's, but again she had found nothing definitive, only now and then a glancing recognition that came into being and was as quickly gone.

"He's his own man," her brother had finally said. "I'll be damned if I can see you in him at all. Does he look like whoever the—?"

"He looks like Gene Gray and nobody else in the whole world."

*   *   *

Dori was like all the rest, Matthew thought, starting with one need, the need for love, for companionship, for sex, and then ending with another, the need for marriage. She didn't plan it, she hadn't it in her to set snares, but it had worked out the same way.

That's right, buddy, blame the other fellow, there you go again. Always the other, never yourself.

He had called her twice more; each time she had said, "Of course, if you want to talk," and he had gone there and she had let him do just that, talk. She had not given him any of the good old stuff about remaining friends, but she had already changed from his Dori into being just Dori, anybody's Dori. She hadn't put on any big madonna act about the baby; he was grateful for that. She scarcely mentioned it at all, except to say she was already telling people she was adopting a baby. She was bringing him home for good next Tuesday.

"Cele's moving his crib and carriage over in the station wagon," she had said. "What I ever would have done without Cele!"

Damn Cele and damn everything. There was no use denying it, at times he even felt, damn the baby, or rather, damn the timing of it, damn the patterns life had followed, damn the schedules and calendars. If it had happened a year later, if it had happened between them, if he had made it happen, the whole story would have been different. Then he would have had to get a divorce; he would never want a child of his brought up without his name and he would have had to get a divorce. By now he would already have had it.

He imagined Joan, listening unbelieving, as he told her he wanted it, and the reason for it. He could see her face, could see Hildy's direct young stare when he told her, see the disbelief and disapproval in her eyes: love and sex at *his* age? Johnny would be the only one on his side. "Wow, Dad, wild." Or would he be?

He was bitter. They were all self-centered, seeing everything their own way, and the hell with putting out any effort to feel what he must be feeling. Even Dori was following her own God-given set of rules; she was through with affairs, she was sick of affairs, she was throwing him out because what they had been having was just an affair and there was no sign from him that it would ever be converted into something more than an affair.

Damn it, the insistence of women. October was coming up; that meant less than a year had passed since they met, and already she had run out of trust, out of patience. She'd rather sit there alone holding the baby—

The split-second image flashed, a woman sitting alone on a sofa, holding a new baby, looking down in silence.

Christ, again! He had been free of it since he had had it out with Dori; now here it was again, a new life for it, a new vitality.

He jumped up, outraged. It was long after midnight and everyone was asleep. Dori was asleep too, or he would call and try once more to make her see that since whatever else she was thinking of was still vague, it might yet prove to be nothing, might fizzle out, might remain vague forever. This time he needed no long period to get things sorted out in his mind; this time he knew at once what was roweling his gut: she had thrown him out, that was it, in the nicest gentlest sort of way, thrown him out. Usually it was he who got out of a relationship when the gears began to grind. Gears had been grinding for months, from the night she had told him about Bob Cox, but he'd had no ear for them.

He should never have let Cox take over on the adoption proceedings, true, but was that anything to hold against him? He should probably never have told her about feeling shut out, or about the damnable word *diminish* and how it crossed half a dozen other lines in his life. He should never have let her hear him phoning Joan to say he wouldn't be home, probably should never even have told her about clearing it with the family that he couldn't make it to Truro over the weekend of the twentieth.

But she had loved him anyway. Nobody was ever better than they were in bed together. Nobody was ever happier than she was when he had come back after the bad time that had strapped him into immobility. And at the end? Had he not been right there to the end, taking her to the hospital, staying up all night and all the next day? If he'd been her own husband out in the hospital corridor—

Playacting. If she called anything playacting that would finish it for her, but there were situations where a little playacting was the only civilized way to manage. Another name for it was tact, diplomacy, even kindness. Dori knew all that, practiced it herself most of the time as any real woman did. But then at other times—God, in the last few months honesty had become an obsession with her. Maybe because she had been living a huge lie and was preparing to live it for the rest of her life.

He felt perceptive to have realized that. It comforted him. There were matters here Dori did not yet comprehend. He could make her see them. Damn it, he would have to make her see them, for he could not bear the idea of giving in to defeat when he wanted her so much.

Behind him a door opened and Joan asked, "Are you okay? Is anything wrong?"

"I'm just reading. I couldn't get to sleep."

"You've been upset lately. I can always tell."

"Nothing special."

"You've been in every night since we got home from Truro."

"I told you, they're painting our offices."

He ought to face her now, ought to stop this play-acting now, ought to say, Yes, something is damn wrong, and the only thing that can make it right is to start over and that means leaving all this here and getting a divorce and saying goodbye to this half-dead marriage. He could imagine her face at the words, imagine the scene that would follow.

"I'm going to make some tea," Joan said. "Do you want some?"

He shook his head and watched her go to the kitchen in her nightgown. The words unspoken too long, the words unspoken forever. He put his head down on his arms.

*   *   *

The station wagon pulled up at the side entrance to the building and Dori said, "You take him, Cele, and I'll get the back elevator man."

Inside she said, "Joe, could you help me with a couple of pieces of furniture I borrowed for the baby's room?"

"Sure, sure."

She had told Bill the doorman a few days ago, leaving it to him to tend the grapevine, and apparently he had done so, for Joe showed no surprise at seeing the crib, the baby carriage, various small cartons and the lady at the wheel holding a well-wrapped-up baby.

Cele handed the baby back to her and they went up the back elevator with the furniture. In the elevator Joe said, "How old is it?" and Dori said, "Ten days, no, eleven," in a voice that held no smallest quaver.

"Boy or girl?"

"Boy. Oh here we are. Cele, have you a dollar?"

Once inside and alone Cele said, "I wouldn't trust you around the corner, madam," and Dori said,

"Thank you for the compliment. I hope the room won't seem too small with the crib in it."

The fourth room in her apartment must originally have been intended as a maid's room since it was an old building, erected in the thirties when nearly all good East Side apartments had built-in maids' rooms, but by a quirk in the architecture, caused by the setback and terrace on the floor below, it was about two feet wider than the usual cell-like space and Dori had always used it as a "guest room for one." A narrow bed, narrower than twin-size but well made and prettily covered, a small dresser and a single chair were all the furniture it contained, but a plaid rug and plaid curtains made it bright and appealing. The miniature bathroom with a tub one could not stretch out in was pretty too, and Dori had measured off the space for the crib with minute care, finding that it would fit easily if one did not mind a bathroom door that would swing open only half its normal arc.

"It goes in my room for now, Joe," she said as he came in with the crib. "He's going in with me until I can get a maid. And better leave the carriage in my front hall."

"There's a carriage room downstairs, alongside the package room."

"Is there? Good, I'll have to find out about things, won't I?"

Joe said, "Sure, sure," pocketed his dollar tip and left.

"Not around the corner," Cele repeated and this time Dori laughed. For the first time she freed the baby from the shielding blanket, held him high up, not forgetting to prop the small head with her entire left hand, but holding him at eye level so that they were face to face. "We're home," she said. "Did you ever think we'd make it?"

*　　*　　*

Two days later the phone rang, and without preamble Cele said, "Dr. Jesskin isn't a widower, and she's not 'conveniently dead.' She's remarried and her name is Summerfield and she lives in Washington—state of, not D.C."

"How do you know?"

"I did what you were too decent to do—I up and asked, and kept on asking."

"Asked whom?"

"Asked everybody, everywhere I went, until I got me an answer."

"From whom?"

"Dr. Baum. Ben Baum, your pediatrician and mine. I should have tried him right off. Every pediatrician in New York knows Dr. Jesskin, or has Jesskin babies for patients. And Ben Baum's been our friend for most of the sixteen years he's been the kids' doctor, so finally I just asked him as gossip, and he told me, as gossip. It's no secret anyway."

"Oh Cele—"

"They were divorced eight or ten years ago. She couldn't stand his hours, the night calls, all that. So they got a divorce." Dori started to speak but Cele interrupted. "Remember what I told you, that time you got sore? Decent men get divorces too, not just rats."

"Oh Cele."

"His children were teen-agers then," she went on dryly, "but they seem to have survived. They each got married about a year ago."

"Did Dr. Baum know how they feel toward their father?"

"Like any young marrieds, I gathered. But Ben did know one more piece of family stuff. Long ago, Dr. Jesskin's sister met his friend Bob Cox at some Harvard regatta and they married a year later. So maybe it's her picture on his desk."

"Oh Cele—"

"You're not being too bright today, Dorr. Your conversation isn't, anyway. Suppose you call me back when you can produce more than 'Oh Cele.' "

"All right."

She stood there clutching the phone after Cele had clicked off. Some tactile memory, apparently in her palm, told her that once, a long time ago, she had kept on gripping the crossbar of this very telephone receiver, gripping it after she had put it back into its cradle, as if at a lever to propel herself into action. She had wanted to just stay there, silent, commanding her mind not to leap ahead, but she had failed and had remained there yielding to her mind's rebellion until the clock had reminded her she had to dress for a concert.

It was that first call she had made to Miss Mack, asking for a special appointment, that's what it was, and she had held on and on, not wanting to break the thread that might connect the glimpse in the mirror to something more than an illusion.

Now again she was holding a thread that might connect a first glimpse to something more. Not that there had been any illusion. He had said all those carefully selected words, and she had heard them, and, when she had finally let herself, had understood them. She had tried not to think too much of them since then, but they had kept speaking to her at odd times, always with the picture of their speaker, standing there at his desk, tall, too thin, his color rising.

"Emotionally preoccupied," he had said. He had remained silent since then, as she had known he would. He was no man of sudden compulsions, he knew life took time to grow and develop, he was giving it time. He was giving her time.

He would wait until she managed some sort of signal. There would be no flowers from him, no note under the door, no telephone calls. He would wait. And she had to wait too. Wait through the fall, perhaps through the winter. She had to get through the guilt that sometimes took her when she thought about Matthew. Guilt? Guilt that she finally had come to ask more of living than she used to ask?

Emotionally preoccupied. If Dr. Jesskin loved anybody with a baby, she thought half angrily, he would marry her and adopt that baby, not just be a father figure to it.

Eugene Cornelius Jesskin—oh God, more daydreaming. But sometimes daydreaming was *for* something. To show the way, to get you ready, to see if you were certain.

The one thing he couldn't be certain about, he had said, was "whether it was all at once there or whether it had been a long time developing." Everything else was clear but not that.

A long time developing? Probably for her it had been a long time developing too, long before the *remarkable patient*. Long long before had she not sat in his office and thought, He is so good and kind I really love him? She had meant it as a patient means it, a synonym for gratitude, a recognition of kindness and human response to a problem. But she had felt it and now, suddenly, was remembering it.

The fall, perhaps the winter. In January the baby would be six months old. Another milestone, a major not a minor. A half year since that night he was born.

Dear Dr. Jesskin, My baby is half a year old—As if she were already writing them, the words took tangible shape on some tablet in her mind, clear and warm, as if there were a sun shining upon them. *And since you haven't seen him since his first week, I wonder if you'd like to come and see him now that he has reached this immense age. He would welcome you and so would I. Always gratefully, Dori Gray.*

She ought to write it down; she liked the tone of it. But she did not move toward her desk. She saw that she was still gripping the crossbar of the telephone receiver and slowly moved her hand away, stretching her fingers, opening out her palm. She didn't have to write anything down. When the time finally came, words wouldn't really matter.

ZANE GREY

To the Last Man

PUBLISHED BY POCKET BOOKS NEW YORK

POCKET BOOKS, a Simon & Schuster division of
GULF & WESTERN CORPORATION
1230 Avenue of the Americas, New York, N.Y. 10020

ISBN: 0-671-82076-1

First Pocket Books printing July, 1971

12   11   10   9   8

Trademarks registered in the United States and other countries.

Printed in the U.S.A.

FOREWORD

IT WAS inevitable that in my efforts to write romantic history of the great West I should at length come to the story of a feud. For long I have steered clear of this rock. But at last I have reached it and must go over it, driven by my desire to chronicle the stirring events of pioneer days.

Even to-day it is not possible to travel into the remote corners of the West without seeing the lives of people still affected by a fighting past. How can the truth be told about the pioneering of the West if the struggle, the fight, the blood be left out? It cannot be done. How can a novel be stirring and thrilling, as were those times, unless it be full of sensation? My long labors have been devoted to making stories resemble the times they depict. I have loved the West for its vastness, its contrast, its beauty and color and life, for its wildness and violence, and for the fact that I have seen how it developed great men and women who died unknown and unsung.

In this materialistic age, this hard, practical, swift, greedy age of realism, it seems there is no place for writers of romance, no place for romance itself. For many years all the events leading up to the great war were realistic, and the war itself was horribly realistic, and the aftermath is likewise. Romance is only another name for idealism; and I contend that life without ideals is not worth living. Never in the history of the world were ideals needed so terribly as now. Walter Scott wrote romance; so did Victor Hugo; and likewise Kipling, Hawthorne, Stevenson. It was Stevenson, particularly, who wielded a bludgeon against the realists. People live for the dream in their hearts. And I have yet to know anyone who has not some secret dream, some hope, however dim, some storied wall to look at in the dusk, some painted window leading to the soul. How strange indeed to find that the realists have ideals and dreams! To read them one would think their lives held nothing significant. But they love, they hope, they dream, they sacrifice, they struggle on with that dream in their hearts just the same as others. We all are dreamers, if not in the heavy-lidded wasting of time, then in the meaning of life that makes us work on.

It was Wadsworth who wrote, "The world is too much with us"; and if I could give the secret of my ambition as a novelist in a few words it would be contained in that quotation. My inspiration to write has always come from nature. Character and action are subordinated to setting. In all that I have done I have tried to make people see how the world is too much with them. Getting and spending they lay waste their powers, with never a breath of the free and wonderful life of the open!

So I come back to the main point of this foreword, in which I am trying to tell why and how I came to write the story of a feud notorious in Arizona as the Pleasant Valley War.

Some years ago Mr. Harry Adams, a cattleman of Vermajo Park, New Mexico, told me he had been in the Tonto Basin of Arizona and thought I might find interesting material there concerning this Pleasant Valley War. His version of the war between cattlemen and sheepmen certainly determined me to look over the ground. My old guide, Al Doyle of Flagstaff, had led me over half of Arizona, but never down into that wonderful wild and rugged basin between the Mogollon Mesa and the Mazatzal Mountains. Doyle had long lived on the frontier and his version of the Pleasant Valley War differed markedly from that of Mr. Adams. I asked other old timers about it, and their remarks further excited my curiosity.

Once down there, Doyle and I found the wildest, most rugged, roughest, and most remarkable country either of us had visited; and the few inhabitants were like the country. I went in ostensibly to hunt bear and lion and turkey, but what I really was hunting for was the story of that Pleasant Valley War. I engaged the services of a bear hunter who had three strapping sons as reserved and strange and aloof as he was. No wheel tracks of any kind had ever come within miles of their cabin. I spent two wonderful months hunting game and reveling in the beauty and grandeur of that Rim Rock country, but I came out knowing no more about the Pleasant Valley War. These Texans and their few neighbors, likewise from Texas, did not talk. But all I saw and felt only inspired me the more. This trip was in the fall of 1918.

BORN ENEMIES!

Suddenly Jean was upon her. His kisses burned and bruised her lips. And then, shifting violently to her neck, they pressed so hard that she choked under them. Then the remorseless binding embraces—the hot and savage kisses—fell away from her. He let her go.

"No—Ellen Jorth," he panted, "I don't—want any of you—that way." And he sank on the log and covered his face with his hands. "What I loved in you—was what I thought—you were."

Like a wildcat, Ellen sprang upon him, beating him with her fists, tearing at his hair, scratching his face.

"Oh! . . . I'll kill you!" she hissed.

"Go ahead. There's my gun," Jean returned. "I'm sick of this feud. . . . Kill me!"

But she was as powerless as if she were still held in his giant embrace. "I—I want to—kill you," she whispered, "but I can't."

The next year I went again with the best horses, outfit, and men the Doyles could provide. And this time I did not ask any questions. But I rode horses—some of them too wild for me—and packed a rifle many a hundred miles, riding sometimes thirty and forty miles a day, and I climbed in and out of the deep cañons, desperately staying at the heels of one of those long-legged Texans. I learned the life of those backwoodsmen, but I did not get the story of the Pleasant Valley War. I had, however, won the friendship of that hardy people.

In 1920 I went back with a still larger outfit, equipped to stay as long as I liked. And this time, without my asking it, different natives of the Tonto came to tell me about the Pleasant Valley War. No two of them agreed on anything concerning it, except that only one of the active participants survived the fighting. Whence comes my title, *To the Last Man*. Thus I was swamped in a mass of material out of which I could only flounder to my own conclusion. Some of the stories told me are singularly tempting to a novelist. But, though I believe them myself, I cannot risk their improbability to those who have no idea of the wildness of wild men at a wild time. There really was a terrible and bloody feud, perhaps the most deadly and least known in all the annals of the West. I saw the ground, the cabins, the graves, all so darkly suggestive of what must have happened.

I never learned the truth of the cause of the Pleasant Valley War, or if I did hear it I had no means of recognizing it. All the given causes were plausible and convincing. Strange to state, there is still secrecy and reticence all over the Tonto Basin as to the facts of this feud. Many descendants of those killed are living there now. But no one likes to talk about it. Assuredly many of the incidents told me really occurred, as, for example, the terrible one of the two women, in the face of relentless enemies, saving the bodies of their dead husbands from being devoured by wild hogs. Suffice it to say that this romance is true to my conception of the war, and I base it upon the setting I learned to know and love so well, upon the strange passions of primitive people, and upon my instinctive reaction to the facts and rumors that I gathered.

ZANE GREY.

Avalon, California,
    April, 1921.

To the Last Man

1

★

AT the end of a dry, uphill ride over barren country Jean Isbel unpacked to camp at the edge of the cedars where a little rocky cañon, green with willow and cottonwood, promised water and grass.

His animals were tired, especially the pack mule that had carried a heavy load; and with slow heaves of relief they knelt and rolled in the dust. Jean experienced something of relief himself as he threw off his chaps. He had not been used to hot, dusty, glaring days on the barren lands. Stretching his long length beside a tiny rill of clear water that tinkled over the red stones, he drank thirstily. The water was cool, but it had an acrid taste—an alkali bite that he did not like. Not since he had left Oregon had he tasted clear, sweet, cold water; and he missed it just as he longed for the stately shady forests he had loved. This wild, endless Arizona land bade fair to earn his hatred.

By the time he had leisurely completed his tasks twilight had fallen and coyotes had begun their barking. Jean listened to the yelps and to the moan of the cool wind in the cedars with a sense of satisfaction that these lonely sounds were familiar. This cedar wood burned into a pretty fire and the smell of its smoke was newly pleasant.

"Reckon maybe I'll learn to like Arizona," he mused, half aloud. "But I've a hankerin' for waterfalls an' dark-green forests. Must be the Indian in me. . . . Anyway, dad needs me bad, an' I reckon I'm here for keeps."

Jean threw some cedar branches on the fire, in the light of which he opened his father's letter, hoping by repeated reading to grasp more of its strange portent. It had been two months in reaching him, coming by traveler, by stage and train, and then by boat, and finally by stage again. Written in lead pencil on a leaf torn from an old ledger, it would have been hard to read even if the writing had been more legible.

1

"Dad's writin' was always bad, but I never saw it so shaky," said Jean, thinking aloud.

GRASS VALLEY, ARIZONA.

SON JEAN,—Come home. Here is your home and here your needed. When we left Oregon we all reckoned you would not be long behind. But its years now. I am growing old, son, and you was always my steadiest boy. Not that you ever was so damn steady. Only your wildness seemed more for the woods. You take after mother, and your brothers Bill and Guy take after me. That is the red and white of it. Your part Indian, Jean, and that Indian I reckon I am going to need bad. I am rich in cattle and horses. And my range here is the best I ever seen. Lately we have been losing stock. But that is not all nor so bad. Sheepmen have moved into the Tonto and are grazing down on Grass Valley. Cattlemen and sheepmen can never bide in this country. We have bad times ahead. Reckon I have more reasons to worry and need you, but you must wait to hear that by word of mouth. Whatever your doing, chuck it and rustle for Grass Vally so to make here by spring. I am asking you to take pains to pack in some guns and a lot of shells. And hide them in your outfit. If you meet anyone when you are coming into the Tonto, listen more than you talk. And last, son, don't let anything keep you in Oregon. Reckon you have a sweetheart, and if so fetch her along. With love from your dad,

GASTON ISBEL.

Jean pondered over this letter. Judged by memory of his father, who had always been self-sufficient, it had been a surprise and somewhat of a shock. Weeks of travel and reflection had not helped him to grasp the meaning between the lines.

"Yes, dad's growin' old," mused Jean, feeling a warmth and a sadness stir in him. "He must be 'way over sixty. But he never looked old. . . . So he's rich now an' losin' stock, an' goin' to be sheeped off his range. Dad could stand a lot of rustlin', but not much from sheepmen."

The softness that stirred in Jean merged into a cold, thoughtful earnestness which had followed every perusal of his father's letter. A dark, full current seemed flowing in his veins, and at times he felt it swell and heat. It troubled him,

2

making him conscious of a deeper, stronger self, opposed to his careless, free, and dreamy nature. No ties had bound him in Oregon, except love for the great, still forests and the thundering rivers; and this love came from his softer side. It had cost him a wrench to leave. And all the way by ship down the coast to San Diego and across the Sierra Madres by stage, and so on to this last overland travel by horseback, he had felt a retreating of the self that was tranquil and happy and a dominating of this unknown somber self, with its menacing possibilities. Yet despite a nameless regret and a loyalty to Oregon, when he lay in his blankets he had to confess a keen interest in his adventurous future, a keen enjoyment of this stark, wild Arizona. It appeared to be a different sky stretching in dark, star-spangled dome over him—closer, vaster, bluer. The strong fragrance of sage and cedar floated over him with the camp-fire smoke, and all seemed drowsily to subdue his thoughts.

At dawn he rolled out of his blankets and, pulling on his boots, began the day with a zest for the work that must bring closer his calling future. White, crackling frost and cold, nipping air were the same keen spurs to action that he had known in the uplands of Oregon, yet they were not wholly the same. He sensed an exhilaration similar to the effect of a strong, sweet wine. His horse and mule had fared well during the night, having been much refreshed by the grass and water of the little cañon. Jean mounted and rode into the cedars with gladness that at last he had put the endless leagues of barren land behind him.

The trail he followed appeared to be seldom traveled. It led, according to the meager information obtainable at the last settlement, directly to what was called the Rim, and from there Grass Valley could be seen down in the Basin. The ascent of the ground was so gradual that only in long, open stretches could it be seen. But the nature of the vegetation showed Jean how he was climbing. Scant, low, scraggy cedars gave place to more numerous, darker, greener, bushier ones, and these to high, full-foliaged, green-berried trees. Sage and grass in the open flats grew more luxuriously. Then came the piñons, and presently among them the checker-barked junipers. Jean hailed the first pine tree with a hearty slap on the brown, rugged bark. It was a small dwarf pine struggling to live. The next one was larger, and after that came several, and beyond them pines stood up everywhere above the lower trees. Odor of pine needles mingled with the other dry smells

3

that made the wind pleasant to Jean. In an hour from the first line of pines he had ridden beyond the cedars and piñons into a slowly thickening and deepening forest. Underbrush appeared scarce except in ravines, and the ground in open patches held a bleached grass. Jean's eye roved for sight of squirrels, birds, deer, or any moving creature. It appeared to be a dry, uninhabited forest. About midday Jean halted at a pond of surface water, evidently melted snow, and gave his animals a drink. He saw a few old deer tracks in the mud and several huge bird tracks new to him which he concluded must have been made by wild turkeys.

The trail divided at this pond. Jean had no idea which branch he ought to take. "Reckon it doesn't matter," he muttered, as he was about to remount. His horse was standing with ears up, looking back along the trail. Then Jean heard a clip-clop of trotting hoofs, and presently espied a horseman.

Jean made a pretense of tightening his saddle girths while he peered over his horse at the approaching rider. All men in this country were going to be of exceeding interest to Jean Isbel. This man at a distance rode and looked like all the Arizonians Jean had seen, he had a superb seat in the saddle, and he was long and lean. He wore a huge black sombrero and a soiled red scarf. His vest was open and he was without a coat.

The rider came trotting up and halted several paces from Jean.

"Hullo, stranger!" he said, gruffly.

"Howdy yourself!" replied Jean. He felt an instinctive importance in the meeting with the man. Never had sharper eyes flashed over Jean and his outfit. He had a dust-colored, sun-burned face, long, lean, and hard, a huge sandy mustache that hid his mouth, and eyes of piercing light intensity. Not very much hard Western experience had passed by this man, yet he was not old, measured by years. When he dismounted Jean saw he was tall, even for an Arizonian.

"Seen your tracks back a ways," he said, as he slipped the bit to let his horse drink. "Where bound?"

"Reckon I'm lost, all right," replied Jean. "New country for me."

"Shore. I seen thet from your tracks an' your last camp. Wal, where was you headin' for before you got lost?"

The query was deliberately cool, with a dry, crisp ring. Jean felt the lack of friendliness or kindliness in it.

"Grass Valley. My name's Isbel," he replied, shortly.

4

The rider attended to his drinking horse and presently rebridled him; then with a long swing of leg he appeared to step into the saddle.

"Shore I knowed you was Jean Isbel," he said. "Everybody in the Tonto has heerd old Gass Isbel sent fer his boy."

"Well then, why did you ask?" inquired Jean, bluntly.

"Reckon I wanted to see what you'd say."

"So? All right. But I'm not carin' very much for what *you* say."

Their glances locked steadily then and each measured the other by the intangible conflict of spirit.

"Shore thet's natural," replied the rider. His speech was slow, and the motions of his long, brown hands, as he took a cigarette from his vest, kept time with his words. "But seein' you're one of the Isbels, I'll hev my say whether you want it or not. My name's Colter an' I'm one of the sheepmen Gass Isbel's riled with."

"Colter. Glad to meet you," replied Jean. "An' I reckon who riled my father is goin' to rile me."

"Shore. If thet wasn't so you'd not be an Isbel," returned Colter, with a grim little laugh. "It's easy to see you ain't run into any Tonto Basin fellers yet. Wal, I'm goin' to tell you thet your old man gabbed like a woman down at Greaves's store. Bragged aboot you an' how you could fight an' how you could shoot an' how you could track a hoss or a man! Bragged how you'd chase every sheep herder back up on the Rim. . . . I'm tellin' you because we want you to git our stand right. We're goin' to run sheep down in Grass Valley."

"Ahuh! Well, who's we?" queried Jean, curtly.

"Wha-at? . . . We—I mean the sheepmen rangin' this Rim from Black Butte to the Apache country."

"Colter, I'm a stranger in Arizona," said Jean, slowly. "I know little about ranchers or sheepmen. It's true my father sent for me. It's true, I dare say, that he bragged, for he was given to bluster an' blow. An' he's old now. I can't help it if he bragged about me. But if he has, an' if he's justified in his stand against you sheepmen, I'm goin' to do my best to live up to his brag."

"I get your hunch. Shore we understand each other, an' thet's a powerful help. You take my hunch to your old man," replied Colter, as he turned his horse away toward the left. "Thet trail leadin' south is yours. When you come to the Rim you'll see a bare spot down in the Basin. Thet'll be Grass Valley."

He rode away out of sight into the woods. Jean leaned against his horse and pondered. It seemed difficult to be just to this Colter, not because of his claims, but because of a subtle hostility that emanated from him. Colter had the hard face, the masked intent, the turn of speech that Jean had come to associate with dishonest men. Even if Jean had not been prejudiced, if he had known nothing of his father's trouble with these sheepmen, and if Colter had met him only to exchange glances and greetings, still Jean would never have had a favorable impression. Colter grated upon him, roused an antagonism seldom felt.

"Heigho!" sighed the young man. "Good-by to huntin' an' fishin'! Dad's given me a man's job."

With that he mounted his horse and started the pack mule into the right-hand trail. Walking and trotting, he traveled all afternoon, toward sunset getting into heavy forest of pine. More than one snow bank showed white through the green, sheltered on the north slopes of shady ravines. And it was upon entering this zone of richer, deeper forestland that Jean sloughed off his gloomy forebodings. These stately pines were not the giant firs of Oregon, but any lover of the woods could be happy under them. Higher still he climbed until the forest spread before him and around him like a level park, with thicketed ravines here and there on each side. And presently that deceitful level led to a higher bench upon which the pines towered, and were matched by beautiful trees he took for spruce. Heavily barked, with regular spreading branches, these conifers rose in symmetrical shape to spear the sky with silver plumes. A graceful gray-green moss waved like veils from the branches. The air was not so dry and it was colder, with a scent and touch of snow. Jean made camp at the first likely site, taking the precaution to unroll his bed some little distance from his fire. Under the softly moaning pines he felt comfortable, having lost the sense of an immeasurable open space falling away from all around him.

The gobbling of wild turkeys awakened Jean, "Chug-a-lug, chug-a-lug, chug-a-lug-chug." There was not a great difference between the gobble of a wild turkey and that of a tame one. Jean got up, and taking his rifle went out into the gray obscurity of dawn to try to locate the turkeys. But it was too dark, and finally when daylight came they appeared to be gone. The mule had strayed, and, what with finding it and cooking breakfast and packing, Jean did not make a very early start. On this last lap of his long journey he had slowed down. He was weary of hurrying; the change from weeks in the glaring sun and dust-laden wind to this sweet cool darkly green and brown forest was very welcome; he wanted to linger along the shaded trail. This day he made sure would see him reach the Rim. By and by he lost the trail. It had just worn out from lack of use. Every now and then Jean would cross an old trail, and as he penetrated deeper into the forest every damp or dusty spot showed tracks of turkey, deer, and bear. The amount of bear sign surprised him. Presently his keen nostrils were assailed by a smell of sheep, and soon he rode into a broad sheep trail. From the tracks Jean calculated that the sheep had passed there the day before.

An unreasonable antipathy seemed born in him. To be sure he had been prepared to dislike sheep, and that was why he was unreasonable. But on the other hand this band of sheep had left a broad bare swath, weedless, grassless, flowerless, in their wake. Where sheep grazed they destroyed. That was what Jean had against them.

An hour later he rode to the crest of a long parklike slope, where new green grass was sprouting and flowers peeped everywhere. The pines appeared far apart; gnarled oak trees showed rugged and gray against the green wall of woods. A white strip of snow gleamed like a moving stream away down in the woods.

Jean heard the musical tinkle of bells and the baa-baa of sheep and the faint, sweet bleating of lambs. As he rode toward these sounds a dog ran out from an oak thicket and barked at him. Next Jean smelled a camp fire and soon he caught sight of a curling blue column of smoke, and then a small peaked tent. Beyond the clump of oaks Jean encountered a Mexican lad carrying a carbine. The boy had a swarthy, pleasant face, and to Jean's greeting he replied, "Buenas dias." Jean understood little Spanish, and about all he gathered by his simple queries was that the lad was not alone—and that it was "lambing time."

This latter circumstance grew noisily manifest. The forest seemed shrilly full of incessant baas and plaintive bleats. All about the camp, on the slope, in the glades, and everywhere, were sheep. A few were grazing; many were lying down; most of them were ewes suckling white fleecy little lambs that staggered on their feet. Everywhere Jean saw tiny lambs just born. Their pin-pointed bleats pierced the heavier baa-baa of their mothers.

Jean dismounted and led his horse down toward the camp, where he rather expected to see another and older Mexican, from whom he might get information. The lad walked with him. Down this way the plaintive uproar made by the sheep was not so loud.

"Hello there!" called Jean, cheerfully, as he approached the tent. No answer was forthcoming. Dropping his bridle, he went on, rather slowly, looking for some one to appear. Then a voice from one side startled him.

"Mawnin', stranger."

A girl stepped out from beside a pine. She carried a rifle. Her face flashed richly brown, but she was not Mexican. This fact, and the sudden conviction that she had been watching him, somewhat disconcerted Jean.

"Beg pardon—miss," he floundered. "Didn't expect to see a—girl. . . . I'm sort of lost—lookin' for the Rim—an' thought I'd find a sheep herder who'd show me. I can't savvy this boy's lingo."

While he spoke it seemed to him an intentness of expression, a strain relaxed from her face. A faint suggestion of hostility likewise disappeared. Jean was not even sure that he had caught it, but there had been something that now was gone.

"Shore I'll be glad to show y'u," she said.

"Thanks, miss. Reckon I can breathe easy now," he replied. "It's a long ride from San Diego. Hot an' dusty! I'm pretty tired. An' maybe this woods isn't good medicine to achin' eyes!"

"San Diego! Y'u're from the coast?"

"Yes."

Jean had doffed his sombrero at sight of her and he still held it, rather deferentially, perhaps. It seemed to attract her attention.

"Put on y'ur hat, stranger. . . . Shore I can't recollect when any man bared his haid to me." She uttered a little laugh in which surprise and frankness mingled with a tint of bitterness.

Jean sat down with his back to a pine, and, laying the sombrero by his side, he looked full at her, conscious of a singular eagerness, as if he wanted to verify by close scrutiny a first hasty impression. If there had been an instinct in his meeting with Colter, there was more in this. The girl half sat, half leaned against a log, with the shiny little carbine across her knees. She had a level, curious gaze upon him, and Jean had never met one just like it. Her eyes were rather

8

a wide oval in shape, clear and steady, with shadows of thought in their amber-brown depths. They seemed to look through Jean, and his gaze dropped first. Then it was he saw her ragged homespun skirt and a few inches of brown, bare ankles, strong and round, and crude worn-out moccasins that failed to hide the shapeliness of her feet. Suddenly she drew back her stockingless ankles and ill-shod feet. When Jean lifted his gaze again he found her face half averted and a stain of red in the gold tan of her cheek. That touch of embarrassment somehow removed her from this strong, raw, wild woodland setting. It changed her poise. It detracted from the curious, unabashed, almost bold, look that he had encountered in her eyes.

"Reckon you're from Texas," said Jean, presently.

"Shore am," she drawled. She had a lazy Southern voice, pleasant to hear. "How'd y'u-all guess that?"

"Anybody can tell a Texan. Where I came from there were a good many pioneers an' ranchers from the old Lone Star state. I've worked for several. An', come to think of it, I'd rather hear a Texas girl talk than anybody."

"Did y'u know many Texas girls?" she inquired, turning again to face him.

"Reckon I did—quite a good many."

"Did y'u go with them?"

"Go with them? Reckon you mean keep company. Why, yes, I guess I did—a little," laughed Jean. "Sometimes on a Sunday or a dance once in a blue moon, an' occasionally a ride."

"Shore that accounts," said the girl, wistfully.

"For what?" asked Jean.

"Y'ur bein' a gentleman," she replied, with force. "Oh, I've not forgotten. I had friends when we lived in Texas. . . . Three years ago. Shore it seems longer. Three miserable years in this damned country!"

Then she bit her lip, evidently to keep back further unwitting utterance to a total stranger, And it was that biting of her lip that drew Jean's attention to her mouth. It held beauty of curve and fullness and color that could not hide a certain sadness and bitterness. Then the whole flashing brown face changed for Jean. He saw that it was young, full of passion and restraint, possessing a power which grew on him. This, with her shame and pathos and the fact that she craved respect, gave a leap to Jean's interest.

"Well, I reckon you flatter me," he said, hoping to put her

9

at her ease again. "I'm only a rough hunter an' fisherman—woodchopper an' horse tracker. Never had all the school I needed—nor near enough company of nice girls like you."

"Am I nice?" she asked, quickly.

"You sure are," he replied, smiling.

"In these rags," she demanded, with a sudden flash of passion that thrilled him. "Look at the holes." She showed rips and worn-out places in the sleeves of her buckskin blouse, through which gleamed a round, brown arm. "I sew when I have anythin' to sew with. . . . Look at my skirt—a dirty rag. An' I have only one other to my name. . . . Look!" Again a color tinged her cheeks, most becoming, and giving the lie to her action. But shame could not check her violence now. A damned-up resentment seemed to have broken out in flood. She lifted the ragged skirt almost to her knees. "No stockings! No shoes! . . . How can a girl be nice when she has no clean, decent woman's clothes to wear?"

"How—how can a girl . . ." began Jean. "See here, miss, I'm beggin' your pardon for—sort of stirrin' you to forget yourself a little. Reckon I understand. You don't meet many strangers an' I sort of hit you wrong—makin' you feel too much—an' talk too much. Who an' what you are is none of my business. But we met. . . . An' I reckon somethin' has happened—perhaps more to me than to you. . . . Now let me put you straight about clothes an' women. Reckon I know most women love nice things to wear an' think because clothes make them look pretty that they're nicer or better. But they're wrong. You're wrong. Maybe it'd be too much for a girl like you to be happy without clothes. But you can be—you are just as nice, an'—an' fine—an', for all you know, a good deal more appealin' to some men."

"Stranger, y'u shore must excuse my temper an' the show I made of myself," replied the girl, with composure. "That, to say the least, was not nice. An' I don't want anyone thinkin' better of me than I deserve. My mother died in Texas, an' I've lived out heah in this wild country—a girl alone among rough men. Meetin' y'u to-day makes me see what a hard lot they are—an' what it's done to me."

Jean smothered his curiosity and tried to put out of his mind a growing sense that he pitied her, liked her.

"Are you a sheep herder?" he asked.

"Shore I am now an' then. My father lives back heah in a cañon. He's a sheepman. Lately there's been herders shot at. Just now we're short an' I have to fill in. But I like shepherdin' an' I love the woods, and the Rim Rock an' all the Tonto. If they were all, I'd shore be happy."

"Herders shot at!" exclaimed Jean, thoughtfully. "By whom? An' what for?"

"Trouble brewin' between the cattlemen down in the Basin an' the sheepmen up on the Rim. Dad says there'll shore be hell to pay. I tell him I hope the cattlemen chase him back to Texas."

"Then— Are you on the ranchers' side?" queried Jean, trying to pretend casual interest.

"No. I'll always be on my father's side," she replied, with spirit. "But I'm bound to admit I think the cattlemen have the fair side of the argument."

"How so?"

"Because there's grass everywhere. I see no sense in a sheepman goin' out of his way to surround a cattleman an' sheep off his range. That started the row. Lord knows how it'll end. For most all of them heah are from Texas."

"So I was told," replied Jean. "An' I heard 'most all these Texans got run out of Texas. Any truth in that?"

"Shore I reckon there is," she replied, seriously. "But, stranger, it might not be healthy for y'u to say that anywhere. My dad, for one, was not run out of Texas. Shore I never can see why he came heah. He's accumulated stock, but he's not rich nor so well off as he was back home."

"Are you goin' to stay here always?" queried Jean, suddenly.

"If I do so it'll be in my grave," she answered, darkly. "But what's the use of thinkin'? People stay places until they drift away. Y'u can never tell. . . . Well, stranger, this talk is keepin' y'u."

She seemed moody now, and a note of detachment crept into her voice. Jean rose at once and went for his horse. If this girl did not desire to talk further he certainly had no wish to annoy her. His mule had strayed off among the bleating sheep. Jean drove it back and then led his horse up to where the girl stood. She appeared taller and, though not of robust build, she was vigorous and lithe, with something about her that fitted the place. Jean was loath to bid her good-by.

"Which way is the Rim?" he asked, turning to his saddle girths.

"South," she replied, pointing. "It's only a mile or so. I'll walk down with y'u. . . . Suppose y'u're on the way to Grass Valley?"

11

"Yes; I've relatives there," he returned. He dreaded her next question, which he suspected would concern his name. But she did not ask. Taking up her rifle she turned away. Jean strode ahead to her side. "Reckon if you walk I won't ride."

So he found himself beside a girl with the free step of a mountaineer. Her bare, brown head came up nearly to his shoulder. It was a small, pretty head, graceful, well held, and the thick hair on it was a shiny, soft brown. She wore it in a braid, rather untidily and tangled, he thought, and it was tied with a string of buckskin. Altogether her apparel proclaimed poverty.

Jean let the conversation languish for a little. He wanted to think what to say presently, and then he felt a rather vague pleasure in stalking beside her. Her profile was straight cut and exquisite in line. From this side view the soft curve of lips could not be seen.

She made several attempts to start conversation, all of which Jean ignored, manifestly to her growing constraint. Presently Jean, having decided what he wanted to say, suddenly began: "I like this adventure. Do you?"

"Adventure! Meetin' me in the woods?" And she laughed the laugh of youth. "Shore you must be hard up for adventure, stranger."

"Do you like it?" he persisted, and his eyes searched the half-averted face.

"I might like it," she answered, frankly, "if—if my temper had not made a fool of me. I never meet anyone I care to talk to. Why should it not be pleasant to run across some one new—some one strange in this heah wild country?"

"We are as we are," said Jean, simply. "I didn't think you made a fool of yourself. If I thought so, would I want to see you again?"

"Do y'u?" The brown face flashed on him with surprise, with a light he took for gladness. And because he wanted to appear calm and friendly, not too eager, he had to deny himself the thrill of meeting those changing eyes.

"Sure I do. Reckon I'm overbold on such short acquaintance. But I might not have another chance to tell you, so please don't hold it against me."

This declaration over, Jean felt relief and something of exultation. He had been afraid he might not have the courage to make it. She walked on as before, only with her head bowed a little and her eyes downcast. No color but the gold-

12

brown tan and the blue tracery of veins showed in her cheeks. He noticed then a slight swelling quiver of her throat; and he became alive to its graceful contour, and to how full and pulsating it was, how nobly it set into the curve of her shoulder. Here in her quivering throat was the weakness of her, the evidence of her sex, the womanliness that belied the mountaineer stride and the grasp of strong brown hands on a rifle. It had an effect on Jean totally inexplicable to him, both in the strange warmth that stole over him and in the utterance he could not hold back.

"Girl, we're strangers, but what of that? We've met, an' I tell you it means somethin' to me. I've known girls for months an' never felt this way. I don't know who you are an' I don't care. You betrayed a good deal to me. You're not happy. You're lonely. An' if I didn't want to see you again for my own sake I would for yours. Some things you said I'll not forget soon. I've got a sister, an' I know you have no brother. An' I reckon . . ."

At this juncture Jean in his earnestness and quite without thought grasped her hand. The contact checked the flow of his speech and suddenly made him aghast at his temerity. But the girl did not make any effort to withdraw it. So Jean, inhaling a deep breath and trying to see through his bewilderment, held on bravely. He imagined he felt a faint, warm, returning pressure. She was young, she was friendless, she was human. By this hand in his Jean felt more than ever the loneliness of her. Then, just as he was about to speak again, she pulled her hand free.

"Heah's the Rim," she said, in her quaint Southern drawl. "An' there's y'ur Tonto Basin."

Jean had been intent only upon the girl. He had kept step beside her without taking note of what was ahead of him. At her words he looked up expectantly, to be struck mute.

He felt a sheer force, a downward drawing of an immense abyss beneath him. As he looked afar he saw a black basin of timbered country, the darkest and wildest he had ever gazed upon, a hundred miles of blue distance across to an unflung mountain range, hazy purple against the sky. It seemed to be a stupendous gulf surrounded on three sides by bold, undulating lines of peaks, and on his side by a wall so high that he felt lifted aloft on the rim of the sky.

"Southeast y'u see the Sierra Anchas," said the girl, pointing. "That notch in the range is the pass where sheep are driven to Phoenix an' Maricopa. Those big rough mountains

13

to the south are the Mazatzals. Round to the west is the Four Peaks Range. An' y'u're standin' on the Rim."

Jean could not see at first just what the Rim was, but by shifting his gaze westward he grasped this remarkable phenomenon of nature. For leagues and leagues a colossal red and yellow wall, a rampart, a mountain-faced cliff, seemed to zigzag westward. Grand and bold were the promontories reaching out over the void. They ran toward the westering sun. Sweeping and impressive were the long lines slanting away from them, sloping darkly spotted down to merge into the black timber. Jean had never seen such a wild and rugged manifestation of nature's depths and upheavals. He was held mute.

"Stranger, look down," said the girl.

Jean's sight was educated to judge heights and depths and distances. This wall upon which he stood sheered precipitously down, so far that it made him dizzy to look, and then the craggy broken cliffs merged into red-slided, cedar-greened slopes running down and down into gorges choked with forests, and from which soared up a roar of rushing waters. Slope after slope, ridge beyond ridge, cañon merging into cañon—so the tremendous bowl sunk away to its black, deceiving depths, a wilderness across which travel seemed impossible.

"Wonderful!" exclaimed Jean.

"Indeed it is!" murmured the girl. "Shore that is Arizona. I reckon I love *this*. The heights an' depths—the awfulness of its wilderness!"

"An' you want to leave it?"

"Yes an' no. I don't deny the peace that comes to me heah. But not often do I see the Basin, an' for that matter, one doesn't live on grand scenery."

"Child, even once in a while—this sight would cure any misery, if you only see. I'm glad I came. I'm glad you showed it to me first."

She too seemed under the spell of a vastness and loneliness and beauty and grandeur that could not but strike the heart.

Jean took her hand again. "Girl, say you will meet me here," he said, his voice ringing deep in his ears.

"Shore I will," she replied, softly, and turned to him. It seemed then that Jean saw her face for the first time. She was beautiful as he had never known beauty. Limned against that scene, she gave it life—wild, sweet, young life—the poignant meaning of which haunted yet eluded him. But she belonged there. Her eyes were again searching his, as if for some lost part of herself, unrealized, never known before. Wondering, wistful, hopful, glad—they were eyes that seemed surprised, to reveal part of her soul.

Then her red lips parted. Their tremulous movement was a magnet to Jean. An invisible and mighty force pulled him down to kiss them. Whatever the spell had been, that rude, unconscious action broke it.

He jerked away, as if he expected to be struck. "Girl— I—I"—he gasped in amaze and sudden-dawning contrition— "I kissed you—but I swear it wasn't intentional—I never thought. . . ."

The anger that Jean anticipated failed to materialize. He stood, breathing hard, with a hand held out in unconscious appeal. By the same magic, perhaps, that had transfigured her a moment past, she was now invested again by the older character.

"Shore I reckon my callin' y'u a gentleman was a little previous," she said, with a rather dry bitterness. "But, stranger, yu're sudden."

"You're not insulted?" asked Jean, hurriedly.

"Oh, I've been kissed before. Shore men are all alike."

"They're not," he replied, hotly, with a subtle rush of disillusion, a dulling of enchantment. "Don't you class me with other men who've kissed you. I wasn't myself when I did it an' I'd have gone on my knees to ask your forgiveness. . . . But now I wouldn't—an' I wouldn't kiss you again, either—even if you—you wanted it."

Jean read in her strange gaze what seemed to him a vague doubt, as if she was questioning him.

"Miss, I take that back," added Jean, shortly. "I'm sorry. I didn't mean to be rude. It was a mean trick for me to kiss you. A girl alone in the woods who's gone out of her way to be kind to me! I don't know why I forgot my manners. An' I ask your pardon."

She looked away then, and presently pointed far out and down into the Basin.

"There's Grass Valley. That long gray spot in the black. It's about fifteen miles. Ride along the Rim that way till y'u cross a trail. Shore y'u can't miss it. Then go down."

"I'm much obliged to you," replied Jean, reluctantly accepting what he regarded as his dismissal. Turning his horse, he put his foot in the stirrup, then, hesitating, he looked across the saddle at the girl. Her abstraction, as she gazed away over

15

the purple depths suggested loneliness and wistfulness. She was not thinking of that scene spread so wondrously before her. It struck Jean she might be pondering a subtle change in his feeling and attitude, something he was conscious of, yet could not define.

"Reckon this is good-by," he said, with hesitation.

"*Adios, señor,*" she replied, facing him again. She lifted the little carbine to the hollow of her elbow and, half turning, appeared ready to depart.

"Adios means good-by?" he queried.

"Yes, good-by till to-morrow or good-by forever. Take it as y'u like."

"Then you'll meet me here day after to-morrow?" How eagerly he spoke, on impulse, without a consideration of the intangible thing that had changed him!

"Did I say I wouldn't?"

"No. But I reckoned you'd not care to after—" he replied, breaking off in some confusion.

"Shore I'll be glad to meet y'u. Day after to-morrow about mid-afternoon. Right heah. Fetch all the news from Grass Valley."

"All right. Thanks. That'll be—fine," replied Jean, and as he spoke he experienced a buoyant thrill, a pleasant lightness of enthusiasm, such as always stirred boyishly in him at a prospect of adventure. Before it passed he wondered at it and felt unsure of himself. He needed to think.

"Stranger, shore I'm not recollectin' that y'u told me who y'u are," she said.

"No, reckon I didn't tell," he returned. "What difference does that make? I said I didn't care who or what you are. Can't you feel the same about me?"

"Shore—I felt that way," she replied, somewhat nonplussed, with the level brown gaze steadily on his face. "But now y'u make me think."

"Let's meet without knowin' any more about each other than we do now."

"Shore. I'd like that. In this big wild Arizona a girl—an' I reckon a man—feels so insignificant. What's a name, anyhow? Still, people an' things have to be distinguished. I'll call y'u 'Stranger' an' be satisfied—if y'u say it's fair for y'u not to tell who y'u are."

"Fair! No, it's not," declared Jean, forced to confession. "My name's Jean—Jean Isbel."

"*Isbel!*" she exclaimed, with a violent start. "Shore y'u

16

can't be son of old Gass Isbel. . . . I've seen both his sons."

"He has three," replied Jean, with relief, now the secret was out. "I'm the youngest. I'm twenty-four. Never been out of Oregon till now. On my way—"

The brown color slowly faded out of her face, leaving her quite pale, with eyes that began to blaze. The suppleness of her seemed to stiffen.

"My name's Ellen Jorth," she burst out, passionately. "Does it mean anythin' to y'u?"

"Never heard it in my life," protested Jean. "Sure I reckoned you belonged to the sheep raisers who're on the outs with my father. That's why I had to tell you I'm Jean Isbel. . . . Ellen Jorth. It's strange an' pretty. . . . Reckon I can be just as good a—a friend to you—"

"No Isbel can ever be a friend to me," she said, with bitter coldness. Stripped of her ease and her soft witsfulness, she stood before him one instant, entirely another girl, a hostile enemy. Then she wheeled and strode off into the woods.

Jean, in amaze, in consternation, watched her swiftly draw away with her lithe, free step, wanting to follow her, wanting to call to her; but the resentment roused by her suddenly avowed hostility held him mute in his tracks. He watched her disappear, and when the brown-and-green wall of forest swallowed the slender gray form he fought against the insistent desire to follow her, and fought in vain.

2

★

BUT Ellen Jorth's moccasined feet did not leave a distinguishable trail on the springy pine needle covering of the ground, and Jean could not find any trace of her.

A little futile searching to and fro cooled his impulse and called pride to his rescue. Returning to his horse, he mounted, rode out behind the pack mule to start it along, and soon felt the relief of decision and action. Clumps of small pines grew thickly in spots on the Rim, making it necessary for

17

him to skirt them; at which times he lost sight of the purple basin. Every time he came back to an opening through which he could see the wild ruggedness and colors and distances, his appreciation of their nature grew on him. Arizona from Yuma to the Little Colorado had been to him an endless waste of wind-scoured, sun-blasted barrenness. This black-forested rock-rimmed land of untrodden ways was a world that in itself would satisfy him. Some instinct in Jean called for a lonely, wild land, into the fastnesses of which he could roam at will and be the other strange self that he had always yearned to be but had never been.

Every few moments there intruded into his flowing consciousness the flashing face of Ellen Jorth, the way she had looked at him, the things she had said. "Reckon I was a fool," he soliloquized, with an acute sense of humiliation. "She never saw how much in earnest I was." And Jean began to remember the circumstances with a vividness that disturbed and perplexed him.

The accident of running across such a girl in that lonely place might be out of the ordinary—but it had happened. Surprise had made him dull. The charm of her appearance, the appeal of her manner, must have drawn him at the very first, but he had not recognized that. Only at her words, "Oh, I've been kissed before," had his feelings been checked in their heedless progress. And the utterance of them had made a difference he now sought to analyze. Some personality in him, some voice, some idea had begun to defend her even before he was conscious that he had arraigned her before the bar of his judgment. Such defense seemed clamoring in him now and he forced himself to listen. He wanted, in his hurt pride, to justify his amazing surrender to a sweet and sentimental impulse.

He realized now that at first glance he should have recognized in her look, her poise, her voice the quality he called thoroughbred. Ragged and stained apparel did not prove her of a common sort. Jean had known a number of fine and wholesome girls of good family; and he remembered his sister. This Ellen Jorth was that kind of a girl irrespective of her present environment. Jean championed her loyalty, even after he had gratified his selfish pride.

It was then—contending with an intangible and stealing glamour, unreal and fanciful, like the dream of a forbidden enchantment—that Jean arrived at the part in the little woodland drama where he had kissed Ellen Jorth and had been

18

unrebuked. Why had she not resented his action? Dispelled was the illusion he had been dreamily and nobly constructing. "Oh, I've been kissed before!" The shock to him now exceeded his first dismay. Half bitterly she had spoken, and wholly scornful of herself, or of him, or of all men. For she had said all men were alike. Jean chafed under the smart of that, a taunt every decent man hated. Naturally every happy and healthy young man would want to kiss such red, sweet lips. But if those lips had been for others—never for him! Jean reflected that not since childish games had he kissed a girl—until this brown-faced Ellen Jorth came his way. He wondered at it. Moreover, he wondered at the significance he placed upon it. After all, was it not merely an accident? Why should he remember? Why should he ponder? What was the faint, deep, growing thrill that accompanied some of his thoughts?

Riding along with busy mind, Jean almost crossed a well-beaten trail, leading through a pine thicket and down over the Rim. Jean's pack mule led the way without being driven. And when Jean reached the edge of the bluff one look down was enough to fetch him off his horse. That trail was steep, narrow, clogged with stones, and as full of sharp corners as a crosscut saw. Once on the descent with a packed mule and a spirited horse, Jean had no time for mind wanderings and very little for occasional glimpses out over the cedar tops to the vast blue hollow asleep under a westering sun.

The stones rattled, the dust rose, the cedar twigs snapped, the little avalanches of red earth slid down, the iron-shod hoofs rang on the rocks. The slope had been narrow at the apex in the Rim where the trail led down a crack, and it widened in fan shape as Jean descended. He zigzagged down a thousand feet before the slope benched into dividing ridges. Here the cedars and junipers failed and pines once more hid the sun. Deep ravines were black with brush. From somewhere rose a roar of running water, most pleasant to Jean's ears. Fresh deer and bear tracks covered old ones made in the trail.

Those timbered ridges were but billows of that tremendous slope that now sheered above Jean, ending in a magnificent yellow wall of rock, greened in niches, stained by weather rust, carved and cracked and caverned. As Jean descended farther the hum of bees made melody, the roar of rapid water and the murmur of a rising breeze filled him with the content of the wild. Sheepmen like Colter and wild girls like Ellen

19

Jorth and all that seemed promising or menacing in his father's letter could never change the Indian in Jean. So he thought. Hard upon that conclusion rushed another—one which troubled with its stinging revelation. Surely these influences he had defied were just the ones to bring out in him the Indian he had sensed but had never known. The eventful day had brought new and bitter food for Jean to reflect upon.

The trail landed him in the bowlder-strewn bed of a wide cañon, where the huge trees stretched a canopy of foliage which denied the sunlight, and where a beautiful brook rushed and foamed. Here at last Jean tasted water that rivaled his Oregon springs. "Ah," he cried, "that sure is good!" Dark and shaded and ferny and mossy was this streamway; and everywhere were tracks of game, from the giant spread of a grizzly bear to the tiny, birdlike imprints of a squirrel. Jean heard familiar sounds of deer crackling the dead twigs; and the chatter of squirrels was incessant. This fragrant, cool retreat under the Rim brought back to him the dim recesses of Oregon forests. After all, Jean felt that he would not miss anything that he had loved in the Cascades. But what was the vague sense of all not being well with him—the essence of a faint regret—the insistence of a hovering shadow? And then flashed again, etched more vividly by the repetition in memory, a picture of eyes, of lips—of something he had to forgot.

Wild and broken as this rolling Basin floor had appeared from the Rim, the reality of traveling over it made that first impression a deceit of distance. Down here all was on a big, rough, broken scale. Jean did not find even a few rods of level ground. Bowlders as huge as houses obstructed the stream bed; spruce trees eight feet thick tried to lord it over the brawny pines; the ravine was a veritable cañon from which occasional glimpses through the foliage showed the Rim as a lofty red-tipped mountain peak.

Jean's pack mule became frightened at scent of a bear or lion and ran off down the rough trail, imperiling Jean's outfit. It was not an easy task to head him off nor, when that was accomplished, to keep him to a trot. But his fright and succeeding skittishness at least made for fast traveling. Jean calculated that he covered ten miles under the Rim before the character of ground and forest began to change.

The trail had turned southeast. Instead of gorge after gorge, red-walled and choked with forest, there began to be rolling ridges, some high; others were knolls; and a thick cedar growth made up for a falling off of pine. The spruce had long disappeared. Juniper thickets gave way more and more to the beautiful manzanita; and soon on the south slopes appeared cactus and a scrubby live oak. But for the well-broken trail, Jean would have fared ill through this tough brush.

Jean espied several deer, and again a coyote, and what he took to be a small herd of wild horses. No more turkey tracks showed in the dusty patches. He crossed a number of tiny brooklets, and at length came to a place where the trail ended or merged in a rough road that showed evidence of considerable travel. Horses, sheep, and cattle had passed along there that day. This road turned southward, and Jean began to have pleasurable expectations.

The road, like the trail, led down grade, but no longer at such steep angles, and was bordered by cedar and piñon, jack-pine and juniper, mescal and manzanita. Quite sharply, going around a ridge, the road led Jean's eye down to a small open flat of marshy, or at least grassy, ground. This green oasis in the wilderness of red and timbered ridges marked another change in the character of the Basin. Beyond that the country began to spread out and roll gracefully, its dark-green forest interspersed with grassy parks, until Jean headed into a long, wide gray-green valley surrounded by black-fringed hills. His pulses quickened here. He saw cattle dotting the expanse, and here and there along the edge log cabins and corrals.

As a village, Grass Valley could not boast of much, apparently, in the way of population. Cabins and houses were widely scattered, as if the inhabitants did not care to encroach upon one another. But the one store, built of stone, and stamped also with the characteristic isolation, seemed to Jean to be a rather remarkable edifice. Not exactly like a fort did it strike him, but if it had not been designed for defense it certainly gave that impression, especially from the long, low side with its dark eye-like windows about the height of a man's shoulder. Some rather fine horses were tied to a hitching rail. Otherwise dust and dirt and age and long use stamped this Grass Valley store and its immediate environment.

Jean threw his bridle, and, getting down, mounted the low porch and stepped into the wide open door. A face, gray against the background of gloom inside, passed out of sight just as Jean entered. He knew he had been seen. In front of the long, rather low-ceiled store were four men, all absorbed,

21

apparenttly, in a game of checkers. Two were playing and two were looking on. One of these, a gaunt-faced man past middle age, casually looked up as Jean entered. But the moment of that casual glance afforded Jean time enough to meet eyes he instinctively distrusted. They masked their penetration. They seemed neither curious nor friendly. They saw him as if he had been merely thin air.

"Good evenin'," said Jean.

After what appeared to Jean a lapse of time sufficient to impress him with a possible deafness of these men, the gaunt-faced one said, "Howdy, Isbell"

The tone was impersonal, dry, easy, cool, laconic, and yet it could not have been more pregnant with meaning. Jean's sharp sensibilities absorbed much. None of the slouch-sombreroed, long-mustached Texans—for so Jean at once classed them—had ever seen Jean, but they knew him and knew that he was expected in Grass Valley. All but the one who had spoken happened to have their faces in shadow under the wide-brimmed black hats. Motley-garbed, gun-belted, dusty-booted, they gave Jean the same impression of latent force that he had encountered in Colter.

"Will somebody please tell me where to find my father, Gaston Isbel?" inquired Jean, with as civil a tongue as he could command.

Nobody paid the slightest attention. It was the same as if Jean had not spoken. Waiting, half amused, half irritated, Jean shot a rapid glance around the store. The place had felt bare; and Jean, peering back through gloomy space, saw that it did not contain much. Dry goods and sacks littered a long rude counter; long rough shelves divided their length into stacks of canned foods and empty sections; a low shelf back of the counter held a generous burden of cartridge boxes, and next to it stood a rack of rifles. On the counter lay open cases of plug tobacco, the odor of which was second in strength only to that of rum.

Jean's swift-roving eye reverted to the men, three of whom were absorbed in the greasy checkerboard. The fourth man was the one who had spoken and he now deigned to look at Jean. Not much flesh was there stretched over his bony, powerful physiognomy. He stroked a lean chin with a big mobile hand that suggested more of bridle holding than familiarity with a bucksaw and plow handle. It was a lazy hand. The man looked lazy. If he spoke at all it would be with lazy speech. Yet Jean had not encountered many men to whom he would

22

have accorded more potency to stir in him the instinct of self-preservation.

"Shore," drawled this gaunt-faced Texan, "old Gass lives aboot a mile down heah." With slow sweep of the big hand he indicated a general direction to the south; then, appearing to forget his questioner, he turned his attention to the game.

Jean muttered his thanks and, striding out, he mounted again, and drove the pack mule down the road. "Reckon I've run into the wrong folks to-day," he said. "If I remember dad right he was a man to make an' keep friends. Somehow I'll bet there's going to be hell." Beyond the store were some rather pretty and comfortable homes, little ranch houses back in the coves of the hills. The road turned west and Jean saw his first sunset in the Tonto Basin. It was a pageant of purple clouds with silver edges, and background of deep rich gold. Presently Jean met a lad driving a cow. "Hello, Johnny!" he said, genially, and with a double purpose. "My name's Jean Isbel. By Golly! I'm lost in Grass Valley. Will you tell me where my dad lives?"

"Yep. Keep right on, an' y'u cain't miss him," replied the lad, with a bright smile. "He's lookin' fer y'u."

"How do you know, boy?" queried Jean, warmed by that smile.

"Aw, I know. It's all over the valley that y'u'd ride in ter-day. Shore I wus the one thet tole yer dad an' he give me a dollar."

"Was he glad to hear it?" asked Jean, with a queer sensation in his throat.

"Wal, he plumb was."

"An' who told you I was goin' to ride in to-day?"

"I heerd it at the store," replied the lad, with an air of confidence. "Some sheepmen was talkin' to Greaves. He's the storekeeper. I was settin' outside, but I heerd. A Mexican come down off the Rim ter-day an' he fetched the news." Here the lad looked furtively around, then whispered. "An' thet greaser was sent by somebody. I never heerd no more, but them sheepmen looked pretty plumb sour. An' one of them, comin' out, give me a kick, darn him. It shore is the luckedest day fer us cowmen."

"How's that, Johnny?"

"Wall, that's shore a big fight comin' to Grass Valley. My dad says so an' he rides fer yer dad. An' if it comes now y'u'll be heah."

"Ahuh!" laughed Jean. "An' what then, boy?"

The lad turned bright eyes upward. "Aw, now, yu'all cain't come thet on me. Ain't y'u an Injun, Jean Isbel? Ain't y'u a hoss tracker thet rustlers cain't fool? Ain't y'u a plumb dead shot? Ain't 'u wuss'ern a grizzly bear in a rough-an'-tumble? . . . Now ain't y'u, shore?"

Jean bade the flattering lad a rather sober good day and rode on his way. Manifestly a reputation somewhat difficult to live up to had preceded his entry into Grass Valley.

Jean's first sight of his future home thrilled him through. It was a big, low, rambling log structure standing well out from a wooded knoll at the edge of the valley. Corrals and barns and sheds lay off at the back. To the fore stretched broad pastures where numberless cattle and horses grazed. At sunset the scene was one of rich color. Prosperity and abundance and peace seemed attendant upon that ranch; lusty voices of burros braying and cows bawling seemed welcoming Jean. A hound bayed. The first cool touch of wind fanned Jean's cheek and brought a fragrance of wood smoke and frying ham.

Horses in the pasture romped to the fence and whistled at these newcomers. Jean espied a white-faced black horse that gladdened his sight. "Hello, Whiteface! I'll sure straddle you," called Jean. Then up the gentle slope he saw the tall figure of his father—the same as he had seen him thousands of times, bareheaded, shirt sleeved, striding with long step. Jean waved and called to him.

"Hi, you prodigal!" came the answer. Yes, the voice of his father—and Jean's boyhood memories flashed. He hurried his horse those last few rods. No—dad was not the same. His hair shone gray.

"Here I am, dad," called Jean, and then he was dismounting. A deep, quiet emotion settled over him, stilling the hurry, the eagerness, the pang in his breast.

"Son, I shore am glad to see you," said his father, and wrung his hand. "Wal, wal, the size of you! Shore you've grown, an' how you favor your mother."

Jean felt in the iron clasp of hand, in the uplifting of the handsome head, in the strong, fine light of piercing eyes that there was no difference in the spirit of his father. But the old smile could not hide lines and shades strange to Jean.

"Dad, I'm as glad as you," replied Jean, heartily. "It seems long we've been parted, now I see you. Are you well, dad, an' all right?"

"Not complainin', son. I can ride all day same as ever," he

24

said. "Come. Never mind your hosses. They'll be looked after. Come meet the folks. . . . Wal, wal, you got heah at last."

On the porch of the house a group awaited Jean's coming, rather silently, he thought. Wide-eyed children were there, very shy and watchful. The dark face of his sister corresponded with the image of her in his memory. She appeared taller, more womanly, as she embraced him. "Oh, Jean, Jean, I'm glad you've come!" she cried, and pressed him close. Jean felt in her a woman's anxiety for the present as well as affection for the past. He remembered his aunt Mary, though he had not seen her for years. His half brothers, Bill and Guy, had changed but little except perhaps to grow lean and rangy. Bill resembled his father, though his aspect was jocular rather than serious. Guy was smaller, wiry, and hard as rock, with snapping eyes in a brown, still face, and he had the bow-legs of a cattleman. Both had married in Arizona. Bill's wife, Kate, was a stout, comely little woman, mother of three of the children. The other wife was young, a strapping girl, red headed and freckled, with wonderful lines of pain and strength in her face. Jean remembered, as he looked at her, that some one had written him about the tragedy in her life. When she was only a child the Apaches had murdered all her family. Then next to greet Jean were the little children, all shy, yet all manifestly impressed by the occasion. A warmth and intimacy of forgotten home emotions flooded over Jean. Sweet it was to get home to these relatives who loved him and welcomed him with quiet gladness. But there seemed more. Jean was quick to see the shadow in the eyes of the women in that household and to sense a strange reliance which his presence brought.

"Son, this heah Tonto is a land of milk an' honey," said his father, as Jean gazed spellbound at the bounteous supper.

Jean certainly performed gastronomic feats on this occasion, to the delight of Aunt Mary and the wonder of the children. "Oh, he's starv-ved to death," whispered one of the little boys to his sister. They had begun to warm to this stranger uncle. Jean had no chance to talk, even had he been able to, for the meal-time showed a relaxation of restraint and they all tried to tell him things at once. In the bright lamplight his father looked easier and happier as he beamed upon Jean.

After supper the men went into an adjoining room that appeared most comfortable and attractive. It was long, and the width of the house, with a huge stone fireplace, low ceiling of hewn timbers and walls of the same, small windows with inside shutters of wood, and home-made table and chairs and rugs.

"Wal, Jean, do you recollect them shootin'-irons?" inquired the rancher, pointing above the fireplace. Two guns hung on the spreading deer antlers there. One was a musket Jean's father had used in the war of the rebellion and the other was a long, heavy, muzzle-loading flintlock Kentucky rifle with which Jean had learned to shoot.

"Reckon I do, dad," replied Jean, and with reverent hands and a rush of memory he took the old gun down.

"Jean, you shore handle thet old arm some clumsy," said Guy Isbel, dryly. And Bill added a remark to the effect that perhaps Jean had been leading a luxurious and tame life back there in Oregon, and then added, "But I reckon he's packin' that six-shooter like a Texan."

"Say, I fetched a gun or two along with me," replied Jean, jocularly. "Reckon I near broke my poor mule's back with the load of shells an' guns. Dad, what was the idea askin' me to pack out an arsenal?"

"Son, shore all shootin' arms an' such are at a premium in the Tonto," replied his father. "An' I was givin' you a hunch to come loaded."

His cool, drawling voice seemed to put a damper upon the pleasantries. Right there Jean sensed the charged atmosphere. His brothers were bursting with utterance about to break forth, and his father suddenly wore a look that recalled to Jean critical times of days long past. But the entrance of the children and the women folk put an end to confidences. Evidently the youngsters were laboring under subdued excitement. They preceded their mother, the smallest boy in the lead. For him this must have been both a dreadful and a wonderful experience, for he seemed to be pushed forward by his sister and brother and mother, and driven by yearnings of his own. "There now, Lee. Say, 'Uncle Jean, what did you fetch us?' " The lad hesitated for a shy, frightened look at Jean, and then, gaining something from his scrutiny of his uncle, he toddled forward and bravely delivered the question of tremendous importance.

"What did I fetch you, hey?" cried Jean, in delight, as he took the lad up on his knee. "Wouldn't you like to know? I didn't forget, Lee. I remembered you all. Oh! the job I had packin' your bundle of presents. . . . Now, Lee, make a guess."

"I dess you fetched a dun," replied Lee.

"A dun!—I'll bet you mean a gun," laughed Jean. "Well, you four-year-old Texas gunman! Make another guess."

That appeared too momentous and entrancing for the other two youngsters, and, adding their shrill and joyous voices to Lee's, they besieged Jean.

"Dad, where's my pack?" cried Jean. "These young Apaches are after my scalp."

"Reckon the boys fetched it onto the porch," replied the rancher.

Guy Isbel opened the door and went out. "By golly! heah's three packs," he called. "Which one do you want, Jean?"

"It's a long, heavy bundle, all tied up," replied Jean.

Guy came staggering in under a burden that brought a whoop from the youngsters and bright gleams to the eyes of the women. Jean lost nothing of this. How glad he was that he had tarried in San Francisco because of a mental picture of this very reception in far-off wild Arizona.

When Guy deposited the bundle on the floor it jarred the room. It gave forth metallic and rattling and crackling sounds.

"Everybody stand back an' give me elbow room," ordered Jean, majestically. "My good folks, I want you all to know this is somethin' that doesn't happen often. The bundle you see here weighed about a hundred pounds when I packed it on my shoulder down Market Street in Frisco. It was stolen from me on shipboard. I got it back in San Diego an' licked the thief. It rode on a burro from San Diego to Yuma an' once I thought the burro was lost for keeps. It came up the Colorado River from Yuma to Ehrenberg an' there went on top of a stage. We got chased by bandits an' once when the horses were gallopin' hard it near rolled off. Then it went on the back of a pack horse an' helped wear him out. An' I reckon it would be somewhere else now if I hadn't fallen in with a freighter goin' north from Phoenix to the Santa Fe Trail. The last lap when it sagged the back of a mule was the riskiest an' full of the narrowest escapes. Twice my mule bucked off his pack an' left my outfit scattered. Worst of all, my precious bundle made the mule top heavy comin' down that place back here where the trail seems to drop off the earth. There I was hard put to keep sight of my pack. Sometimes it was on top an' other times the mule. But it got here at last. . . . An' now I'll open it."

After this long and impressive harangue, which at least augmented the suspense of the women and worked the children into a frenzy, Jean leisurely untied the many knots

27

round the bundle and unrolled it. He had packed that bundle for just such travel as it had sustained. Three cloth-bound rifles he laid aside, and with them a long, very heavy package tied between two thin wide boards. From this came the metallic clink. "Oo, I know what dem is!" cried Lee, breaking the silence of suspense. Then Jean, tearing open a long flat parcel, spread before the mute, rapt-eyed youngsters such magnificent things as they had never dreamed of—picture books, mouth-harps, dolls, a toy gun and a toy pistol, a wonderful whistle and a fox horn, and last of all a box of candy. Before these treasures on the floor, too magical to be touched at first, the two little boys and their sister simply knelt. That was a sweet, full moment for Jean; yet even that was clouded by the something which shadowed these innocent children fatefully born in a wild place at a wild time. Next Jean gave to his sister the presents he had brought her— beautiful cloth for a dress, ribbons and a bit of lace, handkerchiefs and buttons and yards of linen, a sewing case and a whole box of spools of thread, a comb and brush and mirror, and lastly a Spanish brooch inlaid with garnets. "There, Ann," said Jean, "I confess I asked a girl friend in Oregon to tell me some things my sister might like." Manifestly there was not much difference in girls. Ann seemed stunned by this munificence, and then awakening, she hugged Jean in a way that took his breath. She was not a child any more, that was certain. Aunt Mary turned knowing eyes upon Jean. "Reckon you couldn't have pleased Ann more. She's engaged, Jean, an' where girls are in that state these things mean a heap. . . . Ann, you'll be married in that!" And she pointed to the beautiful folds of material that Ann had spread out.

"What's this?" demanded Jean. His sister's blushes were enough to convict her, and they were mightily becoming, too.

"Here, Aunt Mary," went on Jean, "here's yours, an' here's somethin' for each of my new sisters." This distribution left the women as happy and occupied, almost, as the children. It left also another package, the last one in the bundle. Jean laid hold of it and, lifting it, he was about to speak when he sustained a little shock of memory. Quite distinctly he saw two little feet, with bare toes peeping out of worn-out moccasins, and then round, bare, symmetrical ankles that had been scratched by brush. Next he saw Ellen Jorth's passionate face as she looked when she had made the violent action so disconcerting to him. In this happy moment the memory seemed farther off than a few hours. It had crystallized. It annoyed while it drew him. As a result he slowly laid this package aside and did not speak as he had intended to.

"Dad, I reckon I didn't fetch a lot for you an' the boys," continued Jean. "Some knives, some pipes an' tobacco. An' sure the guns."

"Shore, you're a regular Santa Claus, Jean," replied his father. "Wal, wal, look at the kids. An' look at Mary. An' for the land's sake look at Ann! Wal, wal, I'm gettin' old. I'd forgotten the pretty stuff an' gimcracks that mean so much to women. We're out of the world heah. It's just as well you've lived apart from us, Jean, for comin' back this way, with all that stuff, does us a lot of good. I cain't say, son, how obliged I am. My mind has been set on the hard side of life. An' it's shore good to forget—to see the smiles of the women an' the joy of the kids."

At this juncture a tall young man entered the open door. He looked like a rider. All about him, even his face, except his eyes, seemed old, but his eyes were young, fine, soft, and dark.

"How do, y'u-all!" he said, evenly.

Ann rose from her knees. Then Jean did not need to be told who this newcomer was.

"Jean, this is my friend, Andrew Colmor."

Jean knew when he met Colmor's grip and the keen flash of his eyes that he was glad Ann had set her heart upon one of their kind. And his second impression was something akin to the one given him in the road by the admiring lad. Colmor's estimate of him must have been a monument built of Ann's eulogies. Jean's heart suffered misgivings. Could he live up to the character that somehow had forestalled his advent in Grass Valley? Surely life was measured differently here in the Tonto Basin.

The children, bundling their treasures to their bosoms, were dragged off to bed in some remote part of the house, from which their laughter and voices came back with happy significance. Jean forthwith had an interested audience. How eagerly these lonely pioneer people listened to news of the outside world! Jean talked until he was hoarse. In their turn his hearers told him much that had never found place in the few and short letters he had received since he had been left in Oregon. Not a word about sheepmen or any hint of rustlers! Jean marked the omission and thought all the more seriously of probabilities because nothing was said. Altogether the evening was a happy reunion of a family of which all living members were there present. Jean grasped that this fact was one of significant satisfaction to his father.

"Shore we're all goin' to live together heah," he declared. "I started this range. I call most of this valley mine. We'll run up a cabin for Ann soon as she says the word. An' you, Jean, where's your girl? I shore told you to fetch her."

"Dad, I didn't have one," replied Jean.

"Wal, I wish you had," returned the rancher. "You'll go courtin' one of these Tonto hussies that I might object to."

"Why, father, there's not a girl in the valley Jean would look twice at," interposed Ann Isbel, with spirit.

Jean laughed the matter aside, but he had an uneasy memory. Aunt Mary averred, after the manner of relatives, that Jean would play havoc among the women of the settlement. And Jean retorted that at least one member of the Isbels should hold out against folly and fight and love and marriage, the agents which had reduced the family to these few present. "I'll be the last Isbel to go under," he concluded.

"Son, you're talkin' wisdom," said his father. "An' shore that reminds me of the uncle you're named after. Jean Isbell . . . Wal, he was my youngest brother an' shore a fire-eater. Our mother was a French creole from Louisiana, an' Jean must have inherited some of his fightin' nature from her. When the war of the rebellion started Jean an' I enlisted. I was crippled before we ever got to the front. But Jean went through three years before he was killed. His company had orders to fight to the last man. An' Jean fought an' lived long enough just to be that last man."

At length Jean was left alone with his father.

"Reckon you're used to bunkin' outdoors?" queried the rancher, rather abruptly.

"Most of the time," replied Jean.

"Wal, there's room in the house, but I want you to sleep out. Come get your beddin' an' gun. I'll show you."

They went outside on the porch, where Jean shouldered his roll of tarpaulin and blankets. His rifle, in its saddle sheath, leaned against the door. His father took it up and, half pulling it out, looked at it by the starlight. "Forty-four, eh? Wal, wal, there's shore no better, if a man can hold straight." At the moment a big gray dog trotted up to sniff at Jean. "An' heah's your bunkmate, Shepp. He's part lofer, Jean. His mother was a favorite shepherd dog of mine. His father was

30

a big timber wolf that took us two years to kill. Some bad wolf packs runnin' this Basin."

The night was cold and still, darkly bright under moon and stars; the smell of hay seemed to mingle with that of cedar. Jean followed his father round the house and up a gentle slope of grass to the edge of the cedar line. Here several trees with low-sweeping thick branches formed a dense, impenetrable shade.

"Son, your uncle Jean was scout for Liggett, one of the greatest rebels the South had," said the rancher. "An' you're goin' to be scout for the Isbels of Tonto. Reckon you'll find it 'most as hot as your uncle did. . . . Spread your bed inside. You can see out, but no one can see you. Reckon there's been some queer happenin's 'round heah lately. If Shepp could talk he'd shore have lots to tell us. Bill an' Guy have been sleepin' out, trailin' strange hoss tracks, an' all that. But shore whoever's been prowlin' around heah was too sharp for them. Some bad, crafty, light-steppin' woodsmen 'round heah, Jean. . . . Three mawnin's ago, just after daylight, I stepped out the back door an' some one of these sneaks I'm talkin' aboot took a shot at me. Missed my head a quarter of an inch! To-morrow I'll show you the bullet hole in the doorpost. An' some of my gray hairs that're stickin' in it!"

"Dad!" ejaculated Jean, with a hand outstretched. "That's awful! You frighten me."

"No time to be scared," replied his father, calmly. "They're shore goin' to kill me. That's why I wanted you home. . . . In there with you, now! Go to sleep. You shore can trust Shepp to wake you if he gets scent or sound. . . . An' good night, my son. I'm sayin' that I'll rest easy to-night."

Jean mumbled a good night and stood watching his father's shining white head move away under the starlight. Then the tall, dark form vanished, a door closed, and all was still. The dog Shepp licked Jean's hand. Jean felt grateful for that warm touch. For a moment he sat on his roll of bedding, his thought still locked on the shuddering revelation of his father's words, "They're shore goin' to kill me." The shock of inaction passed. Jean pushed his pack in the dark opening and, crawling inside, he unrolled it and made his bed.

When at length he was comfortably settled for the night he breathed a long sigh of relief. What bliss to relax! A throbbing and burning of his muscles seemed to begin with his rest. The cool starlit night, the smell of cedar, the moan of wind, the silence—all were real to his senses. After long weeks of long, arduous travel he was home. The warmth of the welcome still lingered, but it seemed to have been pierced by an icy thrust. What lay before him? The shadow in the eyes of his aunt, in the younger, fresher eyes of his sister— Jean connected that with the meaning of his father's tragic words. Far past was the morning that had been so keen, the breaking of camp in the sunlit forest, the riding down the brown aisles under the pines, the music of bleating lambs that had called him not to pass by. Thought of Ellen Jorth recurred. Had he met her only that morning? She was up there in the forest, asleep under the starlit pines. Who was she? What was her story? That savage fling of her skirt, her bitter speech and passionate flaming face—they haunted Jean. They were crystallizing into simpler memories, growing away from his bewilderment, and therefore at once sweeter and more doubtful. "Maybe she meant differently from what I thought," Jean soliloquized. "Anyway, she was honest." Both shame and thrill possessed him at the recall of an insidious idea—dare he go back and find her and give her the last package of gifts he had brought from the city? What might they mean to poor, ragged, untidy, beautiful Ellen Jorth? The idea grew on Jean. It could not be dispelled. He resisted stubbornly. It was bound to go to its fruition. Deep into his mind had sunk an impression of her need—a material need that brought spirit and pride to abasement. From one picture to another his memory wandered, from one speech and act of hers to another, choosing, selecting, casting aside, until clear and sharp as the stars shone the words, "Oh, I've been kissed before!" That stung him now. By whom? Not by one man, but by several, by many, she had meant. Pshaw! he had only been sympathetic and drawn by a strange girl in the woods. To-morrow he would forget. Work there was for him in Grass Valley. And he reverted uneasily to the remarks of his father until at last sleep claimed him.

A cold nose against his cheek, a low whine, awakened Jean. The big dog Shepp was beside him, keen, wary, intense. The night appeared far advanced toward dawn. Far away a cock crowed; the near-at-hand one answered in clarion voice. "What is it, Shepp?" whispered Jean, and he sat up. The dog smelled or heard something suspicious to his nature, but whether man or animal Jean could not tell.

3

★

The morning star, large, intensely blue-white, magnificent in
its dominance of the clear night sky, hung over the dim, dark
valley ramparts. The moon had gone down and all the other
stars were wan, pale ghosts.

Presently the strained vacuum of Jean's ears vibrated to a
low roar of many hoofs. It came from the open valley, along
the slope to the south. Shepp acted as if he wanted the word
to run. Jean laid a hand on the dog. "Hold on, Shepp," he
whispered. Then hauling on his boots and slipping into his
coat Jean took his rifle and stole out into the open. Shepp
appeared to be well trained, for it was evident that he had a
strong natural tendency to run off and hunt for whatever had
roused him. Jean thought it more than likely that the dog
scented an animal of some kind. If there were men prowling
around the ranch Shepp might have been just as vigilant, but
it seemed to Jean that the dog would have shown less eagerness to leave him, or none at all.

In the stillness of the morning it took Jean a moment to
locate the direction of the wind, which was very light and
coming from the south. In fact that little breeze had borne
the low roar of trampling hoofs. Jean circled the ranch
house to the right and kept along the slope at the edge of
the cedars. It struck him suddenly how well fitted he was for
work of this sort. All the work he had ever done, except
for his few years in school, had been in the open. All the
leisure he had ever been able to obtain had been given to
his ruling passion for hunting and fishing. Love of the wild
had been born in Jean. At this moment he experienced a
grim assurance of what his instinct and his training might
accomplish if directed to a stern and daring end. Perhaps his
father understood this; perhaps the old Texan had some
little reason for his confidence.

Every few paces Jean halted to listen. All objects, of
course, were indistinguishable in the dark-gray obscurity,

except when he came close upon them. Shepp showed an increasing eagerness to bolt out into the void. When Jean had traveled half a mile from the house he heard a scattered trampling of cattle on the run, and farther out a low strangled bawl of a calf. "Ahuh!" muttered Jean. "Cougar or some varmint pulled down that calf." Then he discharged his rifle in the air and yelled with all his might. It was necessary then to yell again to hold Shepp back.

Thereupon Jean set forth down the valley, and tramped out and across and around, as much to scare away whatever had been after the stock as to look for the wounded calf. More than once he heard cattle moving away ahead of him, but he could not see them. Jean let Shepp go, hoping the dog would strike a trail. But Shepp neither gave tongue nor came back. Dawn began to break, and in the growing light Jean searched around until at last he stumbled over a dead calf, lying in a little bare wash where water ran in wet seasons. Big wolf tracks showed in the soft earth. "Lofers," said Jean, as he knelt and just covered one track with his spread hand. "We had wolves in Oregon, but not as big as these. . . . Wonder where that half-wolf dog, Shepp, went. Wonder if he can be trusted where wolves are concerned. I'll bet not, if there's a she-wolf runnin' around."

Jean found tracks of two wolves, and he trailed them out of the wash, then lost them in the grass. But, guided by their direction, he went on and climbed a slope to the cedar line, where in the dusty patches he found the tracks again. "Not scared much," he muttered, as he noted the slow trotting tracks. "Well, you old gray lofers, we're goin' to clash." Jean knew from many a futile hunt that wolves were the wariest and most intelligent of wild animals in the quest. From the top of a low foothill he watched the sun rise; and then no longer wondered why his father waxed eloquent over the beauty and location and luxuriance of this grassy valley. But it was large enough to make rich a good many ranchers. Jean tried to restrain any curiosity as to his father's dealings in Grass Valley until the situation had been made clear.

Moreover, Jean wanted to love this wonderful country. He wanted to be free to ride and hunt and roam to his heart's content; and therefore he dreaded hearing his father's claims. But Jean threw off forebodings. Nothing ever turned out so badly as it presaged. He would think the best until certain of the worst. The morning was gloriously bright, and already the frost was glistening wet on the stones. Grass Valley shone like burnished silver dotted with innumerable black spots. Burros were braying their discordant messages to one another; the colts were romping in the fields; stallions were whistling; cows were bawling. A cloud of blue smoke hung low over the ranch house, slowly wafting away on the wind. Far out in the valley a dark group of horsemen were riding toward the village. Jean glanced thoughtfully at them and reflected that he seemed destined to harbor suspicion of all men new and strange to him. Above the distant village stood the darkly green foothills leading up to the craggy slopes, and these ending in the Rim, a red, black-fringed mountain front, beautiful in the morning sunlight, lonely, serene, and mysterious against the level skyline. Mountains, ranges, distances unknown to Jean, always called to him—to come, to seek, to explore, to find, but no wild horizon ever before beckoned to him as this one. And the subtle vague emotion that had gone to sleep with him last night awoke now hauntingly. It took effort to dispel the desire to think, to wonder.

Upon his return to the house, he went around on the valley side, so as to see the place by light of day. His father had built for permanence; and evidently there had been three constructive periods in the history of that long, substantial, picturesque log house. But few nails and little sawed lumber and no glass had been used. Strong and skillful hands, axes and a crosscut saw, had been the prime factors in erecting this habitation of the Isbels.

"Good mawnin', son," called a cheery voice from the porch. "Shore we-all heard you shoot; an' the crack of that forty-four was as welcome as May flowers."

Bill Isbell looked up from a task over a saddle girth and inquired pleasantly if Jean ever slept of nights. Guy Isbel laughed and there was warm regard in the gaze he bent on Jean.

"You old Indian!" he drawled, slowly. "Did you get a bead on anythin'?"

"No. I shot to scare away what I found to be some of your lofers," replied Jean. "I heard them pullin' down a calf. An' I found tracks of two whoppin' big wolves. I found the dead calf, too. Reckon the meat can be saved. Dad, you must lose a lot of stock here."

"Wal, son, you shore hit the nail on the haid," replied the rancher. "What with lions an' bears an' lofers—an' two-footed lofers of another breed—I've lost five thousand dollars in stock this last year."

35

"Dad! You don't mean it!" exclaimed Jean, in astonishment. To him that sum represented a small fortune.

"I shore do," answered his father.

Jean shook his head as if he could not understand such an enormous loss where there were keen able-bodied men about. "But that's awful, dad. How could it happen? Where were your herders an' cowboys? An' Bill an' Guy?"

Bill Isbel shook a vehement fist at Jean and retorted in earnest, having manifestly been hit in a sore spot. "Where was me an' Guy, huh? Wal, my Oregon brother, we was heah, all year, sleepin' more or less aboot three hours out of every twenty-four—ridin' our boots off—an' we couldn't keep down that loss."

"Jean, you-all have a mighty tumble comin' to you out heah," said Guy, complacently.

"Listen, son," spoke up the rancher. "You want to have some hunches before you figure on our troubles. There's two or three packs of lofers, an' in winter time they are hell to deal with. Lions thick as bees, an' shore bad when the snow's on. Bears will kill a cow now an' then. An' whenever an' old silvertip comes mozyin' across from the Mazatzals he kills stock. I'm in with half a dozen cattlemen. We all work together, an' the whole outfit cain't keep these varmints down. Then two years ago the Hash Knife Gang come into the Tonto."

"Hash Knife Gang? What a pretty name!" replied Jean. "Who're they?"

"Rustlers, son. An' shore the real old Texas brand. The Lone Star State got too hot for them, an' they followed the trail of a lot of other Texans who needed a healthier climate. Some two hundred Texans around heah, Jean, an' maybe a matter of three hundred inhabitants in the Tonto all told, good an' bad. Reckon it's aboot half an' half."

A cheery call from the kitchen interrupted the conversation of the men.

"You come to breakfast."

During the meal the old rancher talked to Bill and Guy about the day's order of work; and from this Jean gathered an idea of what a big cattle business his father conducted. After breakfast Jean's brothers manifested keen interest in the new rifles. These were unwrapped and cleaned and taken out for testing. The three rifles were forty-four calibre Winchesters, the kind of gun Jean had found most effective. He tried them out first, and the shots he made were satisfactory to him and amazing to the others. Bill had used an old Henry rifle. Guy did not favor any particular rifle. The rancher pinned his faith to the famous old single-shot buffalo gun, mostly called *needle* gun. "Wal, reckon I'd better stick to mine. Shore you cain't teach an old dog new tricks. But you boys may do well with the forty-fours. Pack 'em on your saddles an' practice when you see a coyote."

Jean found it difficult to convince himself that this interest in guns and marksmanship had any sinister propulsion back of it. His father and brothers had always been this way. Rifles were as important to pioneers as plows, and their skillful use was an achievement every frontiersman tried to attain. Friendly rivalry had always existed among the members of the Isbel family: even Ann Isbel was a good shot. But such proficiency in the use of firearms—and life in the open that was correlative with it—had not dominated them as it had Jean. Bill and Guy Isbel were born cattlemen— chips off the old block. Jean began to hope that his father's letter was an exaggeration, and particularly that the fatalistic speech of last night, "they are goin' to kill me," was just a moody inclination to see the worst side. Still, even as Jean tried to persuade himself of this more hopeful view, he recalled many references to the peculiar reputation of Texans for gun-throwing, for feuds, for never-ending hatreds. In Oregon the Isbels had lived among industrious and peaceful pioneers from all over the States; to be sure, the life had been rough and primitive, and there had been fights on occasions, though no Isbel had ever killed a man. But now they had become fixed in a wilder and sparsely settled country among men of their own breed. Jean was afraid his hopes had only sentiment to foster them. Nevertheless, he forced back a strange, brooding, mental state and resolutely held up the brighter side. Whatever the evil conditions existing in Grass Valley, they could be met with intelligence and courage, with an absolute certainty that it was inevitable they must pass away. Jean refused to consider the old, fatal law that at certain wild times and wild places in the West certain men had to pass away to change evil conditions.

"Wal, Jean, ride around the range with the boys," said the rancher. "Meet some of my neighbors, Jim Blaisdell, in particular. Take a look at the cattle. An' pick out some hosses for yourself."

"I've seen one already," declared Jean, quickly. "A black with white face. I'll take him."

"Shore you know a hoss. To my eye he's my pick. But the boys don't agree. Bill 'specially has degenerated into a fancier of pitchin' hosses. Ann can ride that black. You try him this mawnin'. . . . An', son, enjoy yourself."

True to his first impression, Jean named the black horse Whiteface and fell in love with him before ever he swung a leg over him. Whiteface appeared spirited, yet gentle. He had been trained instead of being broken. Of hard hits and quirts and spurs he had no experience. He liked to do what his rider wanted him to do.

A hundred or more horses grazed in the grassy meadow, and as Jean rode on among them it was a pleasure to see stallions throw heads and ears up and whistle or snort. Whole troops of colts and two-year-olds raced with flying tails and manes.

Beyond these pastures stretched the range, and Jean saw the gray-green expanse speckled by thousands of cattle. The scene was inspiring. Jean's brothers led him all around, meeting some of the herders and riders employed on the ranch, one of whom was a burly, grizzled man with eyes reddened and narrowed by much riding in wind and sun and dust. His name was Everts and he was father of the lad whom Jean had met near the village. Everts was busily skinning the calf that had been killed by the wolves. "See heah, y'u Jean Isbel," said Everts, "it shore was aboot time y'u come home. We-all heahs y'u hev an eye fer tracks. Wal, mebbe y'u can kill Old Gray, the lofer thet did this job. He's pulled down nine calves an' yearlin's this last two months thet I know of. An' we've not hed the spring round-up."

Grass Valley widened to the southeast. Jean would have been backward about estimating the square miles in it. Yet it was not vast acreage so much as rich pasture that made it such a wonderful range. Several ranches lay along the western slope of this section. Jean was informed that open parks and swales, and little valleys nestling among the foothills, wherever there was water and grass, had been settled by ranchers. Every summer a few new families ventured in.

Blaisdell struck Jean as being a lionlike type of Texan, both in his broad, bold face, his huge head with its upstanding tawny hair like a mane, and in the speech and force that betokened the nature of his heart. He was not as old as Jean's father. He had a rolling voice, with the same drawling intonation characteristic of all Texans, and blue eyes that still held

38

the fire of youth. Quite a marked contrast he presented to the lean, rangy, hard-jawed, intent-eyed men Jean had begun to accept as Texans.

Blaisdell took time for a curious scrutiny and study of Jean, that, frank and kindly as it was, and evidently the adjustment of impressions gotten from hearsay, yet bespoke the attention of one used to judging men for himself, and in this particular case having reasons of his own for so doing.

"Wal, you're like your sister Ann," said Blaisdell. "Which you may take as a compliment, young man. Both of you favor your mother. But you're an Isbel. Back in Texas there are men who never wear a glove on their right hands, an' shore I reckon if one of them met up with you sudden he'd think some graves had opened an' he'd go for his gun."

Blaisdell's laugh pealed out with deep, pleasant roll. Thus he planted in Jean's sensitive mind a significant thought-provoking idea about the past-and-gone Isbels.

His further remarks, likewise, were exceedingly interesting to Jean. The settling of the Tonto Basin by Texans was a subject often in dispute. His own father had been in the first party of adventurous pioneers who had traveled up from the south to cross over the Reno Pass of the Mazatzals into the Basin. "Newcomers from outside get impressions of the Tonto accordin' to the first settlers they meet," declared Blaisdell. "An' shore it's my belief these first impressions never change. Just so strong they are! Wal, I've heard my father say there were men in his wagon train that got run out of Texas, but he swore he wasn't one of them. So I reckon that sort of talk held good for twenty years, an' for all the Texans who emigrated, except, of course, such notorious rustlers as Daggs an' men of his ilk. Shore we've got some bad men heah. There's no law. Possession used to mean more than it does now. Daggs an' his Hash Knife Gang have begun to hold forth with a high hand. No small rancher can keep enough stock to pay for his labor."

At the time of which Blaisdell spoke there were not many sheepmen and cattlemen in the Tonto, considering its vast area. But these, on account of the extreme wildness of the broken country, were limited to the comparatively open Grass Valley and its adjacent environs. Naturally, as the inhabitants increased and stock raising grew in proportion the grazing and water rights became matters of extreme importance. Sheepmen ran their flocks up on the Rim in summer time and down into the Basin in winter time. A sheepman could throw a few thousand sheep round a cattleman's ranch and ruin him. The range was free. It was as fair for sheepmen to graze their herds anywhere as it was for cattlemen. This of course did not apply to the few acres of cultivated ground that a rancher could call his own; but very few cattle could have been raised on such limited area. Blaisdell said that the sheepmen were unfair because they could have done just as well, though perhaps at more labor, by keeping to the ridges and leaving the open valley and little flats to the ranchers. Formerly there had been room enough for all; now the grazing ranges were being encroached upon by sheepmen newly come to the Tonto. To Blaisdell's way of thinking the rustler menace was more serious than the sheeping-off of the range, for the simple reason that no cattleman knew exactly who the rustlers were and for the more complex and significant reason that the rustlers did not steal sheep.

"Texas was overstocked with bad men an' fine steers," concluded Blaisdell. "Most of the first an' some of the last have struck the Tonto. The sheepmen have now got distributin' points for wool an' sheep at Maricopa an' Phoenix. They're shore waxin' strong an' bold."

"Ahuh! . . . An' what's likely to come of this mess?" queried Jean.

"Ask your dad," replied Blaisdell.

"I will. But I reckon I'd be obliged for your opinion."

"Wal, short an' sweet it's this: Texas cattlemen will never allow the range they stocked to be overrun by sheepmen."

"Who's this man Greaves?" went on Jean. "Never run into anyone like him."

"Greaves is hard to figure. He's a snaky customer in deals. But he seems to be good to the poor people 'round heah. Says he's from Missouri. Ha-ha! He's as much Texan as I am. He rode into the Tonto without even a pack to his name. An' presently he builds his stone house an' freights supplies in from Phoenix. Appears to buy an' sell a good deal of stock. For a while it looked like he was steerin' a middle course between cattlemen an' sheepmen. Both sides made a rendezvous of his store, where he heard the grievances of each. Laterly he's leanin' to the sheepmen. Nobody has accused him of that yet. But it's time some cattlemen called his bluff."

"Of course there are honest an' square sheepmen in the Basin?" queried Jean.

"Yes, an' some of them are not unreasonable. But the new

40

fellows that dropped in on us the last few years—they're the ones we're goin' to clash with."

"This—sheepman, Jorth?" went on Jean, in slow hesitation, as if compelled to ask what he would rather not learn.

"Jorth must be the leader of this sheep faction that's harryin' us ranchers. He doesn't make threats or roar around like some of them. But he goes on raisin' an' buyin' more an' more sheep. An' his herders have been grazin' down all around us this winter. Jorth's got to be reckoned with."

"Who is he?"

"Wal, I don't know enough to talk aboot. Your dad never said so, but I think he an' Jorth knew each other in Texas years ago. I never saw Jorth but once. That was in Greaves's barroom. Your dad an' Jorth met that day for the first time in this country. Wal, I've not known men for nothin'. They just stood stiff an' looked at each other. Your dad was aboot to draw. But Jorth made no sign to throw a gun."

Jean saw the growing and weaving and thickening threads of a tangle that had already involved him. And the sudden pang of regret he sustained was not wholly because of sympathies with his own people.

"The other day back up in the woods on the Rim I ran into a sheepman who said his name was Colter. Who is he?"

"Colter? Shore he's a new one. What'd he look like?"

Jean described Colter with a readiness that spoke volumes for the vividness of his impressions.

"I don't know him," replied Blaisdell. "But that only goes to prove my contention—any fellow runnin' wild in the woods can say he's a sheepman."

"Colter surprised me by callin' me by my name," continued Jean. "Our little talk wasn't exactly friendly. He said a lot about my bein' sent for to run sheep herders out of the country."

"Shore that's all over," replied Blaisdell, seriously. "You're a marked man already."

"What started such rumor?"

"Shore you cain't prove it by me. But it's not taken as rumor. It's got to the sheepmen as hard as bullets."

"Ahuh! That accounts for Colter's seemin' a little sore under the collar. Well, he said they were goin' to run sheep over Grass Valley, an' for me to take that hunch to my dad."

Blaisdell had his chair tilted back and his heavy boots against a post of the porch. Down he thumped. His neck

41

corded with a sudden rush of blood and his eyes changed to blue fire.

"The hell he did!" he ejaculated, in furious amaze.

Jean gauged the brooding, rankling hurt of this old cattleman by his sudden break from the cool, easy Texan manner. Blaisdell cursed under his breath, swung his arms violently, as if to throw a last doubt or hope aside, and then relapsed to his former state. He laid a brown hand on Jean's knee.

"Two years ago I called the cards," he said, quietly. "It means a Grass Valley war."

Not until late that afternoon did Jean's father broach the subject uppermost in his mind. Then at an opportune moment he drew Jean away into the cedars out of sight.

"Son, I shore hate to make your home-comin' unhappy," he said, with evidence of agitation, "but so help me God I have to do it!"

"Dad, you called me Prodigal, an' I reckon you were right. I've shirked my duty to you. I'm ready now to make up for it," replied Jean, feelingly.

"Wal, wal, shore that's fine-spoken, my boy. . . . Let's set down heah an' have a long talk. First off, what did Jim Blaisdell tell you?"

Briefly Jean outlined the neighbor rancher's conversation. Then Jean recounted his experience with Colter and concluded with Blaisdell's reception of the sheepman's threat. If Jean expected to see his father rise up like a lion in his wrath he made a huge mistake. This news of Colter and his talk never struck even a spark from Gaston Isbel.

"Wal," he began, thoughtfully, "reckon there are only two points in Jim's talk I need touch on. There's shore goin' to be a Grass Valley war. An' Jim's idea of the cause of it seems to be pretty much the same as that of all the other cattlemen. It'll go down a black blot on the history page of the Tonto Basin as a war between rival sheepmen an' cattlemen. Same old fight over water an' grass! . . . Jean, my son, that is wrong. It'll not be a war between sheepmen an' cattlemen. But a war of honest ranchers against rustlers maskin' as sheep-raisers! . . . Mind you, I don't belittle the trouble between sheepmen an' cattlemen in Arizona. It's real an' it's vital an' it's serious. It'll take law an' order to straighten out the grazin' question. Some day the government will keep sheep off of cattle ranges. . . . So get things right in your mind, my son. You can trust your dad to tell the absolute truth. In

42

this fight that'll wipe out some of the Isbels—maybe all of them—you're on the side of justice an' right. Knowin' that, a man can fight a hundred times harder than he who knows he is a liar an' a thief."

The old rancher wiped his perspiring face and breathed slowly and deeply. Jean sensed in him the rise of a tremendous emotional strain. Wonderingly he watched the keen lined face. More than material worries were at the root of brooding, mounting thoughts in his father's eyes.

"Now next take what Jim said aboot your comin' to chase these sheep-herders out of the valley. . . . Jean, I started that talk. I had my tricky reasons. I know these greaser sheep-herders an' I know the respect Texans have for a gunman. Some say I bragged. Some say I'm an old fool in his dotage, ravin' aboot a favorite son. But they are people who hate me an' are afraid. True, son, I talked with a purpose, but shore I was mighty cold an' steady when I did it. My feelin' was that you'd do what I'd do if I were thirty years younger. No, I reckoned you'd do more. For I figured on your blood. Jean, you're Indian, an' Texas an' French, an' you've trained yourself in the Oregon woods. When you were only a boy, few marksmen I ever knew could beat you, an' I never saw your equal for eye an' ear, for trackin' a hoss, for all the gifts that make a woodsman. . . . Wal, rememberin' this an' seein' the trouble ahaid for the Isbels, I just broke out whenever I had a chance. I bragged before men I'd reason to believe would take my words deep. For instance, not long ago I missed some stock, an', happenin' into Greaves's place one Saturday night, I shore talked loud. His barroom was full of men an' some of them were in my black book. Greaves took my talk a little testy. He said. 'Wal, Gass, mebbe you're right aboot some of these cattle thieves livin' among us, but ain't they jest as liable to be some of your friends or relatives as Ted Meeker's or mine or any one around heah?' That was where Greaves an' me fell out. I yelled at him: 'No, by God, they're not! My record heah an' that of my people is open. The least I can say for you, Greaves, an' your crowd, is that your records fade away on dim trails.' Then he said, nasty-like, 'Wal, if you could work out all the dim trails in the Tonto you'd shore be surprised.' An' then I roared. Shore that was the chance I was lookin' for. I swore the trails he hinted of would be tracked to the holes of the rustlers who made them. I told him I had sent for you an' when you got heah these slippery, mysterious thieves, whoever they were, would shore have hell

43

to pay. Greaves said he hoped so, but he was afraid I was partial to my Indian son. Then we had hot words. Blaisdell got between us. When I was leavin' I took a partin' fling at him. 'Greaves, you ought to know the Isbels, considerin' you're from Texas. Maybe you've got reasons for throwin' taunts at my claims for my son Jean. Yes, he's got Indian in him an' that'll be the worse for the men who will have to meet him. I'm tellin' you, Greaves, Jean Isbel is the black sheep of the family. If you ride down his record you'll find he's shore in line to be another Poggin, or Reddy Kingfisher, or Hardin', or any of the Texas gunmen you ought to remember. . . . Greaves, there are men rubbin' elbows with you right heah that my Indian son is goin' to track down!' "

Jean bent his head in stunned cognizance of the notoriety with which his father had chosen to affront any and all Tonto Basin men who were under the ban of his suspicion. What a terrible reputation and trust to have saddled upon him! Thrills and strange, heated sensations seemed to rush together inside Jean, forming a hot ball of fire that threatened to explode. A retreating self made feeble protests. He saw his own pale face going away from this older, grimmer man.

"Son, if I could have looked forward to anythin' but blood spillin' I'd never have given you such a name to uphold," continued the rancher. "What I'm goin' to tell you now is my secret. My other sons an' Ann have never heard it. Jim Blaisdell suspects there's somethin' strange, but he doesn't know. I'll shore never tell anyone else but you. An' you must promise to keep my secret now an' after I am gone."

"I promise," said Jean.

"Wal, an' now to get it out," began his father, breathing hard. His face twitched and his hands clenched. "The sheepman heah I have to reckon with is Lee Jorth, a lifelong enemy of mine. We were born in the same town, played together as children, an' fought with each other as boys. We never got along together. An' we both fell in love with the same girl. It was nip an' tuck for a while. Ellen Sutton belonged to one of the old families of the South. She was a beauty, an' much courted, an' I reckon it was hard for her to choose. But I won her an' we became engaged. Then the war broke out. I enlisted with my brother Jean. He advised me to marry Ellen before I left. But I would not. That was the blunder of my life. Soon after our partin' her letters ceased to come. But I didn't distrust her. That was a terrible time an' all was confusion. Then I got crippled an' put in a hospital. An' in aboot a year I was sent back home."

At this juncture Jean refrained from further gaze at his father's face.

"Lee Jorth had gotten out of goin' to war," went on the rancher, in lower, thicker voice. "He'd married my sweetheart, Ellen. . . . I knew the story long before I got well. He had run after her like a hound after a hare. . . . An' Ellen married him. Wal, when I was able to get aboot I went to see Jorth an' Ellen. I confronted them. I had to know why she had gone back on me. Lee Jorth hadn't changed any with all his good fortune. He'd made Ellen believe in my dishonor. . . . But, I reckon, lies or no lies, Ellen Sutton was faithless. In my absence he had won her away from me. An' I saw that she loved him as she never had me. I reckon that killed all my generosity. If she'd been imposed upon an' weaned away by his lies an' had regretted me a little I'd have forgiven, perhaps. But she worshiped him. She was his slave. An' I, wal, I learned what hate was.

"The war ruined the Suttons, same as so many Southerners. Lee Jorth went in for raisin' cattle. He'd gotten the Sutton range an' after a few years he began to accumulate stock. In those days every cattleman was a little bit of a thief. Every cattleman drove in an' branded calves he couldn't swear was his. Wal, the Isbels were the strongest cattle raisers in that country. An' I laid a trap for Lee Jorth, caught him in the act of brandin' calves of mine I'd marked, an' I proved him a thief. I made him a rustler. I ruined him. We met once. But Jorth was one Texan not strong on the draw, at least against an Isbel. He left the country. He had friends an' relatives an' they started him at stock raisin' again. But he began to gamble an' he got in with a shady crowd. He went from bad to worse an' then he came back home. When I saw the change in proud, beautiful Ellen Sutton, an' how she still worshiped Jorth, it shore drove me near mad between pity an' hate. . . . Wal, I reckon in a Texan hate outlives any other feelin'. There came a strange turn of the wheel an' my fortunes changed. Like most young bloods of the day, I drank an' gambled. An' one night I run across Jorth an' a card-sharp friend. He fleeced me. We quarreled. Guns were thrown. I killed my man. . . . Aboot that period the Texas Rangers had come into existence. . . . An', son, when I said I never was run out of Texas I wasn't holdin' to strict truth. I rode out on a hoss.

"I went to Oregon. There I married soon, an' there Bill an'

45

Guy were born. Their mother did not live long. An' next I married your mother, Jean. She had some Indian blood, which, for all I could see, made her only the finer. She was a wonderful woman an' gave me the only happiness I ever knew. You remember her, of course, an' those home days in Oregon. I reckon I made another great blunder when I moved to Arizona. But the cattle country had always called me. I had heard of this wild Tonto Basin an' how Texans were settlin' there. An' Jim Blaisdell sent me word to come—that this shore was a garden spot of the West. Wal, it is. An' your mother was gone—

"Three years ago Lee Jorth drifted into the Tonto. An', strange to me, along aboot a year or so after his comin' the Hash Knife Gang rode up from Texas. Jorth went in for raisin' sheep. Along with some other sheepmen he lives up in the Rim cañons. Somewhere back in the wild brakes is the hidin' place of the Hash Knife Gang. Nobody but me, I reckon, associates Colonel Jorth, as he's called, with Daggs an' his gang. Maybe Blaisdell an' a few others have a hunch. But that's no matter. As a sheepman Jorth has a legitimate grievance with the cattlemen. But what could be settled by a square consideration for the good of all an' the future Jorth will never settle. He'll never settle because he is now no longer an honest man. He's in with Daggs. I cain't prove this, son, but I know it. I saw it in Jorth's face when I met him that day with Greaves. I saw more. I shore saw what he is up to. He'd never meet me at an even break. He's dead set on usin' this sheep an' cattle feud to ruin my family an' me, even as I ruined him. But he means more, Jean. This will be a war between Texans, an' a bloody war. There are bad men in this Tonto—some of the worst that didn't get shot in Texas. Jorth will have some of these fellows. . . . Now, are we goin' to wait to be sheeped off our range an' to be murdered from ambush?"

"No, we are not," replied Jean, quietly.

"Wal, come down to the house," said the rancher, and led the way without speaking until he halted by the door. There he placed his finger on a small hole in the wood at about the height of a man's head. Jean saw it was a bullet hole and that a few gray hairs stuck to its edges. The rancher stepped closer to the door-post, so that his head was within an inch of the wood. Then he looked at Jean with eyes in which there glinted dancing specks of fire, like wild sparks.

"Son, this sneakin' shot at me was made three mawnin's

46

ago. I recollect movin' my haid just when I heard the crack of a rifle. Shore was surprised. But I got inside quick."

Jean scarcely heard the latter part of this speech. He seemed doubled up inwardly, in hot and cold convulsions of changing emotion. A terrible hold upon his consciousness was about to break and let go. The first shot had been fired and he was an Isbel. Indeed, his father had made him ten times an Isbel. Blood was thick. His father did not speak to dull ears. This strife of rising tumult in him seemed the effect of years of calm, of peace in the woods, of dreamy waiting for he knew not what. It was the passionate primitive life in him that had awakened to the call of blood ties.

"That's aboot all, son," concluded the rancher. "You understand now why I feel they're goin' to kill me. I feel it heah." With solemn gesture he placed his broad hand over his heart. "An', Jean, strange whispers come to me at night. It seems like your mother was callin' or tryin' to warn me. I cain't explain these queer whispers. But I know what I know."

"Jorth has his followers. You must have yours," replied Jean, tensely.

"Shore, son, an' I can take my choice of the best men heah," replied the rancher, with pride. "But I'll not do that. I'll lay the deal before them an' let them choose. I reckon it 'll not be a long-winded fight. It 'll be short and bloody, after the way of Texans. I'm lookin' to you, Jean, to see that an Isbel is the last man!"

"My God—dad! is there no other way? Think of my sister Ann—of my brothers' wives—of—of other women! Dad, these damned Texas feuds are cruel, horrible!" burst out Jean, in passionate protest.

"Jean, would it be any easier for our women if we let these men shoot us down in cold blood?"

"Oh no—no, I see, there's no hope of—of. . . . But, dad, I wasn't thinkin' about myself. I don't care. Once started I'll —I'll be what you bragged I was. Only it's so hard to—to give in."

Jean leaned an arm against the side of the cabin and, bowing his face over it, he surrendered to the irresistible contention within his breast. And as if with a wrench that strange inward hold broke. He let down. He went back. Something that was boyish and hopeful—and in its place slowly rose the dark tide of his inheritance, the savage instinct of self-preservation bequeathed by his Indian mother, and the fierce, feudal blood lust of his Texan father.

Then as he raised himself, gripped by a sickening coldness in his breast, he remembered Ellen Jorth's face as she had gazed dreamily down off the Rim—so soft, so different, with tremulous lips, sad, musing, with far-seeing stare of dark eyes, peering into the unknown, the instinct of life still unlived. With confused vision and nameless pain Jean thought of her.

"Dad, it's hard on—the—the young folks," he said, bitterly. "The sins of the father, you know. An' the other side. How about Jorth? Has he any children?"

What a curious gleam of surprise and conjecture Jean encountered in his father's gaze!

"He has a daughter. Ellen Jorth. Named after her mother. The first time I saw Ellen Jorth I thought she was a ghost of the girl I had loved an' lost. Sight of her was like a blade in my side. But the looks of her an' what she is—they don't gibe. Old as I am, my heart—Bah! Ellen Jorth is a damned hussy!"

Jean Isbel went off alone into the cedars. Surrender and resignation to his father's creed should have ended his perplexity and worry. His instant and burning resolve to be as his father had represented him should have opened his mind to slow cunning, to the craft of the Indian, to the development of hate. But there seemed to be an obstacle. A cloud in the way of vision. A face limned on his memory.

Those damning words of his father's had been a shock—how little or great he could not tell. Was it only a day since he had met Ellen Jorth? What had made all the difference? Suddenly like a breath the fragrance of her hair came back to him. Then the sweet coolness of her lips! Jean trembled. He looked around him as if he were pursued or surrounded by eyes, by instincts, by fears, by incomprehensible things.

"Ahuh! That must be what ails me," he muttered. "The look of her—an' that kiss—they've gone hard with me. I should never have stopped to talk. An' I'm going' to kill her father an' leave her to God knows what."

Something was wrong somewhere. Jean absolutely forgot that within the hour he had pledged his manhood, his life to a feud which could be blotted out only in blood. If he had understood himself he would have realized that the pledge was no more thrilling and unintelligible in its possibilities than this instinct which drew him irresistibly.

48

"Ellen Jorth! So—my dad calls her a damned hussy! So—that explains the—the way she acted—why she never hit me when I kissed her. An' her words, so easy an' cool-like. Hussy? That means she's bad—bad! Scornful of me—maybe disappointed because my kiss was innocent! It was, I swear. An' all she said: 'Oh, I've been kissed before.' "

Jean grew furious with himself for the spreading of a new sensation in his breast that seemed now to ache. Had he become infatuated, all in a day, with this Ellen Jorth? Was he jealous of the men who had the privilege of her kisses? No! But his reply was hot with shame, with uncertainty. The thing that seemed wrong was outside of himself. A blunder was no crime. To be attracted by a pretty girl in the woods —to yield to an impulse was no disgrace, nor wrong. He had been foolish over a girl before, though not to such a rash extent. Ellen Jorth had stuck in his consciousness, and with her a sense of regret.

Then swiftly rang his father's bitter words, the revealing: "But the looks of her an' what she is—they don't gibe!" In the import of these words hid the meaning of the wrong that troubled him. Broodingly he pondered over them.

"The looks of her. Yes, she was pretty. But it didn't dawn on me at first. I—I was sort of excited. I liked to look at her, but didn't think." And now consciously her face was called up, infinitely sweet and more impelling for the deliberate memory. Flash of brown skin, smooth and clear; level gaze of dark, wide eyes, steady, bold, unseeing; red curved lips, sad and sweet; her strong, clean, fine face rose before Jean, eager and wistful one moment, softened by dreamy musing thought, and the next stormily passionate, full of hate, full of longing, but the more mysterious and beautiful.

"She looks like that, but she's bad," concluded Jean, with bitter finality. "I might have fallen in love with Ellen Jorth if—if she'd been different."

But the conviction forced upon Jean did not dispel the haunting memory of her voice nor did it wholly silence the deep and stubborn voice of his consciousness. Later that afternoon he sought a moment with his sister.

"Ann, did you ever meet Ellen Jorth?" he asked.

"Yes, but not lately," replied Ann.

"Well, I met her as I was ridin' along yesterday. She was herdin' sheep," went on Jean, rapidly. "I asked her to show me the way to the Rim. An' she walked with me a mile or

so. I can't say the meetin' was not interestin', at least to me.
. . . Will you tell me what you know about her?"

"Sure, Jean," replied his sister, with her dark eyes fixed
wonderingly and kindly on his troubled face. "I've heard a
great deal, but in this Tonto Basin I don't believe all I hear.
What I know I'll tell you. I first met Ellen Jorth two years
ago. We didn't know each other's names then. She was the
prettiest girl I ever saw. I liked her. She liked me. She seemed
unhappy. The next time we met was at a round-up. There
were other girls with me and they snubbed her. But I left
them and went around with her. That snub cut her to the
heart. She was lonely. She had no friends. She talked about
herself—how she hated the people, but loved Arizona. She
had nothin' fit to wear. I didn't need to be told that she'd
been used to better things. Just when it looked as if we were
goin' to be friends she told me who she was and asked me my
name. I told her. Jean, I couldn't have hurt her more if I'd
slapped her face. She turned white. She gasped. And then
she ran off. The last time I saw her was about a year ago. I
was ridin' a short-cut trail to the ranch where a friend lived.
And I met Ellen Jorth ridin' with a man I'd never seen. The
trail was overgrown and shady. They were ridin' close and
didn't see me right off. The man had his arm round her.
She pushed him away. I saw her laugh. Then he got hold of
her again and was kissin' her when his horse shied at sight
of mine. They rode by me then. Ellen Jorth held her head
high and never looked at me."

"Ann, do you think she's a bad girl?" demanded Jean,
bluntly.

"Bad? Oh, Jean!" exclaimed Ann, in surprise and embarrassment.

"Dad said she was a damned hussy."

"Jean, dad hates the Jorths."

"Sister, I'm askin' you what you think of Ellen Jorth.
Would you be friends with her if you could?"

"Yes."

"Then you don't believe she's bad."

"No. Ellen Jorth is lonely, unhappy. She has no mother.
She lives alone among rough men. Such a girl can't keep men
from handlin' her and kissin' her. Maybe she's too free. Maybe she's wild. But she's honest, Jean. You can trust a
woman to tell. When she rode past me that day her face was
white and proud. She was a Jorth and I was an Isbel. She
hated herself—she hated me. But no bad girl could look like

50

that. She knows what's said of her all around the valley. But she doesn't care. She'd encourage gossip."

"Thank you, Ann," replied Jean, huskily. "Please keep this—this meetin' of mine with her all to yourself, won't you?"

"Why, Jean, of course I will."

Jean wandered away again, peculiarly grateful to Ann for reviving and upholding something in him that seemed a wavering part of the best of him—a chivalry that had demanded to be killed by judgment of a righteous woman. He was conscious of an uplift, a gladdening of his spirit. Yet the ache remained. More than that, he found himself plunged deeper into conjecture, doubt. Had not the Ellen Jorth incident ended? He denied his father's indictment of her and accepted the faith of his sister. "Reckon that's aboot all, as dad says," he soliloquized. Yet was that all? He paced under the cedars. He watched the sun set. He listened to the coyotes. He lingered there after the call for supper; until out of the tumult of his conflicting emotions and ponderings there evolved the staggering consciousness that he must see Ellen Jorth again.

4
★

ELLEN JORTH hurried back into the forest, hotly resentful of the accident that had thrown her in contact with an Isbel.

Disgust filled her—disgust that she had been amiable to a member of the hated family that had ruined her father. The surprise of this meeting did not come to her while she was under the spell of stronger feeling. She walked under the trees, swiftly, with head erect, looking straight before her, and every step seemed a relief.

Upon reaching camp, her attention was distracted from herself. Pepe, the Mexican boy, with the two shepherd dogs, was trying to drive sheep into a closer bunch to save the lambs from coyotes. Ellen loved the fleecy, tottering little lambs, and at this season she hated all the prowling beast of the forest. From this time on for weeks the flock would be besieged by wolves, lions, bears, the last of which were often bold and dangerous. The old grizzlies that killed the ewes to eat only the milk-bags were particularly dreaded by Ellen. She was a good shot with a rifle, but had orders from her father to let the bears alone. Fortunately, such sheep-killing bears were but few, and were left to be hunted by men from the ranch. Mexican sheep herders could not be depended upon to protect their flocks from bears. Ellen helped Pepe drive in the stragglers, and she took several shots at coyotes skulking along the edge of the brush. The open glade in the forest was favorable for herding the sheep at night and the dogs could be depended upon to guard the flock, and in most cases to drive predatory beasts away.

After this task, which brought the time to sunset, Ellen had supper to cook and eat. Darkness came, and a cool night wind set in. Here and there a lamb bleated plaintively. With her work done for the day, Ellen sat before a ruddy camp fire, and found her thoughts again centering around the singular adventure that had befallen her. Disdainfully she strove to think of something else. But there was nothing that could dispel the interest of her meeting with Jean Isbel. Thereupon she impatiently surrendered to it, and recalled every word and action which she could remember. And in the process of this meditation she came to an action of hers, recollection of which brought the blood tingling to her neck and cheeks, so unusually and burningly that she covered them with her hands. "What did he think of me?" she mused, doubtfully. It did not matter what he thought, but she could not help wondering. And when she came to the memory of his kiss she suffered more than the sensation of throbbing scarlet cheeks. Scornfully and bitterly she burst out, "Shore he couldn't have thought much good of me."

The half hour following this reminiscence was far from being pleasant. Proud, passionate, strong-willed Ellen Jorth found herself a victim of conflicting emotions. The event of the day was too close. She could not understand it. Disgust and disdain and scorn could not make this meeting with Jean Isbel as if it had never been. Pride could not efface it from her mind. The more she reflected, the harder she tried to forget, the stronger grew a significance of interest. And when a hint of this dawned upon her consciousness she resented it so forcibly that she lost her temper, scattered the camp fire, and went into the little teepee tent to roll in her blankets.

Thus settled snug and warm for the night, with a shepherd dog curled at the opening of her tent, she shut her eyes and confidently bade sleep end her perplexities. But sleep did not come at her invitation. She found herself wide awake, keenly sensitive to the sputtering of the camp fire, the tinkling of bells on the rams, the bleating of lambs, the sough of wind in the pines, and the hungry sharp bark of coyotes off in the distance. Darkness was no respecter of her pride. The lonesome night with its emphasis of solitude seemed to induce clamoring and strange thoughts, a confusing ensemble of all those that had annoyed her during the daytime. Not for long hours did sheer weariness bring her to slumber.

Ellen awakened late and failed of her usual alacrity. Both Pepe and the shepherd dog appeared to regard her with surprise and solicitude. Ellen's spirit was low this morning; her blood ran sluggishly; she had to fight a mournful tendency to feel sorry for herself. And at first she was not very successful. There seemed to be some kind of pleasure in reveling in melancholy which her common sense told her had no reason for existence. But states of mind persisted in spite of common sense.

"Pepe, when is Antonio comin' back?" she asked.

The boy could not give her a satisfactory answer. Ellen had willingly taken the sheep herder's place for a few days, but now she was impatient to go home. She looked down the green-and-brown aisles of the forest until she was tired. Antonio did not return. Ellen spent the day with the sheep; and in the manifold task of caring for a thousand new-born lambs she forgot herself. This day saw the end of lambing-time for that season. The forest resounded to a babel of baas and bleats. When night came she was glad to go to bed, for what with loss of sleep, and weariness she could scarcely keep her eyes open.

The following morning she awakened early, bright, eager, expectant, full of bounding life, strangely aware of the beauty and sweetness of the scented forest, strangely conscious of some nameless stimulus to her feelings.

Not long was Ellen in associating this new and delightful variety of sensations with the fact that Jean Isbel had set to-day for his ride up to the Rim to see her. Ellen's joyousness fled; her smiles faded. The spring morning lost its magic radiance.

"Shore there's no sense in my lyin' to myself," she soli-

53

loquized, thoughtfully. "It's queer of me—feelin' glad aboot him—without knowin'. Lord! I must be lonesome! To be glad of seein' an Isbel, even if he is different!"

Soberly she accepted the astounding reality. Her confidence died with her gayety; her vanity began to suffer. And she caught at her admission that Jean Isbel was different; she resented it in amaze; she ridiculed it; she laughed at her naïve confession. She could arrive at no conclusion other than that she was a weak-minded, fluctuating, inexplicable little fool.

But for all that she found her mind had been made up for her, without consent or desire, before her will had been consulted; and that inevitably and unalterably she meant to see Jean Isbel again. Long she battled with this strange decree. One moment she won a victory over this new curious self, only to lose it the next. And at last out of her conflict there emerged a few convictions that left her with some shreds of pride. She hated all Isbels, she hated any Isbel, and particularly she hated Jean Isbel. She was only curious—intensely curious to see if he would come back, and if he did come what he would do. She wanted only to watch him from some covert. She would not go near him, not let him see her or guess of her presence. Thus she assuaged her hurt vanity—thus she stifled her miserable doubts.

Long before the sun had begun to slant westward toward the mid-afternoon Jean Isbel had set as a meeting time Ellen directed her steps through the forest to the Rim. She felt ashamed of her eagerness. She had a guilty conscience that no strange thrills could silence. It would be fun to see him, to watch him, to let him wait for her, to fool him.

Like an Indian, she chose the soft pine-needle mats to tread upon, and her light-moccasined feet left no trace. Like an Indian also she made a wide detour, and reached the Rim a quarter of a mile west of the spot where she had talked with Jean Isbel; and here, turning east, she took care to step on the bare stones. This was an adventure, seemingly the first she had ever had in her life. Assuredly she had never before come directly to the Rim without halting to look, to wonder, to worship. This time she scarcely glanced into the blue abyss. All absorbed was she in hiding her tracks. Not one chance in a thousand would she risk. The Jorth pride burned even while the feminine side of her dominated her actions. She had some difficult rocky points to cross, then windfalls to round, and at length reached the covert she desired. A rugged yellow point of the Rim stood somewhat higher than the spot Ellen wanted to watch. A dense thicket of jack pines grew to the very edge. It afforded an ambush that even the Indian eyes Jean Isbel was credited with could never penetrate. Moreover, if by accident she made a noise and excited suspicion, she could retreat unobserved and hide in the huge rocks below the Rim, where a ferret could not locate her.

With her plan decided upon, Ellen had nothing to do but wait, so she repaired to the other side of the pine thicket and to the edge of the Rim where she could watch and listen. She knew that long before she saw Isbel she would hear his horse. It was altogether unlikely that he would come on foot.

"Shore, Ellen Jorth, y'u're a queer girl," she mused. "I reckon I wasn't well acquainted with y'u."

Beneath her yawned a wonderful deep cañon, rugged and rocky with but few pines on the north slope, thick with dark green timber on the south slope. Yellow and gray crags, like turreted castles, stood up out of the sloping forest on the side opposite her. The trees were all sharp, spear pointed. Patches of light green aspens showed strikingly against the dense black. The great slope beneath Ellen was serrated with narrow, deep gorges, almost cañons in themselves. Shadows alternated with clear bright spaces. The mile-wide mouth of the cañon opened upon the Basin, down into a world of wild timbered ranges and ravines, valleys and hills, that rolled and tumbled in dark-green waves to the Sierra Anchas.

But for once Ellen seemed singularly unresponsive to this panorama of wildness and grandeur. Her ears were like those of a listening deer, and her eyes continually reverted to the open places along the Rim. At first, in her excitement, time flew by. Gradually, however, as the sun moved westward, she began to be restless. The soft thud of dropping pine cones, the rustling of squirrels up and down the shaggy-barked spruces, the cracking of weathered bits of rock, these caught her keen ears many times and brought her up erect and thrilling. Finally she heard a sound which resembled that of an unshod hoof on stone. Stealthily then she took her rifle and slipped back through the pine thicket to the spot she had chosen. The little pines were so close together that she had to crawl between their trunks. The ground was covered with a soft bed of pine needles, brown and fragrant.

In her hurry she pricked her ungloved hand on a sharp pine cone and drew the blood. She sucked the tiny wound. "Shore I'm wonderin' if that's a bad omen," she muttered, darkly thoughtful. Then she resumed her sinuous approach to the edge of the thicket, and presently reached it.

Ellen lay flat a moment to recover her breath, then raised herself on her elbows. Through an opening in the fringe of buck brush she could plainly see the promontory where she had stood with Jean Isbel, and also the approaches by which he might come. Rather nervously she realized that her covert was hardly more than a hundred feet from the promontory. It was imperative that she be absolutely silent. Her eyes searched the openings along the Rim. The gray form of a deer crossed one of these, and she concluded it had made the sound she had heard. Then she lay down more comfortably and waited. Resolutely she held, as much as possible, to her sensorial perceptions. The meaning of Ellen Jorth lying in ambush just to see an Isbel was a conundrum she refused to ponder in the present. She was doing it, and the physical act had its fascination. Her ears, attuned to all the sounds of the lonely forest, caught them and arranged them according to her knowledge of woodcraft.

A long hour passed by. The sun had slanted to a point halfway between the zenith and the horizon. Suddenly a thought confronted Ellen Jorth: "He's not comin'," she whispered. The instant that idea presented itself she felt a blank sense of loss, a vague regret—something that must have been disappointment. Unprepared for this, she was held by surprise for a moment, and then she was stunned. Her spirit, swift and rebellious, had no time to rise in her defense. She was a lonely, guilty, miserable girl, too weak for pride to uphold, too fluctuating to know her real self. She stretched there, burying her face in the pine needles, digging her fingers into them, wanting nothing so much as that they might hide her. The moment was incomprehensible to Ellen, and utterly intolerable. The sharp pine needles, piercing her wrists and cheeks, and her hot heaving breast, seemed to give her exquisite relief.

The shrill snort of a horse sounded near at hand. With a shock Ellen's body stiffened. Then she quivered a little and her feelings underwent swift change. Cautiously and noiselessly she raised herself upon her elbows and peeped through the opening in the brush. She saw a man tying a horse to a bush somewhat back from the Rim. Drawing a rifle from its saddle sheath he threw it in the hollow of his arm and walked to the edge of the precipice. He gazed away across the Basin and appeared lost in contemplation or thought. Then he turned to look back into the forest, as if he expected some one.

Ellen recognized the lithe figure, the dark face so like an Indian's. It was Isbel. He had come. Somehow his coming seemed wonderful and terrible. Ellen shook as she leaned on her elbows. Jean Isbel, true to his word, in spite of her scorn, had come back to see her. The fact seemed monstrous. He was an enemy of her father. Long had range rumor been bandied from lip to lip—old Gass Isbel had sent for his Indian son to fight the Jorths. Jean Isbel—son of a Texan— unerring shot—peerless tracker—a bad and dangerous man! Then there flashed over Ellen a burning thought—if it were true, if he was an enemy of her father's, if a fight between Jorth and Isbel was inevitable, she ought to kill this Jean Isbel right there in his tracks as he boldly and confidently waited for her. Fool he was to think she would come. Ellen sank down and dropped her head until the strange tremor of her arms ceased. That dark and grim flash of thought retreated. She had not come to murder a man from ambush, but only to watch him, to try to see what he meant, what he thought, to allay a strange curiosity.

After a while she looked again. Isbel was sitting on an upheaved section of the Rim, in a comfortable position from which he could watch the openings in the forest and gaze as well across the west curve of the Basin to the Mazatzals. He had composed himself to wait. He was clad in a buckskin suit, rather new, and it certainly showed off to advantage, compared with the ragged and soiled apparel Ellen remembered. He did not look so large. Ellen was used to the long, lean, rangy Arizonians and Texans. This man was built differently. He had the widest shoulders of any man she had ever seen, and they made him appear rather short. But his lithe, powerful limbs proved he was not short. Whenever he moved the muscles rippled. His hands were clasped round a knee—brown, sinewy hands, very broad, and fitting the thick muscular wrists. His collar was open, and he did not wear a scarf, as did the men Ellen knew. Then her intense curiosity at last brought her steady gaze to Jean Isbel's head and face. He wore a cap, evidently of some thin fur. His hair was straight and short, and in color a dead raven black. His complexion was dark, clear tan, with no trace of red.

57

He did not have the prominent cheek bones nor the high-bridged nose usual with white men who were part Indian. Still he had the Indian look. Ellen caught that in the dark, intent, piercing eyes, in the wide, level, thoughtful brows, in the stern impassiveness of his smooth face. He had a straight, sharp-cut profile.

Ellen whispered to herself: "I saw him right the other day. Only, I'd not admit it. . . . The finest-lookin' man I ever saw in my life is a damned Isbel! . . . Was that what I come out heah for?"

She lowered herself once more and, folding her arms under her breast, she reclined comfortably on them, and searched out a smaller peephole from which she could spy upon Isbel. And as she watched him the new and perplexing side of her mind waxed busier. Why had he come back? What did he want of her? Acquaintance, friendship, was impossible for them. He had been respectful, deferential toward her, in a way that had strangely pleased, until the surprising moment when he had kissed her. That had only disrupted her rather dreamy pleasure in a situation she had not experienced before. All the men she had met in his wild country were rough and bold; most of them had wanted to marry her, and, failing that, they had persisted in amorous attentions not particularly flattering or honorable. They were a bad lot. And contact with them had dulled some of her sensibilities. But this Jean Isbel had seemed a gentleman. She struggled to be fair, trying to forget her antipathy, as much to understand herself as to give him due credit. True, he had kissed her, crudely and forcibly. But that kiss had not been an insult. Ellen's finer feeling forced her to believe this. She remembered the honest amaze and shame and contrition with which he had faced her, trying awkwardly to explain his bold act. Likewise she recalled the subtle swift change in him at her words, "Oh, I've been kissed before!" She was glad she had said that. Still—was she glad, after all?

She watched him. Every little while he shifted his gaze from the blue gulf beneath him to the forest. When he turned thus the sun shone on his face and she caught the piercing gleam of his dark eyes. She saw, too, that he was listening. Watching and listening for her! Ellen had to still a tumult within her. It made her feel very young, very shy, very strange. All the while she hated him because he manifestly expected her to come. Several times he rose and walked a little way into the woods. The last time he looked at the westering sun and shook his head. His confidence had gone. Then he sat and gazed down into the void. But Ellen knew he did not see anything there. He seemed an image carved in the stone of the Rim, and he gave Ellen a singular impression of loneliness and sadness. Was he thinking of the miserable battle his father had summoned him to lead—of what it would cost—of its useless pain and hatred? Ellen seemed to divine his thoughts. In that moment she softened toward him, and in her soul quivered and stirred an intangible something that was like pain, that was too deep for her understanding. But she felt sorry for an Isbel until the old pride resurged. What if he admired her? She remembered his interest, the wonder and admiration, the growing light in his eyes. And it had not been repugnant to her until he disclosed his name. "What's in a name?" she mused, recalling poetry learned in her girlhood. " 'A rose by any other name would smell as sweet'. . . . He's an Isbel—yet he might be splendid—noble. . . . Bah! he's not—and I'd hate him anyhow."

All at once Ellen felt cold shivers steal over her. Isbel's piercing gaze was directed straight at her hiding place. Her heart stopped beating. If he discovered her there she felt that she would die of shame. Then she became aware that a blue jay was screeching in a pine above her, and a red squirrel somewhere near was chattering his shrill annoyance. These two denizens of the woods could be depended upon to espy the wariest hunter and make known his presence to their kind. Ellen had a moment of more than dread. This keeneyed, keen-eared Indian might see right through her brushy covert, might hear the throbbing of her heart. It relieved her immeasurably to see him turn away and take to pacing the promontory, with his head bowed and his hands behind his back. He had stopped looking off into the forest. Presently he wheeled to the west, and by the light upon his face Ellen saw that the time was near sunset. Turkeys were beginning to gobble back on the ridge.

Isbel walked to his horse and appeared to be untying something from the back of his saddle. When he came back Ellen saw that he carried a small package apparently wrapped in paper. With this under his arm he strode off in the direction of Ellen's camp and soon disappeared in the forest.

For a little while Ellen lay there in bewilderment. If she had made conjectures before, they were now multiplied. Where was Jean Isbel going? Ellen sat up suddenly. "Well, shore this heah beats me," she said. "What did he have in that package? What was he goin' to do with it?"

It took no little will power to hold her there when she wanted to steal after him through the woods and find out what he meant. But his reputation influenced even her and she refused to pit her cunning in the forest against his. It would be better to wait until he returned to his horse. Thus decided, she lay back again in her covert and gave her mind over to pondering curiosity. Sooner than she expected she espied Isbel approaching through the forest, empty handed. He had not taken his rifle. Ellen averted her glance a moment and thrilled to see the rifle leaning against a rock. Verily Jean Isbel had been far removed from hostile intent that day. She watched him stride swiftly up to his horse, untie the halter, and mount. Ellen had an impression of his arrowlike straight figure, and sinuous grace and ease. Then he looked back at the promontory, as if to fix a picture of it in his mind, and rode away along the Rim. She watched him out of sight. What ailed her? Something was wrong with her, but she recognized only relief.

When Isbel had been gone long enough to assure Ellen that she might safely venture forth she crawled through the pine thicket to the Rim on the other side of the point. The sun was setting behind the Black Range, shedding a golden glory over the Basin. Westward the zigzag Rim reached like a streamer of fire into the sun. The vast promontories jutted out with blazing beacon lights upon their stone-walled faces. Deep down, the Basin was turning shadowy dark blue, going to sleep for the night.

Ellen bent swift steps toward her camp. Long shafts of gold preceded her through the forest. Then they paled and vanished. The tips of pines and spruces turned gold. A hoarse-voiced old turkey gobbler was booming his chug-a-lug from the highest ground, and the softer chick of hen turkeys answered him. Ellen was almost breathless when she arrived. Two packs and a couple of lop-eared burros attested to the fact of Antonio's return. This was good news for Ellen. She heard the bleat of lambs and tinkle of bells coming nearer and nearer. And she was glad to feel that if Isbel had visited her camp, most probably it was during the absence of the herders.

The instant she glanced into her tent she saw the package Isbel had carried. It lay on her bed. Ellen stared blankly. "The —the impudence of him!" she ejaculated. Then she kicked the package out of the tent. Words and action seemed to liberate a dammed-up hot fury. She kicked the package again, and thought she would kick it into the smoldering camp-fire. But somehow she stopped short of that. She left the thing there on the ground.

Pepe and Antonio hove in sight, driving in the tumbling woolly flock. Ellen did not want them to see the package, so with contempt for herself, and somewhat lessening anger, she kicked it back into the tent. What was in it? She peeped inside the tent, devoured by curiosity. Neat, well wrapped and tied packages like that were not often seen in the Tonto Basin. Ellen decided she would wait until after supper, and at a favorable moment lay it unopened on the fire. What did she care what it contained? Manifestly it was a gift. She argued that she was highly incensed with this insolent Isbel who had the effrontery to approach her with some sort of present.

It developed that the usually cheerful Antonio had returned taciturn and gloomy. All Ellen could get out of him was that the job of sheep herder had taken on hazards inimical to peace-loving Mexicans. He had heard something he would not tell. Ellen helped prepare the supper and she ate in silence. She had her own brooding troubles. Antonio presently told her that her father had said she was not to start back home after dark. After supper the herders repaired to their own tents, leaving Ellen the freedom of her camp-fire. Wherewith she secured the package and brought it forth to burn. Feminine curiosity rankled strong in her breast. Yielding so far as to shake the parcel and press it, and finally tear a corner off the paper, she saw some words written in lead pencil. Bending nearer the blaze, she read, "For my sister Ann." Ellen gazed at the big, bold handwriting, quite legible and fairly well done. Suddenly she tore the outside wrapper completely off. From printed words on the inside she gathered that the package had come from a store in San Francisco. "Reckon he fetched home a lot of presents for his folks—the kids—and his sister," muttered Ellen. "That was nice of him. Whatever this is he shore meant it for sister Ann. . . . Ann Isbel. Why, she must be that black-eyed girl I met and liked so well before I knew she was an Isbel. . . . His sister!"

Whereupon for the second time Ellen deposited the fascinating package in her tent. She could not burn it up just then. She had other emotions besides scorn and hate. And memory of that soft-voiced, kind-hearted, beautiful Isbel girl checked

61

her resentment. "I wonder if he is like his sister," she said, thoughtfully. It appeared to be an unfortunate thought. Jean Isbel certainly resembled his sister. "Too bad they belong to the family that ruined dad."

Ellen went to bed without opening the package or without burning it. And to her annoyance, whatever way she lay she appeared to touch this strange package. There was not much room in the little tent. First she put it at her head beside her rifle, but when she turned over her cheek came in contact with it. Then she felt as if she had been stung. She moved it again, only to touch it presently with her hand. Next she flung it to the bottom of her bed, where it fell upon her feet, and whatever way she moved them she could not escape the pressure of this undesirable and mysterious gift.

By and by she fell asleep, only to dream that the package was a caressing hand stealing about her, feeling for hers, and holding it with soft, strong clasp. When she awoke she had the strangest sensation in her right palm. It was moist, throbbing, hot, and the feel of it on her cheek was strangely thrilling and comforting. She lay awake then. The night was dark and still. Only a low moan of wind in the pines and the faint tinkle of a sheep bell broke the serenity. She felt very small and lonely lying there in the deep forest, and, try how she would, it was impossible to think the same then as she did in the clear light of day. Resentment, pride, anger—these seemed abated now. If the events of the day had not changed her, they had at least brought up softer and kinder memories and emotions than she had known for long. Nothing hurt and saddened her so much as to remember the gay, happy days of her childhood, her sweet mother, her old home. Then her thought returned to Isbel and his gift. It had been years since anyone had made her a gift. What could this one be? It did not matter. The wonder was that Jean Isbel should bring it to her and that she could be perturbed by its presence. "He meant it for his sister and so he thought well of me," she said, in finality.

Morning brought Ellen further vacillation. At length she rolled the obnoxious package inside her blankets, saying that she would wait until she got home and then consign it cheerfully to the flames. Antonio tied her pack on a burro. She did not have a horse, and therefore had to walk the several miles to her father's ranch.

She set off at a brisk pace, leading the burro and carrying her rifle. And soon she was deep in the fragrant forest.

62

The morning was clear and cool, with just enough frost to make the sunlit grass sparkle as if with diamonds. Ellen felt fresh, buoyant, singularly full of life. Her youth would not be denied. It was pulsing, yearning. She hummed an old Southern tune and every step seemed one of pleasure in action, of advance toward some intangible future happiness. All the unknown of life before her called. Her heart beat high in her breast and she walked as one in a dream. Her thoughts were swift-changing, intimate, deep, and vague, not of yesterday or to-day, nor of reality.

The big, gray, white-tailed squirrels crossed ahead of her on the trail, scampered over the piny ground to hop on tree trunks, and there they paused to watch her pass. The vociferous little red squirrels barked and chattered at her. From every thicket sounded the gobble of turkeys. The blue jays squalled in the tree tops. A deer lifted its head from browsing and stood motionless, with long ears erect, watching her go by.

Thus happily and dreamily absorbed, Ellen covered the forest miles and soon reached the trail that led down into the wild brakes of Chevelon Cañon. It was rough going and less conducive to sweet wanderings of mind. Ellen slowly lost them. And then a familiar feeling assailed her, one she never failed to have upon returning to her father's ranch —a reluctance, a bitter dissatisfaction with her home, a loyal struggle against the vague sense that all was not as it should be.

At the head of this cañon in a little, level, grassy meadow stood a rude one-room log shack, with a leaning red-stone chimney on the outside. This was the abode of a strange old man who had long lived there. His name was John Sprague and his occupation was raising burros. No sheep or cattle or horses did he own, not even a dog. Rumor had said Sprague was a prospector, one of the many who had searched that country for the Lost Dutchman gold mine. Sprague knew more about the Basin and Rim than any of the sheepmen or ranchers. From Black Butte to the Cibique and from Chevelon Butte to Reno Pass he knew every trail, cañon, ridge, and spring, and could find his way to them on the darkest night. His fame, however, depended mostly upon the fact that he did nothing but raise burros, and would raise none but black burros with white faces. These burros were the finest bred in all the Basin and were in great demand. Sprague sold a few every year. He had made a present of one to Ellen, although he hated to part with them. This old man was Ellen's one and only friend.

Upon her trip out to the Rim with the sheep, Uncle John, as Ellen called him, had been away on one of his infrequent visits to Grass Valley. It pleased her now to see a blue column of smoke lazily lifting from the old chimney and to hear the discordant bray of burros. As she entered the clearing Sprague saw her from the door of his shack.

"Hello, Uncle John!" she called.

"Wal, if it ain't Ellen!" he replied, heartily. "When I seen thet white-faced jinny I knowed who was leadin' her. Where you been, girl?"

Sprague was a little, stoop-shouldered old man, with grizzled head and face, and shrewd gray eyes that beamed kindly on her over his ruddy cheeks. Ellen did not like the tobacco stain on his grizzled beard nor the dirty, motley, ragged, ill-smelling garb he wore, but she had ceased her useless attempts to make him more cleanly.

"I've been herdin' sheep," replied Ellen. "And where have y'u been, uncle? I missed y'u on the way over."

"Been packin' in some grub. An' I reckon I stayed longer in Grass Valley than I recollect. But thet was only natural, considerin'—"

"What?" asked Ellen, bluntly, as the old man paused.

Sprague took a black pipe out of his vest pocket and began rimming the bowl with his fingers. The glance he bent on Ellen was thoughtful and earnest, and so kind that she feared it was pity. Ellen suddenly burned for news from the village.

"Wal, come in an' set down, won't you?" he asked.

"No, thanks," replied Ellen, and she took a seat on the chopping block. "Tell me, uncle, what's goin' on down in the Valley?"

"Nothin' much yet—except talk. An' there's a heap of thet."

"Humph! There always was talk," declared Ellen, contemptuously. "A nasty, gossipy, catty hole, that Grass Valley!"

"Ellen, thar's goin' to be war—a bloody war in the ole Tonto Basin," went on Sprague, seriously.

"War! . . . Between whom?"

"The Isbels an' their enemies. I reckon most people down thar, an' sure all the cattlemen, air on old Gass's side. Blaisdell, Gordon, Fredericks, Blue—they'll all be in it."

64

"Who are they goin' to fight?" queried Ellen, sharply.

"Wal, the open talk is thet the sheepmen are forcin' this war. But thar's talk not so open, an' I reckon not very healthy for any man to whisper hyarbouts."

"Uncle John, y'u needn't be afraid to tell me anythin'," said Ellen. "I'd never give y'u away. Y'u've been a good friend to me."

"Reckon I want to be, Ellen," he returned, nodding his shaggy head. "It ain't easy to be fond of you as I am an' keep my mouth shet. . . . I'd like to know somethin'. Hev you any relatives away from hyar thet you could go to till this fight's over?"

"No. All I have, so far as I know, are right heah."

"How aboot friends?"

"Uncle John, I have none," she said, sadly, with bowed head.

"Wal, wal, I'm sorry. I was hopin' you might git away."

She lifted her face. "Shore y'u don't think I'd run off if my dad got in a fight?" she flashed.

"I hope you will."

"I'm a Jorth," she said, darkly, and dropped her head again.

Sprague nodded gloomily. Evidently he was perplexed and worried, and strongly swayed by affection for her.

"Would you go away with me?" he asked. "We could pack over to the Mazatzals an' live thar till this blows over."

"Thank y'u, Uncle John. Y'u're kind and good. But I'll stay with my father. His troubles are mine."

"Ahuh! . . . Wal, I might hev reckoned so. . . . Ellen, how do you stand on this hyar sheep an' cattle question?"

"I think what's fair for one is fair for another. I don't like sheep as much as I like cattle. But that's not the point. The range is free. Suppose y'u had cattle and I had sheep. I'd feel as free to run my sheep anywhere as y'u were to run your cattle."

"Right. But what if you throwed your sheep round my range an' sheeped off the grass so my cattle would hev to move or starve?"

"Shore I wouldn't throw my sheep round y'ur range," she declared, stoutly.

"Wal, you've answered half of the question. An' now supposin' a lot of my cattle was stolen by rustlers, but not a single one of your sheep. What'd you think then?"

65

"I'd shore think rustlers chose to steal cattle because there was no profit in stealin' sheep."

"Egzactly. But wouldn't you hev a queer idee aboot it?"

"I don't know. Why queer? What're y'u drivin' at, Uncle John?"

"Wal, wouldn't you git kind of a hunch thet the rustlers was—say a leetle friendly toward the sheepmen?"

Ellen felt a sudden vibrating shock. The blood rushed to her temples. Trembling all over, she rose.

"Uncle John!" she cried.

"Now, girl, you needn't fire up thet way. Set down an' don't—"

"Dare y'u insinuate my father has—"

"Ellen, I ain't insinuatin' nothin'," interrupted the old man. "I'm jest askin' you to think. Thet's all. You're 'most grown into a young woman now. An' you've got sense. Thar's bad times ahead, Ellen. An' I hate to see you mix in them."

"Oh, y'u do make me think," replied Ellen, with smarting tears in her eyes. "Y'u make me unhappy. Oh, I know my dad is not liked in this cattle country. But it's unjust. He happened to go in for sheep raising. I wish he hadn't. It was a mistake. Dad always was a cattleman till we came heah. He made enemies—who—who ruined him. And everywhere misfortune crossed his trail. . . . But, oh, Uncle John, my dad is an honest man."

"Wal, child, I—I didn't mean to—to make you cry," said the old man, feelingly, and he averted his troubled gaze. "Never mind what I said. I'm an old meddler. I reckon nothin' I could do or say would ever change what's goin' to happen. If only you wasn't a girl! . . . Thar I go ag'in. Ellen, face your future an' fight your way. All youngsters hev to do thet. An' it's the right kind of fight thet makes the right kind of man or woman. Only you must be sure to find yourself. An' by thet I mean to find the real, true, honest-to-God best in you an' stick to it an' die fightin' for it. You're a young woman, almost, an' a blamed handsome one. Which means you'll hev more trouble an' a harder fight. This country ain't easy on a woman when once slander has marked her."

"What do I care for the talk down in that Basin?" returned Ellen. "I know they think I'm a hussy. I've let them think it. I've helped them to."

"You're wrong, child," said Sprague, earnestly. "Pride an'

66

temper! You must never let anyone think bad of you, much less help them to."

"I hate everybody down there," cried Ellen, passionately. "I hate them so I'd glory in their thinkin' me bad. . . . My mother belonged to the best blood in Texas. I am her daughter. I know *who and what I am.* That uplifts me whenever I meet the sneaky, sly suspicions of these Basin people. It shows me the difference between them and me. That's what I glory in."

"Ellen, you're a wild, headstrong child," rejoined the old man, in severe tones. "Word has been passed ag'in' your good name—your honor. . . . An' hevn't you given cause fer thet?"

Ellen felt her face blanch and all her blood rush back to her heart in sickening force. The shock of his words was like a stab from a cold blade. If their meaning and the stern, just light of the old man's glance did not kill her pride and vanity they surely killed her girlishness. She stood mute, staring at him, with her brown, trembling hands stealing up toward her bosom, as if to ward off another and a mortal blow.

"Ellen!" burst out Sprague, hoarsely. "You mistook me. Aw, I didn't mean—what you think, I swear. . . . Ellen, I'm old an' blunt. I ain't used to wimmen. But I've love for you, child, an' respect, jest the same as if you was my own. . . . An' I *know* you're good. . . . Forgive me. . . . I meant only hevn't you been, say, sort of—careless?"

"Care-less?" queried Ellen, bitterly and low.

"An' powerful thoughtless an'—an' blind—lettin' men kiss you an' fondle you—when you're really a growed-up woman now?"

"Yes—I have," whispered Ellen.

"Wal, then, why did you let them?"

"I—I don't know. . . . I didn't think. The men never let me alone—never—never! I got tired everlastingly pushin' them away. And sometimes—when they were kind—and I was lonely for something I—I didn't mind if one or another fooled round me. I never thought. It never looked as y'u have made it look. . . . Then—those few times ridin' the trail to Grass Valley—when people saw me—then I guess I encouraged such attentions. . . . Oh, I must be—I am a shameless little hussy!"

"Hush thet kind of talk," said the old man, as he took her hand. "Ellen, you're only young an' lonely an' bitter. No mother—no friends—no one but a lot of rough men! It's a wonder you hev kept yourself good. But now your eyes are open, Ellen. They're brave an' beautiful eyes, girl, an' if you stand by the light in them you will come through any trouble. An' you'll be happy. Don't ever forgit that. Life is hard enough, God knows, but it's unfailin' true in the end to the man or woman who finds the best in them an' stands by it."

"Uncle John, y'u talk so—so kindly. Y'u make me have hope. There seemed really so little for me to live for—hope for. . . . But I'll never be a coward again—nor a thoughtless fool. I'll find some good in me—or make some—and never fail it, come what will. I'll remember your words. I'll believe the future holds wonderful things for me. . . . I'm only eighteen. Shore all my life won't be lived heah. Perhaps this threatened fight over sheep and cattle will blow over. . . . Somewhere there must be some nice girl to be a friend—a sister to me. . . . And maybe some man who'd believe, in spite of all they say—that I'm not a hussy."

"Wal, Ellen, you remind me of what I was wantin' to tell you when you just got here. . . . Yestiddy I heerd you called thet name in a barroom. An' thar was a fellar thar who raised hell. He near killed one man an' made another plumb eat his words. An' he scared thet crowd stiff."

Old John Sprague shook his grizzled head and laughed, beaming upon Ellen as if the memory of what he had seen had warmed his heart.

"Was it—y'u?" asked Ellen, tremulously.

"Me? Aw, I wasn't nowhere. Ellen, this fellar was quick as a cat in his actions an' his words was like lightnin'."

"Who?" she whispered.

"Wal, no one else but a stranger jest come to these parts —an Isbel, too. Jean Isbel."

"Oh!" exclaimed Ellen, faintly.

"In a barroom full of men—almost all of them in sympathy with the sheep crowd—most of them on the Jorth side—this Jean Isbel resented an insult to Ellen Jorth."

"No!" cried Ellen. Something terrible was happening to her mind or her heart.

"Wal, he sure did," replied the old man, "an' it's goin' to be good fer you to hear all about it."

68

5

★

OLD John Sprague launched into his narrative with evident zest.

"I hung round Greaves' store most of two days. An' I heerd a heap. Some of it was jest plain ole men's gab, but I reckon I got the drift of things concernin' Grass Valley. Yestiddy mornin' I was packin' my burros in Greaves's back yard, takin' my time carryin' out supplies from the store. An' at last when I went in I seen a strange fellar was thar. Strappin' young man—not so young, either—an' he had on buckskin. Hair black as my burros, dark face, sharp eyes—you'd took him fer an Injun. He carried a rifle—one of them new forty-fours—an' also somethin' wrapped in paper thet he seemed partickler careful about. He wore a belt round his middle an' thar was a bowie-knife in it, carried like I've seen scouts an' Injun fighters hev on the frontier in the 'seventies. That looked queer to me, an' I reckon to the rest of the crowd thar. No one overlooked the big six-shooter he packed Texas fashion. Wal, I didn't hev no idee this fellar was an Isbel until I heard Greaves call him thet.

" 'Isbel,' said Greaves, 'reckon your money's counterfeit hyar. I cain't sell you anythin'.'

" 'Counterfeit? Not much,' spoke up the young fellar, an' he flipped some gold twenties on the bar, where they rung like bells. 'Why not? Ain't this a store? I want a cinch strap.'

"Greaves looked particular sour thet mornin'. I'd been watchin' him fer two days. He hedn't hed much sleep, fer I hed my bed back of the store, an' I heerd men come in the night an' hev long confabs with him. Whatever was in the wind hedn't pleased him none. An' I calkilated thet young Isbel wasn't a sight good fer Greaves' sore eyes, anyway. But he paid no more attention to Isbel. Acted jest as if he hedn't heerd Isbel say he wanted a cinch strap.

69

"I stayed inside the store then. Thar was a lot of fellars I'd seen, an' some I knowed. Couple of card games goin', an' drinkin', of course. I soon gathered thet the general atmosphere wasn't friendly to Jean Isbel. He seen thet quick enough, but he didn't leave. Between you an' me I sort of took a likin' to him. An' I sure watched him as close as I could, not seemin' to, you know. Reckon they all did the same, only you couldn't see it. It got jest about the same as if Isbel hedn't been in thar, only you knowed it wasn't really the same. Thet was how I got the hunch the crowd was all sheepmen or their friends. The day before I'd heerd a lot of talk about this young Isbel, an' what he'd come to Grass Valley fer, an' what a bad hombre he was. An' when I seen him I was bound to admit he looked his reputation.

"Wal, pretty soon in come two more fellars, an' I knowed both of them. You know them, too, I'm sorry to say. Fer I'm comin' to facts now thet will shake you. The first fellar was your father's Mexican foreman, Lorenzo, and the other was Simm Bruce. I reckon Bruce wasn't drunk, but he'd sure been lookin' on red licker. When he seen Isbel darn me if he didn't swell an' bustle all up like a mad ole turkey gobbler.

" 'Greaves,' he said, 'if thet fellar's Jean Isbel I ain't hankerin' fer the company y'u keep.' An' he made no bones of pointin' right at Isbel. Greaves looked up dry an' sour an' he bit out spiteful-like: 'Wal, Simm, we ain't hed a hell of a lot of choice in this heah matter. That's Jean Isbel shore enough. Mebbe you can persuade him thet his company an' his custom ain't wanted round heah!'

"Jean Isbel set on the counter an' took it all in, but he didn't say nothin'. The way he looked at Bruce was sure enough fer me to see thet thar might be a surprise any minnit. I've looked at a lot of men in my day, an' can sure feel events comin'. Bruce got himself a stiff drink an' then he straddles over the floor in front of Isbel.

" 'Air you Jean Isbel, son of ole Gass Isbel?' asked Bruce, sort of lolling back an' givin' a hitch to his belt.

" 'Yes sir, you've identified me,' said Isbel, nice an' polite.

" 'My name's Bruce. I'm rangin' sheep heahaboots, an' I hev interest in Kurnel Lee Jorth's bizness.'

" 'Hod do, Mister Bruce,' replied Isbel, very civil an' cool as you please. Bruce hed an eye fer the crowd thet was now listenin' an' watchin'. He swaggered closer to Isbel.

" 'We heerd y'u come into the Tonto Basin to run us sheepmen off the range. How aboot thet?'

" 'Wal, you heerd wrong,' said Isbel, quietly. 'I came to work fer my father. Thet work depends on what happens.'

"Bruce began to git redder of face, an' he shook a husky hand in front of Isbel. 'I'll tell y'u this heah, my Nez Perce Isbel—' an' when he sort of choked fer more wind Greaves spoke up, 'Simm, I shore reckon thet Nez Perce handle will stick.' An' the crowd haw-hawed. Then Bruce got goin' ag'in. 'I'll tell y'u this heah, Nez Perce. Thar's been enough happen already to run y'u out of Arizona.'

" 'Wal, you don't say! What, fer instance?' asked Isbel, quick an' sarcastic.

"Thet made Bruce bust out puffin' an' spittin': 'Wha-tt, fer instance? Huh! Why, y'u dam half-breed, y'u'll git run out fer makin' up to Ellen Jorth. Thet won't go in this heah country. Not fer any Isbel.'

" 'You're a liar,' called Isbel an' like a big cat he dropped off the counter. I heerd his moccasins pat soft on the floor. An' I bet to myself thet he was as dangerous as he was quick. But his voice an' his looks didn't change even a leetle.

" 'I'm not a liar,' yelled Bruce. 'I'll make y'u eat thet. I can prove what I say. . . . Y'u was seen with Ellen Jorth—up on the Rim—day before yestiddy. Y'u was watched. Y'u was with her. Y'u made up to her. Y'u grabbed her an' kissed her! . . . An' I'm heah to say, Nez Perce, thet y'u're a marked man on this range.'

" 'Who saw me?' asked Isbel, quiet an' cold. I seen then thet he'd turned white in the face.

" 'Yu cain't lie out of it,' hollered Bruce, wavin' his hands. 'We got y'u daid to rights. Lorenzo saw y'u—follered y'u —watched y'u.' Bruce pointed at the grinnin' greaser. 'Lorenzo is Kurnel Jorth's foreman. He seen y'u maulin' of Ellen Jorth. An' when he tells the Kurnel an' Tad Jorth an' Jackson Jorth! . . . Haw! Haw! Haw! Why, hell'd be a cooler place fer yu then this heah Tonto.'

"Greaves an' his gang hed come round, sure tickled clean to thar gizzards at this mess. I noticed, howsomever, thet they was Texans enough to keep back to one side in case this Isbel started any action. . . . Wal, Isbel took a look at Lorenzo. Then with one swift grab he jerked the little greaser off his feet an' pulled him close. Lorenzo stopped grinnin'. He began to look a leetle sick. But it was plain he hed right on his side.

" 'You say you saw me?' demanded Isbel.

" 'Si, señor,' replied Lorenzo.

71

"What did you see?"

" 'I see señor an' señorita. I hide by manzanita. I see señorita like grande señor ver mooch. She like señor keese. She—'

"Then Isbel hit the little greaser a back-handed crack in the mouth. Sure it was a crack! Lorenzo went over the counter backward an' landed like a pack load of wood. An' he didn't git up.

" 'Mister Bruce,' said Isbel, 'an' you fellars who heerd thet lyin' greaser, I did meet Ellen Jorth. An' I lost my head. I— I kissed her. . . . But it was an accident. I meant no insult. I apologized—I tried to explain my crazy action. . . . Thet was all. The greaser lied. Ellen Jorth was kind enough to show me the trail. We talked a little. Then—I suppose— because she was young an' pretty an' sweet—I lost my head. She was absolutely innocent. Thet damned greaser told a bare-faced lie when he said she liked me. The fact was she despised me. She said so. An' when she learned I was Jean Isbel she turned her back on me an' walked away.' "

At this point of his narrative the old man halted as if to impress Ellen not only with what just had been told, but particularly with what was to follow. The reciting of this tale had evidently given Sprague an unconscious pleasure. He glowed. He seemed to carry the burden of a secret that he yearned to divulge. As for Ellen, she was dead-locked in breathless suspense. All her emotions waited for the end. She begged Sprague to hurry.

"Wal, I wish I could skip the next chapter an' hev only the last to tell," rejoined the old man, and he put a heavy, but solicitous, hand upon hers. . . . "Simm Bruce haw-hawed lour an' loud. . . . 'Say, Nez Perce,' he calls out, most insolent-like, 'we air too good sheepmen heah to hev the wool pulled over our eyes. We shore know what y'u meant by Ellen Jorth. But y'u wasn't smart when y'u told her y'u was Jean Isbel! . . . Haw-haw!'

"Isbel flashed a strange, surprised look from the red-faced Bruce to Greaves and to the other men. I take it he was wonderin' if he'd heerd right or if they'd got the same hunch thet'd come to him. An' I reckon he determined to make sure.

" 'Why wasn't I smart?' he asked.

" 'Shore y'u wasn't smart if y'u was aimin' to be one of Ellen Jorth's lovers,' said Bruce, with a leer. 'Fer if y'u hedn't give y'urself away y'u could hev been easy enough.'

72

"Thar was no mistakin' Bruce's meanin' an' when he got it out some of the men thar laughed. Isbel kept lookin' from one to another of them. Then facin' Greaves, he said, deliberately: 'Greaves, this drunken Bruce is excuse enough fer a show-down. I take it that you are sheepmen, an' you're goin' on Jorth's side of the fence in the matter of this sheep rangin'.'

"'Wal, Nez Perce, I reckon you hit plumb center,' said Greaves, dryly. He spread wide his big hands to the other men, as if to say they'd might as well own the jig was up.

"'All right. You're Jorth's backers. Have any of you a word to say in Ellen Jorth's defense? I tell you the Mexican lied. Believin' me or not doesn't matter. But this vile-mouthed Bruce hinted against thet girl's honor.'

"Ag'in some of the men laughed, but not so noisy, an' there was a nervous shufflin' of feet. Isbel looked sort of queer. His neck had a bulge round his collar. An' his eyes was like black coals of fire. Greaves spread his big hands again, as if to wash them of this part of the dirty argument.

"'When it comes to any wimmen I pass—much less play a hand fer a wildcat like Jorth's gurl,' said Greaves, sort of cold an' thick. 'Bruce shore ought to know her. Accordin' to talk heahaboots an' what *he* says, Ellen Jorth has been his gurl fer two years.'

"Then Isbel turned his attention to Bruce an' I fer one begun to shake in my boots.

"'Say thet to me!' he called.

"'Shore she's my gurl, an' thet's why I'm a-goin' to hev y'u run off this range.'

"Isbel jumped at Bruce. 'You damned drunken cur! You vile-mouthed liar! . . . . I may be an Isbel, but by God you cain't slander thet girl to my face!' . . . . Then he moved so quick I couldn't see what he did. But I heerd his fist hit Bruce. It sounded like an ax ag'in' a beef. Bruce fell clear across the room. An' by Jinny when he landed Isbel was thar. As Bruce staggered up, all bloody-faced, bellowin' an' spittin' out teeth Isbel eyed Greaves's crowd an' said: 'If any of y'u make a move it'll mean gun-play.' Nobody moved, thet's sure. In fact, none of Greaves's outfit was packin' guns, at least in sight. When Bruce got all the way up—he's a tall fellar—why Isbel took a full swing at him an' knocked him back across the room ag'in' the counter. Y'u know when a fellar's hurt by the way he yells. Bruce got thet second smash right on his big red nose. . . . I never seen any one so
73

quick as Isbel. He vaulted over that counter jest the second Bruce fell back on it, an' then, with Greaves's gang in front so he could catch any moves of theirs, he jest slugged Bruce right an' left, an' banged his head on the counter. Then as Bruce sunk limp an' slipped down, lookin' like a bloody sack, Isbel let him fall to the floor. Then he vaulted back over the counter. Wipin' the blood off his hands, he throwed his kerchief down in Bruce's face. Bruce wasn't dead or bad hurt. He'd jest been beaten bad. He was moanin' an' slobberin'. Isbel kicked him, not hard, but jest sort of disgustful. Then he faced thet crowd. 'Greaves, thet's what I think of your Simm Bruce. Tell him next time he sees me to run or pull a gun.' An' then Isbel grabbed his rifle an' package off the counter an' went out. He didn't even look back. I seen him mount his horse an' ride away. . . . Now, girl, what hev you to say?"

Ellen could only say good-by and the word was so low as to be almost inaudible. She ran to her burro. She could not see very clearly through tear-blurred eyes, and her shaking fingers were all thumbs. It seemed she had to rush away—somewhere, anywhere—not to get away from old John Sprague, but from herself—this palpitating, bursting self whose feet stumbled down the trail. All—all seemed ended for her. That interminable story! It had taken so long. And every minute of it she had been helplessly torn asunder by feelings she had never known she possessed. This Ellen Jorth was an unknown creature. She sobbed now as she dragged the burro down the cañon trail. She sat down only to rise. She hurried only to stop. Driven, pursued, barred, she had no way to escape the flaying thoughts, no time or will to repudiate them. The death of her girlhood, the rending aside of a veil of maiden mystery only vaguely instinctively guessed, the barren, sordid truth of her life as seen by her enlightened eyes, the bitter realization of the vileness of men of her clan in contrast to the manliness and chivalry of an enemy, the hard facts of unalterable repute as created by slander and fostered by low minds, all these were forces in a cataclysm that had suddenly caught her heart and whirled her through changes immense and agonizing, to bring her face to face with reality, to force upon her suspicion and doubt of all she had trusted, to warn her of the dark, impending horror of a tragic bloody feud, and lastly to teach her the supreme truth at once so glorious and so terrible—that she could not escape the doom of womanhood.

About noon that day Ellen Jorth arrived at the Knoll, which was the location of her father's ranch. Three cañons met there to form a larger one. The knoll was a symmetrical hill situated at the mouth of the three cañons. It was covered with brush and cedars, with here and there lichened rocks showing above the bleached grass. Below the Knoll was a wide, grassy flat or meadow through which a willow-bordered stream cut its rugged boulder-strewn bed. Water flowed abundantly at this season, and the deep washes leading down from the slopes attested to the fact of cloudbursts and heavy storms. This meadow valley was dotted with horses and cattle, and meandered away between the timbered slopes to lose itself in a green curve. A singular feature of this cañon was that a heavy growth of spruce trees covered the slope facing northwest; and the opposite slope exposed to the sun and therefore less snowbound in winter, held a sparse growth of yellow pines. The ranch house of Colonel Jorth stood round the rough corner of the largest of the three cañons, and rather well hidden, it did not obtrude its rude and broken-down log cabins, its squalid surroundings, its black mud-holes of corrals upon the beautiful and serene meadow valley.

Ellen Jorth approached her home slowly, with dragging, reluctant steps; and never before in the three unhappy years of her existence there had the ranch seemed so bare, so uncared for, so repugnant to her. As she had seen herself with clarified eyes, so now she saw her home. The cabin that Ellen lived in with her father was a single-room structure with one door and no windows. It was about twenty feet square. The huge, ragged, stone chimney had been built on the outside, with the wide open fireplace set inside the logs. Smoke was rising from the chimney. As Ellen halted at the door and began unpacking her burro she heard the loud, lazy laughter of men. An adjoining log cabin had been built in two sections, with a wide roofed hall or space between them. The door in each cabin faced the other, and there was a tall man standing in one. Ellen recognized Daggs, a neighbor sheepman, who evidently spent more time with her father than at his own home, wherever that was. Ellen had never seen it. She heard this man drawl, "Jorth, heah's your kid come home."

Ellen carried her bed inside the cabin, and unrolled it upon a couch built of boughs in the far corner. She had forgotten Jean Isbel's package, and now it fell out under her sight. Quickly she covered it. A Mexican woman, relative of Antonio, and the only servant about the place, was squatting Indian fashion before the fireplace, stirring a pot of beans. She and Ellen did not get along well together, and few words ever passed between them. Ellen had a canvas curtain stretched upon a wire across a small triangular corner, and this afforded her a little privacy. Her possessions were limited in number. The crude square table she had constructed herself. Upon it was a little old-fashioned walnut-framed mirror, a brush and comb, and a dilapidated ebony cabinet which contained odds and ends the sight of which always brought a smile of derisive self-pity to her lips. Under the table stood an old leather trunk. It had come with her from Texas, and contained clothing and belongings of her mother's. Above the couch on pegs hung her scant wardrobe. A tiny shelf held several worn-out books.

When her father slept indoors, which was seldom except in winter, he occupied a couch in the opposite corner. A rude cupboard had been built against the logs next to the fireplace. It contained supplies and utensils. Toward the center, somewhat closer to the door, stood a crude table and two benches. The cabin was dark and smelled of smoke, of the stale odors of past cooked meals, of the mustiness of dry, rotting timber. Streaks of light showed through the roof where the rough-hewn shingles had split or weathered. A strip of bacon hung upon one side of the cupboard, and upon the other a haunch of venison. Ellen detested the Mexican woman because she was dirty. The inside of the cabin presented the same unkempt appearance usual to it after Ellen had been away for a few days. Whatever Ellen had lost during the retrogression of the Jorths, she had kept her habits of cleanliness, and straightway upon her return she set to work.

The Mexican woman sullenly slouched away to her own quarters outside and Ellen was left to the satisfaction of labor. Her mind was as busy as her hands. As she cleaned and swept and dusted she heard from time to time the voices of men, the clip-clop of shod horses, the bellow of cattle. And a considerable time elapsed before she was disturbed.

A tall shadow darkened the doorway.

"Howdy, little one!" said a lazy, drawling voice. "So y'u-all got home?"

Ellen looked up. A superbly built man leaned against the

doorpost. Like most Texans, he was light haired and light eyed. His face was lined and hard. His long, sandy mustache hid his mouth and drooped with a curl. Spurred, booted, belted, packing a heavy gun low down on his hip, he gave Ellen an entirely new impression. Indeed, she was seeing everything strangely.

"Hello, Daggs!" replied Ellen. "Where's my dad?"

"He's playin' cairds with Jackson an' Colter. Shore's playin' bad, too, an' it's gone to his haid."

"Gamblin'?" queried Ellen.

"Mah child, when'd Kurnel Jorth ever play for fun?" said Daggs, with a lazy laugh. "There's a stack of gold on the table. Reckon yo' uncle Jackson will win it. Colter's shore out of luck."

Daggs stepped inside. He was graceful and slow. His long spurs clinked. He laid a rather compelling hand on Ellen's shoulder.

"Heah, mah gal, give us a kiss," he said.

"Daggs, I'm not your girl," replied Ellen as she slipped out from under his hand.

Then Daggs put his arm around her, not with violence or rudeness, but with an indolent, affectionate assurance, at once bold and self-contained. Ellen, however, had to exert herself to get free of him, and when she had placed the table between them she looked him square in the eyes.

"Daggs, y'u keep your paws off me," she said.

"Aw, now, Ellen, I ain't no bear," he remonstrated. "What's the matter, kid?"

"I'm not a kid. And there's nothin' the matter. Y'u're to keep your hands to yourself, that's all."

He tried to reach her across the table, and his movements were lazy and slow, like his smile. His tone was coaxing.

"Mah dear, shore you set on my knee just the other day, now, didn't you?"

Ellen felt the blood sting her cheeks.

"I was a child," she returned.

"Wal, listen to this heah grown-up young woman. All in a few days! . . . Doon't be in a temper, Ellen. . . . Come, give us a kiss."

She deliberately gazed into his eyes. Like the eyes of an eagle, they were clear and hard, just now warmed by the dalliance of the moment, but there was no light, no intelligence in them to prove he understood her. The instant separated Ellen immeasurably from him and from all of his ilk.

"Daggs, I was a child," she said. "I was lonely—hungry for affection—I was innocent. Then I was careless, too, and thoughtless when I should have known better. But I hardly understood y'u men. I put such thoughts out of my mind. I know now—know what y'u mean—what y'u have made people believe I am."

"Ahuh! Shore I get your hunch," he returned, with a change of tone. "But I asked you to marry me?"

"Yes y'u did. The first day y'u got heah to my dad's house. And y'u asked me to marry y'u after y'u found y'u couldn't have your way with me. To y'u the one didn't mean any more than the other."

"Shore I did more than Simm Bruce an' Colter," he retorted. "They never asked you to marry."

"No, they didn't. And if I could respect them at all I'd do it because they didn't ask me."

"Wal, I'll be dog-goned!" ejaculated Daggs, thoughtfully, as he stroked his long mustache.

"I'll say to them what I've said to y'u," went on Ellen. "I'll tell dad to make y'u let me alone. I wouldn't marry one of y'u—y'u loafers to save my life. I've my suspicions about y'u. Y'u're a bad lot."

Daggs changed subtly. The whole indolent nonchalance of the man vanished in an instant.

"Wal, Miss Jorth, I reckon you mean we're a bad lot of sheepmen?" he queried, in the cool, easy speech of a Texan.

"No," flashed Ellen. "Shore I don't say sheepmen. I say y'u're a *bad lot*."

"Oh, the hell you say!" Daggs spoke as he might have spoken to a man; then turning swiftly on his heel he left her. Outside he encountered Ellen's father. She heard Daggs speak: "Lee, your little wildcat is shore heah. An' take mah hunch. Somebody has been talkin' to her."

"Who has?" asked her father, in his husky voice. Ellen knew at once that he had been drinking.

"Lord only knows," replied Daggs. "But shore it wasn't any friends of ours."

"We cain't stop people's tongues," said Jorth, resignedly.

"Wal, I ain't so shore," continued Daggs, with his slow, cool laugh. "Reckon I never yet heard any daid men's tongues wag."

Then the musical tinkle of his spurs sounded fainter. A

moment later Ellen's father entered the cabin. His dark, moody face brightened at sight of her. Ellen knew she was the only person in the world left for him to love. And she was sure of his love. Her very presence always made him different. And through the years, the darker their misfortunes, the farther he slipped away from better days, the more she loved him.

"Hello, my Ellen!" he said, and he embraced her. When he had been drinking he never kissed her. "Shore I'm glad you're home. This heah hole is bad enough any time, but when you're gone it's black. . . . I'm hungry."

Ellen laid food and drink on the table; and for a little while she did not look directly at him. She was concerned about this new searching power of her eyes. In relation to him she vaguely dreaded it.

Lee Jorth had once been a singularly handsome man. He was tall, but did not have the figure of a horseman. His dark hair was streaked with gray, and was white over his ears. His face was sallow and thin, with deep lines. Under his round, prominent, brown eyes, like deadened furnaces, were blue swollen welts. He had a bitter mouth and weak chin, not wholly concealed by gray mustache and pointed beard. He wore a long frock coat and a wide-brimmed sombrero, both black in color, and so old and stained and frayed that along with the fashion of them they betrayed that they had come from Texas with him. Jorth always persisted in wearing a white linen shirt, likewise a relic of his Southern prosperity, and to-day it was ragged and soiled as usual.

Ellen watched her father eat and waited for him to speak. It occurred to her strangely that he never asked about the sheep or the new-born lambs. She divined with a subtle new woman's intuition that he cared nothing for his sheep.

"Ellen, what riled Daggs?" inquired her father, presently. "He shore had fire in his eye."

Long ago Ellen had betrayed an indignity she had suffered at the hands of a man. Her father had nearly killed him. Since then she had taken care to keep her troubles to herself. If her father had not been blind and absorbed in his own brooding he would have seen a thousand things sufficient to inflame his Southern pride and temper.

"Daggs asked me to marry him again and I said he belonged to a bad lot," she replied.

Jorth laughed in scorn. "Fool! . . . My God! Ellen, I must

79

have dragged you low—that every damned ru—er—sheep-man—who comes along thinks he can marry you."

At the break in his words, the incompleted meaning, Ellen dropped her eyes. Little things once never noted by her were now come to have a fascinating significance.

"Never mind, dad," she replied. "They cain't marry me."

"Daggs said somebody had been talkin' to you. How aboot that?"

"Old John Sprague has just gotten back from Grass Valley," said Ellen. "I stopped in to see him. Shore he told me all the village gossip."

"Anythin' to interest me?" he queried, darkly.

"Yes, dad, I'm afraid a good deal," she said, hesitatingly. Then in accordance with a decision Ellen had made she told him of the rumored war between sheepmen and cattle-men; that old Isbel had Blaisdell, Gordon, Fredericks, Blue and other well-known ranchers on his side; that his son Jean Isbel had come from Oregon with a wonderful reputation as fighter and scout and tracker; that it was no secret how Colonel Lee Jorth was at the head of the sheepmen; that a bloody war was sure to come.

"Hah!" exclaimed Jorth, with a stain of red in his sallow cheek. "Reckon none of that is news to me. I knew all that."

Ellen wondered if he had heard of her meeting with Jean Isbel. If not he would hear as soon as Simm Bruce and Lorenzo came back. She decided to forestall them.

"Dad, I met Jean Isbel. He came into my camp. Asked the way to the Rim. I showed him. We—we talked a little. And shore were gettin' acquainted when—when he told me who he was. Then I left him—hurried back to camp."

"Colter met Isbel down in the woods," replied Jorth, ponderingly. "Said he looked like an Indian—a hard an' slippery customer to reckon with."

"Shore I guess I can indorse what Colter said," returned Ellen, dryly. She could have laughed aloud at her deceit. Still she had not lied.

"How'd this heah young Isbel strike you?" queried her father, suddenly glancing up at her.

Ellen felt the slow, sickening, guilty rise of blood in her face. She was helpless to stop it. But her father evidently never saw it. He was looking at her without seeing her.

"He—he struck me as different from men heah," she stammered.

80

"Did Sprague tell you aboot this half-Indian Isbel—aboot his reputation?"

"Yes."

"Did he look to you like a real woodsman?"

"Indeed he did. He wore buckskin. He stepped quick and soft. He acted at home in the woods. He had eyes black as night and sharp as lightnin'. They shore saw about all there was to see."

Jorth chewed at his mustache and lost himself in brooding thought.

"Dad, tell me, is there goin' to be a war?" asked Ellen, presently.

What a red, strange, rolling flash blazed in his eyes! His body jerked.

"Shore. You might as well know."

"Between sheepmen and cattlemen?"

"Yes."

"With y'u, dad, at the haid of one faction and Gaston Isbel the other?"

"Daughter, you have it correct, so far as you go."

"Oh! . . . Dad, can't this fight be avoided?"

"You forget you're from Texas," he replied.

"Cain't it be helped?" she repeated, stubbornly.

"No!" he declared, with deep, hoarse passion.

"Why not?"

"Wal, we sheepmen are goin' to run sheep anywhere we like on the range. An' cattlemen won't stand for that."

"But, dad, it's so foolish," declared Ellen, eanrestly. "Y'u sheepmen do not have to run sheep over the cattle range."

"I reckon we do."

"Dad, that argument doesn't go with me. I know the country. For years to come there will be room for both sheep and cattle without overrunnin'. If some of the range is better in water and grass, then whoever got there first should have it. That shore is only fair. It's common sense, too."

"Ellen, I reckon some cattle people have been prejudicin' you," said Jorth, bitterly.

"Dad!" she cried, hotly.

This had grown to be an ordeal for Jorth. He seemed a victim of contending tides of feeling. Some will or struggle broke within him and the change was manifest. Haggard, shifty-eyed, with wabbling chin, he burst into speech.

"See heah, girl. You listen. There's a clique of ranchers

81

down in the Basin, all those you named, with Isbel at their haid. They have resented sheepmen comin' down into the valley. They want it all to themselves. That's the reason. Shore there's another. All the Isbels are crooked. They're cattle an' horse thieves—have been for years. Gaston Isbel always was a maverick rustler. He's gettin' old now an' rich, so he wants to cover his tracks. He aims to blame this cattle rustlin' an' horse stealin' on to us sheepmen, an' run us out of the country."

Gravely Ellen Jorth studied her father's face, and the newly found truth-seeing power of her eyes did not fail her. In part, perhaps in all, he was telling lies. She shuddered a little, loyally battling against the insidious convictions being brought to fruition. Perhaps in his brooding over his failures and troubles he leaned toward false judgments. Ellen could not attach dishonor to her father's motives or speeches. For long, however, something about him had troubled her, perplexed her. Fearfully she believed she was coming to some revelation, and, despite her keen determination to know, she found herself shrinking.

"Dad, mother told me before she died that the Isbels had ruined you," said Ellen, very low. It hurt her so to see her father cover his face that she could hardly go on. "If they ruined you they ruined all of us. I know what we had once— what we lost again and again—and I see what we are come to now. Mother hated the Isbels. She taught me to hate the very name. But I never knew how they ruined you—or why —or when. And I want to know now."

Then it was not the face of a liar that Jorth disclosed. The present was forgotten. He lived in the past. He even seemed younger in the revivifying flash of hate that made his face radiant. The lines burned out. Hate gave him back the spirit of his youth.

"Gaston Isbel an' I were boys together in Weston, Texas," began Jorth, in swift, passionate voice. "We went to school together. We loved the same girl—your mother. When the war broke out she was engaged to Isbel. His family was rich. They influenced her people. But she loved me. When Isbel went to war she married me. He came back an' faced us. God! I'll never forget that. Your mother confessed her unfaithfulness—by Heaven! She taunted him with it. Isbel accused me of winnin' her by lies. But she took the sting out of that. . . . Isbel never forgave her an' he hounded me to ruin. He made me out a card-sharp, cheatin' my best friends. I was disgraced. Later he tangled with me in the courts—he beat me out of property—an' last by convictin' me of rustlin' cattle he run me out of Texas."

Black and distorted now, Jorth's face was a spectacle to make Ellen sick with a terrible passion of despair and hate. The truth of her father's ruin and her own were enough. What mattered all else? Jorth beat the table with fluttering, nerveless hands that seemed all the more significant for their lack of physical force.

"An' so help me God, it's got to be wiped out in blood!" he hissed.

That was his answer to the wavering and nobility of Ellen. And she in her turn had no answer to make. She crept away into the corner behind the curtain, and there on her couch in the semidarkness she lay with strained heart, and a resurging, unconquerable tumult in her mind. And she lay there from the middle of that afternoon until the next morning.

When she awakened she expected to be unable to rise— she hoped she could not—but life seemed multiplied in her, and inaction was impossible. Something young and sweet and hopeful that had been in her did not greet the sun this morning. In their place was a woman's passion to learn for herself, to watch events, to meet what must come, to survive.

After breakfast, at which she sat alone, she decided to put Isbel's package out of the way, so that it would not be subjecting her to continual annoyance. The moment she picked it up the old curiosity assailed her.

"Shore I'll see what it is, anyway," she muttered, and with swift hands she opened the package. The action disclosed two pairs of fine, soft shoes, of a style she had never seen, and four pairs of stockings, two of strong, serviceable wool, and the others of a finer texture. Ellen looked at them in amaze. Of all things in the world, these would have been the last she expected to see. And, strangely, they were what she wanted and needed most. Naturally, then, Ellen made the mistake of taking them in her hands to feel their softness and warmth.

"Shore! He saw my bare legs! And he brought me these presents he'd intended for his sister. . . . He was ashamed for me—sorry for me. . . . And I thought he looked at me bold-like, as I'm used to be looked at heah! Isbel or not, he's shore . . ."

83

But Ellen Jorth could not utter aloud the conviction her intelligence tried to force upon her.

"It'd be a pity to burn them," she mused. "I cain't do it. Sometime I might send them to Ann Isbel."

Whereupon she wrapped them up again and hid them in the bottom of the old trunk, and slowly, as she lowered the lid, looking darkly, blankly at the wall, she whispered: "Jean Isbel! . . . I hate him!"

Later when Ellen went outdoors she carried her rifle, which was unusual for her, unless she intended to go into the woods.

The morning was sunny and warm. A group of shirt-sleeved men lounged in the hall and before the porch of the double cabin. Her father was pacing up and down, talking forcibly. Ellen heard his hoarse voice. As she approached he ceased talking and his listeners relaxed their attention. Ellen's glance ran over them swiftly—Daggs, with his superb head, like that of a hawk, uncovered to the sun; Colter with his lowered, secretive looks, his sand-gray lean face; Jackson Jorth, her uncle, huge, gaunt, hulking, with white in his black beard and hair, and the fire of a ghoul in his hollow eyes; Tad Jorth, another brother of her father's, younger, red of eye and nose, a weak-chinned drinker of rum. Three other limber-legged Texans lounged there, partners of Daggs, and they were sun-browned, light-haired, blue-eyed men singularly alike in appearance, from their dusty high-heeled boots to their broad black sombreros. They claimed to be sheepmen. All Ellen could be sure of was that Rock Wells spent most of his time there, doing nothing but looking for a chance to waylay her; Springer was a gambler; and the third, who answered to the strange name of Queen, was a silent, lazy, watchful-eyed man who never wore a glove on his right hand and who never was seen without a gun within easy reach of that hand.

"Howdy, Ellen. Shore you ain't goin' to say good mawnin' to this heah bad lot?" drawled Daggs, with good-natured sarcasm.

"Why, shore! Good morning, y'u hard-working industrious *mañana* sheep raisers," replied Ellen, coolly.

Daggs stared. The others appeared taken back by a greeting so foreign from any to which they were accustomed from her. Jackson Jorth let out a gruff haw-haw. Some of them doffed their sombreros, and Rock Wells managed a lazy, polite good morning. Ellen's father seemed most significantly struck by her greeting, and the least amused.

"Ellen, I'm not likin' your talk," he said, with a frown.

"Dad, when y'u play cards don't y'u call a spade a spade?"

"Why, shore I do."

"Well! I'm calling spades spades."

"Ahuh!" grunted Jorth, furtively dropping his eyes. "Where you goin' with your gun? I'd rather you hung round heah now."

"Reckon I might as well get used to packing my gun all the time," replied Ellen. "Reckon I'll be treated more like a man."

Then the event Ellen had been expecting all morning took place. Simm Bruce and Lorenzo rode around the slope of the Knoll and trotted toward the cabin. Interest in Ellen was relegated to the background.

"Shore they're bustin' with news," declared Daggs.

"They been ridin' some, you bet," remarked another.

"Huh!" exclaimed Jorth. "Bruce shore looks queer to me."

"Red liquor," said Tad Jorth, sententiously. "You-all know the brand Greaves hands out."

"Nad, Simm ain't drunk," said Jackson Jorth. "Look at his bloody shirt."

The cool, indolent interest of the crowd vanished at the red color pointed out by Jackson Jorth. Daggs rose in a single springy motion to his lofty height. The face Bruce turned to Jorth was swollen and bruised, with unhealed cuts. Where his right eye should have been showed a puffed dark purple bulge. His other eye, however, gleamed with hard and sullen light. He stretched a big shaking hand toward Jorth.

"Thet Nez Perce Isbel beat me half to death," he bellowed.

Jorth stared hard at the tragic, almost grotesque figure, at the battered face. But speech failed him. It was Daggs who answered Bruce.

"Wal, Simm, I'll be damned if you don't look it."

"Beat you! What with?" burst out Jorth, explosively.

"I thought he was swingin' an ax, but Greaves swore it was his fists," bawled Bruce, in misery and fury.

"Where was your gun?" queried Jorth, sharply.

"Gun? Hell!" exclaimed Bruce, flinging wide his arms.

85

"Ask Lorenzo. He had a gun. An' he got a biff in the jaw before my turn come. Ask him?"

Attention thus directed to the Mexican showed a heavy discolored swelling upon the side of his olive-skinned face. Lorenzo looked only serious.

"Hah! Speak up," shouted Jorth, impatiently.

"Señor Isbel heet me ver quick," replied Lorenzo, with expressive gesture. "I see thousand stars—then moocho black—all like night."

At that some of Daggs's men lolled back with dry crisp laughter. Daggs's hard face rippled with a smile. But there was no humor in anything for Colonel Jorth.

"Tell us what come off. Quick!" he ordered. "Where did it happen? Why? Who saw it? What did you do?"

Bruce lapsed into a sullen impressiveness. "Wal, I happened in Greaves's store an' run into Jean Isbel. Shore was lookin' fer him. I had my mind made up what to do, but I got to shootin' off my gab instead of my gun. I called him Nez Perce—an' I throwed all thet talk in his face about old Gass Isbel sendin' fer him—an' I told him he'd git run out of the Tonto. Reckon I was jest warmin' up. . . . But then it all happened. He slugged Lorenzo jest one. An' Lorenzo slid peaceful-like to bed behind the counter. I hadn't time to think of throwin' a gun before he whaled into me. He knocked out two of my teeth. An' I swallered one of them."

Ellen stood in the background behind three of the men and in the shadow. She did not join in the laugh that followed Bruce's remarks. She had known that he would lie. Uncertain yet of her reaction to this, but more bitter and furious as he revealed his utter baseness, she waited for more to be said.

"Wal, I'll be doggoned," drawled Daggs.

"What do you make of this kind of fightin'?" queried Jorth.

"Darn if I know," replied Daggs in perplexity. "Shore an' sartin it's not the way of a Texan. Mebbe this young Isbel really is what old Gass swears he is. Shore Bruce ain't nothin' to give an edge to a real gun fighter. Looks to me like Isbel bluffed Greaves an' his gang an' licked your men without throwin' a gun."

"Maybe Isbel doesn't want the name of drawin' first blood," suggested Jorth.

"That'd be like Gass," spoke up Rock Wells, quietly. "I onct rode fer Gass in Texas."

"Say, Bruce," said Daggs, "was this heah palaverin' of yours an' Jean Isbel's aboot the old stock dispute? Aboot his father's range an' water? An' partickler aboot sheep?"

"Wal—I—I yelled a heap," declared Bruce, haltingly, "but I don't recollect all I said—I was riled. . . . Shore, though it was the same old argyment thet's been fetchin' us closer an' closer to trouble."

Daggs removed his keen hawklike gaze from Bruce. "Wal, Jorth, all I'll say is this. If Bruce is tellin' the truth we ain't got a hell of a lot to fear from this young Isbel. I've known a heap of gun fighters in my day. An' Jean Isbel don't run true to class. Shore there never was a gunman who'd risk cripplin' his right hand by sluggin' anybody."

"Wal," broke in Bruce, sullenly. "You-all can take it daid straight or not. I don't give a damn. But you've shore got my hunch thet Nez Perce Isbel is liable to handle any of you fellars jest as he did me, an' jest as easy. What's more, he's got Greaves figgered. An' you-all know thet Greaves is as deep in—"

"Shut up that kind of gab," demanded Jorth, stridently. "An' answer me. Was the row in Greaves's barroom aboot sheep?"

"Aw, hell! I said so, didn't I?" shouted Bruce, with a fierce uplift of his distorted face.

Ellen strode out from the shadow of the tall men who had obscured her.

"Bruce, y'u're a liar," she said, bitingly.

The surprise of her sudden appearance seemed to root Bruce to the spot. All but the discolored places on his face turned white. He held his breath a moment, then expelled it hard. His effort to recover from the shock was painfully obvious. He stammered incoherently.

"Shore y'u're more than a liar, too," cried Ellen, facing him with blazing eyes. And the rifle, gripped in both hands, seemed to declare her intent of menace. "That row was not about sheep. . . . Jean Isbel didn't beat y'u for anythin' about sheep. . . . Old John Sprague was in Greaves's store. He heard y'u. He saw Jean Isbel beat y'u as y'u deserved. . . . An' he told me!"

Ellen saw Bruce shrink in fear of his life; and despite her fury she was filled with disgust that he could imagine she would have his blood on her hands. Then she divined that Bruce saw more in the gathering storm in her father's eyes than he had to fear from her.

87

"Girl, what the hell are y'u sayin'?" hoarsely called Jorth, in dark amaze.

"Dad, y'u leave this to me," she retorted.

Daggs stepped beside Jorth, significantly on his right side. "Let her alone Lee," he advised, coolly. "She's shore got a hunch on Bruce."

"Simm Bruce, y'u cast a dirty slur on my name," cried Ellen, passionately.

It was then that Daggs grasped Jorth's right arm and held it tight. "Jest what I thought," he said. "Stand still, Lee. Let's see the kid make him showdown."

"That's what Jean Isbel beat y'u for," went on Ellen. "For slandering a girl who wasn't there. . . . Me! Y'u rotten liar!"

"But, Ellen, it wasn't all lies," said Bruce, huskily. "I was half drunk—an' horrible jealous. . . . You know Lorenzo seen Isbel kissin' you. I can prove thet."

Ellen threw up her head and a scarlet wave of shame and wrath flooded her face.

"Yes," she cried, ringingly. "He saw Jean Isbel kiss me. Once! . . . An' it was the only decent kiss I've had in years. He meant no insult. I didn't know who he was. An' through his kiss I learned a difference between men. . . . Y'u made Lorenzo lie. An' if I had a shred of good name left in Grass Valley you dishonored it. . . . Y'u made *him* think I was your girl! Damn y'u! I ought to kill y'u. . . . Eat your words now—take them back—or I'll cripple y'u for life!"

Ellen lowered the cocked rifle toward his feet.

"Shore, Ellen, I take back—all I said," gulped Bruce. He gazed at the quivering rifle barrel and then into the face of Ellen's father. Instinct told him where his real peril lay.

Here the cool and tactful Daggs showed himself master of the situation.

"Heah, listen!" he called. "Ellen, I reckon Bruce was drunk an' out of his haid. He's shore ate his words. Now, we don't want any cripples in this camp. Let him alone. Your dad got me heah to lead the Jorths, an' that's my say to you. . . . Simm, you're shore a low-down, lyin' rascal. Keep away from Ellen after this or I'll bore you myself. . . . Jorth, it won't be a bad idee for you to forget you're a Texan till you cool off. Let Bruce stop some Isbel lead. Shore the Jorth-Isbel war is aboot on, an' I reckon we'd be smart to believe old Gass's talk aboot his Nez Perce son."

6

★

From this hour Ellen Jorth bent all of her lately awakened intelligence and will to the only end that seemed to hold possible salvation for her. In the crisis sure to come she did not want to be blind or weak. Dreaming and indolence, habits born in her which were often a comfort to one as lonely as she, would ill fit her for the hard test she divined and dreaded. In the matter of her father's fight she must stand by him whatever the issue or the outcome; in what pertained to her own principles, her womanhood, and her soul she stood absolutely alone.

Therefore, Ellen put dreams aside, an indolence of mind and body behind her. Many tasks she found, and when these were done for a day she kept active in other ways, thus earning the poise and peace of labor.

Jorth rode off every day, sometimes with one or two of the men, often with a larger number. If he spoke of such trips to Ellen it was to give an impression of visiting the ranches of his neighbors or the various sheep camps. Often he did not return the day he left. When he did get back he smelled of rum and appeared heavy from need of sleep. His horses were always dust and sweat covered. During his absences Ellen fell victim to anxious dread until he returned. Daily he grew darker and more haggard of face, more obsessed by some impending fate. Often he stayed up late, haranguing with the men in the dim-lit cabin, where they drank and smoked, but seldom gambled any more. When the men did not gamble something immediate and perturbing was on their minds. Ellen had not yet lowered herself to the deceit and suspicion of eavesdropping, but she realized that there was a climax approaching in which she would deliberately do so.

In those closing May days Ellen learned the significance of many things that previously she had taken as a matter of course. Her father did not run a ranch. There was absolutely no ranching done, and little work. Often Ellen had to chop wood herself. Jorth did not possess a plow. Ellen was bound to confess that the evidence of this lack dumfounded her. Even old John Sprague raised some hay, beets, turnips. Jorth's cattle and horses fared ill during the winter. Ellen remembered how they used to clean up four-inch oak saplings and aspens. Many of them died in the snow. The flocks of sheep, however, were driven down into the Basin in the fall, and across the Reno Pass to Phoenix and Maricopa.

Ellen could not discover a fence post on the ranch, nor a piece of salt for the horses and cattle, nor a wagon, nor any sign of a sheep-shearing outfit. She had never seen any sheep sheared. Ellen could never keep track of the many and different horses running loose and hobbled around the ranch. There were droves of horses in the woods, and some of them wild as deer. According to her long-established understanding, her father and her uncles were keen on horse trading and buying.

Then the many trails leading away from the Jorth ranch—these grew to have a fascination for Ellen; and the time came when she rode out on them to see for herself where they led. The sheep ranch of Daggs, supposd to be only a few miles across the ridges, down in Bear Cañon, never materialized at all for Ellen. This circumstance so interested her that she went up to see her friend Sprague and got him to direct her to Bear Cañon, so that she would be sure not to miss it. And she rode from the narrow, maple-thicketed head of it near the Rim down all its length. She found no ranch, no cabin, not even a corral in Bear Cañon. Sprague said there was only one cañon by that name. Daggs had assured her of the exact location on his place, and so had her father. Had they lied? Were they mistaken in the cañon? There were many cañons, all heading up near the Rim, all running and widening down for miles through the wooded mountain, and vastly different from the deep, short, yellow-walled gorges that cut into the Rim from the Basin side. Ellen investigated the cañons within six or eight miles of her home, both to east and to west. All she discovered was a couple of old log cabins, long deserted. Still, she did not follow out all the trails to their ends. Several of them led far into the deepest, roughest, wildest brakes of gorge and thicket that she had seen. No cattle or sheep had ever been driven over these trails.

This riding around of Ellen's at length got to her father's ears. Ellen expected that a bitter quarrel would ensue, for she certainly would refuse to be confined to the camp; but her father only asked her to limit her riding to the meadow valley, and straightway forgot all about it. In fact, his abstraction one moment, his intense nervousness the next, his harder drinking and fiercer harangues with the men, grew to be distressing for Ellen. They presaged his further deterioration and the ever-present evil of the growing feud.

One day Jorth rode home in the early morning, after an absence of two nights. Ellen heard the clip-clop of horses long before she saw them.

"Hey, Ellen! Come out heah," called her father.

Ellen left her work and went outside. A stranger had ridden in with her father, a young giant whose sharp-featured face appeared marked by ferret-like eyes and a fine, light, fuzzy beard. He was long, loose jointed, not heavy of build, and he had the largest hands and feet Ellen had ever seen. Next Ellen espied a black horse they had evidently brought with them. Her father was holding a rope halter. At once the black horse struck Ellen as being a beauty and a thoroughbred.

"Ellen, heah's a horse for you," said Jorth with something of pride. "I made a trade. Reckon I wanted him myself, but he's too gentle for me an' maybe a little small for my weight."

Delight visited Ellen for the first time in many days. Seldom had she owned a good horse, and never one like this.

"Oh, dad!" she exclaimed, in her gratitude.

"Shore he's yours on one condition," said her father.

"What's that?" asked Ellen, as she laid caressing hands on the restless horse.

"You're not to ride him out of the cañon."

"Agreed. . . . All daid black, isn't he, except that white face? What's his name, dad?"

"I forgot to ask," replied Jorth, as he began unsaddling his own horse. "Slater, what's this heah black's name?"

The lanky giant grinned. "I reckon it was Spades."

"Spades?" ejaculated Ellen, blankly. "What a name! . . . Well, I guess it's as good as any. He's shore black."

"Ellen, keep him hobbled when you're not ridin' him," was her father's parting advice as he walked off with the stranger.

Spades was wet and dusty and his satiny skin quivered.

He had fine, dark, intelligent eyes that watched Ellen's every move. She knew how her father and his friends dragged and jammed horses through the woods and over the rough trails. It did not take her long to discover that this horse had been a pet. Ellen cleaned his coat and brushed him and fed him. Then she fitted her bridle to suit his head and saddled him. His evident response to her kindness assured her that he was gentle, so she mounted and rode him, to discover he had the easiest gait she had ever experienced. He walked and trotted to suit her will, but when left to choose his own gait he fell into a graceful little pace that was very easy for her. He appeared quite ready to break into a run at her slightest bidding, but Ellen satisfied herself on this first ride with his slower gaits.

"Spades, y'u've shore cut out my burro Jinny," said Ellen, regretfully. "Well, I reckon women are fickle."

Next day she rode up the cañon to show Spades to her friend John Sprague. The old burro breeder was not at home. As his door was open, however, and a fire smoldering, Ellen concluded he would soon return. So she waited. Dismounting, she left Spades free to graze on the new green grass that carpeted the ground. The cabin and little level clearing accentuated the loneliness and wildness of the forest. Ellen always liked it here and had once been in the habit of visiting the old man often. But of late she had stayed away, for the reason that Sprague's talk and his news and his poorly hidden pity depressed her.

Presently she heard hoof beats on the hard, packed trail leading down the cañon in the direction from which she had come. Scarcely likely was it that Sprague should return from this direction. Ellen thought her father had sent one of the herders for her. But when she caught a glimpse of the approaching horseman, down in the aspens, she failed to recognize him. After he had passed one of the openings she heard his horse stop. Probably the man had seen her; at least she could not otherwise account for his stopping. The glimpse she had of him had given her the impression that he was bending over, peering ahead in the trail, looking for tracks. Then she heard the rider come on again, more slowly this time. At length the horse trotted out into the opening, to be hauled up short. Ellen recognized the buckskin-clad figure, the broad shoulders, the dark face of Jean Isbel.

Ellen felt prey to the strangest quaking sensation she had

92

ever suffered. It took violence of her new-born spirit to subdue that feeling.

Isbel rode slowly across the clearing toward her. For Ellen his approach seemed singularly swift—so swift that her surprise, dismay, conjecture, and anger obstructed her will. The outwardly calm and cold Ellen Jorth was a travesty that mocked her—that she felt he would discern.

The moment Isbel drew close enough for Ellen to see his face she experienced a strong, shuddering repetition of her first shock of recognition. He was not the same. The light, the youth was gone. This, however, did not cause her emotion. Was it not a sudden transition of her nature to the dominance of hate? Ellen seemed to feel the shadow of her unknown self standing with her.

Isbel halted his horse. Ellen had been standing near the trunk of a fallen pine and she instinctively backed against it. How her legs trembled! Isbel took off his cap and crushed it nervously in his bare, brown hand.

"Good mornin', Miss Ellen!" he said.

Ellen did not return his greeting, but queried, almost breathlessly, "Did y'u come by our ranch?"

"No. I circled," he replied.

"Jean Isbel! What do y'u want heah?" she demanded.

"Don't you know?" he returned. His eyes were intensely black and piercing. They seemed to search Ellen's very soul. To meet their gaze was an ordeal that only her rousing fury sustained.

Ellen felt on her lips a scornful allusion to his half-breed Indian traits and the reputation that had preceded him. But she could not utter it.

"No," she replied.

"It's hard to call a woman a liar," he returned, bitterly. "But you must be—seein' you're a Jorth."

"Liar! Not to y'u, Jean Isbel," she retorted. "I'd not lie to y'u to save my life."

He studied her with keen, sober, moody intent. The dark fire in his eyes thrilled her.

"If that's true, I'm glad," he said.

"Shore it's true. I've no idea why y'u came heah."

Ellen did have a dawning idea that she could not force into oblivion. But if she ever admitted it to her consciousness, she must fail in the contempt and scorn and fearlessness she chose to throw in this man's face.

"Does old Sprague live here?" asked Isbel.

"Yes. I expect him back soon. . . . Did y'u come to see him?"

"No. . . . Did Sprague tell you anythin' about the row he saw me in?"

"He—did not," replied Ellen, lying with stiff lips. She who had sworn she could not lie! She felt the hot blood leaving her heart, mounting in a wave. All her conscious will seemed impelled to deceive. What had she to hide from Jean Isbel? And a still, small voice replied that she had to hide the Ellen Jorth who had waited for him that day, who had spied upon him, who had treasured a gift she could not destroy, who had hugged to her miserable heart the fact that he had fought for her name.

"I'm glad of that," Isbel was saying, thoughtfully.

"Did you come heah to see me?" interrupted Ellen. She fel that she could not endure this reiterated suggestion of fineness, of consideration in him. She would betray herself— betray what she did not even realize herself. She must force other footing—and that should be the one of strife between the Jorths and Isbels.

"No—honest, I didn't, Miss Ellen," he rejoined, humbly. "I'll tell you, presently, why I came. But it wasn't to see you. . . . I don't deny I wanted . . . but that's no matter. You didn't meet me that day on the Rim."

"Meet y'u!" she echoed, coldly. "Shore y'u never expected me?"

"Somehow I did," he replied, with those penetrating eyes on her. "I put somethin' in your tent that day. Did you find it?"

"Yes," she replied, with the same casual coldness.

"What did you do with it?"

"I kicked it out, of course," she replied.

She saw him flinch.

"And you never opened it?"

"Certainly not," she retorted, as if forced. "Doon't y'u know anythin' about—about people? . . . Shore even if y'u are an Isbel y'u never were born in Texas."

"Thank God I wasn't!" he replied. "I was born in a beautiful country of green meadows and deep forests and white rivers, not in a barren desert where men live dry and hard as the cactus. Where I came from men don't live on hate. They can forgive."

"Forgive! . . . Could y'u forgive a Jorth?"

"Yes, I could."

94

"Shore that's easy to say—with the wrongs all on your side," she declared, bitterly.

"Ellen Jorth, the first wrong was on your side," retorted Jean, his voice full. "Your father stole my father's sweetheart—by lies, by slander, by dishonor, by makin' terrible love to her in his absence."

"It's a lie," cried Ellen, passionately.

"It is not," he declared, solemnly.

"Jean Isbel, I say y'u lie!"

"No! *I* say you've been lied to," he thundered.

The tremendous force of his spirit seemed to fling truth at Ellen. It weakened her.

"But—mother loved dad—best."

"Yes, afterward. No wonder, poor woman! . . . But it was the action of your father and your mother that ruined all these lives. You've got to know the truth, Ellen Jorth. . . . All the years of hate have borne their fruit. God Almighty can never save us now. Blood must be spilled. The Jorths and the Isbels can't live on the same earth. . . . And you've got to know the truth because the worst of this hell falls on you and me."

The hate that he spoke of alone upheld her.

"Never, Jean Isbel!" she cried. "I'll never know truth from y'u. . . . I'll never share anythin' with y'u—not even hell."

Isbel dismounted and stood before her, still holding his bridle reins. The bay horse champed his bit and tossed his head.

"Why do you hate me so?" he asked. "I just happen to be my father's son. I never harmed you or any of your people. I met you . . . fell in love with you in a flash—though I never knew it till after. . . . Why do you hate me so terribly?"

Ellen felt a heavy, stifling pressure within her breast. "Y'u're an Isbel. . . . Doon't speak of love to me."

"I didn't intend to. But your—your hate seems unnatural. And we'll probably never meet again. . . . I can't help it. I love you. Love at first sight! Jean Isbel and Ellen Jorth! Strange, isn't it? . . . It was all so strange. My meetin' you so lonely and unhappy, my seein' you so sweet and beautiful, my thinkin' you so good in spite of—"

"Shore it was strange," interrupted Ellen, with scornful laugh. She had found her defense. In hurting him she could

95

hide her own hurt. "Thinking me so good in spite of—
Ha-ha! And I said I'd been kissed before!"

"Yes, in spite of everything," he said.

Ellen could not look at him as he loomed over her. She
felt a wild tumult in her heart. All that crowded to her lips
for utterance was false.

"Yes—kissed before I met you—and since," she said,
mockingly. "And I laugh at what y'u call love, Jean Isbel."

"Laugh if you want—but believe it was sweet, honorable
—the best in me," he replied, in deep earnestness.

"Bah!" cried Ellen, with all the force of her pain and
shame and hate.

"By Heaven, you must be different from what I thought!"
exclaimed Isbel, huskily.

"Shore if I wasn't, I'd make myself. . . . Now, Mister
Jean Isbel, get on your horse an' go!"

Something of composure came to Ellen with these words
of dismissal, and she glanced up at him with half-veiled
eyes. His changed aspect prepared her for some blow.

"That's a pretty black horse."

"Yes," replied Ellen, blankly.

"Do you like him?"

"I—I love him."

"All right, I'll give him to you then. He'll have less work
and kinder treatment than if I used him. I've got some
pretty hard rides ahead of me."

"Y'u—y'u give—" whispered Ellen, slowly stiffening.

"Yes. He's mine," replied Isbel. With that he turned to
whistle. Spades threw up his head, snorted, and started
forward at a trot. He came faster the closer he got, and if
ever Ellen saw the joy of a horse at sight of a beloved
master she saw it then. Isbel laid a hand on the animal's
neck and caressed him, then, turning back to Ellen, he went
on speaking: "I picked him from a lot of fine horses of my
father's. We got along well. My sister Ann rode him a good
deal. . . . He was stolen from our pasture day before yesterday. I took his trail and tracked him up here. Never lost his
trail till I got to your ranch, where I had to circle till I
picked it up again."

"Stolen—pasture—tracked him up heah?" echoed Ellen,
without any evidence of emotion whatever. Indeed, she
seemed to have been turned to stone.

"Trackin' him was easy. I wish for your sake it'd been
impossible," he said, bluntly.

"For my sake?" she echoed, in precisely the same tone.

Manifestly that tone irritated Isbel beyond control. He misunderstood it. With a hand far from gentle he pushed her bent head back so he could look into her face.

"Yes, for your sake!" he declared, harshly. "Haven't you sense enough to see that? . . . What kind of a game do you think you can play with me?"

"Game! . . . Game of what?" she asked.

"Why, a—a game of ignorance—innocence—any old game to fool a man who's tryin' to be decent."

This time Ellen mutely looked her dull, blank questioning. And it inflamed Isbel.

"You know your father's a horse thief!" he thundered.

Outwardly, Ellen remained the same. She had been prepared for an unknown and a terrible blow. It had fallen. And her face, her body, her hands, locked with the supreme fortitude of pride and sustained by hate, gave no betrayal of the crashing, thundering ruin within her mind and soul. Motionless she leaned there, meeting the piercing fire of Isbel's eyes, seeing in them a righteous and terrible scorn. In one flash the naked truth seemed blazed at her. The faith she had fostered died a sudden death. A thousand perplexing problems were solved in a second of whirling, revealing thought.

"Ellen Jorth, you know your father's in with this Hash Knife Gang of rustlers," thundered Isbel.

"Shore," she replied, with the cool, easy, careless defiance of a Texan.

"You know he's got this Daggs to lead his faction against the Isbels?"

"Shore."

"You know this talk of sheepmen buckin' the cattlemen is all a blind?"

"Shore," reiterated Ellen.

Isbel gazed darkly down upon her. With his anger spent for the moment, he appeared ready to end the interview. But he seemed fascinated by the strange look of her, by the incomprehensible something she emanated. Havoc gleamed in his pale, set face. He shook his dark head and his broad hand went to his breast.

"To think I fell in love with such as you!" he exclaimed, and his other hand swept out in a tragic gesture of helpless pathos and impotence.

The hell Isbel had hinted at now possessed Ellen—body,

97

mind, and soul. Disgraced, scorned by an Isbel! Yet loved by him! In that divination there flamed up a wild, fierce passion to hurt, to rend, to flay, to fling back upon him a stinging agony. Her thought flew upon her like whips. Pride of the Jorths! Pride of the old Texan blue blood! It lay dead at her feet, killed by the scornful words of the last of that family to whom she owed her degradation. Daughter of a horse thief and rustler! Dark and evil and grim set the forces within her, accepting her fate, damning her enemies, true to the blood of the Jorths. The sins of the father must be visited upon the daughter.

"Shore y'u might have had me—that day on the Rim—if y'u hadn't told your name," she said, mockingly, and she gazed into his eyes with all the mystery of a woman's nature.

Isbel's powerful frame shook as with an ague. "Girl, what do you mean?"

"Shore, I'd have been plumb fond of havin' y'u make up to me," she drawled. It possessed her now with irresistible power, this fact of the love he could not help. Some fiendish woman's satisfaction dwelt in her consciousness of her power to kill the noble, the faithful, the good in him.

"Ellen Jorth, you lie!" he burst out, hoarsely.

"Jean, shore I'd been a toy and a rag for these rustlers long enough. I was tired of them. . . . I wanted a new lover. . . . And if y'u hadn't give yourself away—"

Isbel moved so swiftly that she did not realize his intention until his hard hand smote her mouth. Instantly she tasted the hot, salty blood from a cut lip.

"Shut up, you hussy!" he ordered, roughly. "Have you no shame? . . . My sister Ann spoke well of you. She made excuses—she pitied you."

That for Ellen seemed the culminating blow under which she almost sank. But one moment longer could she maintain this unnatural and terrible poise.

"Jean Isbel—go along with y'u," she said, impatiently. "I'm waiting heah for Simm Bruce!"

At last it was as if she struck his heart. Because of doubt of himself and a stubborn faith in her, his passion and jealousy were not proof against this last stab. Instinctive subtlety inherent in Ellen had prompted the speech that tortured Isbel. How the shock to him rebounded on her! She gasped as he lunged for her, too swift for her to move a hand. One arm crushed round her like a steel band; the other, hard across her breast and neck, forced her head

98

back. Then she tried to wrestle away. But she was utterly powerless. His dark face bent down closer and closer. Suddenly Ellen ceased trying to struggle. She was like a stricken creature paralyzed by the piercing, hypnotic eyes of a snake. Yet in spite of her terror, if he meant death by her, she welcomed it.

"Ellen Jorth, I'm thinkin' yet—you lie!" he said, low and tense between his teeth.

"No! No!" she screamed, wildly. Her nerve broke there. She could no longer meet those terrible black eyes. Her passionate denial was not only the last of her shameful deceit; it was the woman of her, repudiating herself and him, and all this sickening, miserable situation.

Isbel took her literally. She had convinced him. And the instant held blank horror for Ellen.

"By God—then I'll have somethin'—of you anyway!" muttered Isbel, thickly.

Ellen saw the blood surge in his powerful neck. She saw his dark, hard face, strange now, fearful to behold, come lower and lower, till it blurred and obstructed her gaze. She felt the swell and ripple and stretch—then the bind of his muscles, like huge coils of elastic rope. Then with savage rude force his mouth closed on hers. All Ellen's senses reeled, as if she were swooning. She was suffocating. The spasm passed, and a bursting spurt of blood revived her to acute and terrible consciousness. For the endless period of one moment he held her so that her breast seemed crushed. His kisses burned and bruised her lips. And then, shifting violently to her neck, they pressed so hard that she choked under them. It was as if a huge bat had fastened upon her throat.

Suddenly the remorseless binding embraces—the hot and savage kisses—fell away from her. Isbel had let go. She saw him throw up his hands, and stagger back a little, all the while with his piercing gaze on her. His face had been dark purple: now it was white.

"No—Ellen Jorth," he panted, "I don't—want any of you —that way." And suddenly he sank on the log and covered his face with his hands. "What I loved in you—was what I thought—you were."

Like a wildcat Ellen sprang upon him, beating him with her fists, tearing at his hair, scratching his face, in a blind fury. Isbel made no move to stop her, and her violence spent itself with her strength. She swayed back from him, shaking so that she could scarcely stand.

"Y'u—damned—Isbel!" she gasped, with hoarse passion. "Y'u insulted me!"

"Insulted you? . . ." laughed Isbel, in bitter scorn. "It couldn't be done."

"Oh! . . . I'll *kill* you!" she hissed.

Isbel stood up and wiped the red scratches on his face. "Go ahead. There's my gun," he said, pointing to his saddle sheath. "Somebody's got to begin this Jorth-Isbel feud. It'll be a dirty business. I'm sick of it already. . . . Kill me! . . . First blood for Ellen Jorth!"

Suddenly the dark grim tide that had seemed to engulf Ellen's very soul cooled and receded, leaving her without its false strength. She began to sag. She stared at Isbel's gun. "Kill him," whispered the retreating voices of her hate. But she was as powerless as if she were still held in Jean Isbel's giant embrace.

"I—I want to—kill y'u," she whispered, "but I cain't. . . . Leave me."

"You're no Jorth—the same as I'm no Isbel. We oughtn't be mixed in this deal," he said, somberly. "I'm sorrier for you than I am for myself. . . . You're a girl. . . . You once had a good mother—a decent home. And this life you've led here—mean as it's been—is nothin' to what you'll face now. Damn the men that brought you to this! I'm goin' to kill some of them."

With that he mounted and turned away. Ellen called out for him to take his horse. He did not stop nor look back. She called again, but her voice was fainter, and Isbel was now leaving at a trot. Slowly she sagged against the tree, lower and lower. He headed into the trail leading up the cañon. How strange a relief Ellen felt! She watched him ride into the aspens and start up the slope, at last to disappear in the pines. It seemed at the moment that he took with him something which had been hers. A pain in her head dulled the thoughts that wavered to and fro. After he had gone she could not see so well. Her eyes were tired. What had happened to her? There was blood on her hands. Isbel's blood! She shuddered. Was it an omen? Lower she sank against the tree and closed her eyes.

Old John Sprague did not return. Hours dragged by—dark hours for Ellen Jorth lying prostrate beside the tree, hiding

100

the blue sky and golden sunlight from her eyes. At length the lethargy of despair, the black dull misery wore away; and she gradually returned to a condition of coherent thought.

What had she learned? Sight of the black horse grazing near seemed to prompt the trenchant replies. Spades belonged to Jean Isbel. He had been stolen by her father or by one of her father's accomplices. Isbel's vaunted cunning as a tracker had been no idle boast. Her father was a horse thief, a rustler, a sheepman only as a blind, a consort of Daggs, leader of the Hash Knife Gang. Ellen well remembered the ill repute of that gang, way back in Texas, years ago. Her father had gotten in with this famous band of rustlers to serve his own ends—the extermination of the Isbels. It was all very plain now to Ellen.

"Daughter of a horse thief an' rustler!" she muttered.

And her thoughts sped back to the days of her girlhood. Only the very early stage of that time had been happy. In the light of Isbel's revelation the many changes of residence, the sudden moves to unsettled parts of Texas, the periods of poverty and sudden prosperity, all leading to the final journey to this God-forsaken Arizona—these were now seen in their true significance. As far back as she could remember her father had been a crooked man. And her mother had known it. He had dragged her to her ruin. That degradation had killed her. Ellen realized that with poignant sorrow, with a sudden revolt against her father. Had Gaston Isbel truly and dishonestly started her father on his downhill road? Ellen wondered. She hated the Isbels with unutterable and growing hate, yet she had it in her to think, to ponder, to weigh judgments in their behalf. She owed it to something in herself to be fair. But what did it matter who was to blame for the Jorth-Isbel feud? Somehow Ellen was forced to confess that deep in her soul it mattered terribly. To be true to herself—the self that she alone knew—she must have right on her side. If the Jorths were guilty, and she clung to them and their creed, then she would be one of them.

"But I'm not," she mused, aloud. "My name's Jorth, an' I reckon I have bad blood. . . . But it never came out in me till to-day. I've been honest. I've been good—yes, *good*, as my mother taught me to be—in spite of all. . . . Shore my pride made me a fool. . . . An' now have I any choice to make? I'm a Jorth. I must stick to my father."

101

All this summing up, however, did not wholly account for the pang in her breast.

What had she done that day? And the answer beat in her ears like a great throbbing hammer-stroke. In an agony of shame, in the throes of hate, she had perjured herself. She had sworn away her honor. She had basely made herself vile. She had struck ruthlessly at the great heart of a man who loved her. Ah! That thrust had rebounded to leave this dreadful pang in her breast. Loved her? Yes, the strange truth, the insupportable truth! She had to contend now, not with her father and her disgrace, not with the baffling presence of Jean Isbel, but with the mysteries of her own soul. Wonder of all wonders was it that such love had been born for her. Shame worse than all other shame was it that she should kill it by a poisoned lie. By what monstrous motive had she done that? To sting Isbel as he had stung her! But that had been base. Never could she have stooped so low except in a moment of tremendous tumult. If she had done sore injury to Isbel what had she done to herself? How strange, how tenacious had been his faith in her honor! Could she ever forget? She must forget it. But she could never forget the way he had scorned those vile men in Greaves's store—the way he had beaten Bruce for defiling her name—the way he had stubbornly denied her own insinuations. She was a woman now. She had learned something of the complexity of a woman's heart. She could not change nature. And all her passionate being thrilled to the manhood of her defender. But even while she thrilled she acknowledged her hate. It was the contention between the two that caused the pang in her breast. "An' now what's left for me?" murmured Ellen. She did not analyze the significance of what had prompted that query. The most incalculable of the day's disclosures was the wrong she had done herself. "Shore I'm done for, one way or another. . . . I must stick to Dad. . . . or kill myself?"

Ellen rode Spades back to the ranch. She rode like the wind. When she swung out of the trail into the open meadow in plain sight of the ranch her appearance created a commotion among the loungers before the cabin. She rode Spades at a full run.

"Who's after you?" yelled her father, as she pulled the black to a halt. Jorth held a rifle. Daggs, Colter, the other

Jorths were there, likewise armed, and all watchful, strung with expectancy.

"Shore nobody's after me," replied Ellen. "Cain't I run a horse round heah without being chased?"

Jorth appeared both incensed and relieved.

"Hah! . . . What you mean, girl, runnin' like a streak right down on us? You're actin' queer these days, an' you look queer. I'm not likin' it."

"Reckon these are queer times—for the Jorths," replied Ellen, sarcastically.

"Daggs found strange horse tracks crossin' the meadow," said her father. "An' that worried us. Some one's been snoopin' round the ranch. An' when we seen you runnin' so wild we shore thought you was bein' chased."

"No. I was only trying out Spades to see how fast he could run," returned Ellen. "Reckon when we do get chased it'll take some running to catch me."

"Haw! Haw!" roared Daggs. "It shore will, Ellen."

"Girl, it's not only your runnin' an' your looks that's queer," declared Jorth, in dark perplexity. "You talk queer."

"Shore, dad, y'u're not used to hearing spades called spades," said Ellen, as she dismounted.

"Humph!" ejaculated her father, as if convinced of the uselessness of trying to understand a woman. "Say, did you see any strange horse tracks?"

"I reckon I did. And I know who made them."

Jorth stiffened. All the men behind him showed a sudden intensity of suspense.

"Who?" demanded Jorth.

"Shore it was Jean Isbel," replied Ellen, coolly. "He came up heah tracking his black horse."

"Jean—Isbel—trackin'—his—black—horse," repeated her father.

"Yes. He's not overrated as a tracker, that's shore."

Blank silence ensued. Ellen cast a slow glance over her father and the others, then she began to loosen the cinches of her saddle. Presently Jorth burst the silence with a curse, and Daggs followed with one of his sardonic laughs.

"Wal, boss, what did I tell you?" he drawled.

Jorth strode to Ellen, and, whirling her around with a strong hand, he held her facing him.

"Did y'u see Isbel?"

"Yes," replied Ellen, just as sharply as her father had asked.

103

"Did y'u talk to him?"

"Yes."

"What did he want up heah?"

"I told y'u. He was tracking the black horse y'u stole."

Jorth's hand and arm dropped limply. His sallow face turned a livid hue. Amaze merged into discomfiture and that gave place to rage. He raised a hand as if to strike Ellen. And suddenly Daggs's long arm shot out to clutch Jorth's wrist. Wrestling to free himself, Jorth cursed under his breath. "Let go, Daggs," he shouted, stridently. "Am I drunk that you grab me?"

"Wal, y'u ain't drunk, I reckon," replied the rustler, with sarcasm. "But y'u're shore some things I'll reserve for your private ear."

Jorth gained a semblance of composure. But it was evident that he labored under a shock.

"Ellen, did Jean Isbel see this black horse?"

"Yes. He asked me how I got Spades an' I told him."

"Did he say Spades belonged to him?"

"Shore I reckon he proved it. Y'u can always tell a horse that loves its master."

"Did y'u offer to give Spades back?"

"Yes. But Isbel wouldn't take him."

"Hah! . . . An' why not?"

"He said he'd rather I kept him. He was about to engage in a dirty, blood-spilling deal, an' he reckoned he'd not be able to care for a fine horse. . . . I didn't want Spades. I tried to make Isbel take him. But he rode off. . . . And that's all there is to that."

"Maybe it's not," replied Jorth, chewing his mustache and eying Ellen with dark, intent gaze. "Yu've met this Isbel twice."

"It wasn't any fault of mine," retorted Ellen.

"I heah he's sweet on y'u. How aboot that?"

Ellen smarted under the blaze of blood that swept to neck and cheek and temple. But it was only memory which fired this shame. What her father and his crowd might think were matters of supreme indifference. Yet she met his suspicious gaze with truthful blazing eyes.

"I heah talk from Bruce an' Lorenzo," went on her father. "An' Daggs heah—"

"Daggs nothin'!" interrupted that worthy. "Don't fetch me in. I said nothin' an' I think nothin'."

"Yes, Jean Isbel *was* sweet on me, dad . . . but he will

never be again," returned Ellen, in low tones. With that she pulled her saddle off Spades and, throwing it over her shoulder, she walked off to her cabin.

Hardly had she gotten indoors when her father entered.

"Ellen, I didn't know that horse belonged to Isbel," he began, in the swift, hoarse, persuasive voice so familiar to Ellen. "I swear I didn't. I bought him—traded with Slater for him. . . . Honest to God, I never had any idea he was stolen! . . . Why, when y'u said 'that horse y'u stole,' I felt as if y'u'd knifed me. . . ."

Ellen sat at the table and listened while her father paced to and fro and, by his restless action and passionate speech, worked himself into a frenzy. He talked incessantly, as if her silence was condemnatory and as if eloquence alone could convince her of his honesty. It seemed that Ellen saw and heard with keener faculties than ever before. He had a terrible thirst for her respect. Not so much for her love, she divined, but that she would not see how he had fallen!

She pitied him with all her heart. She was all he had, as he was all the world to her. And so, as she gave ear to his long, illogical rigmarole of argument and defense, she slowly found that her pity and her love were making vital decisions for her. As of old, in poignant moments, her father lapsed at last into a denunciation of the Isbels and what they had brought him to. His sufferings were real, at least, in Ellen's presence. She was the only link that bound him to long-past happier times. She was her mother over again—the woman who had betrayed another man for him and gone with him to her ruin and death.

"Dad, don't go on so," said Ellen, breaking in upon her father's rant. "I will be true to y'u—as my mother was. . . . I am a Jorth. Your place is my place—your fight is my fight. . . . Never speak of the past to me again. If God spares us through this feud we will go away and begin all over again, far off where no one ever heard of a Jorth. . . . If we're not spared we'll at least have had our whack at those damned Isbels."

7

★

DURING June Jean Isbel did not ride far away from Grass Valley.

Another attempt had been made upon Gaston Isbel's life. Another cowardly shot had been fired from ambush, this time from a pine thicket bordering the trail that led to Blaisdell's ranch. Blaisdell heard this shot, so near his home was it fired. No trace of the hidden foe could be found. The ground all around that vicinity bore a carpet of pine needles which showed no trace of footprints. The supposition was that this cowardly attempt had been perpetrated, or certainly instigated, by the Jorths. But there was no proof. And Gaston Isbel had other enemies in the Tonto Basin besides the sheep clan. The old man raged like a lion about this sneaking attack on him. And his friend Blaisdell urged an immediate gathering of their kin and friends. "Let's quit ranchin' till this trouble's settled," he declared. "Let's arm an' ride the trails an' meet these men half-way. . . . It won't help our side any to wait till you're shot in the back." More than one of Isbel's supporters offered the same advice.

"No; we'll wait till we know for shore," was the stubborn cattleman's reply to all these promptings.

"Know! Wal, hell! Didn't Jean find the black hoss up at Jorth's ranch?" demanded Blaisdell. "What more do we want?"

"Jean couldn't swear Jorth stole the black."

"Wal, by thunder, I can swear to it!" growled Blaisdell. "An' we're losin' cattle all the time. Who's stealin' 'em?"

"We've always lost cattle ever since we started ranchin' heah."

"Gas, I reckon y'u want Jorth to start this fight in the open."

"It'll start soon enough," was Isbel's gloomy reply.

Jean had not failed altogether in his tracking of lost or stolen cattle. Circumstances had been against him, and there was something baffling about this rustling. The summer storms set in early, and it had been his luck to have heavy rains wash out fresh tracks that he might have followed. The range was large and cattle were everywhere. Sometimes a loss was not discovered for weeks. Gaston Isbel's sons were now the only men left to ride the range. Two of his riders had quit because of the threatened war, and Isbel had let another go. So that Jean did not often learn that cattle had been stolen until their tracks were old. Added to that was the fact that this Grass Valley country was covered with horse tracks and cattle tracks. The rustlers, whoever they were, had long been at the game, and now that there was reason for them to show their cunning they did it.

Early in July the hot weather came. Down on the red ridges of the Tonto it was hot desert. The nights were cool, the early mornings were pleasant, but the day was something to endure. When the white cumulus clouds rolled up out of the southwest, growing larger and thicker and darker, here and there coalescing into a black thundercloud, Jean welcomed them. He liked to see the gray streamers of rain hanging down from a canopy of black, and the roar of rain on the trees as it approached like a trampling army was always welcome. The grassy flats, the red ridges, the rocky slopes, the thickets of manzanita and scrub oak and cactus were dusty, glaring, throat-parching places under the hot summer sun. Jean longed for the cool heights of the Rim, the shady pines, the dark sweet verdure under the silver spruces, the tinkle and murmur of the clear rills. He often had another longing, too, which he bitterly stifled.

Jean's ally, the keen-nosed shepherd dog, had disappeared one day, and had never returned. Among men at the ranch there was a difference of opinion as to what had happened to Shepp. The old rancher thought he had been poisoned or shot; Bill and Guy Isbel believed he had been stolen by sheep herders, who were always stealing dogs; and Jean inclined to the conviction that Shepp had gone off with the timber wolves. The fact was that Shepp did not return, and Jean missed him.

One morning at dawn Jean heard the cattle bellowing and trampling out in the valley; and upon hurrying to a vantage point he was amazed to see upward of five hundred steers chasing a lone wolf. Jean's father had seen such a spectacle as this, but it was a new one for Jean. The wolf was a big gray and black fellow, rangy and powerful, and until he

107

got the steers all behind him he was rather hard put to it to keep out of their way. Probably he had dogged the herd, trying to sneak in and pull down a yearling, and finally the steers had charged him. Jean kept along the edge of the valley in the hope they would chase him within range of a rifle. But the wary wolf saw Jean and sheered off, gradually drawing away from his pursuers.

Jean returned to the house for his breakfast, and then set off across the valley. His father owned one small flock of sheep that had not yet been driven up on the Rim, where all the sheep in the country were run during the hot, dry summer down on the Tonto. Young Evarts and a Mexican boy named Bernardino had charge of this flock. The regular Mexican herder, a man of experience, had given up his job; and these boys were not equal to the task of risking the sheep up in the enemies' stronghold.

This flock was known to be grazing in a side draw, well up from Grass Valley, where the brush afforded some protection from the sun, and there was good water and a little feed. Before Jean reached his destination he heard a shot. It was not a rifle shot, which fact caused Jean a little concern. Evarts and Bernardino had rifles, but, to his knowledge, no small arms. Jean rode up on one of the black-brushed conical hills that rose on the south side of Grass Valley, and from there he took a sharp survey of the country. At first he made out only cattle, and bare meadowland, and the low encircling ridges and hills. But presently up toward the head of the valley he descried a bunch of horsemen riding toward the village. He could not tell their number. That dark moving mass seemed to Jean to be instinct with life, mystery, menace. Who were they? It was too far for him to recognize horses, let alone riders. They were moving fast, too.

Jean watched them out of sight, then turned his horse downhill again, and rode on his quest. A number of horsemen like that was a very unusual sight around Grass Valley at any time. What then did it portend now? Jean experienced a little shock of uneasy dread that was a new sensation for him. Brooding over this he proceeded on his way, at length to turn into the draw where the camp of the sheep-herders was located. Upon coming in sight of it he heard a hoarse shout. Young Evarts appeared running frantically out of the brush. Jean urged his horse into a run and soon covered the distance between them. Evarts appeared beside himself with terror.

"Boy! what's the matter?" queried Jean, as he dismounted, rifle in hand, peering quickly from Evarts's white face to the camp, and all around.

"Ber-nadino! Ber-nardino!" gasped the boy, wringing his hands and pointing.

Jean ran the few remaining rods to the sheep camp. He saw the little teepee, a burned-out fire, a half-finished meal—and then the Mexican lad lying prone on the ground, dead, with a bullet hole in his ghastly face. Near him lay an old six-shooter.

"Whose gun is that?" demanded Jean, as he picked it up.

"Ber-nardino's," replied Evarts, huskily. "He—he jest got it—the other day."

"Did he shoot himself accidentally?"

"Oh no! No! He didn't do it—atall."

"Who did, then?"

"The men—they rode up—a gang—they did it," panted Evarts.

"Did you know who they were?"

"No. I couldn't tell. I saw them comin' an' I was skeered. Bernardino had gone fer water. I run an' hid in the brush. I wanted to yell, but they come too close. . . . Then I heerd them talkin'. Bernardino come back. They 'peared friendly-like. Thet made me raise up to look. An' I couldn't see good. I heerd one of them ask Bernardino to let him see his gun. An' Bernardino handed it over. He looked at the gun an' haw-hawed, an' flipped it up in the air, an' when it fell back in his hand it—it went off bang! . . . An' Bernardino dropped. . . . I hid down close. I was skeered stiff. I heerd them talk more, but not what they said. Then they rode away. . . . An' I hid there till I seen y'u comin'."

"Have you got a horse?" queried Jean, sharply.

"No. But I can ride one of Bernardino's burros."

"Get one. Hurry over to Blaisdell. Tell him to send word to Blue and Gordon and Fredericks to ride like the devil to my father's ranch. Hurry now!"

Young Evarts ran off without reply. Jean stood looking down at the limp and pathetic figure of the Mexican boy. "By Heaven!" he exclaimed, grimly "the Jorth-Isbel war is on! . . . Deliberate, cold-blooded murder! I'll gamble Daggs did this job. He's been given the leadership. He's started it.

. . . Bernardino, greaser or not, you were a faithful lad, and you won't go long unavenged."

Jean had no time to spare. Tearing a tarpaulin out of the teepee he covered the lad with it and then ran for his horse. Mounting, he galloped down the draw, over the little red ridges, out into the valley, where he put his horse to a run.

Action changed the sickening horror that sight of Bernardino had engendered. Jean even felt a strange, grim relief. The long, dragging days of waiting were over. Jorth's gang had taken the initiative. Blood had begun to flow. And it would continue to flow now till the last man of one faction stood over the dead body of the last man of the other. Would it be a Jorth or an Isbel? "My instinct was right," he muttered, aloud. "That bunch of horses gave me a queer feelin'." Jean gazed all around the grassy, cattle-dotted valley he was crossing so swiftly, and toward the village, but he did not see any sign of the dark group of riders. They had gone on to Greaves's store, there, no doubt, to drink and to add more enemies of the Isbels to their gang. Suddenly across Jean's mind flashed a thought of Ellen Jorth. "What'll become of her? . . . What'll become of all the women? My sister? . . . The little ones?"

No one was in sight around the ranch. Never had it appeared more peaceful and pastoral to Jean. The grazing cattle and horses in the foreground, the haystack half eaten away, the cows in the fenced pasture, the column of blue smoke lazily ascending, the cackle of hens, the solid, well-built cabins—all these seemed to repudiate Jean's haste and his darkness of mind. This place was his father's farm. There was not a cloud in the blue, summer sky.

As Jean galloped up the lane some one saw him from the door, and then Bill and Guy and their gray-headed father came out upon the porch. Jean saw how he waved the womenfolk back, and then strode out into the lane. Bill and Guy reached his side as Jean pulled his heaving horse to a halt. They all looked at Jean, swiftly and intently, with a little, hard, fiery gleam strangely identical in the eyes of each. Probably before a word was spoken they knew what to expect.

"Wal, you shore was in a hurry," remarked the father.

"What the hell's up?" queried Bill, grimly.

Guy Isbel remained silent and it was he who turned slightly pale. Jean leaped off his horse.

110

"Bernardino has just been killed—murdered with his own gun."

Gaston Isbel seemed to exhale a long-dammed, bursting breath that let his chest sag. A terribly deadly glint, pale and cold as sunlight on ice, grew slowly to dominate his clear eyes.

"A-huh!" ejaculated Bill Isbel, hoarsely.

Not one of the three men asked who had done the killing. They were silent a moment, motionless, locked in the secret seclusion of their own minds. Then they listened with absorption to Jean's brief story.

"Wal, that lets us in," said his father. "I wish we had more time. Reckon I'd done better to listen to you boys an' have my men close at hand. Jacobs happened to ride over. That makes five of us besides the women."

"Aw, dad, you don't reckon they'll round us up heah?" asked Guy Isbel.

"Boys, I always feared they might," replied the old man. "But I never really believed they'd have the nerve. Shore I ought to have figgered Daggs better. This heah secret bizness an' shootin' at us from ambush looked aboot Jorth's size to me. But I reckon now we'll have to fight without our friends."

"Let them come," said Jean. "I sent for Blaisdell, Blue, Gordon, and Fredericks. Maybe they'll get here in time. But if they don't it needn't worry us much. We can hold out here longer than Jorth's gang can hang around. We'll want plenty of water, wood, and meat in the house."

"Wal, I'll see to that," rejoined his father. "Jean, you go out close by, where you can see all around, an' keep watch."

"Who's goin' to tell the women?" asked Guy Isbel.

The silence that momentarily ensued was an eloquent testimony to the hardest and saddest aspect of this strife between men. The inevitableness of it in no wise detracted from its sheer uselessness. Men from time immemorial had hated, and killed one another, always to the misery and degradation of their women. Old Gaston Isbel showed this tragic realization in his lined face.

"Wal, boys, I'll tell the women," he said. "Shore you needn't worry none aboot them. They'll be game."

Jean rode away to an open knoll a short distance from the house, and here he stationed himself to watch all points. The cedared ridge back of the ranch was the one approach by which Jorth's gang might come close without being detected, but even so, Jean could see them and ride to the house in time to prevent a surprise. The moments dragged by, and at the end of an hour Jean was in hopes that Blaisdell would soon come. These hopes were well founded. Presently he heard a clatter of hoofs on hard ground to the south, and upon wheeling to look he saw the friendly neighbor coming fast along the road, riding a big white horse. Blaisdell carried a rifle in his hand, and the sight of him gave Jean a glow of warmth. He was one of the Texans who would stand by the Isbels to the last man. Jean watched him ride to the house—watched the meeting between him and his lifelong friend. There floated out to Jean old Blaisdell's roar of rage.

Then out on the green of Grass Valley, where a long, swelling plain swept away toward the village, there appeared a moving dark patch. A bunch of horses! Jean's body gave a slight start—the shock of sudden propulsion of blood through all his veins. Those horses bore riders. They were coming straight down the open valley, on the wagon road to Isbel's ranch. No subterfuge nor secrecy nor sneaking in that advance! A hot thrill ran over eJan.

"By Heaven! They mean business!" he muttered. Up to the last moment he had unconsciously hoped Jorth's gang would not come boldly like that. The verifications of all a Texan's inherited instincts left no doubts, no hopes, no illusions—only a grim certainty that this was not conjecture nor probability, but fact. For a moment longer Jean watched the slowly moving dark patch of horsemen against the green background, then he hurried back to the ranch. His father saw him coming—strode out as before.

"Dad—Jorth is comin'," said Jean, huskily. How he hated to be forced to tell his father that! The boyish love of old had flashed up.

"Whar?" demanded the old man, his eagle gaze sweeping the horizon.

"Down the road from Grass Valley. You can't see from here."

"Wal, come in an' let's get ready."

Isbel's house had not been constructed with the idea of repelling an attack from a band of Apaches. The long living room of the main cabin was the one selected for defense and protection. This room had two windows and a door facing the lane, and a door at each end, one of which opened into the kitchen and the other into an adjoining and

112

later-built cabin. The logs of this main cabin were of large size, and the doors and window coverings were heavy, affording safer protection from bullets than the other cabins.

When Jean went in he seemed to see a host of white faces lifted to him. His sister Ann, his two sisters-in-law, the children, all mutely watched him with eyes that would haunt him.

"Wal, Blaisdell, Jean says Jorth an' his precious gang of rustlers are on the way heah," announced the rancher.

"Damn me if it's not a bad day fer Lee Jorth!" declared Blaisdell.

"Clear off that table," ordered Isbel, "an' fetch out all the guns an' shells we got."

Once laid upon the table these presented a formidable arsenal, which consisted of the three new .44 Winchesters that Jean had brought with him from the coast; the enormous buffalo, or so-called "needle" gun, that Gaston Isbel had used for years; a Henry rifle which Blaisdell had brought, and half a dozen six-shooters. Piles and packages of ammunition littered the table.

"Sort out these heah shells," said Isbel. "Everybody wants to get hold of his own."

Jacobs, the neighbor who was present, was a thick-set, bearded man, rather jovial among these lean-jawed Texans. He carried a .44 rifle of an old pattern. "Wal, boys, if I'd knowed we was in fer some fun I'd hev fetched more shells. Only got one magazine full. Mebbe them new .44s will fit my gun."

It was discovered that the ammunition Jean had brought in quantity fitted Jacob's rifle, a fact which afforded peculiar satisfaction to all the men present.

"Wal, shore we're lucky," declared Gaston Isbel.

The women sat apart, in the corner toward the kitchen, and there seemed to be a strange fascination for them in the talk and action of the men. The wife of Jacobs was a little woman, with homely face and very bright eyes. Jean thought she would be a help in that household during the next doubtful hours.

Every moment Jean would go to the window and peer out down the road. His companions evidently relied upon him, for no one else looked out. Now that the suspense of days and weeks was over, these Texans faced the issue with talk and act not noticeably different from those of ordinary moments.

At last Jean espied the dark mass of horsemen out in the

113

valley road. They were close together, walking their mounts, and evidently in earnest conversation. After several ineffectual attempts Jean counted eleven horses, every one of which he was sure bore a rider.

"Dad, look out!" called Jean.

Gaston Isbel strode to the door and stood looking, without a word.

The other men crowded to the windows. Blaisdell cursed under his breath. Jacobs said: "By Golly! Come to pay us a call!" The women sat motionless, with dark, strained eyes. The children ceased their play and looked fearfully to their mother.

When just out of rifle shot of the cabins the band of horsemen halted and lined up in a half circle, all facing the ranch. They were close enough for Jean to see their gestures, but he could not recognize any of their faces. It struck him singularly that not one of them wore a mask.

"Jean, do you know any of them?" asked his father.

"No, not yet. They're too far off."

"Dad, I'll get your old telescope," said Guy Isbel, and he ran out toward the adjoining cabin.

Blaisdell shook his big, hoary head and rumbled out of his bull-like neck, "Wal, now you're heah, you sheep fellars, what are you goin' to do aboot it?"

Guy Isbel returned with a yard-long telescope, which he passed to his father. The old man took it with shaking hands and leveled it. Suddenly it was as if he had been transfixed; then he lowered the glass, shaking violently, and his face grew gray with an exceeding bitter wrath.

"Jorth!" he swore, harshly.

Jean had only to look at his father to know that recognition had been like a mortal shock. It passed. Again the rancher leveled the glass.

"Wal, Blaisdell, there's our old Texas friend, Daggs," he drawled, dryly. "An' Greaves, our honest storekeeper of Grass Valley. An' there's Stonewall Jackson Jorth. An' Tad Jorth, with the same old red nose! . . . An', say, damn if one of that gang isn't Queen, as bad a gun fighter as Texas ever bred. Shore I thought he'd been killed in the Big Bend country. So I heard. . . . An' there's Craig, another respectable sheepman of Grass Valley. Haw-haw! . . . An', wal, I don't recognize any more of them."

Jean forthwith took the glass and moved it slowly across the faces of that group of horsemen. "Simm Bruce," he said,

114

instantly. "I see Colter. And, yes, Greaves is there. I've seen the man next to him—face like a ham. . . ."

"Shore that is Craig," interrupted his father.

Jean knew the dark face of Lee Jorth by the resemblance it bore to Ellen's, and the recognition brought a twinge. He thought, too, that he could tell the other Jorths. He asked his father to describe Daggs and then Queen. It was not likely that Jean would fail to know these several men in the future. Then Blaisdell asked for the telescope and, when he got through looking and cursing, he passed it on to others, who, one by one, took a long look, until finally it came back to the old rancher.

"Wal, Daggs is wavin' his hand heah an' there, like a general aboot to send out scouts. Haw-haw! . . . An' 'pears to me he's not overlookin' our hosses. Wal, that's natural for a rustler. He'd have to steal a hoss or a steer before goin' into a fight or to dinner or to a funeral."

"It'll be his funeral if he goes to foolin' 'round them hosses," declared Guy Isbel, peering anxiously out of the door.

"Wal, son, shore it'll be somebody's funeral," replied his father.

Jean paid but little heed to the conversation. With sharp eyes fixed upon the horsemen, he tried to grasp at their intention. Daggs pointed to the horses in the pasture lot that lay between him and the house. These animals were the best on the range and belonged mostly to Guy Isbel, who was the horse fancier and trader of the family. His horses were his passion.

"Looks like they'd do some horse stealin'," said Jean.

"Lend me that glass," demanded Guy, forcefully. He surveyed the band of men for a long moment, then he handed the glass back to Jean.

"I'm goin' out there after my hosses," he declared.

"No!" exclaimed his father.

"That gang come to steal an' not to fight. Can't you see that? If they meant to fight they'd do it. They're out there arguin' about my hosses."

Guy picked up his rifle. He looked sullenly determined and the gleam in his eye was one of fearlessness.

"Son, I know Daggs," said his father. "An' I know Jorth. They've come to kill us. It'll be shore death for y'u to go out there."

"I'm goin', anyhow. They can't steal my hosses out from under my eyes. An' they ain't in range."

"Wal, Guy, you ain't goin' alone," spoke up Jacobs, cheerily, as he came forward.

The red-haired young wife of Guy Isbel showed no change of her grave face. She had been reared in a stern school. She knew men in times like these. But Jacobs's wife appealed to him, "Bill, don't risk your life for a horse or two."

Jacobs laughed and answered, "Not much risk," and went out with Guy. To Jean their action seemed foolhardy. He kept a keen eye on them and saw instantly when the band became aware of Guy's and Jacob's entrance into the pasture. It took only another second then to realize that Daggs and Jorth had deadly intent. Jean saw Daggs slip out of his saddle, rifle in hand. Others of the gang did likewise, until half of them were dismounted.

"Dad, they're goin' to shoot," called out Jean, sharply. "Yell for Guy and Jacobs. Make them come back."

The old man shouted; Bill Isbel yelled; Blaisdell lifted his stentorian voice.

Jean screamed piercingly: "Guy! Run! Run!"

But Guy Isbel and his companion strode on into the pasture, as if they had not heard, as if no menacing horse thieves were within miles. They had covered about a quarter of the distance across the pasture, and were nearing the horses, when Jean saw red flashes and white puffs of smoke burst out from the front of that dark band of rustlers. Then followed the sharp, rattling crack of rifles.

Guy Isbel stopped short, and, dropping his gun, he threw up his arms and fell headlong. Jacobs acted as if he had suddenly encountered an invisible blow. He had been hit. Turning, he began to run and ran fast for a few paces. There were more quick, sharp shots. He let go of his rifle. His running broke. Walking, reeling, staggering, he kept on. A hoarse cry came from him. Then a single rifle shot pealed out. Jean heard the bullet strike. Jacobs fell to his knees, then forward on his face.

Jean Isbel felt himself turned to marble. The suddenness of this tragedy paralyzed him. His gaze remained riveted on those prostrate forms.

A hand clutched his arm—a shaking woman's hand, slim and hard and tense.

116

"Bill's—killed!" whispered a broken voice. "I was watchin'. . . . They're both dead!"

The wives of Jacobs and Guy Isbel had slipped up behind Jean and from behind him they had seen the tragedy.

"I asked Bill—not to—go," faltered the Jacobs woman, and, covering her face with her hands, she groped back to the corner of the cabin, where the other women, shaking and white, received her in their arms. Guy Isbel's wife stood at the window, peering over Jean's shoulder. She had the nerve of a man. She had looked out upon death before.

"Yes, they're dead," she said, bitterly. "An' how are we goin' to get their bodies?"

At this Gaston Isbel seemed to rouse from the cold spell that had transfixed him.

"God, this is hell for our women," he cried out, hoarsely. "My son—my son! . . . Murdered by the Jorths!" Then he swore a terrible oath.

Jean saw the remainder of the mounted rustlers get off, and then, all of them leading their horses, they began to move around to the left.

"Dad, they're movin' round," said Jean.

"Up to some trick," declared Bill Isbel.

"Bill, you make a hole through the back wall, say aboot the fifth log up," ordered the father. "Shore we've got to look out."

The elder son grasped a tool and, scattering the children, who had been playing near the back corner, he began to work at the point designated. The little children backed away with fixed, wondering, grave eyes. The women moved their chairs, and huddled together as if waiting and listening.

Jean watched the rustlers until they passed out of his sight. They had moved toward the sloping, brushy ground to the north and west of the cabins.

"Let me know when you get a hole in the back wall," said Jean, and he went through the kitchen and cautiously out another door to slip into a low-roofed, shed-like end of the rambling cabin. This small space was used to store winter firewood. The chinks between the walls had not been filled with adobe clay, and he could see out on three sides. The rustlers were going into the juniper brush. They moved out of sight, and presently reappeared without their horses. It looked to Jean as if they intended to attack the cabins. Then they halted at the edge of the brush and held a long consultation. Jean could see them distinctly, though they

117

were too far distant for him to recognize any particular man. One of them, however, stood and moved apart from the closely massed group. Evidently, from his strides and gestures, he was exhorting his listeners. Jean concluded this was either Daggs or Jorth. Whoever it was had a loud, coarse voice, and this and his actions impressed Jean with a suspicion that the man was under the influence of the bottle.

Presently Bill Isbel called Jean in a low voice. "Jean, I got the hole made, but we can't see anyone."

"I see them," Jean replied. "They're havin' a powwow. Looks to me like either Jorth or Daggs is drunk. He's arguin' to charge us, an' the rest of the gang are holdin' back. . . . Tell dad, an' all of you keep watchin'. I'll let you know when they make a move."

Jorth's gang appeared to be in no hurry to expose their plan of battle. Gradually the group disintegrated a little; some of them sat down; others walked to and fro. Presently two of them went into the brush, probably back to the horses. In a few moments they reappeared, carrying a pack. And when this was deposited on the ground all the rustlers sat down around it. They had brought food and drink. Jean had to utter a grim laugh at their coolness; and he was reminded of many dare-devil deeds known to have been perpetrated by the Hash Knife Gang. Jean was glad of a reprieve. The longer the rustlers put off an attack the more time the allies of the Isbels would have to get here. Rather hazardous, however, would it be now for anyone to attempt to get to the Isbel cabins in the daytime. Night would be more favorable.

Twice Bill Isbel came through the kitchen to whisper to Jean. The strain in the large room, from which the rustlers could not be seen, must have been great. Jean told him all he had seen and what he thought about it. "Eatin' an' drinkin'!" ejaculated Bill. "Well, I'll be—! That'll jar the old man. He wants to get the fight over."

"Tell him I said it'll be over too quick—for us—unless we are mighty careful," replied Jean, sharply.

Bill went back muttering to himself. Then followed a long wait, fraught with suspense, during which Jean watched the rustlers regale themselves. The day was hot and still. And the unnatural silence of the cabin was broken now and then by the gay laughter of the children. The sound shocked and haunted Jean. Playing children! Then another sound, so faint he had to strain to hear it, disturbed and saddened him—his father's slow tread up and down the cabin floor, to and fro, to and fro. What must be in his father's heart this day!

At length the rustlers rose and, with rifles in hand, they moved as one man down the slope. They came several hundred yards closer, until Jean, grimly cocking his rifle, muttered to himself that a few more rods closer would mean the end of several of that gang. They knew the range of a rifle well enough, and once more sheered off at right angles with the cabin. When they got even with the line of corrals they stooped down and were lost to Jean's sight. This fact caused him alarm. They were, of course, crawling up on the cabins. At the end of that line of corrals ran a ditch, the bank of which was high enough to afford cover. Moreover, it ran along in front of the cabins, scarcely a hundred yards, and it was covered with grass and little clumps of brush, from behind which the rustlers could fire into the windows and through the clay chinks without any considerable risk to themselves. As they did not come into sight again, Jean concluded he had discovered their plan. Still, he waited awhile longer, until he saw faint, little clouds of dust rising from behind the far end of the embankment. That discovery made him rush out, and through the kitchen to the large cabin, where his sudden appearance startled the men.

"Get back out of sight!" he ordered, sharply, and with swift steps he reached the door and closed it. "They're behind the bank out there by the corrals. An' they're goin' to crawl down the ditch closer to us. . . . It looks bad. They'll have grass an' brush to shoot from. We've got to be mighty careful how we peep out."

"Ahuh! All right," replied his father. "You women keep the kids with you in that corner. An' you all better lay down flat."

Blaisdell, Bill Isbel, and the old man crouched at the large window, peeping through cracks in the rough edges of the logs. Jean took his post beside the small window, with his keen eyes vibrating like a compass needle. The movement of a blade of grass, the flight of a grasshopper could not escape his trained sight.

"Look sharp now!" he called to the other men. "I see dust. . . . They're workin' along almost to that bare spot on the bank. . . . I saw the tip of a rifle . . . a black hat . . . more dust. They're spreadin' along behind the bank."

Loud voices, and then thick clouds of yellow dust, coming from behind the highest and brushiest line of the embankment, attested to the truth of Jean's observation, and also to a reckless disregard of danger.

Suddenly Jean caught a glint of moving color through the fringe of brush. Instantly he was strung like a whipcord.

Then a tall, hatless and coatless man stepped up in plain sight. The sun shone on his fair, ruffled hair. Daggs!

"Hey, you —— —— Isbels!" he bawled, in magnificent derisive boldness. "Come out an' fight!"

Quick as lightning Jean threw up his rifle and fired. He saw tufts of fair hair fly from Daggs's head. He saw the squirt of red blood. Then quick shots from his comrades rang out. They all hit the swaying body of the rustler. But Jean knew with a terrible thrill that his bullet had killed Daggs before the other three struck. Daggs fell forward, his arms and half his body resting over the embankment. Then the rustlers dragged him back out of sight. Hoarse shouts rose. A cloud of yellow dust drifted away from the spot.

"Daggs!" burst out Gaston Isbel. "Jean, you knocked off the top of his haid. I seen that when I was pullin' trigger. Shore we over heah wasted our shots."

"God! he must have been crazy or drunk—to pop up there—an' brace us that way," said Blaisdell, breathing hard.

"Arizona is bad for Texans," replied Isbel, sardonically. "Shore it's been too peaceful heah. Rustlers have no practice at fightin'. An' I reckon Daggs forgot."

"Daggs made as crazy a move as that of Guy an' Jacobs," spoke up Jean. "They were overbold, an' he was drunk. Let them be a lesson to us."

Jean had smelled whisky upon his entrance to this cabin. Bill was a hard drinker, and his father was not immune. Blaisdell, too, drank heavily upon occasions. Jean made a mental note that he would not permit their chances to become impaired by liquor.

Rifles began to crack, and puffs of smoke rose all along the embankment for the space of a hundred feet. Bullets whistled through the rude window casing and spattered on the heavy door, and one split the clay between the logs before Jean, narrowly missing him. Another volley followed, then another. The rustlers had repeating rifles and they were emptying their magazines. Jean changed his position. The other men profited by his wise move. The volleys had merged into one continuous rattling roar of rifle shots. Then came a sudden cessation of reports, with silence of relief. The cabin was full of dust, mingled with the smoke from the shots of Jean and his companions. Jean heard the stifled breaths of the children. Evidently they were terror-stricken, but they did not cry out. The women uttered no sound.

A loud voice pealed from behind the embankment.

"Come out an' fight! Do you Isbels want to be killed like sheep?"

This sally gained no reply. Jean returned to his post by the window and his comrades followed his example. And they exercised extreme caution when they peeped out.

"Boys, don't shoot till you see one," said Gaston Isbel. "Maybe after a while they'll get careless. But Jorth will never show himself."

The rustlers did not again resort to volleys. One by one, from different angles, they began to shoot, and they were not firing at random. A few bullets came straight in at the windows to pat into the walls; a few others ticked and splintered the edges of the windows; and most of them broke through the clay chinks between the logs. It dawned upon Jean that these dangerous shots were not accident. They were well aimed, and most of them hit low down. The cunning rustlers had some unerring riflemen and they were picking out the vulnerable places all along the front of the cabin. If Jean had not been lying flat he would have been hit twice. Presently he conceived the idea of driving pegs between the logs, high up, and, kneeling on these, he managed to peep out from the upper edge of the window. But this position was awkward and difficult to hold for long.

He heard a bullet hit one of his comrades. Whoever had been struck never uttered a sound. Jean turned to look. Bill Isbel was holding his shoulder, where red splotches appeared on his shirt. He shook his head at Jean, evidently to make light of the wound. The women and children were lying face down and could not see what was happening. Plain it was that Bill did not want them to know. Blaisdell bound up the bloody shoulder with a scarf.

Steady firing from the rustlers went on, at the rate of one shot every few minutes. The Isbels did not return these. Jean did not fire again that afternoon. Toward sunset, when the besiegers appeared to grow restless or careless, Blaisdell fired at something moving behind the brush; and Gaston Isbel's huge buffalo gun boomed out.

"Wal, what're they goin' to do after dark, an' what're *we* goin' to do?" grumbled Blaisdell.

"Reckon they'll never charge us," said Gaston.

"They might set fire to the cabins," added Bill Isbel. He appeared to be the gloomiest of the Isbel faction. There was something on his mind.

"Wal, the Jorths are bad, but I reckon they'd not burn us alive," replied Blaisdell.

"Hah!" ejaculated Gaston Isbel. "Much you know aboot Lee Jorth. He would skin me alive an' throw red-hot coals on my raw flesh."

So they talked during the hour from sunset to dark. Jean Isbel had little to say. He was revolving possibilities in his mind. Darkness brought a change in the attack of the rustlers. They stationed men at four points around the cabins; and every few minutes one of these outposts would fire. These bullets embedded themselves in the logs, causing but little anxiety to the Isbels.

"Jean, what you make of it?" asked the old rancher.

"Looks to me this way," replied Jean. "They're set for a long fight. They're shootin' just to let us know they're on the watch."

"Ahuh? Wal, what 're you goin' to do aboot it?"

"I'm goin' out there presently."

Gaston Isbel grunted his satisfaction at this intention of Jean's.

All was pitch dark inside the cabin. The women had water and food at hand. Jean kept a sharp lookout from his window while he ate his supper of meat, bread, and milk. At last the children, worn out by the long day, fell asleep. The women whispered a little in their corner.

About nine o'clock Jean signified his intention of going out to reconnoitre.

"Dad, they've got the best of us in the daytime," he said, "but not after dark."

Jean buckled on a belt that carried shells, a bowie knife, and revolver, and with rifle in hand he went out through the kitchen to the yard. The night was darker than usual, as some of the stars were hidden by clouds. He leaned against the log cabin, waiting for his eyes to become perfectly adjusted to the darkness. Like an Indian, Jean could see well at night. He knew every point around cabins and sheds and corrals, every post, log, tree, rock, adjacent to the ranch. After perhaps a quarter of an hour watching, during which time several shots were fired from behind the embankment and one each from the rustlers at the other locations, Jean slipped out on his quest.

He kept in the shadow of the cabin walls, then the line of orchard trees, then a row of currant bushes. Here, crouching low, he halted to look and listen. He was now at the edge of the open ground, with the gently rising slope before him. He could see the dark patches of cedar and juniper trees. On the north side of the cabin a streak of fire flashed in the blackness, and a shot rang out. Jean heard the bullet hit the cabin. Then silence enfolded the lonely ranch and the darkness lay like a black blanket. A low hum of insects pervaded the air. Dull sheets of lightning illumined the dark horizon to the south. Once Jean heard voices, but could not tell from which direction they came. To the west of him then flared out another rifle shot. The bullet whistled down over Jean to thud into the cabin.

Jean made a careful study of the obscure, gray-black open before him and then the background to his rear. So long as he kept the dense shadows behind him he could not be seen. He slipped from behind his covert and, gliding with absolutely noiseless footsteps, he gained the first clump of junipers. Here he waited patiently and motionlessly for another round of shots from the rustlers. After the second shot from the west side Jean sheered off to the right. Patches of brush, clumps of juniper, and isolated cedars covered this slope, affording Jean a perfect means for his purpose, which was to make a detour and come up behind the rustler who was firing from that side. Jean climbed to the top of the ridge, descended the opposite slope, made his turn to the left, and slowly worked up behind the point near where he expected to locate the rustler. Long habit in the open, by day and night, rendered his sense of direction almost as perfect as sight itself. The first flash of fire he saw from this side proved that he had come straight up toward his man. Jean's intention was to crawl up on this one of the Jorth gang and silently kill him with a knife. If the plan worked successfully, Jean meant to work round to the next rustler. Laying aside his rifle, he crawled forward on hands and knees, making no more sound than a cat. His approach was slow. He had to pick his way, be careful not to break twigs nor rattle stones. His buckskin garments made no sound against the brush. Jean located the rustler sitting on the top of the ridge in the center of an open space. He was alone. Jean saw the dull-red end of the cigarette he was smoking. The ground on the ridge top was rocky and not well adapted for Jean's purpose. He had to abandon the idea of crawling up on the rustler. Whereupon, Jean turned back, patiently and slowly, to get his rifle.

Upon securing it he began to retrace his course, this time, more slowly than before, as he was hampered by the rifle. But he did not make the slightest sound, and at length he reached the edge of the open ridge top, once more to espy the dark form of the rustler silhouetted against the sky. The distance was not more than fifty yards.

As Jean rose to his knee and carefully lifted his rifle round to avoid the twigs of a juniper he suddenly experienced another emotion besides the one of grim, hard wrath at the Jorths. It was an emotion that sickened him, made him weak internally, a cold, shaking, ungovernable sensation. Suppose this man was Ellen Jorth's father! Jean lowered the rifle. He felt it shake over his knee. He was trembling all over. The astounding discovery that he did not want to kill Ellen's father—that he could not do it—awakened Jean to the despairing nature of his love for her. In this grim moment of indecision, when he knew his Indian subtlety and ability gave him a great advantage over the Jorths, he fully realized his strange, hopeless, and irresistible love for the girl. He made no attempt to deny it any longer. Like the night and the lonely wilderness around him, like the inevitableness of this Jorth-Isbel feud, this love of his was a thing, a fact, a reality. He breathed to his own inward ear, to his soul—he could not kill Ellen Jorth's father. Feud or no feud, Isbel or not, he could not deliberately do it. And why not? There was no answer. Was he not faithless to his father? He had no hope of ever winning Ellen Jorth. He did not want the love of a girl of her character. But he loved her. And his struggle must be against the insidious and mysterious growth of that passion. It swayed him already. It made him a coward. Through his mind and heart swept the memory of Ellen Jorth, her beauty and charm, her boldness and pathos, her shame and her degradation. And the sweetness of her outweighed the boldness. And the mystery of her arrayed itself in unquenchable protest against her acknowledged shame. Jean lifted his face to the heavens, to the pitiless white stars, to the infinite depths of the dark-blue sky. He could sense the fact of his being an atom in the universe of nature. What was he, what was his revengeful

124

father, what were hate and passion and strife in comparison to the nameless something, immense and everlasting, that he sensed in this dark moment?

But the rustlers—Daggs—the Jorths—they had killed his brother Guy—murdered him brutally and ruthlessly. Guy had been a playmate of Jean's—a favorite brother. Bill had been secretive and selfish. Jean had never loved him as he did Guy. Guy lay dead down there on the meadow. This feud had begun to run its bloody course. Jean steeled his nerve. The hot blood crept back along his veins. The dark and masterful tide of revenge waved over him. The keen edge of his mind then cut out sharp and trenchant thoughts. He must kill when and where he could. This man could hardly be Ellen Jorth's father. Jorth would be with the main crowd, directing hostilities. Jean could shoot this rustler guard and his shot would be taken by the gang as the regular one from their comrade. Then swiftly Jean leveled his rifle, covered the dark form, grew cold and set, and pressed the trigger. After the report he rose and wheeled away. He did not look nor listen for the result of his shot. A clammy sweat wet his face, the hollow of his hands, his breast. A horrible, leaden, thick sensation oppressed his heart. Nature had endowed him with Indian gifts, but the exercise of them to this end caused a revolt in his soul.

Nevertheless, it was the Isbel blood that dominated him. The wind blew cool on his face. The burden upon his shoulders seemed to lift. The clamoring whispers grew fainter in his ears. And by the time he had retraced his cautious steps back to the orchard all his physical being was strung to the task at hand. Something had come between his reflective self and this man of action.

Crossing the lane, he took to the west line of sheds, and passed beyond them into the meadow. In the grass he crawled silently away to the right, using the same precaution that had actuated him on the slope, only here he did not pause so often, nor move so slowly. Jean aimed to go far enough to the right to pass the end of the embankment behind which the rustlers had found such efficient cover. This ditch had been made to keep water, during spring thaws and summer storms, from pouring off the slope to flood the corrals.

Jean miscalculated and found he had come upon the embankment somewhat to the left of the end, which fact, however, caused him no uneasiness. He lay there awhile to listen. Again he heard voices. After a time a shot pealed out. He did not see the flash, but he calculated that it had come from the north side of the cabins.

The next quarter of an hour discovered to Jean that the nearest guard was firing from the top of the embankment, perhaps a hundred yards distant, and a second one was performing the same office from a point apparently only a few yards farther on. Two rustlers close together! Jean had not calculated upon that. For a little while he pondered on what was best to do, and at length decided to crawl round behind them, and as close as the situation made advisable.

He found the ditch behind the embankment a favorable path by which to stalk these enemies. It was dry and sandy, with borders of high weeds. The only drawback was that it was almost impossible for him to keep from brushing against the dry, invisible branches of the weeds. To offset this he wormed his way like a snail, inch by inch, taking a long time before he caught sight of the sitting figure of a man, black against the dark-blue sky. This rustler had fired his rifle three times during Jean's slow approach. Jean watched and listened a few moments, then wormed himself closer and closer, until the man was within twenty steps of him.

Jean smelled tobacco smoke, but could see no light of pipe or cigarette, because the fellow's back was turned.

"Say, Ben," said this man to his companion sitting hunched up a few yards distant, "shore it strikes me queer thet Somers ain't shootin' any over thar."

Jean recognized the dry, drawling voice of Greaves, and the shock of it seemed to contract the muscles of his whole thrilling body, like that of a panther about to spring.

8

★

"I WAS shore thinkin' thet same," said the other man. "An', say, didn't thet last shot sound too sharp fer Somers's forty-five?"

"Come to think of it, I reckon it did," replied Greaves.

"Wal, I'll go around over thar an' see."

The dark form of the rustler slipped out of sight over the embankment.

"Better go slow an' careful," warned Greaves. "An' only go close enough to call Somers. . . . Mebbe thet damn half-breed Isbel is comin' some Injun on us."

Jean heard the soft swish of footsteps through wet grass. Then all was still. He lay flat, with his cheek on the sand, and he had to look ahead and upward to make out the dark figure of Greaves on the bank. One way or another he meant to kill Greaves, and he had the will power to resist the strongest gust of passion that had ever stormed his breast. If he arose and shot the rustler, that act would defeat his plan of slipping on around upon the other outposts who were firing at the cabins. Jean wanted to call softly to Greaves, "You're right about the half-breed!" and then, as he wheeled aghast, to kill him as he moved. But it suited Jean to risk leaping upon the man. Jean did not waste time in trying to understand the strange, deadly instinct that gripped him at the moment. But he realized then he had chosen the most perilous plan to get rid of Greaves.

Jean drew a long, deep breath and held it. He let go of his rifle. He rose, silently as a lifting shadow. He drew the bowie knife. Then with light, swift bounds he glided up the bank. Greaves must have heard a rustling—a soft, quick pad of moccasin, for he turned with a start. And that instant Jean's left arm darted like a striking snake round Greaves's neck and closed tight and hard. With his right hand free, holding the knife, Jean might have ended the deadly business in just one move. But when his bared arm felt the hot, bulging neck something terrible burst out of the depths of him. To kill this enemy of his father's was not enough! Physical contact had unleashed the savage soul of the Indian. Yet there was more, and as Jean gave the straining body a tremendous jerk backward, he felt the same strange thrill, the dark joy that he had known when his fist had smashed the face of Simm Bruce. Greaves had leered—he had corroborated Bruce's vile insinuation about Ellen Jorth. So it was more than hate that actuated Jean Isbel.

Greaves was heavy and powerful. He whirled himself, feet first, over backward, in a lunge like that of a lassoed steer. But Jean's hold held. They rolled down the bank into the sandy ditch, and Jean landed uppermost, with his body at right angles with that of his adversary.

127

"Greaves, your hunch was right," hissed Jean. "It's the half-breed. . . . An' I'm goin' to cut you—first for Ellen Jorth—an' then for Gaston Isbel!"

Jean gazed down into the gleaming eyes. Then his right arm whipped the big blade. It flashed. It fell. Low down, as far as Jean could reach, it entered Greaves's body.

All the heavy, muscular frame of Greaves seemed to contract and burst. His spring was that of an animal in terror and agony. It was so tremendous that it broke Jean's hold. Greaves let out a strangled yell that cleared, swelling wildly, with a hideous mortal note. He wrestled free. The big knife came out. Supple and swift, he got to his knees. He had his gun out when Jean reached him again. Like a bear Jean enveloped him. Greaves shot, but he could not raise the gun, nor twist it far enough. Then Jean, letting go with his right arm, swung the bowie. Greaves's strength went out in an awful, hoarse cry. His gun boomed again, then dropped from his hand. He swayed. Jean let go. And that enemy of the Isbels sank limply in the ditch. Jean's eyes roved for his rifle and caught the starlit gleam of it. Snatching it up, he leaped over the embankment and ran straight for the cabins. From all around yells of the Jorth faction attested to their excitement and fury.

A fence loomed up gray in the obscurity. Jean vaulted it, darted across the lane into the shadow of the corral, and soon gained the first cabin. Here he leaned to regain his breath. His heart pounded high and seemed too large for his breast. The hot blood beat and surged all over his body. Sweat poured off him. His teeth were clenched tight as a vise, and it took effort on his part to open his mouth so he could breathe more freely and deeply. But these physical sensations were as nothing compared to the tumult of his mind. Then the instinct, the spell, let go its grip and he could think. He had avenged Guy, he had depleted the ranks of the Jorths, he had made good the brag of his father, all of which afforded him satisfaction. But these thoughts were not accountable for all that he felt, especially for the bitter-sweet sting of the fact that death to the defiler of Ellen Jorth could not efface the doubt, the regret which seemed to grow with the hours.

Groping his way into the woodshed, he entered the kitchen and, calling low, he went on into the main cabin.

"Jean! Jean!" came his father's shaking voice.

"Yes, I'm back," replied Jean.

"Are—you—all right?"

"Yes. I think I've got a bullet crease on my leg. I didn't know I had it till now. . . . It's bleedin' a little. But it's nothin'."

Jean heard soft steps and some one reached shaking hands for him. They belonged to his sister Ann. She embraced him. Jean felt the heave and throb of her breast.

"Why, Ann, I'm not hurt," he said, and held her close. "Now you lie down an' try to sleep."

In the black darkness of the cabin Jean led her back to the corner and his heart was full. Speech was difficult, because the very touch of Ann's hands had made him divine that the success of his venture in no wise changed the plight of the women.

"Wal, what happened out there?" demanded Blaisdell.

"I got two of them," replied Jean. "That fellow who was shootin' from the ridge west. An' the other was Greaves."

"Hah!" exclaimed his father.

"Shore then it was Greaves yellin'," declared Blaisdell. "By God, I never heard such yells! What'd you do, Jean?"

"I knifed him. You see, I'd planned to slip up on one after another. An' I didn't want to make noise. But I didn't get any farther than Greaves."

"Wal, I reckon that'll end their shootin' in the dark," muttered Gaston Isbel. "We've got to be on the lookout for somethin' else—fire, most likely."

The old rancher's surmise proved to be partially correct. Jorth's faction ceased the shooting. Nothing further was seen or heard from them. But this silence and apparent break in the siege were harder to bear than deliberate hostility. The long, dark hours dragged by. The men took turns watching and resting, but none of them slept. At last the blackness paled and gray dawn stole out of the east. The sky turned rose over the distant range and daylight came.

The children awoke hungry and noisy, having slept away their fears. The women took advantage of the quiet morning hour to get a hot breakfast.

"Maybe they've gone away," suggested Guy Isbel's wife, peering out of the window. She had done that several times since daybreak. Jean saw her somber gaze search the pasture until it rested upon the dark, prone shape of her dead husband, lying face down in the grass. Her look worried Jean.

"No, Esther, they've not gone yet," replied Jean. "I've seen some of them out there at the edge of the brush."

129

Blaisdell was optimistic. He said Jean's night work would have its effect and that the Jorth contingent would not renew the siege very determinedly. It turned out, however, that Blaisdell was wrong. Directly after sunrise they began to pour volleys from four sides and from closer range. During the night Jorth's gang had thrown earth banks and constructed log breastworks, from behind which they were now firing. Jean and his comrades could see the flashes of fire and streaks of smoke to such good advantage that they began to return the volleys.

In half an hour the cabin was so full of smoke that Jean could not see the womenfolk in their corner. The fierce attack then abated somewhat, and the firing became more intermittent, and therefore more carefully aimed. A glancing bullet cut a furrow in Blaisdell's hoary head, making a painful, though not serious wound. It was Esther Isbel who stopped the flow of blood and bound Blaisdell's head, a task which she performed skillfully and without a tremor. The old Texan could not sit still during this operation. Sight of the blood on his hands, which he tried to rub off, appeared to inflame him to a great degree.

"Isbel, we got to go out thar," he kept reepating, "an' kill them all."

"No, we're goin' to stay heah," replied Gaston Isbel. "Shore I'm lookin' for Blue an' Fredericks an' Gordon to open up out there. They ought to be heah, an' if they are y'u shore can bet they've got the fight sized up."

Isbel's hopes did not materialize. The shooting continued without any lull until about midday. Then the Jorth faction stopped.

"Wal, now what's up?" queried Isbel. "Boys, hold your fire an' let's wait."

Gradually the smoke wafted out of the windows and doors, until the room was once more clear. And at this juncture Esther Isbel came over to take another gaze out upon the meadows. Jean saw her suddenly start violently, then stiffen, with a trembling hand outstretched.

"Look!" she cried.

"Esther, get back," ordered the old rancher. "Keep away from that window."

"What the hell!" muttered Blaisdell. "She sees somethin', or she's gone dotty."

Esther seemed turned to stone. "Look! The hogs have broken into the pasture! . . . They'll eat Guy's body!"

Everyone was frozen with horror at Esther's statement. Jean took a swift survey of the pasture. A bunch of big black hogs had indeed appeared on the scene and were rooting around in the grass not far from where lay the bodies of Guy Isbel and Jacobs. This herd of hogs belonged to the rancher and was allowed to run wild.

"Jane, those hogs—" stammered Esther Isbel, to the wife of Jacobs. "Come! Look! . . . Do y'u know anythin' about hogs?"

The woman ran to the window and looked out. She stiffened as had Esther.

"Dad, will those hogs—eat human flesh?" queried Jean, breathlessly.

The old man stared out of the window. Surprise seemed to hold him. A completely unexpected situation had staggered him.

"Jean—can you—can you shoot that far?" he asked, huskily.

"To those hogs? No, it's out of range."

"Then, by God, we've got to stay trapped in heah an' watch an awful sight," ejaculated the old man, completely unnerved. "See that break in the fence! . . . Jorth's done that. . . . To let in the hogs!"

"Aw, Isbel, it's not so bad as all that," remonstrated Blaisdell, wagging his bloody head. "Jorth wouldn't do such a hell-bent trick."

"It's shore done."

"Wal, mebbe the hogs won't find Guy an' Jacobs," returned Blaisdell, weakly. Plain it was that he only hoped for such a contingency and certainly doubted it.

"Look!" cried Esther Isbel, piercingly. "They're workin' straight up the pasture!"

Indeed, to Jean it appeared to be the fatal truth. He looked blankly, feeling a little sick. Ann Isbel came to peer out of the window and she uttered a cry. Jacobs's wife stood mute, as if dazed.

Blaisdell swore a mighty oath. "— — —! Isbel, we cain't stand heah an' watch them hogs eat our people!"

"Wal, we'll have to. What else on earth can we do?"

Esther turned to the men. She was white and cold, except her eyes, which resembled gray flames.

"Somebody can run out there an' bury our dead men," she said.

"Why, child, it 'd be shore death. Y'u saw what happened

131

to Guy an' Jacobs. . . . We've jest got to bear it. Shore nobody needn't look out—an' see."

Jean wondered if it would be possible to keep from watching. The thing had a horrible fascination. The big hogs were rooting and tearing in the grass, some of them lazy, others nimble, and all were gradually working closer and closer to the bodies. The leader, a huge, gaunt boar, that had fared ill all his life in this barren country, was scarcely fifty feet away from where Guy Isbel lay.

"Ann, get me some of your clothes, an' a sunbonnet—quick," said Jean, forced out of his lethargy. "I'll run out there disguised. Maybe I can go through with it."

"No!" ordered his father, positively, and with dark face flaming. "Guy an' Jacobs are dead. We cain't help them now."

"But, dad—" pleaded Jean. He had been wrought to a pitch by Esther's blaze of passion, by the agony in the face of the other woman.

"I tell y'u no!" thundered Gaston Isbel, flinging his arms wide.

"I will go!" cried Esther, her voice ringing.

"You won't go alone!" instantly answered the wife of Jacobs, repeating unconsciously the words her husband had spoken.

"You stay right heah," shouted Gaston Isbel, hoarsely.

"I'm goin'," replied Esther. "You've no hold over me. My husband is dead. No one can stop me. I'm goin' out there to drive those hogs away an' bury him."

"Esther, for Heaven's sake, listen," replied Isbel. "If y'u show yourself outside, Jorth an' his gang will kill y'u."

"They may be mean, but no white men could be so low as that."

Then they pleaded with her to give up her purpose. But in vain! She pushed them back and ran out through the kitchen with Jacobs's wife following her. Jean turned to the window in time to see both women run out into the lane. Jean looked fearfully, and listened for shots. But only a loud, "Haw! Haw!" came from the watchers outside. That coarse laugh relieved the tension in Jean's breast. Possibly the Jorths were not as black as his father painted them. The two women entered an open shed and came forth with a shovel and spade.

"Shore they've got to hurry," burst out Gaston Isbel.

Shifting his gaze, Jean understood the import of his

132

father's speech. The leader of the hogs had no doubt scented the bodies. Suddenly he espied them and broke into a trot.

"Run, Esther, run!" yelled Jean, with all his might.

That urged the women to flight. Jean began to shoot. The hog reached the body of Guy. Jean's shots did not reach nor frighten the beast. All the hogs now had caught a scent and went ambling toward their leader. Esther and her companion passed swiftly out of sight behind a corral. Loud and piercingly, with some awful note, rang out their screams. The hogs appeared frightened. The leader lifted his long snout, looked, and turned away. The others had halted. Then they, too, wheeled and ran off.

All was silent then in the cabin and also outside wherever the Jorth faction lay concealed. All eyes manifestly were fixed upon the brave wives. They spaded up the sod and dug a grave for Guy Isbel. For a shroud Esther wrapped him in her shawl. Then they buried him. Next they hurried to the side of Jacobs, who lay some yards away. They dug a grave for him. Mrs. Jacobs took off her outer skirt to wrap round him. Then the two women labored hard to lift him and lower him. Jacobs was a heavy man. When he had been covered his widow knelt beside his grave. Esther went back to the other. But she remained standing and did not look as if she prayed. Her aspect was tragic—that of a woman who had lost father, mother, sisters, brother, and now her husband, in this bloody Arizona land.

The deed and the demeanor of these wives of the murdered men surely must have shamed Jorth and his followers. They did not fire a shot during the ordeal nor give any sign of their presence.

Inside the cabin all were silent, too. Jean's eyes blurred so that he continually had to wipe them. Old Isbel made no effort to hide his tears. Blaisdell nodded his shaggy head and swallowed hard. The women sat staring into space. The children, in round-eyed dismay, gazed from one to the other of their elders.

"Wal, they're comin' back," declared Isbel, in immense relief. "An' so help me—Jorth let them bury their daid!"

The fact seemed to have been monstrously strange to Gaston Isbel. When the women entered the old man said, brokenly: "I'm shore glad. . . . An' I reckon I was wrong to oppose you . . . an' wrong to say what I said aboot Jorth."

No one had any chance to reply to Isbel, for the Jorth gang, as if to make up for lost time and surcharged feelings

133

of shame, renewed the attack with such a persistent and furious volleying that the defenders did not risk a return shot. They all had to lie flat next to the lowest log in order to keep from being hit. Bullets rained in through the window. And all the clay between the logs low down was shot away. This fusillade lasted for more than an hour, then gradually the fire diminished on one side and then on the other until it became desultory and finally ceased.

"Ahuh! Shore they've shot their bolt," declared Gaston Isbel.

"Wal, I doon't know aboot that," returned Blaisdell, "but they've shot a hell of a lot of shells."

"Listen," suddenly called Jean. "Somebody's yellin'."

"Hey, Isbel!" came in loud, hoarse voice. "Let your women fight for you."

Gaston Isbel sat up with a start and his face turned livid. Jean needed no more to prove that the derisive voice from outside had belonged to Jorth. The old rancher lunged up to his full height and with reckless disregard of life he rushed to the window. "Jorth," he roared, "I dare you to meet me—man to man!"

This elicited no answer. Jean dragged his father away from the window. After that a waiting silence ensued, gradually less fraught with suspense. Blaisdell started conversation by saying he believed the fight was over for that particular time. No one disputed him. Evidently Gaston Isbel was loath to believe it. Jean, however, watching at the back of the kitchen, eventually discovered that the Jorth gang had lifted the siege. Jean saw them congregate at the edge of the brush, somewhat lower down than they had been the day before. A team of mules, drawing a wagon, appeared on the road, and turned toward the slope. Saddled horses were led down out of the junipers. Jean saw bodies, evidently of dead men, lifted into the wagon, to be hauled away toward the village. Seven mounted men, leading four riderless horses, rode out into the valley and followed the wagon.

"Dad, they've gone," declared Jean. "We had the best of this fight. . . . If only Guy and Jacobs had listened!"

The old man nodded moodily. He had aged considerably during these two trying days. His hair was grayer. Now that the blaze and glow of the fight had passed he showed a subtle change, a fixed and morbid sadness, a resignation to a fate he had accepted.

The ordinary routine of ranch life did not return for the Isbels. Blaisdell returned home to settle matters there, so that he could devote all his time to this feud. Gaston Isbel sat down to wait for the members of his clan.

The male members of the family kept guard in turn over the ranch that night. And another day dawned. It brought word from Blaisdell that Blue, Fredericks, Gordon, and Colmor were all at his house, on the way to join the Isbels. This news appeared greatly to rejuvenate Gaston Isbel. But his enthusiasm did not last long. Impatient and moody by turns, he paced or moped around the cabin, always looking out, sometimes toward Blaisdell's ranch, but mostly toward Grass Valley.

It struck Jean as singular that neither Esther Isbel nor Mrs. Jacobs suggested a reburial of their husbands. The two bereaved women did not ask for assistance, but repaired to the pasture, and there spent several hours working over the graves. They raised mounds, which they sodded, and then placed stones at the heads and feet. Lastly, they fenced in the graves.

"I reckon I'll hitch up an' drive back home," said Mrs. Jacobs, when she returned to the cabin. "I've much to do an' plan. Probably I'll go to my mother's home. She's old an' will be glad to have me."

"If I had any place to go to I'd sure go," declared Esther Isbel, bitterly.

Gaston Isbel heard this remark. He raised his face from his hands, evidently both nettled and hurt.

"Esther, shore that's not kind," he said.

The red-haired woman—for she did not appear to be a girl any more—halted before his chair and gazed down at him, with a terrible flare of scorn in her gray eyes.

"Gaston Isbel, all I've got to say to you is this," she retorted, with the voice of a man. "Seein' that you an' Lee Jorth hate each other, why couldn't you act like men? . . . You damned Texans, with your bloody feuds, draggin' in every relation, every friend to murder each other! That's not the way of Arizona men. . . . We've all got to suffer— an' we women be ruined for life—because *you* had differences with Jorth. If you were half a man you'd go out an' kill him yourself, an' not leave a lot of widows an' orphaned children!"

Jean himself writhed under the lash of her scorn. Gaston

135

Isbel turned a dead white. He could not answer her. He seemed stricken with merciless truth. Slowly dropping his head, he remained motionless, a pathetic and tragic figure; and he did not stir until the rapid beat of hoofs denoted the approach of horsemen. Blaisdell appeared on his white charger, leading a pack animal. And behind rode a group of men, all heavily armed, and likewise with packs.

"Get down an' come in," was Isbel's greeting. "Bill—you look after their packs. Better leave the hosses saddled."

The booted and spurred riders trooped in, and their demeanor fitted their errand. Jean was acquainted with all of them. Fredericks was a lanky Texan, the color of dust, and he had yellow, clear eyes, like those of a hawk. His mother had been an Isbel. Gordon, too, was related to Jean's family, though distantly. He resembled an industrious miner more than a prosperous cattleman. Blue was the most striking of the visitors, as he was the most noted. A little, shrunken, gray-eyed man, with years of cowboy written all over him, he looked the quiet, easy, cool, and deadly Texan he was reputed to be. Blue's Texas record was shady, and was seldom alluded to, as unfavorable comment had turned out to be hazardous. He was the only one of the group who did not carry a rifle. But he packed two guns, a habit not often noted in Texans, and almost never in Arizonians.

Colmor, Ann Isbel's fiancé, was the youngest member of the clan, and the one closest to Jean. His meeting with Ann affected Jean powerfully, and brought to a climax an idea that had been developing in Jean's mind. His sister devotedly loved this lean-faced, keen-eyed Arizonian; and it took no great insight to discover that Colmor reciprocated her affection. They were young. They had long life before them. It seemed to Jean a pity that Colmor should be drawn into this war. Jean watched them, as they conversed apart; and he saw Ann's hands creep up to Colmor's breast, and he saw her dark eyes, eloquent, hungry, fearful, lifted with queries her lips did not speak. Jean stepped beside them, and laid an arm over both their shoulders.

"Colmor, for Ann's sake you'd better back out of this Jorth-Isbel fight," he whispered.

Colmor looked insulted. "But, Jean, it's Ann's father," he said. "I'm almost one of the family."

"You're Ann's sweetheart, an', by Heaven, I say you oughtn't to go with us!" whispered Jean.

"Go—with—you," faltered Ann.

136

"Yes. Dad is goin' straight after Jorth. Can't you tell that? An' there 'll be one hell of a fight."

Ann looked up into Colmor's face with all her soul in her eyes, but she did not speak. Her look was noble. She yearned to guide him right, yet her lips were sealed. And Colmor betrayed the trouble of his soul. The code of men held him bound, and he could not break from it, though he divined in that moment how truly it was wrong.

"Jean, your dad started me in the cattle business," said Colmor, earnestly. "An' I'm doin' well now. An' when I asked him for Ann he said he'd be glad to have me in the family. . . . Well, when this talk of fight come up, I asked your dad to let me go in on his side. He wouldn't hear of it. But after a while, as the time passed an' he made more enemies, he finally consented. I reckon he needs me now. An' I can't back out, not even for Ann."

"I would if I were you," replied Jean, and knew that he lied.

"Jean, I'm gamblin' to come out of the fight," said Colmor, with a smile. He had no morbid fears nor presentiments, such as troubled Jean.

"Why, sure—you stand as good a chance as anyone," rejoined Jean. "It wasn't that I was worryin' about so much."

"What was it, then?" asked Ann, steadily.

"If Andrew *does* come through alive he'll have blood on his hands," returned Jean, with passion. "He can't come through without it. . . . I've begun to feel what it means to have killed my fellow man. . . . An' I'd rather your husband an' the father of your children never felt that."

Colmor did not take Jean as subtly as Ann did. She shrunk a little. Her dark eyes dilated. But Colmor showed nothing of her spiritual reaction. He was young. He had wild blood. He was loyal to the Isbels.

"Jean, never worry about my conscience," he said, with a keen look. "Nothin' would tickle me any more than to get a shot at every damn one of the Jorths."

That established Colmor's status in regard to the Jorth-Isbel feud. Jean had no more to say. He respected Ann's friend and felt poignant sorrow for Ann.

Gaston Isbel called for meat and drink to be set on the table for his guests. When his wishes had been complied with the women took the children into the adjoining cabin and shut the door.

137

"Hah! Wal, we can eat an' talk now."

First the newcomers wanted to hear particulars of what had happened. Blaisdell had told all he knew and had seen, but that was not sufficient. They plied Gaston Isbel with questions. Laboriously and ponderously he rehearsed the experiences of the fight at the ranch, according to his impressions. Bill Isbel was exhorted to talk, but he had of late manifested a sullen and taciturn disposition. In spite of Jean's vigilance Bill had continued to imbibe red liquor. Then Jean was called upon to relate all he had seen and done. It had been Jean's intention to keep his mouth shut, first for his own sake and, secondly, because he did not like to talk of his deeds. But when thus appealed to by these somber-faced, intent-eyed men he divined that the more carefully he described the cruelty and baseness of their enemies, and the more vividly he presented his participation in the first fight of the feud the more strongly he would bind these friends to the Isbel cause. So he talked for an hour, beginning with his meeting with Colter up on the Rim and ending with an account of his killing Greaves. His listeners sat through this long narrative with unabated interest and at the close they were leaning forward, breathless and tense.

"Ah! So Greaves got his desserts at last," exclaimed Gordon.

All the men around the table made comments, and the last, from Blue, was the one that struck Jean forcibly.

"Shore thet was a strange an' a hell of a way to kill Greaves. Why'd you do thet, Jean?"

"I told you. I wanted to avoid noise an' I hoped to get more of them."

Blue nodded his lean, eagle-like head and sat thoughtfully, as if not convinced of anything save Jean's prowess. After a moment Blue spoke again.

"Then, goin' back to Jean's tellin' aboot trackin' rustled cattle, I've got this to say. I've long suspected thet somebody livin' right heah in the valley has been drivin' off cattle an' dealin' with rustlers. An' now I'm shore of it."

This speech did not elicit the amaze from Gaston Isbel that Jean expected it would.

"You mean Greaves or some of his friends?"

"No. They wasn't none of them in the cattle business, like we are. Shore we all knowed Greaves was crooked. But

138

what I'm figgerin' is thet some so-called honest man in our settlement has been makin' crooked deals."

Blue was a man of deeds rather than words, and so much strong speech from him, whom everybody knew to be remarkably reliable and keen, made a profound impression upon most of the Isbel faction. But, to Jean's surprise, his father did not rave. It was Blaisdell who supplied the rage and invective. Bill Isbel, also, was strangely indifferent to this new element in the condition of cattle dealing. Suddenly Jean caught a vague flash of thought, as if he had intercepted the thought of another's mind, and he wondered—could his brother Bill know anything about this crooked work alluded to by Blue? Dismissing the conjecture, Jean listened earnestly.

"An' if it's true it shore makes this difference—we cain't blame all the rustlin' on to Jorth," concluded Blue.

"Wal, it's not true," declared Gaston Isbel, roughly. "Jorth an' his Hash Knife Gang are at the bottom of all the rustlin' in the valley for years back. An' they've got to be wiped out!"

"Isbel, I reckon we'd all feel better if we talk straight," replied Blue, coolly. "I'm heah to stand by the Isbels. An' y'u know what thet means. But I'm not heah to fight Jorth because he may be a rustler. The others may have their own reasons, but mine is this—you once stood by me in Texas when I was needin' friends. Wal, I'm standin' by y'u now. Jorth is your enemy, an' so he is mine."

Gaston Isbel bowed to this ultimatum, scarcely less agitated than when Esther Isbel had denounced him. His rabid and morbid hate of Jorth had eaten into his heart to take possession there, like the parasite that battened the life of its victim. Blue's steely voice, his cold, gray eyes, showed the unbiased truth of the man, as well as his fidelity to his creed. Here again, but in a different manner, Gaston Isbel had the fact flung at him that other men must suffer, perhaps die, for his hate. And the very soul of the old rancher apparently rose in passionate revolt against the blind, headlong, elemental strength of his nature. So it seemed to Jean, who, in love and pity that hourly grew, saw through his father. Was it too late? Alas! Gaston Isbel could never be turned back! Yet something was altering his brooding, fixed mind.

"Wal," said Blaisdell, gruffly, "let's get down to business.

. . . I'm for havin' Blue be foreman of this heah outfit, an' all of us to do as he says."

Gaston Isbel opposed this selection and indeed resented it. He intended to lead the Isbel faction.

"All right, then. Give us a hunch what we're goin' to do," replied Blaisdell.

"We're goin' to ride off on Jorth's trail—an' one way or another—kill him—*kill him!* . . . I reckon that'll end the fight."

What did old Isbel have in his mind? His listeners shook their heads.

"No," asserted Blaisdell. "Killin' Jorth might be the end of your desires, Isbel, but it'd never end *our* fight. We'll have gone too far. . . . If we take Jorth's trail from heah it means we've got to wipe out that rustler gang, or stay to the last man."

"Yes, by God!" exclaimed Fredericks.

"Let's drink to thet!" said Blue. Strangely they all turned to this Texas gunman, instinctively recognizing in him the brain and heart, and the past deeds, that fitted him for the leadership of such a clan. Blue had all in life to lose, and nothing to gain. Yet his spirit was such that he could not lean to all the possible gain of the future, and leave a debt unpaid. Then his voice, his look, his influence were those of a fighter. They all drank with him, even Jean, who hated liquor. And this act of drinking seemed the climax of the council. Preparations were at once begun for their departure on Jorth's trail.

Jean took but little time for his own needs. A horse, a blanket, a knapsack of meat and bread, a canteen, and his weapons, with all the ammunition he could pack, made up his outfit. He wore his buckskin suit, leggings, and moccasins. Very soon the cavalcade was ready to depart. Jean tried not to watch Bill Isbel say good-by to his children, but it was impossible not to. Whatever Bill was, as a man, he was father of those children, and he loved them. How strange that the little ones seemed to realize the meaning of this good-by! They were grave, somber-eyed, pale up to the last moment, then they broke down and wept. Did they sense that their father would never come back? Jean caught that dark, fatalistic presentiment. Bill Isbel's convulsed face showed that he also caught it. Jean did not see Bill say good-by to his wife. But he heard her. Old Gaston Isbel forgot to speak to the children, or else could not. He never

140

looked at them. And his good-by to Ann was as if he were only riding to the village for a day. Jean saw woman's love, woman's intuition, woman's grief in her eyes. He could not escape her. "Oh, Jean! oh, brother!" she whispered as she enfolded him. "It's awful! It's wrong! Wrong! Wrong! . . . Good-by! . . . If killing *must* be—see that y'u kill the Jorths! . . . Good-by!"

Even in Ann, gentle and mild, the Isbel blood spoke at the last. Jean gave Ann over to the pale-faced Colmor, who took her in his arms. Then Jean fled out to his horse. This cold-blooded devastation of a home was almost more than he could bear. There was love here. What would be left?

Colmor was the last one to come out to the horses. He did not walk erect, nor as one whose sight was clear. Then, as the silent, tense, grim men mounted their horses, Bill Isbel's eldest child, the boy, appeared in the door. His little form seemed instinct with a force vastly different from grief. His face was the face of an Isbel.

"Daddy—kill 'em all!" he shouted, with a passion all the fiercer for its incongruity to the treble voice.

So the poison had spread from father to son.

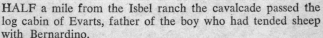

HALF a mile from the Isbel ranch the cavalcade passed the log cabin of Evarts, father of the boy who had tended sheep with Bernardino.

It suited Gaston Isbel to halt here. No need to call! Evarts and his son appeared so quickly as to convince observers that they had been watching.

"Howdy, Jake!" said Isbel. "I'm wantin' a word with y'u alone."

"Shore, boss, git down an' come in," replied Evarts.

Isbel led him inside, and said something forcible that Jean divined from the very gesture which accompanied it. His father was telling Evarts that he was not to join in the Isbel-Jorth war. Evarts had worked for the Isbels a long time, and

141

his faithfulness, along with something stronger and darker, showed in his rugged face as he stubbornly opposed Isbel. The old man raised his voice: "No, I tell you. An' that settles it."

They returned to the horses, and, before mounting, Isbel, as if he remembered something, directed his somber gaze on young Evarts.

"Son, did you bury Bernardino?"

"Dad an' me went over yestiddy," replied the lad. "I shore was glad the coyotes hadn't been round."

"How aboot the sheep?"

"I left them there. I was goin' to stay, but bein' all alone—I got skeered. . . . The sheep was doin' fine. Good water an' some grass. An' this ain't time fer varmints to hang round."

"Jake, keep your eye on that flock," returned Isbel. "An' if I shouldn't happen to come back y'u can call them sheep yours. . . . I'd like your boy to ride up to the village. Not with us, so anybody would see him. But afterward. We'll be at Abel Meeker's."

Again Jean was confronted with an uneasy premonition as to some idea or plan his father had not shared with his followers. When the cavalcade started on again Jean rode to his father's side and asked him why he had wanted the Evarts boy to come to Grass Valley. And the old man replied that, as the boy could run to and fro in the village without danger, he might be useful in reporting what was going on at Greaves's store, where undoubtedly the Jorth gang would hold forth. This appeared reasonable enough, therefore Jean smothered the objection he had meant to make.

The valley road was deserted. When, a mile farther on, the riders passed a group of cabins, just on the outskirts of the village, Jean's quick eye caught sight of curious and evidently frightened people trying to see while they avoided being seen. No doubt the whole settlement was in a state of suspense and terror. Not unlikely this dark, closely grouped band of horsemen appeared to them as Jorth's gang had looked to Jean. It was an orderly, trotting march that manifested neither hurry nor excitement. But any Western eye could have caught the singular aspect of such a group, as if the intent of the riders was a visible thing.

Soon they reached the outskirts of the village. Here their approach had been watched for or had been already reported. Jean saw men, women, children peeping from behind cabins

142

and from half-opened doors. Farther on Jean espied the dark figures of men, slipping out the back way through orchards and gardens and running north, toward the center of the village. Could these be friends of the Jorth crowd, on the way with warnings of the approach of the Isbels? Jean felt convinced of it. He was learning that his father had not been absolutely correct in his estimation of the way Jorth and his followers were regarded by their neighbors. Not improbably there were really many villagers who, being more interested in sheep raising than in cattle, had an honest leaning toward the Jorths. Some, too, no doubt, had leanings that were dishonest in deed if not in sincerity.

Gaston Isbel led his clan straight down the middle of the wide road of Grass Valley until he reached a point opposite Abel Meeker's cabin. Jean espied the same curiosity from behind Meeker's door and windows as had been shown all along the road. But presently, at Isbel's call, the door opened and a short, swarthy man appeared. He carried a rifle.

"Howdy, Gass!" he said. "What's the good word?"

"Wal, Abel, it's not good, but bad. An' it's shore started," replied Isbel. "I'm askin' y'u to let me have your cabin."

"You're welcome. I'll send the folks 'round to Jim's," returned Meeker. "An' if y'u want me, I'm with y'u, Isbel."

"Thanks, Abel, but I'm not leadin' any more kin an' friends into this heah deal."

"Wal, jest as y'u say. But I'd like damn bad to jine with y'u. . . . My brother Ted was shot last night."

"Ted! Is he daid?" ejaculated Isbel, blankly.

"We can't find out," replied Meeker. "Jim says thet Jeff Campbell said thet Ted went into Greaves's place last night. Greaves allus was friendly to Ted, but Greaves wasn't thar—"

"No, he shore wasn't," interrupted Isbel, with a dark smile, "an' he never will be there again."

Meeker nodded with slow comprehension and a shade crossed his face.

"Wal, Campbell claimed he'd heerd from some one who was thar. Anyway, the Jorths were drinkin' hard, an' they raised a row with Ted—same old sheep talk—an' somebody shot him. Campbell said Ted was thrown out back, an' he was shore he wasn't killed."

"Ahuh! Wal, I'm sorry, Abel, your family had to lose in this. Maybe Ted's not bad hurt. I shore hope so. . . . An' y'u an' Jim keep out of the fight, anyway."

"All right, Isbel. But I reckon I'll give y'u a hunch. If this heah fight lasts long the whole damn Basin will be in it, on one side or t'other."

"Abel, you're talkin' sense," broke in Blaisdell. "An' that's why we're up heah for quick action."

"I heerd y'u got Daggs," whispered Meeker, as he peered all around.

"Wal, y'u heerd correct," drawled Blaisdell.

Meeker muttered strong words into his beard. "Say, was Daggs in thet Jorth outfit?"

"He *was*. But he walked right into Jean's forty-four. . . . An' I reckon his carcass would show some more."

"An' whar's Guy Isbel?" demanded Meeker.

"Daid an' buried, Abel," replied Gaston Isbel. "An' now I'd be obliged if y'u'll hurry your folks away, an' let us have your cabin an' corral. Have y'u got any hay for the hosses?"

"Shore. The barn's half full," replied Meeker, as he turned away. "Come on in."

"No. We'll wait till you've gone."

When Meeker had gone, Isbel and his men sat their horses and looked about them and spoke low. Their advent had been expected, and the little town awoke to the imminence of the impending battle. Inside Meeker's house there was the sound of indistinct voices of women and the bustle incident to a hurried vacating.

Across the wide road people were peering out on all sides, some hiding, others walking to and fro, from fence to fence, whispering in little groups. Down the wide road, at the point where it turned, stood Greaves's fort-like stone house. Low, flat, isolated, with its dark, eye-like windows, it presented a forbidding and sinister aspect. Jean distinctly saw the forms of men, some dark, others in shirt sleeves, come to the wide door and look down the road.

"Wal, I reckon only aboot five hundred good hoss steps are separatin' us from that outfit," drawled Blaisdell.

No one replied to his jocularity. Gaston Isbel's eyes narrowed to a slit in his furrowed face and he kept them fastened upon Greaves's store. Blue, likewise, had a somber cast of countenance, not, perhaps, any darker nor grimmer than those of his comrades, but more representative of intense preoccupation of mind. The look of him thrilled Jean, who could sense its deadliness, yet could not grasp any more. Altogether, the manner of the villagers and the watchful pacing to and fro of the Jorth followers and the silent, boding front of Isbel and his men summed up for Jean the menace of the moment that must very soon change to a terrible reality.

At a call from Meeker, who stood at the back of the cabin, Gaston Isbel rode into the yard, followed by the others of his party. "Somebody look after the hosses," ordered Isbel, as he dismounted and took his rifle and pack. "Better leave the saddles on, leastways till we see what's comin' off."

Jean and Bill Isbel led the horses back to the corral. While watering and feeding them, Jean somehow received the impression that Bill was trying to speak, to confide in him, to unburden himself of some load. This peculiarity of Bill's had become marked when he was perfectly sober. Yet he had never spoken or even begun anything unusual. Upon the present occasion, however, Jean believed that his brother might have gotten rid of his emotion, or whatever it was, had they not been interrupted by Colmor.

"Boys, the old man's orders are for us to sneak round on three sides of Greaves's store, keepin' out of gunshot till we find good cover, an' then crawl closer an' to pick off any of Jorth's gang who shows himself."

Bill Isbel strode off without a reply to Colmor.

"Well, I don't think so much of that," said Jean, ponderingly. "Jorth has lots of friends here. Somebody might pick us off."

"I kicked, but the old man shut me up. He's not to be bucked ag'in' now. Struck me as powerful queer. But no wonder."

"Maybe he knows best. Did he say anythin' about what he an' the rest of them are goin' to do?"

"Nope. Blue taxed him with that an' got the same as me. I reckon we'd better try it out, for a while, anyway."

"Looks like he wants us to keep out of the fight," replied Jean, thoughtfully. "Maybe, though . . . Dad's no fool. Colmor, you wait here till I get out of sight. I'll go round an' come up as close as advisable behind Greaves's store. You take the right side. An' keep hid."

With that Jean strode off, going around the barn, straight out the orchard lane to the open flat, and then climbing a fence to the north of the village. Presently he reached a line of sheds and corrals, to which he held until he arrived at the road. This point was about a quarter of a mile from Greaves's store, and around the bend. Jean sighted no one.

The road, the fields, the yards, the backs of the cabins all looked deserted. A blight had settled down upon the peaceful activities of Grass Valley. Crossing the road, Jean began to circle until he came close to several cabins, around which he made a wide detour. This took him to the edge of the slope, where brush and thickets afforded him a safe passage to a line directly back of Greaves's store. Then he turned toward it. Soon he was again approaching a cabin on that side, and some of its inmates descried him. Their actions attested to their alarm. Jean half expected a shot from this quarter, such were his growing doubts, but he was mistaken. A man, unknown to Jean, closely watched his guarded movements and then waved a hand, as if to signify to Jean that he had nothing to fear. After this act he disappeared. Jean believed that he had been recognized by some one not antagonistic to the Isbels. Therefore he passed the cabin and, coming to a thick scrub-oak tree that offered shelter, he hid there to watch. From this spot he could see the back of Greaves's store, at a distance probably too far for a rifle bullet to reach. Before him, as far as the store, and on each side, extended the village common. In front of the store ran the road. Jean's position was such that he could not command sight of this road down toward Meeker's house, a fact that disturbed him. Not satisfied with this stand, he studied his surroundings in the hope of espying a better. And he discovered what he thought would be a more favorable position, although he could not see much farther down the road. Jean went back around the cabin and, coming out into the open to the right, he got the corner of Greaves's barn between him and the window of the store. Then he boldly hurried into the open, and soon reached an old wagon, from behind which he proposed to watch. He could not see either window or door of the store, but if any of the Jorth contingent came out the back way they would be within reach of his rifle. Jean took the risk of being shot at from either side.

So sharp and roving was his sight that he soon espied Colmor slipping along behind the trees some hundred yards to the left. All his efforts to catch a glimpse of Bill, however, were fruitless. And this appeared strange to Jean, for there were several good places on the right from which Bill could have commanded the front of Greaves's store and the whole west side.

Colmor disappeared among some shrubbery, and Jean seemed left alone to watch a deserted, silent village. Watching and listening, he felt that the time dragged. Yet the shadows cast by the sun showed him that, no matter how tense he felt and how the moments seemed hours, they were really flying.

Suddenly Jean's ears rang with the vibrant shock of a rifle report. He jerked up, strung and thrilling. It came from in front of the store. It was followed by revolver shots, heavy, booming. Three he counted, and the rest were too close together to enumerate. A single hoarse yell pealed out, somehow trenchant and triumphant. Other yells, not so wild and strange, muffled the first one. Then silence clapped down on the store and the open square.

Jean was deadly certain that some of the Jorth clan would show themselves. He strained to still the trembling those sudden shots and that significant yell had caused him. No man appeared. No more sounds caught Jean's ears. The suspense, then, grew unbearable. It was not that he could not wait for an enemy to appear, but that he could not wait to learn what had happened. Every moment that he stayed there, with hands like steel on his rifle, with eyes of a falcon, but added to a dreadful, dark certainty of disaster. A rifle shot swiftly followed by revolver shots! What could they mean? Revolver shots of different caliber, surely fired by different men! What could they mean? It was not these shots that accounted for Jean's dread, but the yell which had followed. All his intelligence and all his nerve were not sufficient to fight down the feeling of calamity. And at last, yielding to it, he left his post, and ran like a deer across the open, through the cabin yard, and around the edge of the slope to the road. Here his caution brought him to a halt. Not a living thing crossed his vision. Breaking into a run, he soon reached the back of Meeker's place and entered, to hurry forward to the cabin.

Colmor was there in the yard, breathing hard, his face working, and in front of him crouched several of the men with rifles ready. The road, to Jean's flashing glance, was apparently deserted. Blue sat on the doorstep, lighting a cigarette. Then on the moment Blaisdell strode to the door of the cabin. Jean had never seen him look like that.

"Jean—look—down the road," he said, brokenly, and with big hand shaking he pointed down toward Greaves's store.

Like lightning Jean's glance shot down—down—down—until it stopped to fix upon the prostrate form of a man, lying in the middle of the road. A man of lengthy build, shirt-sleeved arms flung wide, white head in the dust—dead! Jean's recognition was as swift as his sight. His father! They had killed him! The Jorths! It was done. His father's premonition of death had not been false. And then, after these flashing thoughts, came a sense of blankness, momentarily almost oblivion, that gave place to a rending of the heart. That pain Jean had known only at the death of his mother. It passed, this agonizing pang, and its icy pressure yielded to a rushing gust of blood, fiery as hell.

"Who—did it?" whispered Jean.

"Jorth!" replied Blaisdell, huskily. "Son, we couldn't hold your dad back. . . . We couldn't. He was like a lion. . . . An' he throwed his life away! Oh, if it hadn't been for that it'd not be so awful. Shore, we come heah to shoot an' be shot. But not like that. . . . By God, it was murder—murder!"

Jean's mute lips framed a query easily read.

"Tell him, Blue. I cain't," continued Blaisdell, and he tramped back into the cabin.

"Set down, Jean, an' take things easy," said Blue, calmly. "You know we all reckoned we'd git plugged one way or another in this deal. An' shore it doesn't matter much how a fellar gits it. All thet ought to bother us is to make shore the other outfit bites the dust—same as your dad had to."

Under this man's tranquil presence, all the more quieting because it seemed to be so deadly sure and cool, Jean felt the uplift of his dark spirit, the acceptance of fatality, the mounting control of facilities that must wait. The little gunman seemed to have about his inert presence something that suggested a rattlesnake's inherent knowledge of its destructiveness. Jean sat down and wiped his clammy face.

"Jean, your dad reckoned to square accounts with Jorth, an' save us all," began Blue, puffing out a cloud of smoke. "But he reckoned too late. Mebbe years ago—or even not long ago—if he'd called Jorth out man to man there'd never been any Jorth-Isbel war. Gaston Isbel's conscience woke too late. That's how I figger it."

"Hurry! Tell me—how it—happened," panted Jean.

"Wal, a little while after y'u left I seen your dad writin' on a leaf he tore out of a book—Meeker's Bible, as y'u can see. I thought thet was funny. An' Blaisdell gave me a hunch. Pretty soon along comes young Evarts. The old man calls him out of our hearin' an' talks to him. Then I seen him give the boy somethin', which I afterward figgered was

148

what he wrote on the leaf out of the Bible. Me an' Blaisdell both tried to git out of him what thet meant. But not a word. I kept watchin' an' after a while I seen young Evarts slip out the back way. Mebbe half an hour I seen a bare-legged kid cross the road an' go into Greaves's store. . . . Then shore I tumbled to your dad. He'd sent a note to Jorth to come out an' meet him face to face, man to man! . . . Shore it was like readin' what your dad had wrote. But I didn't say nothin' to Blaisdell. I jest watched."

Blue drawled these last words, as if he enjoyed remembrance of his keen reasoning. A smile wreathed his thin lips. He drew twice on the cigarette and emitted another cloud of smoke. Quite suddenly then he changed. He made a rapid gesture—the whip of a hand, significant and passionate. And swift words followed:

"Colonel Lee Jorth stalked out of the store—out into the road—mebbe a hundred steps. Then he halted. He wore his long black coat an' his wide black hat, an' he stood like a stone.

" 'What the hell!' burst out Blaisdell, comin' out of his trance.

"The rest of us jest looked. I'd forgot your dad, for the minnit. So had all of us. But we remembered soon enough when we seen him stalk out. Everybody had a hunch then. I called him. Blaisdell begged him to come back. All the fellars had a say. No use! Then I shore cussed him an' told him it was plain as day thet Jorth didn't hit me like an honest man. I can sense such things. I knew Jorth had a trick up his sleeve. I've not been a gun fighter fer nothin'.

"Your dad had no rifle. He packed his gun at his hip. He jest stalked down thet road like a giant, goin' faster an' faster, holdin' his head high. It shore was fine to see him. But I was sick. I heerd Blaisdell groan, an' Fredericks thar cussed somethin' fierce. . . . When your dad halted—I reckon aboot fifty steps from Jorth—then we all went numb. I heerd your dad's voice—then Jorth's. They cut like knives. Y'u could shore heah the hate they hed fer each other."

Blue had become a little husky. His speech had grown gradually to denote his feeling. Underneath his serenity there was a different order of man.

"I reckon both your dad an' Jorth went fer their guns at the same time—an even break. But jest as they drew, some one shot a rifle from the store. Must hev been a forty-five seventy. A big gun! The bullet must have hit your dad low down, aboot the middle. He acted thet way, sinkin' to his knees. An' he was wild in shootin'—so wild thet he must hev missed. Then he wabbled—an' Jorth run in a dozen steps, shootin' fast, till your dad fell over. . . . Jorth run closer, bent over him, an' then straightened up with an Apache yell, if I ever heerd one. . . . An' then Jorth backed slow—lookin' all the time—backed to the store, an' went in."

Blue's voice ceased. Jean seemed suddenly released from an impelling magnet that now dropped him to some numb, dizzy depth. Blue's lean face grew hazy. Then Jean bowed his head in his hand, and sat there, while a slight tremor shook all his muscles at once. He grew deathly cold and deathly sick. This paroxysm slowly wore away, and Jean grew conscious of a dull amaze at the apparent deadness of his spirit. Blaisdell placed a huge, kindly hand on his shoulder.

"Brace up, son!" he said, with voice now clear and resonant. "Shore it's what your dad expected—an' what we all must look for. . . . If y'u was goin' to kill Jorth before—think how —— —— shore yu're goin' to kill him now."

"Blaisdell's talkin'," put in Blue, and his voice had a cold ring. "Lee Jorth will never see the sun rise ag'in!"

These calls to the primitive in Jean, to the Indian, were not in vain. But even so, when the dark tide rose in him, there was still a haunting consciousness of the cruelty of this singular doom imposed upon him. Strangely Ellen Jorth's face floated back in the depths of his vision, pale, fading, like the face of a spirit floating by.

"Blue," said Blaisdell, "let's get Isbel's body soon as we dare, an' bury it. Reckon we can, right after dark."

"Shore," replied Blue. "But y'u fellars figger thet out. I'm thinkin' hard. I've got somethin' on my mind."

Jean grew fascinated by the looks and speech and action of the little gunman. Blue, indeed, had something on his mind. And it boded ill to the men in that dark square stone house down the road. He paced to and fro in the yard, back and forth on the path to the gate, and then he entered the cabin to stalk up and down, faster and faster, until all at once he halted as if struck, to upfling his right arm in a singular fierce gesture.

"Jean, call the men in," he said, tersely.

They all filed in, sinister and silent, with eager faces turned to the little Texan. His dominance showed markedly.

"Gordon, y'u stand in the door an' keep your eye peeled,"

went on Blue. . . . "Now, boys, listen! I've thought it all out. This game of man huntin' is the same to me as cattle raisin' is to y'u. An' my life in Texas all comes back to me, I reckon, in good stead fer us now. I'm goin' to kill Lee Jorth! Him first, an' mebbe his brothers. I had to think of a good many ways before I hit on one I reckon will be shore. It's got to be *shore*. Jorth has got to die! Wal, heah's my plan. . . . Thet Jorth outfit is drinkin' some, we can gamble on it. They're not goin' to leave thet store. An' of course they'll be expectin' us to start a fight. I reckon they'll look fer some such siege as they held round Isbel's ranch. But we shore ain't goin' to do thet. I'm goin' to surprise thet outfit. There's only one man among them who is dangerous, an' thet's Queen. I know Queen. But he doesn't know me. An' I'm goin' to finish my job before he gets acquainted with me. After thet, all right!"

Blue paused a moment, his eyes narrowing down, his whole face setting in hard cast of intense preoccupation, as if he visualized a scene of extraordinary nature.

"Wal, what's your trick?" demanded Blaisdell.

"Y'u all know Greaves's store," continued Blue. "How them winders have wooden shutters thet keep a light from showin' outside? Wal, I'm gamblin' thet as soon as it's dark Jorth's gang will be celebratin'. They'll be drinkin' an' they'll have a light, an' the winders will be shut. They're not goin' to worry none aboot us. Thet store is like a fort. It won't burn. An' shore they'd never think of us chargin' them in there. Wal, as soon as it's dark, we'll go round behind the lots an' come up jest across the road from Greaves's. I reckon we'd better leave Isbel where he lays till this fight's over. Mebbe y'u'll have more'n him to bury. We'll crawl behind them bushes in front of Coleman's yard. An' heah's where Jean comes in. He'll take an ax, an' his guns, of course, an' do some of his Injun sneakin' round to the back of Greaves's store. . . . An', Jean, y'u must do a slick job of this. But I reckon it'll be easy fer you. Back there it'll be dark as pitch, fer anyone lookin' out of the store. An' I'm figgerin' y'u can take your time an' crawl right up. Now if y'u don't remember how Greaves's back yard looks I'll tell y'u."

Here Blue dropped on one knee to the floor and with a finger he traced a map of Greaves's barn and fence, the back door and window, and especially a break in the stone foundation which led into a kind of cellar where Greaves

151

stored wood and other things that could be left outdoors.

"Jean, I take particular pains to show y'u where this hole is," said Blue, "because if the gang runs out y'u could duck in there an' hide. An' if they run out into the yard— wal, y'u'd make it a sorry run fer them. . . . Wal, when y'u've crawled up close to Greaves's back door, an' waited long enough to see an' listen—then you're to run fast an' swing your ax smash ag'in' the winder. Take a quick peep in if y'u want to. It might help. Then jump quick an' take a swing at the door. Y'u'll be standin' to one side, so if the gang shoots through the door they won't hit y'u. Bang thet door good an' hard. . . . Wal, now's where I come in. When y'u swing thet ax I'll shore run fer the front of the store. Jorth an' his outfit will be some attentive to thet poundin' of yours on the back door. So I reckon. An' they'll be *lookin'* thet way. I'll run in—yell—an' throw my guns on Jorth."

"Humph! Is that all?" ejaculated Blaisdell.

"I reckon thet's all an' I'm figgerin' it's a hell of a lot," responded Blue, dryly. "Thet's what Jorth will think."

"Where do we come in?"

"Wal, y'u all can back me up," replied Blue, dubiously. "Y'u see, my plan goes as far as killin' Jorth—an' mebbe his brothers. Mebbe I'll get a crack at Queen. But I'll be shore of Jorth. After thet all depends. Mebbe it'll be easy fer me to get out. An' if I do y'u fellars will know it an' can fill thet storeroom full of bullets."

"Wal, Blue, with all due respect to y'u, I shore don't like your plan," declared Blaisdell. "Success depends upon too many little things any one of which might go wrong."

"Blaisdell, I reckon I know this heah game better than y'u," replied Blue. "A gun fighter goes by instinct. This trick will work."

"But suppose that front door of Greaves's store is barred," protested Blaisdell.

"It hasn't got any bar," said Blue.

"Y'u shore?"

"Yes, I reckon," replied Blue.

"Hell, man! Aren't y'u takin' a terrible chance?" queried Blaisdell.

Blue's answer to that was a look that brought the blood to Blaisdell's face. Only then did the rancher really comprehend how the little gunman had taken such desperate chances before, and meant to take them now, not with any hope or assurance of escaping with his life, but to live up to his peculiar code of honor.

"Blaisdell, did y'u ever heah of me in Texas?" he queried, dryly.

"Wal, no, Blue, I cain't swear I did," replied the rancher, apologetically. "An' Isbel was always sort of mysterious aboot his acquaintance with you."

"My name's not Blue."

"Ahuh! Wal, what is it, then—if I'm safe to ask?" returned Blaisdell, gruffly.

"It's King Fisher," replied Blue.

The shock that stiffened Blaisdell must have been communicated to the others. Jean certainly felt amaze, and some other emotion not fully realized, when he found himself face to face with one of the most notorious characters ever known in Texas—an outlaw long supposed to be dead.

"Men, I reckon I'd kept my secret if I'd any idee of comin' out of this Isbel-Jorth war alive," said Blue. "But I'm goin' to cash. I feel it heah. . . . Isbel was my friend. He saved me from bein' lynched in Texas. An' so I'm goin' to kill Jorth. Now I'll take it kind of y'u—if any of y'u come out of this alive—to tell who I was an' why I was on the Isbel side. Because this sheep an' cattle war—this talk of Jorth an' the Hash Knife Gang—it makes me sick. I *know* there's been crooked work on Isbel's side, too. An' I never want it on record thet I killed Jorth because he was a rustler."

"By God, Blue! it's late in the day for such talk," burst out Blaisdell, in rage and amaze. "But I reckon y'u know what y'u're talkin' aboot. . . . Wal, I shore don't want to heah it."

At this juncture Bill Isbel quietly entered the cabin, too late to hear any of Blue's statement. Jean was positive of that, for as Blue was speaking those last revealing words Bill's heavy boots had resounded on the gravel path outside. Yet something in Bill's look or in the way Blue averted his lean face or in the entrance of Bill at that particular moment, or all these together, seemed to Jean to add further mystery to the long secret causes leading up to the Jorth-Isbel war. Did Bill know what Blue knew? Jean had an inkling that he did. And on the moment, so perplexing and bitter, Jean gazed out the door, down the deserted road to where his dead father lay, white-haired and ghastly in the sunlight.

"Blue, you could have kept that to yourself, as well as

153

your real name," interposed Jean, with bitterness. "It's too late now for either to do any good. . . . But I appreciate your friendship for dad, an' I'm ready to help carry out your plan."

That decision of Jean's appeared to put an end to protest or argument from Blaisdell or any of the others. Blue's fleeting dark smile was one of satisfaction. Then upon most of this group of men seemed to settle a grim restraint. They went out and walked and watched; they came in again, restless and somber. Jean thought that he must have bent his gaze a thousand times down the road to the tragic figure of his father. That sight roused all emotions in his breast, and the one that stirred there most was pity. The pity of it! Gaston Isbel lying face down in the dust of the village street! Patches of blood showed on the back of his vest and one white-sleeved shoulder. He had been shot through. Every time Jean saw this blood he had to stifle a gathering of wild, savage impulses.

Meanwhile the afternoon hours dragged by and the village remained as if its inhabitants had abandoned it. Not even a dog showed on the side road. Jorth and some of his men came out in front of the store and sat on the steps, in close convening groups. Every move they made seemed significant of their confidence and importance. About sunset they went back into the store, closing door and window shutters. Then Blaisdell called the Isbel faction to have food and drink. Jean felt no hunger. And Blue, who had kept apart from the others, showed no desire to eat. Neither did he smoke, though early in the day he had never been without a cigarette between his lips.

Twilight fell and darkness came. Not a light showed anywhere in the blackness.

"Wal, I reckon it's aboot time," said Blue, and he led the way out of the cabin to the back of the lot. Jean strode behind him, carrying his rifle and an ax. Silently the other men followed. Blue turned to the left and led through the field until he came within sight of a dark line of trees.

"Thet's where the road turns off," he said to Jean. "An' heah's the back of Coleman's place. . . . Wal, Jean, good luck!"

Jean felt the grip of a steel-like hand, and in the darkness he caught the gleam of Blue's eyes. Jean had no response in words for the laconic Blue, but he wrung the hard, thin hand and hurried away in the darkness.

154

Once alone, his part of the business at hand rushed him into eager thrilling action. This was the sort of work he was fitted to do. In this instance it was important, but it seemed to him that Blue had coolly taken the perilous part. And this cowboy with gray in his thin hair was in reality the great King Fisher! Jean marveled at the fact. And he shivered all over for Jorth. In ten minutes—fifteen, more or less, Jorth would lie gasping bloody froth and sinking down. Something in the dark, lonely, silent, oppressive summer night told Jean this. He strode on swiftly. Crossing the road at a run, he kept on over the ground he had traversed during the afternoon, and in a few moments he stood breathing hard at the edge of the common behind Greaves's store.

A pin point of light penetrated the blackness. It made Jean's heart leap. The Jorth contingent were burning the big lamp that hung in the center of Greaves's store. Jean listened. Loud voices and coarse laughter sounded discord on the melancholy silence of the night. What Blue had called his instinct had surely guided him aright. Death of Gaston Isbel was being celebrated by revel.

In a few moments Jean had regained his breath. Then all his faculties set intensely to the action at hand. He seemed to magnify his hearing and his sight. His movements made no sound. He gained the wagon, where he crouched a moment.

The ground seemed a pale, obscure medium, hardly more real than the gloom above it. Through this gloom of night, which looked thick like a cloud, but was really clear, shone the thin, bright point of light, accentuating the black square that was Greaves's store. Above this stood a gray line of tree foliage, and then the intensely dark-blue sky studded with white, cold stars.

A hound bayed lonesomely somewhere in the distance. Voices of men sounded more distinctly, some deep and low, others loud, unguarded, with the vacant note of thoughtlessness.

Jean gathered all his forces, until sense of sight and hearing were in exquisite accord with the suppleness and lightness of his movements. He glided on about ten short, swift steps before he halted. That was as far as his piercing eyes could penetrate. If there had been a guard stationed outside the store Jean would have seen him before being seen. He saw the fence, reached it, entered the yard, glided in the dense shadow of the barn until the black square began to loom

155

gray—the color of stone at night. Jean peered through the obscurity. No dark figure of a man showed against that gray wall—only a black patch, which must be the hole in the foundation mentioned. A ray of light now streaked out from the little black window. To the right showed the wide, black door.

Farther on Jean glided silently. Then he halted. There was no guard outside. Jean heard the clink of a cup, the lazy drawl of a Texan, and then a strong, harsh voice—Jorth's. It strung Jean's whole being tight and vibrating. Inside he was on fire while cold thrills rippled over his skin. It took tremendous effort of will to hold himself back another instant to listen, to look, to feel, to make sure. And that instant charged him with a mighty current of hot blood, straining, throbbing, damming.

When Jean leaped this current burst. In a few swift bounds he gained his point halfway between door and window. He leaned his rifle against the stone wall. Then he swung the ax. Crash! The window shutter split and rattled to the floor inside. The silence then broke with a hoarse, "What's thet?"

With all his might Jean swung the heavy ax on the door. Smash! The lower half caved in and banged to the floor. Bright light flared out the hole.

"Look out!" yelled a man, in loud alarm. "They're batterin' the back door!"

Jean swung again, high on the splintered door. Crash! Pieces flew inside.

"They've got axes," hoarsely shouted another voice. "Shove the counter ag'in' the door."

"No!" thundered a voice of authority that denoted terror as well. "Let them come in. Pull your guns an' take to cover!"

"They ain't comin' in," was the hoarse reply. "They'll shoot in on us from the dark."

"Put out the lamp!" yelled another.

Jean's third heavy swing caved in part of the upper half of the door. Shouts and curses intermingled with the sliding of benches across the floor and the hard shuffle of boots. This confusion seemed to be split and silenced by a piercing yell, of different caliber, of terrible meaning. It stayed Jean's swing—caused him to drop the ax and snatch up his rifle.

"Don't anybody move!"

156

Like a steel whip this voice cut the silence. It belonged to Blue. Jean swiftly bent to put his eye to a crack in the door. Most of those visible seemed to have been frozen into unnatural positions. Jorth stood rather in front of his men, hatless and coatless, one arm outstretched, and his dark profile set toward a little man just inside the door. This man was Blue. Jean needed only one flashing look at Blue's face, at his leveled, quivering guns, to understand why he had chosen this trick.

"Who're—you?" demanded Jorth, in husky pants.

"Reckon I'm Isbel's right-hand man," came the biting reply. "Once tolerable well known in Texas. . . . *King Fisher!*"

The name must have been a guarantee of death. Jorth recognized this outlaw and realized his own fate. In the lamplight his face turned a pale greenish white. His outstretched hand began to quiver down.

Blue's left gun seemed to leap up and flash red and explode. Several heavy reports merged almost as one. Jorth's arm jerked limply, flinging his gun. And his body sagged in the middle. His hands fluttered like crippled wings and found their way to his abdomen. His death-pale face never changed its set look nor position toward Blue. But his gasping utterance was one of horrible mortal fury and terror. Then he began to sway, still with that strange, rigid set of his face toward his slayer, until he fell.

His fall broke the spell. Even Blue, like the gunman he was, had paused to watch Jorth in his last mortal action. Jorth's followers began to draw and shoot. Jean saw Blue's return fire bring down a huge man, who fell across Jorth's body. Then Jean, quick as the thought that actuated him, raised his rifle and shot at the big lamp. It burst in a flare. It crashed to the floor. Darkness followed—a blank, thick, enveloping mantle. Then red flashes of guns emphasized the blackness. Inside the store there broke loose a pandemonium of shots, yells, curses, and thudding boots. Jean shoved his rifle barrel inside the door and, holding it low down, he moved it to and fro while he worked lever and trigger until the magazine was empty. Then, drawing his six-shooter, he emptied that. A roar of rifles from the front of the store told Jean that his comrades had entered the fray. Bullets zipped through the door he had broken. Jean ran swiftly round the corner, taking care to sheer off a little to the left, and when he got clear of the building he saw a line of flashes in the middle of the road. Blaisdell and the others were firing into the door of the store. With nimble fingers Jean reloaded his rifle. Then swiftly he ran across the road and down to get behind his comrades. Their shooting had slackened. Jean saw dark forms coming his way.

"Hello, Blaisdell!" he called, warningly.

"That y'u, Jean?" returned the rancher, looming up. "Wal, we wasn't worried aboot y'u."

"Blue?" queried Jean, sharply.

A little, dark figure shuffled past Jean. "Howdy, Jean!" said Blue, dryly. "Y'u shore did your part. Reckon I'll need to be tied up, but I ain't hurt much."

"Colmor's hit," called the voice of Gordon, a few yards distant. "Help me, somebody!"

Jean ran to help Gordon uphold the swaying Colmor. "Are you hurt—bad?" asked Jean, anxiously. The young man's head rolled and hung. He was breathing hard and did not reply. They had almost to carry him.

"Come on, men!" called Blaisdell, turning back toward the others who were still firing. "We'll let well enough alone. . . . Fredericks, y'u an' Bill help me find the body of the old man. It's heah somewhere."

Farther on down the road the searchers stumbled over Gaston Isbel. They picked him up and followed Jean and Gordon, who were supporting the wounded Colmor. Jean looked back to see Blue dragging himself along in the rear. It was too dark to see distinctly; nevertheless, Jean got the impression that Blue was more severely wounded than he had claimed to be. The distance to Meeker's cabin was not far, but it took what Jean felt to be a long and anxious time to get there. Colmor apparently rallied somewhat. When this procession entered Meeker's yard, Blue was lagging behind.

"Blue, how air y'u?" called Blaisdell, with concern.

"Wal, I got—my boots—on—anyhow," replied Blue, huskily.

He lurched into the yard and slid down on the grass and stretched out.

"Man! Y'u're hurt bad!" exclaimed Blaisdell. The others halted in their slow march and, as if by tacit, unspoken word, lowered the body of Isbel to the ground. Then Blaisdell knelt beside Blue. Jean left Colmor to Gordon and hurried to peer down into Blue's dim face.

"No, I ain't—hurt," said Blue, in a much weaker voice. "I'm—jest killed! . . . It was Queen! . . . Y'u all heerd me—

158

Queen was—only bad man in that lot. I knowed it. . . . I could—hev killed him. . . . But I was—after Lee Jorth—an' his brothers. . . ."

Blue's voice failed there.

"Wal!" ejaculated Blaisdell.

"Shore was funny—Jorth's face—when I said—King Fisher," whispered Blue. "Funnier—when I bored—him through. . . . But it—was—Queen—"

His whisper died away.

"Blue!" called Blaisdell, sharply. Receiving no answer, he bent lower in the starlight and placed a hand upon the man's breast.

"Wal, he's gone. . . . I wonder if he really was the old Texas King Fisher. No one would ever believe it. . . . But if he killed the Jorths, I'll shore believe him."

10
★

TWO weeks of lonely solitude in the forest had worked incalculable change in Ellen Jorth.

Late in June her father and her two uncles had packed and ridden off with Daggs, Colter, and six other men, all heavily armed, some somber with drink, others hard and grim with a foretaste of fight. Ellen had not been given any orders. Her father had forgotten to bid her good-by or had avoided it. Their dark mission was stamped on their faces.

They had gone and, keen as had been Ellen's pang, nevertheless, their departure was a relief. She had heard them bluster and brag so often that she had her doubts of any great Jorth-Isbel war. Barking dogs did not bite. Somebody, perhaps on each side, would be badly wounded, possibly killed, and then the feud would go on as before, mostly talk. Many of her former impressions had faded. Development had been so rapid and continuous in her that she could look back to a day-by-day transformation. At night she hated the sight of herself and when the dawn came she would rise, singing.

Jorth had left Ellen at home with the Mexican woman and Antonio. Ellen saw them only at meal times, and often not then, for she frequently visited old John Sprague or came home late to do her own cooking.

It was but a short distance up to Sprague's cabin, and since she had stopped riding the black horse, Spades, she walked. Spades was accustomed to having grain, and in the mornings he would come down to the ranch and whinny. Ellen had vowed she would never feed the horse and bade Antonio do it. But one morning Antonio was absent. She fed Spades herself. When she laid a hand on him and when he rubbed his nose against her shoulder she was not quite so sure she hated him. "Why should I?" she queried. "A horse cain't help it if he belongs to—to—" Ellen was not sure of anything except that more and more it grew good to be alone.

A whole day in the lonely forest passed swiftly, yet it left a feeling of long time. She lived by her thoughts. Always the morning was bright, sunny, sweet and fragrant and colorful, and her mood was pensive, wistful, dreamy. And always, just as surely as the hours passed, thought intruded upon her happiness, and thought brought memory, and memory brought shame, and shame brought fight. Sunset after sunset she had dragged herself back to the ranch, sullen and sick and beaten. Yet she never ceased to struggle.

The July storm came, and the forest floor that had been so sear and brown and dry and dusty changed as if by magic. The green grass shot up, the flowers bloomed, and along the cañon beds of lacy ferns swayed in the wind and bent their graceful tips over the amber-colored water. Ellen haunted these cool dells, these pine-shaded, mossy-rocked ravines where the brooks tinkled and the deer came down to drink. She wandered alone. But there grew to be company in the aspens and the music of the little waterfalls. If she could have lived in that solitude always, never returning to the ranch home that reminded her of her name, she could have forgotten and have been happy.

She loved the storms. It was a dry country and she had learned through years to welcome the creamy clouds that rolled from the southwest. They came sailing and clustering and darkening at last to form a great, purple, angry mass that appeared to lodge against the mountain rim and burst

160

into dazzling streaks of lightning and gray palls of rain. Lightning seldom struck near the ranch, but up on the Rim there was never a storm that did not splinter and crash some of the noble pines. During the storm season sheep herders and woodsmen generally did not camp under the pines. Fear of lightning was inborn in the natives, but for Ellen the dazzling white streaks or the tremendous splitting, crackling shock, or the thunderous boom and rumble along the battlements of the Rim had no terrors. A storm eased her breast. Deep in her heart was a hidden gathering storm. And somehow, to be out when the elements were warring, when the earth trembled and the heavens seemed to burst asunder, afforded her strange relief.

The summer days became weeks, and farther and farther they carried Ellen on the wings of solitude and loneliness until she seemed to look back years at the self she had hated. And always, when the dark memory impinged upon peace, she fought and fought until she seemed to be fighting hatred itself. Scorn of scorn and hate of hate! Yet even her battles grew to be dreams. For when the inevitable retrospect brought back Jean Isbel and his love and her cowardly falsehood she would shudder a little and put an unconscious hand to her breast and utterly fail in her fight and drift off down to vague and wistful dreams. The clean and healing forest, with its whispering wind and imperious solitude, had come between Ellen and the meaning of the squalid sheep ranch, with its travesty of home, its tragic owner. And it was coming between her two selves, the one that she had been forced to be and the other that she did not know— the thinker, the dreamer, the romancer, the one who lived in fancy the life she loved.

The summer morning dawned that brought Ellen strange tidings. They must have been created in her sleep, and now were realized in the glorious burst of golden sun, in the sweep of creamy clouds across the blue, in the solemn music of the wind in the pines, in the wild screech of the blue jays and the noble bugle of a stag. These heralded the day as no ordinary day. Something was going to happen to her. She divined it. She felt it. And she trembled. Nothing beautiful, hopeful, wonderful could ever happen to Ellen Jorth. She had been born to disaster, to suffer, to be forgotten, and die alone. Yet all nature about her seemed a magnificent rebuke to her morbidness. The same spirit that came out there with the thick, amber light was in her. She lived, and something in her was stronger than mind.

Ellen went to the door of her cabin, where she flung out her arms, driven to embrace this nameless purport of the morning. And a well-known voice broke in upon her rapture.

"Wal, lass, I like to see you happy an' I hate myself fer comin'. Because I've been to Grass Valley fer two days an' I've got news."

Old John Sprague stood there, with a smile that did not hide a troubled look.

"Oh! Uncle John! You startled me," exclaimed Ellen, shocked back to reality. And slowly she added: "Grass Valley! News?"

She put out an appealing hand, which Sprague quickly took in his own, as if to reassure her.

"Yes, an' not bad so far as you Jorths are concerned," he replied. "The first Jorth-Isbel fight has come off. . . . Reckon you remember makin' me promise to tell you if I heerd anythin'. Wal, I didn't wait fer you to come up."

"So," Ellen heard her voice calmly saying. What was this lying calm when there seemed to be a stone hammer at her heart? The first fight—not so bad for the Jorths! Then it had been bad for the Isbels. A sudden, cold stillness fell upon her senses.

"Let's sit down—outdoors," Sprague was saying. "Nice an' sunny this—mornin'. I declare—I'm out of breath. Not used to walkin'. An' besides, I left Grass Valley in the night —an' I'm tired. But excoose me from hangin' round thet village last night! There was shore—"

"Who—who was killed?" interrupted Ellen, her voice breaking low and deep.

"Guy Isbel an' Bill Jacobs on the Isbel side, an' Daggs, Craig, an' Greaves on your father's side," stated Sprague, with something of awed haste.

"Ah!" breathed Ellen, and she relaxed to sink back against the cabin wall.

Sprague seated himself on the log beside her, turning to face her, and he seemed burdened with grave and important matters.

"I heerd a good many conflictin' stories," he said, earnestly. "The village folks is all skeered an' there's no believin' their gossip. But I got what happened straight from Jake Evarts. The fight come off day before yestiddy. Your father's gang rode down to Isbel's ranch. Daggs was seen

162

to be wantin' some of the Isbel hosses, so Evarts says. An' Guy Isbel an' Jacobs run out in the pasture. Daggs an' some others shot them down . . ."

"Killed them—that way?" put in Ellen, sharply.

"So Evarts says. He was on the ridge an' swears he seen it all. They killed Guy an' Jacobs in cold blood. No chance fer their lives—not even to fight! . . . Wal, then they surrounded the Isbel cabin. The fight lasted all thet day an' all night an' the next day. Evarts says Guy an' Jacobs laid out thar all this time. An' a herd of hogs broke in the pasture an' was eatin' the dead bodies . . ."

"My God!" burst out Ellen. "Uncle John, y'u shore cain't mean my father wouldn't stop fightin' long enough to drive the hogs off an' bury those daid men?"

"Evarts says they stopped fightin', all right, but it was to watch the hogs," declared Sprague. "An' then, what d' ye think? The wimminfolks come out—the redheaded one, Guy's wife, an' Jacobs's wife—they drove the hogs away an' buried their husbands right there in the pasture. Evarts says he seen the graves."

"It is the women who can teach these bloody Texans a lesson," declared Ellen, forcibly.

"Wal, Daggs was drunk, an' he got up from behind where the gang was hidin', an' dared the Isbels to come out. They shot him to pieces. An' thet night some one of the Isbels shot Craig, who was alone on guard. . . . An' last—this here's what I come to tell you—Jean Isbel slipped up in the dark on Greaves an' knifed him."

"Why did y'u want to tell me that particularly?" asked Ellen, slowly.

"Because I reckon the facts in the case are queer—an' because, Ellen, your name was mentioned," announced Sprague, positively.

"My name—mentioned?" echoed Ellen. Her horror and disgust gave way to a quickening process of thought, a mounting astonishment. "By whom?"

"Jean Isbel," replied Sprague, as if the name and the fact were momentous.

Ellen sat still as a stone, her hands between her knees. Slowly she felt the blood recede from her face, prickling her skin down below her neck. That name locked her thought.

"Ellen, it's a mighty queer story—too queer to be a lie," went on Sprague. "Now you listen! Evarts got this from

163

Ted Meeker. An' Ted Meeker heerd it from Greaves, who didn't die till the next day after Jean Isbel knifed him. An' your dad shot Ted fer tellin' what he heerd. . . . No, Greaves wasn't killed outright. He was cut somethin' turrible—in two places. They wrapped him all up an' next day packed him in a wagon back to Grass Valley. Evarts says Ted Meeker was friendly with Greaves an' went to see him as he was layin' in his room next to the store. Wal, accordin' to Meeker's story, Greaves came to an' talked. He said he was sittin' there in the dark, shootin' occasionally at Isbel's cabin, when he heerd a rustle behind him in the grass. He knowed some one was crawlin' on him. But before he could get his gun around he was jumped by what he thought was a grizzly bear. But it was a man. He shut off Greaves's wind an' dragged him back in the ditch. An' he said: 'Greaves, it's the half-breed. An' he's goin' to cut you—*first for Ellen Jorth!* an' then for Gaston Isbel!' . . . Greaves said Jean ripped him with a bowie knife. . . . An' thet was all Greaves remembered. He died soon after tellin' this story. He must hev fought awful hard. Thet second cut Isbel gave him went clear through him. . . . Some of the gang was thar when Greaves talked, an' naturally they wondered why Jean Isbel had said 'first for Ellen Jorth.' . . . Somebody remembered thet Greaves had cast a slur on your good name, Ellen. An' then they had Jean Isbel's reason fer sayin' thet to Greaves. It caused a lot of talk. An' when Simm Bruce busted in some of the gang haw-hawed him an' said as how he'd get the third cut from Jean Isbel's bowie. Bruce was half drunk an' he began to cuss an' rave about Jean Isbel bein' in love with his girl. . . . As bad luck would have it, a couple of more fellars come in an' asked Meeker questions. He jest got to thet part, 'Greaves, it's the half-breed, an' he's goin' to cut you—*first for Ellen Jorth*', when in walked your father! . . . Then it all had to come out—what Jean Isbel had said an' done—an' why. How Greaves had backed Simm Bruce in slurrin' you!"

Sprague paused to look hard at Ellen.

"Oh! Then—what did dad do?" whispered Ellen.

"He said, 'By God! half-breed or not, there's one Isbel who's a man!' An' he killed Bruce on the spot an' gave Meeker a nasty wound. Somebody grabbed him before he could shoot Meeker again. They threw Meeker out an' he crawled to a neighbor's house, where he was when Evarts seen him."

Ellen felt Sprague's rough but kindly hand shaking her. "An' now what do you think of Jean Isbel?" he queried.

A great, unsurmountable wall seemed to obstruct Ellen's thought. It seemed gray in color. It moved toward her. It was inside her brain.

"I tell you, Ellen Jorth," declared the old man, "thet Jean Isbel loves you—loves you turribly—an' he believes you're good."

"Oh no—he doesn't!" faltered Ellen.

"Wal, he jest does."

"Oh, Uncle John, he cain't believe that!" she cried.

"Of course he can. He does. You are good—good as gold, Ellen, an' he knows it. . . . What a queer deal it all is! Poor devil! To love you thet turribly an' hev to fight your people! Ellen, your dad had it correct. Isbel or not, he's a man. . . . An' I say what a shame you two are divided by hate. Hate thet you hed nothin' to do with." Sprague patted her head and rose to go. "Mebbe thet fight will end the trouble. I reckon it will. Don't cross bridges till you come to them, Ellen. . . . I must hurry back now. I didn't take time to unpack my burros. Come up soon. . . . An', say, Ellen, don't think hard any more of thet Jean Isbel!"

Sprague strode away, and Ellen neither heard nor saw him go. She sat perfectly motionless, yet had a strange sensation of being lifted by invisible and mighty power. It was like movement felt in a dream. She was being impelled upward when her body seemed immovable as stone. When her blood beat down this deadlock of all her physical being and rushed on and on through her veins it gave her an irresistible impulse to fly, to sail through space, to run and run and run.

And on the moment the black horse, Spades, coming from the meadow, whinnied at sight of her. Ellen leaped up and ran swiftly, but her feet seemed to be stumbling. She hugged the horse and buried her hot face in his mane and clung to him. Then just as violently she rushed for her saddle and bridle and carried the heavy weight as easily as if it had been an empty sack. Throwing them upon him, she buckled and strapped with strong, eager hands. It never occurred to her that she was not dressed to ride. Up she flung herself. And the horse, sensing her spirit, plunged into strong, free gait down the cañon trail.

The ride, the action, the thrill, the sensations of violence

165

were not all she needed. Solitude, the empty aisles of the forest, the far miles of lonely wilderness—were these the added all? Spades took a swinging, rhythmic lope up the winding trail. The wind fanned her hot face. The sting of whipping aspen branches was pleasant. A deep rumble of thunder shook the sultry air. Up beyond the green slope of the cañon massed the creamy clouds, shading darker and darker. Spades loped on the levels, leaped the washes, trotted over the rocky ground, and took to a walk up the long slope. Ellen dropped the reins over the pommel. Her hands could not stay set on anything. They pressed her breast and flew out to caress the white aspens and to tear at the maple leaves, and gather the lavender juniper berries, and came back again to her heart. Her heart that was going to burst or break! As it had swelled, so now it labored. It could not keep pace with her needs. All that was physical, all that was living in her had to be unleashed.

Spades gained the level forest. How the great, brown-green pines seemed to bend their lofty branches over her, protectively, understandingly. Patches of azure-blue sky flashed between the trees. The great white clouds sailed along with her, and shafts of golden sunlight, flecked with gleams of falling pine needles, shone down through the canopy overhead. Away in front of her, up the slow heave of forest land, boomed the heavy thunderbolts along the battlements of the Rim.

Was she riding to escape from herself? For no gait suited her until Spades was running hard and fast through the glades. Then the pressure of dry wind, the thick odor of pine, the flashes of brown and green and gold and blue, the soft, rhythmic thuds of hoofs, the feel of the powerful horse under her, the whip of spruce branches on her muscles contracting and expanding in hard action—all these sensations seemed to quell for the time the mounting cataclysm in her heart.

The oak swales, the maple thickets, the aspen groves, the pine-shaded aisles, and the miles of silver spruce all sped by her, as if she had ridden the wind; and through the forest ahead shone the vast open of the Basin, gloomed by purple and silver cloud, shadowed by gray storm, and in the west brightened by golden sky.

Straight to the Rim she had ridden, and to the point where she had watched Jean Isbel that unforgetable day. She rode to the promontory behind the pine thicket and beheld a scene which stayed her restless hands upon her heaving breast.

The world of sky and cloud and earthly abyss seemed one of storm-sundered grandeur. The air was sultry and still, and smelled of the peculiar burnt-wood odor caused by lightning striking trees. A few heavy drops of rain were pattering down from the thin, gray edge of clouds overhead. To the east hung the storm—a black cloud lodged against the Rim, from which long, misty veils of rain streamed down into the gulf. The roar of rain sounded like the steady roar of the rapids of a river. Then a blue-white, piercingly bright, ragged streak of lightning shot down out of the black cloud. It struck with a splitting report that shocked the very wall of rock under Ellen. Then the heavens seemed to burst open with thundering crash and close with mighty thundering boom. Long roar and longer rumble rolled away to the eastward. The rain poured down in roaring cataracts.

The south held a panorama of purple-shrouded range and cañon, cañon and range, on across the rolling leagues to the dim, lofty peaks, all canopied over with angry, dusky, low-drifting clouds, horizon-wide, smoky, and sulphurous. And as Ellen watched, hands pressed to her breast, feeling incalculable relief in sight of this tempest and gulf that resembled her soul, the sun burst out from behind the long bank of purple cloud in the west and flooded the world there with golden lightning.

"It is for me!" cried Ellen. "My mind—my heart—my very soul. . . . Oh, I know! I know now! . . . I love him—love him—love him!"

She cried it out to the elements. "Oh, I love Jean Isbel—an' my heart will burst or break!"

The might of her passion was like the blaze of the sun. Before it all else retreated, diminished. The suddenness of the truth dimmed her sight. But she saw clearly enough to crawl into the pine thicket, through the clutching, dry twigs, over the mats of fragrant needles to the covert where she had once spied upon Jean Isbel. And here she lay face down for a while, hands clutching the needles, breast pressed hard upon the ground, stricken and spent. But vitality was exceeding strong in her. It passed, that weakness of realization, and she awakened to the consciousness of love.

But in the beginning it was not consciousness of the man. It was new, sensorial life, elemental, primitive, a liberation

167

of a million inherited instincts, quivering and physical, over which Ellen had no more control than she had over the glory of the sun. If she thought at all it was of her need to be hidden, like an animal, low down near the earth, covered by green thicket, lost in the wildness of nature. She went to nature, unconsciously seeking a mother. And love was a birth from the depths of her, like a rushing spring of pure water, long underground, and at last propelled to the surface by a convulsion.

Ellen gradually lost her tense rigidity and relaxed. Her body softened. She rolled over until her face caught the lacy, golden shadows cast by sun and bough. Scattered drops of rain pattered around her. The air was hot, and its odor was that of dry pine and spruce fragrance penetrated by brimstone from the lightning. The nest where she lay was warm and sweet. No eye save that of nature saw her in her abandonment. An ineffable and exquisite smile wreathed her lips, dreamy, sad, sensuous, the supremacy of unconscious happiness. Over her dark and eloquent eyes, as Ellen gazed upward, spread a luminous film, a veil. She was looking intensely, yet she did not see. The wilderness enveloped her with its secretive, elemental sheaths of rock, of tree, of cloud, of sunlight. Through her thrilling skin poured the multiple and nameless sensations of the living organism stirred to supreme sensitiveness. She could not lie still, but all her movements were gentle, involuntary. The slow reaching out of her hand, to grasp at nothing visible, was similar to the lazy stretching of her limbs, to the heave of her breast, to the ripple of muscle.

Ellen knew not what she felt. To live that sublime hour was beyond thought. Such happiness was like the first dawn of the world to the sight of man. It had to do with bygone ages. Her heart, her blood, her flesh, her very bones were filled with instincts and emotions common to the race before intellect developed, when the savage lived only with his sensorial perceptions. Of all happiness, joy, bliss, rapture to which man was heir, that of intense and exquisite preoccupation of the senses, unhindered and unburdened by thought, was the greatest. Ellen felt that which life meant with its inscrutable design. Love was only the realization of her mission on the earth.

The dark storm cloud with its white, ragged ropes of lightning and down-streaming gray veils of rain, the purple gulf rolling like a colored sea to the dim mountains, the glorious golden light of the sun—these had enchanted her eyes with her beauty of the universe. They had burst the windows of her blindness. When she crawled into the green-brown covert it was to escape too great perception. She needed to be encompassed by close tangible things. And there her body paid the tribute to the realization of life. Shock, convulsion, pain, relaxation, and then unutterable and insupportable sensing of her environment and the heart! In one way she was a wild animal alone in the woods, forced into the mating that meant reproduction of its kind. In another she was an infinitely higher being shot through and through with the most resistless and mysterious transport that life could give to flesh.

And when that spell slackened its hold there wedged into her mind a consciousness of the man she loved—Jean Isbel. Then emotion and thought strove for mastery over her. It was not herself or love that she loved, but a living man. Suddenly he existed so clearly for her that she could see him, hear him, almost feel him. Her whole soul, her very life cried out to him for protection, for salvation, for love, for fulfillment. No denial, no doubt marred the white blaze of her realization. From the instant that she had looked up into Jean Isbel's dark face she had loved him. Only she had not known. She bowed now, and bent, and humbly quivered under the mastery of something beyond her ken. Thought clung to the beginnings of her romance—to the three times she had seen him. Every look, every word, every act of his returned to her now in the light of the truth. Love at first sight! He had sworn it, bitterly, eloquently, scornful of her doubts. And now a blind, sweet, shuddering ecstasy swayed her. How weak and frail seemed her body—too small, too slight for this monstrous and terrible engine of fire and lightning and fury and glory—her heart! It must burst or break. Relentlessly memory pursued Ellen, and her thoughts whirled and emotion conquered her. At last she quivered up to her knees as if lashed to action. It seemed that first kiss of Isbel's, cool and gentle and timid, was on her lips. And her eyes closed and hot tears welled from under her lids. Her groping hands found only the dead twigs and the pine boughs of the trees. Had she reached out to clasp him? Then hard and violent on her mouth and cheek and neck burned those other kisses of Isbel's, and with the flashing, stinging memory came the truth that now she would have bartered her soul for them. Utterly she surrendered to the resistlessness of this love. Her loss of mother and friends, her wandering from one wild place to another, her lonely life among bold and rough men, had developed her for violent love. It overthrew all pride, it engendered humility, it killed hate. Ellen wiped the tears from her eyes, and as she knelt there she swept to her breast a fragrant spreading bough of pine needles. "I'll go to him," she whispered. "I'll tell him of—of my—my love. I'll tell him to take me away—away to the end of the world—away from heah—before it's too late!"

It was a solemn, beautiful moment. But the last spoken words lingered hauntingly. "Too late?" she whispered.

And suddenly it seemed that death itself shuddered in her soul. Too late! It was too late. She had killed his love. That Jorth blood in her—that poisonous hate—had chosen the only way to strike this noble Isbel to the heart. Basely, with an abandonment of womanhood, she had mockingly perjured her soul with a vile lie. She writhed, she shook under the whip of this inconceivable fact. Lost! Lost! She wailed her misery. She might as well be what she had made Jean Isbel think she was. If she had been shamed before, she was now abased, degraded, lost in her own sight. And if she would have given her soul for his kisses, she now would have killed herself to earn back his respect. Jean Isbel had given her at sight the deference that she had unconsciously craved, and the love that would have been her salvation. What a horrible mistake she had made of her life! Not her mother's blood, but her father's—the Jorth blood—had been her ruin.

Again Ellen fell upon the soft pine-needle mat, face down, and she groveled and burrowed there, in an agony that could not bear the sense of light. All she had suffered was as nothing to this. To have awakened to a splendid and uplifting love for a man whom she had imagined she hated, who had fought for her name and had killed in revenge for the dishonor she had avowed—to have lost his love and what was infinitely more precious to her now in her ignominy—his faith in her purity—this broke her heart.

11

★

WHEN Ellen, utterly spent in body and mind, reached
home that day a melancholy, sultry twilight was falling.
Fitful flares of sheet lightning swept across the dark horizon
to the east. The cabins were deserted. Antonio and the Mexican woman were gone. The circumstances made Ellen
wonder, but she was too tired and too sunken in spirit to
think long about it or to care. She fed and watered her
horse and left him in the corral. Then, supperless and without removing her clothes, she threw herself upon the bed,
and at once sank into heavy slumber.

Sometime during the night she awoke. Coyotes were yelping, and from that sound she concluded it was near dawn.
Her body ached; her mind seemed dull. Drowsily she was
sinking into slumber again when she heard the rapid clip-
clop of trotting horses. Startled, she raised her head to
listen. The men were coming back. Relief and dread
seemed to clear her stupor.

The trotting horses stopped across the lane from her cabin,
evidently at the corral where she had left Spades. She heard
him whistle. From the sound of hoofs she judged the number
of horses to be six or eight. Low voices of men mingled
with thuds and cracking of straps and flopping of saddles
on the ground. After that the heavy tread of boots sounded
on the porch of the cabin opposite. A door creaked on its
hinges. Next a slow footstep, accompanied by clinking of
spurs, approached Ellen's door, and a heavy hand banged
upon it. She knew this person could not be her father.

"Hullo, Ellen!"

She recognized the voice as belonging to Colter. Somehow
its tone, or something about it, sent a little shiver down her
spine. It acted like a revivifying current. Ellen lost her
dragging lethargy.

"Hey, Ellen, are y'u there?" added Colter, in louder voice.

"Yes. Of course I'm heah," she replied. "What do y'u want?"

"Wal—I'm shore glad y'u're home," he replied. "Antonio's gone with his squaw. An' I was some worried aboot y'u."

"Who's with y'u, Colter?" queried Ellen, sitting up.

"Rock Wells an' Springer. Tad Jorth was with us, but we had to leave him over heah in a cabin."

"What's the matter with him?"

"Wal, he's hurt tolerable bad," was the slow reply.

Ellen heard Colter's spurs jangle, as if he had uneasily shifted his feet.

"Where's dad an' Uncle Jackson?" asked Ellen.

A silence pregnant enough to augment Ellen's dread finally broke to Colter's voice, somehow different. "Shore they're back on the trail. An' we're to meet them where we left Tad."

"Are y'u goin' away again?"

"I reckon. . . . An', Ellen, y'u're goin' with us."

"I am not," she retorted.

"Wal, y'u are, if I have to pack y'u," he replied, forcibly. "It's not safe heah any more. That damned half-breed Isbel with his gang are on our trail."

That name seemed like a red-hot blade at Ellen's leaden heart. She wanted to fling a hundred queries on Colter, but she could not utter one.

"Ellen, we've got to hit the trail an' hide," continued Colter, anxiously. "Y'u mustn't stay heah alone. Suppose them Isbels would trap y'u! . . . They'd tear your clothes off an' rope y'u to a tree. Ellen, shore y'u're goin'. . . . Y'u heah me!"

"Yes—I'll go," she replied, as if forced.

"Wal—that's good," he said, quickly. "An' rustle tolerable lively. We've got to pack."

The slow jangle of Colter's spurs and his slow steps moved away out of Ellen's hearing. Throwing off the blankets, she put her feet to the floor and sat there a moment staring at the blank nothingness of the cabin interior in the obscure gray of dawn. Cold, gray, dreary, obscure—like her life, her future! And she was compelled to do what was hateful to her. As a Jorth she must take to the unfrequented trails and hide like a rabbit in the thickets. But the interest of the moment, a premonition of events to be, quickened her into action.

Ellen unbarred the door to let in the light. Day was break-

172

ing with an intense, clear, steely light in the east through which the morning star still shone white. A ruddy flare betokened the advent of the sun. Ellen unbraided her tangled hair and brushed and combed it. A queer, still pang came to her at sight of pine needles tangled in her brown locks. Then she washed her hands and face. Breakfast was a matter of considerable work and she was hungry.

The sun rose and changed the gray world of forest. For the first time in her life Ellen hated the golden brightness, the wonderful blue of sky, the scream of the eagle and the screech of the jay; and the squirrels she had always loved to feed were neglected that morning.

Colter came in. Either Ellen had never before looked attentively at him or else he had changed. Her scrutiny of his lean, hard features accorded him more Texan attributes than formerly. His gray eyes were as light, as clear, as fierce as those of an eagle. And the sand gray of his face, the long, drooping, fair mustache hid the secrets of his mind, but not its strength. The instant Ellen met his gaze she sensed a power in him that she instinctively opposed. Colter had not been so bold nor so rude as Daggs, but he was the same kind of man, perhaps the more dangerous for his secretiveness, his cool, waiting inscrutableness.

" 'Mawnin', Ellen!" he drawled. "Y'u shore look good for sore eyes."

"Don't pay me compliments, Colter," replied Ellen. "An' your eyes are not sore."

"Wal, I'm shore sore from fightin' an' ridin' an' layin' out," he said, bluntly.

"Tell me—what's happened," returned Ellen.

"Girl, it's a tolerable long story," replied Colter. "An' we've no time now. Wait till we get to camp."

"Am I to pack my belongin's or leave them heah?" asked Ellen.

"Reckon y'u'd better leave—them heah."

"But if we did not come back—"

"Wal, I reckon it's not likely we'll come—soon," he said, rather evasively.

"Colter, I'll not go off into the woods with just the clothes I have on my back."

"Ellen, we shore got to pack all the grub we can. This shore ain't goin' to be a visit to neighbors. We're shy pack hosses. But y'u make up a bundle of belongin's y'u care for, an' the things y'u'll need bad. We'll throw it on somewhere."

173

Colter stalked away across the lane, and Ellen found herself dubiously staring at his tall figure. Was it the situation that struck her with a foreboding perplexity or was her intuition steeling her against this man? Ellen could not decide. But she had to go with him. Her prejudice was unreasonable at this portentous moment. And she could not yet feel that she was solely responsible to herself.

When it came to making a small bundle of her belongings she was in a quandary. She discarded this and put in that, and then reversed the order. Next in preciousness to her mother's things were the long-hidden gifts of Jean Isbel. She could part with neither.

While she was selecting and packing this bundle Colter again entered and, without speaking, began to rummage in the corner where her father kept his possessions. This irritated Ellen.

"What do y'u want there?" she demanded.

"Wal, I reckon your dad wants his papers—an' the gold he left heah—an' a change of clothes. Now doesn't he?" returned Colter, coolly.

"Of course. But I supposed y'u would have me pack them."

Colter vouchsafed no reply to this, but deliberately went on rummaging, with little regard for how he scattered things. Ellen turned her back on him. At length, when he left, she went to her father's corner and found that, as far as she was able to see, Colter had taken neither papers nor clothes, but only the gold. Perhaps, however, she had been mistaken, for she had not observed Colter's departure closely enough to know whether or not he carried a package. She missed only the gold. Her father's papers, old and musty, were scattered about, and these she gathered up to slip in her own bundle.

Colter, or one of the men, had saddled Spades, and he was now tied to the corral fence, champing his bit and pounding the sand. Ellen wrapped bread and meat inside her coat, and after tying this behind her saddle she was ready to go. But evidently she would have to wait, and, preferring to remain outdoors, she stayed by her horse. Presently, while watching the men pack, she noticed that Springer wore a bandage round his head under the brim of his sombrero. His motions were slow and lacked energy. Shuddering at the sight, Ellen refused to conjecture. All too soon she would learn what had happened, and all too soon, perhaps, she herself would be in the midst of another fight.

174

She watched the men. They were making a hurried slipshod job of packing food supplies from both cabins. More than once she caught Colter's gray gleam of gaze on her, and she did not like it.

"I'll ride up an' say good-by to Sprague," she called to Colter.

"Shore y'u won't do nothin' of the kind," he called back.

There was authority in his tone that angered Ellen, and something else which inhibited her anger. What was there about Colter with which she must reckon? The other two Texans laughed aloud, to be suddenly silenced by Colter's harsh and lowered curses. Ellen walked out of hearing and sat upon a log, where she remained until Colter hailed her.

"Get up an' ride," he called.

Ellen complied with this order and, riding up behind the three mounted men, she soon found herself leaving what for years had been her home. Not once did she look back. She hoped she would never see the squalid, bare pretension of a ranch again.

Colter and the other riders drove the pack horses across the meadow, off of the trails, and up the slope into the forest. Not very long did it take Ellen to see that Colter's object was to hide their tracks. He zigzagged through the forest, avoiding the bare spots of dust, the dry, sun-baked flats of clay where water lay in spring, and he chose the grassy, open glades, the long, pine-needle matted aisles. Ellen rode at their heels and it pleased her to watch for their tracks. Colter manifestly had been long practiced in this game of hiding his trail, and he showed the skill of a rustler. But Ellen was not convinced that he could ever elude a real woodsman. Not improbably, however, Colter was only aiming to leave a trail difficult to follow and which would allow him and his confederates ample time to forge ahead of pursuers. Ellen could not accept a certainty of pursuit. Yet Colter must have expected it, and Springer and Wells also, for they had a dark, sinister, furtive demeanor that strangely contrasted with the cool, easy manner habitual to them.

They were not seeking the level routes of the forest land, that was sure. They rode straight across the thick-timbered ridge down into another cañon, up out of that, and across rough, rocky bluffs, and down again. These riders headed a little to the northwest and every mile brought them into wilder, more rugged country, until Ellen, losing count of

175

cañons and ridges, had no idea where she was. No stop was made at noon to rest the laboring, sweating pack animals.

Under circumstances where pleasure might have been possible Ellen would have reveled in this hard ride into a wonderful forest ever thickening and darkening. But the wild beauty of glade and the spruce slopes and the deep, bronze-walled cañons left her cold. She saw and felt, but had no thrill, except now and then a thrill of alarm when Spades slid to his haunches down some steep, damp, piny declivity.

All the woodland, up and down, appeared to be richer, greener as they traveled farther west. Grass grew thick and heavy. Water ran in all ravines. The rocks were bronze and copper and russet, and some had green patches of lichen.

Ellen felt the sun now on her left cheek and knew that the day was waning and that Colter was swinging farther to the northwest. She had never before ridden through such heavy forest and down and up such wild cañons. Toward sunset the deepest and ruggedest cañon halted their advance. Colter rode to the right, searching for a place to get down through a spruce thicket that stood on end. Presently he dismounted and the others followed suit. Ellen found she could not lead Spades because he slid down upon her heels, so she looped the end of her reins over the pommel and left him free. She herself managed to descend by holding to branches and sliding all the way down that slope. She heard the horses cracking the brush, snorting and heaving. One pack slipped and had to be removed from the horse, and rolled down. At the bottom of this deep, green-walled notch roared a stream of water. Shadowed, cool, mossy, damp, this narrow gulch seemed the wildest place Ellen had ever seen. She could just see the sunset-flushed, gold-tipped spruces far above her. The men repacked the horse that had slipped his burden, and once more resumed their progress ahead, now turning up this cañon. There was no horse trail, but deer and bear trails were numerous. The sun sank and the sky darkened, but still the men rode on; and the farther they traveled the wilder grew the aspect of the cañon.

At length Colter broke a way through a heavy thicket of willows and entered a side cañon, the mouth of which Ellen had not even descried. It turned and widened, and at length opened out into a round pocket, apparently inclosed, and as lonely and isolated a place as even pursued rustlers could desire. Hidden by jutting wall and thicket of

176

spruce were two old log cabins joined together by roof and attic floor, the same as the double cabin at the Jorth ranch.

Ellen smelled wood smoke, and presently, on going round the cabins, saw a bright fire. One man stood beside it gazing at Colter's party, which evidently he had heard approaching.

"Hullo, Queen!" said Colter. "How's Tad?"

"He's holdin' on fine," replied Queen, bending over the fire, where he turned pieces of meat.

"Where's father?" suddenly asked Ellen, addressing Colter.

As if he had not heard her, he went on wearily loosening a pack.

Queen looked at her. The light of the fire only partially shone on his face. Ellen could not see its expression. But from the fact that Queen did not answer her question she got further intimation of an impending catastrophe. The long, wild ride had helped prepare her for the secrecy and tactiturnity of men who had resorted to flight. Perhaps her father had been delayed or was still off on the deadly mission that had obsessed him; or there might, and probably was, darker reason for his absence. Ellen shut her teeth and turned to the needs of her horse. And presently, returning to the fire, she thought of her uncle.

"Queen, is my uncle Tad heah?" she asked.

"Shore. He's in there," replied Queen, pointing at the nearer cabin.

Ellen hurried toward the dark doorway. She could see how the logs of the cabin had moved awry and what a big, dilapidated hovel it was. As she looked in, Colter loomed over her—placed a familiar and somehow masterful hand upon her. Ellen let it rest on her shoulder a moment. Must she forever be repulsing these rude men among whom her lot was cast? Did Colter mean what Daggs had always meant? Ellen felt herself weary, weak in body, and her spent spirit had not rallied. Yet, whatever Colter meant by his familiarity, she could not bear it. So she slipped out from under his hand.

"Uncle Tad, are y'u heah?" she called into the blackness. She heard the mice scamper and rustle and she smelled the musty, old, woody odor of a long-unused cabin.

"Hello, Ellen!" came a voice she recognized as her uncle's, yet it was strange. "Yes. I'm heah—bad luck to me! . . . How're y'u buckin' up, girl?"

"I'm all right, Uncle Tad—only tired an' worried. I—"

"Tad, how's your hurt?" interrupted Colter.

177

"Reckon I'm easier," replied Jorth, wearily, "but shore I'm in bad shape. I'm still spittin' blood. I keep tellin' Queen that bullet lodged in my lungs—but he says it went through."

"Wal, hang on, Tad!" replied Colter, with a cheerfulness Ellen sensed was really indifferent.

"Oh, what the hell's the use!" exclaimed Jorth. "It's all—up with us—Colter!"

"Wal, shut up, then," tersely returned Colter. "It ain't doin' y'u or us any good to holler."

Tad Jorth did not reply to this. Ellen heard his breathing and it did not seem natural. It rasped a little—came hurriedly—then caught in his throat. Then he spat. Ellen shrunk back against the door. He was breathing through blood.

"Uncle, are y'u in pain?" she asked.

"Yes, Ellen—it burns like hell," he said.

"Oh! I'm sorry. . . . Isn't there something I can do?"

"I reckon not. Queen did all anybody could do for me —now—unless it's pray."

Colter laughed at this—the slow, easy, drawling laugh of a Texan. But Ellen felt pity for this wounded uncle. She had always hated him. He had been a drunkard, a gambler, a waster of her father's property; and now he was a rustler and a fugitive, lying in pain, perhaps mortally hurt.

"Yes, uncle—I will pray for y'u," she said, softly.

The change in his voice held a note of sadness that she had been quick to catch.

"Ellen, y'u're the only good Jorth—in the whole damned lot," he said. "God! I see it all now. . . . We've dragged y'u to hell!"

"Yes, Uncle Tad, I've shore been dragged some—but not yet—to hell," she responded, with a break in her voice.

"Y'u will be—Ellen—unless—"

"Aw, shut up that kind of bag, will y'u?" broke in Colter, harshly.

It amazed Ellen that Colter should dominate her uncle, even though he was wounded. Tad Jorth had been the last man to take orders from anyone, much less a rustler of the Hash Knife Gang. This Colter began to loom up in Ellen's estimate as he loomed physically over her, a lofty figure, dark, motionless, somehow menacing.

"Ellen, has Colter told y'u yet—aboot—aboot Lee an' Jackson?" inquired the wounded man.

The pitch-black darkness of the cabin seemed to help fortify Ellen to bear further trouble.

"Colter told me dad an' Uncle Jackson would meet us heah," she rejoined, hurriedly.

Jorth could be heard breathing in difficulty, and he coughed and spat again, and seemed to hiss.

"Ellen, he lied to y'u. They'll never meet us—heah!"

"Why not?" whispered Ellen.

"Because—Ellen—" he replied, in husky pants, "your dad an'—uncle Jackson—are daid—an' buried!"

If Ellen suffered a terrible shock it was a blankness, a deadness, and a slow, creeping failure of sense in her knees. They gave way under her and she sank on the grass against the cabin wall. She did not faint nor grow dizzy nor lose her sight, but for a while there was no process of thought in her mind. Suddenly then it was there—the quick, spiritual rending of her heart—followed by a profound emotion of intimate and irretrievable loss—and after that grief and bitter realization.

An hour later Ellen found strength to go to the fire and partake of the food and drink her body sorely needed.

Colter and the men waited on her solicitously, and in silence, now and then stealing furtive glances at her from under the shadow of their black sombreros. The dark night settled down like a blanket. There were no stars. The wind moaned fitfully among the pines, and all about that lonely, hidden recess was in harmony with Ellen's thoughts.

"Girl, y'u're shore game," said Colter, admiringly. "An' I reckon y'u never got it from the Jorths."

"Tad in there—he's game," said Queen, in mild protest.

"Not to my notion," replied Colter. "Any man can be game when he's croakin', with somebody around. . . . But Lee Jorth an' Jackson—they always was yellow clear to their gizzards. They was born in Louisiana—not Texas. . . . Shore they're no more Texans than I am. Ellen heah, she must have got another strain in her blood."

To Ellen their words had no meaning. She rose and asked, "Where can I sleep?"

"I'll fetch a light presently an' y'u can make your bed in there by Tad," replied Colter.

"Yes, I'd like that."

"Wal, if y'u reckon y'u can coax him to talk you're shore wrong," declared Colter, with that cold timbre of voice that struck like steel on Ellen's nerves. "I cussed him good an' told him he'd keep his mouth shut. Talkin' makes him cough an' that fetches up the blood. . . . Besides, I reckon I'm the one to tell y'u how your dad an' uncle got killed. Tad didn't see it done, an' he was bad hurt when it happened. Shore all the fellars left have their idee aboot it. But I've got it straight."

"Colter—tell me now," cried Ellen.

"Wal, all right. Come over heah," he replied, and drew her away from the camp fire, out in the shadow of gloom. "Poor kid! I shore feel bad aboot it." He put a long arm around her waist and drew her against him. Ellen felt it, yet did not offer any resistance. All her faculties seemed absorbed in a morbid and sad anticipation.

"Ellen, y'u shore know I always loved y'u—now don't y'u?" he asked, with suprpessed breath.

"No, Colter. It's news to me—an' not what I want to heah."

"Wal, y'u may as well heah it right now," he said. "It's true. An' what's more—your dad gave y'u to me before he died."

"What! Colter, y'u must be a liar."

"Ellen, I swear I'm not lyin'," he returned, in eager passion. "I was with your dad last an' heard him last. He shore knew I'd loved y'u for years. An' he said he'd rather y'u be left in my care than anybody's."

"My father gave me to y'u in marriage!" ejaculated Ellen, in bewilderment.

Colter's ready assurance did not carry him over this point. It was evident that her words somewhat surprised and disconcerted him for the moment.

"To let me marry a rustler—one of the Hash Knife Gang!" exclaimed Ellen, with weary incredulity.

"Wal, your dad belonged to Daggs's gang, same as I do," replied Colter, recovering his cool ardor.

"No!" cried Ellen.

"Yes, he shore did, for years," declared Colter, positively. "Back in Texas. An' it was your dad that got Daggs to come to Arizona."

Ellen tried to fling herself away. But her strength and her spirit were ebbing, and Colter increased the pressure of his arm. All at once she sank limp. Could she escape her fate? Nothing seemed left to fight with or for.

"All right—don't hold me—so tight," she panted. "Now tell me how dad was killed . . . an' who—who—"

Colter bent over so he could peer into her face. In the darkness Ellen just caught the gleam of his eyes. She felt the virile force of the man in the strain of his body as he pressed her close. It all seemed unreal—a hideous dream—the gloom, the moan of the wind, the weird solitude, and this rustler with hand and will like cold steel.

"We'd come back to Greaves's store," Colter began. "An' as Greaves was daid we all got free with his liquor. Shore some of us got drunk. Bruce was drunk, an' Tad in there—he was drunk. Your dad put away more 'n I ever seen him. But shore he wasn't exactly drunk. He got one of them weak an' shaky spells. He cried an' he wanted some of us to get the Isbels to call off the fightin'. . . . He shore was ready to call it quits. I reckon the killin' of Daggs—an' then the awful way Greaves was cut up by Jean Isbel—took all the fight out of your dad. He said to me, 'Colter, we'll take Ellen an' leave this heah country—an' begin life all over again—where no one knows us.'"

"Oh, did he really say that? . . . Did he—really mean it?" murmured Ellen, with a sob.

"I'll swear it by the memory of my daid mother," protested Colter. "Wal, when night come the Isbels rode down on us in the dark an' began to shoot. They smashed in the door—tried to burn us out—an' hollered around for a while. Then they left an' we reckoned there'd be no more trouble that night. All the same we kept watch. I was the soberest one an' I bossed the gang. We had some quarrels aboot the drinkin'. Your dad said if we kept it up it'd be the end of the Jorths. An' he planned to send word to the Isbels next mawnin' that he was ready for a truce. An' I was to go fix it up with Gaston Isbel. Wal, your dad went to bed in Greaves's room, an' a little while later your uncle Jackson went in there, too. Some of the men laid down in the store an' went to sleep. I kept guard till aboot three in the mawnin'. An' I got so sleepy I couldn't hold my eyes open. So I waked up Wells an' Slater an' set them on guard, one at each end of the store. Then I laid down on the counter to take a nap."

Colter's low voice, the strain and breathlessness of him, the agitation with which he appeared to be laboring, and especially the simple, matter-of-fact detail of his story, carried absolute conviction to Ellen Jorth. Her vague doubt of

181

him had been created by his attitude toward her. Emotion dominated her intelligence. The images, the scenes called up by Colter's words, were as true as the gloom of the wild gulch and the loneliness of the night solitude—as true as the strange fact that she lay passive in the arm of a rustler.

"Wal, after a while I woke up," went on Colter, clearing his throat. "It was gray dawn. All was as still as death. . . . An' somethin' shore was wrong. Wells an' Slater had got to drinkin' again an' now laid daid drunk or asleep. Anyways, when I kicked them they never moved. Then I heard a moan. It came from the room where your dad an' uncle was. I went in. It was just light enough to see. Your uncle Jackson was layin' on the floor—cut half in two—daid as a door nail. . . . Your dad lay on the bed. He was alive, breathin' his last. . . . He says, 'That half-breed Isbel—knifed us—while we slept!' . . . The winder shutter was open. I seen where Jean Isbel had come in an' gone out. I seen his moccasin tracks in Jackson's blood an' tracked it to the winder. Y'u shore can see them bloody tracks yourself, if y'u go back to Greaves's store. . . . Your dad was goin' fast. . . . He said, 'Colter—take care of Ellen,' an' I reckon he meant a lot by that. He kept sayin', 'My God! if I'd only seen Gaston Isbel before it was too late!' an' then he raved a little, whisperin' out of his haid. . . . An' after that he died. . . . I woke up the men, an' aboot sunup we carried your dad an' uncle out of town an' buried them. . . . An' them Isbels shot at us while we were buryin' our daid! That's where Tad got his hurt. . . . Then we hit the trail for Jorth's ranch. . . . An' now, Ellen, that's all my story. Your dad was ready to bury the hatchet with his old enemy. An' that Nez Perce Jean Isbel, like the sneakin' savage he is, murdered your uncle an' your dad. . . . Cut him horrible—made him suffer tortures of hell—all for Isbel revenge!"

When Colter's husky voice ceased Ellen whispered through lips as cold and still as ice, "Let me go . . . leave me—heah—alone!"

"Why, shore! I reckon I understand," replied Colter. "I hated to tell y'u. But y'u had to heah the truth aboot that half-breed. . . . I'll carry your pack in the cabin an' unroll your blankets."

Releasing her, Colter strode off in the gloom. Like a dead weight, Ellen began to slide until she slipped down full length beside the log. And then she lay in the cool, damp shadow, inert and lifeless so far as outward physical move-

182

ment was concerned. She saw nothing and felt nothing of the night, the wind, the cold, the falling dew. For the moment or hour she was crushed by despair, and seemed to see herself sinking down and down into a black, bottomless pit, into an abyss where murky tides of blood and furious gusts of passion contended between her body and her soul. Into the stormy blast of hell! In her despair she longed, she ached for death. Born of infidelity, cursed by a taint of evil blood, further cursed by higher instinct for good and happy life, dragged from one lonely and wild and sordid spot to another, never knowing love or peace or joy or home, left to the companionship of violent and vile men, driven by a strange fate to love with unquenchable and insupportable love a half-breed, a savage, an Isbel, the hereditary enemy of her people, and at last the ruthless murderer of her father—what in the name of God had she left to live for? Revenge! An eye for an eye! A life for a life! But she could not kill Jean Isbel. Woman's love could turn to hate, but not the love of Ellen Jorth. He could drag her by the hair in the dust, beat her, and make her a thing to loathe, and cut her mortally in his savage and implacable thirst for revenge—but with her last gasp she would whisper she loved him and that she had lied to him to kill his faith. It was that—his strange faith in her purity—which had won her love. Of all men, that he should be the one to recognize the truth of her, the womanhood yet unsullied—how strange, how terrible, how overpowering! False, indeed, was she to the Jorths! False as her mother had been to an Isbel! This agony and destruction of her soul was the bitter Dead Sea fruit—the sins of her parents visited upon her.

"I'll end it all," she whispered to the night shadows that hovered over her. No coward was she—no fear of pain or mangled flesh or death or the mysterious hereafter could ever stay her. It would be easy, it would be a last thrill, a transport of self-abasement and supreme self-proof of her love for Jean Isbel to kiss the Rim rock where his feet had trod and then fling herself down into the depths. She was the last Jorth. So the wronged Isbels would be avenged.

"But he would never know—never know—I lied to him!" she wailed to the night wind.

She was lost—lost on earth and to hope of heaven. She had right neither to live nor to die. She was nothing but a little weed along the trail of life, trampled upon, buried in the mud. She was nothing but a single rotten thread in a tangled web of love and hate and revenge. And she had broken.

Lower and lower she seemed to sink. Was there no end to this gulf of despair? If Colter had returned he would have found her a rag and a toy—a creature degraded, fit for his vile embrace. To be thrust deeper into the mire—to be punished fittingly for her betrayal of a man's noble love and her own womanhood—to be made an end of, body, mind, and soul.

But Colter did not return.

The wind mourned, the owls hooted, the leaves rustled, the insects whispered their melancholy night song, the camp-fire flickered and faded. Then the wild forestland seemed to close imponderably over Ellen. All that she wailed in her despair, all that she confessed in her abasement, was true, and hard as life could be—but she belonged to nature. If nature had not failed her, had God failed her? It was there—the lonely land of tree and fern and flower and brook, full of wild birds and beasts, where the mossy rocks could speak and the solitude had ears, where she had always felt herself unutterably a part of creation. Thus a wavering spark of hope quivered through the blackness of her soul and gathered light.

The gloom of the sky, the shifting clouds of dull shade, split asunder to show a glimpse of a radiant star, piercingly white, cold, pure, a steadfast eye of the universe, beyond all understanding and illimitable with its meaning of the past and the present and the future. Ellen watched it until the drifting clouds once more hid it from her strained sight.

What had that star to do with hell? She might be crushed and destroyed by life, but was there not something beyond? Just to be born, just to suffer, just to die—could that be all? Despair did not loose its hold on Ellen, the strife and pang of her breast did not subside. But with the long hours and the strange closing in of the forest around her and the fleeting glimpse of that wonderful star, with a subtle divination of the meaning of her beating heart and throbbing mind, and, lastly, with a voice thundering at her conscience that a man's faith in a woman must not be greater, nobler, than her faith in God and eternity—with these she checked the dark flight of her soul toward destruction.

A CHILL, gray, somber dawn was breaking when Ellen dragged herself into the cabin and crept under her blankets, there to sleep the sleep of exhaustion.

When she awoke the hour appeared to be late afternoon. Sun and sky shone through the sunken and decayed roof of the old cabin. Her uncle, Tad Jorth, lay upon a blanket bed upheld by a crude couch of boughs. The light fell upon his face, pale, lined, cast in a still mold of suffering. He was not dead, for she heard his respiration.

The floor underneath Ellen Jorth's blankets was bare clay. She and Jorth were alone in this cabin. It contained nothing besides their beds and a rank growth of weeds along the decayed lower logs. Half of the cabin had a rude ceiling of rough-hewn boards which formed a kind of loft. This attic extended through to the adjoining cabin, forming the ceiling of the porch-like space between the two structures. There was no partition. A ladder of two aspen saplings, pegged to the logs, and with braces between for steps, led up to the attic.

Ellen smelled wood smoke and the odor of frying meat, and she heard the voices of men. She looked out to see that Slater and Somers had joined their party—an addition that might have strengthened it for defense, but did not lend her own situation anything favorable. Somers had always appeared the one best to avoid.

Colter espied her and called her to "Come an' feed your pale face." His comrades laughed, not loudly, but guardedly, as if noise was something to avoid. Nevertheless, they awoke Tad Jorth, who began to toss and moan on the bed.

Ellen hurried to his side and at once ascertained that he had a high fever and was in a critical condition. Every time he tossed he opened a wound in his right breast, rather high up. For all she could see, nothing had been done for him except the binding of a scarf round his neck and under his arm. This scant bandage had worked loose. Going to the door, she called out:

"Fetch me some water." When Colter brought it, Ellen was rummaging in her pack for some clothing or towel that she could use for bandages.

"Weren't any of y'u decent enough to look after my uncle?" she queried.

"Huh! Wal, what the hell!" rejoined Colter. "We shore did all we could. I reckon y'u think it wasn't a tough job to pack him up the Rim. He was done for then an' I said so."

"I'll do all I can for him," said Ellen.

"Shore. Go ahaid. When I get plugged or knifed by that half-breed I shore hope y'u'll be round to nurse me."

"Y'u seem to be pretty shore of your fate, Colter."

"Shore as hell!" he bit out, darkly. "Somers saw Isbel an' his gang trailin' us to the Jorth ranch."

"Are y'u goin' to stay heah—an' wait for them?"

"Shore I've been quarrelin' with the fellars out there over that very question. I'm for leavin' the country. But Queen, the damn gun fighter, is daid set to kill that cowman, Blue, who swore he was King Fisher, the old Texas outlaw. None but Queen are spoilin' for another fight. All the same they won't leave Tad Jorth heah alone."

Then Colter leaned in at the door and whispered: "Ellen, I cain't boss this outfit. So let's y'u an' me shake 'em. I've got your dad's gold. Let's ride off to-night an' shake this country."

Colter, muttering under his breath, left the door and returned to his comrades. Ellen had received her first intimation of his cowardice; and his mention of her father's gold started a train of thought that persisted in spite of her efforts to put all her mind to attending her uncle. He grew conscious enough to recognize her working over him, and thanked her with a look that touched Ellen deeply. It changed the direction of her mind. His suffering and imminent death, which she was able to alleviate and retard somewhat, worked upon her pity and compassion so that she forgot her own plight. Half the night she was tending him, cooling his fever, holding him quiet. Well she realized that but for her ministrations he would have died. At length he went to sleep.

And Ellen, sitting beside him in the lonely, silent darkness of that late hour, received again the intimation of nature, those vague and nameless stirrings of her innermost being, those whisperings out of the night and the forest and the sky. Something great would not let go of her soul. She pondered.

Attention to the wounded man occupied Ellen; and soon she redoubled her activities in this regard, finding in them something of protection against Colter.

He had waylaid her as she went to a spring for water, and with a lunge like that of a bear he had tried to embrace her. But Ellen had been too quick.

"Wal, are y'u goin' away with me?" he demanded.

"No. I'll stick by my uncle," she replied.

That motive of hers seemed to obstruct his will. Ellen was keen to see that Colter and his comrades were at a last stand and disintegrating under a severe strain. Nerve and courage of the open and the wild they possessed, but only in a limited degree. Colter seemed obsessed by his passion for her, and though Ellen in her stubborn pride did not yet fear him, she realized she ought to. After that incident she watched closely, never leaving her uncle's bedside except when Colter was absent. One or more of the men kept constant lookout somewhere down the cañon.

Day after day passed on the wings of suspense, of watching, of ministering to her uncle, of waiting for some hour that seemed fixed.

Colter was like a hound upon her trail. At every turn he was there to importune her to run off with him, to frighten her with the menace of the Isbels, to beg her to give herself to him. It came to pass that the only relief she had was when she ate with the men or barred the cabin door at night. Not much relief, however, was there in the shut and barred door. With one thrust of his powerful arm Colter could have caved it in. He knew this as well as Ellen. Still she did not have the fear she should have had. There was her rifle beside her, and though she did not allow her mind to run darkly on its possible use, still the fact of its being there at hand somehow strengthened her. Colter was a cat playing with a mouse, but not yet sure of his quarry.

Ellen came to know hours when she was weak—weak physically, mentally, spiritually, morally—when under the sheer weight of this frightful and growing burden of suspense she was not capable of fighting her misery, her abasement,

187

her low ebb of vitality, and at the same time wholly withstanding Colter's advances.

He would come into the cabin and, utterly indifferent to Tad Jorth, he would try to make bold and unrestrained love to Ellen. When he caught her in one of her unresisting moments and was able to hold her in his arms and kiss her he seemed to be beside himself with the wonder of her. At such moments, if he had any softness or gentleness in him, they expressed themselves in his sooner or later letting her go, when apparently she was about to faint. So it must have become fascinatingly fixed in Colter's mind that at times Ellen repulsed him with scorn and at others could not resist him.

Ellen had escaped two crises in her relation with this man, and as a morbid doubt, like a poisonous fungus, began to strangle her mind, she instinctively divined that there was an approaching and final crisis. No uplift of her spirit came this time—no intimations—no whisperings. How horrible it all was! To long to be good and noble—to realize that she was neither—to sink lower day by day! Must she decay there like one of these rotting logs? Worst of all, then, was the insinuating and ever-growing hopelessness. What was the use? What did it matter? Who would ever think of Ellen Jorth? "O God!" she whispered in her distraction, "is there nothing left—nothing at all?"

A period of several days of less torment to Ellen followed. Her uncle apparently took a turn for the better and Colter let her alone. This last circumstance nonplused Ellen. She was at a loss to understand it unless the Isbel menace now encroached upon Colter so formidably that he had forgotten her for the present.

Then one bright August morning, when she had just begun to relax her eternal vigilance and breathe without oppression, Colter encountered her and, darkly silent and fierce, he grasped her and drew her off her feet. Ellen struggled violently, but the total surprise had deprived her of strength. And that paralyzing weakness assailed her as never before. Without apparent effort Colter carried her, striding rapidly away from the cabins into the border of spruce trees at the foot of the cañon wall.

"Colter—where—oh, where are y'u takin' me?" she found voice to cry out.

"By God! I don't know," he replied, with strong, vibrant passion. "I was a fool not to carry y'u off long ago. But I

188

waited. I was hopin' y'u'd love me! . . . An' now that Isbel gang has corralled us. Somers seen the half-breed up on the rocks. An' Springer seen the rest of them sneakin' around. I run back after my horse an' y'u."

"But Uncle Tad! . . . We mustn't leave him alone," cried Ellen.

"We've got to," replied Colter, grimly. "Tad shore won't worry y'u no more—soon as Jean Isbel gets to him."

"Oh, let me stay," implored Ellen. "I will save him."

Colter laughed at the utter absurdity of her appeal and claim. Suddenly he set her down upon her feet. "Stand still," he ordered. Ellen saw his big bay horse, saddled, with pack and blanket, tied there in the shade of a spruce. With swift hands Colter untied him and mounted him, scarcely moving his piercing gaze from Ellen. He reached to grasp her. "Up with y'u! . . . Put your foot in the stirrup!" His will, like his powerful arm, was irresistible for Ellen at that moment. She found herself swung up in front of him. Then the horse plunged away. What with the hard motion and Colter's iron grasp on her Ellen was in a painful position. Her knees and feet came into violent contact with branches and snags. He galloped the horse, tearing through the dense thicket of willows that served to hide the entrance to the side cañon, and when out in the larger and more open cañon he urged him to a run. Presently when Colter put the horse to a slow rise of ground, thereby bringing him to a walk, it was just in time to save Ellen a serious bruising. Again the sunlight appeared to shade over. They were in the pines. Suddenly with backward lunge Colter halted the horse. Ellen heard a yell. She recognized Queen's voice.

"Turn back, Colter! Turn back!"

With an oath Colter wheeled his mount. "If I didn't run plump into them," he ejaculated, harshly. And scarcely had the goaded horse gotten a start when a shot rang out. Ellen felt a violent shock, as if her momentum had suddenly met with a check, and then she felt herself wrenched from Colter, from the saddle, and propelled into the air. She alighted on soft ground and thick grass, and was unhurt save for the violent wrench and shaking that had rendered her breathless. Before she could rise Colter was pulling at her, lifting her to her feet. She saw the horse lying with bloody head. Tall pines loomed all around. Another rifle cracked. "Run!" hissed Colter, and he bounded off, dragging her by the hand. Another yell pealed out. "Here we are,

189

Colter!". Again it was Queen's shrill voice. Ellen ran with all her might, her heart in her throat, her sight failing to record more than a blur of passing pines and a blank green wall of spruce. Then she lost her balance, was falling, yet could not fall because of that steel grip on her hand, and was dragged, and finally carried, into a dense shade. She was blinded. The trees whirled and faded. Voices and shots sounded far away. Then something black seemed to be wiped across her feeling.

It turned to gray, to moving blankness, to dim, hazy objects, spectral and tall, like blanketed trees, and when Ellen fully recovered consciousness she was being carried through the forest.

"Wal, little one, that was a close shave for y'u," said Colter's hard voice, growing clearer. "Reckon your keelin' over was natural enough."

He held her lightly in both arms, her head resting above his left elbow. Ellen saw his face as a gray blur, then taking sharper outline, until it stood out distinctly, pale and clammy, with eyes cold and wonderful in their intense flare. As she gazed upward Colter turned his head to look back through the woods, and his motion betrayed a keen, wild vigilance. The veins of his lean, brown neck stood out like whipcords. Two comrades were stalking beside him. Ellen heard their stealthy steps, and she felt Colter sheer from one side or the other. They were proceeding cautiously, fearful of the rear, but not wholly trusting to the fore.

"Reckon we'd better go slow an' look before we leap," said one whose voice Ellen recognized as Springer's.

"Shore. That open slope ain't to my likin', with our Nez Perce friend prowlin' round," drawled Colter, as he set Ellen down on her feet.

Another of the rustlers laughed. "Say, can't he twinkle through the forest? I had four shots at him. Harder to hit than a turkey runnin' crossways."

This facetious speaker was the evil-visaged, sardonic Somers. He carried two rifles and wore two belts of cartridges.

"Ellen, shore y'u ain't so daid white as y'u was," observed Colter, and he chucked her under the chin with familiar hand. "Set down heah. I don't want y'u stoppin' any bullets. An' there's no tellin'."

Ellen was glad to comply with his wish. She had begun to recover wits and strength, yet she still felt shaky. She observed that their position then was on the edge of a well-wooded slope from which she could see the grassy cañon floor below. They were on a level bench, projecting out from the main cañon wall that loomed gray and rugged and pine fringed. Somers and Colter and Springer gave careful attention to all points of the compass, especially in the direction from which they had come. They evidently anticipated being trailed or circled or headed off, but did not manifest much concern. Somers lit a cigarette; Springer wiped his face with a grimy hand and counted the shells in his belt, which appeared to be half empty. Colter stretched his long neck like a vulture and peered down the slope and through the aisles of the forest up toward the cañon rim.

"Listen!" he said, tersely, and bent his head a little to one side, ear to the slight breeze.

They all listened. Ellen heard the beating of her heart, the rustle of leaves, the tapping of a woodpecker, and faint, remote sounds that she could not name.

"Deer, I reckon," spoke up Somers.

"Ahuh! Wal, I reckon they ain't trailin' us yet," replied Colter. "We gave them a shade better'n they sent us."

"Short an' sweet!" ejaculated Springer, and he removed his black sombrero to poke a dirty forefinger through a bullet hole in the crown. "Thet's how close I come to cashin'. I was lyin' behind a log, listenin' an' watchin', an' when I stuck my head up a little—zam! Somebody made my bonnet leak."

"Where's Queen?" asked Colter.

"He was with me fust off," replied Somers. "An' then when the shootin' slacked—after I'd plugged thet big, red-faced, white-haired pal of Isbel's—"

"Reckon thet was Blaisdell," interrupted Springer.

"Queen—he got tired layin' low," went on Somers. "He wanted action. I heerd him chewin' to himself, an' when I asked him what was eatin' him he up an' growled he was goin' to quit this Injun fightin'. An' he slipped off in the woods."

"Wal, that's the gun fighter of it," declared Colter, wagging his head. "Ever since that cowman, Blue, braced us an' said he was King Fisher, why Queen has been sulkier an' sulkier. He cain't help it. He'll do the same trick as Blue tried. An' shore he'll get his everlastin'. But he's the Texas breed all right."

"Say, do you reckon Blue really is King Fisher?" queried Somers.

191

"Naw!" ejaculated Colter, with downward sweep of his hand. "Many a would-be gun slinger has borrowed Fisher's name. But Fisher is daid these many years."

"Ahuh! Wal, mebbe, but don't you fergit it—thet Blue was no would-be," declared Somers. "He was the genuine article."

"I should smile!" affirmed Springer.

The subject irritated Colter, and he dismissed it with another forcible gesture and a counter question.

"How many left in that Isbel outfit?"

"No tellin'. There shore was enough of them," replied Somers. "Anyhow, the woods was full of flyin' bullets. . . . Springer, did you account for any of them?"

"Nope—not thet I noticed," responded Springer, dryly. "I had my chance at the half-breed. . . . Reckon I was nervous."

"Was Slater near you when he yelled out?"

"No. He was lyin' beside Somers."

"Wasn't thet a queer way fer a man to act?" broke in Somers. "A bullet hit Slater, cut him down the back as he was lyin' flat. Reckon it wasn't bad. But it hurt him so thet he jumped right up an' staggered around. He made a target big as a tree. An' mebbe them Isbels didn't riddle him!"

"That was when I got my crack at Bill Isbel," declared Colter, with grim satisfaction. "When they shot my horse out from under me I had Ellen to think of an' couldn't get my rifle. Shore had to run, as y'u seen. Wal, as I only had my six-shooter, there was nothin' for me to do but lay low an' listen to the sping of lead. Wells was standin' up behind a tree aboot thirty yards off. He got plugged, an' fallin' over he began to crawl my way, still holdin' to his rifle. I crawled along the log to meet him. But he dropped aboot half-way. I went on an' took his rifle an' belt. When I peeped out from behind a spruce bush then I seen Bill Isbel. He was shootin' fast, an' all of them was shootin' fast. That was when they had the open shot at Slater. . . . Wal, I bored Bill Isbel right through his middle. He dropped his rifle an', all bent double, he fooled around in a circle till he flopped over the Rim. I reckon he's layin' right up there somewhere below that daid spruce. I'd shore like to see him."

"Wal, you'd be as crazy as Queen if you tried thet," declared Somers. "We're not out of the woods yet."

"I reckon not," replied Colter. "An' I've lost my horse. Where'd y'u leave yours?"

"They're down the cañon, below thet willow brake. An' saddled an' none of them tied. Reckon we'll have to look them up before dark."

"Colter, what're we goin' to do?" demanded Springer.

"Wait heah a while—then cross the cañon an' work round up under the bluff, back to the cabin."

"An' then what?" queried Somers, doubtfully eying Colter.

"We've got to eat—we've got to have blankets," rejoined Colter, testily. "An' I reckon we can hide there an' stand a better show in a fight than runnin' for it in the woods."

"Wal, I'm givin' you a hunch thet it looked like you was runnin' fer it," retorted Somers.

"Yes, an' packin' the girl," added Springer. "Looks funny to me."

Both rustlers eyed Colter with dark and distrustful glances. What he might have replied never transpired, for the reason that his gaze, always shifting around, had suddenly fixed on something.

"Is that a wolf?" he asked, pointing to the Rim.

Both his comrades moved to get in line with his finger. Ellen could not see from her position.

"Shore thet's a big lofer," declared Somers. "Reckon he scented us."

"There he goes along the Rim," observed Colter. "He doesn't act leary. Looks like a good sign to me. Mebbe the Isbels have gone the other way."

"Looks bad to me," rejoined Springer, gloomily.

"An' why?" demanded Colter.

"I seen thet animal. Fust time I reckoned it was a lofer. Second time it was right near them Isbels. An' I'm damned now if I don't believe it's thet half-lofer sheep dog of Gass Isbel's."

"Wal, what if it is?"

"Ha! . . . Shore we needn't worry about hidin' out," replied Springer, sententiously. "With thet dog Jean Isbel could trail a grasshopper."

"The hell y'u say!" muttered Colter. Manifestly such a possibility put a different light upon the present situation. The men grew silent and watchful, occupied by brooding thoughts and vigilant surveillance of all points. Somers slipped off into the brush, soon to return, with intent look of importance.

"I heerd somethin'," he whispered, jerking his thumb backward. "Rollin' gravel—crackin' twigs. No deer! . . .

193

Reckon it'd be a good idee for us to slip round acrost this bench."

"Wal, y'u fellars go, an' I'll watch heah," returned Colter.

"Not much," said Somers, while Springer leered knowingly.

Colter became incensed, but he did not give way to it. Pondering a moment, he finally turned to Ellen. "Y'u wait heah till I come back. An' if I don't come in reasonable time y'u slip across the cañon an' through the willows to the cabins. Wait till aboot dark." With that he possessed himself of one of the extra rifles and belts and silently joined his comrades. Together they noiselessly stole into the brush.

Ellen had no other thought than to comply with Colter's wishes. There was her wounded uncle who had been left unattended, and she was anxious to get back to him. Besides, if she had wanted to run off from Colter, where could she go? Alone in the woods, she would get lost and die of starvation. Her lot must be cast with the Jorth faction until the end. That did not seem far away.

Her strained attention and suspense made the moments fly. By and by several shots pealed out far across the side cañon on her right, and they were answered by reports sounding closer to her. The fight was on again. But these shots were not repeated. The flies buzzed, the hot sun beat down and sloped to the west, the soft, warm breeze stirred the aspens, the ravens croaked, the red squirrels and blue jays chattered.

Suddenly a quick, short, yelp electrified Ellen, brought her upright with sharp, listening rigidity. Surely it was not a wolf and hardly could it be a coyote. Again she heard it. The yelp of a sheep dog! She had heard that often enough to know. And she rose to change her position so she could command a view of the rocky bluff above. Presently she espied what really appeared to be a big timber wolf. But another yelp satisfied her that it really was a dog. She watched him. Soon it became evident that he wanted to get down over the bluff. He ran to and fro, and then out of sight. In a few moments his yelp sounded from lower down, at the base of the bluff, and it was now the cry of an intelligent dog that was trying to call some one to his aid. Ellen grew convinced that the dog was near where Colter had said Bill Isbel had plunged over the declivity. Would the dog yelp that way if the man was dead? Ellen thought not.

No one came, and the continuous yelping of the dog got

194

on Ellen's nerves. It was a call for help. And finally she surrendered to it. Since her natural terror when Colter's horse was shot from under her and she had been dragged away, she had not recovered from fear of the Isbels. But calm consideration now convinced her that she could hardly be in a worse plight in their hands than if she remained in Colter's. So she started out to find the dog.

The wooded bench was level for a few hundred yards, and then it began to heave in rugged, rocky bulges up toward the Rim. It did not appear far to where the dog was barking, but the latter part of the distance proved to be a hard climb over jumbled rocks and through thick brush. Panting and hot, she at length reached the base of the bluff, to find that it was not very high.

The dog espied her before she saw him, for he was coming toward her when she discovered him. Big, shaggy, grayish white and black, with wild, keen face and eyes he assuredly looked the reputation Springer had accorded him. But sagacious, guarded as was his approach, he appeared friendly.

"Hello—doggie!" panted Ellen. "What's—wrong—up heah?"

He yelped, his ears lost their stiffness, his body sank a little, and his bushy tail wagged to and fro. What a gray, clear, intelligent look he gave her! Then he trotted back.

Ellen followed him around a corner of bluff to see the body of a man lying on his back. Fresh earth and gravel lay about him, attesting to his fall from above. He had on neither coat nor hat, and the position of his body and limbs suggested broken bones. As Ellen hurried to his side she saw the front of his shirt, low down, was a bloody blotch. But he could lift his head; his eyes were open; he was perfectly conscious. Ellen did not recognize the dusty, skinned face, yet the mold of features, the look of the eyes, seemed strangely familiar.

"You're—Jorth's—girl," he said, in faint voice of surprise.

"Yes, I'm Ellen Jorth," she replied. "An' are y'u Bill Isbel?"

"All thet's left of me. But I'm thankin' God somebody come—even a Jorth."

Ellen knelt beside him and examined the wound in his abdomen. A heavy bullet had indeed, as Colter had avowed, torn clear through his middle. Even if he had not sustained other serious injury from the fall over the cliff, that terrible bullet wound meant death very shortly. Ellen shuddered. How inexplicable were men! How cruel, bloody, mindless!

195

"Isbel, I'm sorry—there's no hope," she said, low voiced. "Y'u've not long to live. . . . I cain't help y'u. God knows I'd do so if I could."

"All over!" he sighed, with his eyes looking beyond her. "I reckon—I'm glad. . . . But y'u can—do somethin' for me. Will y'u?"

"Indeed, yes. Tell me," she replied, lifting his dusty head on her knee. Her hands trembled as she brushed his wet hair from his clammy brow.

"I've somethin'—on my conscience," he whispered.

The woman, the sensitive in Ellen, understood and pitied him then.

"Yes," she encouraged him.

"I stole cattle—my dad's an' Blaisdell's—an' made deals—with Daggs. . . . All the crookedness—wasn't on—Jorth's side. . . . I want—my brother Jean—to know."

"I'll try—to tell him," whispered Ellen, out of her great amaze.

"We were all—a bad lot—except Jean," went on Isbel. "Dad wasn't fair. . . . God! how he hated Jorth! Jorth, yes, who was—your father. . . . Wal, they're even now."

"How—so?" faltered Ellen.

"Your father killed dad. . . . At the last—dad wanted to—save us. He sent word—he'd meet him—face to face—an' let thet end the feud. They met out in the road. . . . But some one shot dad down—with a rifle—an' then your father finished him."

"An' then, Isbel," added Ellen, with unconscious mocking bitterness, "your brother murdered my dad!"

"What!" whispered Bill Isbel. "Shore y'u've got—it wrong. I reckon Jean—could have killed—your father. . . . But he didn't. Queer, we all thought."

"Ah! . . . Who did kill my father?" burst out Ellen, and her voice rang like great hammers at her ears.

"It was Blue. He went in the store—alone—faced the whole gang alone. Bluffed them—taunted them—told them he was King Fisher. . . . Then he killed—your dad—an' Jackson Jorth. . . . Jean was out—back of the store. We were out—front. There was shootin'. Colmor was hit. Then Blue ran out—bad hurt. . . . Both of them—died in Meeker's yard."

"An' so Jean Isbel has not killed a Jorth!" said Ellen, in strange, deep voice.

"No," replied Isbel, earnestly. "I reckon this feud—was

hardest on Jean. He never lived heah. . . . An' my sister Ann said—he got sweet on y'u. . . . Now did he?"

Slow, stinging tears filled Ellen's eyes, and her head sank low and lower.

"Yes—he did," she murmured, tremulously.

"Ahuh! Wal, thet accounts," replied Isbel, wonderingly. "Too bad! . . . It might have been. . . . A man always sees— different when—he's dyin'. . . . If I had—my life—to live over again! . . . My poor kids—deserted in their babyhood— ruined for life! All for nothin'. . . . May God forgive—"

Then he choked and whispered for water.

Ellen laid his head back and, rising, she took his sombrero and started hurriedly down the slope, making dust fly and rocks roll. Her mind was a seething ferment. Leaping, bounding, sliding down the weathered slope, she gained the bench, to run across that, and so on down into the open cañon to the willow-bordered brook. Here she filled the sombrero with water and started back, forced now to walk slowly and carefully. It was then, with the violence and fury of intense muscular activity denied her, that the tremendous import of Bill Isbel's revelation burst upon her very flesh and blood and transfiguring the very world of golden light and azure sky and speaking forestland that encompassed her.

Not a drop of the precious water did she spill. Not a misstep did she make. Yet so great was the spell upon her that she was not aware she had climbed the steep slope until the dog yelped his welcome. Then with all the flood of her emotion surging and resurging she knelt to allay the parching thirst of this dying enemy whose words had changed frailty to strength, hate to love, and the gloomy hell of despair to something unutterable. But she had returned too late. Bill Isbel was dead.

197

JEAN ISBEL, holding the wolf-dog Shepp in leash, was on the trail of the most dangerous of Jorth's gang, the gunman Queen. Dark drops of blood on the stones and plain tricks of a rider's sharp-heeled boots behind coverts indicated the trail of a wounded, slow-traveling fugitive. Therefore, Jean Isbel held in the dog and proceeded with the wary eye and watchful caution of an Indian.

Queen, true to his class, and emulating Blue with the same magnificent effrontery and with the same paralyzing suddenness of surprise, had appeared as if by magic at the last night camp of the Isbel faction. Jean had seen him first, in time to leap like a panther into the shadow. But he carried in his shoulder Queen's first bullet of that terrible encounter. Upon Gordon and Fredericks fell the brunt of Queen's fusillade. And they, shot to pieces, staggering and falling, held passionate grip on life long enough to draw and still Queen's guns and send him reeling off into the darkness of the forest.

Unarmed, and hindered by a painful wound, Jean had kept a vigil near camp all that silent and menacing night. Morning disclosed Gordon and Fredericks stark and ghastly beside the burned-out camp-fire, their guns clutched immovably in stiffened hands. Jean buried them as best he could, and when they were under ground with flat stones on their graves he knew himself to be indeed the last of the Isbel clan. And all that was wild and savage in his blood and desperate in his spirit rose to make him more than man and less than human. Then for the third time during these tragic last days the wolf-dog Shepp came to him.

Jean washed the wound Queen had given him and bound it tightly. The keen pang and burn of the lead was a constant and all-powerful reminder of the grim work left for him to do. The whole world was no longer large enough for him and whoever was left of the Jorths. The heritage of blood his father had bequeathed him, the unshakable love for a worthless girl who had so dwarfed and obstructed his will and so bitterly defeated and reviled his poor, romantic, boyish faith, the killing of hostile men, so strange in its after effects, the pursuits and fights, and loss of one by one of his confederates—these had finally engendered in Jean Isbel a wild, unslakable thirst, these had been the cause of his retrogression, these had unalterably and ruthlessly fixed in his darkened mind one fierce passion—to live and die the last man of that Jorth-Isbel feud.

At sunrise Jean left this camp, taking with him only a small knapsack of meat and bread, and with the eager, wild Shepp in leash he set out on Queen's bloody trail.

Black drops of blood on the stones and an irregular trail of footprints proved to Jean that the gunman was hard hit. Here he had fallen, or knelt, or sat down, evidently to bind his wounds. Jean found strips of scarf, red and discarded. And the blood drops failed to show on more rocks. In a deep forest of spruce, under silver-tipped spreading branches, Queen had rested, perhaps slept. Then laboring with dragging steps, not improbably with a lame leg, he had gone on, up out of the dark-green ravine to the open, dry, pine-tipped ridge. Here he had rested, perhaps waited to see if he were pursued. From that point his trail spoke an easy language for Jean's keen eye. The gunman knew he was pursued. He had seen his enemy. Therefore Jean proceeded with a slow caution, never getting within revolver range of ambush, using all his woodcraft to trail this man and yet save himself. Queen traveled slowly, either because he was wounded or else because he tried to ambush his pursuer, and Jean accommodated his pace to that of Queen. From noon of that day they were never far apart, never out of hearing of a rifle shot.

The contrast of the beauty and peace and loneliness of the surroundings to the nature of Queen's flight often obtruded its strange truth into the somber turbulence of Jean's mind, into that fixed columnar idea around which fleeting thoughts hovered and gathered like shadows.

Early frost had touched the heights with its magic wand. And the forest seemed a temple in which man might worship nature and life rather than steal through the dells and under the arched aisles like a beast of prey. The green-and-gold leaves of aspens quivered in the glades; maples in the ravines fluttered their red-and-purple leaves. The needle-matted carpet under the pines vied with the long lanes of silvery grass, alike enticing to the eye of man and beast. Sunny rays of light, flecked with dust and flying insects, slanted down from the overhanging brown-limbed, green-massed foliage. Roar of wind in the distant forest alternated with soft breeze close at hand. Small dove-gray squirrels ran all over the woodland, very curious about Jean and his dog, rustling the twigs, scratching the bark of trees, chattering and barking, frisky, saucy, and bright-eyed. A plaintive twitter of wild canaries came from the region above the treetops—first voices of birds in their pilgrimage toward the south. Pine cones dropped with soft thuds. The blue jays followed these intruders in the forest, screeching their displeasure. Like rain pattered the dropping seeds from the spruces. A woody, earthy, leafy fragrance, damp with the current of life, mingled with a cool, dry, sweet smell of withered grass and rotting pines.

Solitude and lonesomeness, peace and rest, wild life and nature, reigned there. It was a golden-green region, enchanting to the gaze of man. An Indian would have walked there with his spirits.

And even as Jean felt all this elevating beauty and inscrutable spirit his keen eye once more fastened upon the blood-red drops Queen had again left on the gray moss and rock. His wound had reopened. Jean felt the thrill of the scenting panther.

The sun set, twilight gathered, night fell. Jean crawled under a dense, low-spreading spruce, ate some bread and meat, fed the dog, and lay down to rest and sleep. His thoughts burdened him, heavy and black as the mantle of night. A wolf mourned a hungry cry for a mate. Shepp quivered under Jean's hand. That was the call which had lured him from the ranch. The wolf blood in him yearned for the wild. Jean tied the cowhide leash to his wrist. When this dark business was at an end Shepp could be free to join the lonely mate mourning out there in the forest. Then Jean slept.

Dawn broke cold, clear, frosty, with silvered grass sparkling, with a soft, faint rustling of fallen aspen leaves. When the sun rose red Jean was again on the trail of Queen. By a frosty-ferned brook, where water tinkled and ran clear as air and cold as ice, Jean quenched his thirst, leaning on a stone that showed drops of blood. Queen, too, had to quench his thirst. What good, what help, Jean wondered, could the cold, sweet, granite water, so dear to woodsmen and wild creatures, do this wounded, hunted rustler? Why did he not wait in the open to fight and face the death he had meted? Where was that splendid and terrible daring of the gunman? Queen's love of life dragged him on and on, hour by hour, through the pine groves and spruce woods, through the oak swales and aspen glades, up and down the rocky gorges, around the windfalls and over the rotting logs.

The time came when Queen tried no more ambush. He gave up trying to trap his pursuer by lying in wait. He gave up trying to conceal his tracks. He grew stronger or, in desperation, increased his energy, so that he redoubled his progress through the wilderness. That, at best, would count only a few miles a day. And he began to circle to the northwest, back toward the deep cañon where Blaisdell and Bill Isbel had reached the end of their trails. Queen had evidently left his comrades, had lone-handed it in his last fight, but was now trying to get back to them. Somewhere in these wild, deep forest brakes the rest of the Jorth faction had found a hiding place. Jean let Queen lead him there.

Ellen Jorth would be with them. Jean had seen her. It had been his shot that killed Colter's horse. And he had withheld further fire because Colter had dragged the girl behind him, protecting his body with hers. Sooner or later Jean would come upon their camp. She would be there. The thought of her dark beauty, wasted in wantonness upon these rustlers, added a deadly rage to the blood lust and righteous wrath of his vengeance. Let her again flaunt her degradation in his face and, by the God she had forsaken, he would kill her, and so end the race of Jorths!

Another night fell, dark and cold, without starlight. The wind moaned in the forest. Shepp was restless. He sniffed the air. There was a step on his trail. Again a mournful, eager, wild, and hungry wolf cry broke the silence. It was deep and low, like that of a baying hound, but infinitely wilder. Shepp strained to get away. During the night, while Jean slept, he managed to chew the cowhide leash apart and run off.

Next day no dog was needed to trail Queen. Fog and low-drifting clouds in the forest and a misty rain had put the rustler off his bearings. He was lost, and showed that he realized it. Strange how a matured man, fighter of a hundred battles, steeped in bloodshed, and on his last stand, should grow panic-stricken upon being lost! So Jean Isbel read the signs of the trail.

Queen circled and wandered through the foggy, dripping forest until he headed down into a cañon. It was one that notched the Rim and led down and down, mile after mile into the Basin. Not soon had Queen discovered his mistake. When he did do so, night overtook him.

The weather cleared before morning. Red and bright the sun burst out of the east to flood that low basin land with light. Jean found that Queen had traveled on and on, hoping, no doubt, to regain what he had lost. But in the darkness he had climbed to the manzanita slopes instead of back up the cañon. And here he had fought the hold of that strange brush of Spanish name until he fell exhausted.

Surely Queen would make his stand and wait somewhere in this devilish thicket for Jean to catch up with him. Many and many a place Jean would have chosen had he been in Queen's place. Many a rock and dense thicket Jean circled or approached with extreme care. Manzanita grew in patches that were impenetrable except for a small animal. The brush was a few feet high, seldom so high that Jean could not look over it, and of a beautiful appearance, having glossy, small leaves, a golden berry, and branches of dark-red color. These branches were tough and unbendable. Every bush, almost, had low branches that were dead, hard as steel, sharp as thorns, as clutching as cactus. Progress was possible only by endless detours to find the half-closed aisles between patches, or else by crashing through with main strength or walking right over the tops. Jean preferred this last method, not because it was the easiest, but for the reason that he could see ahead so much farther. So he literally walked across the tips of the manzanita brush. Often he fell through and had to step up again; many a branch broke with him, letting him down; but for the most part he stepped from fork to fork, on branch after branch, with balance of an Indian and the patience of a man whose purpose was sustaining and immutable.

On that south slope under the Rim the sun beat down hot. There was no breeze to temper the dry air. And before midday Jean was laboring, wet with sweat, parching with thirst, dusty and hot and tiring. It amazed him, the doggedness and tenacity of life shown by this wounded rustler. The time came when under the burning rays of the sun he was compelled to abandon the walk across the tips of the manzanita bushes and take to the winding, open threads that ran between. It would have been poor sight indeed that could not have followed Queen's labyrinthine and broken passage through the brush. Then the time came when Jean espied Queen, far ahead and above, crawling like a black bug along the bright-green slope. Sight then acted upon Jean as upon a hound in the chase. But he governed his actions if he could not govern his instincts. Slowly but surely he followed the dusty, hot trail, and never a patch of blood failed to send a thrill along his veins.

Queen, headed up toward the Rim, finally vanished from sight. Had he fallen? Was he hiding? But the hour disclosed that he was crawling. Jean's keen eye caught the slow moving of the brush and enabled him to keep just so close to the rustler, out of range of the six-shooters he carried. And so all the interminable hours of the hot afternoon that snail-pace flight and pursuit kept on.

Halfway up the Rim the growth of manzanita gave place to open, yellow, rocky slope dotted with cedars. Queen took to a slow-ascending ridge and left his bloody tracks all the way to the top where in the gathering darkness the weary pursuer lost them.

Another night passed. Daylight was relentless to the rustler. He could not hide his trail. But somehow in a desperate last rally of strength he reached a point on the heavily timbered ridge that Jean recognized as being near the scene of the fight in the cañon. Queen was nearing the rendezvous of the rustlers. Jean crossed tracks of horses, and then more tracks that he was certain had been made days past by his own party. To the left of this ridge must be the deep cañon that had frustrated his efforts to catch up with the rustlers on the day Blaisdell lost his life, and probably Bill Isbel, too. Something warned Jean that he was nearing the end of the trail, and an unaccountable sense of imminent catastrophe seemed foreshadowed by vague dreads and doubts in his gloomy mind. Jean felt the need of rest, of food, of ease from the strain of the last weeks. But his spirit drove him implacably.

Queen's rally of strength ended at the edge of an open, bald ridge that was bare of brush or grass and was surrounded by a line of forest on three sides, and on the fourth by a low bluff which raised its gray head above the pines. Across this dusty open Queen had crawled, leaving unmistakable signs of his condition. Jean took long survey of the circle of trees and of the low, rocky eminence, neither of which he liked. It might be wiser to keep to cover, Jean thought, and work around to where Queen's trail entered the forest again. But he was tired, gloomy, and his eternal vigilance was failing. Nevertheless, he stilled for the thousandth time that bold prompting of his vengeance and, taking to the edge of the forest, he went to considerable pains to circle the open ground. And suddenly sight of a man sitting back against a tree halted Jean.

He stared to make sure his eyes did not deceive him. Many times stumps and snags and rocks had taken on strange resemblance to a standing or crouching man. This was only another suggestive blunder of the mind behind his eyes—what he wanted to see he imagined he saw. Jean glided on from tree to tree until he made sure that this sitting image indeed was that of a man. He sat bolt upright, facing back across the open, hands resting on his knees—and closer scrutiny showed Jean that he held a gun in each hand.

Queen! At the last his nerve had revived. He could not crawl any farther, he could never escape, so with the courage of fatality he chose the open, to face his foe and die. Jean had a thrill of admiration for the rustler. Then he stalked out from under the pines and strode forward with his rifle ready.

A watching man could not have failed to espy Jean. But Queen never made the slightest move. Moreover, his stiff, unnatural position struck Jean so singularly that he halted with a muttered exclamation. He was now about fifty paces from Queen, within range of those small guns. Jean called, sharply, *"Queen!"* Still the figure never relaxed in the slightest.

Jean advanced a few more paces, rifle up, ready to fire the instant Queen lifted a gun. The man's immobility brought the cold sweat to Jean's brow. He stopped to bend the full intense power of his gaze upon this inert figure. Suddenly over Jean flashed its meaning. Queen was dead. He had backed up against the pine, ready to face his foe, and he had died there. Not a shadow of a doubt entered Jean's mind as he started forward again. He knew. After all, Queen's blood would not be on his hands. Gordon and Fredericks in their death throes had given the rustler mortal wounds. Jean kept on, marveling the while. How ghastly thin and hard! Those four days of flight had been hell for Queen.

Jean reached him—looked down with staring eyes. The guns were tied to his hands. Jean started violently as the whole direction of his mind shifted. A lightning glance

204

showed that Queen had been propped against the tree—another showed boot tracks in the dust.

"By Heaven, they've fooled me!" hissed Jean, and quickly as he leaped behind the pine he was not quick enough to escape the cunning rustlers who had waylaid him thus. He felt the shock, the bite and burn of lead before he heard a rifle crack. A bullet had ripped through his left forearm. From behind the tree he saw a puff of white smoke along the face of the bluff—the very spot his keen and gloomy vigilance had descried as one of menace. Then several puffs of white smoke and ringing reports betrayed the ambush of the tricksters. Bullets barked the pine and whistled by. Jean saw a man dart from behind a rock and, leaning over, run for another. Jean's swift shot stopped him midway. He fell, got up, and floundered behind a bush scarcely large enough to conceal him. Into that bush Jean shot again and again. He had no pain in his wounded arm, but the sense of the shock clung in his consciousness, and this, with the tremendous surprise of the deceit, and sudden release of long-damned overmastering passion, caused him to empty the magazine of his Winchester in a terrible haste to kill the man he had hit.

These were all the loads he had for his rifle. Blood passion had made him blunder. Jean cursed himself, and his hand moved to his belt. His six-shooter was gone. The sheath had been loose. He had tied the gun fast. But the strings had been torn apart. The rustlers were shooting again. Bullets thudded into the pine and whistled by. Bending carefully, Jean reached one of Queen's guns and jerked it from his hand. The weapon was empty. Both of his guns were empty. Jean peeped out again to get the line in which the bullets were coming and, marking a course from his position to the cover of the forest, he ran with all his might. He gained the shelter. Shrill yells behind warned him that he had been seen, that his reason for flight had been guessed. Looking back, he saw two or three men scrambling down the bluff. Then the loud neigh of a frightened horse pealed out.

Jean discarded his useless rifle, and headed down the ridge slope, keeping to the thickest line of pines and sheering around the clumps of spruce. As he ran, his mind whirled with grim thoughts of escape, of his necessity to find the camp where Gordon and Fredericks were buried, there to procure another rifle and ammunition. He felt the wet blood dripping down his arm, yet no pain. The forest was too open for good cover. He dared not run uphill. His only course was ahead, and that soon ended in an abrupt declivity too precipitous to descend. As he halted, panting for breath, he heard the ring of hoofs on stone, then the thudding beat of running horses on soft ground. The rustlers had sighted the direction he had taken. Jean did not waste time to look. Indeed, there was no need, for as he bounded along the cliff to the right a rifle cracked and a bullet whizzed over his head. It lent wings to his feet. Like a deer he sped along, leaping cracks and logs and rocks, his ears filled by the rush of wind, until his quick eye caught sight of thick-growing spruce foliage close to the precipice. He sprang down into the green mass. His weight precipitated him through the upper branches. But lower down his spread arms broke his fall, then retarded it until he caught. A long, swaying limb let him down and down, where he grasped another and a stiffer one that held his weight. Hand over hand he worked toward the trunk of this spruce and, gaining it, he found other branches close together down which he hastened, hold by hold and step by step, until all above him was black, dense foliage, and beneath him the brown, shady slope. Sure of being unseen from above, he glided noiselessly down under the trees, slowly regaining freedom from that constriction of his breast.

Passing on to a gray-lichened cliff, overhanging and gloomy, he paused there to rest and to listen. A faint crack of hoof on stone came to him from above, apparently farther on to the right. Eventually his pursuers would discover that he had taken to the cañon. But for the moment he felt safe. The wound in his forearm drew his attention. The bullet had gone clear through without breaking either bone. His shirt sleeve was soaked with blood. Jean rolled it back and tightly wrapped his scarf around the wound, yet still the dark-red blood oozed out and dripped down into his hand. He became aware of a dull, throbbing pain.

Not much time did Jean waste in arriving at what was best to do. For the time being he had escaped, and whatever had been his peril, it was past. In dense, rugged country like this he could not be caught by rustlers. But he had only a knife left for a weapon, and there was very little meat in the pocket of his coat. Salt and matches he possessed. Therefore the imperative need was for him to find the last camp, where he could get rifle and ammunition, bake bread, and rest up before taking again the trail of the rustlers. He had reason to believe that this cañon was the one where the fight on the Rim, and later, on a bench of woodland below, had taken place.

Thereupon he arose and glided down under the spruces toward the level, grassy open he could see between the trees. And as he proceeded, with the slow step and wary eye of an Indian, his mind was busy.

Queen had in his flight unerringly worked in the direction of this cañon until he became lost in the fog; and upon regaining his bearings he had made a wonderful and heroic effort to surmount the manzanita slope and the Rim and find the rendezvous of his comrades. But he had failed up there on the ridge. In thinking it over Jean arrived at a conclusion that Queen, finding he could go no farther, had waited, guns in hands, for his pursuer. And he had died in this position. Then by strange coincidence his comrades had happened to come across him and, recognizing the situation, they had taken the shells from his guns and propped him up with the idea of luring Jean on. They had arranged a cunning trick and ambush, which had all but snuffed out the last of the Isbels. Colter probably had been at the bottom of this crafty plan. Since the fight at the Isbel ranch, now seemingly far back in the past, this man Colter had loomed up more and more as a stronger and more dangerous antagonist than either Jorth or Daggs. Before that he had been little known to any of the Isbel faction. And it was Colter now who controlled the remnant of the gang and who had Ellen Jorth in his possession.

The cañon wall above Jean, on the right, grew more rugged and loftier, and the one on the left began to show wooded slopes and brakes, and at last a wide expanse with a winding, willow border on the west and a long, low, pine-dotted bench on the east. It took several moments of study for Jean to recognize the rugged bluff above this bench. On up that cañon several miles was the site where Queen had surprised Jean and his comrades at their campfire. Somewhere in this vicinity was the hiding place of the rustlers.

Thereupon Jean proceeded with the utmost stealth, absolutely certain that he would miss no sound, movement, sign, or anything unnatural to the wild peace of the cañon. And his first sense to register something was his keen smell. Sheep! He was amazed to smell sheep. There must be a flock not far away. Then from where he glided along under the trees he saw down to open places in the willow brake and noticed sheep tracks in the dark, muddy bank of the brook. Next he heard faint tinkle of bells, and at length, when he could see farther into the open enlargement of the cañon, his surprised gaze fell upon an immense gray, wooly patch that blotted out acres and acres of grass. Thousands of sheep were grazing there. Jean knew there were several flocks of Jorth's sheep on the mountain in the care of herders, but he had never thought of them being so far west, more than twenty miles from Chevelon Cañon. His roving eyes could not descry any herders or dogs. But he knew there must be dogs close to that immense flock. And, whatever his cunning, he could not hope to elude the scent and sight of shepherd dogs. It would be best to go back the way he had come, wait for darkness, then cross the cañon and climb out, and work around to his objective point. Turning at once, he started to glide back. But almost immediately he was brought stock-still and thrilling by the sound of hoofs.

Horses were coming in the direction he wished to take. They were close. His swift conclusion was that the men who had pursued him up on the Rim had worked down into the cañon. One circling glance showed him that he had no sure covert near at hand. It would not do to risk their passing him there. The border of woodland was narrow and not dense enough for close inspection. He was forced to turn back up the cañon, in the hope of soon finding a hiding place or a break in the wall where he could climb up.

Hugging the base of the wall, he slipped on, passing the point where he had espied the sheep, and gliding on until he was stopped by a bend in the dense line of willows. It sheered to the west there and ran close to the high wall. Jean kept on until he was stooping under a curling border of willow thicket, with branches slim and yellow and masses of green foliage that brushed against the wall. Suddenly he encountered an abrupt corner of rock. He rounded it, to discover that it ran at right angles with the one he had just passed. Peering up through the willows, he ascertained that there was a narrow crack in the main wall of the cañon. It had been concealed by willows low down and leaning spruces above. A wild, hidden retreat! Along the base of the wall there were tracks of small animals. The place was odorous, like all dense thickets, but it was not dry. Water ran through there somewhere. Jean drew easier breath. All sounds except the rustling of birds or mice in the willows had ceased.

The brake was pervaded by a dreamy emptiness. Jean decided to steal on a little farther, then wait till he felt he might safely dare go back.

The golden-green gloom suddenly brightened. Light showed ahead, and parting the willows, he looked out into a narrow, winding cañon, with an open, grassy, willow-streaked lane in the center and on each side a thin strip of woodland.

His surprise was short lived. A crashing of horses back of him in the willows gave him a shock. He ran out along the base of the wall, back of the trees. Like the strip of woodland in the main cañon, this one was scant and had but little underbrush. There were young spruces growing with thick branches clear to the grass, and under these he could have concealed himself. But, with a certainty of sheep dogs in the vicinity, he would not think of hiding except as a last resource. These horsemen, whoever they were, were as likely to be sheep herders as not. Jean slackened his pace to look back. He could not see any moving objects, but he still heard horses, though not so close now. Ahead of him this narrow gorge opened out like the neck of a bottle. He would run on to the head of it and find a place to climb to the top.

Hurried and anxious as Jean was, he yet received an impression of singular, wild nature of this side gorge. It was a hidden, pine-fringed crack in the rock-ribbed and cañon-cut tableland. Above him the sky seemed a winding stream of blue. The walls were red and bulged out in spruce-greened shelves. From wall to wall was scarcely a distance of a hundred feet. Jumbles of rock obstructed his close holding to the wall. He had to walk at the edge of the timber. As he progressed, the gorge widened into wilder, ruggeder aspect. Through the trees ahead he saw where the wall circled to meet the cliff on the left, forming an oval depression, the nature of which he could not ascertain. But it appeared to be a small opening surrounded by dense thickets and the overhanging walls. Anxiety augmented to alarm. He might not be able to find a place to scale those rough cliffs. Breathing hard, Jean halted again. The situation was growing critical again. His physical condition was worse. Loss of sleep and rest, lack of food, the long pursuit of Queen, the wound in his arm, and the desperate run for his life—these had weakened him to the extent that if he undertook any strenuous effort he would fail. His cunning weighed all chances.

The shade of wall and foliage above, and another jumble

of ruined cliff, hindered his survey of the ground ahead, and he almost stumbled upon a cabin, hidden on three sides, with a small, bare clearing in front. It was an old, ramshackle structure like others he had run across in the cañons. Cautiously he approached and peeped around the corner. At first swift glance it had all the appearance of long disuse. But Jean had no time for another look. A clip-clop of trotting horses on hard ground brought the same pell-mell rush of sensations that had driven him to wild flight scarcely an hour past. His body jerked with its instinctive impulse, then quivered with his restraint. To turn back would be risky, to run ahead would be fatal, to hide was his one hope. No covert behind! And the clip-clop of hoofs sounded closer. One moment longer Jean held mastery over his instincts of self-preservation. To keep from running was almost impossible. It was the sheer primitive animal sense to escape. He drove it back and glided along the front of the cabin.

Here he saw that the cabin adjoined another. Reaching the door, he was about to peep in when the thud of hoofs and voices close at hand transfixed him with a grim certainty that he had not an instant to lose. Through the thin, black-streaked line of trees he saw moving red objects. Horses! He must run. Passing the door, his keen nose caught a musty, woody odor and the tail of his eye saw bare dirt floor. This cabin was unused. He halted—gave a quick look back. And the first thing his eye fell upon was a ladder, right inside the door, against the wall. He looked up. It led to a loft that, dark and gloomy, stretched halfway across the cabin. An irresistible impulse drove Jean. Slipping inside, he climbed up the ladder to the loft. It was like night up there. But he crawled on the rough-hewn rafters and, turning with his head toward the opening, he stretched out and lay still.

What seemed an interminable moment ended with a trample of hoofs outside the cabin. It ceased. Jean's vibrating ears caught the jingle of spurs and a thud of boots striking the ground.

"Wal, sweetheart, heah we are home again," drawled a slow, cool, mocking Texas voice.

"Home! I wonder, Colter—did y'u ever have a home—a mother—a sister—much less a sweetheart?" was the reply, bitter and caustic.

Jean's palpitating, hot body suddenly stretched still and cold with intensity of shock. His very bones seemed to quiver

210

and stiffen into ice. During the instant of realization his heart stopped. And a slow, contracting pressure enveloped his breast and moved up to constrict his throat. That woman's voice belonged to Ellen Jorth. The sound of it had lingered in his dreams. He had stumbled upon the rendezvous of the Jorth faction. Hard indeed had been the fates meted out to those of the Isbels and Jorths who had passed to their deaths. But no ordeal, not even Queen's, could compare with this desperate one Jean must endure. He had loved Ellen Jorth, strangely, wonderfully, and he had scorned evil repute to believe her good. He had spared her father and her uncle. He had weakened or lost the cause of the Isbels. He loved her now, desperately, deathlessly, knowing from her own lips that she was worthless—loved her the more because he had felt her terrible shame. And to him— the last of the Isbels—had come the cruelest of dooms— to be caught like a crippled rat in a trap; to be compelled to lie helpless, wounded, without a gun; to listen, and perhaps to see Ellen Jorth enact the very truth of her mocking insinuation. His will, his promise, his creed, his blood must hold him to the stern decree that he should be the last man of the Jorth-Isbel war. But could he lie there to hear—to see—when he had a knife and an arm?

14

★

THEN followed the leathery flop of saddles to the soft turf and the stamp of loosened horses.

Jean heard a noise at the cabin door, a rustle, and then a knock of something hard against wood. Silently he moved his head to look down through a crack between the rafters. He saw the glint of a rifle leaning against the sill. Then the doorstep was darkened. Ellen Jorth sat down with a long, tired sigh. She took off her sombrero and the light shone on the rippling, dark-brown hair, hanging in a tangled braid. The curved nape of her neck showed a warm tint of golden tan. She wore a gray blouse, soiled and torn, that clung to her lissome shoulders.

"Colter, what are y'u goin' to do?" she asked, suddenly. Her voice carried something Jean did not remember. It thrilled into the icy fixity of his senses.

"We'll stay heah," was the response, and it was followed by a clinking step of spurred boot.

"Shore I won't stay heah," declared Ellen. "It makes me sick when I think of how Uncle Tad died in there alone—helpless—sufferin'. The place seems haunted."

"Wal, I'll agree that it's tough on y'u. . . . But what the hell *can* we do?"

A long silence ensued which Ellen did not break.

"Somethin' has come off round heah since early mawnin'," declared Colter. "Somers an' Springer haven't got back. An' Antonio's gone. . . . Now, honest, Ellen, didn't y'u heah rifle shots off somewhere?"

"I reckon I did," she responded, gloomily.

"An' which way?"

"Sounded to me up on the bluff, back pretty far."

"Wal, shore that's my idee. An' it makes me think hard. Y'u know Somers come across the last camp of the Isbels. An' he dug into a grave to find the bodies of Jim Gordon an' another man he didn't know. Queen kept good his brag. He braced that Isbel gang an' killed those fellars. But either him or Jean Isbel went off leavin' bloody tracks. If it was Queen's y'u can bet Isbel was after him. An' if it was Isbel's tracks, why shore Queen would stick to them. Somers an' Springer couldn't follow the trail. They're shore not much good at trackin'. But for days they've been ridin' the woods, hopin' to run across Queen. . . . Wal now, mebbe they run across Isbel instead. An' if they did an' got away from him they'll be heah sooner or later. If Isbel was too many for them he'd hunt for my trail. I'm gamblin' that either Queen or Jean Isbel is daid. I'm hopin' it's Isbel. Because if he ain't daid he's the last of the Isbels, an' mebbe I'm the last of Jorth's gang. . . . Shore I'm not hankerin' to meet the half-breed. That's why I say we'll stay heah. This is as good a hidin' place as there is in the country. We've grub. There's water an' grass."

"Me—stay heah with y'u—alone!"

The tone seemed a contradiction to the apparently accepted sense of her words. Jean held his breath. But he could not still the slowly mounting and accelerating faculties

212

within that were involuntarily rising to meet some strange, nameless import. He felt it. He imagined it would be the catastrophe of Ellen Jorth's calm acceptance of Colter's proposition. But down in Jean's miserable heart lived something that would not die. No mere words could kill it. How poignant that moment of her silence! How terribly he realized that if his intelligence and his emotion had believed her betraying, his soul had not!

But Ellen Jorth did not speak. Her brown head hung thoughtfully. Her supple shoulders sagged a little.

"Ellen, what's happened to y'u?" went on Colter.

"All the misery possible to a woman," she replied, dejectedly.

"Shore I don't mean that way," he continued, persuasively. "I ain't gainsayin' the hard facts of your life. It's been bad. Your dad was no good. . . . But I mean I can't figger the change in y'u."

"No, I reckon y'u cain't," she said. "Whoever was responsible for your make-up left out a mind—not to say feeling."

Colter drawled a low laugh.

"Wal, have that your own way. But how much longer are y'u goin' to be like this heah?"

"Like what?" she rejoined, sharply.

"Wal, this stand-offishness of yours?"

"Colter, I told y'u to let me alone," she said, sullenly.

"Shore. An' y'u did that before. But this time y'u're different. . . . An' wal, I'm gettin' tired of it."

Here the cool, slow voice of the Texan sounded an inflexibility before absent, a timber that hinted of illimitable power.

Ellen Jorth shrugged her lithe shoulders and, slowly rising, she picked up the little rifle and turned to step into the cabin.

"Colter," she said, "fetch my pack an' my blankets in heah."

"Shore," he returned, with good nature.

Jean saw Ellen Jorth lay the rifle lengthwise in a chink between two logs and then slowly turn, back to the wall. Jean knew her then, yet did not know her. The brown flash of her face seemed that of an older, graver woman. His strained gaze, like his waiting mind, had expected something, he knew not what—a hardened face, a ghost of beauty, a recklessness, a distorted, bitter, lost expression in keeping with her fortunes. But he had reckoned falsely. She did not look like that. There was incalculable change, but the beauty remained, somehow different. Her red lips were parted. Her brooding eyes, looking out straight from under the level,

213

dark brows, seemed sloe black and wonderful with their steady, passionate light.

Jean, in his eager, hungry devouring of the beloved face, did not on the first instant grasp the significance of its expression. He was seeing the features that had haunted him. But quickly he interpreted her expression as the somber, hunted look of a woman who would bear no more. Under the torn blouse her full breast heaved. She held her hands clenched at her sides. She was listening, waiting for that jangling, slow step. It came, and with the sound she subtly changed. She was a woman hiding her true feelings. She relaxed, and that strong, dark look of fury seemed to fade back into her eyes.

Colter appeared at the door, carrying a roll of blankets and a pack.

"Throw them heah," she said. "I reckon y'u needn't bother coming in."

That angered the man. With one long stride he stepped over the doorsill, down into the cabin, and flung the blankets at her feet and then the pack after it. Whereupon he deliberately sat down in the door, facing her. With one hand he slid off his sombrero, which fell outside, and with the other he reached in his upper vest pocket for the little bag of tobacco that showed there. All the time he looked at her. By the light now unobstructed Jean descried Colter's face; and sight of it then sounded the roll and drum of his passions.

"Wal, Ellen, I reckon we'll have it out right now an' heah," he said, and with tobacco in one hand, paper in the other he began the operations of making a cigarette. However, he scarcely removed his glance from her.

"Yes?" queried Ellen Jorth.

"I'm goin' to have things the way they were before—an' more," he declared. The cigarette paper shook in his fingers.

"What do y'u mean?" she demanded.

"Y'u know what I mean," he retorted. Voice and action were subtly unhinging this man's control over himself.

"Maybe I don't. I reckon y'u'd better talk plain."

The rustler had clear gray-yellow eyes, flawless, like crystal, and suddenly they danced with little fiery flecks.

"The last time I laid my hand on y'u I got hit for my pains. An' shore that's been ranklin'."

"Colter, y'u'll get hit again if y'u put your hands on me," she said, dark, straight glance on him. A frown wrinkled the level brows.

214

"Y'u mean that?" he asked, thickly.

"I shore do."

Manifestly he accepted her assertion. Something of incredulity and bewilderment, that had vied with his resentment, utterly disappeared from his face.

"Heah I've been waitin' for y'u to love me," he declared, with a gesture not without dignified emotion. "Your givin' in without that wasn't so much to me."

And at these words of the rustler's Jean Isbel felt an icy, sickening shudder creep into his soul. He shut his eyes. The end of his dream had been long in coming, but at last it had arrived. A mocking voice, like a hollow wind, echoed through that region—that lonely and ghost-like hall of his heart which had harbored faith.

She burst into speech, louder and sharper, the first words of which Jean's strangely throbbing ears did not distinguish.

"—— —— you! . . . I never gave in to y'u an' I never will."

"But, girl—I kissed y'u—hugged y'u—handled y'u—" he expostulated, and the making of the cigarette ceased.

"Yes, y'u did—y'u brute—when I was so downhearted and weak I couldn't lift my hand," she flashed.

"Ahuh! Y'u mean I couldn't do that now?"

"I should smile I do, Jim Colter!" she replied.

"Wal, mebbe—I'll see—presently," he went on, straining with words. "But I'm shore curious. . . . Daggs, then—he was nothin' to y'u?"

"No more than y'u," she said, morbidly. "He used to run after me—long ago, it seems. . . . I was only a girl then—innocent—an' I'd not known any but rough men. I couldn't all the time—every day, every hour—keep him at arm's length. Sometimes before I knew—I didn't care. I was a child. A kiss meant nothing to me. But after I knew—"

Ellen dropped her head in brooding silence.

"Say, do y'u expect me to believe that?" he queried, with a derisive leer.

"Bah! What do I care what y'u believe?" she cried, with lifting head.

"How aboot Simm Bruce?"

"That coyote! . . . He lied aboot me, Jim Colter. And any man half a man would have known he lied."

"Wal, Simm always bragged aboot y'u bein' his girl," asserted Colter. "An' he wasn't over-particular aboot details of your love-makin'."

Ellen gazed out of the door, over Colter's head, as if the forest out there was a refuge. She evidently sensed more about the man than appeared in his slow talk, in his slouching position. Her lips shut in a firm line, as if to hide their trembling and to still her passionate tongue. Jean, in his absorption, magnified his perceptions. Not yet was Ellen Jorth afraid of this man, but she feared the situation. Jean's heart was at bursting pitch. All within him seemed chaos— a wreck of beliefs and convictions. Nothing was true. He would wake presently out of a nightmare. Yet, as surely as he quivered there, he felt the imminence of a great moment —a lightning flash—a thunderbolt—a balance struck.

Colter attended to the forgotten cigarette. He rolled it, lighted it, all the time with lowered, pondering head, and when he had puffed a cloud of smoke he suddenly looked up with face as hard as flint, eyes as fiery as molten steel.

"Wal, Ellen—how aboot Jean Isbel—our half-breed Nez Perce friend—who was shore seen handlin' y'u familiar?" he drawled.

Ellen Jorth quivered as under a lash, and her brown face turned a dusty scarlet, that slowly receding left her pale.

"Damn y'u, Jim Colter!" she burst out, furiously. "I wish Jean Isbel would jump in that door—or down out of that loft! . . . He killed Greaves for defiling my name! . . . He'd kill *y'u* for your dirty insult. . . . And I'd like to watch him do it. . . . Y'u cold-blooded Texan! Y'u thieving rustler! Y'u liar! . . . Y'u lied aboot my father's death. And I know why. Y'u stole my father's gold. . . . An' now y'u want me—y'u expect me to fall into your arms. . . . My Heaven! cain't y'u tell a decent woman? Was your mother decent? Was your sister decent? . . . Bah! I'm appealing to deafness. But y'u'll *heah* this, Jim Colter! . . . I'm not what y'u think I am. I'm not the—the damned hussy y'u liars have made me out. . . . I'm a Jorth, alas! I've no home, no relatives, no friends! I've been forced to live my life with rustlers—vile men like y'u an' Daggs an' the rest of your like. . . . But I've been good! Do y'u heah that? . . . I *am* good—an', so help me God, y'u an' all your rottenness cain't make me bad!"

Colter lounged to his tall height and the laxity of the man vanished.

Vanished also was Jean Isbel's suspended icy dread, the cold clogging of his fevered mind—vanished in a white, living, leaping flame.

Silently he drew his knife and lay there watching with the

eyes of a wildcat. The instant Colter stepped far enough over toward the edge of the loft Jean meant to bound erect and plunge down upon him. But Jean could wait now. Colter had a gun at his hip. He must never have a chance to draw it.

"Ahuh! So y'u wish Jean Isbell would hop in heah, do y'u?" queried Colter. "Wal, if I had any pity on y'u, that's done for it."

A sweep of his long arm, so swift Ellen had no time to move, brought his hand in clutching contact with her. And the force of it flung her half across the cabin room, leaving the sleeve of her blouse in his grasp. Pantingly she put out that bared arm and her other to ward him off as he took long, slow strides toward her.

Jean rose half to his feet, dragged by almost ungovernable passion to risk all on one leap. But the distance was too great. Colter, blind as he was to all outward things, would hear, would see in time to make Jean's effort futile. Shaking like a leaf, Jean sank back, eye again to the crack between the rafters.

Ellen did not retreat, nor scream, nor move. Every line of her body was instinct with fight, and the magnificent blaze of her eyes would have checked a less callous brute.

Colter's big hand darted between Ellen's arms and fastened in the front of her blouse. He did not try to hold her or draw her close. The unleashed passion of the man required violence. In one savage pull he tore off her blouse, exposing her white, rounded shoulders and heaving bosom, where instantly a wave of red burned upward.

Overcome by the remendous violence and spirit of the rustler, Ellen sank to her knees, with blanched face and dilating eyes, trying with folded arms and trembling hand to hide her nudity.

At that moment the rapid beat of hoofs on the hard trail outside halted Colter in his tracks.

"Hell!" he exclaimed. "An' who's that?" With a fierce action he flung the remnants of Ellen's blouse in her face and turned to leap out the door.

Jean saw Ellen catch the blouse and try to wrap it around her, while she sagged against the wall and stared at the door. The hoof beats pounded to a solid thumping halt just ouside.

"Jim—thar's hell to pay!! rasped out a panting voice.

"Wal, Springer, I reckon I wished y'u'd paid it without spoilin' my deals," retorted Colter, cool and sharp.

217

"Deals? Ha! Y'u'll be forgettin'—your lady love—in a minnit," replied Springer. "When I catch—my breath."

"Where's Somers?" demanded Colter.

"I reckon he's all shot up—if my eyes didn't fool me."

"Where is he?" yelled Colter.

"Jim—he's layin' up in the bushes round thet bluff. I didn't wait to see how he was hurt. But he shore stopped some lead. An' he flopped like a chicken with its—haid cut off."

"Where's Antonio?"

"He run like the greaser he is," declared Springer, disgustedly.

"Ahuh! An' where's Queen?" queried Colter, after a significant pause.

"Dead!"

The silence ensuing was fraught with a suspense that held Jean in cold bonds. He saw the girl below rise from her knees, one hand holding the blouse to her breast, the other extended, and with strange, repressed, almost frantic look she swayed toward the door.

"Wal, talk," ordered Colter, harshly.

"Jim, there ain't a hell of a lot," replied Springer, drawing a deep breath, "but what there is is shore interestin'. . . . Me an' Somers took Antonio with us. He left his woman with the sheep. An' we rode up the cañon, clumb out on top, an' made a circle back on the ridge. That's the way we've been huntin' fer tracks. Up thar in a bare spot we run plump into Queen sittin' against a tree, right out in the open. Queerest sight y'u ever seen! The damn gunfighter had set down to wait for Isbel, who was trailin' him, as we suspected—an' he died thar. He wasn't cold when we found him. . . . Somers was quick to see a trick. So he propped Queen up an' tied the guns to his hands—an', Jim, the queerest thing aboot that deal was this—Queen's guns was empty! Not a shell left! It beat us holler. . . . We left him thar, an' hid up high on the bluff, mebbe a hundred yards off. The hosses we left back of a thicket. An' we waited thar a long time. But, sure enough, the half-breed come. He was too smart. Too much Injun! He would not cross the open, but went around. An' then he seen Queen. It was great to watch him. After a little he shoved his rifle out an' went right fer Queen. This is when I wanted to shoot. I could have plugged him. But Somers says wait an' make it sure. When Isbel got up to Queen he was sort of half hid by the tree.

218

An' I couldn't wait no longer, so I shot. I hit him, too. We all begun to shoot. Somers showed himself, an' that's when Isbel opened up. He used up a whole magazine on Somers an' then, suddenlike, he quit. It didn't take me long to figger mebbe he was out of shells. When I seen him run I was certain of it. Then we made for the hosses an' rode after Isbel. Pretty soon I seen him runnin' like a deer down the ridge. I yelled an' spurred after him. There is where Antonio quit me. But I kept on. An' I got a shot at Isbel. He ran out of sight. I follered him by spots of blood on the stones an' grass until I couldn't trail him no more. He must have gone down over the cliffs. He couldn't have done nothin' else without me seein' him. I found his rifle, an' here it is to prove what I say. I had to go back to climb down off the Rim, an' I rode fast down the cañon. He's somewhere along that west wall, hidin' in the brush, hard hit if I know anythin' aboot the color of blood."

"Wal! . . . that beats me holler, too," ejaculated Colter.

"Jim, what's to be done?" inquired Springer, eagerly. "If we're sharp we can corral that half-breed. He's the last of the Isbels."

"More, pard. He's the last of the Isbel outfit," declared Colter. "If y'u can show me blood in his tracks I'll trail him."

"Y'u can bet I'll show y'u," rejoined the other rustler. "But listen! Wouldn't it be better for us first to see if he crossed the cañon? I reckon he didn't. But let's make sure. An' if he didn't we'll have him somewhar along that west cañon wall. He's not got no gun. He'd never run thet way if he had. . . . Jim, he's our meat!"

"Shore, he'll have that knife," pondered Colter.

"We needn't worry about thet," said the other, positively. "He's hard hit, I tell y'u. All we got to do is find thet bloody trail again an' stick to it—goin' careful. He's layin' low like a crippled wolf."

"Springer, I want the job of finishin' that half-breed," hissed Colter. "I'd give ten years of my life to stick a gun down his throat an' shoot it off."

"All right. Let's rustle. Mebbe y'u'll not have to give much more'n ten minnits. Because I tell y'u I can find him. It'd been easy—but, Jim, I reckon I was afraid."

"Leave your hoss for me an' go ahaid," the rustler then said, brusquely. "I've a job in the cabin heah."

"Haw-haw! . . . Wal, Jim, I'll rustle a bit down the trail an' wait. No huntin' Jean Isbel alone—not fer me. I've had

219

a queer feelin' about thet knife he used on Greaves. An' I reckon y'u'd oughter let thet Jorth hussy alone long enough to—"

"Springer, I reckon I've got to hawg-tie her—" His voice became indistinguishable, and footfalls attested to a slow moving away of the men.

Jean had listened with ears acutely strung to catch every syllable while his gaze rested upon Ellen who stood beside the door. Every line of her body denoted a listening intensity. Her back was toward Jean, so that he could not see her face. And he did not want to see, but could not help seeing her naked shoulders. She put her head out of the door. Suddenly she drew it in quickly and half turned her face, slowly raising her white arm. This was the left one and bore the marks of Colter's hard fingers.

She gave a little gasp. Her eyes became large and staring. They were bent on the hand that she had removed from a step on the ladder. On hand and wrist showed a bright-red smear of blood.

Jean, with a convulsive leap of his heart, realized that he had left his bloody tracks on the ladder as he had climbed. That moment seemed the supremely terrible one of his life.

Ellen Jorth's face blanched and her eyes darkened and dilated with exceeding amaze and flashing thought to become fixed with horror. That instant was the one in which her reason connected the blood on the ladder with the escape of Jean Isbel.

One moment she leaned there, still as stone except for her heaving breast, and then her fixed gaze changed to a swift, dark blaze, comprehending, yet inscrutable, as she flashed it up the ladder to the loft. She could see nothing, yet she knew and Jean knew that she knew he was there. A marvelous transformation passed over her features and even over her form. Jean choked with the ache in his throat. Slowly she put the bloody hand behind her while with the other she still held the torn blouse to her breast.

Colter's slouching, musical step sounded outside. And it might have been a strange breath of infinitely vitalizing and passionate life blown into the well-springs of Ellen Jorth's being. Isbel had no name for her then. The spirit of a woman had been to him a thing unknown.

She swayed back from the door against the wall in singular, softened poise, as if all the steel had melted out of her body. And as Colter's tall shadow fell across the threshold

220

Jean Isbel felt himself staring with eyeballs that ached—straining incredulous sight at this woman who in a few seconds had bewildered his senses with her transfiguration. He saw but could not comprehend.

"Jim—I heard—all Springer told y'u," she said. The look of her dumfounded Colter and her voice seemed to shake him visibly.

"Suppose y'u did. What then?" he demanded, harshly, as he halted with one booted foot over the threshold. Malignant and forceful, he eyed her darkly, doubtfully.

"I'm afraid," she whispered.

"What of? Me?"

"No. Of—of Jean Isbel. He might kill y'u and—then where would I be?"

"Wal, I'm damned!" ejaculated the rustler. "What's got into y'u?" He moved to enter, but a sort of fascination bound him.

"Jim, I hated y'u a moment ago," she burst out. "But now —with that Jean Isbel somewhere near—hidin'—watchin' to kill y'u—an' maybe me, too—I—I don't hate y'u any more. . . . Take me away."

"Girl, have y'u lost your nerve?" he demanded.

"My God! Colter—cain't y'u see?" she implored. "Won't y'u take me away?"

"I shore will—presently," he replied, grimly. "But y'u'll wait till I've shot the lights out of this Isbel."

"No!" she cried. "Take me away now. . . . An' I'll give in —I'll be what y'u want. . . . Y'u can do with me—as y'u like."

Colter's lofty frame leaped as if at the release of bursting blood. With a lunge he cleared the threshold to loom over her.

"Am I out of my haid, or are y'u?" he asked, in low, hoarse voice. His darkly corded face expressed extremest amaze.

"Jim, I mean it," she whispered, edging an inch nearer him, her white face uplifted, her dark eyes unreadable in their eloquence and mystery. "I've no friend but y'u. . . . I'll be—yours. . . . I'm lost. . . . What does it matter? . . . If y'u want me—take me *now*—before I kill myself."

"Ellen Jorth, there's somethin' wrong aboot y'u," he responded. "Did y'u tell the truth—when y'u denied ever bein' a sweetheart of Simm Bruce?"

"Yes, I told y'u the truth."

"Ahuh! An' how do y'u account for layin' me out with every dirty name y'u could give tongue to?"

"Oh, it was temper. I wanted to be let alone."

"Temper! Wal, I reckon y'u've got one," he retorted, grimly. "An' I'm not shore y'u're not crazy or lyin'. An hour ago I couldn't touch y'u."

"Y'u may now—if y'u promise to take me away—at once. This place has got on my nerves. I couldn't sleep heah with that Isbel hidin' around. Could y'u?"

"Wal, I reckon I'd not sleep very deep."

"Then let us go."

He shook his lean, eagle-like head in slow, doubtful vehemence, and his piercing gaze studied her distrustfully. Yet all the while there was manifest in his strung frame an almost irrepressible violence, held in abeyance to his will.

"That aboot y'u bein' so good?" he inquired, with a return of the mocking drawl.

"Never mind what's past," she flashed, with passion dark as his. "I've made my offer."

"Shore there's a lie aboot y'u somewhere," he muttered, thickly.

"Man, could I do more?" she demanded, in scorn.

"No. But it's a lie," he returned. "Y'u'll get me to take y'u away an' then fool me—run off—God knows what. Women are all liars."

Manifestly he could not believe in her strange transformation. Memory of her wild and passionate denunciation of him and his kind must have seared even his calloused soul. But the ruthless nature of him had not weakened nor softened in the least as to his intentions. This weather-vane veering of hers bewildered him, obsessed him with its possibilities. He had the look of a man who was divided between love of her and hate, whose love demanded a return, but whose hate required a proof of her abasement. Not proof of surrender, but proof of her shame! The ignominy of him thirsted for its like. He could grind her beauty under his heel, but he could not soften to this feminine inscrutableness.

And whatever was the truth of Ellen Jorth in this moment, beyond Colter's gloomy and stunted intelligence, beyond even the love of Jean Isbel, it was something that held the balance of mastery. She read Colter's mind. She dropped the torn blouse from her hand and stood there, unashamed, with the wave of her white breast pulsing, eyes black as night and full of hell, her face white, tragic, terrible, yet strangely lovely.

"Take me away," she whispered, stretching one white arm toward him, then the other.

Colter, even as she moved, had leaped with inarticulate cry and radiant face to meet her embrace. But it seemed, just as her left arm flashed up toward his neck, that he saw her bloody hand and wrist. Strange how that checked his ardor—threw up his lean head like that of a striking bird of prey.

"Blood! What the hell!" he ejaculated, and in one sweep he grasped her. "How'd y'u do that? Are y'u cut? . . . Hold still."

Ellen could not release her hand.

"I scratched myself," she said.

"Where? . . . All that blood!" And suddenly he flung her hand back with fierce gesture, and the gleams of his yellow eyes were like the points of leaping flames. They pierced her —read the secret falsity of her. Slowly he stepped backward, guardedly his hand moved to his gun, and his glance circled and swept the interior of the cabin. As if he had the nose of a hound and sight to follow scent, his eyes bent to the dust of the ground before the door. He quivered, grew rigid as stone, and then moved his head with exceeding slowness as if searching through a microscope in the dust—farther to the left—to the foot of the ladder—and up one step— another—a third—all the way up to the loft. Then he whipped out his gun and wheeled to face the girl.

"Ellen, y'u've got your half-breed heah!" he said, with a terrible smile.

She neither moved nor spoke. There was a suggestion of collapse, but it was only a change where the alluring softness of her hardened into a strange, rapt glow. And in it seemed the same mastery that had characterized her former aspect. Herein the treachery of her was revealed. She had known what she meant to do in any case.

Colter, standing at the door, reached a long arm toward the ladder, where he laid his hand on a rung. Taking it away he held it palm outward for her to see the dark splotch of blood.

"See?"

"Yes, I see," she said, ringingly.

Passion wrenched him, transformed him. "All that—aboot leavin' heah—with me—aboot givin' in—was a lie!"

"No, Colter. It was the truth. I'll go—yet—now—if y'u'll spare—*him!*" She whispered the last word and made a slight movement of her hand toward the loft.

"Girl!" he exploded, incredulously. "Y'u love this half-breed—this *Isbel? . . .* Y'u *love* him!"

"With all my heart! . . . Thank God! It has been my glory. . . . It might have been my salvation. . . . But now I'll go to hell with y'u—if y'u'll spare him."

"Damn my soul!" rasped out the rustler, as if something of respect was wrung from that sordid deep of him. "Y'u—y'u woman! . . . Jorth will turn over in his grave. He'd rise out of his grave if this Isbel got y'u."

"Hurry! Hurry!" implored Ellen. "Springer may come back. I think I heard a call."

"Wal, Ellen Jorth, I'll not spare Isbel—nor y'u," he returned, with dark and meaning leer, as he turned to ascend the ladder.

Jean Isbel, too, had reached the climax of his suspense. Gathering all his muscles in a knot he prepared to leap upon Colter as he mounted the ladder. But Ellen Jorth screamed piercingly and snatched her rifle from its resting place and, cocking it, she held it forward and low.

"Colter!"

Her scream and his uttered name stiffened him.

"Y'u will spare Jean Isbel!" she rang out. "Drop that gun —drop it!"

"Shore, Ellen. . . . Easy now. Remember your temper. . . . I'll let Isbel off," he panted, huskily, and all his body sank quiveringly to a crouch.

"Drop your gun! Don't turn round. . . . Colter!—*I'll kill y'u!*"

But even then he failed to divine the meaning and the spirit of her.

"Aw, now, Ellen," he entreated, in louder, huskier tones, and as if dragged by fatal doubt of her still, he began to turn.

Crash! The rifle emptied its contents in Colter's breast. All his body sprang up. He dropped the gun. Both hands fluttered toward her. And an awful surprise flashed over his face.

"So—help—me—God!" he whispered, with blood thick in his voice. Then darkly, as one groping, he reached for her with shaking hands. "Y'u—y'u white-throated hussy! . . . I'll . . ."

He grasped the quivering rifle barrel. Crash! She shot him

224

again. As he swayed over her and fell she had to leap aside, and his clutching hand tore the rifle from her grasp. Then in convulsion he writhed, to heave on his back, and stretch out—a ghastly spectacle. Ellen backed away from it, her white arms wide, a slow horror blotting out the passion of her face.

Then from without came a shrill call and the sound of rapid footsteps. Ellen leaned against the wall, staring still at Colter. "Hey, Jim—what's the shootin'?" called Springer, breathlessly.

As his form darkened the doorway Jean once again gathered all his muscular force for a tremendous spring.

Springer saw the girl first and he appeared thunderstruck. His jaw dropped. He needed not the white gleam of her person to transfix him. Her eyes did that and they were riveted in unutterable horror upon something on the ground. Thus instinctively directed, Springer espied Colter.

"Y'u—y'u shot him!! he shrieked. "What for—y'u hussy? . . . Ellen Jorth, if y'u've killed him, I'll . . ."

He strode toward where Colter lay.

Then Jean, rising silently, took a step and like a tiger he launched himself into the air, down upon the rustler. Even as he leaped Springer gave a quick, upward look. And he cried out. Jean's moccasined feet struck him squarely and sent him staggering into the wall, where his head hit hard. Jean fell, but bounded up as the half-stunned Springer drew his gun. Then Jean lunged forward with a single sweep of his arm—and looked no more.

Ellen ran swaying out of the door, and, once clear of the threshold, she tottered out on the grass, to sink to her knees. The bright, golden sunlight gleamed upon her white shoulders and arms. Jean had one foot out of the door when he saw her and he whirled back to get her blouse. But Springer had fallen upon it. Snatching up a blanket, Jean ran out.

"Ellen! Ellen! Ellen!" he cried. "It's over!" And reaching her, he tried to wrap her in the blanket.

She wildly clutched his knees. Jean was conscious only of her white, agonized face and the dark eyes with their look of terrible strain.

"Did y'u—did y'u . . ." she whispered.

"Yes—it's over," he said, gravely. "Ellen, the Isbel-Jorth feud is ended."

"Oh, thank—God!" she cried, in breaking voice. "Jean—y'u are wounded . . . the blood on the step!"

225

"My arm. See. It's not bad. . . . Ellen, let me wrap this round you." Folding the blanket around her shoulders, he held it there and entreated her to get up. But she only clung the closer. She hid her face on his knees. Long shudders rippled over her, shaking the blanket, shaking Jean's hands. Distraught, he did not know what to do. And his own heart was bursting.

"Ellen, you must not kneel—there—that way," he implored.

"Jean! Jean!" she moaned, and clung the tighter.

He tried to lift her up, but she was a dead weight, and with that hold on him seemed anchored at his feet.

"I killed Colter," she gasped. "I *had* to—kill him! . . . I offered—to fling myself away. . . ."

"For me!" he cried, poignantly. "Oh, Ellen! Ellen! the world has come to an end! . . . Hush! don't keep sayin' that. Of course you killed him. You saved my life. For I'd never have let you go off with him. . . . Yes, you killed him. . . . You're a Jorth an' I'm an Isbel. . . . We've blood on our hands—both of us—I for you an' you for me!"

His voice of entreaty and sadness strengthened her and she raised her white face, loosening her clasp to lean back and look up. Tragic, sweet, despairing, the loveliness of her— the significance of her there on her knees—thrilled him to his soul.

"Blood on my hands!" she whispered. "Yes. It was awful— killing him. . . . But—all I care for in this world is for your forgiveness—and your faith that saved my soul!"

"Child, there's nothin' to forgive," he responded. "Nothin' . . . Please, Ellen . . ."

"I lied to y'u!" she cried. "I lied to y'u!"

"Ellen, listen—darlin'." And the tender epithet brought her head and arms back close-pressed to him. "I know— now," he faltered on. "I found out to-day what I believed. An' I swear to God—by the memory of my dead mother— down in my heart I never, never, never believed what they —what y'u tried to make me believe. *Never!*"

"Jean—I love y'u—love y'u—love y'u!" she breathed with exquisite, passionate sweetness. Her dark eyes burned up into his.

"Ellen, I can't lift you up," he said, in trembling eagerness, signifying his crippled arm. "But I can kneel with you! . . ."